THE LAST DAYS

By Scott Westerfeld

Midnighters
THE SECRET HOUR
TOUCHING DARKNESS
BLUE NOON

PARASITE POSITIVE
THE LAST DAYS

THE RISEN EMPIRE

SCOTT WESTERFELD
THE LAST DAYS

www.atombooks.co.uk

ATOM

First published in the United States in 2006 by Razorbill,
Penguin Group (USA) Inc.
First published in Great Britain in 2007 by Atom
Reprinted 2008

Copyright 2006 © Scott Westerfeld

The moral right of the author has been asserted.

Interior design by Christopher Grassi

A CIP catalogue record for this book
is available from the British Library.

ISBN 978-1-905654-06-2

Typeset in Caxton by M Rules
Printed and bound in the UK by
CPI Mackays, Chatham ME5 8TD

Atom
An imprint of
Little, Brown Book Group
100 Victoria Embankment
London EC4Y 0DY

An Hachette Livre UK Company
www.hachettelivre.co.uk

www.atombooks.co.uk

To Jazza
first reader and best friend

PART I

INFLUENCES

Ever hear this charming little rhyme?

Ring-around-the-rosy.

A pocket full of posies.

Ashes, ashes, we all fall down.

Some people say that this poem is about the Black Death, the fourteenth-century plague that killed 100 million people. Here's the theory: 'Ring-around-the-rosy' was an early symptom of plague: a circular rash of red skin. In medieval times, people carried flowers, like posies, with them for protection against disease. The words 'ashes to ashes' appear in the funeral mass, and sometimes plague victims' houses were burned.

And 'we all fall down'?

Well, you can figure that one out for yourself.

Sadly, though, most experts think this is nonsense. A red rash isn't really a plague symptom, they say, and 'ashes' was originally some other word. Most important, the rhyme is too new. It didn't appear in print until 1881.

Trust me, though: it's about the plague. The words have changed a little from the original, but so have any words carried on the lips of children for seven hundred years. It's a little reminder that the Black Death will come again.

How can I be so sure about this rhyme, when all the experts disagree?

Because I ate the kid who made it up.

NIGHT MAYOR TAPES:
102-130

1. THE FALL

–MOZ–

I think New York was leaking.

It was past midnight and still a hundred degrees. Some kind of city sweat was oozing up through the sidewalk cracks, shimmering with oily rainbows in the streetlights. The garbage piled up outside the restaurants on Indian Row was seeping, leftover curry turning into slurry. The glistening plastic bags would smell jaw-droppingly foul the next morning, but as I walked past that night, they still gave off the perfumes of saffron and freshly thrown-out rice.

The people were sweating too – shiny-faced and frizzy-haired, like everyone had just stepped out of a shower. Eyes were glassy, and cell phones dangled limply on wrist straps, softly glowing, spitting occasional fragments of bubblegum songs.

I was on my way home from practicing with Zahler. It was way too hot to write anything new, so we'd riffed, plowing through the same four chords a thousand times. After an hour the riff had faded from my ears, like it does when you say the same word over and over till it turns meaningless. Finally, all I could hear was the squeak of Zahler's sweaty fingers on his strings and his amp hissing like a steam-pipe, another music squeezing up through ours.

We pretended we were a band warming up onstage, slowly revving the crowd into a frenzy before the lead singer jumps into the spotlights: the World's Longest Intro. But we didn't have a lead singer, so the riff just petered out into rivulets of sweat.

I sometimes feel it right before something big happens – when I'm about to break a guitar string, or get caught sneaking in, or when my parents are *this* close to having a monster fight.

So just before the TV fell, I looked up.

The woman was twenty-something, with fire-engine red hair and raccoon eyes, black makeup streaming down her cheeks. She pushed a television through her third-floor window, an old boxy one, its power cord flailing as it tumbled toward the sidewalk. The TV clipped a fire escape, the deep ringing sound swallowed seconds later by the crash on the pavement twenty feet ahead of me.

A spray of shattered glass skittered around my feet, glittering and sharp, tinkling like colliding chandeliers as shards rolled and skidded to a halt. Fragments of streetlight and sky reflected up from them, as if the television had split into a thousand tiny screens, all still working. My own eye stared back at me from a Manhattan-shaped sliver. Wide and awestruck, it blinked.

The next thing I did was look straight up. You know, in case everyone was throwing out TVs that night, and I should roll under a parked car. But it was just her – she was letting out long, wordless screams now and throwing out more stuff:

Pillows with tasseled edges. Dolls and desk lamps. Books fluttering like crash-landing birds. A jar full of pens and pencils. Two cheap wooden chairs, smashed first against the window frame so they'd fit through. A computer keyboard that sent up a splash of keys and tiny springs. Silverware glittering as it tumbled, ringing on the pavement like a triangle when dinner's ready . . . a whole apartment squeezed out one window. Somebody's life laid bare.

And all the while she was shrieking like a beast above us.

I looked around at the gathering crowd, most of them getting out late from Indian Row, addled by curry. The rapt expressions on their upturned faces made me jealous. The whole time Zahler and I had jammed, I'd been imagining an audience like this one: flabbergasted and electrified, yanked out of the everyday by their ears and eyeballs. And now this crazy woman, with her rock-star hair and makeup, had them mesmerized. Why bother with riffs and solos and lyrics when all the crowd wanted was an avalanche of screams and smashed Ikea furniture?

But once the shock wore off, their rapture faded into something uglier. Soon enough, people were laughing and pointing, a gang of boys shouting, 'Jump, jump, jump!' in rhythm. A camera flash popped, catching a satanic flicker in the woman's eyes. A couple of faces glowed with blue cell-phone light – calling the police, or nearby friends to come and join in? I wondered.

One of the spectators slipped into the impact zone, running half-crouched to snatch a black dress from under a rain of computer cables and extension cords. She backed away, holding it up to her body as if she'd pulled it off a rack. Another ducked in to snag an armload of magazines.

'Hey!' I yelled. I was about to point out that this wasn't exactly Dumpster diving – the woman might want her stuff back after this psychotic meltdown was over – but then the CDs started flying. Glittering projectiles spattered on the street like plastic hail, each one impelled from the window by a shriek.

The looters retreated – the woman was *aiming* now, and the CDs were deadly. I mean, compact discs don't hurt much, but these were still in their cases, giving them extra weight and corners.

Then I saw it: the neck of an electric guitar emerging from the window, then the whole instrument – a mid-seventies Fender Stratocaster with gold pickups and whammy bar, a creamy yellow body with a white pick-guard.

I took a step forward, holding one hand up. 'Wait!'

The madwoman glared down at me, mascara smeared across her face like black blood, clutching the Stratocaster to her chest. Her hands found the strings, as if she was about to play, and then she let out one last terrible howl.

'*No!*' I shouted.

She let the guitar drop.

It spun in the air, delicate tuning hardware glittering in the streetlights. I was already running, tripping on smashed plastic and tangled clothes, thinking that there were four hundred bones in my two hands, wondering how many of them that lacquered hardwood would break after a thirty-foot fall.

But I couldn't just let it smash . . .

Then the miracle: the guitar snapped to a halt in midair. Its strap was caught on a corner of the fire escape, where it hung, spinning perilously.

I skidded to a halt, looking straight up.

'Over here!' someone shouted.

I glanced down for a split second: a girl my age, with short black hair and red-framed glasses, yanking something big and flat from under the clutter, sending silverware scattering in all directions.

'Watch out,' I said, pointing up toward where the Strat was untangling itself. 'It's about to fall.'

'I know! Take the other side!'

I glanced back down at her, frowning. The girl was holding two corners of a blanket she'd rescued from the pile. She unfurled its plaid expanse toward me with a flick, as if we were making a bed. I grabbed for the other corners, finally understanding.

We stepped back from each other, pulling the blanket taut, looking up again. Above us, the guitar spun faster and faster, like a kid unwinding on a swing set.

'Be careful,' I said. 'That's a nineteen seventy-three . . . Um, what I mean is, it's really valuable.'

'With gold pickups?' she snorted. 'Nineteen seventy-five, maybe.'

I looked down at her.

'Incoming!' she yelled.

The guitar slipped free, still spinning, hardware glittering, strap flailing. It landed heavy as a dead body between us, almost jerking the blanket from my fists. Its momentum pulled us both forward a few skidding steps, suddenly face to face.

But there was no awful thud; the Stratocaster hadn't struck pavement.

'We saved it!' Her brown eyes were glowing.

I looked down at the guitar, safely swaddled in plaid. 'Whoa. We did.'

Then the fire escape rang out again. Both of us flinched as we looked up. But it wasn't more stuff falling – it was a pair of human figures, six stories above, descending toward the crazy woman's window. They weren't climbing down the metal stairs, though – they were practically flying, swinging from handhold to handhold, graceful as headlight shadows slipping across a ceiling.

I watched them, awestruck, until the girl next to me shouted two terrifying words:

'*Toaster oven!*'

It was tumbling out the window directly over our heads, glass door hanging open, scattering crumbs . . .

We bundled the Stratocaster into its blanket and ran.

–PEARL–

'You know what the weird thing was?'

The cute guy frowned, still wide-eyed and panting. '*The* weird thing? I can't think of anything that *wasn't* weird about that.'

I smiled, holding out both palms, weighing the weirdness. It was all relative, these days. You had to take your normal where you found it. People went crazy all the time; it was how they went crazy that mattered.

We'd taken the Strat and run around the corner – around a couple of corners, actually – until I'd led the guy to my street without saying so. My building was right across from us, but I wasn't sure I wanted him knowing where I lived – even if he was the sort of boy to consider catching a Fender Stratocaster with his bare hands. And I certainly didn't want my mom coming home late and finding me out on the front steps huddled with some random cute guy and a secondhand plaid bedspread. She might get the wrong idea. In fact, she would make a point of getting the wrong idea.

The stoop we sat on was darkened by scaffolding, protected from the streetlights, invisible. The Strat lay between us, still wrapped in its bedspread, partly to protect it and partly because the guy looked guilty, like he thought someone was going to chase us down and make us give it back.

Like who? Not that crazy woman: she was gone by now. I'd seen angels coming to collect her. That's what happens when you lose it these days: real-life angels, just like Luz had told me about, though I hadn't quite believed her until tonight.

But I didn't want to sound crazy myself, so I said, 'Here's what was weird. That was girl's stuff she was tossing. The clothes coming out the window: dresses and skirts. *Her* stuff.'

He frowned again. 'Why wouldn't it be?'

'Because there's no *story* that way.' I paused and pushed my glasses up my nose, which makes people focus on my eyes, which are dark brown and, frankly, fabulous. 'I could understand if she was throwing all her boyfriend's crap out the window, because he cheated on her or something. That's more or less nonweird: people do that on TV. But you wouldn't throw your own stuff out like that, would you?'

'Maybe. Maybe not.' He thought about it for a few seconds, frowning at someone laughing as she walked past, hands full of CDs in spiderweb-cracked cases. I thought he was about to tell me we should give back the guitar, but instead he said, 'Girls have girlfriends too, you know. And roommates who don't pay the rent.'

'Hmm,' I said. I'd sort of thought the guy was thick, because he'd taken forever to understand my brilliant guitar-saving plan (the way firefighters used to save jumpers). But this answer demonstrated lateral thinking.

Cute *and* lateral. And he knew a Strat when he saw one.

'Maybe a girlfriend,' I admitted. 'But your roommate's stuff?' I'd never really had a roommate except my mom, which doesn't count. 'Wouldn't you sell their crap on eBay?'

He laughed, dark eyes sparkling in the shadows. Then he got

all serious again. 'Probably. But you're right: I think it was hers. She was throwing her whole life away.'

'But why?' I asked softly.

'I don't know, but right before she threw the Strat out she was holding it the right way. The way you really hold a guitar.' He put his hands in air-guitar position, his left fingers playing delicate scales along an imaginary neck.

'Not like some model in a video,' I murmured. 'That drives me crazy.'

'Yeah.' He paused, then shrugged. 'So it was her guitar. And she looked sad up there, not angry. Like someone losing everything she had.'

Whoa. This guy was totally lateral, like he knew something he wasn't saying. 'Wait. You're just guessing, right?'

'Yeah.' He opened his hands and looked down at his palms. 'Just looked that way to me.'

'Well, then . . .' I put my hand on the plaid bundle between us. 'If she *wanted* to throw it out, it's not like we stole it.'

He stared at me.

'What?' I said. 'You want to take it back and toss it on the pile?'

He shook his head. 'No. Someone else would take it. And they'd carry it around unprotected, pretend they were playing it.' He shuddered.

'Exactly!' I smiled. 'What's your name anyway?'

'Moz.'

I must have made an uncomprehending expression.

'Short for "Mosquito,"' the guy said.

'Oh, of course.' He *was* kind of small, like I am. Have you ever noticed that small people are cuter? Like dolls. 'My name's Pearl. Not short for anything, despite its shortness.'

Moz pulled his serious face. 'So, Pearl, don't you think she might want her guitar back after she . . .' His voice drifted off.

'Comes back from wherever they lock her up?'

He nodded, and I wondered if he knew I didn't mean the generic 'they' who lock crazy people up, but the two angels we'd seen on the fire escape. Did he understand what was happening to the world? Most people seemed to know even less than I did – all they saw were the garbage piling up and the extra rats, didn't even notice the rumbling underfoot. But this guy talked like he could sense things, at least.

'We could find out who she is,' he said. 'Maybe ask someone in her building'

'And hang on to it for her?'

'Yeah. I mean, if it was just some crappy guitar it wouldn't matter, but this . . .' His eyes got sparkly again, like the thought of a homeless Strat was going to make him cry.

And right then I had my brain-flash: the realization that had been screaming for my attention since I'd seen Moz running to catch the Stratocaster bare-handed. Maybe this was the guy I needed, a guy with raw heart, ready to throw himself under a falling Fender because it was vintage and irreplaceable.

Maybe Moz was what I'd been waiting for since Nervous System had exploded.

'Okay,' I said. 'We'll keep it for her. But at my place.' I put my arm around the bundle.

'*Your* place?'

'Sure. After all, why should I trust you? You might go and pawn it. Three or four thousand dollars for you, when it was my idea to use the bedspread.'

'But *I'm* the one who wants to give it back,' he sputtered cutely. 'A second ago you were all, "It's not stealing."'

'Maybe that's what you *want* me to think.' I pushed my glasses up my nose. 'Maybe that was just a cover for your devious plans.' It hurt to see his wounded expression, because I was being totally unfair. Moz might have been lateral, but I could already tell that he was nine kinds of nondevious.

'But . . . you were just . . .' He made a strangled noise.

I hugged the Strat closer. 'Of course, you could come over and play it anytime. We could play together. Are you in a band?'

'Yeah.' His wary eyes didn't leave the bedspread. 'Half a band anyway.'

'Half a band?' I smiled, knowing now that my brain-flash had been right on target. 'A band in need of completion? Maybe this is fate.'

He shook his head. 'We've already got two guitarists.'

'What else?'

'Um, just two guitarists.'

I laughed. 'Listen, a drummer and a bass player is half a band. Two guitarists is just a . . .' He frowned, so I didn't finish.' Anyway, I play keyboards.'

'You do?' He shook his head. 'So how do you know so much about guitars? I mean, you called the year on that Strat when it was still in the air!'

'Lucky guess.' And, of course, I *do* play guitar. And keyboards too, and flute and xylophone and a wicked-mean harmonica – there's practically nothing I don't play. But I figured out a while back not to say that out loud; everyone thinks we nonspecialists are amateurs. (Tell that to the nonspecialist currently known as Prince.) I also never show off my perfect pitch or mention the name of my high school.

His dark and gorgeous eyes narrowed. 'Are you sure you don't play guitar?'

I laughed. 'I never said that. But trust me, I absolutely play keyboards. How's tomorrow?'

'But, um, how do you even know we'd . . .' He took a breath. 'I mean, like, what are your— ?'

'Uh!' I interrupted. 'Not that word!' If he asked me what my *influences* were, the whole thing was off.

He shrugged. 'You know what I mean.'

I sighed through clenched teeth. How was I supposed to explain that I was in too much of a hurry to give a damn? That there were more important things to worry about? That the world didn't have time for labels anymore?

'Look, let's say you hated graves, okay?'

'Hated graves?'

'Yeah, detested tombs. Loathed sepulchers. Abhorred any-place anyone was buried. Understand?'

'Why would I do that?'

I let out a groan. Mozzy was being very nonlateral all of a sudden. 'Hypothetically hated graves.'

'Um, okay. I hate graves.' He put on a grave-hating face.

'Excellent. Perfect. But you'd still go to the Taj Mahal, wouldn't you?' I spread my hands in explanatory triumph.

'Um, I'd go where?'

'The Taj Mahal! The most beautiful building in the world! You know all those Indian restaurants around the corner, the murals on the walls?'

He nodded slowly. 'Yeah, I know the one you mean: lots of arches, a pond out front, with kind of an onion on top?'

'Exactly. And gorgeous.'

'I guess. And somebody's buried there?'

'Yeah, Moz, some old queen. It's a total tomb. But you don't suddenly think it's ugly, just because of its *category,* do you?'

His expression changed from tomb-hating to lateral-thinking. 'So, in other words . . .' Brief pause. 'You don't mind if you're in a band that plays alternative death-metal cypherfunk, as long as it's the Taj Mahal of alternative death-metal cypherfunk. Right?'

'Exactly!' I cried. 'You guys can worry about the category. All the death-metal you want. Just be *good* at it.' I picked up the Stratocaster, wrapped it tighter. 'How's tomorrow? Two o'clock.'

He shrugged. 'Okay, I guess. Let's give it a shot. Maybe keyboards are what we need.'

Or maybe I *am*, I thought, but out loud I just told him my buzzer number, pointing across the street. 'Oh, and two more questions, Moz.'

'Sure?'

'One: do you guys really play death-metal cypherfunk?'

He smiled. 'Don't worry. That was hypothetical death-metal cypherfunk.'

'Phew,' I said, trying not to notice how that little smile had made him even cuter. Now that we were going to jam together, it didn't pay to notice things like that. 'Question two: does your half a band have a name?'

He shook his head. 'Nope.'

'No problem,' I said. 'That'll be the easy part.'

3. POISONBLACK

The next day, Zahler and I saw our first black water.

We'd just met outside my building, on our way to Pearl's. A gang of kids across the street was gathered around a fire hydrant, prying at it with a two-foot wrench, hoping to get some relief from the early afternoon heat. Zahler stopped to watch, like he always did when kids were doing anything more or less illegal.

'Check it out!' He grinned, pointing at a convertible coming down the street. If the hydrant erupted in the next ten seconds, the unwitting driver was going to get soaked.

'Watch your guitar,' I said. We were twenty feet away, but you never knew how much pressure was lurking in a hydrant on a hot summer day.

'It's protected, Moz,' he said, but he stood the instrument case upright behind himself. I felt empty-handed, headed to a jam session with nothing but a few guitar picks in my pocket. My fingers were itching to play their first notes on the Strat.

We were sort of late, but the car was a BMW, its driver in a suit and tie and talking on his cell phone. Back when Zahler and I had been little, soaking a guy like that would have been worth about ten thousand fire-hydrant points. We could spare ten seconds.

But the kids were still fiddling as the convertible passed.

'Incompetent little twerps.' Zahler sighed. 'Should we give them a hand?'

'It's already after two.' I turned and headed up the street.

But as I walked I heard the cries behind us change from squeals of excitement to shrieks of fear.

We spun around. The hydrant was spraying black water in all directions, covering the kids with a sticky, shimmering coat. A thick, dark mist rose into the air, breaking the sunlight into a gleaming spectrum, like a rainbow on an oil slick. The screaming kids were stumbling back, bare skin glistening with the stuff. A couple of the little ones just stood in the torrent, crying.

'What the hell?' Zahler whispered.

I took a step forward, but the smell – earthy and fetid and rotten – forced me to a halt. The dark cloud was still rising up between the buildings, roiling like smoke overhead, and the wind was shifting toward us. Tiny black dots began to spatter the street, closer and closer, like a sudden summer rain starting up. Zahler and I backed away, staring down at the pavement. The drops were as luminous as tiny black pearls.

The hydrant seemed to cough once, the gush of black water sputtering, and then the water turned clear. Above us, the cloud was already dissolving, turning into nothing more than a shadowy haze across the sky.

I knelt on the sidewalk, peering down at one of the black drops. It glimmered unsteadily for a moment, reflecting sunlight as the shadow from the cloud overhead faded. And then it boiled away before my eyes.

'What the hell *was* that, Moz?'

'I don't know. Maybe somebody's heating oil leaked into the pipes?' I shook my head.

The kids were staring at the hydrant warily, half afraid the water would turn black again, but also eager to wash themselves. A few stepped forward, and the oily stuff seemed to slide from their skin, dark stains disappearing from their soaked shorts and T-shirts.

A minute later they were all playing in the spray, like nothing weird had happened.

'Didn't look like any oil I've ever seen,' Zahler said.

'Yeah. Probably just old water in the hydrant,' I said, not wanting to think about it. It had disappeared so quickly, I could almost imagine it hadn't happened at all. 'Or something like that. Come on, we're late.'

Pearl's room looked like a recording studio had mated with a junkyard, then exploded.

The walls were lined with egg cartons, the big twelve-by-twelve ones that you see stacked outside restaurants. Sinuous hills rose between the egg-shaped valleys, curving like the sound waves they gobbled.

'Whoa, you've got a ton of gear!' Zahler exclaimed. His voice was echoless, rebounding from the walls with less bounce than a dead cat.

I'd always told Zahler that we could soundproof his room this way so that his parents would stop yelling at us to turn it down. But we'd never had enough motivation to make it happen. Or enough egg cartons.

The floor was covered with spare cables, effects boxes, all the usual fire hazards – we stepped lightly over the spaghetti-junctions of power strips, dozens of adapters squeezed into them, all labeled to show what was plugged in where. Two racks of electronics towered at one end of the room, the cables gathered with twist-ties. The modules were organized neatly into tribes: black and buttonless digital units; flickering arpeggiators; a few dinosaur synths with analog dials and needles, like old science-fiction movie props ready for takeoff.

Zahler was looking around nervously, probably wondering if his cheap little electric was going to get squashed under all that gear. I was wondering why Pearl, if she owned all this keyboard stuff, had risked falling toaster ovens just to save a vintage guitar.

'Where do you *sleep*?' Zahler asked. The bed was covered with scattered CDs, more cables, and a few harmonicas and hand drums.

'The guest room, mostly,' Pearl said proudly. 'I suffer for my art.'

Zahler laughed but rolled me a look. Pearl wasn't exactly suffering. She hadn't showed us all of her mom's apartment, but what we'd seen was already bigger than his parents' and mine put together, the walls crowded with paintings and glass cases full of stuff from all over the world. Stairs led to more floors above, and we'd passed a pair of armed security guards down in the lobby. Pearl had probably seen the Taj Mahal in person.

So why had she contemplated helping herself to the Strat, when she could obviously afford to buy one of her own?

Maybe she was used to everything falling from the sky. She'd looked pretty annoyed when we weren't on time, like this was a job interview or something.

I sifted through the CDs on the bed, trying to peg her influences. What was Pearl really into, besides old Indian tombs, punctuality, and soundproofing? The discs left me clueless. They were hand-labeled with the names of bands I'd never heard of: Zombie Phoenix, Morgan's Army, Nervous System . . .

'Nervous System?' I asked.

Pearl groaned. 'That's this band I was in. Bunch of Juilliard geeks and, um, me.'

I glanced at Zahler: great. Not only did Pearl have lots of real gear, she also knew some real musicians, which meant she might not be too impressed with us. We weren't exactly into virtuosity – we hadn't taken any lessons since sixth grade. This jam session was going to be a bust.

'Did you guys play any gigs?' Zahler asked.

She shrugged. 'We did, at their high school, mostly. But the System had no heart. Or it did, I guess, but then the heart exploded. You guys want to plug in?'

The Stratocaster soothed my nerves.

It swung from my shoulder, featherlight, lacquered back side cool against my thigh. The strings were six strands of spiderweb, with the easiest action my fingers had ever felt. I strummed a quick, unplugged E-major chord and was amazed to hear that even a three-story fall hadn't knocked the Strat out of tune.

Pearl pushed in the power button on a Marshall amp, a hulking old beast with tubes inside. (Why did a keyboardist have a guitar amp handy? Had it also fallen from the sky?) The tubes warmed up slowly, the hiss fading in like a wave breaking.

'You guys have to share this amp,' Pearl apologized. 'Nonoptimal, I know.'

Zahler shrugged. 'That's fool.'

She raised an eyebrow. Zahler says *fool* instead of *cool,* which is kind of confusing. But at least he didn't mention that I'd never owned an amp, so we shared one over at his place too.

Pearl tossed us cords, and I plugged in – a sizzle-snap of connection, then the familiar hum of six open strings. I dampened five of them and plucked a low E. Zahler tuned up to it, booming through his strings one by one, setting off a little plastic chorus of CD cases shivering against one another on the bed.

The Marshall was set to 7, a volume we never dared in Zahler's room, and I hoped Pearl's egg cartons worked. Otherwise, her neighbors were going to feel us in their bones. But I was ready to risk someone calling the police. The Strat was squeaking impatiently as I slid my fingers along its neck, like it was ready too.

Finally Zahler nodded, and Pearl rubbed her hands together, sitting down at the little desk jammed between the two racks of electronics. A computer waited there, cabled to a musical key-board, the kind with elegant black and white keys instead of the usual jumble of letters, numbers, and symbol-junk.

She rested one hand on the keys, the other on a mouse. At her double-click, dozens of lights on the towers flickered to life. 'Play something.'

My fingers were suddenly nervous. It was important to get these notes right, to make a solid first impression on this accidental guitar. Pearl thought that 'fate' had brought us together, but that was the wrong word for it. Fate hadn't made that woman go insane. People had been edgy this whole weird summer, what with the crime wave, the rat wave, and the crazy-making heat. That was bigger than Pearl and Zahler and me.

This guitar wasn't destiny. It was just another symptom of whatever bizarre illness New York City was coming down with, something strange and unexpected like that spout of black water on the way over.

For a moment the Strat felt awkward in my hands.

But then Zahler said, 'Big Riff?'

I smiled. The Big Riff went back a long time, as long as we'd been playing. It was simple and gutsy, and we didn't bother prac-ticing it too much anymore. But the Strat was going to make it new all over again, like playing baseball with bottle rockets.

Zahler started up. His part of the Big Riff is low and growly, his strings muffled with the flesh of his right hand, like something trying to sizzle up out of a boiling pot.

I took a slow, deep breath . . . then jumped in. My part's faster than his, fingers roaming in the high notes halfway up the neck. My part skitters while his churns, blowing sparks from his embers. Mine darts and mutates, keeps changing, while Zahler's stays level and even and thick, filling in all the gaps.

The Strat loved the Big Riff, sliced straight into it. Its spiderweb strings tempted my fingers faster and higher, weightless against Zahler's firmament. If the Big Riff was an army, he was the infantry, the grunts on the ground, and the Strat had turned me into orbital ninjas dropping from the sky, black pajamas under their space suits.

Pearl sat there listening, fingers flexing, mouse twitching, eyes closed. She looked ready to pounce, waiting restlessly for an opening.

We kept going for ten minutes, maybe twenty – it's hard to tell time when you're playing the Big Riff – but she never jumped in . . .

Finally Zahler gave a little shrug and let the Riff peter out. I followed him down, wrapping up with one last plunge from orbit, the Strat skittering into reluctant silence.

'So, what's the matter?' he asked. 'You don't like it?'

Pearl sat silently for another few seconds, thinking hard.

'No, it's excellent. Exactly what I wanted.' Her fingers stroked the keys absently. 'But, um, it's kind of . . . *big.*'

'Yeah,' Zahler said. 'We call it the Big Riff. Pretty fool, huh?'

'No doubt. But, uh, let me ask you something. How long have you guys been playing together?'

Zahler looked at me.

'Six years,' I said. Since we were eleven, playing our nylon-string loaners from school. We'd electrified them with the mikes from his older sister's karaoke machine.

Pearl frowned. 'And all that time, it's been just the two of you?'

'Um, yeah?' I admitted. Zahler was looking at me kind of embarrassed, maybe thinking, *Don't tell her about the karaoke machine.*

She nodded. 'No wonder.'

'No wonder what?' I said.

'There's no room left over.'

'There's no *what*?'

Pearl pushed her glasses up her nose. 'It's totally full up. Like a pizza with cheese, onions, pepperoni, chilies, sausage, M&M's, and bacon bits. What am I supposed to do, add the guacamole?'

Zahler made a face. 'You mean it sucks.'

'No. It's big and raw . . .' She let out a hiss through her teeth, nodding slowly. 'You guys made a whole band out of two guitars, which is very lateral. But if you're going to have a *real* band – like, one with more than two people in it – you're going to have to strip your sound way down. We have to poke some holes in the Big Riff.'

Zahler glanced at me, eyes narrowed, and I realized that if I decided to blow this off right now, he would march out of there with me. And I almost did, because the Big Riff was *sacred*, part of our friendship from the beginning, and Pearl was talking about tearing it up just to make room for her towers of electronic overkill.

I glared up at all those winking lights, wondering how she was supposed to squeeze that much gear into anyone else's sound without squishing it.

'Plus, it's not really a song,' she added. 'More like a guitar solo that doesn't go anywhere.'

'Whoa . . .'I breathed. 'Like a *what*?'

'A guitar solo that doesn't go anywhere,' Zahler repeated, nodding. I stared at him.

'I mean, you guys want to do *songs*, right?' Pearl continued. 'With verses and choruses and stuff? Don't you think the Big Riff could use a B section?'

'Fool idea,' Zahler said. Then he scratched his head. 'What's a B section?'

-ZAHLER-

The new girl was intense. And kind of hot.

She could pull a tune apart like it was *nothing*. Not like Moz, who always talked in circles. Pearl could just hum what she meant, fingers waving little patterns, like she was *seeing* air-notes at the same time. I watched carefully, wishing my fingers could do that.

She was one of those girls who looked better in glasses – all smart and stuff.

The way she stripped down the Big Riff was totally fawesome. Like I knew would happen, she didn't touch my part. My part is basic, the foundation of the Riff. But Moz's jamming could get kind of random, like she'd said about pizza. You know when they have the sundae bar at school where you make your own sundae? I always add toppings until the ice cream disappears, and it winds up kind of disgusting. Give him enough room, and Moz's playing can get like that.

Don't get me wrong – the Mosquito's a genius, a way better player than me, and there was some pretty fool stuff in his Big Riff zigzags. But it took Pearl to pick out his best threads and weave them back together in a way that made sense.

She explained that a B section was a completely different part of a song, like when the chorus has a different riff, or everything slows down or changes key. Me and Moz didn't do that too much, because I'm happy playing the same four chords all day long and he's happy buzzing around on top of them.

But when you think about it, most songs do have B sections, and we sort of hadn't noticed that ours almost never did. So the moral of the story is, you shouldn't be in a band with just two people for six years. Kind of saps your perspective.

Moz was all buzzy at first, like the Big Riff was his pet frog that Pearl was dissecting. He kept looking at me and making faces, but I eyeballed him into submission. Once he saw that I thought Pearl was okay, he sort of had to listen to her. It hadn't been my idea to drag my ax all the way down here, after all.

In the end, Moz was no idiot, and only an idiot would mind listening to a smart, hot girl telling him something that's for his own good. And for the good of the band, which is what the three of us were already turning into.

It was fawesome to watch. All the years Moz and I had been jamming, it was about adding *more* to the riffs. So it felt great to see stuff getting erased, to sweep away all the mosquito-droppings and get back to the foundation.

Which, like I said before, is where I'm happiest.

Once the Big Riff was cleaned up, Pearl started playing. I'd figured she was going to blow us away with some kind of thousand-note-a-minute alternafunk jazz, because she'd been in that Juilliard band. But everything she played was sweet and simple. She spent most of her time poking around with her mouse, diluting the tones flowing from her synthesizers until they were thin enough to sneak through the folds of the Big Riff.

In the end, I realized that Pearl was playing some of the lines she'd erased from Moz's part. Even though she'd simplified them, the whole thing wound up bigger, like an actual band instead of two guitarists trying to sound like one.

And then came the moment when the whole thing finally clicked, totally paranormal, falling into place like an explosion played backwards.

I yelled, 'You know, we should record this!'

Moz nodded, but Pearl just laughed. 'Guys, I've been recording the whole time.' She pointed at the computer screen.

'Really?' Moz skidded us to a halt. 'You didn't say anything about that.'

I eyeballed him to calm down. The Mosquito is always afraid that someone's going to steal our riffs.

Pearl just shrugged. 'Sometimes people choke when you press the red button. So I just keep my hard disk spinning. Here, listen.'

She fiddled with her mouse, popping in and out of the last two hours, little snatches of us, like we'd already been turned into cell-phone ringtones. In a few seconds, she pinned down the one-minute stretch where the New Big Riff had somehow flipped inside out and become perfect.

We all sat there, listening. Moz's and my mouths were open. We'd finally nailed it. After six years . . .

'Still needs a B section,' Pearl said. 'And drums. We should get a drummer.'

'And a bass player,' I said.

She looked at me. 'Maybe.'

'Maybe?' Moz said. 'What kind of band doesn't have a bass?'

She shrugged. 'What kind of band has only two guitarists? One thing at a time. You guys know any drummers?'

Moz shrugged.

'Yeah, they're hard to find,' Pearl said, shaking her head. 'The System had a couple of *percussionists* but no real drummer.

That's part of why we sucked. But I know a few from school.'
She shrugged.

'I know this girl,' I said. 'She's great.'

Moz looked at me, all buzzy again. 'You do? You never told me about any drummer.'

'You never told me we were looking for one.' I shrugged. 'Besides, I don't really know her, just seen her play. She's fawesome.'

'Probably not available, then,' Pearl said, shaking her head. 'There's never enough drummers to go around.'

'Um, I think she might be available,' I said. What I didn't mention was that she didn't exactly have real drums and that I'd never seen her playing with a band, only in Times Square, asking for spare change. Or that she might also be sort of homeless, as far as I could tell. Unless she *really* liked playing in Times Square and wearing the same army jacket and pair of jeans every day.

Totally fool drummer, though.

'Talk to her,' Pearl said. She shot a mean look at the egg-carton-covered door to her room. 'Listen, I think my mom's home, so maybe we should quit. But next time, we'll write a B section for the Big Riff. Maybe some words. Either of you guys sing?'

We looked at each other. Moz can sing, but he wouldn't admit to it out loud. And he's too genius a guitarist to waste in front of a mike.

'Well,' Pearl said. 'I know this really lateral singer who's free right now, sort of. And in the meantime, you can talk to your drummer.'

I smiled, nodding. I liked how in a hurry this girl was, how she was motivating us. And she looked pretty hot doing it, all focused and in charge. Six years of jamming, and all of a sudden it felt like a real band was falling into place. I was looking at the posters on Pearl's wall, already thinking of album covers.

'Drums? In here?' Moz said.

My gaze swept across all the amps, cables, and synths. There was about enough room for us, all this crap, and *maybe* someone playing bongos. No way could a whole drum kit fit in here, even if they weren't exactly drums. And with egg cartons jammed into the windows, the place was already reeking of rehearsal sweat. I could imagine what a hardworking drummer would do to that equation.

That was another reason I'd never bothered to mention her to Moz before. Drummers are way too big and loud for bedrooms.

'I know a place where we can practice,' Pearl said. 'It's pretty cheap.'

Moz and I looked at each other. We'd never paid to rehearse before. But Pearl didn't notice. I guessed she'd shelled out money to rehearse in lots of places. I just hoped she was paying for this one too. I had some money from my dog-walking gig, but Moz was the tightest guy I'd ever met.

'The other thing is, before we start adding a bunch more people, we need to figure out a name for the band,' Pearl said. 'And it has to be the right name. Otherwise, it'll keep changing every time someone new jams with us.' She shook her head. 'And we'll never figure out who we are.'

'Maybe we should call ourselves the B-Sections,' I said. 'That would be fawesome.'

Pearl looked at me, kind of squinting. 'Fawesome? Do you keep saying *fawesome*?'

'Yeah.' I grinned at Moz. He rolled his eyes.

She thought about it for a minute, then smiled and said, 'Fexcellent.'

I laughed out loud. This chick was totally fool.

5. GARBAGE

–PEARL–

'One of those boys was rather fetching.'

'Yeah, I noticed that, Mom. Thanks for pointing it out, though, in case I missed it.'

'A bit scruffy, though. And that dirge you were playing was making the china rattle all afternoon.'

'It wasn't *all* afternoon.' I sighed, staring out the window of the limo. 'Maybe two hours.'

Getting a ride with Mom was nine kinds of annoying. But deepest Brooklyn was such a pain by subway, and I had to see Minerva right away. Her esoterica kept saying that hearing good news helped the healing process. And my news was better than good.

'Besides, Mom, "that dirge" is totally fexcellent.'

'It's feculent?' She made a quiet scoffing sound. 'Don't you know that feculent means *foul*?'

I giggled, reminding myself to tell Zahler that one. Maybe we could call ourselves the Feculents. But that sounded sort of British, and we didn't.

We sounded like the kind of band that rattled the china. The Rattlers? Too country and western. China Rattlers? Too lateral, even for me. The Good China? Nah. People would think we were from Taiwan.

'Will they be coming over again?' my mother asked in a small voice.

'Yes. They will.' I played with my window buttons, filling the limo's backseat with little bursts of summer heat.

She sighed. 'I'd hoped that we were past all this band practice.'

I let out a groan. '*Band practice* is what marching bands do, Mom. But don't worry. We'll be moving our gear to Sixteenth Street in a week or so. Your china will soon be safe.'

'Oh. That place.'

I peered at her, pushing my glasses up my nose. 'Yes, full of musicians. How awful.'

'They look more like drug addicts.' She shivered a little, which made her icicles tinkle. Mom was all blinged out for some fundraiser at the Brooklyn Museum, wearing cocktail black and too much makeup. Her being dressed up like that always creeps me out, like we're headed to a funeral.

Of course, I was creeped out anyway – we were in Minerva's neighborhood now. Big brooding brownstones slid past outside, all tricked out like haunted houses, turrets and iron railings and tiny windows way up high. My stomach started to flutter, and I suddenly wished it was both of us going to some dress-up party, everyone drinking champagne and being clueless, and next year's budget for the Egyptian Wing the big topic of consternation. Or, at worst, talking about the sanitation crisis, instead of staring out the window at it.

Mom detected my flutters – which she's pretty good at – and took my hand. 'How's Minerva doing, poor thing?'

I shrugged, glad now that I'd scrounged a ride. Mom's minor annoyances had distracted me almost the whole way. Waiting for the subway, staring down at the rats on the tracks, would've totally reminded me of where I was going.

'Better. She says.'

'What do the doctors say?'

I didn't even shrug. I wasn't allowed to tell Mom that there were no doctors anymore, just an esoterica. We stayed silent until the limo pulled up outside Minerva's house. Night was falling by then, lights going on. The brownstone's darkened windows made the block look like it was missing a tooth.

The street looked different, as if the last two months had sapped something from it. Garbage was piled high on the streets, the sanitation crisis much more obvious out here in Brooklyn, but I didn't see any rats scuttling around. There seemed to be a lot of stray cats, though.

'This used to be such a nice neighborhood,' Mom said. 'Do you need Elvis to collect you?'

'No. That's okay.'

'Well, call him if you change your mind,' Mom said as the door opened. 'And don't take the train too late.'

I slipped out past Elvis, annoyance rising in me again. Mom knew I hated the subway late at night, and that Minerva's company didn't exactly make me want to dally.

Elvis and I traded our funny little salute, which we've been doing since I was nine, and we both smiled. But then he glanced up at the house, lines creasing his forehead. Something skittered in the garbage bags by our feet – stray cats or not, rats were in residence.

'Are you sure you won't be wanting a ride home, Pearl?' he rumbled softly.

'Positive. Thanks, though.'

Mom likes all conversations to include her, so she scooted closer across the limo's backseat. 'What time did you get in last night anyway?'

'Right after eleven.'

She pursed her lips the slightest discernible amount, showing she knew I was lying, and I gave her the tiniest possible eye-roll to show I didn't care.

'Well, see you *at* eleven tonight, then.'

I snorted a little for Elvis. The only way Mom was coming home before midnight was if they ran out of champagne at the museum, or if the mummies all got loose.

I imagined old-movie mummies in tattered bandages. Nice and nonscary.

Then her voice softened. 'Give my love to Minerva.'

'Okay,' I said, waving and turning away, flinching as the door boomed shut behind me. 'I'll try.'

Luz de la Sueño opened the door and waved me in quick, like she was worried about flies zipping in behind. Or maybe she didn't want the neighbors to see her new decorations, seeing as how Halloween was more than two months away.

My nostrils wrinkled at the smell of garlic tea brewing, not to mention the other scents coming from the kitchen, overpowering and unidentifiable. These days, New York seemed to disappear behind me when I came through Minerva's door, as if the brownstone had one foot in some other city, somewhere ancient and crumbling, overgrown.

'She is much better,' Luz said, ushering me toward the stairs. 'And excited you are visiting.'

'That's great,' I said, but I hesitated for a moment in the foyer. Luz's take on Minerva's illness had always been a bit too mystical for me, but after what I'd witnessed the night before, I figured the esoterica was at least a little noncrazy.

'Luz, can I ask you a question? About something I saw?'

'You saw something? Outside?' Her eyes widened, drifting to the shaded windows.

'No, back in Manhattan.'

'*Sí?*' Luz said. The intensity of her gaze was freaking me out as usual.

I usually understand where people fit, organizing them in my head, like arranging Mom's good china in its case. But I was totally clueless about Luz – where she came from, how old she was, whether she'd grown up rich or poor. Her English wasn't fluent, but her accent was careful, her grammar exact. Her unlined face looked young, but she wore these old-lady dresses, sometimes hats with veils. Her hands were calloused and full of wiry strength, and three fat skull rings grinned at me from her big-knuckled fingers.

Luz was all about skulls, but they didn't seem to mean to her what they meant to me and my friends. She was more gospel than goth.

'There was this woman,' I said. 'Around the corner from us. She went crazy, throwing all this stuff out the window.'

'*Sí.*' Luz nodded. 'That is the sickness. It is spreading now. You are still careful, yes?'

'Yep. No boys for me.' I put my hands up. Luz believed everything was because of too much sex – part of her religious thing. 'But it looked like her own stuff. Not like when Minerva broke up with Mark, hating everything he'd given her.'

'Yes, but it is the same. The sickness, it makes the infected not want to be what they were before. They must throw away everything to make the change.' She crossed herself – *the change* was what she was trying to prevent in Minerva.

'But Min didn't trash all her stuff, did she?'

'Not so much.' Luz fingered the cross around her neck. 'She is very spiritual, not joined to things. But to people, and to *la musica.*'

'Oh.' That made a kind of sense. When Minerva had cracked up, she'd thrown away Mark and the rest of Nervous System first. And then her classes and all our friends, one by one. I'd stuck with her the longest, until everyone hated me for staying friends with her, and then she'd finally tossed me too.

That meant Moz had been right: the crazy woman had been getting rid of her own stuff, throwing her whole life out the window. I wondered how he'd known.

I thought about the mirrors upstairs, all covered with velvet. Min didn't want to see her own face, to hear her own name – suddenly it all made sense.

Luz touched my shoulder. 'That is why it is good you are here. I think maybe now, Pearl, you can do more than I.'

I felt the music player in my pocket, loaded up with Big Riff. I couldn't do anything myself – I wasn't some kind of skull-wielding esoterica – but maybe this fexcellent music . . .

Luz started up the stairs, waving for me to follow.

'One more thing: I think I saw angels.'

She stopped and turned, crossing herself again. '*Angeles de la lucha?* They were fast? On the rooftops?'

I nodded. 'Like you told me to watch for around here.'

'And they took this woman?'

I shrugged. 'I don't know. I got the hell out of there.'

'Good.' She reached out and stroked my face, her fingers rough and smelling of herbs. 'It is not for you, the struggle that is coming.'

'So where do the angels take you?' I whispered.

Luz closed her eyes. 'To somewhere far away.'

'What, like heaven?'

She shook her head. 'No. On an airplane. To a place where they make the change firm in you. So you can fight for them in the struggle.' She took my hand. 'But that is not for you – not for Minerva. Come.'

The rest of the way up, there were lots of new decorations to check out. The stairway walls were covered with wooden crosses, a thousand little stamped-metal figures nailed into each one. The figures were nonweird shapes – shoes, dresses, trees, dogs, musical instruments – but the wild jumble of them made me wonder if someone had put normality into a blender, then set it on disintegrate.

And of course there were the skulls. Their painted black eyes stared down at us from the shadows, every floor a little darker as we climbed. The windows up here were blacked out, the mirrors draped with red velvet. Street noises faded as we climbed, the air growing as still as a sunken ship.

Outside Minerva's room, Luz bent to pick up a towel from the floor, sighing apologetically. 'It is only me tonight. The family are more tired every day.'

'Anything I can do to help?' I whispered.

Luz smiled. 'You are here. That is help.'

She pulled a few leaves from her pocket, crushing them together in her hands. They smelled like fresh-cut grass, or mint. She knelt and rubbed her palms on my sneakers and the legs of my jeans.

I'd always kind of rolled my eyes at her spells before, but tonight I felt in need of protection.

'Maybe you will sing to her.'

I swallowed, wondering if Luz had somehow divined what I'd been planning. 'Sing? But you always said—'

'*Sí.*' Her eyes sparked in the darkness. 'But she is better now. However, to keep you safe . . .'

She pressed a familiar little doll into my hands, stroking its tattered red yarn hair into place. It stared up at me, smiling maniacally, one button eye dangling from two black threads, setting my stomach fluttering again.

The doll was the creepiest of Luz's rituals of protection. But suddenly it made sense. It had always been Min's favorite back when we were little, the only object she'd ever really been attached to, besides the ring she'd thrown at Mark in front of the whole System. I was glad to have the doll tonight, even if Minerva hadn't been violent since her family had given up on drugs and doctors and had switched to Luz.

I wondered how they'd found her. Were esotericas listed in the phone book? Was Esoterica a cool band name, or too lateral? Was the Big Riff in my pocket really a kind of magic—

'Don't be afraid,' Luz whispered. Then she opened the door with one strong hand, the other pushing me into the darkness. 'Go and sing.'

–MINERVA–

Pearl was glowing. Her face shimmered as the door swung closed, setting the candle flickering jaggedly.

'You're shiny,' I murmured, squinting.

She swallowed, licking her upper lip. I could smell her nervous saltiness.

'It's hot out.'

'It's summer, right?'

'Yeah, middle of August.' Pearl frowned, even though I'd been right.

I closed my eyes, remembering April, May . . . all the way up to graduation. Pearl was jealous because she had to go back to Juilliard next year, though everyone else in the Nerv—

The thing inside me flinched.

Zombie made a grumpy noise and rolled over on my belly. His big green eyes opened slowly, surveying Pearl.

'I have good news,' she said softly. When I first got sick, I hated the sound of her voice, but not anymore. I was getting better – I didn't hate Pearl, or anyone human. All I hated now was the Vile Thing she brought every time she visited. It hung from her hands, one eyeball dangling, leering at me.

I tried to smile, but the lenses of Pearl's glasses caught

the candlelight, bright as a camera flash, and I had to turn away.

She raised her voice a little. 'You okay?'

'Sure. It's just a little bright today.' Sometimes I blew out the candle, but that made Luz cross. She said I'd have to get used to it if I was ever going to leave this room again.

But my room was nice. It smelled like Zombie and me and the thing inside us.

'So I met these guys,' Pearl said, talking fast now, forgetting to whisper. 'They've been playing together for a while. They're nine kinds of raw, not like Nervous—'

I must have flinched again, because Pearl went quiet. Zombie *mur-row*ed and dropped heavily to the floor. He started toward her, winding his way through my old toys and clothes and sheet music, all the objects on the floor that crept closer every night while I slept.

'We weren't so bad,' I managed to say.

'Yeah, but these guys are fawesome.' She paused, smiling at herself. Pearl always liked silly, made-up words. 'They're sort of New Sound, like Morgan's Army, but more raw. Like when we started, before you-know-who messed up your head. But without six composers trying to write one song. These two guys are much more . . .'

'Controllable?' I said.

Pearl frowned, and the Vile Thing in her hands glared at me.

'I was going to say *mellow*.'

Zombie had tiptoed up behind Pearl, like he'd been planning to wind through her legs. But he was slinking close to the floor now, sniffing at her shoes suspiciously. He didn't like the smell of anyone but me these days.

'But I was thinking, and maybe this is stupid.' Pearl shifted her weight from one foot to the other. 'If these guys work out, and you keep getting better—'

'I'm already better.'

'That's what Luz says. The three of us aren't ready yet, but maybe by the time we are . . .' Her voice wavered, sounding fragile. 'It would be great if you could sing for us.'

Her words made me close my eyes, something huge moving through my body, half painful, half restless. It took a moment to recognize, because it had been gone for so long.

To twist and turn, spreading out and surrounding people, drowning them – my voice seething, boiling, filling up the air.

I wanted to sing again . . .

A slow sigh deflated me. What if it still hurt, like everything else that wasn't Zombie or darkness? I had to test myself first.

'Could you do something for me, Pearl?'

'Anything.'

'Say my name.'

'Crap, no way. Luz would kick my ass.'

I smelled Pearl's fear in the room and heard Zombie's soft footfalls retreating from her. He jumped up onto the bed, warm and nervous next to me. I opened my eyes, trying not to squint in the candle-brightness.

Pearl was sweating again, pacing like Zombie does because Luz never lets him go outside. 'She said that singing might be okay. But your name? Are you *sure*?'

'I'm not sure, Pearl. That's why you have to.'

She swallowed. 'Okay . . . Min.'

I snorted. 'Shiny, smelly Pearl. Can't even do the whole thing?'

She stared at me for a long moment, then said softly, 'Minerva?'

I shuddered out of habit, but the sickness didn't come. Then she said the name again, and nothing swept through me. Nothing but relief. Even Luz had never managed that.

It felt outlandish and magnificent, as naughty as a cigarette after voice class. I closed my eyes and smiled.

'Are you okay?' she whispered.

'Very. And I want to sing for your band, Pearl. You brought music, didn't you?'

She nodded, smiling back at me. 'Yeah. I mean, I wasn't sure if you . . . But we have this really cool riff.' She reached into her pocket for a little white sliver of plastic, then began to unwind the earphones wrapped around it. 'This is after only one day of practice – well, six years and a day – but there's no chorus or anything yet. You can write your own words.'

'I can do words.' Words were the first thing I'd gotten back. There were notebooks full of scrawl underneath the bed, filled with all my new secrets. New songs about the deep.

Pearl had an adapter in one hand. She was looking around for my stereo.

'I broke it,' I said sadly.

'Your Bang and Olufsen? That's a drag.' She frowned. 'Say, you didn't throw it out the window, did you?'

I giggled. 'No, silly. Down the stairs.' I reached out my hand. 'Come here. We can share.'

She paused for a moment, glancing back at the door.

'Don't worry. Luz went downstairs already.' She was working in the kitchen now, preparing my nighttime botanicas. I could hear the rumble of water through the pipes and smell garlic and mandrake tea being strained. 'She trusts you enough not to listen in.'

'Oh. That's good, I guess.' Pearl put the adapter back in her pocket and took a step closer, the Vile Thing leering at me from her hand.

'But you have to put that *thing* down,' I said, waving one hand.

She paused, and I could smell her start to sweat again.

'Don't you trust me, shiny Pearl?' I squinted up at her. 'You know I would never eat you.'

'Um, yeah.' She swallowed. 'And that's really non-threatening of you, Minerva.'

I smiled again at the sound of my own name, and Pearl smiled back, finally believing how much better I was. She knelt, placing the Vile Thing carefully on the floor, like it might explode.

Taking a deep breath, she began to cross the room with measured steps. Zombie padded away as she grew closer, and I smelled the catnip on Pearl's shoes. That's why he was being so edgy. She smelled like his old toys, which he hated these days.

He went over to sniff the Vile Thing, which suddenly had turned into just some old doll. It looked lifeless and defeated there on the floor, not nearly as vile as it had been.

More relief flowed through me. Just the thought of singing was making me stronger. Even the shiny candlelight didn't seem so jagged.

Pearl sat next to me on the bed, the music player in her hand glowing now. I saw the apple shape on it and flinched a little, remembering that I *had* thrown something out the window – eighty gigs of music that smelly boy had given me.

Pearl reached across, pushing my hair back behind one ear with trembling fingers. I realized how greasy it was, even though Luz made me shower every single Saturday.

'Do I look horrible?' I asked quietly. I hadn't seen myself in . . . two months, if it was August.

'No. You're still beautiful.' She grinned, putting one earphone in her own ear. 'Maybe a little skinny. Doesn't Luz feed you?'

I smiled, thinking of all the raw meat I'd eaten for lunch. Bacon cold and salty, the strips still clinging together, fresh from between plastic. And then the chicken whose neck I'd heard Luz wring in the backyard, its skin still prickly from being plucked, its living blood hot down my throat. And still I was hungry.

As Pearl leaned forward in the Apple glow, I saw the pulse in her throat, and the beast inside me growled.

Mustn't eat Pearl, I reminded myself.

She gave the other earphone to me, and I put it in. We looked into each other's eyes from a few inches away, tethered by the split white cord. It was strange and intense – no one but Luz had dared get this close to me since I'd bitten that stupid doctor.

I could smell coffee on Pearl's breath, the clean sweat of summer heat, the separate scent of fear. Her pupils were huge, and I remembered that to her eyes, my room was dark. My life was spent in shadows now.

There was a hint of moisture between her upper lip and nose, in that little depression the size of a fingertip. I leaned forward, wanting to lick it, to see if it was salty like the bacon had been . . .

Then she squeezed the player, and music spilled into me.

It started abruptly – a rough edit, not even on the downbeat – but the riff was too gutsy to care. One guitar rumbled underneath, simple as a bass part, someone playing with three untutored fingers. Another guitar played up high, full of restless and cluttered energy, seductively neurotic.

Neither was Pearl, I could tell.

Then she entered on keys, spindly and thin but fitting perfectly. She was even leaving room for me, laying low, like she never had back in the System.

That thought made me jealous – little Pearl growing up a bit while I'd been lying here in shadows. Suddenly, I wanted to get up and put on clothes and sunglasses, go out into the world.

Soon, I thought, still listening. The music had me humming, venturing into the spaces Pearl had left open, finding lines to twist and turn. She was right – it was New Sound-ish, like all those indie bands we'd loved last spring. But less frantic, as smooth as water. My whole body wanted to jump into this music.

But when my lips first parted, only random curses spilled out, verses from the earliest, most unreadable scrawl in the notebooks under my bed. Then they sputtered to a halt, like the fading geyser from a shaken beer bottle, and I gradually gained control. I began to murmur a jagged, wordless song across the music.

For a few moments it was beautiful, a savage version of my old self, though with new spells in it. The sound of my own singing made the beast inside me burn, but clever Pearl had cheated it for a few moments: I could only hear myself with one ear. The other was filled with the riff, a dense and splendid protection.

But soon enough the sickness closed my throat, the song choking to a stop. I looked at Pearl, to see if I'd imagined it. Her eyes, inches from mine, glowed like her music player's screen.

Catching my breath, I concentrated on the riff again, listening. She was right: They were way outside the System, this oddball pair of guitarists. They had pulled something out of me, slipped it right past the beast.

'Where did you find them?'

'Sixth Street. Totally random.'

'Hmm. The one who can really play, he sounds . . .' I swallowed .

'Yeah,' Pearl said. 'He's lateral and raw, like I always wanted Nervous System to be. No lessons, or at least not many, and *no* theory classes. He fills up whatever space you give him. Almost out of control, but like you said, controllable. He's the Taj Mahal of random guitarists.'

I smiled. All those things were true, but I hadn't been thinking them.

To me, he sounded more like . . . yummy.

PART II

AUDITIONS

The Plague of Justinian was the first time the Black Death appeared.

Fifteen hundred years ago, the emperor Justinian had just embarked on his greatest work: the rebuilding of the Roman Empire. He wanted to reunite its two halves and place the known world under Roman rule once more.

But as his vast war began, the Black Death came. It swept across the eastern Mediterranean, leaving millions dead in its wake. Thousands died daily in the Byzantine capital of Constantinople, and Justinian was forced to watch his dreams crumble.

Oddly, historians aren't certain what the Black Death was. Bubonic plague? Typhus? Something else? A few historians suggest that it was a random assortment of diseases brought on by one overriding factor: an explosion of the rat population fostered by the Roman army's vast stores of grain .

That's close, but not quite.

Whatever caused it, the Black Death's effects were clear. The Roman Empire slipped into history at last. Much of the mathematics, literature, and science of the ancients was lost. A dark age descended on Europe.

Or, as we said back then, 'Humanity lost that round.'

NIGHT MAYOR TAPES:
142-146

–ZAHLER–

My dogs were acting paranormal that day, all edgy and anxious.

The first bunch seemed fine when I picked them up. In the air-conditioned lobby of their fancy Hell's Kitchen building, they were full of energy, eager to be walked. Ernesto, the doorman, handed over the four leashes and an envelope stuffed with cash, my pay for that week. And then – like every Monday, Wednesday, and Friday – I headed one block uptown to pick up three more.

I got the idea of being a dog walker from an old trick of mine. Whenever I was totally bummed, I'd go over to the Tompkins Square Park dog run – a big open space that's just for dogs and owners – and watch them jumping on one another, sniffing butts and chasing balls. Huge dogs and tiny ones, graceful retrievers and spastic poodles were all jumbled together and all fawesomely ecstatic to get out of their tiny, lonely New York apartments and into a chase, a growling match, or a mad dash to nowhere in particular. No matter how depressed I was, the sight of scrappy puppies facing off with German shepherds always made me feel much better. So why not be paid to get cheered up?

You don't make much per dog per hour, but if you can handle six or seven at a time, it starts to add up. Most times it's easy money.

Sometimes it's not.

Straight out the door, the heat and stink seemed to get to them. The two Doberman brothers who usually kept order were nipping at each other, and the schnauzer and bull terrier were acting all paranoid, zigzagging every time a car door slammed, too jittery even to sniff at piles of garbage. As we battled down the street, their leashes kept tangling, like long hair on a breezy day.

Things only got worse when I picked up the second pack. The doorman realized that the owner of the insanely huge mastiff had forgotten to leave money for me and buzzed up to ask her about it. While I waited, the two packs started tangling with each other, nipping and jumping, their barking echoing off the marble walls and floor of the lobby.

I tried to unwind them and restore order, one nervous eyeball on the elevator. It would be totally unfool for my customers to see their dogs brawling when they were supposed to be getting exercise. So when nobody answered the doorman's buzzing, I didn't stick around to complain, just hauled them out of there and back into the heat.

I was already wishing I hadn't been in such a hurry to show Moz our possible drummer. A trip to the anarchy of Times Square was exactly what my unruly dog pack didn't need.

Here's what I've learned about dogs:

They're a lot like pretty girls. Having one or two around makes everything more fun, but when you get a whole bunch together, it turns into one big power struggle. Every time you add or subtract from the pack, everything gets rearranged. The top dog might wind up number two or fall all the way to the bottom. As I watched the Doberman brothers trying to stare down the mastiff, I was starting to wonder if being in a band was pretty much the same thing – more Nature Channel than MTV.

And really, all the jostling was a big waste of time, because Pearl was clearly the right girl to run things.

Don't get me wrong, the Mosquito was my oldest and best friend. I would never have picked up a guitar if it hadn't been for him, and he was the fawesomest musician I'd ever seen. But Moz wasn't cut out to be in charge. Of *anything*. He'd never held on to even the crappiest job because any kind of organized activity – waiting in line, filling out forms, showing up on time – made him all buzzy. There was no way he could keep five or six unruly musicians on their leashes and pull them all in the same direction.

As for me, I thought the little dogs had the right attitude. The schnauzer didn't really care whether the mastiff or the Dobermans took charge: he just wanted to sniff some butt and get on with the walk.

He just wanted the struggle to be over.

Today, though, nobody was in control – certainly not me. The seven leashes in my hand didn't mean squat. Each time we got to an intersection, I'd try to pull us toward Times Square, but the pack kept freaking out about every stray scent, surging off in random directions. I'd let them wander a bit until they got it out of their system, then pull them back toward the way I wanted us to go. We weren't going to set any crosstown speed records, but at least there was plenty of time before we were supposed to meet Moz, who, like I just mentioned, was probably going to be late anyway.

The weird thing was how much the vacant lots scared them. Even the mastiff was slinking past open spaces, when normally she would have charged straight in for a run.

How weird was that? A creature the size of a horse who'd been cooped up in a Manhattan apartment all day, and all she wanted to do was cling to me, shivering like a wet poodle.

In this mood, the commotion of Times Square was going to turn my pack into a portable riot. It seemed like Moz and I might have to see my drummer some other day.

Then we passed the mouth of a dark alley, and things really got paranormal.

The bull terrier – who always has to pee on everything – took advantage of the anarchy to pull us all in. He trotted to the piss-stained wall, cocked his leg halfway, then suddenly froze, staring into the darkness. The yapping of the other dogs choked off, like seven muzzles had been strapped on all at once.

The alleyway was full of eyes.

Hundreds of tiny faces gazed up at us from the shadows. Behind me trucks rushed past, and I could feel the warmth of sunlight on my back, the reassuring pace and movement of the real world. But in the alley everything was frozen, time interrupted. The bulbous bodies of the rats were motionless, huddled against garbage bags, their teeth bared, heads poking out of holes and crannies. Nothing moved but a shimmer of whiskers as a thousand nostrils tested the air.

In the farthest corner, a lone cat was perched high on a leaking pile of garbage. It stared down at me, unimpressed by my small army of dogs, offended by my presence in the alley. I felt tiny under its arrogant gaze – like some street kid who'd stumbled into a five-star restaurant looking for a place to pee.

The cat blinked its red eyes, then yawned, its pink tongue curling.

This is totally unfool, I thought. If my Dobermans spotted that cat, they'd go after it, dragging me and the whole pack deep into the alley. I could imagine myself returning seven rat-bitten, half-rabid canines to the doormen and never seeing another dime of dog-walking money again.

'Come on, guys, I murmured, gently pulling the fistful of leashes backward. 'Nothing to see here.'

But they were paralyzed, transfixed by the galaxy of eyes.

The cat opened its mouth again, letting out a long, irritated *mrrr-row* . . .

And the Dobermans ran like scaredy-cats.

They both leaped straight up, twisting around in midair, and charged past me toward the sunlight. The others followed in a mob, wrapping their leashes around my legs and dragging me stumbling into the street.

It was all I could do to stay on my feet as the mastiff charged ahead, opening up into her full gallop. She pulled the rest of us straight out onto the road, where a yellow flash of taxi screeched past dead ahead of us. A squat little delivery van squealed around us, horn blaring, scaring the mastiff into a sharp left turn.

We were headed down the middle of the street now, a garbage truck thundering along in front of us, the delivery van behind. We were *in traffic*, as if I'd decided to take a dog-powered chariot out for a little spin.

Unfortunately, I'd sort of forgotten to bring the chariot, so I was stumbling and staggering, seven leashes still tangled around my legs. And if I fell down, I knew the mastiff would keep going, galloping along until my face had been rubbed off completely on the asphalt. Even if my face friction somehow brought the pack to a halt, the pursuing delivery van would squash us all flat.

It was still blaring its horn, because that was *clearly helping*, and the two guys on the back of the garbage truck were laughing, pointing their giant-gloved fingers at me. A pair of bike messengers shot past in polka-dotted Lycra, me and my dogs just another bunch of clowns at the rodeo.

The whole procession swerved around some street work ahead, and suddenly my feet were slipping across an expanse of loose sand. I spotted an abandoned pizza box and planted my sneakers on it. Then I was skidding, my free hand in the air, riding the box like it was a boogie board at the beach.

Just when it was getting fun, the garbage truck began to slow, pulling up in front of a big apartment building with long, turd-shaped garbage bags piled outside. The truck filled the whole street, leaving nowhere for the pack to go.

Our momentum stalled, and the pack's energy wrapped itself into a tightly wound bundle of nipping and barking. By now the little dogs could hardly even stand, reduced as they were to a spaghetti mishmash of leashes and legs. Even the mastiff was tired out, her long, curving tongue lapping at the air.

One of the garbage guys swung himself down to work a big lever on the side of the truck, its huge maw opening in front of us with a metal screech. The other jumped off and shouted at me through the din.

'Hey, boss! You didn't take those pooches into that alley back there, did you?' He pointed over my shoulder but I knew which one he meant.

'Um, yeah?'

He shook his head. 'Bad idea. Even we don't go down there no more. Not worth it.'

I blinked, still trying to catch my breath. 'What do you mean?'

'Didn't you hear about the crisis? Way things are going, you got to be respectful. Let the rats have some of the city back, you know?' He laughed, patting the rumbling metal expanse with his gloved hand. 'Especially if you don't got a big truck to protect you. Bunch of pooches isn't enough these days.'

He turned to the pile of bags behind him and kicked one viciously. Waiting for a second to make sure no tiny creatures scattered from it, he shouldered the bag and began to feed its length into the giant steel maw.

I blew out a slow breath, knelt down, and started to untangle my dogs, wondering what they and the Sanitation Department knew that I didn't. Moz had said some paranormal stuff about the woman who'd tossed him her guitar – that she was part of something bigger – and I'd read there was a crime wave now, to go along with the heat and the garbage.

But wasn't it always like this in the middle of every long summer, brains beginning to zigzag in the fawesome temperatures?

Of course, the day before, Moz and I had watched that black water spraying out of a fire hydrant, as if something old and rotten had been dredged up beneath the city. Despite the heat bouncing off the asphalt, I shivered, thinking about what I'd seen back in that alley. That cat was *in charge* of all those rats, one glance had told me. Like my dogs, those glowing eyes were one big pack, but the feline had total control, no jostling or butt-sniffing required, like they were all family. And that just wasn't natural.

The delivery truck guy blared his horn at me one more time – like it was me in his way and not the garbage truck – so I gave him the finger. On the other side of his glass, his face broke into a smile, as if a little disrespect was all he'd been looking for.

Before the garbage truck was done, I got the pack unwound and back onto the sidewalk. We headed across town, toward the bottom end of Times Square, where we were supposed to meet Moz.

Maybe we could see my drummer after all. The hundred yard dash had finally worn my dogs out, and the mastiff trotted ahead, tail high, having taken over through the mysteries of dog-pack democracy. Maybe it was because she'd led us down the street to safety, or because the Dobermans had fled first from the rat-infested alley.

Whatever. At least it was all decided now, and someone other than me was in charge.

8. CASH MONEY CREW

–MOZ–

Times Square was buzzing.

Even in broad daylight, the battery of lights and billboards rattled me, rubbing my brain raw. Huge video screens were wrapped around the curving buildings over my head, shimmering like water in the rain, ads for computers and cosmetics flickering across them. News bites scrolled past on glittering strips, punctuated by nonsense stock-ticker symbols.

I was an insect in a canyon of giant TVs, mystified and irrelevant.

And penniless.

I'd never felt poor before, never once. I'd always thought it was moronic to ogle car ads and store windows, but now that I needed it, I saw money everywhere – in silver initials on thousand-dollar handbags, woven like gold threads into suits and silk scarves, and in the flickering images overhead. On the subway coming up here, I'd coveted the dollars invisibly stockpiled in magnetic strips on MetroCards, even the change rattling in beggars' paper cups.

Money, money, everywhere.

I couldn't go back to my piece-of-crap guitar after that Stratocaster. I had to own that same smooth action, those purring depths and crystal highs. Of course, maybe it didn't have to be a '75 with gold pickups. In the music stores on Forty-eighth Street, I'd found a few cheaper guitars I could live with, but I still needed to scrape together about two thousand bucks before the crazy woman returned.

Problem was, I had no idea how.

I'm not lazy, but money and me don't mix. Every time I get a job, something always happens. The boss tells me to smile, pretending I want to be at work when I'd rather be anywhere else. Or makes me call in every week to ask for my hours, and it turns into a whole extra job finding out when I'm supposed to be at my job. And whenever I explain these issues, someone always asks me the dreaded question, *If you hate it so much, why don't you just quit?*

And I say, 'Good point.' And quit.

In that flickering canyon of advertising, two thousand dollars had never seemed so far away.

Zahler was waiting at the corner where he'd said to meet, seven dogs in tow.

He was panting and sweaty, but his entourage looked happy – gazing up at the signs, sniffing at tourists passing by. It was all just flickering lights to them.

No jobs, no money. Lucky dogs.

'How much you get paid for that, Zahler?'

'Not enough,' he panted. 'Almost got killed on the way down here!'

'Yeah, sure,' I said. One of the little ones was nibbling me, and I knelt and petted him. 'This guy looks deadly.'

'No really, Moz. There was this alley . . . and this cat.'

'An alley cat? And you with only seven dogs.' One of which was gigantic, like a horse with long, flowing hair. I stroked its head, laughing at Zahler.

Still panting, he pointed his free hand at one of the little ones. 'It's all his fault, for peeing.'

'Huh?'

'It was just— never mind.' He frowned. 'Listen, you hear that drumming? It's her. Come on.'

I grabbed the monster-dog's leash from Zahler, and then two more, pulling the three of them away from a pretzel cart whose ripples of heat smelled like seared salt and fresh bread. 'So, you think Pearl will approve of this drummer?'

'Sure. Pearl's all about talent, and this girl is fexcellent . '

'But she plays on the street, Zahler? She could be homeless or something.'

He snorted. 'Compared to Pearl, you and me are practically homeless. Didn't you see that apartment?'

'Yeah, I saw that apartment.' I could still smell the money crammed into every corner.

'*And* there were stairs. More floors than we even saw.'

'Sure, Pearl's insanely rich. And this is supposed to convince me she can deal with a homeless drummer?'

'We don't know that this girl's homeless, Moz. Anyway, all I'm saying is that if Pearl can deal with you and me, she's no snob.'

I shrugged. *Snob* wasn't the word I would've used.

'Are you still bummed because of what she did to the Riff?'

'No. Once I got used to the idea of flushing all those years of practice down the toilet, I got over it.'

'Dude! You *are* still bummed.'

'No, I mean it.'

'Look, I know it hurts, Moz. But she's going to make us *huge*!'

'I *get* it, Zahler.' I sighed, angling my dogs away from a hot-dog cart. Of course, practicing yesterday had hurt – but so did getting a tattoo, or watching a perfect sunset, or playing till your fingers bled. Sometimes you just had to sit there and deal with the pain.

Pearl had rubbed me raw, but she knew how to listen. She could hear the heart of the Big Riff, and she hadn't done anything I wouldn't have if I'd been listening. I'd had six years to figure out what she'd recognized in six minutes. That's what made me cringe.

That and the whammy she'd put on Zahler. He wouldn't shut up about how brilliant Pearl was, how she was going to make us big, how things were finally going to happen. Like all those years with just the two of us had been a waste of time.

Zahler had a total crush on Pearl – that was obvious. But if I said so out loud, he'd just roast me with his death stare. And talk about wasting time: girls like her were about as likely to hook up with boys like us as Zahler's dogs were to pull him to the moon.

'Okay, I thought you said she was a drummer.'

'What?' Zahler cried above the rumble. 'You don't call that drumming?'

'Well, she's got drumsticks. But I thought drummers were to supposed to have *drums*.' I shook my head, trying to keep my three curious dogs from surging into the rapt crowd of tourists, Times Square locals, and loitering cops surrounding the woman.

'Yeah, well, imagine if she did have drums. Listen to how much sound she's getting out of those paint cans.'

'Those are actually paint *buckets*, Zahler.'

'What's the diff?'

I sighed. Painting had been one of my shorter-lived jobs, because they just gave you the colors to use, instead of letting you decide. 'Paint cans are the metal containers that paint comes in.

Paint buckets are the plastic tubs you mix it up in. Neither of them are drums.'

'But *listen*, Moz. Her sound is huge!'

My brain was already listening – my mouth was just giving Zahler a hard time out of habit and general annoyance – and the woman really did have a monster sound. Around her was arrayed every size of paint bucket you could buy, some stacked, some upside down, a few on their sides, making a sort of giant plastic xylophone.

It took me a minute to figure out how a bunch of paint buckets could have so much power. She'd set up on a subway grate, suspending herself over a vast concrete echo chamber. Her tempo matched the timing of the echoes rumbling up from below, as if a ghost drummer were down there following her, exactly one beat behind. As my head tilted, I heard other ghosts: quicker echoes from the walls around us and from the concrete awning overhead.

It was like an invisible drum chorus, led effortlessly from its center, her sticks flashing gracefully across battered white plastic, long black dreadlocks flying, eyes shut tight.

'She's pretty fool, Zahler,' I admitted.

'Really?'

'Yeah. Especially if we could rebuild this chunk of Times Square every place we played.'

He let out an exasperated sigh. 'What, the echoes? You never heard of digital delay?'

I shrugged. 'Wouldn't be the same. Wouldn't be as big.'

'Doesn't have to be as big, Moz. We don't want her playing a gigantic drum solo like this; we want her smaller, fitting in with the rest of the band. Didn't you learn *anything* yesterday?'

I glared at him, the anger spilling out from the place I thought I'd had it tucked away, rippling through me again 'Yeah, I did:

that you're a total sucker for every chick who comes along with an instrument. Even if it's a bunch of *paint buckets*!'

His jaw dropped. 'Dude! That is totally unfool! You just said she was great. And you know Pearl's fexcellent too. Now you're going to get all boys-only on me?'

I turned away, thoughts echoing in my brain, like my skull was suddenly empty and lined with concrete. Between the Stratocaster that wasn't mine, the other guitars I couldn't afford, Pearl's demolition of the Big Riff, and now the thought of *paint buckets*, it'd been too many adjustments to make in forty-eight hours.

I almost wished it was just Zahler and me again. We'd been like a team that was a hundred points behind – we weren't going to win anything, so we could just play and have fun. But Pearl had changed that. Everything was up in the air, and how it all came down *mattered* now.

Part of me hated her for that and hated Zahler for going along so easily.

He kept quiet, wrangling the dogs while I calmed myself down.

'All right,' I finally said. 'Let's talk to her. What have we got to lose?'

We waited till she was packing up, stacking the buckets into one big tower. Her muscles glowed with sweat, and a few splinters from a stick she'd broken rolled in the breeze from a subway passing underneath.

She glanced at us and our seven dogs.

'You're pretty good,' I said.

She jutted her chin toward a paint bucket that was right side up and half full of change and singles, then went back to stacking.

'Actually, we were wondering if you wanted to play with us sometime.'

She shook her head, one of her eyes blinking rapidly. 'This corner is mine. Had it for a year.'

'Hey, we're not moving in on you,' Zahler spoke up, waving his free hand. 'We're talking about you playing in our band. Rehearsing and recording and stuff. Getting famous.'

I cringed. "Getting famous" had to be the lamest reason for doing anything.

She shrugged, just a twitch of her shoulders. 'How much?'

'How much . . . what?' Zahler said.

But it was obvious to me. The same thing that had been obvious all day.

'Money,' I answered. 'She wants money to play with us.'

His eyes bugged. 'You want *cash*?'

She took a step forward and pulled a photo ID card from her pocket, waved it in Zahler's face. 'See that? That's from the MTA. Says I can play down in the subway, legal and registered. Had to sit in front of a review panel to get that.' As she put the card away, a little shiver went through her body. 'Except I don't go down there anymore.'

She kicked the upturned paint bucket, the pile of loose change clanking like a metallic cough. 'Seventy, eighty bucks in there. Why would I play for free?'

'Whoa, sorry.' Zahler started to pull his dogs away giving me a look like she'd asked for our blood.

I didn't move, though, staring at the bucket, at the bills fluttering on top. There were *fives* in there – it probably totaled a hundred easy. She had every right to ask for money. The world was all *about* money; only a lame-ass bunch of kids wouldn't know that.

'Okay,' I said. 'Seventy-five a rehearsal.

Zahler froze, his eyes popping again.

'How much for a gig?'

I shrugged. 'I don't know. One-fifty?'

'Two hundred.'

I sighed. The words *I don't know* had just cost me fifty bucks. That's how it worked with money: you had to know, or at least act like you did. 'Okay. Two hundred.'

I held out my hand to shake, but she just passed me her business card.

'Are you crazy, Moz? Pearl's going to freak when she finds out she has to pay for a drummer.'

'She's not paying anyone, Zahler. I am.'

'Yeah, right. And where are you going to get seventy-five bucks?'

I looked down at the dogs. They were staring in all directions at the maelstrom of Times Square, gawking like a bunch of tourists from Jersey. I tried to imagine rounding up customers, going door-to-door like Zahler had, putting up signs, making schedules. No way.

My plan was much better.

'Don't worry about it. I've got an idea.'

'Yeah, sure you do. But what about the Strat? You can't save up for a guitar if you're paying out seventy-five bucks two or three times a week.'

'I'll figure that out when its owner shows up again. If she shows up.

Zahler let out his breath, not sure what to make of this. I looked down at the card: *Alana Ray, Drummer.* No address, just a cell-phone number, but if she could make a hundred bucks a day in cash, somehow I doubted she was homeless.

It had been so simple hiring her, a million times simpler than

I'd imagined. No arguing about influences, getting famous, or who was in charge. Just a few numbers back and forth.

Money had made it easy.

'Moz, you're freaking me out. You're, like, the tightest guy I know. You never bought your own amplifier, and I've only seen you change your strings about twice in the last six years.'

I nodded. I'd always waited until they rusted out from under my fingers.

'And now you're going to pay out hundreds of dollars?' Zahler said. 'Why don't we find another drummer? One who's got real drums and doesn't cost money.'

'One who's that good?'

'Maybe not. But Pearl said she knew a few.'

'We don't have to run to her. We said that we'd handle this. So I'll pay.' I turned to him. 'And don't tell Pearl about the money, okay?'

Zahler groaned. 'Whoa, now I get it. You want to pay this girl so she owes you, right? You want her to be your drummer, not Pearl's.' He shook his head. 'That is some dumb-ass logic at work, Moz. We're supposed to be a band.'

'Pearl's already paying for rehearsal space.'

'Which is no big deal for her. You're getting into a spending contest with a girl who lives in an apartment that has *stairs*. Whole other *floors*!'

I looked down at my tattered shoes. 'It's not a contest, Zahler. It's just business.'

'Business?' He laughed. 'You don't know jack about business.'

I looked up at him, expecting to feel the death stare, but he was just confused. I didn't understand myself, not completely, but I knew I had to get some part of this band under control. If I let Pearl decide everything and pay for everything, Zahler and I would wind up just a couple of sidekicks along for the ride. 'Just don't tell her about the money, okay?'

He blinked, his dogs winding around his feet in disarray. I saw him wondering if I'd gone insane, wondering if I was going to screw this whole thing up, and knew I was right on the edge of losing him.

Which was fine, if he really thought I was that hopeless. Maybe it was better to walk away now than later.

But finally, he exhaled. 'Okay. Whatever. I won't tell Pearl you're paying. I guess I can pitch in some of my dog money too.'

I shook my head. 'I've got it covered.'

'But maybe we should warn Pearl . . . before we all show up for rehearsal.'

I frowned. 'Warn her about what?'

'Um, that our new drummer drums on paint buckets . . .'

-PEARL-

I took the subway to Brooklyn, so Mom wouldn't find out from Elvis.

Skittering sounds wafted up from the tracks as I waited for a train, the shuffling of tiny feet among discarded coffee cups and newspapers. The platform was empty except for me, the tunnels murmuring with echoes. The subways sounded wrong these days, almost alive, like there was something big down here. Something breathing.

I hated facing the subway on Sunday mornings, with no rush-hour crowds to protect me, but we didn't have much choice about when to rehearse. Minerva said that church was the only thing that kept Luz away till after noon.

This would all be much easier when we didn't have to sneak Minerva out of her room, but she needed to join the band now. Lying around in bed all day was never going to cure her. She had to get out of that dark room, meet some new people, and, most of all, sing her brains out.

Moz, Zahler, and I had rehearsed together four times now – we had a B section for the Big Riff and two more half-formed songs. We were better every time we played, but we needed structure: verses and choruses, a drummer too. We didn't have time to wait for Min to get completely well. The world was in too much of a hurry around us.

Except for the F train, of course. Ten minutes later, it still hadn't come, and I hoped it wasn't broken down again. The subways were having some kind of weird trouble this summer. Minor earthquakes, they said on TV – Manhattan's bedrock settling.

That was also the official explanation for the black water infecting the pipes. They said it wasn't dangerous, even if they didn't know exactly *what* it was – it evaporated too quickly for anyone to find out. Most people were drinking bottled water, of course. Mom was bathing in Evian. I wasn't sure I believed any of it, but in any case, I didn't have time for earthquakes today. The rehearsal space was reserved in my name, on my credit card – the others couldn't get in without me. If I was late getting up to Sixteenth Street, everything would fall apart.

I fished out my cell phone. It searched for a signal, until a tremulous *7:58 A.M.* appeared. One hour to get to Brooklyn and back.

Still hovering on the screen was the last number I'd called the night before – Moz's – to remind him again about this morning.

Lonely and nervous on the empty platform, I pressed send.

'Yeah?' a croaky voice answered.

'Moz?'

'Mmm,' came his annoyed grumble. 'Pearl? Crap! Am I late?'

'No, it's only eight.'

'Oh.' He scratched his head so hard I could hear it over the cell-phone crackle. 'So what's up?'

'I'm on my way out to Brooklyn to pick up Minerva. I was wondering if . . . you wanted to come.'

'To *Brooklyn*?'

That's how he said it: *Brooklyn?* Like I wanted to drag him to Bombay.

I should have given up. For two weeks now I'd been trying to connect with Moz, but he always kept his distance. If only I hadn't messed up that first rehearsal, the one where I'd pulled the Big Riff apart. I should have gone slowly, respecting what had been conjured between us when the Strat had fallen from the sky. But instead I'd decided to dazzle him with nine kinds of brilliance. *Clever, Pearl.*

Eight A.M. was probably not the best time to break my losing streak, but for two seconds I'd imagined that maybe this morning – the morning we became a real band – might be different.

I kept talking, trying to make it sound fun. 'Yeah. I didn't explain this before, but it's kind of a ninja mission, getting her out of there.'

'Kind of a *what?*'

'Kind of tricky. Her parents have this thing about . . .' Insanity? Abduction? 'Well, let's just say I could use your help.'

I hadn't said much about Min to anyone yet, except what a lateral singer she was. It wouldn't hurt if Moz got used to her weirdness before she met the rest of them. And it would be nice just having someone beside me on the way out there, even if he only waited outside while I snuck in to get her.

'Look, uh, Pearl . . .' he said. 'I just woke up.'

'I sort of figured that. But I'm at the F station down from your house. You could get here in five minutes.'

Silence crackled in my ear; a breeze stirred newspapers on the tracks.

I sighed. 'Look, it's no big deal. Sorry to wake you up.'

'That's okay. My alarm's about to go off anyway. See you at nine.'

'Yeah. You're going to love Minerva. And a drummer! It's going to be fawesome, huh?'

'Sure. Totally.'

I felt like I was supposed to say more, something to get him revved up for our first real rehearsal. 'Don't forget your Strat.'

'It's not mine. But yeah, see you soon.' Click.

I slipped the phone back into my pocket, letting another sigh slip through my teeth. I'd let him take the Stratocaster home after the second rehearsal, but that hadn't changed anything between us. I was still Boss Pearl.

The newspapers stirred on the tracks again, one rolling over restlessly. I felt the platform rumbling under my feet, and my stomach tightened. As the sound steadily grew into a roar, it pushed all the thoughts from my head, thundering across me as if something huge was about to burst from the tunnel, over-powering all my plans.

But it was just the F train pulling in.

In the past two weeks, Minerva's block had gotten worse. The garbage had been massed into a few huge, leaking mountains. Like how you deal with snow: push it into piles, then wait for the sun to make it go away.

Except garbage doesn't melt, and snow doesn't smell bad.

It was more than weird. Mom always bitched about this or that neighborhood going to seed, but I'd figured that took decades, longer than I'd been alive anyway. Until this summer, New York had always looked pretty much the same to me. But this part of Brooklyn seem to change every time I saw it, like someone dying of a disease before my eyes.

Luz always talked about 'the sickness' like it wasn't just Minerva but the whole city – maybe the whole world – that was afflicted, all of it a prelude to the big struggle. Only she never said what the struggle was actually about. Good versus evil? Angels versus demons? Crazy versus sane?

Crazy Versus Sane. Now *there* was a band name that fit us like a glove.

The early morning shadows stretched down the block, sunlight spattering the asphalt through the leaves, dancing with the breeze. I crept past the garbage mountains, trying not to listen to the things inside them and wishing I didn't have the Taj Mahal of hearing. No people were on the street, not even any dogs. Just the occasional red flash of cats' eyes watching me from overgrown front yards.

The front-door key was where Min had told me her mom kept it, under an iron boot-wipe by the door. It was covered with grime and stained my fingertips a red-brown rusty color when I tried to wipe it off. But it fit smoothly into the lock, the bolt sliding across with a soft *click*.

The door swung open onto a silent audience of skulls.

I took slow, careful steps into the darkness, listening for any noise from the wooden planks underfoot. According to Minerva, her parents were deep sleepers – her little brother, Max, was the one we had to worry about. I just hoped Min was awake and dressed, not surfing some nightmare that would make her scream when I opened her door.

I took the stairs slowly, my soft-soled fencing shoes pressing on the edges of the steps, not in the creaky middles. As a little kid, I'd once gotten up at midnight and pushed down every key of our baby grand from top to bottom, pressing so delicately that the hammers never struck the strings, making not a whisper of sound the whole way. Once you've managed that, you can pretty much do anything without waking the grown-ups.

The house creaked and settled around me, like a huge old instrument in need of tuning. I passed the blenderized-reality crucifixes, her parents' room, my slow, trembling steps carrying me silently to Min's door. Staring at the heavy sliding bolt that locked her in, I suddenly wished I didn't have to touch the scroll-work symbols carved into the bolt: cat's eyes and centipedes, worms with eyes and spindly legs, and, of course, more skulls.

I swallowed as my fingertips grasped the cool metal then slid the bolt slowly across. I opened the door and slipped inside.

Minerva was still under the covers, still asleep.

'Min!' I hissed.

A cold hand fell on the back of my neck.

–MINERVA–

Pearl was shiny, glistening, smelling of fear. There was lightning in her eyes – like Zombie when you rub his fur the wrong way hard.

She made sputtering noises, so I put a finger to my lips. 'Shhh, Pearl. Mustn't wake Maxwell.'

'Jesus, Min!' she hissed. 'You scared the *crap* out of me!'

I giggled. I'd been giggling for half an hour, waiting in that corner to make her jump. That was the first thing being sick taught me: it's fun to scare people.

'Look!' I pointed at the Min-shaped bundle in my bed. 'It works like magic.'

'Yeah, nine kinds of supernatural.' As her breathing slowed, Pearl's eyes swept up and down me, still flashing. I was dressed in cocktail black and dark glasses, more Saturday night than Sunday morning, but it felt fantastic to be in real clothes after months of pajamas. The dress squeezed me tight, shaping my body, embracing me. My four thickest necklaces lay tangled against my breasts, and my nails were painted black.

I shook my head, making my earrings tinkle.

'Cute,' she whispered. 'You look like an Egyptian princess crossed with a twelve-year-old goth.'

I stuck my tongue out at her and snapped for Zombie.

He scampered over and jumped into my arms. 'Let's go. I want to make music.'

Pearl glared at him, still pissy. 'You can't bring a *cat* to rehearsal, Min!'

'I know, silly.' I giggled softly, stroking Zombie's head. 'He's just going out to play.'

She frowned. 'But Luz says he's not supposed to go out.'

'We can't leave poor Zombie in here. He'll be all lonely.' I stared into his eyes and pouted. 'What if he starts scratching on my door and yowling? Could wake up Daddy.'

Pearl pushed her glasses up her nose, which she does when she's being bossy. 'Luz will freak if she sees him outside.'

'Luz is mean to Zombie,' I said, pulling him closer to kiss his little triangular cat-forehead.

'She'll be even meaner to me if she figures out I took you into Manhattan.'

'She won't. It'll be okay, Pearl. We'll bring him in when we get back. He'll come when his mommy calls.' I smiled.

Her breath caught. My teeth had gotten pointy lately. Certain things kept happening, no matter what Luz did to stop them.

'I just don't see how Zombie escaped that whole throwing-things-away bit,' Pearl muttered. 'You got rid of your boyfriend, your band, your fexcellent German stereo, and me – but not your stupid *cat*?'

'Not stupid.' I turned Zombie around and looked into his eyes. He knew things. Big things.

Pearl was being pissy at her phone now. 'Crap. It's past eight-thirty. I don't suppose there are any taxis around here on Sunday morning?'

'No taxis ever.' I frowned. 'Daddy says they won't bring him home from work anymore.'

Pearl swore under her breath, closing her eyes. 'I'm going to have to call Elvis, or we'll be late.' She looked at me, all serious. 'Can you try to act normal in front of him?'

'Of course, Pearl. No need to get all shiny.'

'Are you sure you're ready for this?'

I smiled my pointy smile and turned to face my desk. 'Watch this . . .'

I leaned across to blow out the candle, and smoke poured up, sandalwood turning instantly to the smell of ashes. Reaching out with my free hand, I tugged at one corner of the fabric draped across the mirror, and velvet flowed down onto the desk like water.

'*Minerva!*' Pearl hissed.

There was my face, trapped inside the mirror frame, but it didn't make me scream. I didn't faint or suddenly want to throw Zombie out the window.

Luz had put the beast inside me to sleep, and everything was easier now.

My skin was pale and flawless, glowing softly in the candlelight. Two months uncut, my dark hair flowed raggedly around my features. Cheeks, chin, brow – everything was sharper and finer now, as if my flesh had tightened. When I pulled off my sunglasses, my eyes were radiant and wide, stuck in an expression of bewilderment and wonder.

Zombie purred softly in my arms.

'Still pretty,' I whispered. And something more than pretty now.

I hadn't told Luz yet that I could do this: look at my own reflection. It would make her too happy, like she was winning. Luz wanted to strip away my new senses, file down my pointy teeth, turn me back into the boring old Minerva.

But Pearl was going to help me stop that from happening – Pearl and her music. I slipped my glasses back on and, Zombie's weight shifting in my other arm, lifted the notebooks from the desk. Inside them were secrets, ancient words I'd heard in the worst of my fever. Singing the old mysteries would keep me the way I was: not crazy anymore, but so much more than boring.

Halfway cured was best.

Pearl was talking on her phone, wheedling Elvis until he promised not to mention this little trip to her mom.

When she hung up I pouted. 'But I wanted to go on the subway.' Luz had told me never, ever to go down in the earth again. But I could feel it calling me, rumbling underfoot. It wanted me.

'There's no time for a train,' shiny Pearl whispered, opening the door. 'Come on. And try to be quiet on the stairs.'

Stairs, I thought happily. Finally, I was headed down, out of this attic prison and down toward the earth. I wanted to go down into basements, into tunnels and chasms and excavations. I wanted to sing my way down to the things waiting there for me.

'*Ah, la musica,*' I whispered. 'Here I come.'

–ALANA RAY–

I got there early, just to watch.

I'd been to the Warehouse plenty of times. It's an old factory building in Chelsea, hollowed out and loaded up with rehearsal spaces, foam spread across the walls to kill the echoes, forty-eight power plugs in every room. There's a recording studio in the basement – sixty dollars an hour, one dollar a minute – but it's full of junk and strictly for the kids.

I watched the place fill up, random guitar chops and drumbeats filtering out, bouncing up and down the block. Sixteenth is a narrow street, about thirty-five feet from wall to wall, so it takes a tenth of a second for sound to cross over and jump back. At 150 beats per minute, that's a sixteenth-note lag.

I clapped my hands and listened to the echo, then drummed softly on my jeans in tempo as I watched.

From the stoop of the empty FedEx office down the block, I could catalog all the faces going in, concentrating so I'd remember the new people I was meeting upstairs. I always try to see people before they see me, same way as animals want to be upwind, not down.

At the school I went to, where we all had special needs, some of the other kids couldn't recognize faces very well. They learned to identify people by their posture or their walk, which seemed like a good idea to me. I can understand faces just fine, but I don't trust people till I've seen the way they move.

A long gray limousine slid up in front of the Warehouse. A big Jamaican guy in a gray uniform got out and glanced up and down the block, making sure it was safe. But he didn't see me.

The bulge of a shoulder holster creased his jacket. Times Square was getting more like that every day, armed guards appearing at the entrances of the big stores. More policemen too.

Satisfied, the driver opened the limo's door for two girls.

They looked about the same age as the boys who'd hired me nearly two weeks ago, seventeen or eighteen, but I figured these limo-girls couldn't possibly know them. Those dog-walking boys didn't have limo money – not even *taxi* money.

Also, the boys hadn't been druggies, and one of these girls definitely had a problem. Skin pale as an oyster, she unfolded from the limousine and stood there holding on to the door, shaky from the ride. Though her long arms were thin and wiry, her muscles were almost as defined as mine.

What kind of junkie works out? I wondered as she made her way around the car to the entrance of the Warehouse. Her movements were slow and pointy, articulated in the wrong spots. I couldn't take my eyes off her: it was like watching a stick insect walk along a branch.

A minute later the two dog-boys showed up, and it turned out they did know one another – or at least the boys knew the other girl, the little one with eyeglasses. She introduced them to the junkie girl; then they all went inside except the boy who'd hired me. He waited outside, like he'd said he would.

His name was Moz: M-o-z I remembered that because I'd written it down.

I watched him wait, doing a nervous little dance, never putting his guitar case down. His fingers ran through practice patterns, flickering against his thigh, and I matched his tempo for a while on my knees.

I wondered how they'd come together: a junkie, a rich girl, two scruffy boys, all of them younger than me, probably too young to be serious about their music. Maybe they were *all* rich, and the boys had dressed down just to hire me cheap.

That was a dirty trick if they had, and I don't play with people who trick me. But I wasn't sure yet.

When my watch said sixteen seconds left, I picked up my duffel bags and crossed the street.

'Hey, Alana,' he said. 'You made it.'

'Alana Ray,' I corrected him. 'Nine o'clock on Sunday morning.'

'Yeah. Pretty messed up, huh?' He shrugged and rolled his eyes, like the time had been someone else's idea. Someone annoying.

'You got my eighty bucks?' I asked, still drumming two fingers against the strap of one duffel bag.

'Sure . . . um, eighty?' His eyes narrowed a bit.

I smiled. 'Seventy-five. Just messing with you.'

He laughed in a way that said five bucks meant something to him, and the money came out of his pockets in crumpled singles and fives, even ten dollars' worth of quarters rolled by hand.

I relaxed a little. This boy was dirt poor. There wasn't any kind of rich person who'd go to that much trouble to trick me.

'Those all your drums . . . um, buckets?' he asked, staring at the duffel bags.

'Don't take up much space, do they?' I said. But really I hadn't brought everything, not for the first time. No sense hauling forty-two pounds of gear if all these kids wanted was a drum machine with dreadlocks.

'Must be easier to carry than a real set.'

I nodded. I've never carried a real drum set, but it seemed like it would be hard.

He counted up to seventy-five, which seemed to clean his pockets out. I felt a little bad about my eighty-dollar trick, and my feet started tapping.

'Um, there's one thing,' he said, shouldering his guitar and screwing up his face, nervous and flickering again. He was kind of cute, all uncomfortable like this. I felt myself worrying about him, like a kid walking down the street with one shoelace untied.

'What is it?' I said.

'It'd be better if you didn't mention the money to Pearl.'

'Who's Pearl?'

'She's the . . .' He frowned. 'Just don't mention it to anyone, I guess. Okay?'

'Fine with me.' I shrugged. 'Money's the same, whoever gives it to you.'

'Yeah, I guess it is.' He nodded, his face serious like I'd said something profound instead of simply logical. That was the *point* of money, after all: crisp and clean or wrinkled or disintegrated into quarters – a dollar was always worth a hundred cents.

We headed on in.

Upstairs was like every practice room: distracting. Four walls and a ceiling of undulating foam, the pattern shimmering in the corners of my vision. The disconcerting tangle of cables on the floor. The stillness hovering around us, the air robbed of echoes.

The small girl with eyeglasses took over, introducing me to everyone.

'This is Zahler. He plays guitar.' The big burly dog-boy smiled broadly. He hadn't wanted to pay me, I remembered.

'And Minerva. It's her first time too. She's going to sing for us.'

The junkie girl took off her dark glasses for two seconds, squinting in the fluorescent lights and smiled at me.

She was wearing a long black velvet dress, as shiny as the streets after it rains, a tangle of necklaces, and dangling earrings. Her long black nails glistened, dazzling me like the undulating ceiling.

'She's a singer?' I asked. 'Huh . . . I'd have figured she was a roadie.'

They all laughed at my joke, except for Minerva, whose smile curled tighter. Her teeth sent a little shiver toward me. I touched my forehead three times, blinked one eye, then the other to still the air.

'And I'm Pearl: keyboards,' the other girl said. 'You're Alana, right?'

'Alana Ray. One name,' I said, my voice tremulous from Minerva's stare.

'Cool,' she said. 'Hyphenated?'

I grinned. I'd known the little rich girl was going to ask that. It bugs some people, me having two first names that are invisibly stuck together.

'No. *Carbonated.* Just a little bubble of air.'

No one laughed, but no one ever does. That joke was just for me.

Setup was quick. The boys just had to plug in and tune, and Pearl had only one small keyboard. She balanced it on the room's mixing console, where she could control everyone else's sound. The junkie girl adjusted her microphone stand higher, then fiddled with the light switches, her movements still jerky and insectlike. Even though she was still wearing those dark glasses, she turned down the lights till I could hardly see.

I didn't complain, though. Her glare had made me shiver once already.

I set up in one corner, two walls of foam padding at my back, twenty-one paint buckets arranged before me, the stacks growing taller from right to left, one to six buckets high. ($S_6 = 21$)

I pulled out six contact microphones, my own mixer and effects boxes, and went to work. I don't like rehearsal spaces or recording studios as much as the open air – but at least I can bring my own echoes.

Pearl watched me clip the mikes to my stacks of plastic, run their cables into the mixer, then route them out through the effects.

'Paint cans, huh?' she asked.

'Paint buckets,' I corrected, and saw Moz smile for the first time.

'Uh, sure. How many channels you need?' she asked, fingering the sliders on the mixing board. 'Six? Twelve?'

'Just two. Left and right.' I handed her the cables.

Pearl frowned as I turned away from her. This way, she couldn't control my mix from her board. It was like she wanted me to give her my eggs, my cheese, and my chives all in separate bowls. But instead I was handing her the whole omelet, cooked just the way I liked it.

She didn't argue, though, and I saw that Moz was still grinning.

'Everybody ready?' Pearl asked. Everyone was.

Minerva swallowed and walked up to grasp her mike with one pale hand. The other held a notebook, which I could see was open to a page of chaos, like the handwriting of the unluckiest kids back at my special school.

Moz just nodded, not looking up at Pearl, flicking his cords around on the floor with one toe.

The burly boy (whose name I'd already forgotten; should have written it down) was the only one who smiled. He leaned his head down to stare closely at his strings, setting his fingers carefully. Then, concentrating hard, he began to play. It was a simple riff, thick and dirty.

Pearl did something on the board, and the sound softened.

I listened for a moment, then tuned my echoes to ninety-two beats per minute. Moz started playing, high and fast. I thought it was a strange way to start, too complicated, like a guitar solo bursting out of nowhere. But then Pearl entered, playing a gossamer melody that wrapped a shape around what he was doing.

I listened for a while, not sure what to do. I had a lot of choices. Something simple and lazy, to give the music more backbone? Or should I swing the beat, a little off-kilter, to loosen it up? Or follow Moz's superquick fluttering, like rain against the roof?

I always relished this moment, right before starting to play. It was the one time my fingers didn't tremble or drum against my knees, when I could hold my hands out steady. No reason to hurry.

Also, I didn't want to make a mistake. There was something fragile about this music, as if it would fly apart if pushed in the wrong direction. Pearl, Moz, and the other boy thought they knew one another already, but they didn't yet.

I began carefully, only a downbeat at first, building the pattern one stroke at a time – simple to complicated, less to more. Then, just before it got too crowded, I slipped sideways, subtracting one stroke for each I added, gradually shifting the music around us, but leaving it still tenuous, directionless.

For a moment I thought I'd made a mistake. These were just kids. Maybe they needed to be pushed in one direction or another, or maybe they'd wanted a drum machine, after all.

But then the junkie girl came in.

There were no words, though she held one of the notebooks open in front of her. With the microphone pressed close to her lips, she was humming, but the melody emerged from the speakers sharp-edged and keening, cutting through the mass of intricacies we'd built.

Suddenly the music had focus, a beating heart. She wrapped the rest of us around herself, piercing my gradual shadows with a single ray of light.

I smiled, having a rare moment of absolute comfort in my own skin, every compulsion satisfied, the clockwork of the whole world clicking into place around my drumming. Even if they were young and flawed, these four had something. Maybe a happy accident was happening here, like the first time I'd ever noticed the echoes from the street matching my footsteps . . .

Then the strangeness began, something I hadn't seen since I was little. The air started to glitter wildly, my eyelids fluttering. This was more than ripples of heat from summer asphalt, or the shimmers I saw when someone was angry at me.

Shapes were forming on the cable-strewn floor, and faces materialized in the patterns of the soundproofing: I glimpsed expressions of hurt and fear and fury at the edges of my vision, as if my medication was failing.

I imagined dropping my sticks, reaching into my pocket, and spilling out my pills to count them. But I was positive I'd taken one that morning, and the labels always warned that they built up slowly in the bloodstream: weeks to take effect, weeks to fade away. Never stop, even if you think you don't need them anymore.

Minerva was glowing, her pale skin luminous in the darkness. Her movements had smoothed out, no longer insectlike. She was singing now, teeth jammed close to the microphone, her incomprehensible song sputtering for a moment as she turned a page of the notebook.

The practice room was seething, phantasms filling up the spaces between objects, demons with long tails riding the sound waves in the air.

I was afraid, but I couldn't stop. I couldn't bring my drumming to a halt any more than I could smother the tapping of my foot or the twitches in my face. I was trapped here, caught in the pattern I'd helped shape.

Then reality shifted once more, like the sprockets of a film finally catching, and I saw something I'd almost forgotten . . . *what music looked like.*

Moz's guitar notes were scattered like Christmas lights across the ceiling, shimmering in and out, Pearl's sinuous melody linking and electrifying them. The dog-boy's riff spread out underneath, solid and steady, and my drumming was the scaffolding that held it aloft, all of it pulsating at ninety-two beats per minute, alive and connecting us.

I stared at the apparition, awestruck. This was the way I'd been born to see music, before the doctors had taught me to separate my senses, to grab objects and faces and hold them in place. Before they'd cured me of these visions with therapy and pills.

How had this other reality returned? Every sense conjoined, complete and undivided . . .

But then my eyes dropped to the floor, and I saw Minerva's song.

It was tangled around our feet, twisting its way through cords and cables, plunging in and out of the floor, like loops of Loch Ness monster in the water. It was a worm, blind and horned, its rippling segments pushing it through the earth, rearing up a hungry maw teethed with a ring of knives.

And suddenly I knew that Minerva's curse was something a thousand years older than heroin or crack.

I let out a gasp, and she turned her head toward me, *saw* me seeing it. She dropped the notebook and pulled off her glasses in one brittle motion, her song dissipating into a long, furious hiss. The architecture of the music shattered overhead, my drumsticks spinning from my hands.

The rest of them stumbled to a halt. Pearl was staring at her friend, alarmed. Moz was staring at Minerva too and for a moment his expression was unmistakable: the boy was dripping with desire.

'Why'd you two stop, man?' the burly dog-boy cried. 'That shit was *paranormal*!'

I blinked, looking down at empty hands. No trembling, just like after any good session. I felt no need to tap my feet or touch my forehead. There was nothing in the air but the hiss of amplifiers, a barely visible ripple in the corners of my eyes.

But I still felt it in the soles of my feet, the beast we'd been playing. Something was rumbling in the earth, deeper than six stories below. Answering Minerva's song.

'You can smell it too, can't you?' she whispered to me.

'No . . . not smell. But sometimes I see things I shouldn't.' I swallowed, clutching at my pill bottle through my jeans, by reflex spilling out the speech they made us memorize at school, in case the police ever thought we were on drugs: 'I have a neurological condition that may cause compulsive behavior, loss of motor control, or hallucinations.'

Minerva raised an eyebrow, then curled back her lips in a sneer that showed too many pointed teeth. *'Spasticus . . . autisticus.'*

I nodded. That was more or less me.

But what the hell was she?

–MOZ–

Her uncovered face was radiant, shining with a brilliance that liquefied me.

She'd worn her shades until that moment – a total poser, I'd figured. But I could see now that she *had* to wear them, not for her protection, but for ours, to shield us from her eyes.

What she had wasn't beauty, it was something a thousand times scarier, something that gnawed at my edges. I'd already heard it in the music, felt it in the way she'd wrenched us all into her wake – the whole band sucked up and totaled by her magnetism, or whatever you'd call it. Something *charisma* was too small a word for.

Something overriding, bottomless.

Suddenly, this was *her* band, not mine or Pearl's. And just as suddenly, I didn't mind.

Minerva put her sunglasses back on.

I picked up her notebook from where it had fluttered to the floor.

What covered the open pages wasn't writing, more like the scroll from a lie detector, or one of those machines that inscribes the shapes of earthquakes. Ragged black lines undulated in impenetrable columns, smeared and spattered with drops of water. A few smudges were rusty brown, like old blood.

I offered it to her, but Minerva was still staring at Alana Ray – *glaring*, her gaze dangerous even through dark glasses. I felt like I should say something to calm her down, since I'd brought Alana Ray here and Minerva was angry at her about . . . something.

Because Alana Ray had dropped her sticks? But Minerva had freaked out before the Big Riff had broken down. I opened my mouth but found myself silenced by the memory of Minerva's naked eyes.

'Min?' Pearl said.

I closed my mouth. Let Pearl handle this.

'You okay, Min?'

'Yeah, sure.' Minerva leaned across to take the note book from my hand, pressed it close against her chest. 'Sorry about that. Didn't mean to have a hissy fit. I was just kind of . . . into that song.'

'I'm sorry too,' Alana Ray said quietly. 'My condition sometimes leads to performance complications.'

I swallowed, trying to remember what Alana Ray had confessed about herself . . . something wrong with her brain? All of a sudden, she was talking funny, with microscopic pauses between her words. Little twitches traveled across her body as she stared back at Minerva, as if her nervous system was unraveling inside. I opened my mouth again to say something.

'Hey, no problem,' Zahler said first. 'You were fawesome. We were *all* totally paranormal' He turned to Pearl 'Right?'

'Yeah,' Pearl said softly. 'We were.' She gave me a questioning look.

I held her gaze, something I hadn't done in two weeks.

It had all clicked – our music, this band. Pearl's strange electric friend had pulled us together and forged us into something as brilliant as she was.

'That was great,' I said, nodding at Pearl. 'Good going.'

Her face brightened in the dark practice room. 'Well okay, then.' She turned to Alana Ray. 'You need to take a break?'

Alana Ray blinked one eye, then the other, then shook her head like she had water in her ear 'No. I'd rather keep playing. I think my . . . complication is over. But maybe a different song? Sometimes the same stimulus can provoke the same reaction.'

'Uh, sure,' Pearl said, then shrugged. 'How about Piece Two?'

Zahler and I just nodded, but Minerva smiled, pulling the microphone closer to her mouth. Low, soft laughter touched with reverb, scattered about the room.

'No problem, Alana Ray,' she whispered, opening her notebook. 'I've got about a million stimuli to go.'

Nobody freaked out for the rest of rehearsal.

We played Piece Two, a long jam wrapped around a looped sample from an old vinyl record of Pearl's, then our third song, which didn't even have a working title yet. Alana Ray never stumbled again, just accompanied us with psychic comprehension. With every new section she'd follow along for a while, then slowly start to build us up, adding structure and form, staring at invisible sheet music hovering in the air, somehow *seeing* what we needed her to do.

I didn't catch a single word Minerva sang, but every time she opened her mouth, she injected us with brilliance. Her voice had an uncanny magnitude, as if her notebooks were full of incantations for making the ground beneath us rumble. I couldn't take my eyes off her, except when I closed them and listened hard.

Between songs, I kicked myself for not having gone out to

Brooklyn that morning. I finally saw how stupid the struggle between Pearl and me had been. Neither of us were rock stars – we were backups, sidekicks, allies. Good musicians, maybe, but Minerva was luminous.

The anger that had been dogging me the last two weeks was spent, leaving nothing but contentment. I had an awesome band, a place to rehearse with no one yelling, 'Turn it down!' and a 1975 Strat with gold pickups in my hands. I'd even cracked the money thing and was saving a few bucks for myself every day. I couldn't remember why being miserable had seemed so import-ant.

Minerva had changed everything.

After an hour and a half, we'd played every song we knew as many times as we could and ground to a reluctant halt.

'Hey,' Zahler said. 'We need some new tunes, don't we?'

'Yeah.' I looked at Pearl. 'We should get together soon. Work on some more stuff for next Sunday.' Suddenly I had fragments of a million songs in my head.

Pearl smiled happily. 'More tunes? No problemo.'

Minerva frowned. '*Problema. Pero masculino.*'

'Huh?' I said, glancing at Pearl.

'Um, Min's been studying Spanish, sort of.' Pearl pulled out her cell phone and frowned at it. 'Speaking of which, I think we need to get back to Brooklyn for your, um, lesson.'

'You're studying Spanish?' Zahler said, grinning. '*Mas cervezas!*'

'*Prefiero sangre,*' Minerva said, her teeth glimmering in the darkness.

'Yeah, okay.' Pearl turned to Alana Ray. 'Listen, it was great to meet you. You were brilliant. I mean, especially for paint cans.'

'Paint buckets,' Alana Ray said. 'It was good to meet you too.'

'So . . . you want to play with us again?'

Alana Ray looked at me, and I nodded – at seventy-five bucks she was a bargain. She smiled. 'Yes. This was very . . . involving.'

'That's us. Involving.' Pearl swallowed. 'Sorry that Min and I have to run, but you've got the room until eleven. If I go reserve it for next week, can you guys handle breaking down?'

'What about your mixing board?' Zahler said.

'They keep it locked up downstairs. Here's my key.'

She threw a glittering chain across the room to Zahler and grabbed Minerva's hand. 'Come on, Min. We really have to motor.'

Zahler shouted goodbye, but Pearl was already pulling Minerva out of the door, yanking her along like a five-year-old who didn't want to leave the zoo.

I followed them into the hall, running ahead to stab the elevator button.

'Thanks,' Pearl said. 'Sorry to leave you guys to clean up. It's just . . .' Her voice faded into a sigh.

'Smelly Spanish lessons,' Minerva said. From all around us, the mutterings of bands leaked out, the thump of drums, muffled stabs of feedback.

'Don't worry about it.' I wondered what their mysterious rush was really all about. Not Spanish lessons, obviously. I tried to remember what Pearl had said on the phone that morning. Something about *ninjas*? 'You've done everything so far, Pearl. It won't kill us to put some stuff away.'

'Not everything. You guys found Alana Ray. She's incredible.'

'Yeah, I guess she is.' I smiled. 'Listen, I'm sorry I was so sleepy when you called this morning. Next time, I'll be glad to help out . . .' I glanced at Minerva. 'With whatever.'

'Oh, cool,' Pearl said softly, her smile growing. She was staring down at the floor. 'That's great.'

The elevator came, and when they stepped on, I did too, wanting a few more seconds with Minerva. 'I'll come down with you guys, if you don't mind, and then ride back up.'

'We don't mind,' Minerva said.

It was quiet in the big freight elevator, the walls padded with movers' blankets to protect them from the ravages of dollies, amps, and drums.

I cleared my throat. 'Listen, Pearl, I've been kind of a dick-head.'

'About what?' Pearl said, and Min's eyebrows rose behind dark glasses.

'About everything; about you. But this band is finally coming together, and I feel kind of stupid about the way I've been acting. So . . . I'm okay now.'

'Hey, Moz. It's my fault too.' Pearl turned to me, her face a little pink, almost blushing. 'I know I can be sort of bossy.'

'She's got a point there,' Minerva said.

I laughed. 'Nah. You just know what you're doing.' I shrugged. 'So me and Zahler should come over tomorrow? Get some new tunes worked up before next Sunday?'

Pearl nodded, still grinning. 'Perfect.'

'You coming?' I asked Minerva. 'I mean, you're the singer and everything.' I pointed at the notebooks she still clutched to her chest.

'Um, probably not,' Pearl said. 'She's kind of – '

'It's very *intensive* Spanish,' Minerva said.

'Oh. Sure.'

The elevator doors opened, and we stepped out into the lobby, Pearl still pulling Minerva along. A couple of guys were rolling a dolly full of turntable decks into the building, negotiating the bump between stairway ramp and marble floor with extreme care.

Pearl stepped up to the front desk, pulling out a credit card and talking to the guy about next week.

Minerva turned to me and said softly, 'See you next week.'

I nodded, swallowing, suddenly glad she was wearing those dark glasses. I wondered how many fewer stupid things I'd have said in my life if all pretty girls wore them. 'I'll totally be there.'

Okay, maybe not that many.

But Minerva just laughed and reached out with the hand Pearl wasn't holding. Hot as a freshly blown-out match, her fingertip traced my arm from wrist to elbow. Between her parted lips, I could see teeth sliding from left to right against each other, and then she mouthed a silent word.

Yummy.

She turned away from my shiver, back to Pearl just as she finished up and flicked open her phone.

'Elvis? We're ready.' Pearl snapped the phone shut and looked at me. 'See you guys tomorrow. Call me?'

'Yeah. I'll tell Zahler.' My breath was short, the line Minerva had traced along my arm still burning. 'See you.'

They waved, and I watched them walk through the door and out, then make their way toward a huge gray limo – a *limo*? – that slid into view. Minerva's mouthed word still echoed in my head, so unexpected, more like a daydream than something that had actually *happened.* My brain couldn't get hold of it, like a guitar lick I could hear but that my fingers couldn't grasp.

But she turned back toward me just before she ducked into the car and stuck her tongue out. Then her smile flashed, wicked and electric.

The limo slid away.

I swallowed, turned, and ran back to catch the elevator's closing doors. The guys with turntables were piled inside, leaving just enough space for me to squeeze in. As we rode up, I was rocking on the balls of my feet, humming one of the strange fragments Minerva had left in my brain, bouncing off the blanketed wall behind me.

I glanced over at the two guys and noticed they were watching my little dance.

'Fresh tunes?' one said, grinning.

'Yeah, very.' I licked my lips, tasting salt there. 'Things are going *great*.'

PART III

REHEARSALS

The Black Death had a distant twin.

At the same time the Plague of Justinian was raging across the Roman world, a great empire in South America, that of the Nazca, was also disappearing. The Nazca temples were suddenly abandoned, their cities emptied of life. Historians have no clue why this vast and sophisticated culture, thousands of miles away from plague-ridden Rome, vanished at exactly the same historical moment.

Most people haven't heard of the Nazca, after all. That's how thoroughly they disappeared.

It wasn't until the 1920s that the outside world discovered their greatest legacy. Airplanes flying over the arid mountaintops of Peru spotted huge drawings scratched into the earth. Covering four hundred square miles were pictures of many-legged creatures, vast spiders, and strange human figures. Archaeologists don't know what these drawings mean. Are they images of the gods? Or of demons? Do they tell a story?

Actually, they're a warning.

It is often noticed how they were built to last, cut into mountaintops where rain hardly ever falls and where there's almost zero erosion. Amazingly, they're still clearly visible after fifteen hundred years. Whatever they're trying to say, the message is designed to last across the centuries.

Maybe the time to read them is now.

NIGHT MAYOR TAPES:
282-287

–PEARL–

The halls of Juilliard seemed wrong on that first day back to school.

This was my fourth year here, so the place was pretty familiar by now. But things always felt strange when I returned from summer break, as if the colors had changed slightly while I was gone. Or maybe I'd grown some fraction of an inch over the last three months, shifting everything imperceptibly out of scale.

Today I couldn't get used to how empty the hallways felt. Of course, it made sense. All my friends in Nervous System (or *ex*-friends, really, thanks to Minerva's meltdown) had graduated last year, leaving the school full of acquaintances and strangers. That was what I got for hanging out with so many seniors when I was a junior.

I picked up my schedule from the front office and checked over the signs saying which classes and ensembles had been canceled due to lack of interest. No baroque instruments class this year. No jazz improv group. No *chamber choir*?

That was kind of lateral.

But all my planned classes were still scheduled. They made you take four years of composition and theory, after all, and my morning was full of required academics: English, trig, and the inescapable advanced biology.

So it wasn't until lunch that I began to see how much had really changed.

The cafeteria was the biggest room at school. It doubled as a concert hall, because even fancy private schools like Juilliard couldn't take up infinite space in the middle of Manhattan. My third-period AP bio class was just next door, prime real estate for getting to the front of the food line. Walking in ten seconds after the lunch bell, I was happy to see all the vacant tables. The familiar floury smell of macaroni and cheese *à la Juilliard,* one of the nonfeculent dishes here, made me smile.

Even if the System was gone, it was good to be back.

I got a trayful and looked around for anyone I could sit with, especially someone with useful musical skills. Moz and I might want to bring in backup musicians one day.

It only took a few seconds to spot Ellen Bromowitz all alone in the corner. She was in my year and a fawesome cellist, first chair in the orchestra. We'd been temporary best friends in our early freshman days, back when neither of us knew anyone else.

I took a seat across from her. Cellos could be cool even if Ellen sort of wasn't. Besides, there was hardly anyone else there.

She looked up from her macaroni, a little puzzled. 'Pearl?'

'Hey, Ellen.'

'Didn't expect to see you here.' She raised an eyebrow.

'Well . . .' I wasn't quite sure what she meant. 'Haven't seen you in a while. Just thought I'd say hi.'

She didn't answer, just kept looking at me.

'How's it going?' I asked.

'Interesting question.' A wry little smile played across her face. 'So, you don't have any friends to sit with either?'

I swallowed, feeling more or less busted. 'I guess not. The rest of Nervous System were seniors. All your friends graduated too, huh?'

'Graduated?' She shook her head. 'No. But no one's back yet.'

'Not back from where?'

'Summer.' She looked around the cafeteria.

The place still hadn't filled up. It seemed so quiet, not like the lunchtime chaos I remembered. I wondered if it had always been this spacious and peaceful in here, and if this was just another of those little summer-shifted perceptions making everything feel wrong.

But that didn't quite make sense. Things seeming smaller every year, I could understand. But *emptier*?

'Well, it was a pretty feculent summer,' I said. 'Between the sanitation crisis and the rats and stuff. Maybe not everyone's back from Switzerland or wherever else they escaped to.'

Ellen finished swallowing some mac and cheese. 'My friends don't go to Switzerland in the summer.'

'Oh, right.' I shrugged, remembering how scholarship students always hung out together. 'Well, Vermont, or whatever.'

She made a little sighing sound.

'Still, it's great to be back, huh?' I said.

Her eyes narrowed. 'You're in an awfully good mood. What's that all about? Got a new boyfriend or something?'

I laughed. 'No boyfriend. But yeah, I'm really happy. The weather's finally cooler, the subways are working this week, and I'm getting another band together.' I shrugged. 'Things are going great, I guess. And . . .

'And what?'

'Well, *maybe* there's a boy. Not sure yet if it's a good idea, though.'

I felt an embarrassingly nonsubtle grin growing on my face.

True, I wasn't sure whether it was a good idea at all, but at least the downright feculence between me and Moz had finally ended.

Having a band had wrung all the resentment out of him. He never complained about our early Sunday morning rehearsals anymore, just showed up ready to play. Moz could be so amazing when he was like this – like my mom said, totally fetching – focused when he played, intense when he listened to the rest of us.

So maybe sometimes I imagined distilling that concentration down to just the two of us, putting his newfound focus to work in other ways. And maybe, writing songs in my bedroom, I occasionally had to remind myself that it wasn't cool to jump the bones of your bandmates.

Mark and Minerva had shown me how much trouble that could cause. I'd heard he'd cracked up completely over the summer. Must be tough, losing your girlfriend and your band on the same day.

So I bit my tongue when Moz starting looking really intense and fervent, reminding myself it was for the good of the band, which was more important to me than any boy.

But that didn't mean I never thought about it.

The band had changed Minerva too. She could be nine kinds of normal these days. Maybe she still wore dark glasses, but the thought of going out in the sun didn't terrify her anymore. Neither did her own reflection – mirrors were her new best friends. Best of all, she loved dressing up and sneaking out to rehearsals. Her songs evolved every time we played, the formless rages slowly taking shape, bent into verses and choruses by the structure of the music.

One day soon, I figured, the words might actually start making sense.

The funny thing was, Alana Ray seemed to help Min the most. Her fluttering patterns wrapped around Minerva's fury, lending it form and logic. I suspected that Alana Ray was guiding us all somehow, a paint-bucket-pounding guru in our midst.

I'd gone online a few times, trying to figure out what exactly her condition was. She twitched and tapped like she had Tourette's, but she never swore uncontrollably. A disease called Asperger syndrome looked about right, except for those hallucinations. Maybe Minerva had called it during that first rehearsal, and Alana Ray was a little bit autistic, a word that could mean all kinds of stuff. But whatever her condition was, it seemed to give her some special vision into the bones of things.

So now that we had a drummer-sage and a demented Taj Mahal of a singer, the band only had two problems left: (1) we didn't have a bass player, which I knew exactly how to fix, and (2) we *still* didn't have a name . . .

'How does Crazy Versus Sane sound to you?' I asked Ellen.

'Pardon me?'

'For a band name.'

'Hmm,' she said. 'I guess it makes sense; you're going to be all New Sound, right?'

'Sort of, but better.'

She shrugged. 'It's a little bit trying-too-hard; the word *crazy*, I mean. Like in *Catch-22*. Anyone who tells you they're crazy really isn't. They're just faking, or they wouldn't know they were crazy.'

'Okay.' I frowned, remembering why hanging out with Ellen

could be a drag sometimes. She had a tendency toward non-enthusiasm.

But then she smiled. 'Don't worry, Pearl. You'll think of something. You playing guitar for them?'

'No, keyboards. We've got one too many guitarists already.'

'Too bad.' She pulled up an acoustic guitar case from the floor, sat it in the chair next to her. 'Wouldn't mind being in a band.'

I stared at the guitar. 'What are you doing with that?'

She shrugged. 'Gave up the cello.'

'What? But you were first chair last year!'

'Yeah, but cellos . . .' A long sigh. 'They take too much infrastructure.'

'They do what?'

She sighed, rearranging the dishes on her tray as she spoke. 'They need infrastructure. Most of the great cello works are written for orchestra. That's almost a hundred musicians right there, plus all the craftsmen to build the instruments and maintain them and enough people to build a concert hall. And to pay for that, you're talking about thousands of customers buying tickets every year, rich donors and government grants . . . That's why only really big cities have orchestras.'

'Um, Ellen? You *live* in a really big city. You're not planning to move to Alaska or something, are you?'

She shook her head. 'No. But what if big cities don't *work* anymore? What if you can't stick that many people together without it falling apart? What if . . .' Ellen's voice faded as she looked around the cafeteria once more.

I followed her gaze. The place still was only two-thirds full, with entire tables vacant and no line at all for food. It was like nobody had been scheduled for A-lunch.

It was starting to freak me out. Where the hell *was* everyone?

'What if the time for orchestras is over, Pearl?'

I let out a snort. 'There've been orchestras for centuries. They're part of . . . I don't know, *civilization*.'

'Yeah, civilization. That's the whole problem . . .' She touched the neck of the guitar case softly. 'I was so sick of carrying that big cello around, like some dead body in a coffin. I just wanted something simple. Something I could play by the campfire, whether or not there's any civilization around.'

A weird tingle went down my spine. 'What happened to you this summer, Ellen?'

She looked up at me and, after a long pause, said, 'My dad went away.'

'Oh. Crap.' I swallowed, remembering when my parents had divorced. 'I'm really sorry. Like . . . he left your mom?'

Ellen shook her head. 'Not right away. You see, someone bit him on the subway, and he . . . got different.'

'*Bit* him?' I thought of the rumors I'd heard, that some kind of rabies was spreading from the rats – that you could see people like Min on the streets now, hungry and wearing dark glasses.

She nodded, still stroking the guitar case's neck. 'At least I'm still on a full scholarship. So I can switch to guitar before—'

'But you're a great *cellist*. You can't give up on civilization yet. I mean, New York City's still around.'

She nodded. 'Mostly. There are still concerts and classes and baseball games going on. But it's kind of like the *Titanic*: there's really only enough lifeboats for the first class passengers.' She scanned the room. 'So when I see people not showing up, I sort of wonder if those passengers are already leaving. And then the floor's going to start tilting, the deck chairs sliding past.'

'Um . . . the what?'

Ellen turned to me with narrowed eyes. 'Here's the thing,

Pearl. I bet your friends are already off in Switzerland, or some-place like that.'

I shrugged. 'They mostly just graduated.'

'I bet they're in Switzerland anyway. Most people who can afford it are already gone. But my friends . . .' She shook her head, then shrugged. 'They don't have drivers or bodyguards, and they have to ride the subway to school. So they're in hiding, sort of.'

'You're here.'

'Only reason is that we live around the corner. I don't have to ride the subway. Plus . . .' She smiled, touching the case in the seat next to her. 'I really want to learn to play guitar.'

We talked more – about her father, about all the stuff we'd seen that summer. But my mind kept wandering to the band.

Listening to Ellen, it had occurred to me that bands like ours needed a lot of infrastructure too, as much as any symphony orchestra. To do what we did, we needed electronic instruments and microphones, mixing boards and echo boxes and stacks of amplifiers. We needed nightclubs, recording studios, record com-panies, cable channels that showed music videos, and fans who had CD players and electricity at home.

Crap, we *needed* civilization.

I couldn't exactly see Moz and Min jamming around a camp-fire, after all.

What if Luz's fairy tales were true, then, and some big struggle was coming? And what if Ellen Bromowitz had it right, and the time for orchestras was over? What if the illness that had ripped apart Nervous System was going to bring down the infrastructure that made having our kind of band even possible?

I straightened up in my chair. It was time to get moving. I had to quit patting myself on the back just because Moz was happy and Minerva was relatively noncrazy and rehearsals were going well.

We needed to become world-famous soon, while there was still that kind of world to be famous in.

14. THE REPLACEMENTS

–ZAHLER–

We churned out one fawesome tune after another – me, Moz, and Pearl, meeting two or three times a week at her place. After we'd used up all our old riffs, we started basing stuff on Pearl's loopy samples, and the Mosquito didn't even buzz about it. Ever since the band had gotten real – with a drummer, a singer, even separate amps for Moz and me – he'd finally realized that this wasn't a competition.

What he hadn't realized was how hot Pearl was or that she had a major crush on him.

All I could do was shake my head about that last part. The problem for Pearl was, she'd really given Moz something. She'd stripped away his shell, had shown him a way to get everything he really wanted, had helped him find a focus that he'd been too lame to discover for himself.

He was never going to forgive her for that.

Me, I still thought Pearl was hot. But for now, there was nothing I could do about it. And actually, I was happy with things the way they were. My best friend and the foolest girl in the world had finally quit fighting, the music was fexcellent, and Pearl loved the band, which meant she wasn't going anywhere without me tagging along.

It was all going so good, I should have known something was about to explode.

We were working on the B section of one of the new tunes, called 'A Million Stimuli to Go.' It was totally complicated, and no matter how hard I tried, I just couldn't play it. Moz kept showing me how on his Strat, but for some reason it didn't work on my fingers.

At least, it didn't until Pearl jumped in. She swept aside the CD cases and a harmonica scattered across her bed and sat down next to me. Unhooking the strap of my guitar, she pulled it over into her lap.

'Let me, Zahler,' she said.

Then, like it was no big deal, she started playing the part.

Normally, sitting that close to her would have been pretty fool. But at that moment I was too dumbfounded to appreciate it.

'See?' she said, her fingers practically smoking as they cruised across the strings. 'You've just got to use your pinky on that last bit.'

Moz laughed. 'He hates using his pinky. Says it's his retarded finger.'

I didn't say anything right then, just watched her play, nodding like a moron. She was dead on about how to make the part work, and now that I could see it from behind the strings, it didn't even look that hard. When Pearl handed me back my guitar, I managed to get it right the first time.

She stood up and went back to her keyboards, tweaking her stacks while I ran through it a dozen more times, pushing the riff deep into my brain.

I didn't say anything more about it till later, when it was just me and the Mosquito.

*

'Moz, did you see what happened back there?'

We were wandering through late-night Chinatown, surrounded by the clatter of restaurant kitchens. The thick sweat of fry-cooking rolled along the narrow streets, and the metal doors of fish markets were rumbling down, the briny smell of guts lingering in the air.

It was pretty quiet at night since the pedestrian curfew had been imposed. Moz and I always ignored the curfew, though, so it was like we owned the city.

'See what?' Moz twisted his body to peer down the alley we'd just passed.

'No, not down there.' Since that day with my dogs, I didn't even *glance* into alleys anymore. 'Back at Pearl's. When she showed me that riff.' My hands lifted into guitar position, fingers fluttering. The moves were in me now, too late to save me from humiliation.

'Oh, the one you had trouble with? What about it?'

'Did you see how Pearl just *did* it?'

He frowned, his own fingers tracing the pattern. 'That's how it's supposed to be played.'

I groaned. 'No, Moz, not *how* she played it. *That* she played it, when it was driving me nuts!'

'Oh,' he said, then waited as a garbage truck steamed past, squeaking and groaning. For some reason, there were six guys hanging onto the back, instead of the usual two or three. They watched us warily as the truck rumbled away. 'Yeah, she's pretty good. You didn't know that?'

'Hell, no. When did that happen?'

'A long time before we met her.' He laughed. 'You never noticed how her hand moves when she calls out chords?' His left hand twitched in the air. 'And I told you how she spotted the Strat, same as me.'

'But—'

'And that stuff in her room: the flute, the harmonicas, the hand drums. She plays it all, Zahler.'

I frowned. It was true, there were a lot of instruments lying around at Pearl's. And sometimes she'd pull one down and play something on it, just for a joke. 'I never noticed any guitars, though.'

He shrugged. 'She keeps them under the bed. I thought you knew.'

I looked down and swung my boot at the fire hydrant squatting on the curb, catching it hard in one of its little spouty things. It clanked and I hopped back, remembering I didn't mess with hydrants anymore. 'That doesn't bug you?'

'Bug me? I don't care if she keeps them in the attic, as long as I get to play the Strat.'

'Not that. Doesn't it bug you that *I'm* supposed to be our guitarist, and I don't even play guitar as well as our *keyboard player*?'

'So? She's a musical genius.'

I groaned. Sometimes the Mosquito could be spectacularly retarded. 'Well, doesn't that sort of imply that the "musical genius" should be our second guitarist, and not me?'

He stopped, turned to face me. 'But Zahler, that won't help. You don't play keyboards at all.'

'Ahhh! That's not what I mean!'

Moz sighed, put his hands up. 'Look, Zahler, I know she plays guitar better than you. And she understands the Big Riff better than I do, just like she does most music. She probably drums better than a lot of drummers – maybe not Alana Ray, though. But like I said, she's a musical genius. Don't worry. She and I were talking about you, and Pearl's already got a plan.'

'Talking about me? A plan?'

'Of course. Pearl's always got a plan – that's why she's the boss.' He smiled. 'I got over it, why can't you?'

'Why can't I *get over it*?' I stood there, breathing hard, hands flexing, looking to grab something by the throat and choke it. 'You weren't over *jack* until a couple of weeks ago! And that's only because you think that weird junkie friend of hers is hot!'

He stared at me, eyes wide, and I glared back at him. It was one of those things I hadn't known until I'd blurted it out. But now I could see that it was totally true. The only reason Moz had been so fool lately was that Minerva had clicked the reset button on his brain.

I'd already told Moz what I thought of her. She was a junkie, or an ex-junkie, or a soon-to-be junkie, and was bad news. Even before she'd freaked out at Alana Ray during that first rehearsal, the whole dark glasses and trippy singing had been totally paranormal.

I'm not saying she wasn't a good singer, just that I like my songs with *words*. And I like my skinny, pale chicks with veiny arms as far away as possible.

'Min's not a junkie,' he said.

'Oh, yeah? How do you know?'

He spread his hands. 'Well, how do you know she *is*?'

'Listen, I don't know *what* she is.' I slitted my eyes. 'All I know is that it's something that they only let out for two hours a week! That's why we rehearse early Sunday morning, right? And why those two run back to Brooklyn? Because visiting hours are over?'

Moz frowned. 'Yeah, I don't really know what that's about.' He turned away and started walking again, like I hadn't just been yelling at him. 'I think Pearl likes to keep Minerva to herself. They've been friends since they were little kids, and Min's kind of . . . fragile.

I snorted. Junkies might be easy to knock down, but they're never fragile. They have souls like old leather shoes studded with steel, and they're about as much good as friends.

From the fish store across the street, a big Asian guy was eyeing us, a baseball bat in one hand. When I waved and smiled, he nodded and went back to tossing out bucketfuls of used ice, spreading them across the asphalt to let them melt. The icy splinters glittered in the streetlights, and I walked over to crush some under my feet.

Stupid Pearl. Stupid Moz. Stupid guitar.

Against the street, the ice looked black. People said that if you got black water into the freezer fast enough, it would freeze up instead of evaporating, and you'd have black ice. Of course, they never said why you'd *want* anything like that in your fridge. When I went over to Moz's, I still crossed the street so I didn't get too close to that hydrant, even though it had one of those special caps on it now to keep kids out.

'There's something I should tell you about, though.' Moz's boots crunched through the ice behind me. 'But you can't tell anyone else.'

'Great,' I murmured, smashing more ice. 'Just what this band needs, more secrets.' Moz still hadn't told Pearl he was paying Alana Ray, or me where he was getting the money from. And apparently Pearl and Moz had their own secret plans for me . . .

'Min gave me her phone number.'

I spun toward him. He was smiling. 'Dude! You *do* think she's hot!'

He laughed, kicking a glittering spray of hail toward me. 'Zahler, let me explain something to you. Minerva isn't *hot*. She's way past hot. She's a fifty-thousand-volt plasma rifle. She's a jet engine.'

I closed my eyes and groaned. When Moz started talking this

way about a girl, it was all over. His obsessions were like an epic guitar solo playing in his brain, endless skittering riffs without any particular logic.

'She's luminous. A rock star. So of course she's a little strange.' He sighed. 'But, yeah, you're right. It might be weird with Pearl . . .'

When he said those last words, that's when I probably should have tried to talk him out of it, but at that moment I was all tangled up about the guitar thing – deeply pissed with Moz and Pearl. They could have at least *told* me I was a worthless doofus instead of thinking it behind my back and making plans.

I opened my eyes. 'So, you're plasma-rifle serious? Jet-engine serious?'

'Yeah, man. She's hot.'

I shrugged. It wasn't my fault if Moz decided to screw everything up. 'When did she give you her number?'

'Sunday before last?'

'Ten days ago?' I rolled my eyes, wanting to make him feel stupid. 'Don't you think you should maybe *do* something about it?'

He swallowed, rocking on his feet a little. 'It was kind of funny, though. She handed me her number so Pearl couldn't see, and she told me to call at one in the morning. Exactly. She even set my watch to hers.'

'So she's weird. We knew that, right?'

'I guess. Yeah, I should call her.' He started walking again, kind of twitchy, like Alana Ray before rehearsals.

I sighed, even more miserable now. Here I'd pushed Moz into going after a weird junkie chick, and it hadn't even made me feel any better. I stopped next to a row of mini-Dumpsters outside a restaurant kitchen door and jumped up onto the edge of one, sitting there and pounding my boot heels against its metal side.

'Anyway,' Moz said. 'What does that have to do with Pearl playing guitar?'

'Can't remember. All I know is that this sucks. I mean, what good is it being the third-best guitarist in a band? Or does Minerva play guitar too?'

He laughed, jumping up beside me. 'Listen, Zahler. You're important to the band. You give us energy.'

'What, like a puppy?'

'Don't you remember that first day? If you hadn't been there, me and Pearl wouldn't have lasted ten minutes.'

'So what? You two are past all that stuff. You don't need me anymore.' I looked at him, frowning. 'So what's this plan of Pearl's?'

'Well, she figures it's not really New Sound, having more than one guitar.'

'Oh.' My throat closed up, and my feet stopped swinging, freezing in midair.

I was toast. Gone.

'Pearl was going to tell you this, but I guess I have to now. Um, the thing is . . . we want you to play bass.'

'*What?*'

'We need a bassist. And with this band, anytime we add some-body, everything goes haywire.' He shook his head. 'I mean, I don't want to have to explain Alana Ray to someone new.' His voice dropped. 'Or Min, for that matter.'

One of my heels hit metal. A soft *boom*. 'But Moz, I've spent the last six years playing guitar.'

'Zahler, you've spent the last six years playing guitar *like a bass*.' He moved his fingers all spastically. 'You never noticed that every part I've ever written for you is on the bottom four strings, with hardly any chords? You could switch over in about five minutes. I would've told you to change years ago, except you and me *didn't have a bass.*'

'But Moz,' I said, my world crumbling. 'We still don't have a bass.'

'Yeah, we do. Pearl's got one under her bed.'

I yelled, pounding both heels against booming metal. 'But doesn't that mean she *plays*? Better than me, probably, seeing as how I never even touched one except one time in a music store?'

'Don't you worry about her.' He smiled and half-turned, held out his palm toward me. 'Come on.'

I stared at his hand. 'Come on what?'

'Put your hand up to mine.'

I frowned, then did it. My fingers stuck out almost an inch longer than Moz's. Big, fat, clumsy fingers.

'Whoa,' he said. 'That is fawesome. You should try this with Pearl sometime. She's got really tiny hands.'

'She does?' I remembered playing the bass that time in the store, slapping at strings thick as steel worms. The frets were miles apart.

'Yeah. She can hardly get her left hand around the neck.'

I looked down at my big, fat, fawesome fingers and laughed.

'Can't even hold a bass, huh? Some musical genius.'

15. THE NEED

–MOZ–

It felt weird, waiting for one A.M. exactly.

I've always hated clocks and schedules, but this felt different – more like the sensation I'd gotten just before the TV had shattered on the street in front of me. My magic powers were screaming that something was about to happen.

As if I didn't know that already.

I sat there in the kitchen with no lights on, the window wide open and trying to suck in some late September coolness. My parents' apartment is on the sixth floor, and all night long leftover heat filters up from the rest of the building, like we live in the top of a steam cooker. The ancient refrigerator was humming, rattling mightily as it tried to keep beer cold and milk from going sour. An occasional whoop of siren leaped up from the street, along with the staticky pops of police radios.

The darkness was buzzing around me, my skin tingling, fingers drifting over my unplugged Stratocaster's strings, pulling small noises from them. I imagined the notes amplified and her voice singing over the lines I played.

The whole one o'clock thing didn't make sense. Minerva had said something about not waking her parents up, but if they were the problem, why call in the middle of the night?

I wondered if her mom and dad were some kind of religious freaks, the kind who didn't let her talk to boys on the phone. Was that why she only went out on Sunday mornings? Did they think Pearl was taking her to church?

Wouldn't that be perfect? If rehearsal was our church, Minerva was the high priestess.

I skidded one fingernail down my lowest string, making the sound of a tiny jet plane crashing to the ground. I was always edgy calling a girl the first time, even a normal girl with normal parents. Even one who'd never screamed holy sacraments while I played guitar.

Minerva had handed me her number when no one else was looking, had whispered her instructions. She knew this was a bad idea, and I knew too – the sort of thing that broke up bands. The badness of it was all over me in the darkness, hovering an inch from my skin, like a cloud of mosquitoes getting ready to bite.

And one A.M., which had seemed, like, *forever* away fifteen minutes ago, was almost here . . .

I placed the Strat on the kitchen table, took the phone from the wall, and pulled out the number she'd given me. Her handwriting was sloppy, almost as bad as Zahler's, the paper crumpled from ten days in my pocket, crammed against keys and coins and guitar picks.

I dialed slowly, telling myself it didn't really count until I pressed the last digit. After all, I'd gone this far a few other nights, only to choke.

But this time, five seconds before the hour, I finished the spell.

She picked up before it even rang.

'Ooh, no dial tone,' she said softly, which didn't make any sense at first.

'Minerva?'

'You finally did it, Mozzy,' she whispered.

I licked my lips, which felt as dry and rough as burnt toast. 'Yeah, I did.'

'I've been sitting here waiting, ten nights in a row.'

'Oh. Sorry it took so long.' I found myself whispering back at her, even though my parents' room was at the other end of the apartment.

'I've been really good every night, picking up exactly at one.' She sighed. 'And every time . . . *buzzzz*.'

'Oh, a dial tone.' I cleared my throat, not sure what to say.

'A dial tone instead of you,' she said, her voice slipping out of its whisper. Minerva talked like she sang, low and growly, a tone that penetrated the rumble of the fridge and the whir of cars down on the street.

I reached over to the Strat and plucked an open string. 'Doesn't your phone have a ringer?'

'Yes, it has a ringer.' I heard a distant clank on her end, like she'd kicked something. 'But it rings in my parents' room and downstairs too. Only Pearl and Luz are supposed to know this number.'

'That sucks.' I wondered who Luz was. Another friend? 'And the worst thing is, Luz took all my numbers away.'

'Took your numbers? You mean she stole your address book?'

Minerva giggled. 'No, silly Moz. The little buttons with numbers. There's no way for me to dial out.'

'Crap. Really?' What was the *deal* with her parents? Or Luz, whoever she was?

'Smelly phone.' Another soft *clank*. 'So I've been sitting here waiting every night, hoping you would call. Wanting you to, but all nervous in case a little ring squirted out. Picking up exactly at one, and all I get is *buzzzz* . . . like some horrible bee.'

'Sorry about that.' I shifted my weight on the kitchen chair, remembering staring at my own phone at one o'clock, wishing I'd had the guts to call. 'Well, I'm talking to you now.'

'Mmm. It's yummy too. We finally get to talk with no one else around.'

'Yeah, it's cool.' My throat was dry, and the badness was clinging to my skin now, like an itch all over me. It reminded me of hiding in the closet when I was little, excited but scared that someone would open the door. 'So, can I ask you something, Min?'

'Sure. You get to ask me anything, now that no one's listening.'

'Um, yeah.' The fridge turned itself off, leaving me in sudden silence. My voice dropped as I asked, 'So, when you and Pearl leave early? You're not really going to Spanish lessons, are you?'

She giggled softly. 'No. We have to get back before Luz knows I'm gone.'

'Oh. Luz again.' I noticed that my right hand was all twisted up in the phone cord, my fingers strangled white and bloodless. I started to unwind it. 'But that's, like, a Spanish name, right?'

'It means *light*. "Let there be Luz."'

'So she's your Spanish teacher.' Or whatever.

'*Sí. Y un problema grande.*'

Even I could figure out that bit of Spanish. Luz was a big problem. But what *was* she? A nanny? Some sort of religious homeschooling tutor? A shrink?

'What are you thinking?'

I shifted around on my chair, skin itching again. 'I'm wondering about you.'

'Mmm,' she purred. 'If I'm crazy? If I'm *bad*?'

I swallowed. 'No. But I don't really know you, outside of practice.'

'I think you do know me, Mozzy. That's why I wanted you to call. Because you know things.'

'Um, I do?'

'Sure. Just close your eyes.'

I did, and she started humming, the sound barely carrying over the wires. I imagined her singing in the practice room, drawing me into her slipstream as we played. Fragments of her songs echoed in my head. It felt like I was being pulled somewhere.

She stopped humming, but her breathing still reached my ears.

'Where do you get those words, Min? For our songs?'

She laughed softly. 'From underneath.'

'Like, from underneath your conscious mind or something?'

'No, silly,' she whispered. 'Underneath my *house*.'

'Uh, really?' With my eyes closed, she seemed so close, like she was whispering in my ear. 'You write in your basement?'

'I did at first, back when they let me go down there. I had fevers and could feel something under the house. Something rumbling.'

'Yeah.' I nodded. 'I know what you mean. I can feel something kind of . . . underneath us when you sing.'

'Something in the ground.' She was breathing harder now. 'You *do* know things.'

'Sometimes I feel like my music's just buzzing around in the air. But you pull it down, tie it to something that's real.'

'Mmm. It's realer than you think.' She breathed slowly for a while, and I just listened until she said, 'Do you want more, Moz?'

I swallowed. 'How do you mean?'

'Do . . . you . . . want . . . more? I can give you the rest of it. You're only tasting a little tiny fraction.'

I opened my eyes. The darkness in the kitchen was suddenly sharp. 'A fraction of what?'

'Of what I have. Come over, and I'll show you.'

The table seemed to tremble: my heart beating in my fingertips. 'Come over . . . now?'

'Yes, Mozzy. Come rescue me and Zombie.'

'Um . . . Zombie?'

'He's my undead slave.'

I swallowed. 'Yeah?'

She let out a giggle, just above a whisper. 'And his breath smells like cat food.'

'Oh.' I let out a slow breath. 'Zombie has whiskers too, doesn't he?'

'Yeah, and he also knows things. But . . . Moz?'

'What?'

'I'm *hungry*.'

I laughed. She was so skinny, I never thought of Minerva getting hungry. She ate a lot of beef jerky at rehearsal, but I figured that was for her voice or something.

'You want to go and get something? I'll wait.' I wanted to sit there in silence for a minute or two, just to recover. Just to scratch myself all over.

'Can't.'

'Why not?'

'See, here's the thing. The door of my room has this smelly lock. On the outside.'

'Really?' I blinked. 'Like, your parents keep you locked in at night?'

'Daytime too. Because I was sick before.'

I closed my eyes again. A new layer of hovering badness sprang up all around me, filling the room with a buzzing sound.

'That's why you have to come rescue me,' she said. 'Come let me out and I'll show you everything.'

I bit my lip. 'But you live in . . . Brooklyn, right?'

She groaned. 'Don't be lame. Just take the F train. Half an hour.'

Just half an hour. Plus however long it took the train to come, maybe an hour total. Not forever; I wasn't afraid of the subways yet.

And if I didn't go see her, how long would it take to fall asleep in my room all alone? A thousand hours, at least.

Every time I'd watched her sing, her songs moving through my hands as I played, I'd gone to bed that night with her cries still echoing in my brain. Every time, I'd imagined a thousand ways of following her back to Brooklyn, and now she was inviting me.

If I said no, this itch would never leave my skin.

'Everyone's asleep here,' she was saying. 'And I can show you where my music comes from.'

'Okay, Min. I'll come.' I stood up, like I was heading out the door right then, but my head started to spin. I sat back down. 'But how are you going to get out?'

'You're going to rescue me. It's easy. Pearl does it all the time.'

'Um, am I supposed to climb up to your window or something?'

'No, silly. Just walk up the stairs.' She giggled. 'But first, you have to find the magic key . . .'

16. LOVE BITES

—MINERVA—

Mozzy was taking for*ever*.

I was dressed up so pretty, it was killing me just sitting here at my desk, staring at myself in the mirror. Zombie was pacing, knowing from the tinkle of my earrings that we were going out.

'Not long now,' I said softly. My stomach rumbled.

The thought of Moz coming over had changed the balance inside me – the hungry thing had woken up, stirred from the sleep Luz had forced upon it. I'd already chewed through all my emergency beef jerky, trying not to think of the way he smelled. So yummy and intense.

I took a bite of pork rind, letting its unctuous texture coat my mouth. Zombie wandered over and *mur-row*ed, so I gave him my fingers to lick.

'You can go play with your little friends soon.'

I looked at the clock: after two. Smelly Moz. What if he'd chickened out? I wanted to get closer to the earth. Singing felt wonderful, but I needed to feel the dirt under my fingernails, to smell and taste the things down there.

I needed to learn more, to put flesh on the words in my notebooks.

My stomach rumbled again, and I felt funny in a way I hadn't for a while. Like before Luz came along – kind of . . . inhuman. That wasn't good.

Mustn't eat Mozzy, I thought, and peeled a clove of garlic. It was fresh, the way Luz said was best, the papery skin still flecked with purple. The clove split between my teeth, sharp and hot as fresh chicken blood. My next breath sucked the flavor into my lungs, and my nerves steadied.

'That'll teach you,' I whispered to the hungry thing inside me, then took a swig from the little bottle of tequila Pearl had smuggled in, swishing it around my mouth. Didn't want to taste funny for Moz.

In the clarity of my garlic buzz, I took off my dark glasses and stared into the mirror, wondering in which direction I was headed tonight.

Some things, like Luz's teas and tinctures, made me better, more boring and sensible. Others, like singing with Pearl's band, brought out the magnificent beast inside me and summoned the big things underground. It was the same old balancing act – how far to go with boys, with booze, with dangerous places – but magnified until the whole earth shook.

I wasn't sure yet which way Moz was going to take me. I knew that both halves of me wanted badly to take him under the ground, but I was pretty certain they had different ideas about what to *do* with him down there.

I gnashed another clove of garlic, swilled another shot of tequila, just in case.

The stairs creaked . . . *Moz*.

I stood up, crossed to the door, and pressed my ear against it. He was down at the very bottom, making his slow way up. My thirsty hearing swept through the house: Max's heart beating in the room next door, Daddy snoring low and even, no pages turning from my mother reading late in bed. Silence, except for the slow, cautious feet creeping up the stairs, the occasional crinkle of the house cooling down.

Zombie did figure eights around my feet.

'No purring,' I hissed. 'Mommy's listening.'

I slid my cheek along the door, put my nose up to the crack. Sniffed.

Moz was still too far downstairs to smell. I counted my own heartbeats to a thousand, spread my palms out on the door, pressed my anxious weight against it, groaning. Even shiny Pearl didn't climb the stairs this slowly.

Finally he reached the top floor and I caught his scent, nervous and unsure.

And *hungry*. I smiled.

He turned the hasp free, the faint vibrations traveling through wood and into my thirsty skin. The metal bolt slid across.

I took a step back, dizzy. Being rescued was *much* better when it was Mozzy doing it.

The door opened the tiniest crack.

'Min?' On a little puff of air, smelling of yummy Moz breath.

I didn't answer, just stood there behind the door, Zombie warm against my ankle. Everything was tingling.

The door pushed open another nervous inch. 'Minerva?'

'Mozzzz,' I buzzed.

'*Jesus.*' His face peeked through, shiny in the candle light, expressions squirming across it.

I put my hand out to stroke his cheek. Brought it back and licked my fingers. Nervous-tasting, but Mozzy.

He pushed through into my room, leaned back to softly shut the door. Closed his eyes. 'Jesus, Min. Those are some creaky-ass stairs.'

I giggled, slipping a hand through the unzipped top of his jacket, pressing my palm against his chest. His heart was pounding deliciously. If he hadn't been breathing so hard, I could have heard the warm blood rushing through his veins.

Don't think naughty thoughts, I scolded myself.

'You made it, though.'

His eyes opened, a relieved grin making his face shimmer. 'Yeah.'

I pulled my hand back from the hothouse of his jacket, pressed fingers against the door. 'No one heard you. Relax.'

Mozzy nodded but didn't relax at all. His expression was so naked, tension transforming into excitement, his own hunger rumbling. His eyes rolled across my tight black dress and boots, growing wider, about to burst.

'You're all dressed up.'

I smiled. 'Well, we're going somewhere special, you know.'

'Oh.' He glanced down at himself: T-shirt under leather jacket, jeans. 'I didn't think . . .I mean, it's two in the morning.'

'Shush, Moz. You look delicious.' I bent down and swept up Zombie. 'Come on. Time for the creaky-ass stairs again.'

'Okay . . .' He frowned. 'The cat's coming?'

I sighed. Why was everyone always giving Zombie funny looks? He never stuck his nose into *their* business. Zombie had things to do, places to be. Zombie needed rescuing too. And he knew things.

If he could talk, Zombie would've told us what was coming.

But all I said was, 'He's got a date with a tree.'

'Oh, sure.' Moz smiled and softly opened the door.

With no smelly sun wrecking everything, outside was much better.

In beautiful soft starlight, I could see the dead leaves scattered on the ground, the spiderwebs sparkling in the grass, captured insects making them dance. The unburnt air was moist, thick with scents and sounds.

I put Zombie down, watched him slip in among the glistening piles of plastic bags. Those garbage mountains were alive in the darkness, the steady breeze carrying messages from deep inside.

I put my hand against one, felt its cool slickness. It had a scent like my room, my bedclothes, like something that Zombie and I shared. Little tremblings were rampant in the pile's depths, answering my presence.

'Family,' I murmured, rustles of understanding moving through me.

'Um, yeah. Your family,' Moz whispered, glancing nervously back at my house, as if the porch light was about to pop on, Daddy emerging with a shotgun. 'Where're we going anyway?'

His anxious smell made hunger bubble up inside me again, and I wished I'd brought more garlic. I turned and took his hand, pulling him down the street. 'This way. I'm taking you where I can show you things.'

'Oh, okay.' He followed in a silent trance, obedient in my grasp. As we neared the first intersection, though, my steps slowed. Everything was muddled.

I'd grown up on this street, but somehow things had changed. A new world had descended on my old neighborhood – a terrain of smells, skittering sounds, and territorial boundaries. The old maps inside my head had crumbled over the last two months, turning the street signs into gibberish.

'Which way's the F stop, Moz?'

'We're going somewhere by *subway*? It's, like, two-thirty, Min!'

I frowned. 'We're not getting on a train. Just need to remember.' I squeezed his hand, looking up into his bulging, thirsty eyes. 'I've been locked up for a while, you know.'

'Oh, right.' His throat rippled with a swallow. 'Sure. It's back this way.'

I followed him, familiar landmarks seething with the new reality – the vacant lot one block over, alive now with shivering forms; my old preschool, playground swings creaking in the breeze; the best Lebanese restaurant in Brooklyn, its garbage smelling of rancid honey and chickpeas, trembling with movement.

Luz has been robbing me of all this, I thought. She wanted to cure me of my new senses, to lock me away from this sumptuous half-lit world. Every step I took, I was finding out more . . . I still had enough crazy left to understand.

Moz took me to the F station down the block, and I pulled him to the lip of the stairs, breathed in the subterranean hum for a dizzy and exultant moment, like when *la musica* traveled through me. The beast rumbled, twisting happily in my guts.

'But I thought we weren't—'

'We're not taking the train,' I said. 'This is just a shortcut.'

'A shortcut?' he said, not quite believing.

'You can only get what you want underground, Mozzy. But believe me, you'll love the way it tastes.'

He blinked, then nodded. I smiled, covering my eyes as I pulled him down into the fluorescent lights, his pulse fluttering under my fingers.

Every step we took, the pull was getting stronger

Moz could sense it too, as if its influence traveled through my skin and into his, an electric current of desire. Or maybe he could smell it on me – here underground I felt myself glowing with it, the beast inside me doing back flips, screaming that it was almost loose. Whatever was down here had freed it from Luz's restraints. My tongue ran across my teeth uneasily.

Must. . . not. . . eat. . . Mozzy.

But I couldn't stop moving forward either.

Behind me Moz was panting, eyes glittering like wet glass. When I jumped down from the platform onto the empty subway tracks, he didn't say a word, just paused for a moment before following. His lips were full of blood, and I could see his heart racing in his throat. It was all I could do not to take him right there, but I knew it would only get better the farther down we went. I pulled him into the darkness of the tunnel.

Gravel crunched under our feet, and the skitters and smells of tiny things were all around us. My friends, my family.

Then a shiver traveled up into my toes . . . *danger*.

Moz pulled me to a stop. He'd felt it too. 'Crap! Is that a train?'

I knelt, put one hand on a rail.

'Watch out! That's—'

'Don't be scared, Moz.' I pointed with my free hand. '*That's* the electric one. This one's just for listening . . .' The smooth, cold metal under my palm was trembling, but not with the approach of a train. Everything around us shivered: gravel, iron beams, the work lights hanging from their cords. The earth was shuddering in fear.

Calling me to the struggle – *la lucha*. Calling Moz too.

And suddenly I knew something that Luz's cures had hidden from me, something I'd only glimpsed in my songs. The thing underground, the thing that made the earth rumble, was our *enemy*.

The beast inside me had been created to fight it.

'We have to be careful. It's close.'

He sucked in deep breaths through his nose. 'I've heard this, Min, at practice. It's in your music.'

'Clever Mozzy.'

He shook his head. 'But how come it has a . . . *smell*?'

I shrugged. 'Because it has a body. It's real and dangerous. And I don't think we want to meet it just yet, so shush.' I dragged him farther into the tunnel, toward the trail that the old enemy had left behind – the perfect place to quicken the beast inside me.

As we grew nearer, I felt the rest of Luz's restraints stripped away, the lures and tangles and spores of the beast spilling through my system. Finally I understood how it worked. Down here, the beast inside me didn't want to eat Mozzy, it wanted to spread itself.

The old enemy somehow made it . . . *horny.*

Here was the hole, chewed and broken earth, like a wound in the side of the man-made tunnel, stained with the black stuff the enemy used to melt the earth. The ancient enemy was huge, I realized now, big enough to make its own tunnels, though it loved the subway's free ride.

I dragged Moz into the gashed stone of its trail, pushed him against the crumbling edge, easily holding his shoulders in a grip he couldn't break.

His pupils were as big as starless skies. 'Min . . .'

'Shhh.' I put one ear against the tunnel wall and listened . . . The enemy was drifting away, my bad hunger growing as its influence faded. My teeth wanted to pull Moz to pieces, to sate my hunger in a way no chicken blood could touch . . .

'I need to give it to you *now*,' I said.

'But what—'

'Mozzy . . .' I put my hand over his mouth. 'Here's the thing: if we stand here talking, I think I'll eat you.'

His eyes wide, he nodded.

Pulling away my hand, I leaned forward, my mouth covering his, and the beast exploded. It struggled to filter through my skin, trying to wring itself out every pore, squeezing itself into my sweat and spit and blood, saturating every drop of me.

Infecting Moz, injecting him.

The kiss took long seconds, and when it was over I was dripping.

I pushed myself back from Moz and stared into his glittering eyes. He was panting, beautiful, infected. Relief swept through me, and I kissed him softer this time, finally certain that he was safe. Just this once, sane had beaten crazy.

After that first kiss, the hungry beast inside me didn't want to consume this new warrior in the struggle. It was satisfied.

But me . . . I was only getting started.

–PEARL–

I'd bought a new dress just for this, and nine kinds of makeup. My hair had been redone that afternoon, cut and blown and sculpted with goo. I was dripping borrowed bling and staring at my bathroom mirror, a contact lens balanced on the tip of my finger.

Color my mother ecstatic.

'You can do it, Pearl.' She was hovering behind me, similarly glammed.

'That's not the question.' I stared at the contact lens, which shimmered like a tiny bowl of light. A dreadful, painful glow. 'The question is whether I *want* to.'

'Don't be silly, darling. You said you wanted to look your best tonight.'

'Mmm.' Foolish words that had sent Mom into a spending rampage.

Back a million years ago when she was seventeen, she'd actually had a coming-out party, like a real old-fashioned debutante. She still had the pictures. And we'd stayed in New York City no matter how high the garbage got, no matter how dangerous the streets – because this was where the parties were. So she probably hoped this was the beginning of a new era of Pretty Pearl, no more blue jeans or glasses or bands.

'I could just go there blind.'

'Nonsense. To be truly lovely, one must make eye contact. And I don't want you stumbling all over the art.'

'She's a photographer, Mom. Photos are traditionally hung on the wall; you can't stumble on them.' Typical. It was my mother who always got invited to these things, but she never bothered to Google the artist. Which was lucky, I guess. A glance would have revealed who else was on the guest list tonight, giving away the real reason I wanted to go.

'Quit stalling, Pearl. I know you can do this.'

'And how do you know that, Mom?'

'Because I wear contact lenses and so did your father. You've got the genes for it!'

'Great,' I said. 'Thanks for passing on those sticking-a-finger-in-your-eye genes to me. Not to mention the crappy-eyesight genes.' I stared at the little lens gradually drying to razor-sharpness on my fingertip, imagining all my totally lateral caveman ancestors jamming rocks and sticks into their eyeballs, none of them realizing the whole thing would pay off a thousand generations later when I had to look good at an art gallery opening.

'Okay, guys, this is for you,' I said, taking a breath and prying my left eye open wide. As my finger approached, the little transparent disk grew until it blotted out everything, dissolving into a fit of blinking.

'Is it in?' my mother asked.

'How the hell should I know?' I opened one eye, then the other, squinting at myself in the mirror.

Blurry Pearl, clear Pearl, blurry Pearl, clear Pearl . . .

'Hey, I think it's in.'

'See?' my mother said. 'That was easy as pie.'

'Pi squared, maybe. Let's get going.' I scooped new makeup into my brand-new handbag, its silver chain glittering softly in my blurry eye.

My mother frowned. 'What about the other one?'

I alternated eyes again – blurry mother, clear mother – and shrugged. 'Sorry, Mom. I don't think I've got the genes for it.'

As long as I could recognize faces, the demimonde was good enough for me.

Out on the street, Elvis made a big deal about my new look, acting like he didn't recognize me, trying to get me to blush. The older I got, the more he thought his job was to make me feel ten years old. Lately, he was tragically good at it.

The weird thing was, though, by the time we arrived at the gallery, I felt twenty-five. There weren't any cameras popping as Elvis swung the limousine door open for me, but there was a guy with a clipboard and headset, other blinged-up art lovers sweeping into the entrance, their bodyguards piling up out in the street, the clink and chatter coming from the crowd inside . . . It was almost like going onstage.

Even with everything going on, New York still had *gallery openings.* Civilization was still kicking ass, and here I was, in costume and in character. Ready to charm.

Once inside the gallery, the first trick was extricating myself from Mom. She kept showing me off to friends, all of them dutifully not recognizing me and dropping their jaws, reading from the same script as Elvis. Soon Mom was striking up conversations with strangers, dropping 'my daughter' comments and clearly craving 'Not your sister?' in response.

And she wonders why I don't dress up more.

Finally, though, I weaseled out of her orbit with the lame excuse of wanting to look at, you know, the *art.* Her fingers trailed on my shoulder as I slipped away, reminding everyone one more time that I was her daughter.

I made my way straight to a table full of champagne, rows and columns of it bubbling furiously, and smiled. The open bar: where else would a record company rep hang out at an art opening?

I snagged a glass and hovered near the table, keeping an eagle eye (just one) out for the face I'd downloaded that morning. My trap was finally set – I was ready. All my lines were memorized; I was dressed ravishingly and standing in the perfect spot. There was nothing more I could do but wait.

So I waited . . .

Twenty minutes later, my enthusiasm had faded.

No record company talent scout had materialized, the glass was empty, and my feet were unhappy in their new shoes. The party buzzed around me, ignoring my little black dress and borrowed bling, like I was some kind of nonentity. Bubbles rattled unpleasantly in my head.

All my life I'd wondered how my mother's sole life purpose could be going to parties, even while the world was crumbling around her. Finally Google had shown me the answer: her reason for existence was to get *me* into *this* party. Astor Michaels, Red Rat Records' most fawesome talent scout, was also the biggest collector of this photographer's work. He'd discovered the New Sound, signing both Zombie Phoenix and Morgan's Army – not huge, commercial bands, but gutsy bands like us.

It was a perfect match, like when Moz and I had been brought together. Surely this was fate playing with my mother's social calendar.

But as I picked up my second glass and wandered through the crowd, squinting at two hundred half-blurry faces and recognizing none of them, I started to consider an awful possibility: could fate be *messing with me*?

What if Astor Michaels was out of town? Or busy scouting bands at some undiscovered club instead of here? What if Google had lied to me? All my efforts tonight would be wasted – in fact, my mother's whole *life* would be wasted . . .

I stood there, dizzy on my feet, staring at a half-empty glass and realizing something equally dismaying: the champagne gene was another one my mom hadn't passed on. Maybe it was my half-blurry vision or the buzz of the uncaring crowd around me, but I felt like reality was in a blender.

I had to get control.

I took a deep breath and pulled myself out of the crowd, wandering to the party's edge to look at the pictures. They were gigantic photos of the sanitation crisis: glimmering mountains of plastic bags, garbage guys on strike, lots of rats. All were dramatic and weirdly beautiful, almost life-size, as if you could walk straight into them. Which begged the question: Why would you want this stuff on your wall when it was all happening right outside?

The crowd seemed to agree. People were crowded into the middle of the room, shrinking from the images of decomposition. Only a few of us hovered at the fringes of the party, sullen and extraneous, like sophomore guys at the senior prom.

Poor art lovers, I thought, and then, in a fit of champagne-stoked genius, I realized where Astor Michaels had been hiding.

He wasn't here for the prom; he was here for the art. He was one of the sophomores.

I started to circle the room, ignoring the crowd in the middle this time, the ones who looked well connected and happy and cool. I looked for the lonely guys, the losers.

Halfway around, I spotted him out of the corner of my eye –

my good eye, luckily. He was ogling a vast photo of a shrine built by sanitation workers out in the Bronx: praying hands and crosses and skulls (*again!*) all jumbled up to provide protection on their route.

I took a deep drink of champagne to steady myself, my lines beginning to tumble through my head.

'*What am I listening to? Oh, just this lateral new band.*'

My fingers fumbled with the sticky clasp of my new handbag, scrambling around inside until they found my music player at the very bottom. Its earphones were non-helpfully tangled with makeup and hair goo and a million other things I never normally carried. After long seconds of unwinding, I managed to drag the player out and get the phones into my ears. But where was my neck strap? I peered down into the bottomless handbag in horror, realizing I hadn't brought it.

I flashed back to my hours spent at the Apple store looking for just the right strap: sleek black leather with a shiny steel USB connector. I could see it in my mind's eye, still in its packaging, sitting on my bed with all the other *crap.*

And of course this stupid cocktail dress, like all stupid cocktail dresses, had no pockets. It would look way too obvious just carrying the music player in my hand, and a pair of earphones snaking out from my handbag wasn't going to make me look like the hip young trendsetter I was supposed to be. The kind who says things like . . .

'*No, they're not signed. Everyone just* knows *about them.*'

I squeezed my eyes shut, trying to think.

There was only one place to put it.

I took a gulp of champagne, switched the music player on, and dropped it down my cleavage. It fit perfectly and was kind of warm down there. *Really* warm – I looked down and realized that while scrabbling in my handbag I'd locked the screen backlight on.

Framed by the black velvet of my dress, my breasts glowed softly blue.

In my champagne haze, it was kind of cool looking. Carrying your music this way might not be the Taj Mahal of class, but it was definitely going to get the guy's attention.

I moved closer.

'What language is she singing in? I don't think it is one, really.'

The player was set to shuffle our four best songs – long, intense rants of Minerva's peppered with Moz's cleanest, simplest lines, Alana Ray shattering it all into a thousand glittering shapes, Zahler finally playing a proper bass underneath. As I drew nearer, the music began to synchronize with the bubbles in my bloodstream, my footsteps falling with the beat. I was cool and connected, seventeen and covered with bling, a record company's dream demographic in the flesh.

The world began to shift around me, just like when we played, my fingers twitching with the keyboard parts. Huge photographs rolled past my shoulder, a galaxy of rats' and cats' eyes flickering on my blurry side.

'What's their name? I don't think they have a name yet, actually . . .'

By the time I walked up beside Astor Michaels, swirling one last smidgen of champagne in the bottom of my glass, I was cool and predatory and confident, the embodiment of our music.

He turned and looked at me, his eyes following the white cords from my ears down into my glowing cleavage. His gaze flashed a little, reflecting the soft blue light.

Then Astor Michaels smiled at me, and his teeth were pointy, a hundred times sharper than Minerva's . . .

All my lines flew from my head, and I pulled my earphones out, pushing them toward him with quivering hands.

'You've got to listen, man,' I said. 'This shit is paranormal.'

PART IV

THE DEAL

About seven hundred years ago, the disease that finished the Roman Empire returned.

Humanity was already in a bad way. China had just suffered a brutal civil war, Europe had endured a destructive famine, and the Little Ice Age was descending. Across the world, temperatures dropped, crops failed, and whole countries fell into poverty. Wars were sparked by what little wealth remained.

Then a relentless and deadly plague appeared in Asia. In some parts of China, nineteen out of every twenty people perished. The disease was carried to Europe and the Middle East, where it killed a third of the population. The most intense part of the outbreak lasted only five years, but worldwide it left 100 million dead.

Historians once assumed that the Black Death was bubonic plague, a bacterium spread by rats. But that never quite added up: too many people died too quickly. According to some, it might have been a new form of anthrax transmitted from animals to humans. Others believe that an Ebola-like virus suddenly evolved to become airborne, spreading across the world via handshakes and coughs, then disappeared.

But what was the Black Death really, and how did it come and go so quickly?

Keep your ears open, and you'll find out.

NIGHT MAYOR TAPES:
313-314

18. ANONYMOUS 4

–ZAHLER–

The offices of Red Rat Records were fawesome.

Maybe they weren't the biggest label in the world – Red Rat was only an independent – but they had an old town house in the East Twenties all to themselves. Astor Michaels took us inside, saying that the richest family in New York City had once lived there. The ground floor was still fitted out like a money-counting room: antique brass bars guarding the receptionist's desk, the doors solid oak, thick as dictionaries.

There were a bunch of kids waiting in line to deliver CDs and press packets by hand, most of them in full stage dress: black eyeliner and fingernails, ripped clothes and Mohawks. All of them were trying to look fool, but they stared wide-eyed as the five of us were ushered past the brass bars and inside. I got a weird jolt, thinking, *We're rock stars, and they're not.*

I'd always known Pearl would take us places, but I hadn't thought it would be this fast. I didn't feel ready for it, especially since I'd only been playing my new instrument a week.

But Pearl was unstoppable. She'd even managed some kind of deal with Minerva's parents, getting her into Manhattan on a workday. The two of them were supposedly out buying Minerva new clothes, something about her birthday coming up.

We tromped downstairs to the basement, where Astor Michaels's personal office occupied the steel cube of an old walk-in safe, lit only by the flickering glow of a computer screen. It was as big as a one-car garage, the walls lined with rows of safe-deposit boxes. The foot-thick metal door looked too heavy to move – I hoped it was anyway. If anyone shut it, I would've started screaming.

Huge photographs hung from the walls, artsy pictures of garbage-strewn alleys, gushing black water, and rats.

Yes: rats. And that wasn't the weirdest thing about Astor Michaels.

Our new rep licked his lips a lot, and when he smiled, his teeth never showed. He kept his sunglasses on until we got down into the darkness, and once he took them off, I wished he'd put them back on again. His eyes were way too wide and spent a lot of time lingering on the three girls, especially Minerva.

It was creepy, but I guess when you're a record company rep, you get to ogle all the girls you want. And anyway, it didn't matter whether I liked the guy or not. We were *signed.*

Well, almost. Pearl said her lawyer was still going over the contract. That's right – she said 'my lawyer,' the way she'd say 'my gardener' or 'my driver' or 'my house in Connecticut.' Like a lawyer was something you kept in a drawer along with the double-A batteries and spare apartment keys.

'In a few minutes, we'll all go upstairs,' Astor Michaels said. 'Marketing is dying to meet you. They love the music, of course, but they want to make sure you really have it.'

What's 'it'? I almost asked. But I figured that if you did have it, you probably didn't need to ask what it was, which meant I didn't, so I should just shut up.

'Should we have dressed up for this?' Pearl asked, which didn't make any sense because she looked fexcellent in her tight black dress, a thin choker of diamonds around her neck. The only bad thing was that her glasses were missing, which made her look less smart and in charge.

Still, she looked amazing.

Astor Michaels waved a hand. 'Just be yourselves.'

What if myself happens to be a big sweaty ball of nerves today? I wanted to ask, but that also didn't sound like a very 'it' thing to say.

We went upstairs, where a bunch of people with six-hundred-dollar haircuts sat around a conference table shaped like a long, curvy swimming pool. Pearl took charge, of course. She talked about our 'influences', naming a bunch of bands I'd never heard of except for seeing their CDs on Pearl's bed.

Minerva sat at the head of the table, shimmering, sucking up all the compliments that came her way. She obviously had it – even I could see that now, reflected in the marketing people's gazes. Ever since Minerva and Moz had secretly hooked up, her junkie vibe was slowly changing into something else – whether less creepy or more, I couldn't tell.

But the haircuts ate it up.

Moz also seemed to make an impression on them, like he had it too. As if Minerva had given it to him. He was much more intense these days, his eyes radiating confidence and a new kind of hungriness that I couldn't understand.

That was the weird thing: as Minerva got less junkie-like, she seemed to push Moz in the opposite direction, so we were really only breaking even.

Me and Alana Ray stayed quiet, like a rhythm section should. I was a bass player now, after all, and we don't say too much.

*

After a while we headed back down to the safe, leaving the haircuts upstairs to talk about us. Astor Michaels said we'd done a good job, then gave us some fexcellent news.

'We want you to play a showcase. Four Red Rat bands in a little club we're renting.' He licked his lips. 'In two weeks . . . I hope that's not too soon.'

'Soon is good,' Pearl said, which was probably the smart thing to say, but a wave of panic was rolling through me. Two more Sunday rehearsals with my new instrument didn't seem like enough. I practiced hours every day, of course, but that was nothing like playing with the whole band. Those big bass strings still felt clumsy under my fingers, like playing with gloves on.

'There's one issue, though,' Astor Michaels was saying. 'We're printing the posters tomorrow. Taking out ads as well.'

'Oh, crap.' Pearl cleared her throat. 'And we don't have a name yet.'

'We've been meaning to come up with one,' I blurted. 'But there hasn't been time.'

'Can't agree on anything,' Moz growled.

Pearl shifted uncomfortably next to me on Astor Michaels's big leather couch. 'Can't we just be "Special Guests" or something?'

He shook his head, lips parting, a little glimpse of teeth slipping into view. 'Posters and ads cost money, Pearl. That money's wasted if your name is missing.'

'Yeah, I guess so.' She looked around at us.

'Here's what we'll do,' Astor Michaels said. 'I'll leave you five to discuss this while I go and have lunch. When I come back in an hour, you give me a name you all agree on. Not a list, not suggestions or ideas: one name. Either it'll be perfect or it won't be.'

Pearl swallowed. 'So what if it's not?'

He shrugged. 'Then the deal's off.'

'What?' Pearl said, eyes widening. 'No showcase?'

'No nothing.' Astor Michaels stood and headed out. 'If you five can't agree on a name, then how are you supposed to tour together? How are you supposed to make records? How can Red Rat commit to you for five years if you can't commit to one simple name?' He stood in the doorway, slipping sunglasses over his laughing, too-wide eyes. 'So unless you agree on something perfect, the whole deal's off.'

'But . . . not really,' Pearl said. 'Really?'

'Really. You have an hour.' Astor Michaels looked at his watch. 'How's that for motivation?'

We sat there in silence for a moment, the blown-up photos of rats staring down at us. The room was full of guilt, like we'd all committed some terrible crime together.

'Was that meant ironically?' Alana Ray asked.

'Um . . . I don't think so,' Pearl said.

'Crap,' Moz said. 'What are we going to do?'

Pearl turned to me and Moz, suddenly angry. 'I *knew* we should have figured this out when it was just us three, in that first rehearsal. Now it's all *complicated*!'

'Hey, man,' I said, holding up my hands. 'That's the day I said we should call ourselves the B-Sections. Why don't we go with that?'

Moz and Pearl just stared at me.

'What?' I said. 'Don't you remember? B-Sections?'

Pearl glanced at Moz, then turned to me. 'Yeah, I remember. But I didn't want to be the one to explain that band names based on musical terms – the F-Sharps, the Overtones, the Tapeloops – are in fact the lamest. Thing. Ever.'

Moz shrugged. 'I just thought you were kidding, Zahler. I mean, for one thing, being plural is stupid.'

I frowned. 'Being what?'

'Plural. With an *s* at the end. Makes us sound like some fifties band, like the Rockettes or something.'

Minerva let out a giggle. 'The Rockettes are dancers, Moz. They have long, tasty legs.'

Okay, maybe she wasn't totally normal yet.

'Whatever,' Moz said. 'I don't want to be a plural band. Because if we're the B-Sections, then what's one of us? *A* B-Section? "Hello, I am a B-Section. Together, me and my friends are many B-Sections."'

Minerva giggled again, and I said, 'You know, Moz, anything sounds retarded if you say it a bunch of times in a row. So what's your great idea?'

'I don't know. A "The" in front is cool, as long as the next word isn't plural.' He kicked Astor Michaels's desk in front of him. 'Like, the Desk.'

'*The Desk?*' I groaned. 'Now that's just a genius band name, Moz. That's much better than the B-Sections. Let's go upstairs and tell them we want to be the Desk.'

Moz rolled his eyes. 'It was just an example, Zahler.'

I sank back into the big leather couch. I could see how this was going to go. It was that old classic, the Moz Veto. Like whenever we're trying to figure out what movie to see, Moz never suggests anything, so I have to keep coming up with suggestions while he goes, 'No,' 'Not interested,' 'That sucks,' 'Seen it,' 'Subtitles are lame . . .'

Pearl leaned forward. 'Okay, guys, we don't have to panic about this.'

'Panic!' I said. 'We could be the Panic!'

'I'd rather be the Desk,' Moz said quietly.

'Hang *on!*' Pearl said. 'One idea at a time. A couple of weeks ago, I thought of something.'

Moz swung his veto gaze toward her. 'What?'

'How about Crazy Versus Sane?'

'Pearl, darling,' Minerva said. 'Don't you think that's kind of . . . pointed?' She looked at Alana Ray, not noticing that everyone else was looking at her.

'It's not about *us*,' Pearl said. 'It's about all the weird stuff going on. Like the black water, the sanitation crisis, the crime wave. Like that crazy woman who dropped the Stratocaster on me and Moz . . . That's how this band got started.'

'I don't know,' Moz said. 'Crazy Versus Sane. Sounds kind of artsy-fartsy to me.'

Score another one for the Moz Veto.

I tried to think, random words and phrases spilling through my head, but Pearl had been right. Band names only got harder the longer you waited to pick one. The deeper the music got into your brain, the more impossible it became to describe it in two or three words.

The silence was broken by the shriek of some metal band's demo tape echoing out of another scout's office. The steel walls of the safe seemed to be closing in, the air growing stale. I imagined Astor Michaels shutting the door, giving us until we ran out of oxygen to come up with a name.

I thought of the growling, thumping rehearsal building on Sixteenth Street and wondered if all the bands in there had names. How many bands were there in the whole world? Thousands? Millions?

Looking up at the ranks of safe-deposit boxes surrounding us, I wondered if we should all just get numbers.

'Why don't we just pick something simple?' I said. 'Like . . . Eleven?'

'Eleven?' Moz said. 'That's great, Zahler. But it's no "the Desk."'

Minerva sighed. 'That's the problem with Crazy Versus Sane: it's false advertising, seeing as how we're kind of short on sane.'

'What's not sane is making us choose a name this way,' Pearl said, glaring up at the rat photos.

'Is this sort of ultimatum normal for record companies?' Alana Ray asked.

'No. It's totally *para*normal,' I said.

Pearl's eyes lit up. 'Hey, Zahler, maybe that's it. We should call ourselves the Paranormals!'

'Plural,' Moz said. 'Do you guys not *get* the plural thing?'

'Whatever,' Pearl said. 'Paranormal? *The* Paranormal, if you want to be all *the* about everything.'

'*Paranormal* can mean two things,' Alana Ray said.

We all looked at her. Those rare times Alana Ray actually said something, everybody else listened.

'*Para* can mean *beside*,' she continued. 'Like paralegals and paramedics, who work beside lawyers and doctors. But it can also mean *against*. Like a parasol is against the sun and a paradox against the normal way of thinking.'

I blinked. That was just about the most words Alana Ray had said in a row since that first rehearsal. And like everything she said, it was very weird and kind of smart.

Maybe Paranormal *was* the right name for us.

Pearl frowned. 'So what's a parachute against?'

Alana Ray's eyebrows twitched. 'The chute of gravity.'

'Gravity sucks,' I said softly.

'So if we go with Paranormal,' Alana Ray said, 'we should figure out whether we are *beside* normal or *against* it. Names are important. That's why I ask you all to call me by my whole first name.'

'Hey, I just thought Ray was your last name,' Moz said, then frowned. 'What is your last name anyway?'

I held my breath. With Alana Ray, asking her last name was practically a personal question. But after a few seconds, she said, 'I don't have a real last name.' She didn't continue right away, her hands flickering nervously.

'How do you mean?' Pearl asked.

'At my school, they gave us new last names, ones that anyone could spell. That way, when we told our names to people, no one would ever ask us to spell them. It was to save us from embarrassment.'

'You have trouble spelling?' Pearl asked. 'Like, dyslexia?'

'Dyslexia,' Alana Ray answered. 'D-y-s-l-e-x-i-a. Dyslexia.'

'Dude,' I said. 'I couldn't spell that.'

She smiled at me. 'Only some of us had trouble spelling. But they renamed us all.'

'Maybe it doesn't matter,' Minerva said softly, and everyone turned toward her. 'As long as the music's good, people will think the name's brilliant too. Even if it's just some random word.'

Moz nodded. 'Yeah, the Beatles had a pretty stupid name, if you think about it. Didn't hurt them much.'

'Dude!' My jaw dropped open. 'They did *not* have a stupid name! It's a classic!'

'It's lame,' Minerva said. '*Beatles*, like the insect, except spelled like *beat*, because it's music?'

Pearl cleared her throat. 'Had to do with Buddy Holly and the Crickets, actually.'

'Whatever,' Minerva said. 'It's a really pathetic pun. *And* it's plural.' She smiled at Moz.

'Whoa . . . really?' I blinked. But they were right: *beetle* didn't have an *a* in it. They'd spelled it wrong.

Moz and Minerva were laughing at me, and he said, 'You never noticed that?'

I shrugged. 'I just figured they spelled it that way in England.

I mean, I read this English book once, and all kinds of stuff was spelled wrong.'

Now *everyone* was laughing at me, but I was thinking maybe Minerva was right. Maybe it didn't matter what we called ourselves: the Paranormals, the F-Sharps, or even the Desk. Maybe the music would grow around the name, whatever it was.

But we kept arguing, of course.

When Astor Michaels came back expecting an answer, Pearl pulled out her phone. 'It's only been forty minutes! You said an hour.'

He snorted. 'I've got work to do. So what do we call this band?'

We all froze. We'd come up with about ten thousand ideas, but nobody could agree on a single one. Suddenly I couldn't remember any of them.

'Come on!' Astor Michaels snapped his fingers. 'It's do-or-die time. Are we in business or not?'

Naturally, everyone looked at Pearl.

'Um . . .' The silence stretched out. 'The, uh, Panics?'

'The Pa*nic*,' Moz corrected. 'Singular.'

Astor Michaels considered this for a moment, then burst out laughing. 'You'd be amazed how many people come up with that.'

'With what?' Pearl said.

'Panic. Whenever I give bands the Name Ultimatum, they always wind up calling themselves something like the Panic, the Freakout, or even How the Hell Should We Know?' He laughed again, his teeth flashing in the semi-darkness.

'So . . . you don't like it?' Pearl asked softly.

'It's crap,' he chuckled. 'Sound like a bunch of eighties wannabes.'

No one else was asking, so I did: 'Does this mean we're dumped?'

He snorted. 'Don't be silly. Just trying to motivate you and have a little fun. Lighten up, guys.'

Minerva was giggling, but the rest of us were ready to kill him.

Astor Michaels sat down behind his desk, his smile finally showing all his teeth, a row of white razors in the darkness. 'Special Guests it is!'

–ALANA RAY–

When the doorman heard our names, he didn't bother to check the list or use his headset. He didn't even meet our eyes, just waved us in.

Pearl and I walked straight past the line of people waiting to have their IDs checked, to be patted down and metal-detected, to pay forty dollars (a thousand dollars for every twenty-five people) to get in. It had all happened just as Astor Michaels had promised. We were underdressed, unpaying, and in Pearl's case underage, but we were getting in to see Morgan's Army.

'Our names,' I said. 'They worked.'

'Why shouldn't they?' Pearl grinned as we followed the long, half-lit entry hall toward the lights and noise of the dance floor. 'We're Red Rat talent.'

'Almost Red Rat talent,' I said. The 'almost' part was making me twitchy. Pearl's lawyer was still arguing about details in the recording contract. She said that we would thank her for this diligence in a few years, when we were famous. I knew that details were important in legal documents, but right now the delay made the world tremble, like going out the door without a bottle of pills in my pocket.

'Whatever,' Pearl said. 'Our band is nine kinds of real now, Alana Ray – and real musicians don't pay to see one another play.'

'We were already real,' I said as we crossed the dance floor, the warm-up DJ's music making my fingers want to drum. 'But you're right. Things do feel different now.'

I looked at one twitching hand in front of me, mottled with the pulsing lights of the dance floor. Flashing lights usually made me feel disassociated from my own body, but tonight everything seemed very solid, very real.

Was it because I'd (almost) signed a record deal? My teachers at school always said that money, recognition, success – all the things normal people had that we didn't – weren't so important, that no one should ever use them to make us feel less than real. But it wasn't exactly true. Getting my own apartment had made me feel more real, and making money did too. The night I'd gotten my first business cards, I'd taken them out of the box one by one, reading my name again and again, even though they were all exactly the same . . .

And now my name had gotten me to the front of a long line of people with more-expensive clothes and better haircuts, people who hadn't gone to special-needs schools. People with real last names.

I couldn't help but feel that was important.

Pearl was beaming in the dance-floor lights, as if she was feeling more real too. It was illegal for her to be here, and I'd expected the doorman to know she was only seventeen, even if Astor Michaels had said it wouldn't be a problem.

That thought made me nervous for a moment. At my school they'd taught us to obey the law. Our lives would be complicated enough without criminal records, they liked to point out. Of course, saying that people like us couldn't afford to break the law suggested that other people could. Maybe Pearl and I were more like those other people now.

My fingers started to itch and pulse, but not because of the flashing lights: I wanted to sign that record deal soon. I wanted to grab this realness and put it on paper.

As we waited for the first band to start, I looked around for Astor Michaels. He made me shiver sometimes, even though he seemed to like me, always asking my opinions about music. He also asked about my visions, which didn't upset him the way they did Minerva. Of course, I never saw Astor Michaels upset by anything. He didn't care that his smile made people nervous, and he only laughed when I told him that he moved like an insect.

I found him easier to talk to than most people, just not to look at.

'Too bad Moz couldn't make it,' Pearl said. 'What did he say he was doing tonight?'

'He didn't,' I answered, though I had guesses in my head.

Moz was different now. In the last month he'd started borrowing things from the rest of us – Astor Michaels's smile, my twitchiness, Minerva's dark glasses – as if he wanted to start over.

He and Minerva whispered when Pearl wasn't looking, and the two sent messages to each other while we played. When my visions were strong enough, I could see their connection: luminous filaments reaching up from Minerva's song to Moz's fluttering notes, pulling them down toward the seething shapes beneath the floor.

I tried not to watch. Moz still paid me and said he would keep paying until Red Rat Records had actually given us money. He had never broken his promises to me, so I didn't want to tell my guesses to Pearl.

And I didn't want to make her sad tonight, because it was nice of her to have asked me along to see her favorite band.

The opening act had just been signed by Astor Michaels – like us, except for our 'almost'. But they already had a name. *Toxoplasma* was stenciled on their amps.

'What does that word mean?' I asked Pearl.

'Don't know.' She shrugged. 'Don't quite get it.'

Neither did I, but I also didn't understand why Zahler never used his first name, or why Moz had started saying 'Min' instead of 'Minerva', or why no one ever called Astor Michaels anything but 'Astor Michaels'. Names could be tricky.

After his little joke, Astor Michaels had said it didn't matter what we called ourselves, that our real audience would find us by smell, but that sounded unlikely to me. I hoped we would come up with our own name soon. I didn't want one tacked onto us, like 'Jones' had been to me.

'How did Morgan's Army get their name?' I asked. 'Did Astor Michaels give it to them?'

'No.' Pearl shrugged. 'They're named after somebody called Morgan.'

'Their singer?'

She shook her head. 'No. Her name's Abril Johnson. There are a lot of rumors about who Morgan is, but nobody knows for sure.'

I sighed. Maybe Zahler was right, and bands should just have numbers.

Toxoplasma was four brothers covered with tattoos. I liked the singer's voice – velvet and lazy, smoothing the words out like a hand across a bedspread. But the other three were brutally efficient, like people cooking on TV, chopping things apart in a hurry. They wore dark glasses and scattered the music into little pieces. I wondered how one brother could be so different from the others.

When their first song was done, I felt myself shiver – Astor Michaels was hovering behind us in the crowd. Pearl saw me glance back at him and turned and smiled. He handed her a glass of champagne.

That was illegal, but I didn't worry. Here in the flashing lights, the law felt less real.

'So what do you think of Toxoplasma?' he asked.

'Too thrashy for me,' Pearl said.

I nodded. 'I think three insects is too many for one band.'

Astor Michaels laughed and his hand touched my shoulder. 'Or maybe too few.'

I pulled away a little as the second song began; I don't like people touching me. That makes it hard to go to clubs sometimes, but it's always important to see what new music people are inventing.

'Just think,' he said. 'In a week you'll be playing in front of a crowd as big as this one. Bigger.'

Pearl's smile widened, and I could tell she was feeling realer by the minute. I turned to watch the audience. It wasn't like when I played in Times Square, where people could come and go as they pleased, some watching intently, some throwing money, others just passing by. Everyone here was focused on the band, judging them, waiting to be impressed, demanding to be energized. These weren't a bunch of tourists already wide-eyed just from being in New York.

Toxoplasma was making an impression. Rivulets of people were streaming forward, pressing toward the stage, dancing with the same chopping fervor as the three insect brothers. They hadn't looked much different from the rest of the crowd until now, but suddenly they all moved like skinheads, a wiry strength playing over the surface of their bodies.

They were insects too, and my heart started beating f aster, my fingers drumming. I'd never seen so many together before.

I already understood that there were different kinds of insects – Astor Michaels was very different from Minerva, after all, and I had seen many other kinds back when I'd played down in the subway – but the ones in front of the stage made me nervous in a new way.

They seemed dangerous, ready to explode.

My vision was starting to shimmer, which almost never happened with music I didn't like. But the air was rippling around Toxoplasma, like heat rising from a subway grate in winter. In front of the band they'd started moshing, which is why I always stay away from the stage. Shock waves seemed to travel from their slamming bodies outward through the crowd, their twitches spreading like a fever across the club.

'Mmm. Smell that,' Astor Michaels said, tipping back his head with closed eyes. 'I should have called *these* guys the Panic.' He giggled, still amused by his little joke on us.

I shivered, blinked my eyes three times. 'I don't like this band. They're *against* normal, not beside it.'

'They won't last long anyway,' he said. 'Maybe a couple of weeks. But they serve their purpose.'

'Which is what?' Pearl asked.

He smiled, wide enough to show the Minerva-like sharpness of his teeth. 'They shake things up.'

I could see what he meant. The tremors spreading from the insectoid moshers were changing things inside the club, making everyone edgy. It felt like when news of some strange new attack broke once while I was playing Times Square, and the crowd seemed to turn all at once to read the words crawling by on the giant news tickers. Most of the audience didn't like Toxoplasma's music any more than Pearl and I, but it tuned their nervous systems to a higher setting. I could see it in their eyes and in the quick, anxious motions of their heads.

And I realized that Astor Michaels was good at manipulating crowds. Maybe that was what made *him* feel more real.

'The audience expects something big to happen now,' I said.

'Morgan's Army,' Astor Michaels answered, letting his teeth slip out again.

It worked: Morgan's Army shook things up more.

Abril Johnson held an old-fashioned microphone, clutching it in two hands like a lounge singer from long ago. Her silver evening dress glittered in the three spotlights that followed her, covering the walls and ceiling of the club with swirling pinpricks. As the band slid into their first song, she didn't make a sound. She waited for a solid minute, barely moving, like a praying mantis creeping closer in slow motion before it pounces.

Bass rumbled through us from the big Marshall stacks, setting the floor trembling. Glasses hanging over the bar began to shudder against one another – my vision already shimmering, the sound looked like snow in the air.

Then Abril Johnson started singing, low and slow. The words were barely recognizable; she was stretching and mangling them in her mouth, as if trying to twist them into something inscrutable. I closed my eyes and listened hard, trying to pick out the half-familiar, half-alien words entwined in the song.

After a moment I realized where I'd heard them before: the strange words were shaped from the same nonsense syllables that Minerva always sang. But Abril Johnson had hidden them in her drawl, interweaving them with plain English.

I shook my head. I'd always thought that Minerva's lyrics were random, made-up, just leftover ravings from her crazy days. But if she shared them with someone else . . . were they another language?

My eyes opened, and I forced myself to look at the floor. Minerva's beast was moving underneath us. Its Loch Ness loops rose and fell among the feet of the unseeing crowd – but much, much bigger than in our little practice room, as thick as the giant cables of the Brooklyn Bridge. It had been made huge by the stacks of amps and the focus of the spellbound throng, and I could see details in the creature now. There were segments along its length, like a sinuous earthworm testing the air.

'How's that for intense?' Pearl murmured, her empty champagne glass clutched tightly in both hands, echoing the singer's grip on the microphone.

'Very.' Astor Michaels cocked his head. 'But not as intense as you'll be, my dears. Not as authentic.'

I shuddered a little, knowing what he meant. Minerva's songs were purer, unadulterated by English. Our spell would be stronger.

The beast coiled faster, and the floor of the nightclub rumbled under my feet, as if some droning bass note had found the resonant frequency of the room. I thought of how wineglasses could shatter from just the right pitch and wondered if a whole building might disintegrate when filled by some low and perfectly chosen note.

Pearl suddenly looked up, her eyes wide. 'It's them!'

I followed her gaze and saw a pair of dark figures on the catwalks high above us, climbing gracefully among the rigging of stage lights and exhaust fans.

'*Those* people.' Astor Michaels shook his head. 'New fad: physical hacking, climbing around on roofs and airshafts and down in the subways. Can't keep them out of the clubs anymore. They especially like the New Sound.'

'Angels,' Pearl said.

'Assholes,' Astor Michaels corrected. 'Takes away from the music.'

The song moved into its B section, and I dropped my gaze back to the floor, catching the last flicker of the worm disappearing. The hallucinations faded as the music grew faster, the air returning to stillness, the lyrics to ordinary English.

'She lost it,' I said.

'Yeah.' Pearl frowned. 'Kind of blew the momentum there.'

Astor Michaels nodded. 'The Army never gets that transition right, for some reason. It always feels like something is about to break through.' He clicked his tongue against his teeth. 'But it never does.'

'Are you sure you want it to?' I asked. 'What if it's . . .?'

Dangerous? I thought of saying. *Monstrous?*

'Not commercial?' Astor Michaels laughed. 'Don't worry. I've got a feeling that whatever it is, it's going to be the Next Big Thing. That's why I signed you guys.'

Pearl looked annoyed. 'Because we sound like Morgan's Army?'

He shook his head, pulling her empty champagne glass from her hands. 'No, you sound like yourselves. But someone has to take the New Sound to the next level. And I'm pretty sure it will be you.'

He turned toward the bar to get her more champagne, and the band slowed into the A section again, as if trying to call back my visions. But they'd lost their grasp on the beast, and Abril Johnson's lyrics were just normal words now. I saw that she wasn't an insect at all; she was just imitating them, mimicking the madness she'd seen on the subway and in the streets.

I realized that Minerva was more real than her.

And I wondered: what if one day the beast under the floor turned real?

20. GRIEVOUS ANGELS

–MOZ–

The noise in my body never stopped. All night I lay awake, tissues struggling against one another, blood simmering. I could feel the beast fighting against everything I'd been, trying to remake me into something else, trying to replace me. Even my sweat raged, squeezing angrily from my pores, like a bar fight spilling out onto the street.

When I looked in the mirror, I didn't see my face. It wasn't just that I was thinner, cheekbones twisting at new angles, eyes widening – it was something deeper, pushing up from beneath my skin, remote and contemptuous of me.

As if someone else's bones were trying to emerge.

The crazy thing was, part of me was dying to know what I was changing into. Sometimes I just wanted to get it over with, to let go and slip across the edge. I'd almost said yes tonight when Pearl had asked me to the Morgan's Army gig, wondering what hundreds of bodies pressed in close would do to my hunger, already halfway to uncontrollable. I imagined their scents tilling the air, the crowd noise mingling with the roar inside me . . .

But not yet – not without Min. In her arms, I still felt like myself. Besides, I had plenty more to learn down here, playing for quarters underground.

*

A woman was watching me, listening carefully, clutching her purse with both hands. She wasn't sure yet whether to open it and reach in, risking that extra tendril of connection with the strange boy playing guitar in the subway. But she couldn't pull herself away

Union Square Station was almost empty at this hour, my music echoing around us. The red velvet of my guitar case was spattered with silver, and more coins lay on the concrete floor. All night, people had thrown their quarters from a distance and moved on. Even through dark glasses they could see the intensity leaking out of my eyes. They could smell my hunger.

But this woman stood there, spellbound.

I'd always wondered if charisma was something in your genes, like brown eyes or big feet. Or if you learned it from the sound of applause or cameras snapping. Or if famous people glowed because I'd seen so many airbrushed pictures of them, their beauty slammed into my brain, like advertising jingles with faces.

But it had turned out that charisma was a *disease*, an infection you got from kissing the right person, a beast that lived in your blood. Connecting with this woman, drawing her closer, I could feel how I'd been magnetized.

She took a step forward, fingers tensing on the purse clasp. It popped open.

I didn't dare stare back into her spellbound eyes. There were no police down here anymore, not late at night. No one to stop me if I lost it.

Her fingers fumbled inside the purse, eyes never leaving me. She stepped closer, and a five-dollar bill fluttered down to lie among the coins. A glance at her pleading expression told me that she was paying for escape.

I stopped playing, reaching into a pocket for my plastic bag of garlic. The spell broken, the woman turned and headed for the stairs, the last strains of the Strat echoing into silence. She didn't look back, her steps growing hurried as she climbed away.

Something twisted inside me, angry at me for letting her go. I could feel it wrapped around my spine, growing stronger every day. Its tendrils stretched into my mouth, changing the way things tasted, making my teeth itch. The urge to follow the woman was so strong . . .

I put the plastic bag to my face and breathed in the scent of fresh garlic, burning away the noises in my head, smoothing the rushing of my blood.

Min had given me the bag for emergencies, but I used it all the time now. I'd even tried to make Luz's disgusting mandrake tea, which Mom said stank up the apartment. Nothing soothed the beast like meat, though, and nothing – not even Min – tasted as good. Raw steak was best, but there was a shortage these days, the price climbing higher all the time, and plain hamburger ripped out of the plastic still fridge-cold was almost as wonderful.

I stood there inhaling garlic, listening.

Min was right – you could learn things down here. Secrets were hidden in New York's rhythms, its shifts of mood, the blood flow of its water mains. Its hissing steam pipes and the stirrings of rats and wild felines all rattled with infection, like a huge version of the illness inside my body.

My hearing could bend around corners now, sharper every day, filling my head with echoes. I could hear our music so much better, could almost *see* the beast that Minerva called to when she sang.

And I knew it was down here, somewhere . . . ready to teach me things.

A little after eleven-thirty, its scent came and found me. The smell was drifting up from below, carried on the stale, soft breeze of passing trains. I remembered it from that first night I'd gone out to Brooklyn, when Minerva had led me down the tracks and pushed me into that broken section of tunnel; the scent made me angry and horny and hungry, all at once.

Then I heard something, a low and shuddering note, more subtle than any subway passing underfoot. Like when Minerva made the floor rumble beneath us as we played.

I scooped up the glittering change and stuffed it into my pockets, shut the Stratocaster safely into its case, snatched up the little battery-powered amplifier. By then the smell had faded, pulled away by the random winds of the subway, and I stood there uncertainly for a moment. Union Square sprawled around me, a warren of turnstiles and token booths and stairways down to half the subway lines in the city.

I half closed my eyes and walked slowly through the station, catching whiffs of perfume and piss, the bright metal tang of disinfectant, the blood-scent of rust everywhere. Finally, another dizzying gust welled up from the stairs leading down to the F train. Of course.

F *for* fool, I thought. *Or* feculent.

Downstairs the platform was empty, silent except for the skitter of rats on the tracks. The push-pull wind of distant trains stirred loose bits of paper and kept the scent swirling around me, the way the world spins when you've had too much beer.

I pulled off my dark glasses and stared into the tunnel depths. Nothing but blackness.

But from the uptown direction came the faintest sound.

Walking toward that end of the platform, a cluster of new smells hit me: antiperspirant and freshly opened cigarettes, foot powder and the chemical sting of dry-cleaned clothing . . .

Someone was hiding behind the last steel column on the platform, breathing nervously, aware of me. just another late-night traveler scared to be down here.

But from the tunnel beyond, the other scent was calling.

I took another step, letting the man see me. He wore a subway worker's uniform, his eyes wide, one hand white-knuckled around a flashlight. Had he heard the beast too?

'Sorry,' I said. 'I'm just . . .' I shrugged tiredly, adjusting the weight of my guitar and amp. 'Trying to get home. '

His eyes stayed locked on mine, full of glassy terror. 'You're one of them.'

I realized I'd taken my sunglasses off; he could see straight through to the thing inside me. 'Uh, I didn't mean to . . .'

He raised one hand to cross himself, drawing my eyes to the silver crucifix at his throat. He looked like he wanted to run, but my infection held him in place – the way I moved, the radiance of my eyes.

An itch traveled across my skin, like the feeling I got climbing the stairs to Minerva's room. I was salivating.

The fear in the man's sweat was like the scent of sizzling bacon crawling under your bedroom door in the morning – irresistible.

'Stay away from me,' he pleaded softly.

'I'm *trying*.' I put down the amp and guitar and fumbled in my jacket for the plastic bag of garlic. Pulling out a clove, I scrabbled to peel it, fingernails gouging the papery skin. The pearly white flesh poked through at last, smooth and oily in my fingers. I shoved it in my mouth half-peeled and bit down hard.

It split – sharp and hot – juices running down my throat like straight Tabasco. I sucked in its vapors and felt the thing inside me weaken a little.

I breathed a garlicky sigh of relief

The man's eyes narrowed. No longer transfixed, he shook his

head at my torn T-shirt and grubby jeans. I was just a seventeen-year-old again, tattered and weighted down with musical equipment. Nothing dangerous.

'You shouldn't litter,' he snorted, glaring at the garlic skin I'd dropped. 'Someone's got to clean that up, you know.'

Then he turned to walk briskly away, the scent of fear fading in his wake.

I breathed garlic deep into my lungs.

Mustn't eat the nice people, Minerva's voice chided in my head.

I was going to try that mandrake tea again. Even if it did taste like lawn-mower clippings, that was probably better than the taste of—

Down the tunnel the darkness shifted restlessly, something huge rolling over in its sleep, and I forgot all about my hunger.

It was down there, the thing that rumbled beneath us when we played.

I grabbed my Strat – leaving the amp behind – and jumped down onto the tracks. The smell carried me forward into the darkness, the tunnel walls echoing with the crunch of gravel, like Alana Ray's drumbeats scattering from my footsteps. The scent grew overpowering, as mind-bending as pressing my nose against Minerva's neck, drawing me closer.

The ground began to swirl, the blackness suddenly liquid underfoot. As my eyes adjusted, I realized it was a horde of rats flowing like eddies of water around my tennis shoes, thousands of them filling the tracks.

But the sight didn't make me flinch – the rats smelled familiar and safe, like Zombie sleeping warm on my chest.

The scent led me to a jagged, gaping hole in the tunnel wall, big enough to walk into, just like the cavity where Minerva and I had first kissed. It led away into pitch-blackness, its sides glistening. The rats swirled around me.

I could smell danger now, but I didn't want to run. My blood was pulsing, my whole body readying for a fight. I listened for a moment and knew instinctively that the hole was empty, though something had passed this way.

I reached out to touch the broken granite, and a dark gunk as thick as honey came off on my fingers. Like the black water, it shimmered for a moment on my skin, then faded into the air.

But its scent left behind a word in my mind . . . *enemy*. Just like Min always said: *I call the enemy when I sing*.

The ground rumbled underfoot, and the rats began to squeak.

I started running down the subway tunnel, feet crunching on gravel, the rats following, anger rippling across my skin. My tongue ran along my teeth, feeling every point. My whole body was crying out to fight this thing.

Then all at once I heard it, smelled it, saw it coming toward me . . .

A form moved against the darkness, shapeless except for the tendrils whipping out to grasp the tunnel's support columns. It dragged itself toward me – without legs, with way too many arms.

I staggered to a halt, a nervous garlic burp clearing my head for a few seconds. I realized how big it was – like a whole subway car rolling loose – and how *unarmed* I was . . .

But then the thing inside me tightened its grip on my spine, flooding me with anger. I pulled the Stratocaster from its case and held its neck with both hands, bringing it over one shoulder like an ax. Steel strings and golden pickups flashed in the darkness, and suddenly the beautiful instrument was nothing but a weapon, a hunk of wood for smashing things.

The rats flowed around me, scrambling up the walls and columns.

The thing refused to take any shape in the darkness, but it

was heading toward me faster now, its body spitting out gravel to both sides. It lashed at the dangling subway work lights, popping them one by one as it grew closer, like a rolling cloud of smoke bringing darkness.

Then something glimmered wetly at its center, an open maw ringed with teeth like long knives – and me with an electric guitar. Some small, rational part of my mind knew that I was very, *very* screwed . . .

It was only twenty yards away. I swung the Stratocaster across myself; its weight made my feet stumble.

Ten yards . . .

Suddenly human figures shot past me out of the darkness, meeting the creature head on. Bright metal weapons flashed, and the monster's screech echoed down the tunnel. Someone knocked me to one side and pinned me against the wall, holding me there as the beast streamed past. Cylinders of flesh sprouted from its length, grasping the steel columns around us, ending in sharp-toothed mouths that gnashed wetly. Human screams and flying gravel and the shriek of rats filled the air around us.

And then it was gone, sucking the air behind it like a passing subway train.

The woman who'd shoved me against the wall let go, and I stumbled back onto the tracks. The monstrous white bulk was receding into the darkness, leaving a trail of glistening black water. The dark figures and a stream of rats pursued it. Weapons flickered like subway sparks.

I stood there, panting and clutching the Strat like I was going to hit something with it. Then the creature slipped out of sight, disappearing into the hole I'd found, like a long, pale tongue flickering into a mouth.

The hunters followed, and the tunnel was suddenly empty, except for me, a few hundred crushed rats, and the woman.

I blinked at her. She was a little older than me, with a jet-black fringe of bangs over brown eyes, a scuffed leather jacket and cargo pants with stuffed-full pockets.

She eyed the guitar in my hands. 'Can you talk?'

'Talk?' I stood there for another moment, stunned and shaking.

'As in *converse*, dude. Or are you crazy already?'

'Um . . .' I lowered the Strat. 'I don't think so.'

She snorted. 'Yeah, right. So, like, dude, are you *trying* to get yourself killed?'

She led me to an abandoned subway stop farther up the tracks, a darkened ghost station. The stairways were boarded over, the token booth trashed, but the graffiti-covered platform was abuzz with hunters regrouping after the chase. They slipped up from the tracks, as graceful as the dark figures climbing down the fire escape that night I'd met Pearl.

Angels was what Luz called the people in the struggle. But I'd never figured on angels carrying backpacks and walkie-talkies.

'Easy with that thing,' the woman who'd saved me said. 'We're all friends here.'

'What? . . . Oh, sorry.' I was still clutching the Stratocaster like a weapon. The shoulder strap dangled from one end, so I slung the guitar over my back.

Confusion was finally setting in. Had I really just seen a giant monster? And wanted to *fight* it?

I looked at her. 'Um . . . who *are* you?'

'I'm Lace, short for Lacey. You?'

'Moz.'

'You can say your own name? Not bad.'

'I can do what?'

Instead of answering, she pulled a tiny flashlight from a pocket and shone it in my eyes. The light was blinding.

'Ouch! What are you *doing*?'

She leaned closer, sniffing at my breath. 'Garlic? Clever boy.'

A guy's voice came from behind me. 'Positive? Or just some wack-job?'

'Definitely a peep, Cal. But a self-medicator, by the looks of it.'

'Another one?' Cal said. His accent sounded southern. 'That's the third this week.'

Tracers from the flashlight still streaked my vision, but I could see Lace's silhouette shrug. 'Well, garlic *is* in all the folklore. Who told you to eat that stuff, Moz?'

I blinked. 'Um, this woman called Luz.'

'A doctor? A faith healer?'

'She's, uh . . .' What was Min's word? 'An esoterica?'

'What the hell's that?' Cal said. My vision returning, I noticed he was wearing a Britney Spears T-shirt under his leather jacket, which seemed weirdly out of place.

'Probably something esoteric,' Lace said.

I shook my head. I'd never met Luz face-to-face. 'She's a healer. Some kind of Catholic, I guess. She uses tea and stuff.'

'Amateur hour,' Lace said in a singsong voice. 'So, Moz, how long have you had an appetite for rare meat?'

I thought of Min's kiss. 'Three weeks and four days.'

Cal raised an eyebrow. 'That's pretty precise.'

'Well, that's when I first . . .' My voice faded. It didn't seem like a good idea, telling them about Min. 'Who *are* you guys anyway?'

Lace snorted. 'Dude. We're the guys who saved your butt. You almost got flattened by that worm, remember?'

I swallowed, watching as two angels lifted a third onto the platform. He was bleeding from a huge gash on one leg, black water dripping from the wound. He didn't cry out, but his face was knitted in pain, his teeth clenched.

And I'd been about to fight that thing *alone*?

'Uh, thanks.'

'Uh, you're welcome.' Her eyes narrowed. 'Have you got any girlfriends? Any roommates? Cats?'

'Cats?' I thought of Zombie's strange gaze. 'Listen, I don't know what you're talking about. Or what that thing was! What's going on here?'

'He doesn't know anything, Lace,' Cal said. 'Just bag him and let's get moving. That beastie's only wounded; it might swing back around.'

The woman stared at me for another moment, then nodded. 'Okay. So here's the thing, Moz. Old-fashioned folk remedies aren't going to keep your head together for much longer. Very soon, you're going to do unpleasant things to your friends and neighbors. So we're taking you for a little trip to New Jersey.'

'*New Jersey?*'

'Yeah, Montana's full.' Lace smiled, pulling a small, thin object from her cargo pants. A needle glistened in the darkness at its tip. 'This won't hurt a bit, and you shouldn't be there more than a week or two, thanks to your esoterica friend. Got to admit, she kept you in pretty good shape.'

'Hey, wait a second.' I backed away, holding up my hands. 'I'm not going anywhere. I've got a gig next week.'

'A gig?' Lace glanced at the guitar on my back and shrugged. 'Cool. But I'm afraid you're going to miss it. We need to train you.'

'Train me for *what*?'

'Saving the world,' Cal said.

I swallowed. 'You mean Luz is right? There really is a struggle?'

'She told you about the . . .?' Lace's voice faded, and she closed her eyes, sniffing the air. 'Hey, Cal – did you feel that?'

I had. My magic powers were spinning. I took a step away.

'Not so fast, Moz!' Lace grabbed my arm, thrusting the needle closer.

As I pulled free from her grip, the ground broke open beneath us . . .

Columns of flesh tore themselves up from the concrete of the platform, rings of teeth flashing in the darkness. One whipped past me, leaving my jacket sleeve in ribbons. I was already running, dodging through the flailing tendrils, stumbling over broken concrete.

The angels fought back, swords whistling through the air around me, as deadly as the gnashing teeth.

I jumped from the platform, then glanced back. Lace was spinning in place, her long sword slicing low through the air, cutting through columns of flesh as they thrust up from the ground. Black water spewed from the ragged stumps.

My hands reached for the neck of my Strat again, itching to pull it off my back. I was dying to run back and rejoin the fight, but I shut my eyes, yanked out the garlic, and bit straight into an unpeeled clove.

The burning sharpness cleared my head: I didn't want to be part of any struggle. I didn't want to go to some camp in New Jersey. All I wanted was to stay here, be in my band, play gigs, and get famous!

I turned away from the battle and dashed down the tracks, running back toward Union Square Station. As I passed the gash in the tunnel, a storm of rats spilled out, headed back toward the fight. I danced like a barefoot kid on hot asphalt as they swept past.

Finally the lights of the station glimmered in front of me. I leaped up onto the platform and kept running, climbing stairs and slanting tunnels until I'd dashed into the open air.

My pockets were heavy, jingling with enough change to catch a taxi out to Brooklyn. I had to tell Min what I'd seen. The enemy was just like she'd said: something monstrous. There really were angels, and they were recruiting, taking infected people away to . . . *New Jersey*?

Whatever. The struggle was real.

I hailed a cab and gave the driver Minerva's street name. When he said he didn't go to that part of Brooklyn anymore, I leaned forward and bared my teeth, asking him to reconsider. He turned, met my demented rock-star gaze, and changed his mind.

Once the cab was speeding up the Williamsburg Bridge, climbing away from the earth, my nerves began to calm. I was headed toward Minerva, to safety. I'd escaped the angels, and as long as I stayed out of the subways, they'd never find me again . . .

Then I remembered that my guitar case and amp were back there, underground. I sank down into the vinyl seat, eyes squeezing shut.

The amp didn't matter – I didn't need it anymore – but the *case*. If the angels came looking for me, they'd find it on the tracks. Inside was a polite note, asking anyone who found this guitar to please call Moz at this number. Big Reward!

And, of course, the note gave my address as well.

-MINERVA-

I pulled out Astor Michaels's birthday present right before midnight, just like he'd told me to.

It was wrapped in silver foil, my own face gazing back at me in the candlelight, blurry and twisted. Zombie jumped up onto the bed and sniffed the package, then looked up at me, his little face worried.

Astor Michaels wasn't family to me and Zombie – and now Moz. He was more like a distant relative, part of the clan who spelled their last names differently. It made him smell funny.

'It's okay, Zombie. Astor's going to make Mommy a rock star.'

When I pulled on the red ribbon, its knot only tightened, so I lifted the box to my mouth. The ribbon tensed for a moment as my teeth closed, then relaxed, like a chicken when Luz broke its neck.

Teeth were useful for all sorts of things these days. Mozzy could open beer bottles with his.

I slid the box out from its wrapping, checking the clock. Ten seconds.

I counted down, hoping the present wasn't something heart-shaped. *Eww*. Astor Michaels knew I was with Mozzy. He'd spotted it faster than anyone else, except maybe smelly Alana Ray – and Zahler, of course, who

Moz had told before he'd even called me. (Okay, really it was only Pearl who didn't know. Poor little Pearl.)

My fingernails slit the box open, and I smiled.

It was a cell phone, shiny and microscopic. Lifting it up, hefting the insubstantial weight, I felt its shape fitting into my palm. What a very excellent idea . . .

Zombie, who'd been batting at the red ribbon, came over for another sniff, and at that moment the phone buzzed silently against my palm, like a housefly trapped in my fist. Zombie looked up at me and meowed.

'Must be for me,' I said.

I kept Astor Michaels waiting for three vibrations before I pushed the big green button.

'Aren't you clever?'

'It's my job to keep the talent happy.'

'Mmm.' I was already wondering when Mozzy would be home from playing down in the subway. He was supposed to call me exactly at one; I could phone him right before and give him a little surprise . . . I giggled.

'Sounds like I've succeeded,' Astor Michaels said.

'Very much so.' Then I frowned. 'Why didn't Pearl ever give me one of these?'

'Maybe she thought you'd get yourself into trouble.'

'Hmph.' Pearl probably liked being the only one with my number. Showed what she knew. 'It's about time. Luz stole my buttons, you know.'

'So you said. You needed a real phone, Min. In fact, it's about time you had a real life.'

Zombie stared up at me, as if listening.

'What do you mean by that, Astor Michaels?'

'Why don't you move out, Min?'

'Move . . . out?' My eyes swept the candlelit darkness around me.

'Red Rat has a few apartments set aside for our special artists, for when they come to town to record. Nicely furnished and in Manhattan. You could move in anytime.'

I swallowed, reaching out to stroke Zombie. His fur had the shivers. 'But what about—'

'Your parents?' He made a disappointed noise. 'You're eighteen in two weeks, Min. You can disappear for that long, can't you? Do you think the police will spend much time looking for a runaway who's about to turn legal?'

I didn't answer. I didn't care about the police, or my parents much either. But I wasn't sure how long I could go without Luz. She could be a total pain, but she'd cured me, more or less.

And Mozzy needed her even more than I did. I was splitting Luz's medicines with him, making sure he got through the first stages of the illness. So far, he was keeping it together just fine, but I didn't want him to turn all bitey.

'Min?'

I covered up the microphone. 'What do you think, Zombie?'

His eyes opened wide, glistening, nervous but . . . excited. Mozzy needed to get well, but *we* needed things too – to breathe the air outside at night, sucking in the smells and the moonlight. To go down in the subway, like Mozzy got to *every night.*

I wanted to learn more . . . to make my songs stronger.

In a couple of weeks I could call up Luz and have her come to my new place. She could make birthday mandrake tea for both of us. Once I was eighteen, it wouldn't matter if she told my parents where I was.

Me and Moz could make it for that long, couldn't we? We knew to eat lots of garlic. Probably all those other smelly herbs were just for show.

Zombie meowed, still staring at me with gleaming eyes. In our own place, he could go play with his little friends whenever he wanted.

Astor Michaels was talking again. 'Once you're out of that room, the band can rehearse every day. Think what that would do for you, especially with your first gig coming up.'

I bit my lip. Pearl had been complaining about having only one more Sunday to rehearse. Zombie stared at me, tail twitching, anxious.

'Okay. I'll move.'

'I thought you might say that,' Astor Michaels said, and I could hear his smile. It slid through the airwaves like a needle. 'Go pack.'

'What, right now? But it's midnight.'

'Best time to run away, don't you think? I'm on the road as we speak, coming over to collect you.'

'Um, but Moz said he was going to call later.'

He filled my ear with a little sigh. 'You can call *him* instead, Min. Remember my little present? The one we're talking on?'

'Oh, right.' I giggled. 'Clever Astor Michaels.'

'I'll see you in twenty minutes. Pack light.'

Pack light? Puh.

I needed lots of dresses – all my black ones, for wearing onstage. All my necklaces and rings too, even though my old jewelry box was pink and tattered. Only a few pairs of shoes, because I really had to buy all new ones; none of mine were very rock star. I packed every bit of the underwear me and Pearl had bought the day we'd gone to Red Rat Records, but no pajamas, because I was so bored of lying around all day. Bored of sleeping.

Never again, I thought as I stuffed my two suitcases full. I could save up all my sleeping for the grave.

I packed my notebooks, of course. I'd memorized most of the

songs in them, but they smelled good, and I liked to stare at my old handwriting. It was sweet how only I could read the songs, all of them in my own special language.

Zombie trilled from the top of the dresser, reminding me to bring cat food and a place for him to pee. I grabbed his bag of dry food and promised to get him a litter box. And big piles of bones – Moz and I were going to need lots of meat, especially without Luz's tinctures and teas to help us.

I wondered if he would come and stay with me . . .

The thought made me shiver a little, and I looked around my room again, the place I'd lived for almost eighteen years. It was time to grow up, after all.

The illness had emptied this room of meaning. Luz had cleared all my old possessions out, back when they'd made me scream. She was reintroducing familiar things one by one, but none of them held any significance now. Everything from before the disease smelled like old toys from childhood, sugary with memories, a little embarrassing.

Better to let my parents keep it all.

Mommy and Daddy would be upset, but I could call them from my new phone and tell them how happy I was.

I snapped the suitcases shut, then crossed to the door, closing my eyes to listen. Maxwell was sleeping loudly down the hall. He'd started snoring lately, puberty making him prickly and restless. He'd be much happier without a crazy big sister sucking up everyone's attention.

I listened harder, trying to hear through Max's snuffling. The slightest creak of settling sounded below . . . was it Astor Michaels on the stairs? But he didn't know about the secret key.

The phone vibrated again, like a tiny, nervous animal in my hand.

'I'm ready,' I whispered.

'Excellent. We're just pulling up now. Heavens, this neighborhood's seen better days.'

'It's not our fault. The mean garbagemen won't come here anymore.'

'Well, I'm glad I'm taking you away.'

I frowned. Suddenly I wished it wasn't Astor Michaels helping me escape. Maybe this wasn't such a great idea, rushing off with him. Mozzy could help me instead . . .

But I couldn't imagine unpacking my bags, putting everything back into closets and drawers and under the bed, defeated.

One more day, even one more hour, was too long to stay here.

'Okay,' I whispered. 'First you have to get the key. Then you sneak to the top of the stairs without making any noise—'

He laughed. 'Just a moment, darling Min. I don't *do* sneaking.'

'But . . . there's a lock on my door.'

'Yes. And you can break it.'

'The lock?'

'The *door*. You've had the condition for five months, Minerva. You can feel your strength, right? I've broken doors down *by accident*. Just hit it with the palm of your hand. Hard.'

I touched the door softly, thinking of all the nights I'd tried to stare holes in it. But knock it down?

'It'll make noise,' I whispered. 'Wake them all up.'

'You'll be down and out the front door while they're still wondering what's going on. Don't be shy. Just hit it, Min.'

I remembered how I'd lifted Pearl's mixing board with one hand last Sunday, making her eyes as round as buttons.

But bash down my own door?

'Do you want to stay in your room forever?' he said.

I hissed at the phone. Astor Michaels and his little tests. Were we mature enough to stay together? Tough enough to face a nasty audience? Strong enough to . . . bash things down?

Fine.

I hung up, scooped Zombie from the floor, and placed one palm against the wood. Drew my arm back . . .

And smashed it into smithereens.

Moz stood just outside, his jaw open.

'Mozzy!' I cried.

His smell rushed into the room, and Zombie struggled to jump down and say hi.

I stared at my stinging palm. 'I'd have heard you coming up except for smelly Astor Michaels distracting me.'

'Um, I . . .

'Poor Mozzy. You look frazzled.'

'Something happened to me. Something weird.' He looked down at the bits of wood around him. 'Why did you do that?'

I bent to pick up a suitcase. 'I'll tell you on the way.'

'What way? The way where?'

'My new place,' I said. 'Quit squirming! Not you, Mozzy. Grab that, would you?'

He blinked a few times, then saw my other suitcase and gripped its handle.

I paused for a moment, listening. Maxwell was definitely awake, his snores shattered into little pieces, just like my door. I could hear him twisting on his bed, snuffling with confusion.

Downstairs in my parents' room, the floor was creaking with footsteps.

'Come on,' I hissed.

We didn't bother sneaking. The stairs complained, but it felt so good not to be worrying over every squeak of the cranky old steps. We were past my parents' room, almost at the front door, when Daddy flicked on the lights above us.

'Minerva?' he called softly. 'Max?'

I pulled open the front door. The outside smells rushed in: the garbage mountains, the rotting leaves of fall, Zombie's little friends skittering in the dark.

'Bye, Daddy,' I called up, trying to sound a little sad at leaving. 'Don't worry, please. I'll call you soon.'

'What are you doing? Who *is* that?'

Moz looked very embarrassed to be stared at. But it was Daddy in his pajamas who looked silly.

'Tell Max and Mommy goodbye and that I'll see you all on my birthday, okay?'

'Minerva! You can't just leave . . . You're not well! Where are you—?'

'I said I'd call you!' Daddy never *listens*. I stomped out the door.

'How are we going to get anywhere?' Moz sputtered, running after me. 'Won't they call the cops? I sent my cab away, and we can't take the subway! There's this thing down—'

'It's okay, Moz. Look, there he is!'

Astor Michaels was half a block away, standing next to his limo, looking surprised to see Mozzy. His driver hovered close to him, scanning the piles of garbage nervously, one hand in his pocket like he was getting ready to shoot some of Zombie's little friends.

We ran up, and I handed Astor Michaels my suitcase. 'Take this; Zombie has his claws in my dress.'

'You're bringing your cat,' he said flatly, staring at Moz.

'And Mozzy too!' I said.

'Yes, I see that.' Astor Michaels sighed tiredly. 'Hello, Moz.'

'What's going on here?' Moz said, sounding all manly and jealous, which made me giggle.

But then Daddy yelled something, and we all got in the limo, dragging the suitcases in behind us instead of opening the trunk. The driver put the car into gear and whisked us away.

I waved to Daddy out the back window.

'We're going to our new place, Moz,' I explained. 'You should come stay there with me.'

'Um . . .' Astor Michaels said.

'I can't go home,' Mozzy said, staring out at midnight Brooklyn rushing past. 'I saw this thing down in the subway, and the angels caught me. They almost took me away, like Luz always says.'

'Angels?' I asked. For the first time, I noticed how shaky Moz was. He was pale with shock, twitching and sweating like he'd seen something much worse than my door exploding.

'It's real, Min,' he said softly. 'The struggle's real.'

I wrapped my arms around him. 'Don't worry, Mozzy. We'll take you someplace safe.'

'By all means,' Astor Michaels said. 'Must keep the talent happy.'

22. CROWDED HOUSE

-PEARL-

The morning after the Morgan's Army gig, my phone rang – Astor Michaels calling.

'You gave me a hangover,' I answered, still feeling all the glasses of champagne he'd brought me. Mom gave me a stern look across the breakfast table, but I ignored her. Stupid champagne genes.

Astor Michaels laughed at me from the other end. 'Well, at least we have something to celebrate. They're finally ready.'

I squinted in the sunlight streaming into the dining room. 'The contracts?'

'In my hand.'

'Your lawyer works on Saturday morning?'

'They were ready yesterday.'

Mom was pretending not to listen, but I tried not to swear too loud. Everyone had been nine kinds of bugging me to get the negotiations over with, like the delay was all my fault. 'And you didn't mention this last night *why*?'

'I had a very busy evening in front of me.'

'Oh. Your mysterious errand.' He'd left me and Alana Ray at the club before the gig had ended, smiling like he had a dirty secret.

'And after that, things got even busier.' Astor Michaels

sighed tiredly. 'If you meet me downtown in two hours, I'll explain everything.'

'Explain whatever you want,' I said. 'Just bring the contracts.'

'Contracts?' my mother said the moment I hung up. 'Does this mean you're really going through with all this?'

I looked down at my hands, which were quivering a little – half hangover, half excitement. 'Yeah, I really am.'

She looked out the window. 'Why we wasted all that money on school, I don't know, if you were just going to do something like this.'

'Juilliard wasn't a waste, Mom. Not hardly. But it's . . . over.'

She looked at me, trying to muster up a look of disbelief, but she knew I was right. Fewer students showed up for classes every day, and those that were still around were all planning some kind of escape from the city. Ellen Bromowitz had called it exactly right: one week ago, the senior orchestra had been officially put on hold for the rest of the year. The infrastructure was already failing.

'Plus,' I said, 'this *is* my lifelong dream and everything.'

'Lifelong? You're only seventeen, darling.'

I looked up at her, about to reply with some snark, but her eyes had turned shiny in the sunlight. Suddenly I saw something I'd never even imagined before: my indestructible mother looking fragile, as if she really was worried about the future.

I wondered if her friends were all doing the same as mine – heading to Switzerland, leaving the city behind. What if no one bothered anymore to raise money for museums and dance companies and orchestras? What if all the parties she lived for had no more reason to exist and simply stopped happening, leaving all her diamonds and black cocktail dresses useless?

Mom needed her infrastructure too, I suddenly realized, and she was watching it crumble away.

So all I said was, 'Seventeen years is a long time, Mom. I just hope this isn't too late.'

I called Moz's house right away to tell him to come along. The two of us had started the band, after all. This was our moment of success.

His mother hadn't seen him that morning. She wasn't sure if he'd come home the night before and didn't sound very happy about it. Maybe sometimes in the past Moz hadn't made it home on Friday nights, she kept saying, but the way things were these days, he really should know better . . .

I hung up a little worried, hoping Moz wasn't going to go all lateral on me. Except for Alana Ray and almost-eighteen Min, all our parents had to countersign the Red Rat contracts. With our first gig only six days away, now was not the time to pick a fight.

I called Zahler's house next, but there was no answer, and my brain started to spin with every imaginable reason the two of them might have gone missing. The police were investigating a lot of disappearances lately, especially underground; there was talk of shutting the trains down altogether. But Moz and Zahler wouldn't be stupid enough to go down into the *subway*, would they?

Not now, when we were this close . . .

Astor Michaels had given me the address of a huge block of apartments on Thirteenth Street. I got there right on time and found him waiting in the lobby, an alligator-skin briefcase clutched under one arm.

'Shall we go on up?' he said.

'You live here?' I frowned. The lobby carpet was a bit thread-bare in spots, and two security guards sat in reclining chairs behind the doorman, eyeing us carefully, shotguns across their laps.

'Heavens, no. Red Rat owns a few apartments here. I thought you might want to see one.'

I didn't know what he meant by that, but I looked at his brief-case. 'Whatever.'

The elevators were the old-fashioned kind, zoo cages on cables. An ancient guy in uniform slid the door closed after we stepped in, then wrenched a huge lever to one side. The machine began to rise, the floors passing just through the bars. My hang-over started to grumble about the three cups of coffee I'd had.

Astor Michaels turned to me, clutching his briefcase a little tighter. 'Pearl, I've been doing this since the New Sound was really new.'

'That's why I tracked you down.'

'And I've signed fifteen bands in that time. But yours has something special. You know that, right?'

As I watched the floors slide past, I let myself smile, remem-bering how thrilled I'd been to find Moz and Zahler. 'We've got heart, I guess.'

'That heart is Minerva, Pearl. *She* is what makes you special.'

We came to a stomach-jerking halt. I swallowed, my heart beating harder, wondering where Astor Michaels was going with this. Did he not want to sign the rest of us? Was he trying to make me jealous of Min?

The elevator man was nudging his lever one way and then the other, bouncing us up and down to align our feet with the red-carpeted floor on the other side of the bars. I tried to remem-ber how many glasses of champagne Astor Michaels had bought me last night.

'I know Minerva is special,' I said carefully. 'I grew up with her.'

'Indeed.'

Finally the elevator lurched and bumped its way to a halt, and we stepped off into a long hallway. The cage rattled shut and slipped away.

Astor Michaels just stood there. 'Of my fifteen bands, Pearl, eleven have self-destructed so far.'

I nodded. That was pretty famous, how Red Rat bands tended to explode. 'All part of the New Sound, I guess.'

'And why do you suppose that is?'

'Uh, I don't know. Drugs?'

He shook his head. 'That's what we usually tell the press. But it's rarely true.'

I narrowed my eyes. 'You mean, you cover up the truth by saying it was *drugs*? Isn't it supposed to be the other way around?'

'Generally. But certain things are worse than drugs.' He shivered. 'Late last night, Toxoplasma had something of a meltdown. Right after their very first gig too. Those boys never really got along, you know.'

I saw a line of sweat roll down his forehead. It was the first time I'd ever seen Astor Michaels looking discomposed.

'What happened?'

'Who knows, exactly? It was all very stressful. And expensive to clean up.' He looked down at his free hand, picking under the fingernails with his thumb. 'And messy.'

'They broke up?'

'Not exactly.' He didn't smile. 'As you say, that's *always* been the problem with the New Sound. Toxoplasma had heart, but they only lasted a single gig. *One gig!* He let out a long sigh. 'Morgan's Army may last forever, but of course they're not the real thing.'

'Hey, maybe they weren't perfect last night, but I thought they played a great set. What do you mean, "not real"?'

Astor Michaels glanced up and down the empty hall. 'I'll tell you inside.'

He turned and walked away, and as I followed, my stomach started to roil again. My knees felt shaky, as if someone was adjusting the exact height of the floor beneath me. What were we *doing* here?

Reaching an apartment door, he rapped on it twice sharply, then waited a moment. 'Don't want to disturb the tenants, but I think they're out.'

'Whose place *is* this?'

He pulled out a key, opened the door.

Zombie was waiting just inside.

'I could always see them,' Astor Michaels began. 'Even before it happened to me.'

I was staring at the couch, where half of Min's clothes were draped: black dresses and shawls and stockings strewn across the room. Two open suitcases lay on the floor.

My stomach twisted again. Minerva lived here now. Astor Michaels had installed her here, his special girl.

'They were coming to the clubs, leaking sex out of their eyeballs, only a few of them at first. But once they got onstage . . .' He shook his head. 'They're natural stars, charismatic as hell. Except for that one little problem.'

'They're bug-ass crazy?' I said harshly, looking at the dresser – the old pink jewelry box I'd bought Min when she was twelve was splayed open, full of shiny things.

'Crazy? I work for a record company, Pearl. Crazy I could deal with.' He leaned forward. 'But they're bloody cannibals.'

I looked up into his eyes. Had he just said *cannibals*?

But then I remembered how Min had hospitalized one of her doctors in the days before Luz. I thought of all the raw meat she ate, the way her teeth grew sharper every day.

Almost as sharp as Astor Michaels's.

There in the darkened apartment, something cold crawled down my spine. 'Why did you bring me here?'

He looked puzzled for a moment, then let out a snort. 'Please, I never even *tried* it, not once. I'm different than the rest of them.' His eyes twitched; he still looked nervous. 'Sane. And I wouldn't hurt you for the world, my dear little Pearl. You've done me such a huge favor.'

'A favor?'

'For the last two years, I've been looking for someone like me – someone who's infected but immune to the hunger. A singer who can get onstage and take the New Sound to the world without . . .' He looked down at his fingernails again, then shrugged. 'Quite so much cannibalism.'

I wondered again what exactly had happened with Toxoplasma the night before. Probably nothing a rehab clinic could fix.

'That's why I was so thrilled when you brought me Minerva,' Astor Michaels said. 'She's *real*, don't you see? Not a mimic, like Abril Johnson. But not like those lost boys in Toxoplasma either.' Zombie jumped onto his lap, and he stroked the cat's head. 'She's immune to the hunger.'

'I wouldn't go that far,' I said, looking at the clothes strewn around the room. 'She had it pretty bad there for a while.'

'Then somehow you've kept her together, Pearl.'

'But it wasn't me. Her parents hired this . . . esoterica. Someone who knew what to do for her.' I looked around the apartment, wondering how Min was going to get what she needed now. How long would she last without Luz's medicines?

'Well, if someone's figured out how to cure this thing, we really do need to move fast. Won't be long before they bottle it and *everyone's* a rock star.' He shivered. 'What a disaster.'

I looked at his hands, with their long, sharp, manicured nails. 'And it never made you . . .'

'Crazy? A cannibal?' He shook his head. 'Just hungry for raw meat sometimes. And horny, always.'

'Horny?' My skin was crawling now.

'Of course.' He giggled. 'That's how it spreads, you know. It's nothing but a disease, Pearl. Just some new bug in the water. And as far as I can tell, it's sexually transmitted. It makes you want to spread it.'

I closed my eyes. So Luz had been right about boys. What else was she right about? I wondered where her angels were, now that I needed them . . .

Then I remembered that Mark had cracked up too. Had he given it to her? Or vice versa? One of them had to have been cheating . . .

Zombie jumped up onto my lap, and I opened my eyes.

Astor Michaels was still talking. 'I've been shagging wannabe singers for two years now, trying to find someone who could keep it together after the charisma set in, and every single one went nuts. *Fifteen bands*, Pearl. And finally you bring me a rock star already made!' He leaned back, rubbing his palms across Min's dresses and sighing. 'After all my labors.'

I sat there, stroking Zombie, trying not to scream as what he'd just said sank in. Astor Michaels had intentionally spread this disease; he'd been making more casualties like Minerva, broken people stuck in attics by their families, or lying huddled on the street, on subway platforms . . .

We were in business with a monster. The New Sound was the music of monsters.

I took a deep breath, reminding myself about the contracts. This didn't have to change anything. Artists had been bat-shit crazy before; it was what you did with your insanity that mattered. We were still a good band, a *great* band even, even if our whole style of music was based on . . . a disease.

As long as we were the Taj Mahal of cannibal bands, maybe it wasn't so bad.

'Okay,' I said.

It wasn't really, but sometimes saying that word helps.

Astor Michaels smiled. 'So we're in this together, right, Pearl? We have to keep Min healthy, so that all our hard work – yours and mine – finally pays off. Even if she does something that makes you really, really angry. Okay?'

I looked at him through narrowed eyes. 'Like what?'

'You know, something she's not necessarily . . . in control of.' He shrugged. 'The disease makes people crazy, violent, and especially horny. Sometimes even I can't control myself.'

'Doesn't sound like you've been trying that hard.'

He smiled, revealing his razor teeth to the gums. 'A small price to pay for art.'

Zombie's ear perked up, and he jumped from my lap and ran to the door. A second later came the jingling of keys outside.

'Ah. They're home,' Astor Michaels said, eyes twitching. 'Just remember, we all want this band to be a success. So don't get mad at poor Min. I've seen the change happen with my own eyes, and she's been through more than you can imagine. So be nice, all right?'

I nodded, but my head was spinning again.

They're home, he'd said.

They.

The door opened, and Minerva breezed in. Moz followed behind, carrying a threadbare duffel bag.

'Mozzy! Look who's here!' Min cried, beaming all the wattage of her fawesome beauty at me, her cannibal-rock-star charisma. Moz just stood there staring, looking a little surprised, a lot guilty.

With a twist in my stomach, I remembered his mother's anxious voice on the phone that morning.

He took a slow breath, then shrugged the duffel bag from his shoulder. It thumped to the floor like a dead body – stuffed full.

He was moving in.

'Hey, Pearl. How's it going?'

I tried to answer, but my gut was writhing now, squeezing the taste of stomach-ripe champagne up into the back of my throat. Minerva moved a step closer to Moz, five pale fingers wrapping protectively around his arm.

He was hers now. Completely.

With the three of them here together, I could finally see the changes in Moz, all the clues I'd managed to blind myself to: the luster of his skin, the beautiful, inhuman angles of his face. Just like Min back in spring – when the hunger was first welling up – he'd grown a heart-twisting shade more fetching.

Even slitted against the dim candlelight, his eyes glowed, full of pity for me. He must have known what I'd wanted.

But *she'd* taken it instead.

Suddenly the desolate feeling in my stomach was swept away by fury: Minerva had done it *again*, hooked up with someone in the band – in my band. Even after what had happened with Mark and the System, after everything Luz had told her, Min had done this to me *again*. I clenched my fists. Of course she would throw it in my face now, when we were *this* close, the contracts near enough to touch, ready to be signed.

I felt Astor Michaels's gaze, willing me to keep it together. For the good of the band. For the good of the New Sound . . . the music of monsters.

He snapped open the locks on his briefcase, pulled out his pen.

I swallowed my screams whole. They went down my throat as sharp-cornered and cold as ice cubes.

'Hi, guys,' I said. 'Nice place.'

PART V

THE GIG

Study the Black Death, and you'll understand one truth: when things start to go wrong, human beings always find ways to make them worse.

The year the Death came to Europe, a city called Caffa on the doorstep of Asia was under siege. When the attackers found themselves coming down with a strange new disease, they wisely decided to run. But first they catapulted plague-ridden corpses over the walls of the city – so both sides would get the disease. Brilliant move.

When the Black Death was at its worst, the church decided to look for someone to blame and began to persecute heretics, Muslims, and Jews. As people fled these attacks, the disease fled with them. Nice work.

England and France had gone to war one year before the Black Death struck, but instead of making peace while the pandemic raged, they kept on fighting. In fact, they kept on fighting for 116 years, keeping their people poor, malnourished, susceptible to disease. Now that's commitment.

The Black Death was helped along by war, by panic, even by the weather, but it had no greater ally than human stupidity. Sometimes, you wonder how our species has made it this far.

Not without a lot of help, I assure you.

NIGHT MAYOR TAPES:
411–421

23. MORAL HAZARD

-ALANA RAY-

I still hadn't made a decision, but my hands were steady.

I'd been here at the nightclub more than three hours and hadn't needed to drum my fingers or touch my forehead even once. Like being suspended in that moment before playing, the cadence of the universe around me needed no adjustments.

The club was at one end of a long alleyway in the meatpacking district, one free of garbage, the walls painted with giant murals and tagged with graffiti. I'd come in through a huge loading dock, trucks full of equipment rumbling in a tight line, waiting to disgorge.

Inside, the space was more than three hundred feet from stage to back wall, the echoes returning lazily, almost a whole second late – two beats at 120 beats per minute. Useless for playing, but that was fine with me. I liked my fake echoes with this band, just to be in control of *something*. My visions, my emotions, even the patterns I played all seemed to spring unbidden from the air, but at least my echo boxes obeyed me.

Astor Michaels had asked me to come early for sound check, so that the engineers could get used to my paint buckets. I'd brought thirty-six to arrange in eight stacks ($S_8 = 36$), along with my special buckets: unusual sizes and thicknesses, even the broken ones that gave off the buzz of cracked plastic.

Unlike Pearl, the engineers here thanked me when I ran only two channels from my board to theirs. They had four bands to worry about tonight – each with its own array of treble, bass, effects, and volume settings – and wanted things as simple as possible. They let me hang out for the whole sound check, watching as they plastered the club's huge mixing board with notes scribbled on masking tape. Its backside sprouted a tangle of cables, four bands' worth of musical specificities sculpted in color-coded spaghetti.

I was still watching them work when I felt Astor Michaels behind me.

'Miss Jones,' he said, a sheaf of papers in his hand.

'I prefer Alana Ray.'

He smiled. 'Sorry to be formal, but we have business to conduct.' The papers rustled, making the air ripple. 'You're the only one who hasn't signed yet. Not embarrassed about your penmanship, are you?'

'Top of my class,' I said, then shrugged. 'The competition was less than average.'

'Ah. Didn't mean it that way.' He pulled out a thick fountain pen. 'I'm sure your signature's more legible than Zahler's – or his mother's, for that matter.'

The drummer on stage started a long fill, rolling across his whole set, the sound phasing and twisting as engineers played with their settings. For a few moments, we couldn't speak.

When the drumroll stuttered to a halt, Astor Michaels spread the contracts out on the mixing board. 'Shall we?'

I stared down at them, all those carefully chosen, hair-splitting words. When I'd read the contract, it had made a tangle in my mind, the numbered and cross-referenced paragraphs twisted around one another like the theme of a fugue.

'What's wrong?'

'I'm concerned about . . . the ethics of signing.'

'Ethics?' He laughed. 'Good God, Alana Ray. This band has four minors, two of whom are bat-shit crazy. Minerva had to forward-date her contract to next week. We've got a simpleton and a control freak as well. The ethics of *you* signing? You're practically the only one of sound mind!'

I didn't like how he was talking about the others, but first I had to explain: 'I'm not concerned about my own competence. I am worried about tonight.'

'Stage fright?' His voice softened. 'Is it tough with your condition?'

I shook my head. 'This is not about me. What if signing this contract risks harm to others? In the law, that is called a moral hazard.'

'I don't follow you.'

I looked up from the mass of words spread out across the mixing board, finally meeting Astor Michaels's eyes. 'I think that something dangerous may happen here tonight, because of us. Because of what Minerva is.'

'Oh.' He blinked. 'So you've . . . seen something?'

'Only what I always see when she sings.'

'Your little Loch Ness hallucination?' He smiled.

'I also saw it at the Morgan's Army gig, but stronger.' The drummer hit his snare, its echo bouncing across the vast club. There would be a thousand people here tonight. Huge stacks of amplifiers waited on either side of the stage, buzzing in the silence, crinkling the air. 'More people makes the beast bigger; more sound makes it bigger.'

'I hope so, Alana Ray, but that doesn't make it real.' Astor Michaels frowned. 'You know that, don't you?'

'Do I?'

He stared at me for a moment, genuinely puzzled. Then he shook his head. 'We've both seen strange things in our lives, I'll grant you that. We've both had . . . *conditions* to deal with. But both of us made something from them. That's why we're sitting here across this contract, you and me.'

I looked at his teeth, remembering what Pearl had told me on the phone last night. How Astor Michaels had made a career out of making more insects.

He stabbed at the papers with one long fingernail. 'What you have right here is real, and your visions aren't. You know that.'

I was suddenly angry. 'How can you be certain? This is in *my* head, not yours. No one else can see the things I do.'

His stare held me coolly. 'But you're the most logical person I've ever met, Alana Ray. And you wouldn't have come here for a sound check if you weren't going to play tonight, and you wouldn't play tonight if you weren't going to sign. So you don't really believe in monsters, do you?'

I swallowed, looking down at my hands – perfectly still, ready to play. I had dreamed of drumming all last night, of being under the spotlights. 'But you say Minerva is going to change things. What if she makes the beast real?'

'I've watch this epidemic roll across New York City for two years, and I've never seen anything like what you describe.'

I stared at him, wanting to believe. Astor Michaels had discovered the New Sound, after all. Maybe he knew what he was talking about.

'Don't you trust me?' he said, the pen flickering in his hand. 'Don't you think I'll do right by you?'

'I think it was right, what you did for Minerva.'

He let out a snort. 'Finally somebody thanks me.'

'Yes. Thank you,' I said. Minerva's freedom had frightened Pearl, but I'd watched too many schoolmates graduate into mental institutions, into group homes and jails, and I knew that locking people up was paranormal – *against* normal, not beside it. Locks didn't cure; they strangled.

'Well, then.' He held out the pen, eyes glinting. 'I don't think you're afraid of me or afraid of monsters. I think you're just afraid of your own success.'

I shook my head. Astor Michaels was very wrong about that. That morning, I'd thrown my change bucket away. Moral hazard or not, I wanted to be more real than someone begging on the streets.

So I signed, as he'd always known I would.

–ZAHLER–

The crowd was filling the main room now – a thousand people, Astor Michaels said, but it sounded like millions. Here in the backstage dressing room the noise was smoothed to a hum, like a hive of bees just waiting for someone to poke it with a stick.

The more I listened, the more they sounded like they were ready to boo somebody off the stage. Especially some lame bassist who'd only been playing for about four weeks . . .

I swallowed. *Nobody* had ever been this nervous before.

This was real. This was actual. This was happening *right now.*

Under the dressing room fluorescent lights was the worst place to practice, but I sat there in my chair slapping at the strings. Maybe I would get a little bit better, maybe just enough to save myself from humiliation.

Sometimes, playing my new instrument, my fingers moved more gracefully than they ever had across a guitar. Lately I'd been dreaming of the whole world expanding from guitar-size to bass-size, everything suddenly scaled just right for me and my big, fat, clumsy hands. But right now, the strings of Pearl's bass felt an inch thick, dragging at my fingers like quicksand in a nightmare.

Moz didn't look much happier. He was standing in one corner of the dressing room, wearing dark glasses and trembling. A sheen of sweat covered his face and bare arms.

'You look like you got the flu, Moz,' I said.

He shook his head. 'Just need my cup of tea.'

'Almost ready, Mozzy.' A teakettle was plugged into the wall next to where Minerva sat doing her makeup. She had some weird herbs waiting to be brewed.

'Your *cup of tea*?' I shook my head. Living with a girl had turned Moz totally lame. And it was all my fault because I'd told him to call Minerva, because I'd been so mad at him for wanting me to switch instruments . . .

It was all the stupid bass's fault!

Alana Ray stood right in the center of the room, staring at her own outstretched hands. Their rock-steadiness made her look incomplete, as if Moz had stolen all her twitchiness.

She'd traded her usual army jacket for this fawesome Japanese kimono over jeans. No one had told *me* we were supposed to dress up. I looked down at my same old unfool T-shirt. Would the crowd boo me for wearing it? They sounded really impatient now. The whole thing was starting an hour late, which Astor Michaels kept saying would make everything really intense . . .

But what if it just pissed them off?

Pearl was in the opposite corner from Moz, in the same dress she'd worn to Red Rat Records. She looked fawesome, I could tell, even if my brain was melting.

But she didn't look happy. She kept swearing under her breath: 'Special Guests? More like Special Retards. I can't *believe* we're going out as "Special Guests." Why don't we just call ourselves Special Education?'

'The band going on first is called Plasmodium,' Moz said. 'How much does that name suck?'

Pearl looked at him, gave Minerva a two-second glare, then said quietly, 'Sounds a lot like Toxoplasma.'

'We should pick a real name soon,' Minerva said, staring at her reflection in the mirror, applying makeup with steady hands. She was wearing a long evening gown, lots of jewelry, and didn't look nervous at all. She didn't notice the looks Pearl had been giving her. 'If we let Astor Michaels choose one, it'll have the word *plasma* in it.'

'What does *plasma* even mean?' Moz asked.

'It can mean two things,' Alana Ray said. 'Electrified gas or blood.'

'Gee,' Pearl muttered. 'Which one do you think he was going for?'

The teakettle suddenly spit out a crooked screech, the sound fading into a moan as Minerva unplugged it. She poured the boiling water into her cup of herbs, and the smell of compost heap filled the room. 'Here you go, Mozzy.'

An explosion of sound came from the walls, a thudding from the floor beneath us.

'Crap!' I hissed. 'It's the first band. We're the second band. That means we're next!'

'That is correct,' Alana Ray said.

My stomach started roiling like that time when I was little and I swallowed part of my chemistry set. We were going to face a possibly homicidal crowd in . . . *'Half an hour.'*

'Plus changeover time,' Alana Ray said.

I shut my eyes and listened. The crowd wasn't booing yet. Maybe they weren't such a nasty bunch after all. But Plasmodium sounded tight, not like they'd been forced to switch instruments, say, in the last month or so . . .

'Listen to that,' I said. 'Their bass player is way faster than me. Everyone's going to think I suck.'

'You don't suck, Zahler,' Moz said. 'And he sounds *too* fast to me.'

'Be dead by tomorrow at that speed,' Pearl said, staring down at her fingernails.

'Dead?' I said. 'What do you mean?' Did people ever *die* on stage? I wondered. Like from heart attacks? Or the audience killing them because they sucked?

'Relax, Zahler.' Moz was sipping his tea now, still trembling, Minerva mopping at the sheen of sweat across his face with a towel. 'You've got half an hour to get yourself together.'

Great. I was being told to chill out by a guy who looked like he was dying of Ebola fever. Maybe Moz was about to collapse, and then we could do this whole Special Guest thing *after* he recovered – and I got some more practice in. Alana Ray was still staring at her hands. She'd hardly moved the whole time, like some kind of kung-fu Zen master contemplating destiny. I was thinking how maybe I should have worn something Japanese – then I'd at least *look* fool. Well, actually, I already looked fool. In the usual sense of the word.

'Time is a strange thing, Zahler,' Alana Ray said. 'If you focus your mind, thirty minutes can seem like five hours.'

But it didn't. It seemed like five seconds.

Then Astor Michaels came in and said that it was showtime.

A thousand of them waited out there, all just looking at us.

Random shouts filtered up from the audience – they weren't heckling us exactly, just bored and ready for another band to start. We didn't have any fans yet – the few friends Moz and I had invited were too young to get in. The sight of the unfriendly crowd made me realize one big thing missing from my rock-star dreams:

In all my fantasies about being famous, I was *already* famous, so I never had to *get* famous. I never had to walk out in front of a crowd for the first time, unknown and defenseless. In my dreams, this awful night had already happened.

I looked over at Moz, but he was staring down at his feet and still trembling, like he was having a seizure. Behind her paint buckets, Alana Ray's eyes were shut, and Pearl was peering down at her keyboards, flicking switches as fast as she could, like she was about to take off in a spaceship. Nobody looked back at me, like they were all suddenly embarrassed to be in the same band.

It's not my fault! I wanted to shout. *I never wanted to play the bass!*

Minerva was the only one who looked happy to be onstage. She was already leaning over her mike stand, talking to a bunch of tattooed guys down in front, flirting with them, flicking at their grasping hands with spike-heeled black boots. Even through her dark glasses you could see that her eyes were scary-wide and glowing, sucking energy from the crowd before she'd sung a single note.

Pearl gave me a low E, and I took a deep breath and tuned up. The sound boomed out from my bass like a foghorn, rumbling through the club. A few howls from the audience answered the noise, as if I'd interrupted someone's conversation and they were pissed.

The guys flirting with Minerva had big muscles and tattoos on their shaved heads. I'd read the night before about a big riot in Europe, a whole crowd at some soccer game going crazy all at once, attacking one another. Hundreds had died, and nobody knew why.

What if that happened here, right now? The whole crowd turning into deadly maniacs? I knew exactly who everyone would choose to kill first.

The half-assed bass player in the lame T-shirt. That's who.

When we were all tuned up, the stage lights lowered.

Total darkness, like I'd suddenly gone blind from freaking out. More impatient shouts filtered up from the crowd, and someone yelled, 'You suck!' which people laughed at, because we hadn't even started yet.

We were so dead.

I swallowed, waiting to begin . . .

'Zahler!' Pearl hissed.

Oh, right. We were doing the Big Riff first. *I* was supposed to start.

My fingers groped for the strings, and I heard the amps squeak with the sweat on my fingers. I tried to remember what to play.

And I couldn't.

No, this wasn't happening . . .

I'd been playing this riff for six years, and yet it had somehow disappeared from my brain, from my fingers, from my whole body.

I stood there in silence, waiting to die.

–MOZ–

Zahler had frozen up.

Perfect.

My head was burning, sweat running into my eyes, heart pounding like something in a cage. But it wasn't stage fright; it was the beast gone wild in me. I'd been anxious all day, too nervous to eat, and now the hunger had caught up with me all at once.

Garlic and mandrake tea wasn't cutting it. I needed flesh and blood.

'*Play, Zahler!*' I heard Pearl hiss, trying to get him going.

The crowd was growing impatient, a restless hum building before us, but at least the delay gave me a few more seconds of darkness. My vision had been doing weird things all day: I hadn't been able to look at Min, as if her face were made of sharp angles that cut into my eyes. Even the smell of her clothes and perfume was making my head spin, as if living together had somehow given me an overdose of her.

But here in the darkness I felt alone, almost under control.

Zahler still wasn't starting the Big Riff, though, which left only me. I could play his old guitar part and wait for him to come in. But once the music began, the lights would pop back on, so bright, so sharp . . .

And then the hunger would take control again.

I could run offstage right now, slip out of the club and into some all-night store, wolf down a slab of raw meat. Probably a better idea than taking a chunk out of someone right here in front of a thousand witnesses.

But even with the beast ravenous inside me, I had to stay. I couldn't let Zahler live forever with the shame of having blown it tonight.

I took a deep breath, and just as my fingers moved . . . Zahler finally began to play.

Six years of practice took over: the Big Riff grabbed me, coiled around my spine and out my fingers, my nervous system responding as automatically as breathing. Pearl followed, then Alana Ray came in, the echoes of her paint buckets making the space huge around us.

The lights came up, and the crowd was suddenly cheering. *Good move, Zahler*, I thought. *Making them wait for it.*

Minerva kept them waiting too, left the Big Riff grinding for a solid minute before she brought the microphone anywhere near her lips. But you could tell she hadn't frozen up – her whole body moved with the beat, drawing every eye in the crowd, gulping in their energy.

She played with them, drawing the microphone close, then pushing it away, grinning behind dark glasses. The Big Riff could hypnotize you, I knew all too well – Zahler and I some-times played it for hours at a stretch. When Minerva let it flow through her body, she was as spellbinding as a swaying cobra.

Then she pulled off her glasses, braving the spotlights to peer into the audience, to fix them with her gaze. I saw their faces ignite with the light reflected from her, as if somehow she'd made eye contact with everyone.

That was when she started to sing, and when I started to feel *really* funny.

The words that Minerva had scrawled down in her basement tumbled out of her, as lunatic as the first time she'd played with us – incomprehensible, ancient, and wild. They dredged up weird pictures in my mind, the skulls and centipedes carved into the iron lock on her bedroom door.

The ground began to rumble.

Maybe it was just my stomach, the gnawing hunger changing into something sharper. It felt as if all the raw hamburger I'd consumed over the last few weeks had gotten to me at last, my iron gut finally succumbing to food poisoning.

The sight of Minerva with her glasses off made my head spin, the spotlights flashing from her face like crystal. I felt the garlic leaving my body in a hot sweat, as if giant hands were squeezing me, wringing out every protection I had against the beast inside.

Disgust was leaking into me, a loathing for everything that had put me on this stage: Minerva, this band, the Stratocaster in my hands. The whole insane idea of fame and adulation and even *music itself* . . .

I wanted to throw it all away, to run from all these pointless complications and let the beast inside take over. To hide in some distant, shadowy place and gnaw on nothing but flesh and bones – perfectly sated, an animal.

But my fingers kept playing. The music held me there, balanced between love and hatred.

I stared down at the stage, not looking at Minerva, but I couldn't keep her song out of my ears. It kept pouring from the amplifiers, echoing back and forth across the club, building like feedback in my head.

The cables at my feet were moving, shivering like dizzying snakes across the floor. I tore my eyes from them, glaring out into the darkness of the nightclub.

I saw it start out there.

A shape moved through the crowd, a swell of hands thrown up into the air, like a stadium wave carrying itself along, traveling toward us from the back of the club. It broke against the stage, shattering into wild cries of surprise.

The ground rumbled under my feet.

Then the swell appeared again, moving from right to left this time, carrying screams along with it. That's when I realized this wasn't something innocent, like upraised arms at a baseball game . . . Reality was bending before my eyes.

The floor itself was surging up, the bulge moving like a rat scurrying under a rug. More violent this time – the people in its path were thrown into the air, tossed up to fall into the outstretched arms of the crowd, like stage-jumpers.

My sharp ears caught a thin scream behind me, and I glanced back to see Alana Ray crying out, 'No, no, no . . . ,' unheard in the booming beat of the Big Riff. But she kept playing: the music had also captured her, locking her hands into their fluttering patterns.

The moving surge of floor turned again, growing stronger. As I watched, the ground began to split, the earth opening like a huge zipper, vomiting up black water and cracked pieces of concrete. A choking smell filled my nostrils.

It was headed toward the stage, but none of us stopped playing.

A few people began to scramble away from its path, trying to run through the crowd, but most were staring raptly up at us, too mesmerized by Minerva to move.

It was the enemy, of course, the same beast I'd seen down in the subway. She had finally called it up.

The Stratocaster burned my fingers, my whole body rejecting the music we were making, but still I couldn't stop.

Screams filled the nightclub now. More of the crowd fought to scramble over one another for safety, trying to avoid the snapping maws of the beast. It grew closer and closer to us.

And then angels started falling.

They dropped from the ceiling on thin filaments, cables that sparkled in the spotlights, descending toward the creature and onto the stage. One angel swung to the top of each set of amplifiers, swords flashing in their hands. They rappelled down the stacks, stabbing each speaker right in its center, every thrust bringing forth a high-pitched shriek from the equipment – a squealing counterpoint to the Big Riff.

Dozens of them dropped onto the beast and into the crowd, pushing people away. They brought the creature to a halt, hacking with swords and stabbing with long, telescoping spears. Its cries of pain joined the squawking of the amplifiers, until the music finally began to stumble . . .

Minerva's voice faltered, and the spell was shattered.

I broke free, pulling the Stratocaster's strap from my shoulder and grabbing the guitar by its neck, despising it with every fiber of my being. I raised it over my head and swung it down against the stage, smashing it again and again, its strings snapping, its broken neck twisting like a dying chicken's. The guitar buzzed and squeaked out a last few tuneless notes, its death cries leaking from the surviving amps.

Around me, the others had ground to a halt. In tears, Alana Ray threw her sticks aside, kicking wildly at her paint buckets. Zahler just stood there open-mouthed, staring at the battle on the nightclub floor. I couldn't look at Minerva anymore.

Stepping back from the broken guitar, my hands bent into claws, I started to stomp at it with my boots. It peeped and squawked.

Then an angel landed on the stage in front of me, dressed in commando black, trailing a thin cable from her waist. She held a small object in one hand.

I recognized her: Lace.

I turned to run, to escape her and everything else: this band, this music, the monstrous thing we'd called up. But after a few steps, before I'd even reached the edge of the stage, she'd caught up with me, grabbing my arm and spinning me around, her needle flashing in the spotlights.

I felt a pinprick at my neck, then her arms supporting me.

'Say good night, Moz,' Lace said.

The sound of my own name almost made me vomit, and then nausea and pain melted into darkness.

PART VI | THE TOUR

There has never been a better time for a pandemic.

Airplanes can carry people across the globe in a single day, and half a billion people fly every year. Cities are far larger and more crowded than at any point in history.

The last great disease was Spanish flu, which appeared at the end of World War I. (Pandemics love wars.) It spread across the planet faster than any previous disease. Within one year, one billion people were infected, a third of the world's popula-tion. Its spread was so frighteningly quick that one U.S. town outlawed shaking hands.

And all this was before airplanes could fly across oceans, before most people owned a car. These days, any pandemic would travel much, much faster. We've got it all these days: dense cities, instant transportation, and all the wars you could want. For the worms, that's motive, means, and opportunity.

When the last days come, they will come quickly.

NIGHT MAYOR TAPES END HERE.

–MINERVA–

The smelly angels took us all away.

I tried to explain to them that I was fine – had been for weeks – and that Zahler, Pearl, and Alana Ray weren't even infected. But one look at sweaty, frothing, guitar-smashing Mozzy convinced them we were all insane.

That was the angels' big problem: they thought they knew *everything*.

I could have run. I was as fast and strong as them now – I could shatter bedroom doors with a single blow, after all. With the angels busy protecting a thousand bystanders and catching Astor Michaels and killing the giant worm that I'd called up (okay . . . *oops*), disappearing would have been a cinch.

But that would have meant leaving Moz and the others behind, and we really were a band now; I couldn't let them be kidnapped without me. So I let the angels stick me with their stupid needles . . .

And woke up all the way across the river in New Jersey. They'd put me in a locked room, a cross between a cheap hotel and a mental hospital. Nothing to do but watch the world fall apart on TV.

Smelly angels.

'We're very interested in you, Minerva.'

'Really, Cal?' I batted my eyelashes. He was kind of hand-some – in a boring, clean-cut way – and had a cute southern accent. Not as yummy as Mozzy, of course, but I liked how Cal turned pink when you flirted with him. 'Then why don't you let me out of here? It's not like I'm *dangerous*, after all.'

His eyes narrowed. Cal never wore sunglasses, like the other angels did. They were all infected, of course, and only sane because they took their meds. The angels had a big pill factory out here. No skulls or crucifixes on the walls, though – they were very scientific.

But Cal was different. He didn't need pills and smelled a little bit like Astor Michaels. Fellow freaks of nature.

'We can't let you go because we don't know what you *are*,' Cal's girlfriend said.

I glared at her. Her name was Lace-short-for-Lacey, and she'd stuck Mozzy with her needle.

'But I'm *cured*. You can see that.' They'd tried to give me their smelly angel medicine, but I was refusing it. Fresh garlic was enough for me now.

Cal scratched his head. 'Yeah, you told us about your esoter-ica already. We're checking her out.'

'You be nice to Luz,' I warned. 'She knows things.'

'We know things too,' he said.

Lace got all bossy then, hands on hips and voice too loud. 'We've been around for centuries, cured a lot more peeps than Luz ever will. Your friend might know a few folk remedies, but the Watch has this stuff down to a science.'

'Science, huh?' I ran one finger down the side of my neck, making Cal all squirmy. 'So what *am* I, then?'

Lace frowned. 'What you are is freaky.'

'We've been watching Astor Michaels for a while now,' Cal said. 'We knew he was spreading the parasite, but this whole *singing* thing . . . It kind of caught us by surprise.'

I didn't say how the worm had caught me by surprise too. I'd always felt it rumbling when we played, but I'd never thought it would come *visit*.

Even humming made me nervous now. Smelly underground monsters.

I shrugged. 'Why don't you ask Astor Michaels about it, then?'

'He doesn't know any more than wc do,' Lace said. 'He's just some record producer, trying to find the Next Big Thing. He's immune to the parasite's worst effects, but that's more common than you'd think.'

'I'm a carrier myself.' Cal smiled, all proud of himself. He'd already come by my room to explain how he was naturally immune and how he'd been a badass vampire-hunter even before the crisis. Now he worked for something called the Night Watch, which was run by someone called the Night Mayor. Oooh! Spooky.

I batted my eyes again. 'Did you get up to tricks like Astor Michaels did, Cal? Were you *bad*?'

'No.' He swallowed, then Lace gave him a look. 'Well, not on that scale. And never on purpose . . .'

'Did you infect *her*?' I asked, pointing at Lace-short-for-Lacey. I'd seen them being all kissy through the bars of my window.

'No,' he said in a tiny voice. 'My cat did.'

'Your cat?' I blinked. 'Kitties can do that?'

'Felines are the major vector,' Cal said. 'The parasite hid in the deep-dwelling rat population for centuries, until the worms drove them up to the surface . . .'

As Cal went on with his parasite-geek lecture, which he *loved* to do, I remembered back to before I got sick. As the sanitation crisis had settled over our street, Zombie started spending a lot of time outside. And every night he'd come home and sleep on my chest, breathing his cat-food breath into my face.

That was how I'd gotten sick? From *Zombie*?

That meant that Mark wasn't such a dirty dog after all. He hadn't given the nasty to me; I'd given it to him . . .

'Oops,' I said softly.

I wondered where Zombie was now. I always left the apartment window open so he could visit his little friends, but Manhattan looked pretty bad on TV. The whole island had been sealed off by Homeland Security, like *that* was going to keep the parasite from spreading.

Cal had explained to me how clever the parasite was: it turned infected people horny, hungry, bitey – anything to pass on its spores – and made them despise everything they'd loved before. That's why I'd thrown away Mark and my dolls and my music, why Moz had smashed his Stratocaster to bits. The anathema, as Cal called it, pushed infected people to run away from home and head to the next town over, and the next town after that . . .

It wouldn't be long before the whole world had it.

There were full-scale riots in most big cities now, blood-thirsty maniacs running around doing vile things – and not all of them were infected, you could totally tell. Schools were shutting down, the roads were choked with refugees, and the president kept making speeches telling everyone to pray.

No shit.

But the news never mentioned cat food supplies, not that I ever saw. So what was Zombie eating now? He didn't *mind* birds and mousies, but he always puked them up.

'Anyway,' Lace said, noticing I wasn't listening. 'We don't really care how you got the disease or how your voodoo friend cured you. This is about your songs.'

I smiled. 'They make the ground rumble. Want me to sing one for you?'

'Um, not really,' Cal said, then he frowned. 'That worm was probably just a coincidence anyway. But certain people around here are interested. They've been listening to recordings from that night, and they want to know where you got those lyrics.'

'You need my help? But I thought you had this stuff down to a science.'

Lace took a slow breath. 'Maybe what happened that night wasn't strictly science.'

Cal turned to her. 'What do you mean by that?'

'Dude! You saw what happened! That shit was . . .' Her voice faded.

'Paranormal?' I looked down at my fingernails, which needed a manicure. They were still growing faster every day, even though I was cured. 'Okay. I'll tell you everything I know . . . *if* you let me see Mozzy and the others. I want us to be together. We're a band, you know.'

'But the other three tested parasite-negative,' Cal said.

'I told you they would.'

He frowned. 'Yeah, I guess you did. But if we let you see them, you can't do anything that would compromise their health.'

'Eww! I wouldn't kiss any of *them*.'

'Kissing's not the only vector.'

I tried not to roll my eyes. Anything to get out of this smelly room. 'Okay, I promise not to share my ice cream.'

'Cal,' Lace said. 'If she really wanted to infect them, she could have already.' She turned to me. 'But Moz is still dangerous.'

'I can handle Mozzy. He just needs his tea.'

'He's getting better stuff than tea,' she said. 'But he's still in bad shape. It's not pretty.'

I snorted. 'I've been tied to a bed in a nuthouse, screaming and trying to bite my doctors' fingers off. And then locked in my room for three months, hating myself and eating dead chickens raw. Don't talk to *me* about pretty, Miss Lace-short-for-Lacey.'

The two of them looked at each other all seriously, then argued for a while longer, but I knew that eventually I'd get my way. They wanted to know about my songs real bad.

And like Astor Michaels always said, you had to keep the talent happy.

-PEARL-

The Night Watch stuck me, Zahler, and Alana Ray in one of their 'guest rooms', a little cluster of cabins at the forested edge of the compound. We were free to go where we wanted in the compound, except the hospital where Moz was, but outside our door a tall fence stretched in both directions. Razor wire coiled down its length, reminding us that we were prisoners; not because they wouldn't let us out, but because outside was too deadly for us now. Special Guests all over again.

There wasn't much to do except watch the world end on TV.

Thanks to jet planes, overcrowded schools, and the sheer six billion of us all crammed together, the disease was spinning out of control. It hit critical mass in New York City in that first week we were out in Jersey, spreading faster than anyone could contain, conceal, or comprehend what was happening.

The talking heads all went lateral, of course, blaming terrorists or avian flu or the government or God. All nonsense, though at least they'd stopped pretending this was just a sanitation problem. But none of them seemed to get that the world was ending.

Sometimes they'd interview people in small towns, where everything was weirdly normal, the disease invisible so far. They were all smirking at New York, like we'd had it coming. But the boondocks wouldn't be fun for very long. Credit cards, phones, and the Internet were already starting to fail. Hardly anyone was making contact lenses, movies, medicines, or refined gasoline anymore. Even in the smallest towns, they'd miss all that infrastructure when it was gone.

Ellen Bromowitz had been right: there weren't going to be any symphony orchestras for a while. No celebrity interviews in magazines, no album cover photo shoots or music videos. And the biggest hit on local radio these days was 'Where's the National Guard Camp Nearest You?'

No way to get famous.

Of course, now that I knew the scale of what was happening, becoming a rock star seemed less important. In fact, it seemed just plain stupid, unbelievably self-centered, and nine kinds of deluded.

I'd seen this coming. Even back when all I'd had to go on was Min's craziness and Luz's strange tales, I'd understood somehow that the world was about to break. So what had I done? Tried to escape reality by becoming *famous*. As if the world couldn't touch me then, as if bad things didn't happen to people with record deals. As if I could just leave all the nonfamous people behind.

What a joke. A sad, demented joke.

So that was me now: depressed and deflated in New Jersey, shell-shocked that our first gig had turned into a bloodbath, that the world was crumbling, and that my lifelong dream had turned out to be the Taj Mahal of shallow.

I never wanted to go onstage again, never wanted to play another instrument . . . and just when I'd finally thought of a really fexcellent band name.

How's that for annoying?

*

Every morning the Night Watch brought in truckloads of peeps – parasite positives – they'd captured the night before. They treated as many as would fit in their hospital, an empty elementary school they'd taken over. Hundreds of them, reborn as angels, trained on the assembly field every day. Their swords glittered like a host of flashbulbs popping in unison.

An army was building here.

Cal said that in all of human history, this was the fastest the infection had ever spread – those jet planes again. And what nobody but the Watch realized yet was that the worst part was yet to come. The creature that Min had summoned, the worm, was one of thousands rising up to attack humanity. Just like Luz had said, the sickness was merely a sign that a great struggle was about to begin.

When Cal visited to give us his geeky lectures, he'd offer the scientific version. It was all a chain reaction: the rising worms upset deep-dwelling rats, who carried the parasite to the surface; they infected felines, who gave it to their humans, who turned into peeps and spread it to still more humans. The disease made people stronger and faster, vicious and fearless – the perfect soldiers to fight the worms.

Through most of history, vampires were rare; but every few centuries, humanity needed tons of them. This epidemic was our species' immune system gearing up, peeps like killer T-cells multiplying in our blood, getting ready to repel an invader. Of course, as Cal liked to point out, immune systems are dangerous things: lupus, arthritis, and even asthma are all caused by our own defenses. Fevers have to be controlled.

That's where the Watch came in, to organize the peeps and keep them from doing too much damage. Like your mom bringing you aspirin and cold compresses and chicken soup – but with ninja uniforms.

*

Early one morning a week after we'd arrived, they finally let us see the others.

Moz was in a hospital bed, looking worse than I'd expected. His arms and legs were restrained, and long IV tubes snaked into both arms, dripping yellowish liquids into his bloodstream. Electronic monitors were taped all over his bare, pale chest. A plastic shunt jutted from his throat, so they could inject things without opening up a vein.

Moz's eyes looked bruised, his skin stretched taut across his cheekbones. The room was dark and smelled vaguely like garlic and disinfectant.

Minerva sat silent beside him. The sight of her sent a tremor of rage through me: *she'd* done this to him, infected him with her kiss.

Cal said she'd been partly under the parasite's control.

Always trying to spread itself, it made its hosts horny, greedy, irrational. But I was still pissed off. Parasite-positive or not, you should never, *ever* hook up with anyone in your band.

Not twice in a row.

'Hey,' I said. They'd warned us not to say his name, because of the anathema. He'd only just recovered enough to look at our faces.

'Hey, man,' Zahler said. 'How's it going, Minerva?'

Minerva pointed to her own mouth, then made a key-turning gesture. *My lips are sealed.*

Of course . . . Moz had been in love with Min. Her sultry, beautiful voice would burn his ears. I noticed that he looked at Zahler and Alana Ray and me, but kept his gaze averted from Min.

Not that I could look at her myself.

'Hey,' Moz said hoarsely.

'You look like crap!' Zahler said.

'Feel like crap too.'

'At least you aren't smashing things,' Alana Ray said.

She tried to smile, but her head jerked to one side instead. Since the gig, she was twitchier than I'd ever seen her.

Moz winced, as if remembering the wreckage he'd left of the Strat. He must have loved the guitar more than Minerva, I realized, half smiling. He hadn't smashed *her* to pieces, after all.

Small favors.

'Pretty intense gig, though, huh?' Moz said.

I nodded. 'Yeah, fawesome. For most of one song anyway.'

'That crowd thought we were totally fool.' Zahler sighed. 'Too bad about the, uh . . . giant worm, though.'

'Yeah. That part sucked,' Moz said.

We were all quiet for a while. The Watch hadn't told us anything about that night, and the news had much bigger things to talk about, but we all were pretty sure that people had been killed. Of course, so had the beast we'd raised – one less underground monster.

That was why the Night Watch was interested in us.

They knew the secret history of how worms and peeps had always appeared together and had a grip on modern science as well. Cal said they'd known before anyone else that this apocalypse was coming. They had cures and treatments for turning maniacs into soldiers to fight the enemy. They had cool worm-killing swords.

But we could do something they couldn't.

We could sing the worms up. We could bring them out of hiding and to the surface, which made them a lot easier to destroy . . .

After we'd been talking for a while, Min handed me a note. Her handwriting was still a mess, but I could understand it. More or less.

'So, Moz, we have to leave for a while,' I said. 'Just for a day or so. We'll be back before you're out of bed.'

'Where?' he croaked.

My fingers folded the note up small. 'Manhattan.'

'Are you kidding?' Zahler said. 'It's dangerous back there! And I promised my mom I'd stay right here!'

I nodded. Local phones were mostly still working, so we knew that my mom was safe in the Hamptons, Elvis at her side, and that Zahler's parents were at a Guard camp in Connecticut. Minerva's family had been scooped up by the Night Watch, who'd wanted to check and see if they also carried her weird monster-calling strain of the disease. But Moz's parents, like most New Yorkers, were holding out in their building. And they'd said things looked ugly down on the street.

'Sorry, Zahler. But there's someone the Night Watch wants us to meet.'

'Can't this someone come out to Jersey?' he asked.

I crumpled the note and shrugged. 'Apparently not.'

'Well, screw that!' Zahler said. 'New York is one big Maniac City! They can't *make* us go, can they?'

'Pearl,' Alana Ray said. 'Does it say what they want to talk about?'

'Only that maybe we can help. What happened that night – we might be able to use it to save people.' I turned to each of them as I spoke, pushing my glasses up my nose, like this was a rehearsal and I wanted to get them to stop tuning up and playing riffs and listen to me. 'These Night Watch guys are the only people in the world who aren't clueless about what's going on. When that thing turned up at our gig, they were the ones who stopped it from killing everybody, remember? It won't hurt us to listen to them.'

'It's not the listening that I'm—'

'I am sorry to interrupt, Zahler,' Alana Ray said, tapping her forehead twice, a shiver moving across her. 'But I agree with Pearl. We called that creature up; we were responsible.'

'We didn't know it was going to happen!' Zahler cried.

'Whether that is true or not . . .' Alana Ray's eyes dropped to the floor, as if she saw something there. 'It would be unethical not to help if we can.'

I looked at the others. Minerva nodded silently, trying to catch my eye. Moz crooked one thumb into the air, and Zahler let out a defeated sigh.

–ZAHLER–

There was a checkpoint at the Jersey end of the Holland Tunnel, swarming with New York cops and Guardsmen and guys in khaki toting machine guns. It didn't look to me like they were letting anyone through.

I figured this was the end of the trip – too bad, we'd tried – and that was fine by me. But then Lace zipped down her window, flashed a badge, and said, 'Homeland Security.'

The unshaven Guardsman stared at the badge, his eyes red. He looked like he'd been awake for days, like he'd seen some scary shit, and like he thought we were crazy.

But he waved us through.

'Homeland Security?' I asked. 'Are you guys, like, *really* Homeland Security? Some sort of paranormal branch?'

'Please.' Lace snorted. 'Those guys can't even handle *natural* disasters.'

Our convoy slid into the tunnel. We were in two big military-looking vehicles, a bunch of angels riding on the outside. I wondered what the cops thought of them. But I guessed everyone had seen much weirder stuff than black ninja suits and swords lately.

The tunnel was completely dark. Lace flicked on the

headlights and drove straight down the middle, ignoring the lane dividers. As I watched the entrance disappear behind us through the back window, blackness swallowed everything except the red tinge of our taillights. It felt like sinking to the core of the earth.

'Aren't there worms down here?' I asked.

'They'd never attack us here,' Lace said. 'The whole Hudson River's balanced over our heads. They breach this tunnel, and a million tons of water gush down on us *and* them.'

'Oh. Fawesome,' I said, reminding myself to shut up forever, as of now.

'Are they that smart?' Alana Ray asked.

Lace shrugged. 'It's all instinct. They evolved underground.'

I swallowed, thinking about how much earth there was below us. Room for all kinds of weird stuff to be brewing, and I'd never even thought about it.

'Okay, let's get a few things straight about Dr. Prolix,' Cal said. 'There's a red line painted on the floor of her office. Whatever you do, don't step across it.'

'A line on the floor?' Pearl said. 'Doesn't she like musicians?'

'She's a carrier, like me,' he explained. 'A really old one, so she's got a few diseases that aren't around much anymore. Typhus and stuff. Bubonic plague. If you get too close to her, we sort of have to . . . burn your clothes.'

I looked at the others, wondering if I'd really heard him say that. These angels or Night Watch guys or whatever were always saying stuff that was just messed up. Talking to Cal was like watching some psycho version of the History Channel that only showed the nasty parts – epidemics, massacres, and inquisitions, twenty-four/seven.

'Burn our clothes?' Minerva said. 'But this is my last nice dress! Shouldn't you put *her* in a glass bubble or something?'

Cal shook his head. 'The whole house is set up for negative

air-pressure prophylaxis, so the germs around Dr. Prolix can't get to where you'll be standing. Just don't cross the line.'

'Bubonic plague?' Alana Ray repeated. A shudder traveled through her body, and she pressed her hands together. 'Exactly how old is this woman?'

'Old,' he said.

In Manhattan, the streets were still alive.

Rats moved among leaking piles of garbage, stray cats sliding under smashed and motionless cars. You could see long ripples in the asphalt where the worms had passed, leaving gleaming stains of black water in the high sun. A few gaping holes showed where they'd burst through the surface. I wondered if anyone had been standing right there when they had . . .

According to Cal, it was all natural: they were hunters and we were their prey.

Nature can blow me.

'There are no bodies,' Alana Ray said.

'The peeps are cannibals,' Lace said. 'And the worms are human-eaters.'

'Much neater than your usual epidemic,' Cal said.

A flash of disbelief went through me; this wasn't *really* the Manhattan I'd grown up in. For a moment, it was all a big movie set – a giant, evil version of Disney World. There weren't really any monsters under our feet, or crazy people hiding in the dark-ened buildings, and all our parents were actually back in the real Manhattan, wondering where we were.

But then we passed an empty school yard, the concrete ripped and torn from one end to the other. An ice-cream truck waited beside it – split almost in half, ripped open from underneath. It was bleeding white goo into the street, and the breeze carried a smell like spoiled milk and burnt sugar through the open windows.

A basketball sat abandoned in the middle of the playground. It stirred in the wind, and the realness of everything settled over me again.

Our convoy weaved slowly downtown, avoiding the worst streets and any people we spotted. Small groups were scurrying from place to place, carrying water and food and other stuff they must have looted from the stores. Smashed and gaping windows were everywhere.

'Are all these people infected?' Pearl asked.

'If they are, they're not symptomatic yet,' Cal said. 'Peeps can't stand direct sunlight.'

I looked out the back window, twisting my neck to see up. It was almost noon, the sun reaching down into the narrow canyons of downtown. The angels all wore dark glasses, except for Cal.

The problem was, this close to winter the sun went down early in New York. An hour from now the shadows of the empty skyscrapers would begin to lengthen.

I hoped this wasn't going to be a long conversation.

We made our way down to the Stock Exchange. It was the worst part of the city we'd seen, the streets empty and broken. Papers and trash blew in little cyclones around us, and Lace honked her horn to scatter a big posse of rats. I guessed the stock market wasn't going to open back up anytime soon.

Lace turned the vehicle's engine off, rolling the last dozen yards to a silent halt. The angels climbed carefully down, drawing their swords and forming a circle around us. The asphalt was pitted and gouged, as if worms popped through all the time around here.

'Everybody out,' Lace said. 'Step lightly, though. The worms can hear our footsteps.' I opened my door and stared down at the street. It was stained with black water, with old gum, and with something viscous and red.

Crap, I thought. All my life I'd been at the top of the food chain and had never really appreciated it. Peeps were bad enough, even worse than junkies, I figured. But the worms – something about the ground opening up and swallowing people was just *wrong*.

I lowered one foot softly to the street, then the other, a shiver of nerves traveling through my body. The asphalt felt fragile, like the ice on the Central Park Reservoir does when you sneak onto it in early spring. As I took my first step, my foot resisted, and I almost screamed, imagining a hungry mouth bursting through to grab my leg.

But it was just the old wad of gum, softened to stickiness by the sun. It tugged at my sole with every step, making a sucking sound.

The angels led us into a long, crooked alley. The old-fashioned cobblestones were broken and bulging, with a few gaping holes that seethed with rats. I shivered at the sight of all those furry bodies. Cal and Lace talked about rats like they were on our side, something about them storing the parasite and bubbling up to spread it when the worms began to rise. But how that was a good thing, I had *no* idea . . .

We crept slowly down the alley, keeping clear of the worm-holes. At the end was an old town house, its stoop covered with silent, watchful cats.

Their red eyes followed us as we went in.

There really was a red line on the floor.

A breeze pushed me toward it, like a gentle hand pressing against my back. Cal had explained that all the air in the house moved toward Dr. Prolix, sucking her ancient germs away from us and down into a big, germ-killing furnace. She was immune to all her own diseases, being infected like the rest of the angels, but we'd be dead meat if we got too close. Even Cal and Lace kept away from the line. Didn't want their fexcellent ninja suits burned, I guess.

I stayed against the back wall, as far away as I could get. Not just to stay away from the Plague Lady but to be farther from the weird old dolls that lined the shelves of her office. Real-looking hair sprouted from their crumbling heads, and all their faces were painted with smiles.

Kids in the old days must have loved nightmares or something .

'You're the one who sings,' Dr. Prolix said, her gaze dismissing the rest of us and locking onto Minerva. Her voice was dry and raspy, like two sheets of paper rubbing together. Her unwrinkled face didn't look that old, except for the thinness of her skin and the stiffness of her smile. She looked like one of her own dolls, decorated with glowing human eyes.

'Yeah, that's me,' Minerva said in a small voice.

'And where did you learn these songs, young woman?'

'When I first got sick, I felt something down in my basement calling me, making me sort of . . .' She let out a giggle.

'Sexually aroused?' Dr. Prolix asked.

'Yeah, I guess. When I went there in my fevers, I could hear whispering from the cracks.' Minerva shrugged. 'So I started writing down what they said.'

I swallowed. I'd never really thought about where her lyrics had come from, but then, Minerva had never mentioned that they'd bubbled up from underground. That seemed like the kind of thing you might *mention*.

'Perhaps I might hear a few words?' Dr. Prolix said.

'Um, is that a good idea?' Pearl asked softly.

'Don't sing, dear,' the old woman said. 'Just speak them.'

Minerva paused a moment, then cleared her throat.

A few syllables came from her mouth, at first halting and tangled, like someone trying to imitate the sound of a sink gurgling. But then she started speaking in rhythm, and the weird sounds smoothed into words.

Then Minerva fell into the verses and choruses Pearl had built around the nonsense syllables, pitching her voice in a singsong way. I recognized a few phrases from Piece Two, and my fingers moved half-consciously, playing the bass line in the air, so I didn't notice when she started singing.

Maybe the floor trembled a little.

'Stop that!' Dr. Prolix snapped.

Minerva came to a halt, shaking her head as though she were snapping out of a daydream. Then she shrugged. 'Sorry.'

'I always wondered how that worked,' Dr. Prolix said softly from behind her desk.

'How what worked?' Cal said. 'What *is* that?'

'The last time the enemy came was seven hundred years ago, before I was born. But the Night Mayor was born toward the end of those times.'

I blinked. Okay, this woman was talking about centuries – about being alive for *centuries*. I felt my brain trying to switch off, like when a crazy person is ranting on the subway and you totally don't want to hear it, but you can't stop listening.

Dr. Prolix spread her hand on her desk. 'Have you ever considered, Cal, how the previous invasions were dealt with? Without seismographs? Without walkie-talkies and cell phones?'

'Um . . . I thought maybe they didn't deal so well?' he said. 'Of course, they didn't have Homeland Security in the way, making it hard to move medicine into regions suffering outbreaks, and there weren't any subway tunnels for the enemy to slide around in. But it must have been hard. What did they lose last time? Two hundred million people?'

'And yet humanity survived.' She folded her hands. 'Legend has it that they didn't have to wait for the worms to come up. Certain peeps, called "singers", were able to bring them forth. So the Watch set traps and ambushes and killed the enemy at will.'

Cal breathed out a little sigh. 'And we believe this?'

Dr. Prolix nodded. 'The Night Mayor saw it happen when he was a child. He saw a woman call up a worm.' Her glowing eyes swept across the rest of us. 'Along with fifteen drummers and bell-ringers and a man with a conch horn, with a great throng watching, waiting for the kill.'

Conch horn? I thought. Oh, great. I was going to have to switch instruments *again*.

'Dude,' Lace said, punching Cal in the shoulder. 'How come you never told me about this?'

'First I've heard of it,' he muttered.

'Some of the old ways were lost.' Dr. Prolix looked down at her hands. 'Many of us burned in the Inquisition.'

'Those guys again,' Cal said.

'But the knowledge was not completely lost, it seems.' Dr. Prolix looked at Minerva. 'Where do you live, child?'

'Um, Boerum Hill.'

The doctor nodded. 'Some of the old families are buried there.'

'Buried?' Minerva said. 'Eww.'

My jaw dropped. 'You mean, like, we were doing songs that *dead people* wrote?'

'Excellent point, Zahler,' Cal said. 'Come on, Dr. Prolix, this is just wishful thinking. Even if the Watch used to know how to call worms back in the old days, the information's lost, burned at the stake. Why would it be sitting around waiting for some kid in a basement, especially here in the New World?'

'I don't know, Cal.'

He shook his head. 'We only saw it happen once, and that was hardly a controlled experiment. More like a coincidence. The enemy loves to feed in big crowd situations, like that riot the other day in Prague.'

Dr. Prolix was silent for a moment, and I dared to relax a little. Maybe they were going to forget this whole Minerva thing and take us back to New Jersey. We'd only been here half an hour; the sun would still be bright outside . . .

'No,' Alana Ray spoke up. 'It was not a coincidence.'

Everyone looked at her, and she shivered. Then she touched her own chest three times and pointed a quivering finger at Dr. Prolix.

'I can see things. I have a neurological condition that may cause compulsive behavior, loss of motor control, or hallucinations. But sometimes they are *not* hallucinations, I think, but the realness that comes from the patterns of things. I can see how music works, and I often saw something happening as we rehearsed, and when Morgan's Army played . . .'

'Morgan's Army?' Lace said. 'Isn't their guitarist infected?'

'By Morgan herself,' Cal said softly.

'But not their singer,' Alana Ray said, her head jerking toward Minerva. 'That's why *we* made it real, not them.'

Great, I thought. Ten thousand bands in New York City and I had to be in the monster-calling one.

'Alana Ray's right.' Pearl stepped right up to the red line. 'It's not just Minerva. Everyone in the New Sound has stumbled on bits and pieces of this.' She turned to Cal. 'You're always saying how nature stores things: in our genes, in the diseases we carry, even in our pets. Everything we need to fight the worms is all around us. So maybe music's a part of that.'

'Music?' Cal said. 'Music isn't biology.'

I nodded. 'Yeah, Pearl. We're not talking about some force of nature. We're talking about *us*.'

She shook her head. 'What *I'm* talking about is whenever a thousand people gather in one spot and move together, all focused on the same beat, mouthing the same words, riding the same twists and turns. I'm talking about the Taj Mahal of human rituals: a huge crowd hanging on the edge together, waiting for a single note to be played. It's lateral and magic and irresistible, even if you happen to be a giant worm.'

'In other words, music *is* biology.' Minerva smiled. 'Just ask Astor Michaels about that, Cal.'

He rolled his eyes. 'And dead people wrote your lyrics?'

'I don't know where Min's words came from, okay?' Pearl said. 'Maybe they're passed on through the disease somehow, and Min just imagined them coming out of the walls. Or maybe they're really nonsense, and it's the melodies that count. But they work, don't they?'

Alana Ray nodded. 'They make the air shiver.'

'They're something I thought we'd lost,' Dr. Prolix said softly. 'We can't fight what we can't find, after all. But if we could call the worms to a place of our choosing, this war might be much shorter.'

'Maybe it's worth a controlled experiment, Cal,' Lace said. 'A little science, a little art.'

Cal looked at them one by one, then sighed. 'You're the boss, Doctor. Once their guitarist gets well, I'll set it up.'

'Hang on!' I said. 'You're not saying that we're actually going to play those songs *again*?'

Minerva let out a giggle. 'Let's put on a show!'

-ALANA RAY-

We set up in an old amphitheater in the East River Park.

Surrounded by the crumbling and graffiti-covered concrete, thick grass reaching up through the cracks, it felt as if the world had ended long ago. This place had been abandoned by the city early in the sanitation crisis, but it showed how all of Manhattan would look in a few years: nothing but a ruin in the weeds.

Along one edge of the park the FDR Drive sat empty, the whole city strangely silent behind it. I saw only faint movements in the windows that faced us, the barest pulses of life.

The Night Watch angels set to work, bringing us everything we'd asked for, looting equipment and instruments from the music stores in Midtown. They brought me a brand-new set of Ludwig drums and Zildjian cymbals, but Cal wanted a controlled experiment, as few differences as possible from our first gig. So Lace and three other angels and I made our way to an East Village hardware store, hurrying to make it before the sun started to go down.

The windows were all smashed in, and the angels stepped through without hesitation. My sneakers skidded on shattered glass; I was blind in the darkness inside. As my eyes adjusted, I saw that the shelves were almost empty, every tool looted, every can of spray paint gone.

I listened for anyone, or anything, hiding in the wreckage.

As the angels searched, I stood in the broken window, terrified to step in from the sunlight but not wanting to stand out in the street alone. I drummed my fingers against my thighs, watching the way the fragmented glass reflccted sunlight on the ceiling.

Finally Lace shouted that she'd found what we needed. Luckily, no one had bothered to steal the paint buckets.

As we emerged, a pair of young boys called to us from a window overhead. They needed food, they said, and more flashlights to drive the peeps away from their doors and windows at night. Their parents had gone out and hadn't come back.

The angels climbed up and gave them the few remaining batteries they'd found in the store. Then other people started yelling at us from other windows, asking for help. My hands opened, as if they were offering something. But we had nothing else to give.

I felt helpless, the world shimmering with guilt. I'd signed Astor Michaels's contract, had written my name into that tangle of words and consequences. And the monster I'd seen had really come; people had died that night, scores of them. Maybe hundreds.

And I was accountable.

The moral hazard was still following me, slithering underfoot like Minerva's beast, half visible in the corner of my eye. It stirred the grass out in New Jersey and rattled in the drain when I took showers. But it was growing bigger here in the city, drinking in the energy of shattered glass and empty streets. It never left my side.

I knew it was just a hallucination, a trick of my mind as I began to ration my last bottle of pills. But standing there, the blank expanse of First Avenue stretching in both directions as far as I could see, my moral hazard felt more real than I did.

*

Moz wasn't completely recovered yet, but he could hear his own name without wincing and could look at Minerva, even touch her. The two of them waited in the shadow of the amphitheater's shell, Moz limbering his fingers up on a new guitar.

'As good as your Strat?' I asked, knowing the answer.

He winced at the memory and shook his head.

We did a short sound check as the shadows lengthened, pulling electricity from one of the Night Watch's military vehicles. It had a powerful engine, enough to run the instruments, the mixing board, and the thirsty stacks of amplifiers.

The angels had constructed a tower for stage lights on either side of the amphitheater. Once night had fallen in darkened Manhattan, our lights would be visible for miles, a beacon of safety. We were hoping to lure a crowd from among the millions of survivors left in the city.

An audience was necessary, I was certain: it focused Minerva's music, made it more human, and that was what the enemy hungered for.

Once the angels were ready, we gathered onstage and waited for the sun to go down. The worms would never rise up in broad daylight, not long enough for us to kill them.

The park began to come alive. Cats moved among the broken concrete, and the scurrying of smaller creatures stirred the weeds. Lace told Pearl, Zahler, and me to sit on top of one of the Night Watch vehicles, so that we wouldn't be bitten by an infected rat. That seemed wise. Bands with too many insects, like Toxoplasma, could only play fast and twitchy music.

And I didn't want to become a peep. I didn't want to hate my drums and my friends, my own reflection. Lace said that peeps who'd been devout Christians even feared the sight of the cross. Would I be terrified of my own pills? Of paint buckets? Of the sight of music?

The sky changed from pale pink to black, and I saw human forms moving in the near distance, parasite-positives out hunting, looking for the uninfected. They shied away from the bright band shell for now, but I wondered if a few spotlights and a dozen angels could really protect us from an entire city full of cannibals.

I drummed on my thighs and tried to remember that the worms were the real enemy: incomprehensible, inhuman. They came from some unlit place we'd never even imagined existed.

But peeps were still people.

Moz and Minerva were my friends and were human enough to be in love. The infection had made Moz sweaty and sick and violent at first, but I'd seen normal love do that. He was already playing his guitar again; maybe soon he would become like the angels, powerful and sure.

I remembered Astor Michaels talking happily about all the bands he'd signed. He thought of the peeps as *more* than human, as gods, as rock stars. He'd even tried to give them a new kind of music.

Of course, if Pearl was right, the New Sound wasn't new at all. Despite our keyboards and amps and echo boxes, the songs shimmering nervously through my head might be like the struggle itself: very, very old.

I'd never seen Manhattan pitch-black before. Normally the pink glow of mercury-vapor streetlights filled the sky, the rivers sparkled with lights from the other side, the windows of buildings shone all night. But the grid was failing now, and outside the band shell's radiance, the only light trickled down from the strange profusion of stars.

Lace joined us up on the truck. 'I can think of one problem with this whole idea.'

'Only one?' Zahler asked.

'Well, one big one.' Lace pointed across the highway toward the darkened city. 'These people have seen their whole world fall apart, and they've only survived this long by being very careful. So why would they leave their barricaded apartments for something as random as a free concert?'

I looked up at the lightless rows of windows. 'Before we had a name, Astor Michaels said that our real audience would find us by smell.'

'Smell?' She sniffed the air. 'The parasite improves your senses, you know. But aren't we talking about people who *aren't* infected?'

I frowned. Astor Michaels had been ethically broken, a tangled maze of moral hazards, but he knew brilliantly how crowds worked. Even if the people hiding in the city were terrified, they still needed some kind of hope to cling to.

'Don't worry,' I said, tapping my forehead. 'They'll come.'

By ten P.M. the wind had grown stronger, cutting slices of cold salt air from the East River.

The angels had disappeared, hidden among the trees and up in the light towers, perched across the arched top of the amphitheater – watching over us, just like at the nightclub. Ready to descend.

And hopefully to protect us, if this all went horribly wrong.

Pearl switched on her mixing board, and the columns of speakers began to buzz. She gave Zahler a low E and he tuned his bass, the stage rumbling beneath me. Moz and Minerva came out of the shadows to take their places, trembling in the cold.

We waited for a moment, looking at one another. Pearl had finally come up with the perfect name for us, but there was no one to announce it.

So we just started playing.

This time Zahler didn't freeze. He began the Big Riff, the bass notes thundering out across the park, bouncing lazily back from the wall of housing projects along Manhattan's edge. The rest of the lights came up, bright white instead of the colored gels we were used to, as harsh as a movie set. We were blinded now to anything out there in the darkness, terrifyingly exposed. We had only our angels to trust in.

It was Moz who froze this time, his body shuddering for a long moment as he fought the anathema of his own music. But finally his fingers danced into motion on the strings, years of practice beating aside the parasite inside him.

I started drumming, muscles falling into familiar patterns, but the motion of my hands didn't calm me. It wasn't the blank and empty darkness before me, or the thousands of deadly, infected maniacs all around us. It wasn't even the thought of those huge, human-eating creatures we were trying to summon.

What scared me was being drawn again into the engine of our music. I remembered playing, unable to stop, while the worm had rampaged through the crowd, cutting them down while they watched us, mesmerized. My moral hazard still lurked in the corners of my vision, watching me and waiting.

If the world wasn't cured soon, that vision would become too real. I was running out of pills, the last bottle shaking half empty in my pocket, more depleted every day. I wasn't being heroic, risking my life here on the cold edge of Manhattan. I was being logical.

I was one of those people who needed civilization simply to survive.

Minerva began to sing, her voice searching the darkness, keening through the empty and weed-choked park around us. Calling.

The air began to glisten, and soon I could see the music: Moz's notes hovering in the air, Pearl's piercing melody like a thin spotlight moving among them, making them sparkle. Minerva's song wound through it all, stretching out into the darkness, and Zahler and I played with a fierce determination, as tight as fingers locked together, like sentries afraid to turn their heads.

We played the whole piece through, hoping someone would hear.

When we reached the end, no cheers or applause answered us, not even a lonely shout of encouragement. No one had come.

Then the lights faded around us, and I looked out at where the audience should have been.

A galaxy of eyes reflected back at me. Night-seeing eyes.

Peeps.

They stared at us, transfixed, undead. Not like the angels or Minerva or even trembling Moz, not sane or reasonable or human. These had been fully taken by the disease. They wore filthy and tattered clothes, logos ripped from them as the anathema had taken hold. Many were barely covered, shivering in ragged pajamas and sweatpants – the sort of clothes you'd wear to bed when you felt feverish and half-crazy, coming down hard with the flu. Their fingernails were long and shone black, as if they'd glued the husks of dead beetles to their fingers. A hundred of them stood there. Motionless.

The survivors hadn't gathered to hear us. The vampires had.

Astor Michaels had been all too right. Our real audience had found us by smell.

'Oh, crap,' Zahler said next to me.

A stir moved through them, forms shifting in the silence, the spell of the song fading. Glimmers of hunger flashed in their eyes.

'We have to keep playing,' I said.

'We have to *run*,' Zahler hissed. He started to back away.

The crowd stirred again. One of them was shambling toward the stage, squinting his eyes against the light.

'Zahler, stop,' Moz said. 'It's like your dogs. Don't show them you're afraid.'

'My dogs don't *eat people*!'

I heard more sounds in the darkness behind us. Of course, the peeps weren't just in the audience in front of us. They were all around us . . .

'Alana Ray's right. We need to keep playing,' Minerva said. 'We don't want to disappoint the fans.' She pulled the microphone to her lips and began to hum.

The eerie melody crept from the amps, a nameless, shapeless tune that we'd made into our slowest song: 'A Million Stimuli to Go.'

The peeps began to settle down.

Pearl joined Minerva, her fingers spreading across her keyboards to hold down long, lush chords. Then Moz came in on top, quick notes flirting with Minerva's hummed melody, pushing her toward words.

I began to play, rolling the sticks softly across my paint buckets, breaking into a slow beat. Finally Zahler reluctantly joined us, his bass rumbling through the darkness.

The peeps remained motionless, staring at us, unblinking.

We played the whole song, trying to forget our ghastly audience, but we wound up going faster toward the finish, our fear finally showing in the music. We ended with a brutal thrashing of the same chord again and again, finally rattling into silence.

I looked out into the dark.

There were five times as many of them now.

'Spot the problem,' Zahler said.

A ripple went through the ragged army before us. One of them let out a low, hungry moan. A drop of sweat crawled down my back, as cold as the night air.

'We can't stop playing!' I said.

'What?' Zahler hissed. 'You want *more* of them to come?'

Moz took a step back, his hands quivering. 'Yeah, and what if no worm ever shows up?'

'Boys,' Minerva said straight into the microphone, her words echoing through the park, 'I don't think we have a choice.'

A few of the peeps had begun to advance, teeth glittering in the moonlight, hands flexing into claws.

'Min's right,' Pearl murmured.

'"Piece Two"?' Zahler said, and started before anyone could answer.

We all jumped in, playing hard.

Even terrified, I wondered how we sounded to the peeps, whether they really liked the music or whether certain kinds of sound waves calmed them down, like plants and Mozart. They weren't exactly dancing or moshing or singing along. Why were they listening instead of eating us?

I started pushing the tempo, coaxing the others along, almost as fast as a Toxoplasma song – music for insects.

Then Minerva came in, howling her nonsense syllables, setting my vision shimmering, like the glitter of weeping-willow fireworks fading in the air.

Something rippled through the crowd, a sudden wave of motion, and for a terrible moment I wondered if our spell was breaking. But the ragged army didn't rush to attack us; instead the whole mass of them turned together, like a vast flock of birds wheeling as one.

For a second, I thought the peeps were dancing . . . but it was something much better. Or worse, depending on what happened next. The ground had finally begun to shudder.

They were getting ready. They smelled something: the hated worm rising up toward the surface. Sane or not, the parasite inside them knew the scent of its natural enemy.

The rumbling grew, and I pushed the tempo still faster.

The worm broke through just as we hit the first chorus, scattering dirt and black water, tossing a handful of bodies into the air. But these were peeps, not clueless kids in some nightclub, and the crowd didn't panic or run. They came at the beast from every angle, setting upon it with flashing claws, tearing into its pulsing sides with their razor teeth.

The angels didn't stand back and watch. They shot out of the trees, dropping from the amphitheater roof, swords drawn. Jumping into the throng, they fought side by side with the peeps, the great worm screaming and twisting in its trench.

We played and kept playing. When we ran out of verses, we started over without pausing a single beat, the air warping around me. Minerva's voice had a new shape now, shimmering lines of strength that bound peeps and angels into a single force. Zahler's low thumping notes were tendrils reaching down, squeezing the earth shut below the enemy, trapping it here on the surface. I could feel the battle in my muscles, my sticks flashing like the swords below.

Some endless time later the song finally stumbled to a halt, all five of us exhausted, the engine of our music out of steam at last.

I looked down into the park.

The peeps had torn the worm to pieces. Fragments of its huge carcass were spread out across the broken concrete, still twitching as if trying to burrow back into the earth.

A few of the peeps were scrabbling over the remains, *eating* them . . .

'What now?' Zahler said as the last echoes faded. The army of peeps had grown bigger than the crowd at our first gig – more than a thousand of them summoned by our music and the death cries of the worm.

Most of them still looked hungry.

The handful of angels stood out in the audience, covered with blood and black water. They glanced nervously at the peeps around them, their bloodlust fading.

"Dudes!" Lace yelled up at us. 'Keep going!'

So we did.

Altogether we killed five worms that night, playing until dawn began to break at last.

Light filtered across the sky, pink clouds brightening to orange, and finally our grisly audience began to disperse. They faded into the trees, driven back into the dark alleys of the city, sated by the fight.

Up onstage, we collapsed one by one. Zahler's fingers were bleeding, and Minerva had practically croaked her way through our last song. Even the angels looked unsteady on their feet. Covered with black water, blood, and chunks of gelatinous flesh, they cleaned their swords with shaking hands.

I curled up on the concrete stage, shivering in the predawn chill. My hands ached, my body thrummed with echoes, and shimmering hallucinations colored everything I saw.

But I was smiling. About halfway through the concert, my moral hazard had slunk into the darkness.

And *this* felt very real.

EPILOGUE: THE CURE

–MOZ–

Being on tour wasn't all it was cracked up to be. There were too many long bus trips, we were in a new town almost every night, and I hated living out of suitcases and trailers for months on end. Most hotels didn't have much staff anymore – most didn't have *sheets*. Room service was a thing of the ancient past.

But we did it for the fans.

At every new town they'd give us a heroes' welcome, having hiked in from miles away or squandered their last few gallons of gasoline to drive from farther. They brought their homemade weapons and homemade liquor, ready to fight the enemy and party, to sing along, basically to have a good time. Local angels and regular people, even a few wild peeps wandered in most nights – everyone wanted to see us perform.

We'd become famous after all, even though the old ways of manufacturing fame – television, magazines, movie sound tracks – hardly existed anymore. There was still a lot of radio around, ten thousand backyard stations juiced with solar power, so everyone knew our songs.

They knew our name too, thanks to Pearl, who'd finally come up with the three perfect words to describe

us. Even if it is a stupid plural. I mean, it doesn't really make
sense without the *s* at the end.

The Last *Day*? Come on. That's as bad as the Desk.

So you probably know how the rest of the story goes:

We toured like crazy, hitting the big cities all over the world,
playing one show after another until the local population of the
enemy had been destroyed. Then we did our famous Heartland
Tour, playing every small town that had ever spotted a worm-
sign in the distance and a few that hadn't.

We were just as popular overseas. One good thing about
singing in a language that's been dead for seven centuries:
nobody feels left out.

Especially not the worms.

Everywhere we and our two dozen superhuman bodyguards
went, the enemy came, called up from the bowels of the earth by
their ancient hunger, unable to resist a thousand tasty humans
swaying to Minerva's songs, as tempting as the smell of bacon
sizzling in the morning.

Our fans and the angels kept slaying them, until the last few
survivors got canny enough to slither back into the depths. The
crisis slowly began to subside, the deep-dwelling rats retreating
into their unlit warrens, taking the spores of the parasite with
them. Thanks, guys, till next time.

Of course, things took a while to get back to normal.

There were cities and societies that had to be rebuilt, and the
Night Watch still had to mop up the last few untreated peeps.
They scoured the wilderness for those that the anathema had
pushed into lonely existences, healing the vampires one by one
until they became creatures of legend again. And then the Watch
itself disappeared back into the shadows.

The earth was cured – or at least we humans thought so.

No one knew what the worms thought, or if they thought anything at all. We'd killed practically all of them ... except for the most intelligent ones, Cal always pointed out. The ones who somehow figured out that our music was deadly. So the next time the worms rise up, they'll *all* be descendants of those clever enough to escape. They probably get smarter with every invasion of the surface: wormy evolution in action.

Fexcellent.

But the next crisis won't happen for at least a few hundred years, and I'll be too old to tour by then.

Angels don't live forever, after all.

Along the way, Min and I broke up and got back together about fifteen times, and that's if you don't count the breakups that lasted less than two hours. Zahler became a fawesome bass player, and Alana Ray stayed exactly the way she was: ethical, logical, collected. And Pearl is, as you know, running for Mayor of New York again, but that's a whole other story.

By now, we've all been interviewed a million times about the tour. One of Cal Thompson's books covers it the best; he was there watching our backs the whole way. Most of what he says is true, as far as I can remember.

The only really new thing I can add to all those stories is this:

It happened in a small town outside Tulsa, about halfway through the Heartland Tour. That night's gig had been fawesome, us thrashing through a twenty-minute version of 'Piece Two' while the crowd killed the local enemy, a giant bull worm whose death throes tore up that Sears parking lot like a rabid dog does a newspaper.

At the after-party, one of the local angels came up to me. She had short hair, wild makeup, and intense eyes. Her broadsword was strapped across her back like a guitar.

She stood there for a second, eyes flashing in the light of the bonfire. The comforting smell of burning wormflesh filled the air.

'Hey, good work tonight,' I said, raising my hand. 'You guys in the Oklahoma Watch are *great*!'

I was sort of expecting her to say, 'No, *you're* great!' But she didn't answer, just stared at me.

After a moment, I said, 'Tough old worm, though, huh?'

'You owe me a Strat,' she said.

I blinked, finally recognizing her.

She was that crazy woman, the one who'd thrown her life out the window onto Sixth Street the night Pearl and I had met. We'd seen the angels taking her away, to New Jersey – or maybe even Montana, because it was that far back – so of course she'd been cured and had become one of them . . .

I wondered how she'd wound up way out here. Maybe she'd loved New York too much to go back home; the anathema hangs on real hard sometimes. I've seen angels cower at the sight of old friends or flinch when they hear the chorus of a favorite song. Hell, I *still* don't look in mirrors much.

'Wow,' I said, starting to smile. 'It's you.'

Her dark eyes flashed. 'You broke it, one of your bodyguards told me. Smashed it on the stage, like you're Jimi Hendrix or something?'

I shook my head. 'It wasn't like that. I was going through the anathema.'

'That was a nineteen seventy-five Strat with gold pickups and hardware,' she said slowly. 'Do you know how hard those are to find? Especially these days?'

I knew exactly. I'd been looking for another one since we'd started touring. The last few in existence were so valuable even *I* didn't have enough money for one. Here was me helping save the world, and I couldn't even afford a decent ax. How messed up was that?

But I'd had about enough of her attitude. 'Hang on a second. Last thing I saw, you were throwing it out a window!'

'Yeah, well, I was nuts then!'

'*So was I when I smashed it!*'

'Um, Moz?' It was Pearl walking up, carrying two precious bottles of pre-crisis beer. She frowned. 'Is there a problem here?'

The woman glared at me, then her hands unbent from claws and she shook her head. 'No problem.'

The acid scent of angels about to get into a fistfight faded from the air.

I let out a sigh, muttering, 'She says I owe her a Stratocaster.'

Pearl's eyes widened slowly. 'Whoa . . . it's *you*.' Her face broke into a smile. 'Well, I guess you get Moz's beer, then.'

The woman snorted, then took the offered bottle. Homemade liquor was common enough by then, but nobody ever turned down the civilized stuff.

I stood there and watched as Pearl told her how fawesome the local Watch had been tonight. Pearl asked if we could tell headquarters about anything they needed, already the politician, effortlessly charming – saving me once again.

Now that I thought about it, I'd always meant to find this woman, at least to say how much the Strat had meant to me, maybe to explain how it had met its end. But I'd never quite gotten around to it.

It was like Zahler said: Pearl was always fixing the things I'd smashed or dropped or just let slip into disrepair. She'd even helped me and Minerva patch things up more than a few times – anything for the good of the band.

Their conversation paused when another hunk of worm was thrown onto the pyre, making a rattling hiss like a radiator in a

New York winter, a fresh scattering of sparks spitting forth and lifting into the sky, another round of drunken cheers.

'Thanks,' I said to the woman.

'For what?'

'For dropping that guitar at exactly the right moment.' I smiled at Pearl. 'For bringing us together.'

Pearl grinned back at me.

'Well, you've got a funny way of repaying me,' the woman said.

'For what it's worth,' Pearl said, 'I was there, and he *was* batshit crazy at the time.'

'You only break the things you love,' I said.

The woman shook her head slowly. 'But don't you get it, Moz? Anathema or not, it wasn't yours to fall in love with.'

I swallowed, not knowing what to say, and Pearl came to my rescue again. 'We don't always get to choose what we love.'

The woman just scowled, sighing heavily as we turned together toward the blaze. It was growing hotter, its center turning blue as the beast's fat and muscle rendered, dripping down into the bonfire's sizzling core. Pearl's fingers wrapped gently around my arm and drew me closer.

The worm kept burning.

AUTHOR'S NOTE

In case you haven't noticed, all the chapter titles in *The Last Days* are band names. Some of them are great bands, some lame, and a few I've never actually heard play – I just needed their names for chapter titles, okay? But for your edification, and so that you can see that I didn't just make them up, here's the list of all chapter names, with a little info about each band.

Enjoy.

Chapter 1: The Fall
Prolific not-quite-punk band from Manchester, U.K. Founded 1976.

Chapter 2: Taj Mahal
Ageless bluesman. First album in 1967.

Chapter 3: Poisonblack
Finnish gothic-doom metal. (Yes, *really.*) Founded 2000.

Chapter 4: New Order
Surviving members of Joy Division, Manchester, U.K. Founded 1980.

Chapter 5: Garbage
Madison, Wisconsin-based mega-band. Founded 1994.

Chapter 6: Madness
London ska band. Formed 1976, but not popular until the eighties.

Chapter 7: Stray Cats
Rockabilly band from Massapequa, New York. Formed 1979.

Chapter 8: Cash Money Crew

Old school hip-hop collective (later a label). Formed late 1970s, NYC.

Chapter 9: Fear

Los Angeles punk band. Formed 1977.

Chapter 10: The Music

Alt-rock band from Leeds, U.K. Formed 1999.

Chapter 11: Sound Dimension

Reggae session band. Formed in Jamaica in the 1970s.

Chapter 12: The Temptations

A Motown singing group – from Detroit, of course. Formed 1960.

Chapter 13: Missing Persons

L.A. electronic pop band. Formed 1980.

Chapter 14: The Replacements

Punk, then alternative, then splintered into solo acts. Formed 1979 in Minneapolis.

Chapter 15: The Need

Queercore duo from Olympia, Washington. Formed 1996.

Chapter 16: Love Bites

All-girl U.K. teen band. Formed 2005.

Chapter 17: Foreign Objects

Melodic death-metal band from West Chester, Pennsylvania. Formed 1995.

Chapter 18: Anonymous 4

Medieval vocal quartet. Formed 1986.

Chapter 19: The Impressions

Drum-oriented group from Melbourne, Australia. Formed 2002.

Chapter 20: Grievous Angels

Canadian alternative country (Northern Ontario). Formed 1986.

Chapter 21: The Runaways

Joan Jett's first band: proto-punk and all-girl. Formed in L.A., 1975.

Chapter 22: Crowded House

Two-thirds Australian, one-third New Zealand pop band. Formed 1986.

Chapter 23: Moral Hazard

Underground band from Ottawa, Canada. Formed 2000.

Chapter 24: 10,000 Maniacs

Jamestown, New York, punk band. Formed 1981.

Chapter 25: Massive Attack

Trip-hop collective from Bristol, U.K. Formed 1991.

Chapter 26: Hunters and Collectors

Band from Melbourne, Australia. Formed 1980.

Chapter 27: Faithless

London trip-hop trio (and sometimes quartet). Formed 1995.

Chapter 28: Doctor

Indie band from Toronto, Canada. Formed 2004.

Chapter 29: The Kills

Minimalist garage duo from London and Florida. Formed roughly 2000.

Epilogue: The Cure

Post-punk band from Sussex, U.K. Formed 1976.

ACKNOWLEDGEMENT

Thanks to Morgan Butts and her pals for 'fawesome.'

ABOUT THE AUTHOR

Scott Westerfeld is a software designer, composer and writer. He has written several acclaimed novels for adults and teenagers, including the *Midnighters* series for which he won an Aurealis Award. Scott lives with his partner, writer Justine Larbalestier, and they divide their time between New York City and Sydney. Visit his website at www.scottwesterfeld.com

For more information about Scott Westerfeld and other Atom authors visit www.atombooks.co.uk

A PREVIEW OF ANOTHER FANTASTIC ATOM BOOK . . .

THE TIME OF THE
REAPER
ANDREW BUTCHER

Certain aspects of Travis's breakfast routine had not altered with time. He still tended to sit in front of the television munching his way through a bowl of cornflakes. Mum continued to call from the kitchen for him to hurry up or he'd be late for school. But there was no more cartoon fodder for Travis. For the past six years he'd switched on *Breakfast News*. He watched the news at six o'clock as well, and again at ten, and more often than not dipped into the satellite news channels between times for good measure. It was important – vital – for him to keep up to date with what the Bad Guys were doing. In fact, it was pretty much an obsession with him, and had been since the loss of that other major element of mornings in the Naughton household. His father.

Today, *Breakfast News*'s Natalie Kamen was wearing her serious face. '. . . The latest developments as the flu outbreak continues to sweep the country,' she was saying. 'The government's Chief Medical Officer will be in the studio and we'll have reports from hospitals across the nation. We'll also be travelling further afield, to Europe, the United States and China, to find out how they're coping with what is rapidly becoming one of the most far-reaching global pandemics in history. But if you're already suffering with the snuffles at home, we've got just the tonic for you: coming up a little later, Melody Summers with this year's British Eurovision Song Contest entry, "Wake Up To The World".'

Travis thought he'd rather wake up to Natalie Kamen if that was OK. Somehow, though, it didn't seem right that news presenters should be so *hot*. They should be like librarians: bookish, prim, big glasses, and kind of grey. How was he supposed to concentrate on the headlines with Natalie Kamen's legs to distract him?

'She's too old for you. She's too rich for you. She's too pretty for you.' Jane Naughton poked her head around the sitting-room door. Travis often wondered whether all mothers were in possession of psychic powers or just his own. 'And if you don't get to school, Travis, she'll also be too well educated for you.'

'You ever thought of going into motivational speaking, Mum?' grinned Travis.

'I have enough to do making sure you're fit to leave the house in the morning,' his mother said. 'Let alone . . .' The phone rang. 'Who's that calling at this hour?'

'Natalie Kamen,' predicted Travis. 'She *wants* me.'

Actually, he didn't really have time to care *who* was on the phone, not if he wanted to get to Mel's early enough for what he intended. Travis gulped coffee.

'It's Grandma,' Jane Naughton announced. 'She wants to know if we're all right. Are we showing any symptoms of the Sickness.'

'The Sickness? Like with a capital S?' On the television a reporter was standing in a hospital corridor in Leeds somewhere. 'It's only some kind of flu, isn't it? It's not the Plague. How are *they*?'

'We're both fine, Mum,' certified Jane Naughton. 'How are *you*?'

'. . . The number of patients overwhelming,' the reporter was saying. 'Every ward in the hospital has been full since last night but still the sick arrive, to be left on trolleys in corridors like this one because there is simply nowhere else to put them.' Coughing, groaning patients in white smocks and languishing on wheeled beds shunted up against the walls provided graphic testimony to the correspondent's words. Medical staff rushed in and out of camera shot behind him, harassed and confused. 'And it's the same increasingly chaotic story in every hospital in the city.'

'Grandma says they're both well,' Jane Naughton supplied. 'They've had their flu jabs. It seems Grandad doesn't think the jabs will do any good, though. He reckons this isn't a flu epidemic at all.'

'Some of my mates' parents think the same,' Travis mused. 'What does Grandad think it is, then?' The *Sickness*.

'What does Dad think it is, Mum?'

Breakfast News had cut back to the studio. The luscious Natalie was questioning an expert in communicable diseases about the illness.

'Grandad thinks this is all the result of an accident or something in some secret government installation for the development of biological weapons.'

'Does he?' Travis said without humour.

The expert in communicable diseases was talking death rates.

'Mum, where does he get these ideas from?' Jane Naughton scolded amusedly. 'Tell Dad he should read fewer science fiction books and maybe help you out with the housework a . . . I know he does his share, Mum, I was only . . .'

There were deaths. People were dying. Not just in countries where people were always dying in disasters of one kind or another but here, in British cities, on British streets. A small number only, the expert in communicable diseases was explaining. A *small* number. The luscious Natalie seized on that as if viewers should be reassured. Travis knew better. It didn't matter how insignificant the total was statistically speaking if you or someone you loved were among the fatalities. Take the annual casualty rate for serving police officers, for example . . . That was the trouble with experts. They saw information, not people.

'Mum, I don't think that's necessary. I told you we're both fine. Not even a runny nose between us.'

Deaths. To the Sickness. In every country in the world.

Apparently, the government's plan to administer vaccine from huge centralised stockpiles protected by the police from possibly over-eager citizens was in full swing. Apparently, entertainment was being laid on at their locations because the queuing might take a while, though there was certainly plenty of vaccine for everyone.

Travis, rather uncomfortably, thought of the band playing 'Nearer My God To Thee' as the *Titanic* went down.

'Trav,' his mother hissed across the room, 'Grandma and Grandad want us to go to Willowstock.' The small village a hundred-plus miles away where they lived. 'They think we'll be safer there.' She shook her head tolerantly. 'Don't they worry over nothing.'

'Sure, Mum,' said Travis.

Apparently, the cheering prospect of Melody Summers and 'Wake Up To The World' was having to be postponed. Apparently, Melody was a little under the weather just now. The luscious Natalie hoped she'd feel better soon.

'We'll leave it at that, then, Mum.' Jane Naughton strove valiantly to bring the call to an end. 'If the situation gets worse, we'll think about it, but I really don't . . . Yes. Travis? Do you want a word with Grandma?'

Sadly, there was someone else he needed a word with first. His heart hardened inside him. 'Can't. Sorry. Got to get to Mel's.'

'Now?' his mother marvelled. 'But it's still only—'

'Yeah. Sorry. Tell Grandma I'll call her tonight.'

'Travis . . .'

He turned off the TV on his way to the hall. Natalie Kamen blinked out of existence. Travis didn't know it then, but that was the last he'd ever see of her.

'I mean it.' The soldier's eyes stared wildly at the teenagers. 'You move. I fire.' His finger trembled on the trigger. His whole body shook.

'OK. All right. Take it easy,' Ash soothed. 'We're not moving. See?' Linden for one felt herself frozen to the spot. 'Take it easy.'

'Good. That's good. I don't want to hurt anyone.' The soldier's lips quivered like those of a little boy on the brink of tears.

Linden felt her fear receding. 'Why don't you put the gun down? That way—'

'No. *No.*' A feverish urgency seized the young soldier again. He waved the rifle at them more threateningly.

'Oh, nice one, Lin,' muttered Ash.

'If I put the gun down you'll run and if you run you won't listen and you have to listen to me. Everybody has to listen to me.'

'We're all ears,' confirmed Ash.

The soldier's voice was racked with sobs. 'It's coming. We won't be able to stop it. It's coming for all of us. It's coming for *you*.'

'What is?' Linden said. 'What's coming?'

'If they knew I was here . . . But people have to listen to me. It's coming and it'll mean the end.'

'The end?' A chill deeper even than that of being held at gunpoint by a clearly mentally unbalanced soldier frosted Linden's heart.

'Of everything. Of *every*thing.' The soldier sagged where he stood as if stricken with grief. 'I've got to get home. I need to find my way home before it's too—'

'Lin!' said Ash, warningly.

The soldier's head snapped up and a cry of despair rose from his throat as other soldiers materialised among the woodland shadows, seeming to solidify only as they stepped forward to surround their younger colleague and the two Children of Nature. They were maybe a dozen strong and twice that number of metres away and Linden hadn't heard their approach at all. Combats. Automatic weapons. Faces blanked out by what looked like gas masks. Guns levelled at a trio of targets.

'Listen, we . . . we don't know this guy.' Ash appealed to the silent soldiers. 'We don't want any trouble.'

'Don't let them take me,' the young soldier begged Linden desperately. 'I want to go home. I don't want to go back. It won't do any good. *Tell* them.'

But Linden was speechless.

The soldiers moved in.

'Remember what I said!' the young man entreated. 'It's *coming*!'

And as he swung his rifle Linden felt sure he was going

to fire on the masked soldiers, go down in a blaze of glory. Then she realised what he was really about to do. He thrust the barrel of the gun under his chin. He squeezed the trigger. A single shot reverberated through the forest.

Followed by Linden's scream, Ash's cry of shock.

The masked soldiers made no sound.

The teenagers clasped each other and Linden was glad she'd closed her eyes at the last moment. But she didn't dare to keep them closed now. Better that they were open if she was going to have to plead for her life. Which looked likely. While some of the soldiers attended to the body of the suicide, others kept their weapons trained on her and Ash.

'Please,' she begged, 'don't kill us. We're nothing to do with . . . any of this.'

Maybe they believed her. Possibly that was why, when the young man's body had been lifted from the ground and carried into the forest out of sight, the rest of the soldiers backed away too, still without a word, as though their tongues had been removed along with their faces. They melted into the undergrowth. They vanished like ghosts. In seconds it was as if they'd never been there, as if the entire incident had been a grisly dream.

'My God,' breathed Ash.

Mel's mum opened the door, a little nervously, it seemed. But then, everything Mel's mum did was nervous. She was a singularly pale, bloodless woman who appeared to have been made out of paper. 'Travis,' she said with the twitch of a smile.

'Morning, Mrs Patrick. Monday's here again.'

'Come in,' the woman invited. 'Mel's almost ready.'

'No, she is not!' Mel was on the stairs, heading up. Her school clothes were as black and as baggy and as smothering as the most liberal interpretations of the uniform code would allow. 'What time do you call this, Trav? School starting early this week or something?'

'I couldn't stop thinking about you,' Travis quipped.

'Urgh. Excuse me while I go vomit.' Mel bounded up the remainder of the stairs.

Good, Travis thought. That was her out of the way for the next five minutes. Five minutes were all it would take.

'Would you like to . . . come through to the kitchen, Travis?' asked Mel's mum.

'Could I wait in the living room if that's all right with you, Mrs Patrick?' Travis said.

'Gerry's in the living room,' the woman mentioned, as though this was not a recommendation.

'Yeah.'

In the living room. In his armchair. Watching satellite sport. A bottle of lager in one hand. Fresh butt-ends in the ashtray in front of him. Unshaven and overweight. If ever one man could provide the definition of slob, that man was Gerry Patrick. He was living proof that all clichés were founded in truth. Living proof.

And Travis remembered a line from Shakespeare that his English teacher had raved about once. From *King Lear*, she'd said. The old king mourning over the corpse of his favourite daughter: 'Why should a dog, a horse, a rat have life, and thou no breath at all?' For once, Travis had known what the Bard was getting at. The unfairness of existence, the injustice of life and death. His own dad dead, killed struggling to bring order to society, murdered trying to do good. Filth like Gerry Patrick alive, prospering, abusing the very concept of fatherhood. It was almost more than he could bear.

Only with difficulty could he keep the contempt from his face.

Patrick himself didn't bother. 'You again,' he grunted as Travis entered the living room and shut them both in. 'Still sniffing around our Melanie, I see.'

'Morning, Gerry,' Travis said through tight lips.

'Gerry? It's Mr Patrick to you, boy. Where's your respect?'

'Respect has to be earned these days, haven't you heard, Gerry? And you ain't earned it.'

'Why, you cheeky little . . .' If the man's intention had been to leap to his feet, he failed. The blubbery ballast bulging at his waist restricted him to a lumber rather than a leap, like an irate walrus.

Travis wasn't impressed. Neither did he retreat. 'What, you want to hit me, Gerry? Like you hit Mel?'

The man paused. 'I don't know what you're talking about.'

'Yes, you do. We both know. I've seen the bruises.'

Gerry Patrick sneered squalidly, an 'I bet you have' sneer. 'She walked into a door. She's always walking into doors. She's clumsy.'

'Yeah? Well, why don't you sit back down? We haven't got long but I just thought we should have a quick chat about Mel's "clumsiness".'

Gerry Patrick glared at Travis but he did resume his seat. He might have been a brute, but he wasn't stupid. 'Get on with it, then, and then get out.'

'A pleasure, on both counts. You see, Gerry,' Travis said, 'I kind of want Mel to become less clumsy, as you put it. For her own good. I don't want to hear about her walking into doors from now on, or falling down the stairs, maybe, or off a chair. I want health and safety to be a big issue in this house, and I expect you to take a lead. Because' – Travis felt his anger building – 'if I see any more marks on Mel, any more bruises, any more evidence of any kind of her being knocked about and hit, as *I* put it, then I'm likely to report the guy responsible to the relevant authorities, and I don't think you'd like me to do that, would you, Gerry?'

Patrick stared expressionlessly at Travis for a few seconds. Then he gave a short, harsh laugh. 'I couldn't care less what you do, boy. Report me if you like. I *dare* you. Nobody'll believe you anyway and you want to know why? Because Melanie'd never tell tales against her old dad. Nor would my darling wife. I know that. You probably know that. You'd never get any charges to stick.'

'We'll see. You want to take that risk?'

'And Melanie'd never talk to you again. You want to take *that* risk, Travis, boy?' Gerry Patrick evidently felt that the whip hand belonged to him. 'I bet she doesn't know you're trying to threaten her old dad in your prissy, self-righteous little way, does she? Course not. She wouldn't like it.'

Travis sought to ignore the truth in Patrick's words. He had to focus on what was right. 'I want you to stop . . .'

'Little boy,' scoffed Patrick. 'Meddling in matters that don't concern you. Just like your old man, PC Plod. And look what happened to him. Stuck his interfering nose in where it wasn't wanted and got a knife between the ribs for his trouble. Shame and all that but—'

'Shut up,' Travis gritted through clenched teeth. His eyes blazed blue fire. 'You're not fit to mention my dad.'

The bitterness, the rage, they were still in him, they were part of him now, and sometimes it seemed his fury and his grief would overwhelm him. '*Why should a dog, a horse, a rat have life, and thou no breath at all?*'

Gerry Patrick chuckled coldly, swigged beer, changed channels on the TV.

But Travis steadied himself, controlled himself. To become consumed by loss, to be crushed by grief, to rail against a past that could not be reversed or to fret for ever over what could not be understood, that way madness lay. His father's death had been a senseless tragedy, an affront to justice, but Dad wouldn't want it to destroy Travis, too. And Travis would not be destroyed. He would survive. He would be strong.

He wouldn't take crap from the likes of Gerry Patrick.

'You might be right . . .' he admitted.

'What? You still here, boy?'

And gaining in confidence. 'You might be right: Mel and her mum won't testify to what a piece of filth you are, Gerry. You've had years to scare them and intimidate them and I'm not going to blame them for that. I'm blaming *you*. And I'm promising you this, if you *ever* touch Mel again, I mean *ever*, I won't inform the social services or report it to the police officially, I'll go and have a quiet word with some of my dad's mates who are still on the force. And they don't like scumbags like you, Gerry, and they'll like you even less when I tell them what you think of my dad and his sacrifice, and I reckon that between them they'll be able and more than happy to fit you up on some other charge, where Mel won't need to give evidence. And then you can say goodbye to your armchair and hello to a prison cell. I'll do it. I promise.'

Gerry Patrick glanced into Travis's eyes and saw something there, a steel, a commitment. Fearlessness. He wasn't chuckling or sneering or scoffing now. 'OK,' he capitulated grudgingly. 'OK. I get the picture.'

'One finger on her and you go down.'

'Whatever.'

'And I don't want Mel to know about our little exchange of views.'

A terse nod of the head from Gerry Patrick.

As Mel rushed into the living room, shoes and jacket on. Her gaze darted tensely between Travis and her father as though she'd anticipated trouble. 'You all right, Travis?' she said cautiously.

Travis turned to her and grinned. 'Never better,' he said.

The school bus was late. Then it was very late.

'Looks like it's not coming,' Mel observed.

'Looks like it,' said Travis, still in truth a little preoccupied by his confrontation with her father. *Had he done enough? Had he succeeded in putting an end to Gerry Patrick's abuse? Or – and here was an unsettling possibility given that it was now too late to do anything about it – had he only made the situation worse?*

'I guess the driver might have the flu and hasn't turned up.' Mel looked around her. 'Maybe he's not the only one.' The gathering of students at the bus stop was sparser than normal, even for a Monday.

'Maybe.' An odd thought suddenly occurred to Travis. 'But you know, Saturday night, the others were talking about people's parents and the owners of Alison's stables or whatever, teachers, coming down with the bug, but no kids. All adults. That strike you as weird?'

'Kids are healthier than adults,' Mel stated. 'It's that high-fat, high-sugar, no-portions-of-fruit-and-veg-a-day diet we're not supposed to have keeping us going.'

'Seriously, Mel,' Travis said. 'Do we know anybody our own age or younger who's caught this flu?'

'What about the kids who aren't here now?'

'Looking after sick family. Skiving. Using the flu as an excuse.' The *Sickness*. 'Anyone we know for *sure?*'

Mel shrugged. 'Ask me one on pop music.'

'Mel . . .' Travis shook his head in exasperation.

'OK. Well, the real puzzler is, do we discuss your far-out theories while we walk to school like good, eager little students, or do we do it – discuss your theories – at your house over coffee and CDs because the system's let us down and stranded us at the bus stop and—'

'Neither,' said Travis. 'We're being rescued.'

A car was indicating before pulling into the bus stop's lay-by. Mr Lane's car. He was driving; Jessica, in a school uniform that could have been bought new that morning, occupied the front passenger seat.

She activated the electric window as Travis and Mel crossed to the vehicle. 'Bus not turned up? Fancy a lift?'

They climbed into the back, said their thank-yous and good-mornings to Mr Lane, repeated how much they'd enjoyed Jessica's party.

After all of which, 'Don't expect to see too many buses on the road today,' their chauffeur warned. 'It's been on the radio. Service cut down to the bone. Drivers phoning in unwell. This flu bug. Good excuse for lazy employees to throw a sickie.' Mr Lane was a director of a company that made disposable containers. Sometimes it showed.

'Dad,' disapproved Jessica.

'I think it might be more than that, Mr Lane,' said Travis. 'If you listen to the news it's hitting pretty hard. Everywhere. There've been some deaths.'

Jessica winced at the word. Death was a change unthinkable.

'I reckon it's going to get worse before it gets better.'

'That's what everyone seems to be saying, Travis,' agreed Mr Lane. 'Though I'd still be a little sceptical if I were you. Governments have a habit of preparing us for worst-case scenarios so that when things don't turn out to be *quite* as bad as predicted the same governments can then take the credit. Having said that,' he conceded as he nosed the car from minor to major road without the usual wait for a kindly fellow motorist to flash him out, 'there *does* seem to be less rush-hour traffic this morning.'

'Dad's paper's started to call the flu the Sickness,' said Jessica, with a shudder. 'It starts like flu – coughs and aches and a temperature and stuff, those are the first symptoms – but it isn't flu. Not according to Dad's paper. After a while you develop these disgusting crimson circles all over your body, like a kind of rash. According to the paper. I don't fancy that much, do you?'

'I don't know where the paper is getting its information from,' said Mr Lane sceptically.

'*Breakfast News* hasn't said anything like that,' Travis frowned.

'Exactly. Probably a total fabrication.'

'Or the truth they'd rather we didn't hear.' Not that Travis liked to think the luscious Natalie had been holding out on him.

'Chill, anyway,' shrugged Mel. 'Say it's true. A red rash. We've all had those, haven't we? I mean, what I *mean* is it could be worse. Could be like the Black Death. Stinking, suppurating buboes – swellings – in your armpits and, well, other places. Catch that and it was pretty much all over for you. People thought the arrival of the disease meant the end of the world, the time of the Reaper, when the Grim Reaper, Death himself, would walk among them and punish them for their sins. The Black Death, 1348–50. Wiped out half of Europe.'

'I wasn't aware you were a history buff, Melanie,' Mr Lane remarked a little frostily.

'Only the gross parts,' Mel admitted. 'Which is most of them.'

'Well, I seriously question the relevance of the Black Death to the present situation,' said Mr Lane. 'You're broadly right about the depopulation that happened in the fourteenth century, Melanie, but this is the twenty-first century now. Medical science has moved on. We have drugs. We have cures. We have preventative measures that can be called upon in public-health emergencies. It is simply inconceivable for any disease in this day and age to cause the number of casualties for which the Black Death was responsible. Impossible.'

Travis hoped so. But what about AIDS? As he was a guest in Mr Lane's car, he thought it best not to mention the spread of AIDS. And for another, what about that guy on the bike they'd just passed? He was wearing a mask. All Travis saw of his face were his eyes. Frightened eyes.

Medical science might well have moved on since the 1340s. But what if disease had as well?

That evening the Naughtons received an unexpected but welcome visitor. 'Phil!' Jane Naughton exclaimed, delighted, opening the front door wide. 'What a lovely surprise. Come in.'

'How are you, Jane?' Phil Peck hugged her, kissed her in the way of old friends. 'Good to see you, too.'

'Come on through. Is this a flying visit or have you got time for a coffee? It's been a while.'

'Yeah, I'm sorry about that. Things have been busy, particularly lately.' Phil Peck's brow creased involuntarily. 'But yeah, I'd love a coffee.' He stood in the lounge and glanced around uneasily, almost as if he hadn't been there at least once a month since Keith had been killed. 'Is Travis around?'

'Upstairs. Supposed to be doing homework. Probably playing computer games. I'll call him. He'll be pleased to see you. Phil, chairs are in their usual places, you know.'

Travis *was* glad to see Uncle Phil. Phil Peck wasn't his biological uncle, of course, no blood relation at all (unless it counted that he'd had Dad's blood all over him that terrible day, that he'd held Dad at the last, cradled him in the street while he died). He'd been Dad's long-term partner in the police and was still on the force now. He always took care of his appearance, did Uncle Phil, always kept his beard and moustache neatly trimmed, but tonight Travis thought he was looking haggard, worn, as if he hadn't slept for a week. He also seemed to have little patience for the niceties of conversation, taking his coffee from Mum with scarcely a thank-you.

'This isn't exactly a social call,' he said. 'I suppose you could say I've come to warn you.'

'Warn us?' Jane Naughton said blankly. 'About what?'

Travis studied Uncle Phil's face. It was set in the same expression he'd worn six years ago in Shelley's study, the emotion of being the bearer of unimaginable tidings contained and controlled by training.

'It's the Sickness,' he said.

'That's what it's being called officially now?' Travis asked.

'You mean the flu.' His mother preferred to use a more familiar term, one that seemed somehow safer.

'Sickness. Flu. They don't know what to call it because they don't know what it is,' said Uncle Phil grimly. 'Nobody does. Doctors. Scientists. The government's long line of experts. They know what it does, though.'

'Phil, are you all right?' Jane Naughton was growing concerned.

'What I'm about to tell you, both of you, it's off the record, you hear me?' Glancing pointedly from mother to son and back. 'I shouldn't be telling anyone this, not even Marion. But I owe it to you to give you a chance. If – well, if the situation had been reversed, I know Keith would have gone to Marion with the same information.'

'Uncle Phil' – Travis leaned forward – 'what does the Sickness do?'

'It kills you,' said Phil Peck simply. 'If you contract it, you die.'

'Phil, really,' Jane Naughton objected, startled. 'I don't think there's any need to talk like that with Travis in the room.'

'*Mum.*' Travis clearly felt otherwise.

'And besides, isn't that what's called scaremongering? Have they been working you too hard, Phil? You don't look . . . I mean, on the news they've acknowledged some deaths, but surely . . .'

'If they told you the truth, the whole truth and nothing

but the truth,' Phil Peck said, with a brief ironic smile, 'there'd be greater unrest than there already is. The authorities don't want that, especially with coppers going down with this infection as quickly as everyone else. What the media are being allowed to report, Jane, let me tell you – I've seen it – the reality is ten times worse, and the situation is deteriorating by the day. Soon they won't be able to cover up the truth, there'll be too many bodies to hide in the mortuaries and the funeral homes, and then the brown stuff will definitely hit the fan.'

'But surely, even if things *are* bad, like you say, Phil,' argued Jane Naughton, 'they'll find a cure, a treatment, *something*. They always do, don't they? Surely they can learn from those who've recovered from the Sickness.'

'To my knowledge, Jane,' and Phil Peck shook his head darkly, 'nobody *has* recovered from the Sickness. As far as I know, the mortality rate is one hundred per cent. So if they're going to find a vaccine, let's hope they do it soon.'

'I don't – I can't believe it,' persisted Jane Naughton defensively. 'What about the vaccine they're already distributing? The stockpiles at hospitals and medical centres?'

'It doesn't work,' Peck said. 'It's a placebo, a pretence. It allows the government to look like it's doing something, like it's got everything under control. It hasn't. It just doesn't want people to realise it hasn't and panic. Keep people ignorant and they're less likely to take to the streets.'

'Take to the streets?' Jane Naughton looked worried. 'What for?'

Her late husband's partner declined to answer. 'There's something else that's not been announced officially,' he pursued. 'Something else that'll soon be obvious, though. The Sickness only seems to affect adults.'

'I *thought* so.' Travis's heart thumped. 'I was talking about that with Mel . . .' He trailed off awkwardly. Uncle Phil was looking at him and he couldn't tell whether it was with envy or pity.

'Again, as far as I'm aware, and I've been in all the local hospitals at one time or another over the past few days, not a single sufferer has been under eighteen. Not one. Looks like the Sickness is shaping up to be an adults-only experience.'

'I don't understand,' said Travis's mother. 'How is that possible?'

'DNA. Genes. Cell development. I don't have a clue. How is *any* of this whole bloody nightmare possible?' sighed Uncle Phil. 'It just *is*. Still, maybe we shouldn't be surprised, the mess we've made of the world. Maybe it's all we deserve.'

'That's not fair, Phil. Some of us have tried our best to live right,' Jane maintained. 'You have. Keith did.'

'Yeah. Sorry. It's just a little bit hard to take, that's all.'

'Grandma and Grandad phoned this morning, Uncle Phil,' Travis said. 'Invited us to Willowstock while the Sickness is still spreading. What do you think?'

Phil Peck shrugged defeatedly. 'What do I know? Maybe you should consider taking them up on their offer. Disease spreads more rapidly in areas of high population density, that's for sure. And the government's only operating Stage One of its emergency plan at the moment: reassurance, however hollow, making a play of carrying on as normal. Stage Two'll be with us soon. In some areas I hear it's already starting. Scapegoating. Pointing the finger of blame at minority groups. Terrorist suspects. Anarchists. Activists. Muslims. All fair game. They'll all be rounded up – while we've got the manpower to round anyone up. Maybe they'll deploy the army, if they can fetch them back from Iraq and Afghanistan and God knows where else in time. Yeah, they'll need the army for Stage Three.'

'What's Stage Three?' Travis prompted.

'Anarchy. Chaos. The total breakdown of order. The collapse of society. Martial law. What your mum and dad said, Jane? I'd give it serious thought if I were you. Out in the country you might be safer. But if you're going to go, do it quickly before the curfews and the quarantines start to be imposed. I know I'd go if I could.'

'If you could?' ventured Travis.

'I'm still a police officer,' said Uncle Phil. 'I'm needed here, to protect the public. Besides, Marion hasn't been feeling too well today. Seems she's got a touch of the flu.' Neither Travis nor his mother could meet the man's gaze. 'Listen, I'd better be off. I've said too much already but I thought . . . well, anyway, I could be wrong. Probably am. You were right, Jane. I've been under a lot of stress lately. Police leave cancelled. Covering for absent colleagues. They've probably found a cure already and the world'll be back to normal by the end of the week. I just thought you should know . . . it might not be. And listen, here's my police mobile number. You know my other, don't you? Call me if you need anything, if anything happens . . . You look after yourselves, all right?'

'All right,' said Travis. But he had a sinking feeling it wouldn't be.

RADIX

"A consistent effort that persuades the
its energy and voluminous detail, a nove ....
in a few huge gulps, so that the reader may be engulfed
by the author's crushing imagination and uninterrupted
by reality. It evokes memories of H.P. Lovecraft and A.
Merritt. A dazzling first effort."
                                    – DONALD MOFFIT
                           Author of *The Jupiter Theft*

Thirteen centuries in the future, after streams of energy
from other universes have brought devastation to Earth
and genetic change to mankind, humanity trembles on
the brink of oblivion. One man is destined to prevent
disaster: Sumner Kagan, beset by enemies but as yet
unaware of the true enemy, fights for his selfhood.

As a fearful and rebellious teenager, Sumner wages war
against guerrilla bands of *distorts* who haunt the ruined
city, attacking all who, like Sumner, carry the "white
card", symbol of their untained human genes. Sumner
is captured but survives the brutality of the police camps
and allows himself to be trained by the elite troops in
the service of the Masseboth. These are privileged rulers,
whose attempt to preserve a pure gene pool has become
a weapon of oppression to all "outsiders".

As these experiences test his physical strength, his
mental abilities are challenged by his contact with the
voors, extraterrestrial beings with telepathic powers,
who make use of human bodies in their present
existence. Sumner must doubt their motives as Corby,
once his physical son and now master of the voors,
struggles to become an alien presence in his body.

Haunted by the voor and stalked by Nefandi, an
artificial man programmed as a killer by the mysterious
intelligence who threatens destruction, Sumner is ready
for his destiny. He encounters Bonescrolls, a *yawp*,
whose tribe has evolved to human species, and Ardent
Fang and Drift, members of a tribe of distorts.

From Bonescrolls he learns of his alter ego, the Delph, a godmind containing the crystallization of human experience and surviving over eons in the brain of one man. From Ardent Fang and Drift he learns friendship and humanity, and with them sets out to wake the godmind from its dreaming.

As he approaches the centre of the godmind's power, he must elude Nefandi and the troops sent by the Masseboth. And he must use the voorish powers within him to battle against telephathic forces that seek to cloud his mind and his vision of the truth.

On the success of Sumner's quest hangs the future of humankind.

RADIX offers a complete world, brilliantly realized by the most talented new writer since Frank Herbert.

A.A. Attanasio was born in Newark, New Jersey, in 1951, graduated from the University of Pennsylvania in 1973, received an M.F.A. in creative writing from Columbia University in 1975 and an M.A. in linguistics from NYU in 1976. He now lives in Hawaii.

Radix

A.A. Attanasio

CORGI BOOKS

A DIVISION OF TRANSWORLD PUBLISHERS LTD

RADIX

A CORGI BOOK 0 552 99004 3

First publication in Great Britain

PRINTING HISTORY
Corgi edition published 1982

Copyright © A. A. Attanasio 1981

This book is set in 9½/10 Baskerville

Corgi Books are published by
Transworld Publishers Ltd.,
Century House, 61–63 Uxbridge Road,
Ealing, London W5 5SA

Printed and bound in Great Britain by
Cox & Wyman Ltd, Reading

For
LIGHTWORKERS
across time and space

Acknowledgments

The inwardness of this effort has indebted me to many people. I am particularly grateful to my family for their compassionate support; the poet Jon Lang for sharing his visions and for allowing me to transmogrify his poem "The Other" into the Voor Litany (pages 303-304); the editor Maria Guarnaschelli for ennobling this book with her clarity and caring; the composer Victor Bongiovanni for permission to use a voice from his musical composition "Berceuse from Suite for Piano Four-Hand"* as Sumner's undersong (page 444); and the copy editor Betsy Cenedella for closing the circle.

Robert Silverberg published an early and greatly re-visioned excerpt of "The Blood's Horizon" in his *New Dimensions 7* (Harper & Row, 1977).

I also want to thank Artie Conliffe for the map of the hemisphere and Fred Marcellino for the cover art.

* "Berceuse from Suite for Piano Four-Hand" copyright © 1979 by Victor Bongiovanni.

Contents

Things can be—
and their Being is grounded
in *Nothing's* ability to *noth*.

—KENNETH BURKE,
Language as Symbolic Action

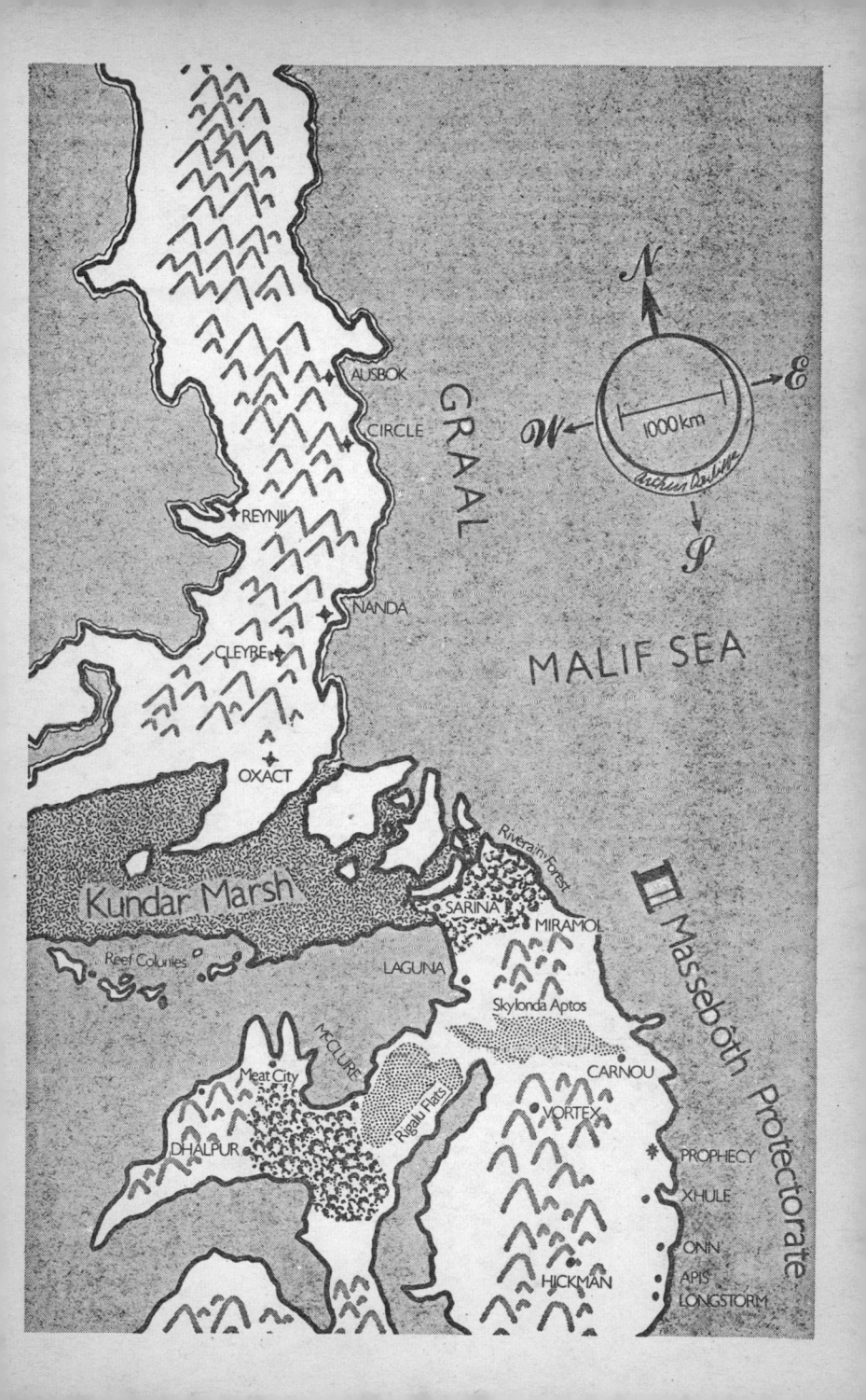

AUSBOK

CIRCLE

GRAAL

REYNII

NANDA

CLEYRE

OXACT

MALIF SEA

N

W   E

1000km

Archeus Aestiva

S

Kundar Marsh

Riverain Forest

SARINA

MIRAMOL

Reef Colonies

LAGUNA

Skylonda Aptos

Masseboth Protectorate

McCLURE

Meat City

CARNOU

Rigalu Flats

VORTEX

DHALPUR

PROPHECY

XHULE

ONN

APIS

LONGSTORM

HICKMAN

Distorts

No man knows himself.

—*I* CHING

Firstness

Blinded by the headlights, Sumner Kagan lunged off the road and slid down the dirt embankment into the dark. Above and behind him braking tires squealed furiously. Savage voices yowled as the Nothungs, in leather streetgear, rolled out of their Death Crib and chased after him. They were five viper-thin men with blood-bruised eyes and teeth filed to points.

'Run, Wad—run!' the Nothungs yelled.

At the bottom of the incline Sumner veered into the marsh. He looked like a spooked cow in the dark, waddling heftily from side to side, with only the Death Crib's headlights shimmering off his smudged and tattered shirt. He pushed into the tall grass, arms flailing wildly. His night vision had returned and he could see clearly the squat silhouette of the alkaloid factory on the horizon. He knew there was a packed dirt path somewhere around here.

Not far behind, the Nothungs were whistling chains through the air, howling, and cracking stones together. If he merely stumbled he would be torn to pieces—the police could search the marshes for weeks and still they wouldn't find all of him.

He thrashed through a brake of cattails, and then his feet hit hard earth. It was the path, a straight run to the alkaloid factory. In the west the Goat Nebula was rising. He screwed his mind into that brilliant green spark and kept his thick legs pumping.

When he reached the chain-link fence of the factory the Nothungs were close enough to pelt his broad, stoop-shouldered back with scattered handfuls of gravel. There was barely time to find the hole that he had sheared through the fence earlier that day. He found it beneath the massive and mud-streaked billboard: NO GO! TRESPASSERS SHOT!

He bellycrawled through and had to strain to haul his corpulent body to its feet. He banged up a long metal ramp toward a broad staircase that ascended into the dark galleries of the factory.

It was bad planning, he told himself, to have to climb stairs after such a long run. It might all end here. *Rau!* His feet and legs were numb with fatigue and his heart was slamming in his throat. He fixed his eyes on the dark shadows at the head of the stairs and ignored the pain that stabbed him more sharply with each step.

17

Just as he made it to the top, one of the Nothungs clutched at his pants and ripped off his back pocket. Desperately, spastically, he sprawled forward and kicked free. Struggling with his own pendulous weight, he pulled himself to his feet as the Nothungs came bellowing over the top.

Exhaustion staggered him but he fought against it. The big vat was up ahead. He could see it below through the wire mesh of the ramp.

The Nothungs were now coming up strong directly behind him, ricocheting their chains off the pipes on either side. They thought they had him trapped. Alone, in an abandoned factory. That appealed to their imaginations. Sumner had known it would.

The silver scars on the metal post, where the DANGER sign had once been, blurred past him, and Sumner took its cue and leaped. The knotted rope was there all right, and its stiff threads stung his pulpy hands as he swung heavily to the other side. There were two sharp screams behind him, two splashes.

Swiftly he looped the rope around the railing and, plodding off into the darkness, found the broad pipe that would carry him back to the other side. He staggered along it, adjacent to the ramp where three silent Nothungs were meekly peering down into the darkness. An emergency waterhose was just where he had left it. He had tested it that morning.

One of the Nothungs was yelling across the darkness: 'We'll find you, fat boy! We'll rip you!'

'Aw, blow it out, screwfaces,' Sumner said, just loud enough to be heard. He had already turned the waterpower on, and as three rage-dark faces spun around, he opened the valve. The blast clipped their legs out from under them and logrolled them off the ramp, their wails lost in the hiss and bang of water hitting acid.

Sumner listened deeply to the hissing water as he crouched with fatigue over the limp hose. His breath was tight in his throat, and his leg muscles were spasming from the hard run. He paused only briefly before taking a canister of red spraypaint from its hiding place beside the waterhose. With an unsteady arm he mist-scrawled on one of the broad overhead pipes: SUGARAT.

Sumner didn't stop to rest until he got to his car in a lot behind the factory. It was a standard bottle-green electric car, square-backed, with three small hard rubber tires and two scoop seats. He loved it more than anything else. It was his home, more of a place of fealty and comfort than the rug-walled residence he shared with his mother.

He slumped over and laid his head and arms on the cool metal roof. When he caught his breath he opened the door and dropped into the driver's seat, his head lolling back against the headrest. One hand fingered the wooden steering wheel and the other dangled over a carton of stale crumbcake. He stuffed a morsel in his mouth, and though it was dry and powdery, a fossil of its original flavor spread over his tongue. He closed his eyes to savor it. He hadn't eaten in two days. He had had to settle this thing with the Nothungs, and he couldn't enjoy eating when he was thinking about killing. But now that was over. It was time for the Tour. His stomach grumbled in anticipation.

Stuffing another block of cake in his mouth, he slid the starter chip into the ignition slot. He felt a warmth spread over him as he opened the clutch, set the car in gear, and wheeled out through the elephant grass.

Sumner and his car had a lot in common. They were both bulky, squarebacked, and sloppy. Dunes of crumbs drifted out of the corners and over stains of beer, gravy, and pastry fillings. Shreds of wrapping paper, crushed cookie cartons, a bedraggled sock, and numerous bottle caps were wedged between the seats and under the dash. And there, beneath the particolored triangular Eye of Lami—which Jeanlu the witch-voor had given him to protect him from his enemies—were three words: BORN TO DREAD. Their ambiguity pleased him. Besides eating, the thing he did most consistently and with the most fervor was dread.

Anxiety sparked through him constantly. And though he hated its hot taste in the back of his throat, he accepted it as one of the necessary indignities of life. So he ate, as if his dread were something that could be smothered somewhere deep in his gut, broken down, and digested.

But his real obsession wasn't food or anxiety. He wanted to be dreaded. He wanted to be the legendary Dark One—magic shining through his ugliness, indifferent to loneliness, deep and calm with violence. He wanted everyone to know he was dangerous.

The problem was that no one ever witnessed his daring deceptions. He was the Sugarat. And no one knew.

In the past six years the Sugarat had achieved a notoriety that fringed on myth. At first he had singled out streetgangs who had humiliated or abused him. He had trapped and destroyed them for his own gratification, never considering that there would be repercussions. But his first few kills had created such a power imbalance among the many gangs of McClure that street warfare raged as it never had before. Rival gangs warred to fill the vacancies the Sugarat had opened up. Firebombs exploded in the homes of gang leaders. Assassinations bloodied commuter trains. Hand to hand combat in the markets and shops became commonplace in the days that followed each of the Sugarat's vendettas.

Sumner thrived on this power. He began to kill more often, for insults and slights he wouldn't have noticed before. He had become important. He had found a way of shaking the world. Of course, there

19

was always the very real likelihood that one of his ploys would backfire, but the dread of being mauled by a gang in no way matched the loathing he felt for himself when he was alone and bored. It was only dread and a little luck that had kept him alive this long.

But now the police wanted Sugarat, and that was something else. For six years they had known he was behind the spasms of violence wrenching the city. They wanted him at any price, but there was nobody, not one weaselly informer, not one witness or skinnyshanked clue to point him out. Nobody knew the Sugarat.

That was why Sumner needed the Tour—to feel what he had done in the past, to know who he was now.

He drove first along a rutted dirt road that smoothed into a causeway and arced out of the industrial district. In a few moments he was at the edge of his hometown, McClure. He parked the car in a dirt field crowded with the hulks of convoy trucks and ambled into The Bent Knife. Ignoring the stares of the dogfaced truckers, he wedged himself into a phone stall and called the police.

'Zh-zh,' he hissed when the phone was picked up. The officer at the other end groaned, recognizing the ritual greeting of the Sugarat. Sumner smiled and in a mumbled whisper told the police where they could find the Nothung corpses. Then he hung up and, tucking his torn shirt in as he went along, lumbered over to the counter and ordered six sandwiches to go.

He liked his sandwiches wide open and sloppy: horseneck clams with miso and seaweed; chunks of veal blanketed in a mushroom sauce of puffballs and chicken-of-the-woods. At The Bent Knife, however, he settled for egg gumbo on toast and barley rolls stuffed with hot pressed tongue.

He drove back into the ancient, burned-out factory district. He didn't touch his food but let its steamy odors graze his nostrils with the seductive promise of heartburn.

The Tour began at the site of the first kill of his life. It was a fire-gutted warehouse, just a sunken-in crater with three scorched aluminum walls tottering around it. He parked his car where he could clearly see the seared white ash of the interior and, on one of the ribbed aluminum walls, streaked with mud and smoke, the huge scrawled letters SUGARAT.

He broke out one of the egg sandwiches, sniffed it appreciatively, then devoured it as he reminisced. He had killed seven members of the Black Touch here. The hardest part had been getting the gasoline. It was expensive, and he had had to starve himself to be able to afford enough of it. As for the liquid detergent, he had simply waited for a shipment to come in to the local mart and then, in his old delivery boy outfit, rolled off a barrel of it. Mixed together, the gasoline and the thick detergent made an extremely viscous incendiary. He had stacked three drums of it in the rafters of the warehouse. The strategy had been the same. When the razor-fisted headbreakers of the Black Touch chased him into the building, he had doused them with the firegun and touched them off with a torch flare. The burn had been beautiful, the screaming brief. It was his best kill. A perfect dupe. Everything he had done in the six years since was derivative.

Sumner cruised his kill-sites, enjoying his food and replaying his strategies. Stacked vertically on the I-beam of a broken trestle were the letters SUGARAT. Beside it was a black tumulus of rail gravel. This was where Sumner had lured a whole gang of Bigbloods beneath the drop-site of a gravel loader. When the chute opened they had been sighting him with their makeshift nail-slings. They never got off a shot.

At another table, with the dank susurrus of a bog twirling about him, he sat on the hood of his car nibbling a barley roll. He gazed into the darkness and the shape of dead trees where the Slash headbreakers had pursued him over a swampbridge. The bridge had been tricked to collapse, of course. But the real shocker for the headbreakers came after they sloshed into the bog—when Sumner ignited the firegum coating the mud they were in.

When his last sandwich was eaten, Sumner was parked again outside the alkaloid factory. He figured the police had come and gone, because the Death Crib had been taken away.

He only vaguely remembered why he had killed the Slash, the Black Touch, and the Bigbloods. It was hard to remember. He didn't think about it much. He wasn't one to brood, though his problems loomed larger each day. He had been out of work for a year and, at seventeen, was already the father of a five-year-old boy he was terrified of. Yet he rarely mulled over his life. He was motivated by a muscular intuition, an urging in the meat of his body to eat, to kill, to find sex. It was his dread.

For Sumner, finding sex was a lot more difficult than setting up a kill. He was big and ugly: six foot five, with rolls of fat bagging under his eyes, coiling around his neck, swaying like tits under his shirt. His face was glazed with the seepings of subcutaneous grease and crusty with eruptions that never went away but only migrated across his features. He had tried to grow a beard, but it came in mangy and made him look diseased. It disgusted him to see himself, so he had ripped out the rearview mirror in his car and kept apart, even from himself.

On the way back into McClure, Sumner picked up some pastries and cruised through the residential streets, eyeing the houses of all the women he desired.

McClure was an old city, maybe four hundred years old, and like most of the towns that had cropped up this deep in the interior, it was made of stone. At least the older buildings were. It was a matter of necessity, since the weather was dangerously unpredictable. Fierce

21

cyclones—raga storms—with winds of four hundred kilometers an hour swooped across the country with little warning. Whole cities were sometimes lost, coastlines reshaped. Nonetheless, wooden houses were perched on hills in the more affluent sections. They were status symbols in the truest sense, meant to be abandoned when the raga storms came.

As part of the nexus of McClure's society, the wealthy had been able to reserve cubicles in the Berth, a massive citadel in the center of town. Even if the Berth were to be completely buried by a raga storm, there was enough oxygen, food, and water inside to sustain thousands of people until they could dig themselves out.

Sumner packed a honeytwist into his mouth and farted when he passed the orange nite-glo sign with the Massebôth symbol on it. It marked the inner city limits and declared that the area was under Massebôth protection.

The symbol was two pillars. One was supposed to be ivory and the other black obsidian. The ivory one, as Sumner remembered from his grim two years of mandatory civil education, represented cultural preservation and advancement. The secrets of petroleum refinement, vulcanized rubber, antibiotics, transistor circuitry, and too much else that had been taken for granted for years were forgotten after the apocalypse that ended the kro-culture. Those that had survived the holocaust and the dark centuries that followed were many generations past any memory of civilization. Only a handful had preserved snatches of the old technology and culture. In time they got together and assembled a civilized community. Centuries later, the Massebôth Protectorate emerged. The white pillar was the symbol of its heritage.

The obsidian pillar stood for the muscle of the Protectorate. Though the Massebôth were confined to the eastern seacoast, with only a few settlements like McClure in the interior, they had the military strength to dominate a much larger empire. What confined them was not the threat of the tribes to the north and west but something that was wrong with the human race. Distorts—people who were genetically malformed—were more the rule than the exception these days, and the Massebôth, who liked things the way they were, had their hands full keeping their population strong.

Also, most of the planet was still unmapped. The Protectorate just didn't have the resources to cope with the vastness and strangeness of their own continent, let alone the rest of the world. A lot was left unexplained—like devas. Military reports, two famous film clips, and rumors described the awesome power of the devas. No one knew what they were, or even if they were intelligent. They had apparently saved endangered explorer-craft, but they had also smashed mapping-balloons that had journeyed too far north. Vast funnels of light were how they were invariably witnessed. But always deep in the unmapped north.

Sumner took the word of his teachers that there had been a time

22

before devas and distorts and raga storms. He didn't think about it much, but he liked to feel that he was informed. That's why he hated going through center-city McClure. There on the massive time-stained walls of the Berth, which housed the university and all the administrative buildings, were scrawls, graffiti, cerebral vomit. Instead of the streetnames or gang slogans that were brightly streaked throughout his neighborhood, the Berth walls were roweled with nonsense—

YOU ARE THE PERPETUAL STRANGLE
    BELIEVE IN NEVER NOTHING ALWAYS
  AMNESTY FOR THE DEAD!

It was infuriating. But there was no way for Sumner to get to where he was going without passing the Berth. Tonight, as the walls loomed closer, their smoky searchlights swinging overhead, he spotted a new scrawl, much larger than the rest—

GIVE UP
YOUR ENDOCRINE INFATUATION
BEFORE YOUR FIRST THRILL
ON MALIGNANCY HILL

Sumner used to wonder who it was that went around writing this stuff and how they did it without getting caught. One night he left his car at home and walked into center-city. He lurked for hours in the dank, gloomy alleys, peering out at a long sweep of the Berth walls. Eventually, a kid maybe fifteen years old strolled past. Large glossy letters began to appear, spraypainted on *backwards* as he went by. Sumner waited until he was done, then lunged out and snagged him. At first he thought it was a voor, but when he held him to the light he could plainly see it was only a nervous kid.

'What the rauk is this supposed to mean?' Sumner demanded, lifting the punk toward the still dripping paint—FIRSTNESS.

The boy looked at him apprehensively, thinking perhaps that Sumner was a Massebôth cop. When he saw that he was just an ugly face, he pulled himself loose and straightened his shirt. His hair was close-cropped, his ears unpierced, his clothes plain, and there was a listless, chalky look on his face. He was obviously a student.

'Spill it,' Sumner ordered. He despised students because they were pithless White Pillar lackeys who thought they had the inside view of reality.

'Where're you from?' the boy asked, pulling himself up and looking Sumner straight in the eyes.

'Right here in McClure, slip. Down by the Point.'

'Nuh,' the student said. 'I mean before that.'

'Wha? I've always lived in the city.'

The student shook his head sadly. 'Think about it, tud. Where

23

were you before McClure?' He turned to go, and then looked back once, a little annoyed, a little bemused. 'Don't stop thinking about it.'

The only thing Sumner had been thinking about at that moment was grabbing the boy by his ankles and bashing his head against his scrawl. But he had held back. This was Massebôth territory, and the last thing he had wanted was a run-in with the police, especially over a sapless student.

Sumner had no respect for the White Pillar. They were stringent scientists and yet they worshipped Mutra, a deity that rebirthed humans until they attained genetic perfection.

Absurd turds, Sumner thought, banking his car through the nightshadow of the Berth. Most of the city—most of the world, as far as he knew—were distorts. They were categorized by color code and allowed to live and propagate so long as their distortions were not visible. Brown cards were the low rung, people too genetically scrambled to have children. They worked the slow-kill jobs in the shale factories. Green and yellow cards could have families, but the Pillars monitored them carefully since most of their offspring were nerve- and bone-warped. Blue cards were the lucky ones. They coupled at will, and most mates were happy to have them, since the majority of their progeny were clean.

Only the white cards were wholly free of distortion. They were the privileged ones for whom bordello-clinics had been established to receive their unmarred genetic material at any time of day or night. Sumner was a white card.

After passing the Berth, Sumner cruised the neighborhoods of the women he desired. These were women to be seen from a distance, coming or going, on lunch break by the factories, or at night with their escorts. Sumner never fantasized about having sex with them. That was inconceivable because of his physical repugnance. But their presence, the fact that such creatures existed, was important. Their beauty and their fulfillment as people balanced the violence, the hunger, and the continual dread of the world. After a kill, like tonight, or when the muscular tension of living got too intense, he would drive around looking to look at women. The mystery of living and dying was visible for him in the sway of a beautiful woman's walk, and the arousal he felt, because it was hopeless, was mystical. Seeing women, lean and filled with peace, strolling home beneath the soft weight of evening, he felt the psychic tension that corded at the root of his neck loosen for a while.

At ease with himself, Sumner felt poised enough to stop at Mutra's Parlor, the bordello outside center-city. The place was a nondescript brick-peaked building between an abattoir and a saloon. This late at night the street was dark and empty, and Sumner parked his car at the front door.

'It's the fat boy again,' the red-haired woman at the one-way window said after Sumner entered the vestibule. A matron was handing him a towel and a Mutric prayer book. He left the book on the plastic table there and walked through the double-pillared door toward the showers.

'Kagan, right?' another woman asked. She was older, her heavily kohled eyes looted. 'He's been around a lot lately.'

'Tud,' the redhead spit. 'White cards shouldn't get it free. Not when they're that ugly.'

'Tell it to Mutra,' the older woman said. They were the only two on call that night, and the dowdy dressing room where they sat was sad with the other women's absence: vacant dressing stalls hung with lingerie and shadows. She opened a blue vial, propped her foot on a small table, and began painting her toenails. 'Got your bag in?'

For white card men, the women wore diaphragms designed to catch and hold the valuable sperm. Later, the seminal fluid was transferred to special ampules and sent to the birth camps where would-be mothers were inseminated. The work was Mutra's holy mission, and all the women involved were well paid. Even so, the redhead was reluctant to service Sumner. 'If only he weren't so gross. I've had him the last three times. My luck must be dead. Do you think—'

'No.' The older woman scowled and shook her head. 'This flop is yours.'

Scrubbed down, Sumner went to the narrow room where a redhead in traditional lingerie was sitting on the edge of the cot. He had been with her several times before, and he was familiar with her moves. Like all the others she was revulsed by his obesity, so he didn't dawdle. The disgust in her face was dulled by the dim light, but Sumner could feel how her flesh tightened under his touch. When he mounted her he looked at her breasts and her firebright hair but not her eyes. He rutted mechanically, the way he masturbated. Within moments, spurred by the cold lust of having killed, hot with the memory of almost being killed, he was seized by an orgasm.

The redhead squeezed herself out from under him. Only after the door glared open and darkened behind her did Sumner realize they hadn't said a word to each other.

Sumner dressed clumsily and lumbered out to his car, sexually hollowed and emotionally abraded. He hated seeing his ugliness in the way the prostitutes handled him. That was always harder than looking in a mirror, but he needed the relief, especially after a kill. As he drove off he thought about the kill and how close he had come to losing himself.

When he got home, the triumph of duping the Nothungs was all spooled out. The Tour had given him a relentless dose of heartburn, and the unfathomable writing on the Berth walls had started his dread smoldering again. Not even cruising the love streets and getting laid had eased him. He wanted to be alone, but he knew that his gawky mother with her sharp face and piercing voice would be waiting up for him.

Reluctantly, Sumner chained and bolted the low garage door and took a long look down the street to steel himself for the inevitable. The avenue was made of packed dirt with wooden planks laid over it. It was narrow and lined on both sides with tall thin buildings of rough black stone. It was late, and no one was sitting out on the stoops. Down at the far end of the street, among the rusted supports of the elevated train, a pack of dogs moved from alley to alley like a breeze of specters.

Sumner opened the heavy door with his latchkey and stood for a moment in the foyer. He let the fusty odor of clove incense settle in on him and adjusted his eyes to the papery light of the globe lanterns that dangled above. Behind the steep stairway with its frayed red carpet was a small room that led into the basement. There his mother held her spirit sessions. A sharp voice called out: 'Is that you, pudding?'

Sumner grunted and started up the stairs. On the third step a woman's face appeared between the slim posts of the banister. It was the color of clouded silver with pink rubbery lips and radiant black eyes. She was framed in a halo of fire-frizzed hair. 'Where're you going, pudding?'

'Nowhere, Ma,' Sumner replied.

'Nowhere isn't a place,' his mother reminded him. She stepped around the banister and stood at the foot of the stairs. She was small, thin as a needle, with flat, wrinkled dugs just barely covered by a crinkled blue shift. The red paint of her eyelids was so thick it smeared as her eyes widened to take in Sumner's mud-knobbed boots, his splattered pants, and the mushroom-pale midriff bulging over his belt.

'What in the name of Mutra have you been doing?' she shrilled, clutching at the two black feathers that hung beneath the folds of her neck. 'Work those boots off now and leave them outside. The wangol you drag home is moody enough without lugging the flesh of the planet through here.'

Sumner's mother made her living as a spirit guide. She conversed with the dead in people's shadows and was reputed to be almost as receptive as a voor, though Sumner knew for a fact that she wasn't. Nonetheless, she had an awesome reputation in the neighborhood, maintained by being meticulous about the influences—or wangol— that entered her home. Mud, a veritable broth of primal wangol, was strictly forbidden.

As Sumner sat on the stoop removing his boots she went over to the sludge he had dragged in and sprinkled it with a white powder from a small horn she kept strapped to her thigh. She said it was elk marrow dust that neutralized unfamiliar wangol, but Sumner had found out

26

long ago that it was nothing but detergent and bread crumbs.

It wasn't that his mother was a blatant charlatan. She really believed it was elk marrow dust. But Sumner knew the old crone who sold his mother her wangol supplies. She used to be a whore, years and years ago, but when she lost her leg plying her trade in a toolshed where an electric swivel-saw had been left carelessly plugged in, she resorted to a life of wangol worship. Once, as a little kid, Sumner had hidden himself in a root cellar of the old crone's house. There, leaning on a stuffed crocodile, surrounded by long strings of garlic, and bottles and vials of various luck powders, he peered through a knothole and watched her prepare her neomancy stash: Rusty water became Getaway Lotion, grease and sawdust became Wangol Oil, and commercial detergent and bread crumbs were concocted into elk marrow dust. Even in those fargone days Sumner was a loner. He had never told his mother what he had seen.

It probably wouldn't have made much difference. Zelda was devout. She had a blue rose tattoo on her lower left buttock, something Sumner spied in his first explosive days of puberty, and she went out twice a week to commune with other spirit guides from all over the city. Besides, without the zords that her shadow-reading brought in, they would both probably starve.

The only thing that absolutely infuriated Sumner was Zelda's professed capacity to speak directly and authoritatively to his dead father. The business about all the terrible wangol he hauled around was tolerable. The four times a year that she set her hair on fire and ran through the house to clear out evil powers were smelly but amusing. And the warty, liver-spotted old men she let use her body to help commune with their dead wives were merely disgusting. But when she would stop in midsentence to consult his dead father, Sumner had to bite his tongue to keep from strangling her.

With his boots off, Sumner trudged up the stairs, carefully averting his eyes from the cheap rugs that hung from the ceiling. Insipid scenes of misty bogs and full moons over mirror-slick seas covered the scabby, mildewed walls. Zelda was hopping along right behind him. 'What have you done to yourself, pudding? You come home sludged as a corpse and not a word out of your sad mouth for your mother. You've been to the whorehouse again, haven't you? Look at your hair, it's still wet. Don't you have any respect for yourself? Do you want children you'll never see by women you'll never see? Why throw your seed at Mutra when you could marry the way your father did. He was a blue card, and he didn't drop his seed foolishly. Where would you be now if he did? In some Mutra camp without parents, with a government name, never knowing who you were. Do you want that for your children? You're a white card, Sumner. You're rare—a spirit blessing. If you cleaned yourself up and lost some weight, you could marry into a wealthy family. You could open your life. You could do something for your mother—instead of *this*.' She poked his expansive gut. 'Tell me what happened to you. Was it an accident? It wasn't an accident! Not in your father's car!'

'It's my car, Ma. It's been mine for years.' Sumner reached the top of the stairs and had to shove aside old Johnny Yesterday, who fell asleep night after night at the head of the stairs, reliving an early childhood habit. Johnny Yesterday was the boarder they had had in their house for the past eight years—since Sumner's father had died. He was half deaf, senile, and blind in one eye. But worst of all, a distort characteristic was just beginning to surface. In his case it was a deep mind distortion: He could move physical objects telekinetically.

In McClure, as in every Massebôth city, distorts of all types were efficiently and painlessly done away with. Johnny Yesterday's deep mind capacity had bloomed just after he had been laid off at the factory, two weeks away from his fifty-year pension. There, for forty-nine years, he had been relentlessly punching holes in the cardboard panels that swung under his nose on their way to becoming circuit boards at the far end of the assembly line. Sumner was convinced the layoff had precipitated the distortion, but Zelda couldn't have cared less. She stopped charging him rent (he didn't have any zords anyway) and discreetly incorporated his rare talent in her spirit guide business.

Sitting in the kitchen behind a thick curtain, amused and stimulated by glass beads and snake vertebrae necklaces that Zelda stored in crates for prospective clients, he performed on cue. When Zelda was ready to start her heavy oaken table thumping or have the flowers in the great brazen coiled-snake vase leap out and dance, she would enunciate very loudly Johnny Yesterday's mother's name: 'Christabel Mira!' She had learned that whenever old Johnny Yesterday heard that name, his deep mind capacity went rogue.

The power was so rare that even when the thick curtain was itself blown away by Johnny's intense telekinetic nostalgia, no one suspected that it was the leering, glassy-eyed old man with the twitching ears who animated the whole show. But Zelda had to be careful in her use of Johnny Yesterday's gift. The Massebôth were always alert to reports of deep mind powers. Once word got around that this was happening, they would haul her away for a quick and painless end.

Zelda, though cautious, was fearless. Convinced by several years of catering to people who needed miracles, whose emptiness could only be filled by the impossible, she truly believed that the Powers were communicating through Johnny Yesterday. That's why when Sumner shoved him aside at the head of the stairs, she became stricken.

'Be gentle, pudding. He's been like a father to you.'

It was a lie. Johnny Yesterday and Sumner had never exchanged a word. By an unspoken agreement they completely ignored each other.

The old man didn't even break the rhythm of his snoring as Sumner propped him back up against the wall and stepped over him into the living room.

It was an expansive room with strange, forbidding hunks of furniture. Almost all of it had been given to Zelda by her patrons, either for services rendered or because nobody else would take it. A behemoth throne, complete with escutcheon-bearing dragons carved into the side panels and a tasseled canopy of royal indigo, occupied the far wall. It was flanked on both sides by peacock-blue urns big enough to stand in, and in which Johnny Yesterday usually did. There was also a massive bronze bust of somebody who looked furious; a candelabra whose candles stuck out at every possible obtuse angle; an ancient metal sea chest that had long ago fused shut and had never been opened, despite a muffled rattling whenever it was moved; and phalanges of imitation ostrich feathers bowing shyly above a metallic-green shag sofa that had gone bald years before it had come here to die. The floor was covered with a giant oval rug with a life-size camel embroidered into it. Here and there were stools with wood-carved monkey feet; a settee shaped like a maw, replete with tiny bamboo teeth and leather lips; and a squat table with brocaded legs and a filigreed surface depicting an angel whose once beatific smile had faded with age to a demented leer.

Sumner maneuvered himself through the clutter of stools to a narrow door beside the furious bust, but before he could open it Zelda grabbed him by the arm.

'Aren't you going to tell me what happened, pudding? You look just terrible.'

'Nothing happened, Ma.'

'Nothing happened?' she whined, and pulled the last two buttons off his shirt. 'You think I'm zaned? Look at you.' She slapped the bellyroll drooping over his belt and flopped one of his tits. 'Pigging it,' she said with disgust; then her eyes narrowed. 'You're not beating up little boys for food money anymore, are you?'

'Ma!' Sumner gently pushed her off and moved to open his door, but Zelda put her hand on the doorknob.

'Hold on, you. You're always squirming, always itching to be someplace else. Stand still a minute and get a good taste of yourself.'

Sumner sighed and scratched his belly. 'What do you want, Ma?'

Her voice sharpened. 'I want you to stand still a minute and look at yourself. What have you ever crafted?' She slapped his belly again. 'Just this. That's all you're good for, taking food and turning it into—'

'Ma!'

'When was the last time you brought home anything but mud and moody wangol? Ha! Last time? There hasn't been a first time.'

'Ma, I want to be alone.'

'When aren't you alone? All I see of you is the mud you leech behind. Where do you go? What do you do? I'm your mother and I don't know. I feed you and I don't know.'

Sumner turned to go, but Zelda grabbed his shoulder and, throwing her whole weight against him, turned him around. He felt her eyes grind into him, and he wondered if he would have to belt her. Instead, he started picking his nose.

Zelda stabbed him with a finger. 'You're a half-witted rundi, running all over town, day after day. For what? Answer me! For what?'

'Ma, it's *my* business—'

'*Your* business?' Her whole face clenched. 'Take your finger out of your nose and listen to me. You don't own anything here. You've never earned even a slice of bread that wasn't for yourself. Don't go telling me what my business is. *You're* my business. I've given you everything you have. This house is mine. That car is mine. Those clothes are mine. And this gumbo is mine!'

She grabbed two big handfuls of Sumner's voluminous midriff and yanked at it until he shoved her off. 'It's *mine*, I say!' She stared at him with apoplectic rage. 'I created it, and I've fed it. What have you ever done? There's nothing—'

She stopped abruptly and her fury became an immense sadness. It happened so quickly that Sumner, even though he knew what was going to happen, was left waiting. 'Klaus! Is this our son? Is this the boy we created?' She cocked her head as if she were listening to somebody behind her.

Sumner bit his tongue and shoved into his room, slamming the door behind him. Alone, he crumbled onto the beat-up mattress and its clutter of heaped clothes and bedding and covered his eyes with his arm. He heard the door snick open. Swiftly he tugged a shoe out from behind the mattress and hurled it at the blanched, shriveled face appearing in the doorway, missing it by inches. The door banged shut, and Sumner covered his eyes again.

Alone. But he was too keyed up to sleep. He stirred restlessly from side to side and finally heaved himself to his feet and started throwing the scattered clothes on his bed all over the small, dark room. The place, like everything else about Sumner, was a sloppy mess. There was a broken chair in one corner, a mattress with a feathery rent in another corner, and a desk propped up by zucchini crates against the one wall with a window. The window itself was cracked, thickened with grime, and splattered with paint. On the desk there was a moil of beat-up tools, stacks of crackling yellowed papers, springs, clips, rocks, mementoes, balled-up tissues, crumbs, a torn shirt, three toothbrushes, several broken pens, a dirty glass, and a gleaming chrome-plated scansule with a sixteen-inch screen and a push-button console.

Next to food, the scansule was the main reason Sumner spent time at home. It was, indirectly, a gift from Klaus, Sumner's dead father. Klaus had been a very successful plant foreman. He had seemed to understand what life was all about, though he had died before Sumner could ask. Sumner was ten at the time, but already his father had put enough money aside for his education. He had had dreams of his son becoming a craftsman, but Sumner was too reclusive and short-tempered to go to school. After Sumner's two years of mandatory civil education and another two years in nine different training programs, Zelda succumbed to the swarm of disciplinary sheets that followed him from one classroom to another and withdrew him from school. She rented a scansule, a self-study device that was connected to McClure's university center. It was with this device that Sumner learned how to make firegum and gunpowder. Otherwise, he wasn't interested in learning.

The other things that fascinated him about the scansule, apart from the sex-ed programs he played back now and then, were the tectonic displays—structural programs in which students could analyze various stoichiometric combinations: crystal stress patterns, principles of wave propagation, and maze properties. Sumner enjoyed sitting in front of the screen and letting those abstract patterns lull him into a soporific trance. It was a form of self-hypnosis, a way of getting beyond his dread and relaxing enough to sleep.

He despised sleep. Slumped out in the sag of his filthy mattress, he was prey to nightmares and their garble of screamshapes and barely heard whispers. He much preferred the slow descent in the pale light of the scansule, letting the meaningless but intricately beautiful patterns ease him into a sprawled slumber. His dreams were tamer then, and he woke without thrashing or howling.

Sumner caressed the cool metal rim of the scansule. He flicked on the power switch, waited a moment, then banged the set, waited another moment, then physically lifted and dropped the set. He waited a final moment before urgently looking around for something to ram through the screen. Fortunately, the only thing handy was a frayed toothbrush, and he decided instead to check the battery. It was missing.

He thought about it for a moment and then realized with a pang of humiliation that there was only one answer. The battery was too securely connected for Zelda or Johnny Yesterday to have removed it. Only a scansule agent could have taken it out, which meant, quite simply, that his dead father's funds were exhausted.

He leaned against the voided scansule and rubbed his eyes, trying to absorb the full import of his situation. For months he had been fearing this day, but now that his father was truly gone, no longer represented even by his zords, the sadness was thicker than dread. Soon they would be coming not only for the scansule but the car. It

31

had belonged to Klaus while he was alive, but like most everything else in Massebôth society, it was on loan from the government. As long as there were funds to pay for its upkeep and recharging, it was Sumner's to do with as he pleased. Now there wouldn't even be enough to cover the three traffic violations he had picked up over the last two months.

Sumner gazed forlornly at the two tickets taped above his desk and reached into his back pocket to pull out the latest one. He had gotten it two days before for speeding down a residential street. One of the women he admired had abruptly appeared at her doorstep.

He froze—hand to fabric-torn hip—and an iciness gripped him so severely he couldn't breathe.

The ticket was gone. It had been in the pocket that one of the Nothungs had ripped off, and it was probably left lying on the wire mesh ramp below the broad steam pipe on which he had defiantly sprayed SUGARAT.

He moaned aloud and dropped to his knees. It was *all* over. Lazy nights blinking out to the scansule, slow drives down the love streets, the Tour—all of it, gone. And worst, most horrible of all, the Sugarat was through.

Sumner swayed to his feet, grabbed the edge of his desk, and heaved it over. The scansule tube exploded, and before the crash and bang thinned out, the door to his room swung open. Zelda stood ready to swoop over him, but when she saw the fury on his face she clutched her two black feathers and quietly closed the door.

Sumner couldn't think. He needed some air. He thudded out of the room and stood for a moment beside the bust with the furious expression. Zelda was leaning against the table with the brocaded legs, still clutching her feathers.

'Who are you?' she demanded with indignation. 'Who are you?' She reached between her legs and pulled out her horn of elk marrow dust. Swinging her arm in a wide arc, afraid to get too close, she tried to scatter the dust on her son. 'Out mind-mauler! Out nerve-squelcher! Get out of the body I created! In the name of Mutra. Out!'

Sumner swung past her and went to the door that led up to the roof.

'No!' Zelda shrieked. 'I won't let you kill my son!' She ran up to him and emptied the detergent and bread crumbs on his head.

Sumner jerked aside the bolt, kicked open the door, and spun around. Zelda leaped back and, casting a warding sign with her thumb and little finger, mumbled something under her breath.

'Ma! Relax!'

'*Me* relax?'

'I'm just a little wound up. I need some air. I'll be all right.'

'Why go up on the roof? It's windy up there. You could get sick.'

Sumner turned and bounded up the stairs, his mother calling after him. 'If you jump, I'll never forgive you. I'll trap your wangol in a jar and torment it as long as I live. We can renew the scansule. We can buy a new one. Don't—'

Sumner banged through the outer door and stepped out of sight onto the roof.

Zelda sighed and threw up her hands. *He'll kill me yet*, she thought. *Why does he have to be such a loner? And foul-tempered, too.* She shook her head. 'It's all your fault,' she said silently to her husband. 'You were the one that wanted him to be free. You trained him that way. Not me. I wanted him to play with other boys. Be sociable. Make friends, I told him. But no. There'll be time for that later, you said. Now he's got to be self-reliant. He has to learn to be comfortable with himself. That's the way it is in this world. You're on your own. Nobody's going to help you. Ha!' She leaned back against the filigreed table, suddenly feeling very heavy. 'Well, I wish you were here now, Klaus. I wish you could see what he's become.'

Zelda sighed again and pushed away from the table. It was time to see how the chowder was doing. She went down two flights of stairs to a small, cramped kitchen where a heavy-bottomed pot was purring on the stove. She always had something cooking down there. Food was the only way she had of reaching her son. 'And that's your fault, too,' she told Klaus, 'going Beyond like that when he was so young. What am I supposed to do? He only listens to me when I have something to eat.'

She lifted the top off the pot and let the steam billow out before sniffing the broth. It smelled good. From experience she knew that Sumner would be hungry soon, so she took down a bowl from a heat-faded wood cabinet and ladled out the thick clam chowder. She selected from the spice rack two jars marked Onion Salt and Turnip Chips. They were really powdered John the Conqueror Root (for energy and defense against sickness) and wangol e-z brew (for calming nerves). Gingerly she sprinkled some of both into the bowl.

Zelda was a good mother. It was her responsibility, she knew, to reform her son, to undo all the harm that Klaus had done. But so far she was getting nowhere. Talking was useless. He never listened to her. So she had resorted to herbal cures and wangol fortifiers. Yet even these hadn't helped. Sumner was as close-minded and reclusive as ever.

Soon she would have to do something drastic. It was wrong to go on protecting him like this—feeding and housing him, treating him like a child, or an old man. *No*, she scolded herself. *I won't do this anymore. He's got to get ahold of his own life.*

Up on the roof Sumner breathed deeply to clear his head. With the glare of the Berth lights and the blue crowns of fire from the refinery stacks in the south, few stars were to be seen. He walked around to the back of the house and stared north. There were three rows of rooftops and then darkness ranging to the horizon, where a faint green glow was suffusing from Rigalu Flats. He stared for a long time at that spectral light and thought of Jeanlu the witchvoor and his son, Corby. He would have to go to them soon for zords, and that thought made his fear all the more palpable. Voors were the madness of the world, distorts with alien strengths and too-knowing minds. He didn't want to go to the voors. They had abused him before, and he feared them. But the police were coming and unless the voors helped him, the Massebôth would kill him.

A moan welled up from his thick body, and he reached for his back pocket. He stood that way for a long minute, his hand on the torn seat of his pants, gazing north fish-eyed and heavy-hearted. Gradually shame and anger opened in him, and a disfigured cry lurched in widening circles through his chest but could find no way out.

When the pain finally dulled he went inside and sulked over a bowl of clam chowder that was steamy and thick and smelled of someplace far away.

Pictures of the Real Universe

Realitysharing

The morning was still dark when Sumner left home in his bottlegreen car. All his important possessions were wrapped in a torn shirt and thrown in the back. Zelda was fluttery with concern and tried to stop him, first with threats about her poor health and then with food. But it was no good. Sumner's dread far outstripped both his guilt and his hunger. He told Zelda he would be back later in the day, though he had no intention of ever seeing her again.

He had a large breakfast at an all-night convoy stop on the outskirts of the city. He allowed himself to dwell on his life with Zelda because this was the last time he would remember her exactly as she was. Their life together had been very good compared to what passed for living in most of the households of their neighborhood. Klaus had freed them from the factories. All his life, Sumner had been allowed to come and go as he pleased, even though Zelda was always there to interrogate him when he got back. Still, he remembered, she never knew what was really going on. And her cooking—Mutra, that was fine! A little heavy on the wangol spices now and then, but fine. He sighed. Too bad she was swayed by all that spirit yak.

Though he was fond of his mother, he was glad that he was finally getting away from her. She was always trying to change him, and he was happy as he was. Or as he had once been, he reminded himself. From now on, it was life on the road. Zelda was gone—but then, so was his life as the Sugarat. More than security, he had lost his very identity.

His destination was Jeanlu's cottage, 189 kilometers away, on the far edge of Rigalu Flats. It was a lonely ride—lonelier still knowing that he would never be going back—but the voors had things he wanted.

He smiled, remembering his first journey outside McClure. How old had he been then? Ten? No. It was just after his first kill. He must have been eleven.

It would be at least an hour before he reached Rigalu Flats, and it was a straight, unbroken road until then. He eased his mind back six years to the memories he had of his first lonely ride into the wilderness—

*　　*　　*

35

Hunger had led Sumner to the fish stalls by the river where he had hoped to scrounge a free meal. He watched closely as thickarmed men in blood-grimed aprons whacked off the heads of perch and mullet, shook out their guts, and then tossed the cut pieces onto mounds of flaked ice. He searched diligently for the misaimed chunks of meat that fell along the stalls. But the competition was too tough—large wild cats that had been bred to fend off rats—and soon he wandered out to the empty wharves to wait for the returning ships.

Watching the inky water slap the dock pilings, he thought about barbecued fish. Its imaginary aroma and flaky dark crust were so real that he didn't notice the old man until he spoke: 'You want to get laid, kid?'

Sumner spun around; his eyes snapped to the old man's face. It was brown and wrinkled as a crumpled bag, the ears doughy, the hair filthy and tangled.

'What're you talking about, wheeze? I got no money for whores.'

The old man stepped closer. 'But you have a white card.'

Sumner's heart skipped two beats. Just a week before, he had gone for his mandatory medical exam. All children at puberty were required by Massebôth law to have their genes tested. After an exhausting series of scrapings, injections, and embarrassing probes, Sumner was issued a white card—the most highly coveted genetic status. He was one in a thousand with unmangled genes.

Yet—how did this crust of a man know about his white card? Sumner looked more closely at the old man's face. He had a straight, fierce mouth and incongruously dreamy eyes. Eventually Sumner would learn to recognize a voor by those searchless eyes. At the time, though, he thought the old man was just a river pirate. He was hard enough, with bead-rings in the tops of his ears, a black bandana across his forehead, and strange, smoky scents lufting off his clothes.

'You want to get laid, waddle? Yes or no?'

Sumner stood his ground gamely, hands on his hips, both excited by the mysterious prospect of sex and frightened by this uncanny pirate. 'How do you know I have a white card?'

A shadow of a smile crossed the old man's rumpled face and softened it. 'I'm a voor, waddle. I know.'

Sumner's whole body clenched. Voors could craze you with a glance. They were the most alien of the distorts and known to have deep mind powers. And if those weren't good enough reasons to stay clear of them, there was a long-standing Unnatural Creatures Edict posted against them by the Massebôth. People were hanged for talking with voors.

Sumner tried to back away, but the water was behind him and there was no one else down by the wharves. Three hundred meters away the fish stalls were bustling with activity, and he realized too late that no one would hear him if he screamed.

36

With a whimper he lunged past the old voor and scurried down the wharf. A beat-up scavenger truck suddenly wheeled out from behind a row of tarred bollards and cut him off. A cowled man leaped out of the cab, and Sumner froze. The man's outstretched hands were blueshelled and barbed.

Distort! Sumner silently screamed. He tried to fight, but the hooded voor was eerily swift. He accurately anticipated all of Sumner's blows and cornered him between the truck and the water. Sumner's fear overwhelmed his revulsion and he went for the creature's eyes, but the voor snagged his hand in an icy grip and guided him to the back of the truck, where the old voor opened the thin metal doors. They threw him in and banged the doors shut.

Sumner raged. He had heard that voors cracked open the skulls of their victims and devoured their brains. He swung around in the tight compartment looking for a weapon. But there was nothing in the back except rust stains and dents. Screaming, he threw himself against the doors, and they buckled.

Before he could hurl his body at the doors again, they squealed open. The claw-handed voor was there, the cowl of his mantle thrown back, revealing a shaved head that was oddly misshapen. The face was moronic, the forehead round and bulging, filling up the sockets so that his baleful yellow eyes had to stare up from under his skull. An idiot's face.

'Sit still, waddle,' the old voor's voice spoke from somewhere beside the truck.

Sumner backed away, feeling his aggression congeal to cold fear. He couldn't tear his eyes away from the cretin face with its cushiony flesh and glossy lips. Its grotesqueness drained him, and he slumped back against the far wall.

With a jolt the antique truck lurched to a start, and he was thrown across the rusted floor. Fighting the sway of the truck, he crawled to the front of the compartment and laced his fingers through the wire mesh of the window that was there. The two voors paid no attention to him, and he looked beyond them, through the bug-splattered windshield at the empty wharf road they were bumping down.

He hung to the wire mesh and gazed intently, hoping to spot some landmark that would give him an idea of where they were taking him. But that was hopeless. The cowled driver seemed to be turning corners randomly, backtracking on himself again and again. At first, Sumner thought they were trying to confuse him, but that didn't make sense. *They'd hood me if I wasn't supposed to know,* he reasoned.

It was only after he glimpsed, at the far end of one street, a gray car with black and white pillars on its hood, that he understood what was happening. The voors were using their telepathy to elude the police. They were looking for a gap in the stop-and-search patrols that ringed the city. After a few minutes of circling, they found one.

Sumner had never been outside of McClure. Most people spent their whole lives in the city and never left. There was no reason to leave. Outside was wilderness where hind rats and distort tribes ruled. Other cities were far off, and unless you were a merchant or convoy driver they offered nothing that couldn't be found in McClure.

Awed, Sumner watched the dark gaunt buildings of McClure bob off into the distance. All around them was desert—flat and empty as an ancient seabed. 'Where're you taking me?' Sumner demanded.

'You're going to get laid, waddle,' the old voor said. 'Nothing more.'

Sumner knew from the tone of the voor's voice that it was hopeless to ask more questions. He was sure that they were taking him someplace desolate where they could cannibalize him at their leisure.

After more than an hour of being jostled and thrown about, Sumner felt the road smooth out. On the left was black rock, immense palisades. On the right, a yawn of space. They were on a ledge road, bucking along at almost top speed. Sumner was so nervous that he didn't even glance to the right. When he did, he gasped.

Down below, for as far as he could see, was a desert of pale green sand laced with swirls of black ash. Everywhere there were broken domes, spires, and turrets fantastically honeycombed, pocked, cratered, and smoothed by wind erosion. The place was a labyrinth of arabesque shapes, echoes of radiance and scaled colors. It took Sumner a long while to perceive that the broken honeycombs were buildings: The whole colossal landscape was—had been—a city!

'It was called Houston,' the old voor said. 'Or Dallas. I'm not sure which anymore.'

Sumner stared dumbfounded at the ghost city and its phantasmagoric shapes until the rickety truck suddenly swung off the rimroad. White chalk cliffs blocked his view of the Flats as they careened along a rutted dirt track. In a cluster of old big-boled trees, they jerked to a stop.

Beyond the trees was a small whitewashed adobe cottage with coral-pink tiles scaling a swayback roof. Blue gentians bloomed in wooden troughs beneath oval clear glass windows. Behind the cottage was a cirque of tamarind trees bowing over a crystal blue pool that had formed in the basin of an old bomb crater.

The two voors, one on either side, led Sumner along a micaflecked path to the edge of the pool. A large wooden tub was there brimming with sudsy water.

'Off with your clothes, waddle.'

Sumner nervously obeyed. When he was naked, the old voor scooped a bulky sponge out of the tub and threw it at him. 'Wash,' he ordered. When he had lathered himself all over, they shoved him into the pool. The water was deep but warm, and he clung to the side while the voors sudsed and soaked his clothes and then beat them dry on a large sunbaked boulder.

He dressed, and the voors walked him back to the front of the cottage. The old voor motioned Sumner toward the house.

Sumner fidgeted.

'Just get over there, howlie,' the old voor said, his voice severe. 'You want to go home, right? Then do what I say.'

Sumner walked up to the cottage and climbed the three polished cedar steps to the door. He moved to knock, but before his hand came down, the door opened.

A woman stood in the doorway wearing a flinty-blue dress with threads of gold at the cuffs and a wide-throated collar. She was gorgeous—tall, with a musical body and black rambling hair. Her eyes, liquid and dreamy as any voor's, were smoke-blue and sparked with many strawberry-gold flecks. She ran a slender hand along the doorjamb and gestured for Sumner to come in.

There was something selcouth about the place. Beer-colored shafts of sunlight filled the room, threading through dense curtains of drying roots and flowers. Brown Indian pipes, swamp violets, groundsel, bloodweed, wind apples, and ice-clear stalks of kiutl hung from thick, well-seasoned rafters.

'My name's Jeanlu,' the woman said.

Sumner stammered out his name and lingered in the doorway until Jeanlu closed the door and offered him a seat.

'Sit down, please.' Her voice was gentle and unhurried, and she trailed a delicate musky scent that set her apart from the brassy aroma of the plants. Sumner sat down, his eyes torn between her and the colorful carpet.

'This is my veve,' she said, gesturing at the carpet, a patchwork of eleven different landscapes: a red sea combed by wind; dark sheol-flowers sprouting beneath two moons; blue-barked pines, and a series of brilliant images that could have come from a scansule crystal display. 'Do you know what a veve is?'

Sumner shook his head.

'Every voor has one, in some form or other. It shows our lineage—where we're from.' She pointed to a black square pinpointed with white flecks. 'This is a planet we call Unchala. It doesn't exist anymore. An eternity ago it was the home of all voors, in a galaxy you don't have a name for.'

Sumner wasn't listening. He expected the other voors to come in any moment. 'How come there are eleven?' he asked, afraid of a silence.

'That's all any voor remembers. We all remember a different eleven. It's sharing that holds the brood together.' She walked over to the stove. 'Would you like something to drink?'

He shook his head and began cracking his knuckles nervously. His hands were large and fat, scabby with dirt that even the sudsy bath couldn't get out. They were a testament to his perpetual anxiety, the nails chewed to nubs.

'Something to eat, perhaps?' She held out a pastry glistening with honey and studded with almonds. He couldn't refuse.

While he worked on the pastry, he studied Jeanlu. She was very attractive, and he began to wonder if maybe the old voor had been telling the truth. *What if she does want me?* he thought with a pang of fear. He had never been intimate with a woman before.

'Don't worry about it,' Jeanlu said with a handsome smile. 'I'm sure you'll catch on quickly.'

Sumner's ears flared red. She was so beautiful he had forgotten she was a voor. She could read his thoughts as easily as the embarrassment on his face. 'But why me?' he managed to blurt out, trying to cover his lapse. 'I'm . . .' He was going to say ugly, but instead mumbled, '. . . just a kid. I'm only eleven.'

'I don't care,' she said sincerely. 'You have a white card. That's all that matters to me.'

Sumner swallowed the last morsel of pastry and shifted uncomfortably in the chair.

'Strong genes are rare,' she went on. 'But they're important to me. You see, I want to have a baby.'

'A baby?' His eyes gauged her. He didn't think she was lying.

'Yes. Voors can't mate with one another. Didn't you know that?'

He shook his head. The sex-ed program that was part of the gene test hadn't covered voor sexual behavior.

'We're distorts, you know. Our children are only strong when we mate with outsiders. If our race is to survive, we need new genes.'

Sumner popped his knuckles.

'Finding someone as unmarred as you is difficult. These are unsteady times. Howlies—people like yourself who have to make sounds to be heard—are dangerous. We have to make the best—' She stopped short and her eyes narrowed, 'I didn't know that. You're so young.' She seemed to look more closely at him. 'You've killed recently.'

'Yes,' Sumner said, knowing it was useless to lie. Three weeks before, he had doused the Black Touch marauders in homemade firegum. His first kill.

Jeanlu shook her head and said with mock gravity, 'So young. And so scared.'

'I'm not scared,' Sumner slammed back. He stared at her sullenly, his legs swinging. It made him uneasy to know that she was watching him think. 'I burned them because they abused me. You can't let people abuse you or they'll never stop.'

Jeanlu nodded compassionately. 'That's what your father used to say, isn't it?'

40

Sumner glared. His father had died almost a year ago. He was a large, powerful man, a man who always got his way. Every week he would take Sumner downtown to play pins or kili. One day he went out hunting and never came back. He had been chasing a pangolin with a loaded shotgun when he tripped. The gunstock hit the ground and the charge went off, blowing away the top of his head. Sumner went berserk when he found out, and Zelda had to tie him down. Weeks later when he was able to control himself again, he went downtown to play pins and forget about his grief. On the way back he was cornered by the Black Touch gang, slinky, mushroom-skinned distort kids who never left the shadows when he went through their neighborhood with his father. Now that he was alone, they dragged him into a back alley, shit-smeared him, and left him hanging upside down for a whole afternoon. He was sick for days afterwards and spent the bedtime wondering how his father would have handled it. It was then that he decided to kill them.

Just thinking about it infuriated him, and he could feel his heart thudding.

'I'm sorry—I didn't mean to bring up such painful memories.' Jeanlu sounded genuinely contrite. 'You were brave to do what you did. Fear is a tool in the hands of a clever man.'

Sumner nodded, feeling his anger cool in the face of being called a man.

Jeanlu laughed and clapped her hands. 'I wonder if you're going to be as fiery in bed?'

Sumner stiffened, feeling a twinge between his legs. There was a spreading warmth pulsing over his belly that turned positively hot when Jeanlu leaned forward and rested a hand on his knee. 'But I want you to know I won't force you into this. If you don't want to be with me, you can go home now.'

The offer was almost too good to believe, and he almost moved to go. But the sensual warmth in Jeanlu's hand was magnetic. At first he thought it was the afterglow of his anger, until it swirled tighter and fired his loins into a sudden heat. The feathery scent of Jeanlu's hair misted over him, and he knew for sure that something wonderful was going to happen. 'N-no,' he stammered. 'I'd like to stay.'

Her smile was radiant. 'Wonderful.' She stood up and loosened the cord holding the front of her dress shut. 'But I have to tell you before you finally decide—' The cream white curves of her breasts appeared between the blue edges of her dress. 'The pastry you ate was laced with a mild aphrodisiac. Nothing to take your wits away. Just something to make your first time more memorable.'

Sumner couldn't have cared less. He writhed in the chair as she ran a finger down between her breasts to the cloud of hair below She took his arm and coaxed him out of the chair and over to the bed. His reluctance evaporated when her cool hands moved under his shirt and

41

over his body. Her touch was electric. In a few minutes he was struggling out of his clothes.

Naked, Jeanlu's body wasn't as attractive as it had promised to be beneath the folds of her dress. It was firm yet soft and well proportioned. But there were large dark scales on her thighs and stomach. She said they were nothing to be concerned about, not a disease, nothing contagious, just a deformity. Sumner looked at them only once and then fixed his attention on the strawberry-gold flecks of her eyes and made love to her as best his cumbersome inexperienced body could.

Jeanlu was patient. She guided their slewed bodies craftily, helping Sumner discover for himself how to please her with his turgid strength. Lust immixed with his uncertainty, and soon he was wauling with pleasure, doing things he had never thought possible. He did them again and again, until the mist rose blue in the tamarind trees and the spiderwebs started shining in the falling light.

Sumner was orgasm-wearied but exultant and proud, and as the room fogged into crepuscular shadows he was ready to urge himself on again. But Jeanlu had become silent. She lay in the bed, her eyes glazed over, her breath soft. As Sumner bent over her and stroked the sweat-strung hair from her eyes, the door swung open and the two voors stepped in.

'Get your clothes on, waddle,' the old voor said. 'Time to go.'

Sumner slunk out of the bed and tugged his clothes on quickly. The old voor led him out by his elbow, and he glanced back only once. Jeanlu was lying on her back, staring up mute-eyed, her face serene and pale as ivory.

He was still buttoning his shirt when the metal doors of the truck banged shut behind him. He got a good grip on the wire mesh before they jolted off into the dusk.

The ride back was uneventful. In the dark, Rigalu Flats was a lattice of shadows suffused with a dusty green light. Sumner asked what made it glow, but the old voor shrugged and the cowled driver was silent.

Without asking where he lived they drove him right to his doorstep. As soon as he hopped out, they sped off.

A Small Time-Drenched World

Sumner ran a hand over his face, feeling the memories stirring just an inch behind his eyes. He sighed and glanced at the dashboard. The battery was well charged, enough to run continuously for perhaps three days. In that time he could make it to one of the large eastern cities—Vortex, Prophecy, maybe even Xhule. All three of them were larger than McClure, and he was hoping to find work there. But doing what? He wasn't trained or licensed to do anything. He had a white card, and though that would certainly get him cash for sperm donations, it would also expose him to the police. And if they caught him, they would kill him. At least he hoped they would, because if they didn't, he would wind up in the dorga pits.

Dorgas were the lowest rung in Massebôth society. They were the corpse-carriers, garbage burners, and street workers. Legally, they didn't exist. They were functional distorts, criminals, or captured and conditioned tribesfolk. When they worked they were made to wear drone straps, headbands that amplified their strength at the same time that they dulled their minds. The characteristic X-scars on dorga brows came from the drone straps and so did their sullen lethargy. Most dorgas lived many years as mindnumbed zombies.

Sumner shivered and brought his attention firmly back to the road in front of him. *Sure I'm a renegade,* he admitted to himself. *But I know I can make it. There's still Jeanlu. I'm not dorga meat yet.*

He reached for an apple and bit off a large chunk. The crisp, cool flavor eased him, and he breathed deeply. A strohlkraft, one of the Massebôth vertical-ascent planes, was cruising about ten kilometers to the south and five kilometers high. It was a silver spark moving against the brisk, high wind that was brooming the sky and advancing a line of cumulus. He wondered if they could see him, or if they would be curious about a three-wheeler heading for the Flats.

With angry chomps he finished the apple and dismissed the fear. *Too late to be tailtucked,* he told himself, though he was still spellbound with dread.

He flicked the core out of the window and fixed his mind on Jeanlu again. Perhaps she would have some brood jewels for him. Maybe some kiutl she wanted moved. It would be a start, a way to earn some zords. Maybe enough for him to buy a new name—to join a craft's league and become a carpenter. He was still young enough.

One hand low on the wheel and the other groping in the greasy bag of beef strips, Sumner thought back to his first experience with brood jewels and kiutl—and Corby. He laughed softly at himself, remembering his ignorance, his initial fear—

He was sixteen when he went to see Jeanlu again. It had been five years since his last visit, but he remembered the route exactly. Everything was as it had been, except that now there was a neat round hut with a blue tile roof beyond the tamarind trees and the crater pool.

When he got out of his car, Jeanlu was standing in the doorway. She waved happily, and the timidity that had been building in him since he left McClure dissolved. He had wanted to see Jeanlu again for a long time. He needed answers to some questions that had been bothering him, but he had been too afraid of the voors to seek her out. He wasn't sure if she would be living in the same place, and he worried that the two voors who had kidnapped him might be around.

But one day, that seemed not to matter. He was bigger and smarter. And danger had become a lot more familiar—something his dread needed. So he had driven out, and now here she was, older-looking, her hair clawed with gray, her face lined, but as beautiful and gracious as he remembered her.

'I've been expecting you,' she said as he stepped up the cedar steps. She was wearing a sacklike dress of ruddy brown that dropped to her ankles and was wide open at the sleeves. 'What took you so long?'

Sumner looked at her quizzically. He was a head taller than she now, and she looked small and frail.

'I've been trying to get you here for the past week.'

The interior of the cottage looked smaller, too. Everything was where it had been, only the dense curtains of drying herbs, flowers, and roots were gone. In their place were hundreds of small, delicate-looking ornaments. They were deep brown and black and obviously woven from the dried plants. To Sumner they looked like trinkets: circles, stars, all manner of geometric shapes, from rectangles and squares to the intricate oddity of a latticed cone within a latticed cube within a latticed sphere.

She offered him a chair. 'How about something to eat or drink?'

Sumner fought back an immediate surge of hunger. 'No thanks.' He remembered the almond pastry spiked with the aphrodisiac.

'You think I'd hurt you?' She tightened her face with mock-annoyance.

'I came to ask some questions,' Sumner replied, sticking to his plan to be absolutely straightforward with her. 'But you said you've been trying to get me here?'

'Not to hurt you. Relax.' She removed a bone-white plate from the stove. It had sliced green peppers and strips of fish on it. 'Redfish sizzled in tangerine juice. I think you'll like it.'

Sumner couldn't turn it down, though he had already promised himself that he would refuse anything she offered him. It was very good—tart with a sweet afterglow. The crisp peppers were perfect between bites of fish. 'My questions can wait,' he said around a mouthful. 'Why did you want me here?'

'I have something for you.' She reached behind and took a large bundle of black crushed leather from one of the shelves. When she unwrapped it, he saw three packages inside covered with faded chamois. She arranged them next to each other on the table. 'These are retribution, or a gift, if you will, for your part in the creation of our son.'

Sumner glanced at the packages and then looked up at Jeanlu.

'Yes,' she said. 'We have a son. I've named him Corby.'

Sumner began to speak, but she raised a hand. 'There's so much to do today, there's no sense dragging this on and on. I know what you're thinking. Let me answer your questions.'

44

Sumner sat back, swamped with uncertainty.

'I called you here because I want you to participate in a timeless ritual that will probably make little sense to you. It may even frighten you. But it means a lot to Corby, and I beg you to be patient and accept my assurance that no harm will come to you.'

Rauk! Sumner wriggled in his chair. He hated being manipulated, and the fact that he had been called here by a power beyond his comprehension only made his dread that much worse.

'Please relax.' Jeanlu smiled, and for the first time Sumner noticed that the gold flecks in her eyes had expanded since the last time he had seen her. Her irises were like polished gold rings rimmed with turquoise.

'It's a custom among voors,' she continued, 'for the child to experience the lives of its parents. Because both Corby and I are voors, he's known my life since before he was born. But to him, you're strange. He knows you only through your chromosomes. Fortunately, considering how violently you live, you're still alive, and now may be his only chance to know you directly. In exchange for your cooperation, I'd like you to have these.'

She carefully unwrapped one of the packages, revealing a small triangular ornament similar to the many geometric shapes dangling throughout the room. 'It's a stalk charm. I made it myself from plant fiber. That's my job—working with sunlight.'

'Your job?' Sumner asked, trying to move his mind past his anxiety.

'Yes. Every voor has a specific function. Mine is crafting stalk charms—forms of shaped-energy that we use for different purposes. This particular shape is called an Eye of Lami. It wards off influences that are detrimental to its possessor.'

The stalk charm was a tight weave of brown, yellow, and green fibers with a faded red flower netted at its center. He held it in his hand, and its nubbled texture pleased him. Coming away with gifts was more than he had expected when he traveled out here. Suddenly his mind was swarming with questions, but the idea of shaped-energy reached the tip of his tongue.

'Each shape has its own potential,' Jeanlu responded. 'Geometry is essential—from the molecular bonds in your cells to the star-bridges. But just how this particular shape works requires an understanding not only of geometry but of plants. And there's no time for that now. Trust me.'

She unfolded the second package, the largest one, and it crackled as she nudged it toward him. Inside was a thick sheaf of crisp leaves the color of dried blood. 'Kiutl,' she said. 'When you drink the tea made from these leaves, you'll understand better what it is to be a voor.'

Kiutl! Sumner winced with excitement. Kiutl was a psiberant, a telepathic drug from the far north that voors smuggled south. It was much coveted in Massebôth society—but because telepathy was anarchy to the government, kiutl was outlawed. On the black market the quantity of voorweed before him would make Sumner a wealthy man. It was virtually impossible to keep his mind off the vellum shirt and the snakeskin ankleslung boots he had been coveting for months. He tore his eyes away from the red leaves and stared at the final package, wondering what it was, knowing that very little could compare with what was already before him.

Jeanlu handed the package to Sumner to open. It felt heavy and hard in his hand, and he opened it curiously. When he saw the vapor-blue stone within, he sucked in his breath. The jewel caught the light and warped it into a luminous star whose fine, bright threads of energy thinned out and re-formed with the quivering of his hand. 'A brood jewel,' he whispered.

He had seen one on display in the Berth archives. They were very rare and, on the right market, priceless.

'Before you make plans to sell it,' Jeanlu said, 'consider what it is. Like the stalk charm, its secret is geometry, but it's not designed to extend or ward off influences. Its function is more internal. If you gaze into it long enough, you'll be able to see yourself—your inner self—or the true self of anyone reflected in it. It's necessary, though, to have a clear mind. Any kind of distraction or mental fix will distort what you see. Also, keep in mind that it's extremely fragile. It takes very little to destroy a brood jewel.'

Through Sumner's mind flashed all the possible merchants he might dare approach with it. Possession of a brood jewel was damning evidence of association with voors, but he knew that there were many who would risk their lives to own such a rarity. Then it occurred to him that the jewel wasn't his yet. He had hardly heard what Jeanlu had said to him, and he looked up at her inquisitively.

'Shall we go meet Corby now?' she asked.

Sumner balked. The gifts were more than tempting—they were provocative. He would do anything for them, yet: *Is it a ruse?* Unlikely, but there was no way to know. He needed some clear answers to the questions he had come to ask.

Before he could speak, Jeanlu answered him: 'No. Yes. No.'

'Huh?'

'The answers to your questions,' she replied ingenuously. 'No, I can't tell you what voors are, where we're from, or why we're here. It would take too much time. And yes, you're safe with us. I'm not trying to deceive you. After all, you're the father of my son. Finally, no, a voor wouldn't use deep mind to kill anyone.'

'But *can* a voor kill with deep mind?'

Jeanlu shrugged. 'Yes,' she said, then added quickly, 'but it never happens. Mind is too sacred.'

'Even if you were threatened?'

'We have other ways to defend ourselves.'

46

'But what if—'

'Sumner, please.' Jeanlu's face darkened. 'You're safe here. Believe me.' Her eyes locked on his, and they softened. 'Let's go see our son.'

Sumner nodded. He folded the chamois cloth over the brood jewel and handed it back to her. When she reached for it, the wide sleeves of her dress rode up on her arms. For an instant Sumner glimpsed the crusty scales on her elbows that he had seen once on her belly. He looked away quickly.

'Don't be disturbed,' she told him, getting to her feet. She put the three chamois parcels back in the crushed leather wrap, folded it, and returned it to the lacquered shelf. 'I told you the last time you were here that I have a deformity. Not much to do about it. Voors sometimes have trouble shaping their bodies.'

She went out the door and led Sumner around to the back. When they got to the edge of the crater pool they stopped, facing toward the hut with the blue tile roof. Sumner looked into the west above the hut where the sky was threaded with clouds. He was charged with nervous energy, not sure what to expect. *My son.* The thought was unreal to him. He wet his lips with his tongue, wondering what they were waiting for, and how weird the kid might be, and just what was going to happen, and how long it was going to take.

Then the hut door opened, and he glimpsed a completely vacant interior before a small boy in white baggy pants and a green collarless shirt stepped out. His face was white as wax and his eyes colorless. As he approached, Sumner thought he heard a sighing in his ears like the whispering draw of the tides. Closer now, the boy's small features seemed luminous. His hair was white-gold, tousled like Sumner's, but unlike Sumner he was slender, a mere sliver of life.

When he was an arm's length away, looking up with eyes pale as glass, he spoke, and his voice was soft and almost deep: 'I'm glad you're here, Father. I have a lot to show you. And'— his small features moved with a gentle, scarcely perceptible smile—'there's so much more I want you to show me.'

Sumner shuffled from foot to foot, his hands jammed into his pockets. The dim noise he had heard was gone, and all his attention was on the calm, seemingly mindless face before him—the skin marble-white.

Sumner tried to force a smile, but it wavered on his face only an instant before slipping off. There was a long awkward silence during which the boy just stared at him blankly. An ugly feeling squeezed down his throat and into his stomach, and he wanted to scream in his mind: *You stink-pissy little distort. What do you want me to do? Fart?* But he remembered the brood jewel and the kiutl waiting for him back in the cottage, and he throttled his inner voice.

The boy's eyes glittered, cold as stone. 'My name's Corby.'

Sumner nodded and looked to Jeanlu for some kind of cue. A smile flicked at the corners of her mouth. 'Why don't you show your father who you are.'

A sense of alarm trilled through Sumner. 'What do you mean?' he asked, his hands squirming in his pockets.

'Don't worry,' the boy said, stepping closer. 'I'm going to show you wonderful things. It'll be easiest to do that out there because it's so open.' He nodded toward the tract of broken ground that started near the cottage and limped off into the Flats. 'It's empty, so we can fill it.'

Sumner's confusion clouded his eyes.

Jeanlu laid a reassuring hand on his shoulder. 'Just go with him,' she urged. 'Everything will be all right.'

'It looks dangerous out there,' he said, wanting to kick himself for having said it.

'There's always danger,' she replied. 'Everywhere. But here there's no threat.'

Sumner swallowed his anxiety. He turned to face his son, who was reaching out to him. He overrode his fear and took the boy's six-fingered hand. It was radiantly cold, almost electric, and he pulled away with a ridiculous whoop and careened clumsily into Jeanlu.

'Easy.' Jeanlu steadied him, then gently veered him toward Corby, who was watching emotionlessly.

'I'm sorry—I'm different,' the boy said in a bruised voice. He led Sumner toward the desert. 'I don't want to frighten you.'

'I'm okay.' Sumner tried to swallow but his throat was tacky. 'It's my fault. I'm edgy. We're family, right?' His words sounded frail, and he tried to swallow again.

'No, you're not to blame. You can't feel—I mean, not the way a voor does. So you really don't know if I'm going to hurt you. I understand.'

Sumner had both his hands in his pockets, afraid to touch the boy again. He gazed up at the sky to calm himself and watched a strong wind fanning a sheet of stratus clouds across the east. 'Why do we have to go out there?' he asked, looking ahead to where the gray shattered rocks ended and the green sand began. There was a rise a few hundred meters off. On the other side of it was a steep incline that dropped into the Flats.

'Because there's no life there,' Corby answered. 'It's hard for me to feel you with all this going on.' He waved at the clumps of sparse scrag-grass withering among the ashy gravel.

'Oh.' Sumner kicked a dried clump of dirt out of his way.

'When you first got here I tried to reach you, but it was impossible with all the stalk charms Jeanlu's got racked in her house. Then, just now by the pool, I tried again. It was better but not clear enough, because I want you to see me as well.'

'I see you.'

'No you don't. But you wouldn't know.'

They came to the rise, and Corby reached out for Sumner's hand. Sumner took it reluctantly and felt his skin crawl and his insides jump when the bright iciness coursed through him. Corby guided him up a footpath that curled along the curve of the rise toward the top. At the ridge-peak, Sumner looked back toward the cottage. Jeanlu was still standing where they had left her, watching after them. The wind dropped down to nothing, and leaf-shadows of the tamarind trees smoothed out to sheets of blue haze at her feet. Turning about, Sumner could see the weird expanse of Rigalu Flats—a huge, tumbling plain rising here and there to clumps of withered ruins, wind-eaten husks of stone—all of it glimmering a hysterical green in the sunlight. *Mutra, it's hell,* he thought, feeling his dread turning inside him. He wanted to dash back to his car, and it took all his strength to stand still and listen to what the boy was saying.

'It *was* hell for the people who lived here at the end.'

Corby started down a couloir that sliced through the steep incline of the rise and descended abruptly to the basin below. It was a cumbersome descent for Sumner, and when he got to the bottom he was sweat-washed, his hands nastily scratched from the tumbles he had taken.

Corby leaned into a sandwalk, moving toward a jumble of rock that had once been buildings. Sumner exerted himself to stay in stride. When they slogged into the ruins, Corby went over to a jut of speckled green concrete and sat down. His features looked malevolent: the eyes too large and flat, the nose and mouth too small, almost fetal, compressed beneath that unreal curve of brow, and the skin like a glaze, like a dead child.

Sumner's dread thickened, and he knew he was going to collapse unless he started his mind moving again. *Get ahold of yourself, twitch.* He ran a shuddering hand over his face. 'I'm going back.'

The boy's eyes frosted and seemed to change color. He smiled vaguely. 'Why are you so scared of me?' He leaned forward and looked deeply at him, a shadow moving in his face. 'Don't try to get ahold of yourself. Let yourself go. Selfishness and fear are the same thing.'

Sumner clenched his fists to master his dread. He looked out over the stretch of sand they had just crossed and watched dust devils whirling in the heated air currents. When the trembling stopped he looked back at the boy.

'That's good,' the child said. 'You're stronger than I thought.'

The compliment washed over Sumner like a cool breeze, and he unclenched his fists.

'Look.' Corby held up a hand white as winter, and Sumner was seized in an icy nervelock. His eyes bulged. Emptiness was spinning out of the pores of his vision, and darkness loomed through him with a deaf-and-dumbness dense as stone. Time parsed into nothingness and an awesomely still I. An aeon sifted by.

Sumner snapped alert, abruptly free of his paralyzing vision. Corby was sitting as if nothing had happened. The cloud patterns behind him cut the sky as before. Only an instant had passed.

'You went deep,' Corby said, the wide glow of his eyes watching him emotionlessly. 'Remember what you can.'

Sumner was fixated by those chatoyant eyes. Light was naked in them, still as ice, unverbed. No way to know what the brain behind that gaze was knowing. Sumner backed off, then turned and started walking toward the cottage, willing himself not to break into a mad scramble.

Surprisingly, his anger matched his terror. He was sure he would lose his mind if he stayed, and he was furious that Jeanlu had duped him. *Voor rauk!* He was stoking his rage, needing it to keep himself above the bog of his fear.

Before he got very far Corby stepped out in front of him, and he staggered into a backstep.

'What's wrong with you?' Corby snapped. 'I didn't hurt you. I was just trying to show you another way of looking at things.'

'I'm not interested.' Sumner waved his hand, motioning the boy aside.

Corby frowned and stepped closer, his six-fingered hands reaching out for him. Sumner tried to turn and run, but he couldn't move. A winter breeze was streaming through him, and he was abruptly aware of standing outside himself. For a prolonged moment he was immersed in a pounding deafness. Then reality squeezed tighter around him.

He was looking at Corby, his ears humming slightly with the trembling warmth of his blood. The vertigo had passed as swiftly as it had come. It had somehow shaken him loose from his dread and left him feeling as calm as a matchflame. Everything had slowed, and for the briefest instant he wondered why he had been so frantic when obviously, if you just stood still, things returned to their places, seconds creaked by, the silence gathered.

Sumner was able to look closely at Corby without trembling. He focused on the hairline, so much like his own, and the wide calm jaw that was his father's. He wondered about what kind of brain was floating beneath the ice of that face.

Corby went over to his concrete perch and sat down. The telepathic bond between them was thickening. Sumner paid him no attention. He was caught up in the experience of time passing slowly. Like a jewel, his life was gradually taking shape in the rocks around him. He could make whatever he wanted of himself.

Energized by the voor, everything he saw was different. The sunlight, he decided, was turtlelight, moving slow and green. The ruins were a river in which the turtlelight was immersed: a river of time, the silt of centuries gathering on the desert floor. Bending, he saw himself in the river. He *was* the shattered rocks, the jade sand, the turtlelight. There was no other life here but him and—his son. In the river of time they were themselves a current, a continuous stream of life flowing from—where? He didn't know where life began, but he knew that with this new voor-power in him he could remember if he tried.

He closed his eyes and imagined himself looking back to the hairy and slobbery jungle lives of his first human ancestors, back to when language was still shut in behind bars of teeth. But that wasn't where the lifestream began. He had to go further back, past the scurrying lemur lives and the slimy and raw slug lives, feeling back millions of years to the eyeless, mouthless beginnings of the cell. Yet instinctively he knew that wasn't the stream source either. To find the beginning he had to dream back far beyond the steaming swampferns, even further, past the burning seas, back to when the whole planet was vaster but less dense, back to when it was a hanging garden of gases and plasma: a phosphorescent cloud swirling in on itself, neither alive nor dead, turning slowly around the star that was dreaming it.

That was the source, he thought to himself, feeling Corby's astral energy turning in him.

Or was it? Where did the gases come from that condensed to these rocks? Other stars. And they? Where did the first stars come from? Was there a living origin beyond beginning and end? Or was that the first myth? The first to be taken up and the last to be put down?

'That's very impressive,' Corby said. 'But none of it is true. You've made it all up.'

Sumner turned to face the boy. He swayed under a mild spell of vertigo.

'Evolution's a fascination,' the voor said. 'It's all constraint. Who are you really? Where are you really from?'

Sumner shivered at the tone of his voice. 'I don't know.'

Corby clapped his hands like a schoolmaster. 'Of course you do. Don't you remember? These were your lives before you had this shape—'

Again Sumner was chilled by an icy breeze. This time, he sensed the psychic energy's direction. The power was streaming directly out of Corby. He could almost see the iridescent tracings of the current as they swirled from a point below the boy's navel and curled through the air toward him. All the warmth of his body smoked away, vision wobbled like bucketwater light, and suddenly he was falling again, caught up in the voor's telepathy. The visible world melted into the darkness of a bottomless plunge. He opened his mouth to scream, but the vast emptiness around him absorbed whatever pitiful sound he made.

When he was alert again, the air was smudged with a greasy odor.

51

Something to eat. He followed the dark taint on the air through a brake of river reeds, over a rotten stump, past trees and shrubs, and down a leaf-strewn slope. There were other scents, sticky plant odors, frayed animal spoors, but his hunger sealed them out. For him, there was only one odor, an oily smell of something living, something small, and not too far away. His skullrooted teeth clamped and unclamped in rhythm with his loping cadence. Then he saw it. That dark brown smallthing, white in its ears and underneath, gladdening itself on bright green, serried grass.

Watching the smallthing perched in the tall grass, eyes alert and wily, ears pricked, Sumner's mouth widened in adoration and a spindly thread of saliva drooled to the ground. Then he was off, and the smallthing bolted. There was a long chase under the grass-head-waves and the tranquil hills and the clouds like mountains. When it ended, it ended quickly. The skullrooted teeth ripped flesh, and there was a hot, sticky smell of blood, and a squeal that jarred the air for a moment.

Sumner tried to get ahold of himself. *What's happening to me?* he bawled, but his cry was lost in a glare of light. The glare splintered to an aerial view, valleyward—a straggle of trees, the curled ribbon of a river. He was flying, the air's buoyancy and the wind's force bending joint and tendon, lifting him up, widening the arc of his circular flight. One eye was soft and swivel-searching the clouds for others like himself. The other eye was keen and downward gazing, feeling the textures of the leaf-dapples and grass shadows far below, hunger giving it clarity. The sun was behind him, the hooked feet pulled in, the hooked head turning, searching. Grasses wavered and hid. He watched his shadow trawling the green rumpled earth. Nothing stirred. But he went on looking. Watching. Watching. A wryneck sailed out of a tree and swooped low over the bent grass. The movement was spotted immediately, and he folded his wings in on themselves and dropped for the kill.

Sumner tried to shrug himself awake, but he couldn't break the fall. He plunged from one dream into the next. He was a shark slendering up toward a glassy-grained surface where smaller fish glittered like stars. Suddenly he was a cloud-feathered gull eyeing a fish's hidden light among the rocks. Then he was an owl living by the claws of his brain. Then a spider watching a fly tangled in mouth-glue, whining its wings.

Of all the dreams that blurred through him, one was particularly vivid. He was whiskering through the stalks of tall plants, trailing a foodscent. Only this time, he was unusually tired and hungry and alone. He was willing to go where he had never gone before—across stubble fields thick with strange scents. Far ahead was a farmhouse, though he didn't recognize it as such. At the time, it was just a mysterious break in the horizon, filled with watery lights and

52

unfamiliar sounds. Nearer was another such thing but more familiar, heavy with the smell of birds.

He approached slowly, gutsack hugging the ground, nostrils flared for danger scents. There was a tall opening, but it was hot with the spoor of something he didn't recognize. So he circled the nest area until he found a small crawlspace. The birds already sensed him and they were clucking nervously as he dragged himself through. He pounced on the nearest bird, snapping its neck, shaking the life out of it. He pulled his kill after him, out through the crawlspace, hurried by the squall of the other birds and a distant barking. Outside he stalled for an instant. A tall creature had spotted him and was making a thin, incomprehensible sound, waving a stick at him. It was too far away to be a threat, so he picked up his kill and jaunted off. But not far. The stick flared brightly, and a crushing blow swamped his eyes with darkness.

Darkness.

Sumner snapped his eyes open and squinted against the turtlelight. With a hand to his face, he tried to clear his mind. *What's happening to me?*

A voice reached him: 'You'll be all right.' It was Corby. His mind unclenched, and he saw that he was standing. Only a few seconds had passed.

Sumner sat down in the dust and rested his head in his hands. Only after several long minutes was he able to look up again. He sat still and rooted his feet and fingers in the sand as if the slightest movement might shatter his delicate hold on sense.

'It's over now,' Corby said. But it wasn't over for Sumner. Every rock, every twisted bolt of steel, every dust mote stood out clear and strong. Even the sunlight and its green reflectant haze shimmering in the air was distinct, detached from the ruins and the sky. He understood. 'I'm alive,' he whispered to himself. 'Alive!'

Overwhelmed by a mingling of awe and fear, euphoric with the cosmic energy that the voor had channeled through him, he rolled to his stomach and began to crawl through the sand. Drifts of sunlight wavered over his body, the heat flowing from the warmed rocks into his whole being. Creation was caressing him, and he writhed in the sand trying to embrace all of it.

When he looked up again, it was night. The skyfires, vibrant auroras, were streaming above him, and by their brilliant light he could see that his clothes and hands were thick with dirt. Around him the ruins were glowing, effusing a dim green pallor. His head felt wide and clear as the sky, sparking with lights. And he realized he was looking at the sky—he *was* the sky!

No—this voor-dreaming had gone far enough. He stopped himself. Corby was sitting on the same jut of concrete he had gone to hours

53

before. Remarkably, he felt no fear of the boy, not a strand of anxiety.

Corby hopped off his perch and took him by the arm. There was no spasm of energy, no jolt. Just the meager grip of a child. 'Let's go home,' he said, sounding tired.

They picked their way among the ruins and dragged through the sand toward the rock escarpment hiding Jeanlu's cottage. Looking at the stars echoing through the coronal lacings of the skyfires, he sought out a particular pattern: the ancient, swayback Lion. When he had found its fierce eye and inferred its tussling mane and lowhung, cold belly, a small voice opened in him: *A wind blows through the Lion's belly.* It was Corby's voice, diminutive, distant, arising from somewhere in the back of his head. Sumner was amazed at first, but what he was hearing swiftly overwhelmed his surprise:

A fire-wind blows through the Lion's belly, so old and far-traveled its beginnings are forgotten. When it reaches this small time-drenched world, it flares in the ozone and scatters. But some of it sifts through the atmosphere. Some of it takes on the shapes that it finds and becomes voors, simply by arriving. We are older than you know. We've been on this planet before. Perhaps this time we'll stay until the sun mists over and the fire-wind, our journey and life, pushes on, scattering us into the future.

They came to the rocky rise, and the inner voice slipped away. At his side, Corby was stalling, too tired to climb. Sumner looked up at the rise. The supple energy of the trance was still coursing through him, and he knew he could make it to the top. He bent down and let Corby straddle his shoulders, then he started climbing. He felt exhilarated, full of strength, and the rock face seemed to conspire with his need to ascend. He thought about the words that had drifted across his mind and wondered how many other worlds the fire-wind of the voors had crossed—how many others like himself had fathered alien flesh.

About three-quarters of the way to the top he pulled up short. On the ground in front of him, where his eyes had been assiduously picking out a trail in the broken rock, was a shadow—a human shadow. He looked up, expecting to see Jeanlu or a voor waiting to help them, and he shrieked. Klaus, his dead father, was standing there, one eye and most of his forehead missing, violently ripped away. The one good eye, set in a face of mottled gray flesh, gazed down at him sadly. The lips were pulled back in a berserk grimace.

Sumner shrieked again and jerked back violently, sending Corby flying off his shoulders. Instinctively he spun about to catch the boy, but it was too late. Corby dropped into the darkness head first, careening toward a jagged ridgerock. Sumner gasped and looked quickly over his shoulder. The specter of his father was gone. Corby walked up from where he had landed, looking a little shaken.

'I—I'm sorry,' Sumner said shrilly. He looked again to where he had seen his father. There was nothing but rocks and ragged shadows, hazy in the dull glow from the Flats.

'It's my fault,' Corby said, taking the lead toward the top of the rise. 'The bond is still strong between us: You're seeing the world like a voor. You'll be all right tomorrow.'

Sumner wiped the cold sweat from his neck and face and plodded after the boy. All his strength was gone, and his legs felt gelatinous. But he didn't stop at the crown of the rise. He saw his car was where he had parked it, and he walked at a steady lumbering pace toward it. When he was leaning against the hood he looked over his shoulder. Corby was still standing on the rise. Before getting into the car, he waved, but the boy didn't wave back.

Sumner didn't wait to catch his breath before shoving the starter chip in and wheeling onto the road. He felt nauseous and sticky with fear, and he was grateful for the solidity of the wooden wheel.

The ride home was maddening. Eerie shadows flickering out of the Flats made him swerve and jam on the brakes several times. Twice he saw his father standing by the side of the road, his hands and the mangled flesh of his face burning with a blue phosphorescence.

When he finally pulled into the driveway at home he was shivering uncontrollably and vomited twice in the street before he was steady enough to put the latchkey in the lock. He crept as silently as he could up the stairs. At each creak of the old wood he expected to hear Zelda's piercing voice. But he made it to his room alone, his heart booming in his ears.

He woke at midday and fell back in a drowse. It was evening before he was able to get out of bed. His hands, face, and clothes were crusted with dirt, but even so he found it hard to believe that he had been with Jeanlu and Corby. His thoughts of the previous day were mistrustfully dark and charged with fear. Recalling the strange hours he had spent on the Flats with Corby made him tremble, and he had to splash his face with cold water to calm himself. *Hallucination,* he rationalized. *That gopping fish I ate.* But Corby was real, and the boy's face, with its dead whiteness and ghostly resemblance to his own, loomed in his memory.

After cleaning himself up he went downstairs to the kitchen. Zelda had some stew prepared, and he ate hungrily. When he was finished she opened a cabinet, lifted out a bundle of black crushed leather, and laid it on the table.

Sumner nearly threw up. 'Where'd you get that?'

'Don't get excited,' she warned him. 'You'll throw up.'

'Ma!'

'I found it in your car. Which was missing with you in it all day yesterday.'

Sumner picked up the package and tried to feel its contents through the leather. He reasoned that Jeanlu had put it in the car while he was with Corby. 'Did you open it?'

55

'Of course not. How do I know what moody wangol you've got in there?'

Sumner inhaled deeply, wondering if he could believe her. 'It's not wangol, Ma. It's film. I didn't want it exposed.'

'Well, if it's exposed, it wasn't me that opened it.'

He decided to believe her. *She'd be crawling all over me now if she'd seen the brood jewel*, he figured.

She was frowning. 'What film do you have in there anyway? You don't have a camera.'

Sumner got up and stuck the package under his arm. 'They're photos. I'm going to get them developed. A friend of mine'll do it for free.'

Zelda thinned her eyes suspiciously. 'Photos? Photos of what?'

Sumner smiled. 'Naked girls, Ma. And people in rut.' He hopped out of the kitchen before she could snag him.

He hung the stalk charm from the ceiling in his car to remind himself that his nightmare of Corby and the Flats was real. The experience had been like a dream—vivid, colorful, and full of malevolent beauty—so that finally he had to believe it *was* a hallucination. There was no other way to come to grips with it. And besides, he had some kiutl and a brood jewel to move.

Sumner toyed with the idea of trying the kiutl himself, but he was leery, and eventually his dread won out. Just to see how potent it was, though, he crumbled one of the leaves and boiled it until the water was wine-red. It smelled sweet, even tempting. So he gave it to Johnny Yesterday. The old man took it eagerly and drank it all off in a few gulps.

Sumner watched him closely for an hour. Nothing happened. A while later, he gave up on it and went out in his car for a cruise. When he came back, old Johnny Yesterday was floating cross-legged above the stairs, oranges and pears drifting around his head. His ears were twitching, and a wicked smile was smeared across his face.

As best as he could time it, the stuff lasted six hours. He figured it was potent enough to sell. But he didn't know how to move it.

He had the same problem with the brood jewel. Just gazing into its receding depths, the blue facets splintering with fans of curved light, he knew it was exceptional. At first, he thought he might be able to use it himself. If it really could reveal the true nature of people, perhaps it would offer up secrets he could cash in on. But that dream was short-lived.

Sitting bent over the jewel, he saw nothing but hazings of shadowlight and his own bulging reflection. Then slowly, a form began shaping itself out of the coal-blue depths. When the skin at the back of his neck crawled in a chill breeze of recognition, he tried to pull away. He was seeing himself dead, sprawled face up, hair droozed with blood, a white curve of bone pushing through the split skin of his jaw. But he couldn't move. Transfixed, he sat looking for hours at the crushed mouth, the violet bruises, the puffed bellybutton, the gelled eyes. . . . The daylight faded and he sagged away, crazed with revulsion and fear.

Later he picked up the jewel and thrust it under a heap of soiled clothes. He wanted to get rid of it quickly. It was a devilstone, another of Jeanlu's evil tricks. Clearly, he realized, the safest thing to do would be to crush it and scatter its dust into the sewer. But it *was* a rarity, even if a monstrous one. The least he could do was get some zords for it. Mutra knew he deserved it.

After a month of seeding questions in a dozen port taverns, Sumner learned of a man in McClure who sometimes bought unusual items from strangers. His name was Parlan Camboy. He was a shipping magnate with out-of-town connections. His office was in a turret of the Commerce building in center-city.

Sumner went there and waited in a posh anteroom several hours before being turned away for the day. The next day was the same. And the next. On the fourth day he told the spectacled, pigeonchested man who was the merchant's secretary that he had some information. 'One of Camboy's ships is going to be pirated. I know how and when.'

A few minutes later he was invited into the main office. The room was opulent. There were cedar rafters with lux-tubes built into them, latticed wall-panels, amber-glossed paintings of naval heroes, deep leather chairs, an intricate parquet floor, and richly carved molding.

Parlan Camboy was sitting behind a dark crimson desk backed by a semicircle of mullioned windows. He appeared to be in his fifties. His sparse hair was the color of hemp, brown and yellow streaked with gray. His face was granite like his eyes—a well-used face. A gold ring hung from his left ear and a shiny scar creased his right cheek.

When Sumner walked in, an undisguised look of disgust crossed Camboy's face. Sumner was dressed as he usually was, in a sweatringed, crumpled shirt and dirty sag-seat pants.

Camboy motioned for him to sit down, and Sumner moved toward one of the leather chairs. Camboy's eyes widened. 'Not there,' he snapped. He pointed to a wooden stool that Sumner hadn't noticed. After he was seated, the merchant turned and opened a window. He adjusted his chair so that there was a draft between them. Then he growled 'Where and when?' Both his hands were under the table.

'I lied,' Sumner confessed, flinching as Camboy's eyes hardened. 'But I had to speak with you. I have something to sell.'

'What is it?' His question was a lash.

'A brood jewel.'

Camboy's face softened, but his eyes remained flinty. 'When can I see it?'

'Now, if you like.'

Sumner smiled inside at the surprise that showed on the merchant's face. 'Now? You brought it with you?'

'I want to sell it quickly.' He reached into his pocket, and Camboy tensed. When he brought out the jewel the older man leaned forward.

'Let me see that.' He held out his hand, but Sumner shook his head.

'First this.' He pulled out a handwrench whose jaws had been fitted with cloth. He worked the jewel between the jaws and held it up. 'You try to jooch me and I'll crush it.'

Camboy smirked. 'You're the kind who would.' He stood up and bent closer.

'Hands behind your back,' Sumner ordered. Camboy reluctantly complied, and Sumner brought the jewel up close enough to be inspected.

The merchant's face remained impassive, but Sumner heard awe in his voice: 'Where'd you get this?'

'Where do you think?'

'You have voor connections?' The scar along his cheek was writhing. 'How much do you want?'

Sumner smiled.

'Five thousand zords,' Camboy offered.

Sumner almost dropped the stone. *Five thousand!* That was five times more than he had hoped to get. 'Ten thousand,' he said, keeping the excitement out of his voice.

Camboy's eyes were fixed on the jewel, and Sumner thought he saw them smile. 'Why're you selling it?'

'I need the money.'

Camboy sighed sadly. 'This is such an exquisite jewel. Don't you see anything in it?'

'I never looked.' He moved the jewel closer to the merchant. 'What do *you* see in it?'

After a lengthy pause Camboy replied: 'A frightened boy who lives with his mother. She's a spirit guide, isn't she? Zelda, I believe?'

Sumner's jaw sagged.

'I also see you have a white card. Congratulations. And that you've been living off your father's savings all your life. And what's this? Sugar?'

Sumner squeezed down hard on the wrench, but that instant the edge of the desk whipped up and forward and caught him in the belly. The impact kicked the wind out of him and sent him hurtling backwards. The wrench and the jewel flew out of his grip, and he landed on his rump against the far wall.

The jewel dropped into Camboy's hand, and he held it between his fingers appreciatively.

Sumner's fury boiled up. The jubilant smile on the merchant's face burned into him, and he flung himself toward the desk with a howl. Camboy caught his striking hand without effort and twisted the thumb far back. With a squeal, Sumner submitted. Powerful hands bent him close to the desktop and thrumped his head against the wood several times—hard. 'The next time you lose control, I'll gouge out your eyes.' He shoved him back to the floor.

Sumner wanted desperately to restrain his rage and pain, but his eyes fogged and soon his grimy face was streaked with tears. He had been dominated, and the feeling was worse than the throb in his head or the deep, aching bruise inside his thumb.

'Get up,' Camboy ordered, his voice metallic.

Sumner pulled himself to his feet by the edge of the desk. Rising, he saw the secret insides of the panel that had struck him. He glimpsed a glint of metal and realized that Camboy, obviously using a foot pedal, could just as easily have released a slashing blade from the desk. He sat on the stool and tried to rub the pain out of his hand.

'You know, you're a lune to sell a jewel as fine as this,' Camboy said, opening a drawer. 'But seeing as you *are* a lune, I can't blame you for not being able to look at yourself. Here—' He counted out ten thousand zords in hundred-zord bills and threw the money onto the desk. 'Take what you asked for.'

Sumner was stunned. He forgot the pain and humiliation and just stared at the cash.

'Take it,' Camboy barked. 'You don't expect me to give you a sight draft. Brood jewels are illegal, you know.'

Sumner had never seen that much money before. Ten thousand zords would be enough for him and Zelda to live well for two years. He picked up the bills with excited fingers and backed out of the office.

On the street, he put the humiliation in Camboy's office out of his head and walked past the window shops feeling proud, eyeing goods he knew he could buy if it suited him. *Ten thousand zords! Mutra, that's enough to start my own shop.* He mused about business and the kind of work he would like to do. A restaurant was what he wanted. Only the best food.

He was pondering what he would have on his menu when three men in black hoods stepped out from an alley and surrounded him. It happened very quickly. One of the hoods was on either side of him, and when he stumbled back a pace they seized both his arms. He tried to yank himself free, but the third one drew a stiletto from his belt and held it to Sumner's throat. It broke the skin, and a trickle of blood threaded over his chest. His knees jellied, his legs trembled, and he felt a squelch in his bowels as he dumped in his pants.

Swiftly, the two men at his sides searched him. When they found the money, one of them shoved him backwards and another tripped him into the gutter. The next instant they were gone, running off into the maze of alleys behind the shops.

Sumner got shakily to his feet and looked around. The avenue was crowded as usual, and there were dozens of people staring at him.

Most of the faces were shocked, but a few were amused and almost jeering. 'Did you see the wad that dingo had on him?' he heard a woman say as he bolted into an alley.

He ran wildly. When he was exhausted he siled to his knees and leaned back against a lamp obelisk. The stench of his slimed pants fluffed around him, and he wept openly.

The Great Space Within

Sumner's stomach quivered as he remembered that day. Thinking about it had made him speed up angrily. Now he slowed and opened his window. The sun was proud over the blue-haze horizon, and there were watery heat mirages on the road. He wiped his sweat-lapped face with his sleeve.

No way that'll happen to me again, he insisted to himself. *I'll be dead before I'm a dingo.* But he wasn't so sure. What could he do now if the police suddenly appeared? *Suicide? Wog!* The thought disgusted him, but still it was less revulsive than the idea of getting caught.

Several times in the past hour he had seen distant strohlkraft glinting in the contrails of dawn. For the moment, the sky was empty, but half of it was blocked off by a wide arc of monolithic buttes. The buttes were bluff-red, streaked with draperies of black organic stains. He imagined a strohlkräft swinging out from the top of them and dropping in front of him to block his escape. *I'll ram it! I'll trash the car before I let them take me.*

His conviction comforted him, and after a while he relaxed again. Soon he was thinking back to the time he worked so remorselessly on his revenge.

He was sure that Parlan Camboy had set him up. *Who else knew about the zords? The secretary? Maybe. But he was a wiff.* It was Camboy that Sumner had wanted.

The day after he was robbed, he got a job painting traffic pyramids in center-city. Zelda was pleased with him, even though he never brought any of the money home. He told her he was paying off a debt. Actually, he was saving everything he earned. There were some expensive items the Sugarat needed.

Zelda was even more pleased at how her son was using his spare time. For hours on end he sat before the scansule with the door to his room open. He had nothing to hide. He was just a curious kid learning about electricity.

When he had enough money and all the information he needed, he stopped going to work and spent a day cruising McClure. He was looking for a desolate spot close to Camboy's office. He found one six blocks away: a wide courtyard separating two shipping warehouses. Down its middle ran a high chain-link fence so that only half the court was open to the street.

Three days later he had bought all the necessary material and had set his trap. Twice during those days he had almost killed himself. The first time was underground in the sewer that doubled as a conduit for the area's power lines. There, setting up a circuit breaker to tap into the trunk line, he had lost his grip on the thick wire. He had almost dumped the charged cable into the sludge he stood knee-deep in. The second time was after he had connected a lead-off line to the chain-link fence. When he tested it, one of the wires broke loose and snaked dangerously through the air. He caught it just as its hot end whipped toward him.

Although the risks were high, the reward promised to be measureless. Weeks had gone by without Sumner being able to eat properly. The slow acid of his rage had made it impossible for him to enjoy his food.

But he was patient. As soon as everything was in place he spent a day and a night on one of the warehouse roofs watching to make sure no one had seen him wire the fence. He had been careful to cut the power lines in the first few hours of morning. Within thirty minutes the lines were connected again with the circuit-switch attached. Still, he had to be certain that no one reported the brief blackout.

He watched the courtyard carefully from the roof. No inspectors or troubleshooters from the power company showed up that day. The next day, back in his room, Sumner took a leaf of the kiutl, rolled it into a cigarette, and smoked it. He gagged, but the aftertaste of the smoke had a pleasant nut flavor.

Zelda was out of the house, so he didn't bother to open a window. Through the coils of smoke he gazed around his room, waiting for the change to overtake him. Nothing happened. He sat back and finished the last of the cigarette.

It was necessary to be sure that Camboy had set him up. The only way to find out, he reasoned, was to look inside his head. *If this muckel really works.*

The greatest danger would come from the brood jewel, if it was still in the office. He would have to be careful not to get too close to it or his real intentions would be as prominent as his bellyroll.

A few minutes after he finished the cigarette an expansive calm settled over him. The light in the room brightened. Outside the window there was a gold-leaf sky. Furtive movements flicked at the edge of his vision, vanishing when he moved. He was sure the room was full of subtle turnings visible to any eyes less stubborn than his own.

A voice lilted in his ears (Yas, the islands be moving inward—the cliffs fall away), and he vaguely recognized it. It seemed to be coming from outside his door (Fore and aft, the cliffs of the fogbound Farallones), but it sounded like a whispering in the back of his head. He went over and opened his door. (The halyards are secure and the

61

mainsails still reefed.) Johnny Yesterday was standing in one of the large blue urns, his eyes closed (Bos'un! Bring arms aloft. Deck watch! Prepare cannon. Load grape!), his ears twitching.

Sumner suppressed a gleeful whoop and closed the door. (Action stations!) He was hearing Johnny Yesterday's thoughts. *Hau! The senile wheeze is playing admiral!* He laughed aloud (The hawsers—be they chanteyed tight?) and picked up the stuffed envelope on his desk. It was time to speak with Parlan Camboy. (If the sea wants you, lad, your time has come.)

Sumner rode the elevated train into center-city, not trusting himself to drive. Sitting in the metallic and captive air of the train, his envelope in his hand, his mind was overrun with sounds. The inner voices of everyone around him sweeled about his head.

It was an insane chorus that made it impossible to think. He looked down the aisle and fixed his mind on a young woman who was reading (How important is form?). She was small and shapely (Art, like society, requires a stringent discipline) with a defiant curl at the edge of her lips. He let his eyes trail down to her legs (Without it, we would lose ourselves in the squalor of the imagination) and linger on the curve of her calves. (However, do not make the timeless error of believing that form is necessarily definition.) There was a honey tone to them that excited him. (Narn! I knew that fat boy was staring at me.)

Sumner lifted his eyes quickly and caught an annoyed glance from the woman. *Fat boy!* The insult galled him, but his hurt was smothered by the sudden rush of muttering voices. For the rest of the trip he flicked his attention quickly from one passenger to another, avoiding any prolonged contact. By the time he stepped to the platform he had gotten used to keeping his mind moving and was able to hold the gibberish down to a distant chattering.

At Parlan Camboy's office the secretary was curt. 'What do you want now?' (Lard ball.)

Sumner bit back a curse and stepped up to the desk. 'I have something for Mr. Camboy.' He tore open the envelope he was holding and thrust it under the secretary's nose. It was a thick sheaf of kiutl—half of everything Jeanlu had given him.

(By Mutra's hind tit! Kiutl!) The secretary disguised his astonishment well. He got up, motioned Sumner to have a seat, and went into the office. Hard as he tried, Sumner couldn't pick up any thoughts from the next room. In a few minutes the door opened, and the secretary cheerfully beckoned him in.

Camboy already had a window open and the wooden stool before his desk. He was seated with his hands under his desk, and Sumner sensed that he was surrounded by hidden weapons. He looked around quickly for the brood jewel, but it wasn't in sight and he relaxed. (Looks nervous. Is he going to try something?)

He opened the envelope fully and scattered the dark red leaves on the desk. (It's voor muckel, all right.) 'I've got fifteen pounds of this,' he said, warming to see the disbelief in Camboy's eyes. (Fifteen? Where'd this dragass steal that much muckel?) 'My voor contact's been generous. But with my white card, I don't want to use this stuff. It might distort me. You're the only merchant I know who can move it.'

Camboy's eyes darkened. (Is he lying? If it's all as good as this stuff looks, that's three thousand, easy.)

Sumner kept his face empty.

'What'd you have to do for all this kiutl?' Camboy asked.

'I've been using my white card.'

'You must rut a lot of voors to earn that much kiutl.' He frowned. 'How much do you want?'

'A thousand zords.'

Camboy smiled. (A rube.) 'Five hundred.'

Sumner shook his head. 'A thousand. You can get three times that in the city fringes.'

(So he knows the market.) 'I'd have figured the ten I gave you last time would have held you over.' (Does he know? Look closely. His eyes are kind of vague. Is that a smile?)

'I lost it. I was pushed over.'

'Gambling?'

'No. On the street. After I left.'

Camboy shook his head, his voice filled with scorn. 'You had it all in one pocket. Right?'

'Ya. So what?'

'Kid, two dozen and one thieves watch this building day and night. A lot of money passes hands here. When you left, they saw the bulge in your pocket and they hit you.'

Sumner clenched his teeth and shook his head with feigned anger. 'I should have had you drop it. I was bonebrained to take the zords.' (He doesn't know. Good. We'll hit him a little harder this time.) 'This isn't my game. But I have the kiutl, and I want to unload it. The zords are important—I'm sick of screwing distorts. You'll give me a thousand?'

Camboy let himself be persuaded. 'When will you bring it by?'

'I'm not,' Sumner answered with finality. 'I got bruised once in this neighborhood. If you want the fifteen pounds, you'll pick it up where I tell you, tonight at midnight.'

(He knows. Why try to lure me away—except to jooch me? Should I dump him now?) Sumner hurriedly told him about the courtyard. 'It's wide open, so you can see me and I can see you.'

Camboy thought about it a moment: (I know that place. It's perfect. Close enough to keep an eye on the hit, and if it's a setup, there's room to move.) 'All right. We'll do it. Tonight at midnight.' He opened his drawer and took out some bills to pay for the kiutl on his desk.

'Don't bother,' Sumner said indifferently. 'That's just a sample. We'll do real business tonight.' He turned and walked out, hearing as he left: (Nobody *gives* away muckel—unless there's plenty more. What a slimwit.)

Alone on the street, Sumner was elated. He stopped for a moment on the steps and beamed seraphically at the squat stone buildings around him. It was dark and the lux-globes on the corners were lit. Most of the shops were closed, and there were only a few merchants in their mushroom-colored longcoats striding down the avenue. Overhead the skyfires were waving, their ghostly sheets of green and yellow muted by the city lights.

A gap of five hours lay between him and his appointment with Camboy, and he decided to spend two or three of them in a cozy tavern. But as he stepped out onto the street he changed his mind. The kiutl was still with him. Though the street appeared virtually empty, his heightened senses picked out a crowd of churning minds that ranged the length of the avenue.

None of the thoughts he felt around him were distinct, but he knew they were there. He could hear their sibilant mumblings in the shadows of narrow alleys and in the darkened doorways on both sides of the street. Malefic, hissing whispers streamed through his mind as he traipsed down the avenue. The darkness seemed to heighten them, and soon he no longer pretended to be indifferent. He scuttled from corner to corner, trying to stay in the pools of light.

You're acting like a drool-mouth, he told himself, wanting to ease the apprehension coiling tighter in his gut. *It's the kiutl. Just pimps and whores your mind's picking up. Nothing to wet your pants about.* He forced himself to slow down to an easy amble. About five blocks ahead was a blaze of gold light. It was the center-city Mall and the northside of the Berth. The area was always crowded with students and people out for a good time. Two music halls, a theater, and a string of amusement stands circled the Mall. Gusts of laughter and music breezed down the street. The wind carried the aromas of barbecued fish and fresh, steaming breads, and Sumner forgot the mind-squabble in the shadows and quickened his step again.

From out of a cloister of shadows to his right, a bulky man swerved. He was half a block away and heading straight for him, arms swinging wide at his side. Sumner flinched but wasn't sure what to do. He didn't want to run wildly down the street, and there were no stores open to slip into. The man wasn't carrying a weapon, and he wasn't actually threatening him.

He had decided to stay calm and keep walking when a voice crackled in his mind: (If that jiggle-belly squeals, I'll crack his head—I swear I'll bust him open.)

Aow! Sumner pulled up. He turned to skip across the road, but it

64

was too late. The stranger was shuffling urgently toward him, leaning close to the curb, ready to cut off his run.

Sumner dashed anyway, and the man lunged forward and caught him by the shoulder. Sumner spun around and nearly fell to the pavement. In the halflight from a lamp obelisk, he saw that the stranger had broad shoulders, a square nose, thin lips crusted like a lizard, and there, between his flat eyes, the X-brand from a drone strap.

Sumner whined, backing off. He lurched into the street, his eyes fixed on the angry features of the dorga. His legs were stiffening, and in a moment he knew he was going to lose his nerve and freeze. The dorga came at him, and Sumner wobbled backwards. A screech and a squawling horn staggered him. A car yawing around the corner slashed by, missing him by inches and cutting off the dorga's advance.

'Clot-heads!' the driver yelled, but Sumner barely heard him. He had already pivoted and was scrambling down the street.

He raced toward the Mall until he was sure the dorga wasn't following him; then he stopped to gather his strength. The sudden rush of adrenalin sharpened the effect of the kiutl, and a distant roar of voices swept over him. The chattering was loudest toward the Mall, so he rounded a corner and slumped off into the shadows.

Sticking close to the walls, senses alert, he hurried from street to street until he had made it to the courtyard where he was to meet Camboy. His head was snapping with sounds, and though the night was warm he was shivering.

This part of town was truly deserted, and gradually the static in his mind subsided. Feeling better, he climbed a series of fire ladders to the roof of an adjacent warehouse. From there he could look out over the city. To the south was the bay, splattered with the red and blue lights of the fishing fleet. The waterfront was dark and peaceful. A strohlkraft grumbled overhead. When its drone faded, another nightmurmur followed—a freight train clanking along the curve of the bay, its boxcars empty, the bay lights winking through them. It was a sleepy, melancholy scene, and he lay back on the cool stones to rest. Above him the skyfires fluttered.

He was glad to be off the streets, glad to have gotten away from that dorga. He understood then that the kiutl was affecting him more profoundly than he had at first thought. Even now, as he lay face up, his body heat leaking into the stones below him, he could feel its strange chemistry in his blood. His heart was rattling and his leg muscles jumping with more than just dread-energy.

After he closed his eyes and breathed deeply for a few minutes, his muscles calmed down and a languid wonder composed him. His mind was empty. The sky above him had a weight, a reality he had never before experienced. It was holding him securely in place. And though

65

it was keeping his eyelids pressed tight, he was grateful for its embrace.

Thoroughly at ease, he looked into the great space within himself and confronted the clouded presences drifting there. A wafer of light separated from the mistings and shimmered before him. It pulsed with his breathing and slowly coalesced to a scene.

It was a gullied, packed-dirt alley with rust-streaked walls. At the far end, under a boast of light, two men were struggling. It was a woeful fight. One man was already on his knees, trying to protect his neck. The other was slugging him viciously on the back of the head, again and again. The kneeling man keeled over, and Sumner glimpsed a wretched look on his face before the other man stooped over him and started plundering his pockets. When he was done he rose and turned, and a whine curled in Sumner's throat. It was the dorga he had just escaped.

He struggled to wake, but his efforts only drew him closer to the bigboned face. Helpless, he watched as the flat eyes and the dark, cracked lips flecked with spit loomed closer. A spasm of fear wrenched through him (Broke him open—damn chit-eater), and suddenly he was seeing and hearing inside the dorga's head.

(What've I got here?) He had crumpled bills, some change, and a few personal trinkets in his hand. The bills and change he stuffed in his pocket. The trinkets he gazed at, turning them over and over, considering them like a lune. (What're these fart-cutters?) Lodge-key, starter chip, dental floss dispenser, and gold charm engraved: *You will live as long as you love—Estella.* (Pig-eyed chit-eater.) He threw away everything but the gold charm. (Wasn't worth the trouble. Got to knock somebody else now. Gotz! I should've slammed that fat boy coming out of Commerce. He'd a had something. Eat like that, got to have something.)

Sumner's insides jumped when he saw his own fear-stretched face in the dorga's mind. He snapped his eyes open. The smoky green skyfires hung overhead. He was back in his body, his fear a hot wire in his stomach. He still couldn't move. For a while he strained, trying to coax his muscles into action, but it was hopeless. The whole weight of the sky was on him. At last he submitted and just lay there staring up through the pressure to where lights were unfolding and vanishing across the blackness.

After his fear dissolved he felt dispirited, vacant as a bone. His flesh was stitched to the cold stones underneath, and he had lost his peripheral vision. The billowing colors were all he could see, and they dazzled him. When he closed his eyes they were still there, vaulting through the great space that was his mind: *How open a man's mind is, after all. A huge stadium. Wide open. Ready to be filled with anything that drops into it.*

Vertigo and fear seized him. Colors vapored, his center fell away again, and he soared. Depthless silence surrounded him and increased his apprehension. *Get a hold!* he bawled. *Get a hold!* The

66

burning sky was rushing through the cavernous space inside him, and he clutched at random thoughts (if the sea wants you, lad), images (a gullied, packed-dirt alley)—*Anything! Get ahold of anything!* Honey-toned legs: long and slinky—it was the woman he had seen on the train, the one with the shapely legs, muscles pliant, not rippling with the vibrations of the car. At the moment their gazes met he had flinched. Her eyes were gray as cement, cold as newsprint. Her life was private and sealed.

Then.

But now—now the whole lucid, vacuous sky was falling through him. He was wide open.

Clarity. He exhaled softly. He was voided—vast and hollow as a cathedral. His dread subsided. The gentle composure he had known before was coming back, and with it came the face of the woman he had seen on the train. It floated before him, pale and slender as a gas. There was nothing private or sealed about it now.

He immediately recognized the indifference of her eyes as a defense. With his present lucidity there was no trouble facing them or even approaching and sliding past them. Behind the arched cheekbones and the defiant curl of lips, she was light and soft, almost watery.

An irresistible anxiety nailed him when he realized that he wasn't just imagining this. His mind had found this woman somewhere in the city and now he was inside her. He could hear the deep sound of her blood—wump-wump-ump—um-wump—like the deep bass tocking of a frog. Her thoughts were nebulous, a diffused sepia light swirling sporadically into dark tide pools, blood-red, fierce.

Sumner couldn't tell what was happening to her at first. *Is she scared? Angry?* He was disoriented until the beating of her heart quickened to an unreal tempo. Then he heard it for what it was. Not her heart at all but—the thump of a bed. *Hau! She's rutting!* A nerve-shearing pang of orphaned loneliness and rage stabbed him. *I don't want to feel her rut,* he cried to himself. Nonetheless, a hot weaseling between his legs urged him to linger, and he had to struggle to pull himself away. As he withdrew, her body climaxed, and a windburst of feathered light and radiant petals surrounded him.

When he was himself again, the sky pressing down, fusing him to the cool rock, his muscles were tightsewn, angry. He felt gnarled with lust, shabby, smelling of sweat. An afterimage idled among the mistings inside his eyelids: rounded shadows of buttocks and breasts, glimpsed quickly as he had spun away.

Again he tried to get up, but he was held down, this time it seemed not by the sky but by the jealous anger locked in his muscles. He kept his eyes closed, uneasy about looking again into the furling skyfires. And soon he was drifting, too irate to care where the telepathic drug was taking him.

An animal face wheeled out of the darkness and stopped to

confront him. It was a wolf, its eyes crystal-bright, silver hairs radiating off its muzzle, shifting with an animated lucency. The jewel eyes, too savage to know fear, watched him, taut with purpose. The gaze was vast as star-silence.

Transfixed by it, Sumner's anger shriveled. Immediately the sharp lines of the wolf's face unknotted, became transparent, and another face was revealed. It was his own. Seeing its beefy shape, the cheeks paunched around the small, squat nose, the jaw slack, the eyes moist and edgy, he recoiled and churned awake, sweat-soaked and trembling.

With a whimper of surprise and relief he saw that he was sitting up. The paralysis had passed. And though his muscles were heavy and soft as wet sand and his insides were icy with fear, he was able to pull himself to his feet. It was then that he sensed more time had passed than he thought. The Goat Nebula was burning brightly in the west. In a short while it would be midnight.

Sumner was grateful that he had been meticulous in his preparations, for he was too hollowed out now to think. Everything he needed was already positioned and tested. All that remained was timing and, as usual, luck. A lot of luck.

After a few minutes of walking tight circles to limber his legs and loosen the fisted muscles in his back, he clambered down the fire ladders. The trickster-sack he had prepared was waiting in the shadowed alcove where he had left it. The sack was burlap and bulky, as if it did contain fifteen pounds of kiutl. He lugged it across the courtyard, staying close to the chain-link fence. The kiutl had thinned out of his blood. The dense shadows draping the buildings around him were empty of inner voices, but he knew that he was being watched. The presence of other people was palpable as blood. In the center of the courtyard, the fence had a gate that he had jimmied hours before. He checked the lock to be certain it would open, and then he turned to face the street.

There were some fugitive movements in a splash of shadows a hundred meters away. Then stillness. He kept his eyes slack, looking for any movement. Veils of light from spotlights at either end of the fence illuminated the whole courtyard. Even the roofs were visible, and he kept a good eye on them in case sniping was to be part of the game.

Abruptly the shadows came alive. A pack of angry dogs charged across the court. Close behind them were five men in hoods. Sumner was surprised by the dogs, and he barely had enough time to get through the gate and pull his cumbersome sack after him. On the other side, he looped the chain through and locked the gate as the dogs snapped wildly at his fingers. Done, he plodded off with the sack in his arms.

At the fence the hoods mumbled curses and pulled out guns. When they fired there was no noise. Metal clattered at his heels, and then a barb of pain twisted in his shoulder. He reached back and tore loose a dart. A watery white liquid was oozing out of it. *Poison?* he was wondering when another dart slammed into him. He yanked it from his buttock quickly, before all the toxin could be injected. For once he was grateful to be bulky. *They've got to get a lot of that sap in me before I go down.*

He glanced over his shoulder and saw that all five hoods were scaling the fence. He kept one eye on them and one on the manhole a few meters away. He had uncovered it earlier, and now he prayed his timing would be right. The sack was more clumsy than he had expected, and he had to let it go early. By the time he squeezed through the manhole and dropped into the fetid atmosphere of the sewer, one of the hoods was over the fence and scrambling toward him.

He fumbled with the protective cloth he had thrown over the circuit breaker and threw the switch. There were no screams, just the clatter of shoes as the one hood who had made it over ran up to the manhole. Sumner splashed into the darkness, groping for the penlight he had brought along. He got it out and flicked it on in time to see the fork in the conduit.

Behind him the hood had splashed into the duct and was kicking through the water, the glint of a knife in his hand. At the fork Sumner stopped running and bent down, his light stabbing left and right. He had left a canister near here hours ago, but the wash of sludge at his knees was stronger now than before. The canister had been knocked over. He sloshed the slimy water until his fingers closed on a slick metal handle. As he lifted it out, he broke the cork seal and let the gasoline gush into the running stream.

The hood was closing in on the fork in the conduit when he smelled the fuel. Without waiting for Sumner to ignite it, he scurried back the way he had come.

Sumner rushed deeper into the duct. Farther on he found the exit manhole he had prepared. Whatever the stunner darts had hit him with was beginning to work. He was feeling drowsy and nauseous. Still he had enough strength to haul himself out of the sewer.

He came out at the far end of the courtyard and could see the chain-link fence. Four bodies were hanging on it. Below them a shower of sparks was dropping off the gate hinges where the metal resistance varied. The dogs were moving in slow circles, whining forlornly.

All the streetlamps and warehouse lights were out. The whole area was dark except for the flashings at the fence. Even so, Sumner was able to spot the one hood who had chased him. He had gone back up the manhole and retrieved the sack Sumner had left behind. He had thrown it over his shoulder and was huddling across the courtyard to a narrow gate. In a few moments, the lock clacked open, and he was through.

Sumner grinned evilly. The sack contained fifteen pounds of explosives wrapped in a thin sheet of kiutl leaves. It was rigged to explode when it was opened.

After the hood was gone, Sumner walked slowly over to the fence and stared at the bodies. Three of them were draped over the top and one was dangling by a leg. All of them were smoking. A nauseating odor of burnt cloth and flesh roiled around them. Where metal buttons or zippers touched the fence, sparks were sporadically shooting out and pattering to the ground.

Sumner took the can of spraypaint from where he had hidden it in a corner of the court. With a sweeping, inspired arm, he scrawled on the asphalt: SUGARAT.

He turned and swayed across the yard to a back gate that he had left open. His car was parked a few blocks away. After napping a couple of hours to wear down the dart-toxin, he was ready for the Tour.

The next day he tuned his scansule into the current-events station. There was a weather report, a catalogue of ships that had arrived during the night, an account of an unexplained blackout in the business district, and a report of an explosion that had gutted the offices of Camboy Shipping. Mr. Camboy and two unidentified persons had been killed in the blast.

Teeth Dreams

Sumner stretched contentedly, savoring a straight run of clean road. The last time he had looked, there had been a flowing stream alongside him, cutting grooves, scoops, and potholes in the rock. But while he had been immersed in his memories it had thinned to a rill, then a trickle, then flat land cracked and shrunken in the sun.

Spires and arcs of windeaten stone blazed an electric green beneath the strong sun, and large cloudshadows migrated over the desert floor. In the inflamed distance, far to the northwest, an isolated storm raged over the Flats: It was a mass of purple clouds, veined with lightning, trawling curtains of rain.

The sway of the terrain was a drowse, and he didn't see the stranger standing in the road until he was less than a hundred meters away. The figure stood motionless in a calligraphy of shadows. All Sumner could see of him was a serape of wild harlequin colors and a beat-up brown leather hat with its wide brim set low over his face. Sumner decided not to stop. There was something belligerent about the way he wore his hat and the way he was standing, feet wide apart, hands hidden beneath the serape. *A convoy pirate!* Sumner thought. He floored the accelerator and bent low over the wheel.

Suddenly a whine highpitched from the rear of the car, and the console lights went out. Sumner pumped the accelerator furiously. He yanked the starter chip out and slammed it back in. He pounded on the steering wheel and kicked the console, but all in vain. The car slowed down remorselessly, gliding gently over the road. It came to a stop exactly where the stranger stood.

Wog!

Sumner groped for the tire iron under his seat, but before he could heft it the stranger's hands appeared from under the serape. He was holding a short silver-gold sword with a thin curved blade. Adroitly he twirled it from hand to hand.

He stepped to the side so that Sumner had a clear view through his open window. Then he took an orange from beneath his serape and rolled it into the air. With a blurred flourish, his thin sword crisscrossed the fruit, and juice sparked in the sunlight. The stranger snapped the sword back into its scabbard, letting the still-whole orange drop into his palm.

He walked over to Sumner and offered him the fruit. Sumner wiped his sweat-runneled face on his sleeve and reached out to accept it. The orange opened like a blossom in his hand.

He looked up at the man to search out his face, a squelchy pain twisting his bowels. He was a big mongrel with the feral air of a dorga renegade. His skin was dark and taut, minutely etched with fine, nervelike wrinkles at the corners of his mouth and eyes. Both his ears were bone-pierced, and his natty hair twisted out from beneath the brim of his hat in spikes and loops. His good left eye was meat-colored and curiously slanted. The empty socket of his right eye was fitted with a shard of mirror, a luminous hole in a rippled, glossy scar that flared from his scalp to the corner of his mouth.

'I'm Nefandi,' he said in accented Massel. His voice was coarse as his face, but there was a humorous glint in his one eye. He reached out quickly and grabbed Sumner by the ears. Sumner tried to pull away, but Nefandi had a firm hold. He squeezed the boy's ears as he brought his eye up close. Sumner tried not to flinch as the dark features pressed near enough for him to see jaundiced smoke in the one eye. A balmy mix of sweat and some musky fragrance like champaca misted around him. Abruptly Nefandi let him go and helped himself to a wedge of the orange in Sumner's hand.

Sumner tried to gather his wits, but the squelchy feeling in his bowels had become an urgent cramp. 'I'm Sumner Kagan. I—'

'Pleased,' Nefandi acknowledged, taking another piece of orange. He grinned crazily, his mouth stuffed with fruit.

Sumner squeezed his thighs together to suppress a diarrheic shiver. 'My car—'

'Small machine to drag this far into the desert. Where you going?'

'Uh, nowhere right now. It stalled on me.' Sumner clenched his whole body to keep from soiling himself. 'I have to dump,' he said meekly.

'Go ahead, radoo. You might as well be at ease.'

Nefandi opened the car door and pulled Sumner by an ear. 'Right this way, tud. Haul it out.' His hands playfully squeezed Sumner's shoulders, arms, and belly as he guided him from the car.

Outside, Sumner scurried off between two talons of green rock, tugged his pants down, and squatted. Nefandi watched him for a moment and then looked around warily. His hand was beneath his serape, clutching the haft of his sword. He wondered if he should kill the fat boy. His eyes filtered the sky along the horizon. It was empty, and his hand relaxed. *There's still time*, he told himself.

His right eye—the mirrored one—was fitted with a sensex that could scan the full electromagnetic spectrum. To the southeast he had seen several infrared spots. Those would be strohlkraft—and that would explain the weak radio noise from there.

He swept the horizon again, slower, with the sensex open to the

72

biospectral range. East, there was an orange haze from the plantlife outside the Flats. North and west, there was nothing, just the lifeless stretches of Rigalu Flats. The green terrain looked gray in the sensex. The only bioresponse was a faint pink efflorescence low in the sky from the interaction of airborne bacteria.

He looked west again. Static prickled over his cheek and brow as he strained the sensex to its limits. He was looking for psynergy, the lifeforce. A dim blue energy glowed for an instant over the gray waste. It was about forty kilometers away. Perhaps it was the voorchild he had been sent to destroy.

Since he had been dropped into Rigalu Flats, he had been sensing a strong psynergy in the area. He felt it as a furtive muscular sensation, definitely biospectral in nature, but until now he hadn't been able to see it or accurately assess its proximity.

Biospectral energy, psynergy or kha, as the voors called it, permeated everything. That was how he had first spotted Sumner—a scarlet pinpoint in the distance. When the car was in sight he had known by its shimmering luster that it wasn't going to slow down. So he stalled its engine with the field-inducer in the haft of his sword.

Was it worth it? he wondered, knowing that every time he used the inducer he revealed his exact location to every timeloose distort in the desert.

He allowed himself a moment to clear his mind. Clarity, he knew, was his only hope of finding the voor he was stalking. After two days of circling through this ghost city he was nerve-weary and dreamy, and he gazed down into the dust patina of his boots, hoping to drain his mind.

Nefandi was an artificial man, designed and bioengineered by the eo, a powerful technocracy four thousand kilometers to the north. There, a dreamworld had intrigued into reality—a world without distorts, dissatisfactions, or death. It was an outpost of a cosmic empire vaster than human thought, where the starkest pleasures were open to everyone. Nefandi's favorite rapture was coobla, a drugless midbrain stimulator that cramped him with bliss.

Psyfactored by his creators to emphasize pleasure over indivi- duation, Nefandi had known the immense ravishment of coobla countless times and was always irreplete without it. He was a total product of his society. His body had been grown by the eo in the id forest outside the biotectured city of Cleyre to serve as an ort, a handservant. He remembered nothing of his time as an ort, for only his body had existed then. Centuries later, after those whom he had been created to serve no longer needed him, the eo allowed his mind to emerge. He lived free for a time while the eo watched to see what he would be useful for. He could have traveled and explored the world that had created him. He could have devoted himself to the immense culture around him and expanded his awareness and his social value.

But his psyfactoring was stronger than his free will, and he gave himself over to coobla, the beatitude of nervelocked joy.

A lifetime of unmitigated delight slunk by before his common resources were spent and the eo took the coobla from him. To return to his ecstasy trance he needed a benefactor, someone who had a use for him and who could pay with coobla. And that was why he served the godmind called the Delph.

The Delph at one time had been the strongest being on the planet. A century before Nefandi was created, the Delph had a span of will huge as the earth. He was the gateway to the multiverse, and the contours of the manifested world were the shape of his whim. This was so because the Delph had been able to receive and conduct the subtle psynergy radiating from the galactic core. But the psynergy he relied on was directional and shifting. As starpatterns changed, the galactic psynergy slimmed, and the Delph had become again no more than a man. He was still the Delph in title, and he souled a technology unmatched anywhere on the planet, yet his only real power was his mystery.

To protect himself against godminds with other sources of power until his own starchanneled psynergy returned, he shaped Nefandi into a killer. For many years now, Nefandi had been fulfilling the Delph's will by stalking timeloose distorts, rogue eo, and voors whose psychic reach fringed on godmind. At the completion of each kill he returned to Cleyre or Nanda or Reynii and was allowed to lose himself again in coobla for a few years.

That was Nefandi's story: pleasure as fetish. And why not? he often pondered. Who was he anyway?—a motherless, fatherless ort. Consciousness was delirium, he had come to believe, and sometimes he frenzied himself wondering if he was whole or if his soul was just hunger. *Useless to ponder. Destiny is too huge to be held by any one mind.*

Thoughts and hunger thinned away from Nefandi as he relaxed himself, and he sensed once more a strong, steady pulse of kha somewhere to the west. He looked about, but there was nothing to see.

Kha sometimes was elusive, especially in the blue regions. The shorter the wavelength, the more advanced the intelligence behind it. Usually. The sun in the biospectral range looked dazzlingly blue. Kiutl plants and harpy eagles were also blue. So were voors.

Humans glowed with a shifting yellow-green. Which is why he finally decided not to kill the fat boy. Sumner's kha was sunburst gold. *His soma's strong and unmarred,* Nefandi could see as Sumner pulled his pants over his broad, quavering buttocks. *Senseless to destroy such a rare creature.*

When he had first grabbed Sumner's ears, he had felt the pulse in his throat and fingered the glands there. The boy had a strong heart, and though he was overweight, it was a layered obesity. The adipose

74

tissue cells had not yet begun to break the fascial symmetry of his body. So it was clear that it was a neurotic and not a biological problem. Helping him out of the car, Nefandi had probed a few neural ganglia and had tried to release some of the somatic tension locked in the surrounding muscles. It was useless. Beneath the fat, the boy was tight as brick.

As he cinched his pants, Sumner thought of bolting, but the idea was zaned. He would never survive the walk back to McClure. He would be easy prey for the hind rats and the poison lizards, and that thought urged him back to the car.

Nefandi was eating the orange that Sumner had left on the console. He spoke around the fruit: 'I want you to take me to your voors.'

Sumner stiffened, and the breath of a lie snagged in his throat: Nefandi was fingering the Eye of Lami that had been dangling inside his car, the sun flashing like wisdom in his mirror-eye.

'The car's bust,' Sumner mumbled.

Nefandi grinned, and one hand slipped beneath his serape. The car jumped to a start.

Sumner's heart shook. 'Who are you?'

'There's a lot to tell. Get in the car.'

Sumner stooped in and squeezed behind the steering wheel. Nefandi threw his hat in the back and eased into the passenger seat. He leaned close to Sumner, and his breath was hot and dark: 'Tell me everything about the voors.'

Sumner shrugged and stepped on the accelerator. 'They're just some friends I have down the road.'

'Voors are never friends.'

Sumner flinched at the animosity in Nefandi's voice.

'Voors look after themselves.' Nefandi finished the orange and hurled the skin out the window. 'They're a brood. That's what they call themselves. Not tribe or family. A brood.'

His voice was sharp, and Sumner tried to change the subject. 'How'd you get out here?'

'It wouldn't mean a croc to you.' Nefandi spit a seed out the window. 'Tell me about the voors.'

'A woman and her boy,' Sumner muttered. 'Jeanlu and Corby. She makes charms.'

'And the boy? Is he timeloose?'

Sumner frowned ignorantly.

'Does the child have deep mind?' Nefandi pressed. 'Does he have powers?'

Sumner shrugged, and the one-eyed man punched him in the ear. 'Tell me!' The car swayed, and Nefandi put one hand on the wheel and the other on Sumner's throat. 'And don't lie.'

Sumner gagged a stiff breath and rasped: 'Corby's strong.'

Nefandi released him and sat back, a shade of satisfaction in his eye.

75

Shame congested Sumner's breathing, and his vision darkened. He debated taking advantage of what little power he had. One sudden swerve at the right moment and both of them would pass Beyond quickly. *Would that be better?* He faced Nefandi and saw himself in the mirror-eye. He was surprised to see that there was no fear in his reflection. The bright beads that were his eyes gazed tonelessly above his chubby cheeks. He was pleased with himself, for he knew that this man might kill him.

Nefandi took out a cheroot and lit it. The sharp, mousy odor of the car and of the boy was nauseating even with the windows open. It made it harder to believe that such a unique kha belonged to this corpulent creature. *Radiant gold,* he marveled. *No doubt he has a white card.*

'You fathered Corby, didn't you?' he asked, and the boy's tight silence was his answer. He watched the rolls of fat in Sumner's legs and hips jiggling with the vibrations of the car. *All hunger and fear.* 'Why're you going back?'

'I need zords.'

'You mean kiutl and brood jewels.' He turned his face into the windowdraft for a drag of fresh air. The road arced out of the Flats, and they passed a draw whose canyon walls were shimmering with cottonwood, tamarisk, and willow. Then they were riding into the green ruins again, and he pulled his head back in.

'I'm a voor-killer, tud. Corby may be the one I'm looking for.' Nefandi took a long draw on his cheroot and let the smoke snake through his nostrils. 'I'm telling you this because you may have to help me. And if you balk, I'll kill you.'

Sumner's knuckles blanched on the steering wheel. 'Who are you?'

'I've been sent here by the Delph, an old Power—the same Power which first shaped the Massebôth Protectorate. We watch over what's left of humanity and keep the voors and distorts from overpopulating.' He tongued a smoke ring. 'If you cooperate with me, I'll reward you well.'

The terror slackened to fear in Sumner, and he seemed to sink into his seat. 'What can I do?'

'For now, just drive.'

Nefandi hung his head out of the window again, and Sumner relaxed his grip on the wheel. He fetched about for a casual comment and settled for a question to fill the silence: 'Can you tell me what all this is?'

Nefandi leaned out of the draft. 'What?'

'Rigalu Flats. What is it?'

'An ancient city, nuh?'

'But why's it green? And why's it glow?'

Nefandi worked the cheroot to the corner of his mouth. 'The green comes from salts and halides like plutonium oxychloride and sodium and ammonium diuranates. The night glow is solar-excited zinc sulfide. And the rigidity and aridity are a result of the subquantal displacement of the hot waste that was spewed all over here.'

Sumner's look was blank as an egg.

'Rigalu Flats was a kro city once,' Nefandi went on. 'One of the largest on the continent. But the quakes and the raga storms leveled it overnight. The nuclear reactors, and there were lots of them, were just so much cardboard in the wind.'

'Reactors?'

'Power stations. The Massebôth have outlawed them. The kro used radioactive material just to heat water to run turbines. Smallvisioned, no? This whole area was hot.' He flicked ash into the mess at his feet. 'And it would have stayed hot for tens of thousands of years.'

Sumner grunted. 'That was stupid. Who cleaned it up?'

'The Delph before he was fully developed. This was the best he could do at the time.'

'Tell me about the people who lived here.'

'The kro were like the Massebôth. Like all people.' He bit down on his cheroot and spoke through his teeth. 'A hot fuse of ambitions and ideas burning from generation to generation. Victims of memory.'

'But who were they?'

Nefandi took out his cheroot and studied the glowing end. 'They liked football.' He nudged the cold ash to the floor. 'Of course, there was more time for amusement in those days. Distorts were rare, and there were no voors at all. North was south for the kro—' Nefandi broke off. The road had swung out of the Flats a little ways back. Now they were winding past isolate pinyon and solitary junipers in a haunted landscape of sandstone knobs, domes, turrets, and coves.

Sumner followed Nefandi's gaze, and then he saw it too. Behind a loose wall of scrag was a hefty pangolin. It was eyeing them pugnaciously, pawing the ground and snorting.

'Moody beast,' Nefandi whispered. 'This must be its backyard.'

Sumner slowed down and began to pull to the side.

'No,' Nefandi warned. 'It's going to attack whether we stand still or move. Hold to the middle of the road. There's less chance of breaking an axle. And don't slow down.'

Sumner was going to object, but that instant the short sword seemed to fly to Nefandi's hand. Sumner leaned forward and gripped the wheel with all his strength.

When they passed the pangolin, it lunged at them across the highway. Sumner wanted to speed up, but the road was particularly broken down along this stretch, and he knew he would lose control if he went too fast. His head whipped back and forth as he tried to watch both the road and the pangolin.

'Just drive,' Nefandi ordered. 'Keep your speed steady. And when I tell you, brake hard.'

The pangolin galloped up to the driver's side, dipped its head, and charged.

'Now!' Nefandi cried, but Sumner was afraid to slow down. He floored the accelerator—too late. The tough bottlenose rammed into the door. Sumner fought the steering wheel as the car swerved violently toward an escarpment. His right fender squealed against the rocks, then pulled away. But before he could get control of the car the pangolin, its brass-red scales rippling with its run, charged again. With an explosive screech the fender tore away and went winging out of sight. Sumner pulled hard on the wheel. The car swayed sickeningly and eased back to the middle of the road.

'Do what I say!' Nefandi barked. 'Hold it steady—steady!'

The pangolin rumbled alongside and dipped its head for another charge. 'Brake!'

The wheels whined, and the car jolted to a stop and stalled. Nefandi was pushed up against the windshield, and he saw the pangolin first. It had glanced off the front of the car and was doubling back to charge again. 'Get this shoebox moving!'

Sumner was frantic. His hands fumbled with the starter chip. Twice the engine misfired; then, as the pangolin was swinging toward them, the car bolted off. The ram-nose caught the rear fender, and the car swiveled to one side, then righted itself.

Sumner thought he could feel the beast's charge through the seat of his pants, but Nefandi urged him not to go too fast. The pangolin came up on the passenger side, and Sumner waited anxiously for Nefandi's cue to brake. He didn't want to look. He heard the creature's heavy grunting, and the dust kicked up by its clawed hooves hazed around him, and that was enough. He locked his eyes on the road and keyed himself for Nefandi's order. The order never came. The pangolin bent forward for the ram, and Nefandi's arm lashed out through the window. The flat of the sword slapped the beast's eye, and it collapsed in an explosion of dust.

'Relax,' Nefandi said, his sword vanishing again under the serape. Sumner pried his hands off the wheel and glanced back. The pangolin had rolled to its feet and was shrugging itself off, watching after them glumly.

'Mutra, that was close,' Sumner said, his voice cracking.

Nefandi took out another cheroot. As he lit it Sumner noticed how steady his hands were, and he gnawed his lower lip jealously.

Nefandi took a moment to gather his thoughts. He was grateful that he hadn't had to activate the sword. Surprise was an essential element in stalking voors. But the boy's fear had almost cost him. The crumbling road was dipping back into the Flats. A four-winged dragonfly tapped against the door, then pulled up and vanished as the green sand hissed beneath the tires.

'You've got to learn to be steady-fingered, tud.'

Sumner nodded, wiping the sweat off his face with his sleeve. He glanced over his shoulder to be sure the pangolin wasn't following.

'I said "learn." I hope you noticed.' He took a few puffs on the cheroot and then wedged it into the console so that its smoke coiled between them. 'It's natural to be scared when you're threatened. You've got to teach yourself to be calm. The secret is separating the facts from the teeth dreams.'

Sumner pursed his lips and flicked a questioning look at him.

'You know what I mean,' Nefandi said, his voice like jagged metal. 'Static thoughts. Nervous fantasies. Nightmare-gnashed molars. Teeth dreams.'

'I know,' Sumner said cautiously.

'You're tripping over your own shadow. Relax.'

Sumner bobbed his head. He wanted very much to change the subject. 'This Power that cleaned up Rigalu Flats—the Delph. What created it?'

Nefandi didn't respond. He gazed out the window, sucking meditatively on his cheroot. Sumner sensed that their conversation was over, and he gnawed his lip and turned his stare toward the plated curves of the road. Ahead, vision doubled in the heat scheming over the rocks.

To their left, dunes of chrome-green sand sloped around sleek, storm-polished arches. On the right, two hundred meters of chalk rock leaned over them. Spangles of fire grass, cane, and salt cedar covered the skull-rocks.

The turn-off appeared from around a tight bend. Sumner wheeled into it, swung the car into an alcove of big-boled trees and killed the engine. The scene beyond the trees was nightmared. The adobe cottage with the coral swayback roof was barely recognizable behind veils of dodder and vetch that had swarmed over its walls. The bottoms of the flower troughs beneath the windows had fallen out, dried mud clotted the cedar steps, and the roof was tattered, missing most of its tiles. The crater pool and the blue-roofed hut couldn't be seen through the miasmic vapors that were steaming softly out of the ground at the side of the cottage. Sumner's heart sank.

But Nefandi was excited. Fear and eagerness competed in him as he opened the car door. The muscular sensation that had been haunting him for days lay all around him. There were definitely voors nearby, and he clutched his sword as he stepped out. Manhigh grass, crackled and yellow, swayed over what was once a garden. The white sand beds in front of the cottage were banked against the walls and littered with dead leaves.

In the shade, he noticed, the land was not dried out but was black and glistening. He looked at the ground around him and saw that it wasn't mud that was catching the light but glossy black worms.

Patches of them were everywhere, crawling and writhing in the shadows. A movement made him look up. It was smoke—no, it was a breeze of flies swarming out of the trees and swooping toward him.

His hand under the serape quickly twisted the hilt of his sword. The weak field that came on around him deflected the swarm, but a few of the more savage flies got through and stung his flesh. He killed one of them. It was long and sick green with huge mouthparts and red eyes.

The fear in him overcame his eagerness, and he looked around carefully. Queer fungi sprouted on all the trees, and an iridescent sheen glazed many of the limbs and trunks. The yellow-brown vapors billowing out of the earth near the cottage were blowing away, but nauseating whiffs still reached them. A rushing wind brought with it a pall that smelled like vomit and a sound of clothes flapping on a line.

A darktime hovel, he thought, scanning with the sensex. Two transparent beings passed slowly over the cottage. They were so close that he could see their clear-spiked combs and the cilia rippling along the hems of their bodies: Among the cilia, he spotted two pendulous sacs studded with quills. ·

Raels! he cried, almost aloud. *What the rauk are raels doing this far south?*

The raels drifted away from him, and he overrode the impulse he had felt to dive back into the car. Raels were a lifeform created centuries ago by the eo to protect their first settlements. They had been designed to carry nematodarts. The darts were small and thin, but they could be fired across a long distance, and they pumped a neurotoxin that was instantly lethal.

Nefandi continued to watch the raels as he looked around. He couldn't believe that voors were living like this. He had always known them to be meticulous about what was theirs except in old age, when they withdrew into their darktime and lost power. But if the algid psynergy rippling over his skin was to be trusted, this was not a place of old voors.

Scanning the yard and the cottage with his sensex, Nefandi detected no blue biospectral energy, just an orange glimmering from the plant-life. He was perplexed. His tingling flesh told him there were at least six or seven voors ahead of him, but none of them were leaking kha. *That's impossible*, he told himself, tempering his fear.

'Mutra!' It was Sumner. He was just crawling out of the car and had stopped in the door.

Nefandi followed his gaze into the sky and stiffened. One of the raels was directly overhead, glistening among the trees—a gelatinous shape, big as a man. It was formlessly intricate: a mass of clear jelly-ruffles rippling in the sunlight. The wind shifted, and it turned, vanishing into its transparency.

'What was *that*?' Sumner cried. For just an instant, he thought he had seen a bloodspot netted by a fine blue tracery inside a bulbous, frilled thing.

80

'Don't know,' Nefandi lied, watching it and its companion in his sensex as they circled the cottage. *That rael was close enough to kill me*, he realized. *Stay alert!*

But there were too many uncertainties to assess at once. Why *wasn't* he dead? The raels and the eo had been opposed to the Delph's autocracy since the godmind's power had begun to diminish. What were those raels doing here if not hunting him? Where were the voors he felt but couldn't see? All his senses screamed danger, and he had to stare deep into the sky's nothingness to calm himself.

Sumner tagged along behind Nefandi as he approached the cottage. For some reason the flies weren't bothering Nefandi, and he stuck close. The reek of dead things and the vapors rising from the earth set his teeth on edge. He wanted desperately to get away. His heart was pounding, and the flies and the blue and green fungi clumped big as quartz crystals on the tree trunks made his dread even more acute.

At the cottage Sumner saw that the door was shut. It was slashed with a large patch of gloss, as if a giant slug had slimed across it. He was relieved when Nefandi didn't try to enter. The windows were splattered with mud and dust, closing off the interior. Flies whined around them, and the sound of laundry thrashing in the wind grew louder and then receded.

Sumner searched about for anything that had retained its naturalness. But the whole yard was languishing with decay: All the tree barks were puffed and graying, the sod around them sagging away into cracked dirt. Even the grass was crazed with nodules of blue fungus or shining with slime and worms.

'Let's go to the other side.' Nefandi's voice startled Sumner. It sounded low and gentle, almost surprised. There seemed, perhaps, to be a hint of fear in it. Sumner hesitated, but the flies clouded over him as Nefandi moved away. Waving his hands about his head, he scurried after him.

Behind the cottage, under the tamarind trees that ringed the crater pool, Corby sat naked in the tall grass. The mud of the pool-rim, shiny and black as frogskin, mottled his body. He sat with his legs crossed, his eyes half closed. The earth around him was dark with the sinking of things: rumpled, decayed weeds, the purple droppings of some birds, a narrow trail where a snake had slithered. A tiny flower hung like a flame against the dark mulch, its red petals tilted and tattered by the wind.

Corby's whole mind was on it. He was trying to shut out the sickness, the alternating waves of fear and lassitude. One moment he had been slumped out in the mud, trembling with grief because his mother was dead and his house was in darktime. The next, he was sitting up, bewildered by his anguish. Wasn't he a voor? Hadn't he been shaped out of light, time and time again, on countless worlds?

How many mothers and children and lovers had he known and lost? Nothing could change that. And nothing could keep what he was now from dissolving into the future.

His reasoning eased him into a mindless languor. But it would last only a few minutes. Then the fear of going on alone would build up in him again. To break out of it, he centered himself wholly on this flower beside his leg. Gradually his vision wavered and thinned as the tensions inside him slackened. The wind shifted, and the laundry on a line strung between the trees stopped fluttering. A dead calm settled for a moment over the pool. Somnolent odors of wet stone and still water thickened, but he didn't notice. His awareness was fixed on the flower.

Soon nothing was left of him but a skein of energy wound about the thread-stem and its petals. Inside, he was alone, the sunlight singing softly, the warmth flowing through him. His querulous mind was quiet, dazzled by the drone of the plant-life, fibers grained with sunlight.

Deeper, another, quieter self blinked into awareness. It was the mage, the timeless part of him, the nomad spirit that remembered many bodies, many worlds. Now that the mind was fixed, furled deep into the tiny plant, kha opened into its own world: a vast granular mindarkness seething with life energies.

In that bright darkness, Corby lingered. From here he could move into any reality. He looked about. A blood chill was blowing out from a corner of the darkness where the unspirited voor dead endlessly relived their lives as the brood soul. He recognized an area where the darkness was inky thick. That was the cellular core of his life, the route into the body. But he didn't want to drop into that swamp. He had fixed his mind on the flower to escape his sickness. A descent into the slow-burn of the body, with its bog of cells and its muscular energy, would just start his thoughts turning again. And he couldn't subject himself to the waves of rootless desires, deathsmells, and garbled memories that surged out of the darkness of the voor dead.

Instead, he waited—his mind coiled into the flower, his kha aware but still. As long as he could keep himself poised like this, conscious but not acting, he was himself—his true self. Neither a howlie nor a voor. It was a delicate state of being, easily lost. But for the brief moment that it lasted, he was able to see himself for what he was: pure sentience, exultant, measureless. It was his body—whatever form it might have—and the patterns of energy sparking through his body that limited his awareness. Only now, for just this instant, was he free. No thoughts. No sensations. Just sentience, lucid and solitary as space.

Corby relished his freedom until his kha began to stir. It was restless. It wanted to shapeshift through his memories or shadowshoot with the thoughts in other people's brains. But he restrained it a while longer. The tension between his human neurology and his voor consciousness was exhilarating. A moment ago the same difference had been an anguish. Now at least the two parts of him were easier to control. He could amuse his mind with the lifespark of the flower, while his kha went on a tour of remembered worlds. Which life would it be this time?

He projected backwards through his deepest memories. Soon he found what he was seeking, and he willed his kha to an ancestral world where only a handful of voors were strong enough to go.

The world was called Unchala. It was the oldest voor memory. So old that only those with extraordinary kha could summon it up. Those who could returned often, for the beauty of the place was consuming. Experiencing it, even once, left strong, nameless desires that took months to quell.

The sky of Unchala, as he remembered it, was a cascade of stellar energy: pearled light, glassy and shifting. The first ancestral voors lived on that energy, absorbing it like plants, feeling it like music. The long outward curve of actinic energy sifted through them and created a perception full of distance, flow, and color. Silence unfurled and stretched into gulfs of streaming light. Hues, shadings, blends, followed. Voor sentience, as it evolved on Unchala, was continually opening up, becoming aware of wider ranges of possibility. There was music in the starlight, thinning out with distance, melling with other energies in a liquid sound: the gentle, faraway songs of other galaxies. And there was orgasm, flares, starbursts of sensation, as Unchala swung around to face its unique sun.

But no— Corby didn't want to remember daytime on Unchala. Such memories were deliriously intense, draining. Far better to stay with the night, where energies were separable and tight with shape.

Night on Unchala was a contemplative time. Voor awareness expanded and deepened, listening with all its scope for the faint and lonely rim songs, or feeling far into the narrow starlanes for the looser, wilder forces pulling the universe apart. Yet, the more the first voors strained, the deeper the distances plunged. There was no boundary to perception—it widened beyond grasp, beyond all the images and sensations of the voor experience. And it possessed the voors with awe and an indomitable serenity. The universe was infinite, a multiverse, its form the shape of constant change.

Seeing the universe in that way, limits were gone and everything was possible. In time, the voors evolved beyond time. When Unchala's orbit eventually decayed and the planet fell into the collapsar that was its sun, the voors had evolved to the point where they could leave their physical forms behind. Disembodied, the voor awareness merged with the radiation that was streaming into the black hole, and they became the longest traveling light that shines through the multiverse—psynergy itself. That flow of radiation which carried their psynergy-patterns across infinity, they called Iz.

Something snapped, and Corby was yanked out of his reverie. The wind strode in from over the water and loomed through the high grass. The flower he had been focused on was pressed into the shadows. The plant-drone dimmed, and his mind reeled back into himself.

The shadows were the same. Only an instant had passed. He rubbed his face with his hands and stretched. His anxiety was gone. The few moments he had spent in Iz living his past had eased him.

Settling into his new calm, he was amazed as always by the regenerative powers of his kha. He wondered if he would ever be able to merge it with his mind so that he could know many of the things that now he could only feel. What would it be like if he could translate his memories into human sensory images?

He lay back in the cool mud and looked up at a nickel-gray plateau of clouds. From what he remembered of his past, he contemplated how his howlie senses would perceive his ancestral home-world.

Nothing much was to be seen in that corner of the universe. Unchala's galaxy had been old a billion years before the planet formed. All the neighboring stars had fallen in on themselves long ago. The sky, night and day, would be black to howlie eyes. Four or five distant white dwarfs were all that burned against a dense wall of hydrogen clouds—a husk of stellar gas thrown off during the galaxy's death throes.

The most spectacular sight would be Unchala's sun. Seeing it from a distance, it would certainly look puzzling: two fountains of rainbow energy shooting in opposite directions. Bridging the blind gap between them were incandescent arcs of plasma dropping away from the main jets. The two torrents of light blazed like auroras: a smoky red at the sides where the plasma streams shot out and fell back, and an iridescent blue-green, ice-bright, along the central currents pulling away from each other. It looked like a misshaped binary, but it was actually a single star.

The blackness between the sprays of light was the collapsed body of the star. Once, a hundred million years before there was life on Unchala, the dark star had been a red supergiant. A companion white dwarf distorted it into a football shape so that when, at the end of its life, it collapsed, it formed an enormous thread-shaped discontinuity—a black hole. Everything that approached was snatched by the collapsar's immense gravity field—photons, asteroids, curtains of interstellar gas. Inside, the discontinuity decreased all of it.

At the poles, however, the gravity field was weakest, and an unusual thing had happened. The fabric of space-time had not completely closed in on itself, and energy streamed out—geysers of high-frequency photons surging against the blackness of the dying galaxy, light from the core of infinity.

Located above one of these poles was Unchala. She was a rock half

84

the size of the Earth. At one time she had been the football star's outer planet. Now she was held in place by a counterbalance of the collapsar's weak polar gravity and other nearby dark stars tugging to set her adrift. Caught between these forces, she hovered directly in line with the exposed core of the black hole, rotating slowly. Every point on her surface faced the collapsar regularly and was washed by the torrent of radiation.

The surface of Unchala was barren. Nothing could survive the intense radiation. But below the heated shell of the planet, micro-organisms flourished in the energy-rich, carbonaceous interior. Some of them mutated and adapted for life in the hotter layers of the crust. In time, an organism protected by silica armor appeared on the surface. The creature was the first voor ancestor. It was microscopic and short-lived, its life locked within a minute replica of the planet's shell.

Five hundred million years later, the surface of Unchala was no longer crater, flat, or airless. Vast calcite-silica reefs had accumulated like coral, dominating the landscape. Soon they began to climb into the black sky, and the gaseous metabolic wastes of the metazoa living inside them leached out, forming, over aeons, a rudimentary cloud ceiling.

With an atmosphere to breathe and to filter out some of the stronger energy, rubiplasts evolved—highly complex cells that used the collapsar's blue-green light for photosynthesis.

An explosion of new evolutionary forms followed, all of it contained within the immense reefs. Only the rubiplasts could expose themselves to the exterior, and even they couldn't survive long without backup cells within the silica shell.

By this time the reefs soared thirteen thousand meters above the surface. They were pitted, tubular structures with colossal knobby branches. The interiors were intricately convoluted and filled with a dense humus of living systems, all symbiotically integrated around the light-catching capacity of the rubiplasts. Sentience began shortly after a manifold array of lenses developed just inside the apertures at the tops of the reefs. With these starprisms, the first voors selectively filtered out cosmic radiation, and as their awareness opened, they watched the universe unfold.

Corby laughed out loud imagining a human standing beside a fully evolved voor. The howlie probably wouldn't even realize that the mountains around him were alive. Huge, unmoving. Yes, but how awesome life was inside those silent reefs. Endless awareness, hundreds of millions of years long. Impossible to grasp with a howlie brain.

Ah, well—

He pitched to his feet and stood there swaying a moment. From where he was, he could see the luff of brown vapors rising from the plot where he had buried Jeanlu's stalk charms. The charms, festering with a strange bacteria that had mutated from his fear-psynergy, were releasing methane, ammonia, and sulphide fumes. He would be happy when he could leave this doomed place. Weird, savage flies, black worms, and putrescent fungi had appeared since Jeanlu died, drawn, perhaps even created, by an imbalance of his powerful kha. *Fear shapes.* Soon the surrounding area would be completely uninhabitable.

The clothes on the line were dry. He sniffed their cleanness and walked past them to a metal tub at the pool's lip. Flies moaned around him, but none landed. He ignored them as he examined the large basin of water. It was tepid and sudsy. With a small kick he smothered the twigfire that was crackling in the sand below and began lathering himself with a soaked sponge.

Above, visible beyond the tangle of tree branches, a rael was circling. Its whorl of thoughtforms was urgent: *Come to center. Come to center and extent.*

Corby waved it off, an exasperated grimace on his child-face. *Go away. Didn't I tell all of you to leave me alone? Why are you still here?*

The rael glittered above the pond, its transparent body casting no shadow on the rippled water. *Come to center, Corby.*

Corby turned his back on the creature. *I am at center. What do you want?*

To protect and serve. I can't leave you. To go's to stay. So you've told us.

To stay is to go. Get out of here.

You are my guide, my teacher. I can't go.

The others left. They understood what I was talking about. Go with them. Come to center and extent.

Corby turned back to face the rael. He looked down at the mudlip of the pool where lank strings of weed were tangled in an almost recognizable script. After a moment, he had acquired the calmness necessary to hear out the rael. *Center and extent. Express.*

The rael gleamed as it tilted in the wind. *The man who's come is dark—a wanderer of the void's edge.*

I'm aware of the man. He's no threat to me.

A threat known to me. Indifferent to life. He's a voor-slayer and well armed. Let me kill him.

No! Corby stared fixedly at the rael, trying to probe its deepest intentions. But, like other artificial intelligences he had encountered, its awareness was incomplete, muffled as wool. All he sensed for sure was that it hated the man who had just arrived with Sumner—Nefandi. But Corby couldn't allow it to kill him. That didn't feel right to the mage within him. *Get out of here. The man's no threat. I'll deal with him in my own way. But you've got to go, or you'll provoke him. Do you understand? My purpose is bigger than Nefandi. Go.*

The rael was silent. From around the cottage another rael floated toward them. It had been waiting in ambush, waiting for the word to kill Nefandi.

Corby focused on the vivid tangle of scents blowing in off the pond. He was annoyed that these small-lifes were lingering, disturbing the clarity he needed to deal correctly with his father and the killer ort. When he had his anger in check, he looked up at the two raels hovering before him. *It's hard for you, I know. You're human-made. Biological artifacts, designed to spy and kill. But you're learning. If you shave the world down small enough for you to be the center, you're left with nothing—alone. Specialization limits expression. Give it up. I've explained all this before. Don't you understand? Event is extent. Go and contemplate this. We'll discuss it later.*

The two raels drifted off, desultory. Soon the brisk wind took them; they rose swiftly and were gone. Corby felt a momentary misting of pity. Raels, beyond their designed function, were helpless. They had no heritage, no ancestral precedents—no culture. They had been created by the same technology that had shaped Nefandi. Questions of essence and meaning meant a lot to them. And, because his was the most powerful kha they had known, they believed he had answers.

Most of his childhood he had spent with them and the deva, another artificial being. They had been his playfriends, and in the telepathic union they had shared with him, he had shown them Unchala and the long voor-wanderings of Iz. And they had shown him what little they knew of the culture that had crafted them. Eo, their creators were called, and they lived in a private kingdom of their own far to the north. Nothing more about them had been left extant in the memories of the raels.

He diverted his mind from them and continued to lather himself. He had much to do now. There was no time to ponder the raels' anomie.

On the other side of the cottage, Sumner and Nefandi were moving around. He could feel their fear, and that made him smile. All morning he had been sensing their approach, and now that they were finally here he could relax. The ritual would take place as planned, and Jeanlu would have her chance to be fulfilled.

Corby dropped the sponge into the tub and waded out into the pool. He kicked forward and rolled to his back so that the water lapped over him. Floating face up, watching huge galleons of clouds sailing over him, he thought about Nefandi.

Though he had never met him, he saw the taut, one-eyed face clearly: shiny scar, roistering beard, coiled hair, and bloody eye. It was as if he had known him all his life. And in a way he had. When in trance, his mage-self alert in its cellular darkness, all voor memories were his—every thought crafted by his people was open to him. Iz. So it was called. A mysterious sameness that linked all voor minds. A dimension broader than time, changing, shadowy, impossible to comprehend.

Iz revealed Nefandi to him. He knew the man and his treacheries well—but now was not the time to dwell on memories. *Memories begin and end in the blood*, he reminded himself. *Stay close to the blood.*

He did no more thinking until Nefandi, followed timidly by Sumner, edged around from the front of the cottage. Then he slipped under the water to get the last of the suds out of his hair. When he surfaced, they were staring at him.

Nefandi was startled by the creature rising out of the pool. It was white as porcelain, small as a child, moving slow and lissom through the green water. The tamarind trees along the bank were leafing the sunlight so that the mud-rim of the pool sparked. In that dappled light the creature seemed to waver like a mirage. Closer, its features stood out from the blank white of its face, an unknowable mask: colorless eyes, flat and mindless beneath a heavy bone-build of brow; nose, lips, and chin of a doll. *Where's his kha? Why does he have no kha?*

The sensex wasn't responding to the boy at all. He appeared as a gray shade, devoid of biospectral energy. *As if he's dead*, Nefandi thought. *Or—* He strained his sensex, and as the boy stepped to shore he saw through him, his child-body clear as air.*— or retaining all his psynergy. But that's not possible. He has to use something to keep his body alive.*

Then he saw it. The distort looked at him, its head transparent, except for a black seed deep in its brain.

Go into the house. I'll come for you later.

The words crisped in Nefandi's mind, and he whirled toward the house and started walking. Before he knew what he was doing, he had rounded the corner of the cottage. The thought-command had been as vivid and compelling as his own will. It was only after he had gotten to the doorstep that he was able to assess what had happened: *Lami! The voor's a godmind!* Corby had compacted all his power to a point so violet it looked black. *Is it possible?* Nefandi was numb. He opened the cottage door and entered without thought. *Complete control of me. Complete!*

Inside, the compulsion tensing his muscles snapped, and he was himself. *How? No physical form can sustain a kha with that high a frequency. Impossible. But it's happened. I just saw it. Damn, I—* He broke off. For the first time in many years his thoughts were scrambling without direction. It was a frightening sensation, for it meant that he was losing control. *Lost control. It's already happened. Mother of Time, that thing out there—* He seized control of his mind, focused on the moment. His muscles unlocked fluidly, and he looked about him.

The room was spacious and filled with delicate creatures of windowlight. Smoky scents of seasoned wood and drying plants lingered in the air, though there were no stalk charms to be seen. From one of the thick-grained rafters, a multihued carpet hung. Nefandi identified it immediately as a veve. The traditional eleven scenes were embroidered on it, all but one of which he recognized as voorish ancestral homes. The rest of the room was commonplace—table, bed, oilstove. He walked over to a shelf above the stove and selected a tin filled with yellow tea. At a ritual pace he took down a small pot from a row of utensils hanging above a narrow bed, filled it with water he found in a jug beside the table, and lit the stove.

It was important, he understood, to stay calm. Not only because an anxiety-riddled mind was no help, but especially because he knew that everything he felt and thought was being remembered by this room. In his sensex he could still see the electric yellow glow fringed red where he had first stood upon entering the room. The rest of the place was empty of psynergy, smooth and blank, as if no one lived there.

To keep his own psynergy contained, Nefandi shifted his mind into selfscan. Waiting for the water to boil, he stood at the window beside the stove, hearing the trees that rattled in the wind, letting the sound fill him and unlitter his mind.

The last of his tension drifted away, leaving him entirely what he was—so much cheese-soft flesh, so many gravity-thick bones. He watched the dim attenuation of afternoon light, dust motes rising and falling in the windowgleam. A jay flashed through the dead branches outside, and he looked out at clouds that plumed the wind, feathering over a chain of hills. Beside the crater pool, the voor child was walking off with Sumner. Before he could think to wonder, he focused on the mist rising from the soaked mudbank, rising and knotting in the shadows, dissolving in the air.

The pot on the stove clattered to life, and Nefandi turned his attention to it. He found a hard clay cup among others on the windowsill. It was glazed a ruddy brown with a black sea squid tangled in its own tentacles etched on the side. He put several pinches of tea in the cup and poured in the steaming water. The brew swirled up green and smelled spicy. He brought the cup to the table and sat down by a front window. A live cloud of flies swarmed back and forth between the scabby trees. Several of them banged against the window so viciously they dropped to the sill, their small jeweled bodies rolling crazily for a moment before flying off. The rusty trees looked tormented, the earth-skin of their bark peeling off, knobby with fungi.

He sipped the tea, and the fluid warmth filled his whole chest. Thoughts were trying to muscle through the sheen of sensations that occupied him. *What's happening with the fat boy? Where was he being led? What's going to happen to me?* But he gave them no focus, and they shadowed away. The skin of the tea with its satin light caught his eye, and he studied the blend of color and scent and warmth. His face was islanded in the green water. There was nothing to think about.

Sumner was terrified. As soon as he saw the white child's head break the surface of the pool, his insides tightened, and he asked himself

89

again but with more fervor than ever: *What am I doing here? I must've been luned to come back here.*

And when Nefandi suddenly lurched about and stalked off, Sumner was overwhelmed by a desperate urge to flee. But he was rooted. Corby's black-gummed smile was a gash in his white face, his pale eyes unsmiling, cold as fever. He slogged to shore, and an odor of muscadine rose around him. 'Welcome back. I've missed you,' he said in his soft, sincere voice. He held out his hand, but Sumner refused to take it.

'Where's Jeanlu?' Sumner asked.

Corby's face was emotionless in the freckled light. 'She's dead.'

Sumner looked down at the long, soft fingers of mud reaching into the water. He searched but could find nothing to say.

'Would you like to see her?' Corby asked.

Sumner looked dismayed. 'Her body?'

'Her body's waiting. Back there.' He nodded toward a trellis overgrown with red moss and the furry shafts of shagbark vine.

'Waiting?' Sumner said. 'For what?'

'For you.' Corby motioned Sumner to follow him. 'You were the only consort she conceived by. I've been calling for you since she died.'

Sumner didn't move. His hands were jammed in his pockets, his fingers furiously clenched. The wind freshened, and he breathed deeply. If he didn't fear Corby so much, he would have hated him. *Manipulating me like I was a machine—foc!* He looked over his shoulder to find Nefandi, but the man was gone. A hysterical laugh coiled tightly inside him. *First sign of a real voor and he tucks his tail.*

'All of Jeanlu's brood jewels are yours,' Corby said easily. 'She has six or seven.'

Wog! Sumner's heart thudded. He picked a pebble out of the mud and whipped it sidewise over the pool so that it skipped five times before sinking. A smile warmed his face, and he thought: *You knew that's what I came for, didn't you?*

Corby nodded. 'I put the thought there myself. I had to get you here somehow.'

Sumner nodded back at him, both frightened and reassured. *Six or seven brood jewels! What do you want me to do?*

'That's between you and Jeanlu. First, you should see her.'

Sumner toed a stubborn root in the mud. *I thought you said she was dead.*

'She is. But her body is waiting. You'll be the last to see her.'

A spasm of uncertainty writhed in Sumner's belly. *I don't understand.*

'Of course not. You're a howlie.' Corby's mute eyes could have been mocking or indifferent or anything.

The boy led him through the tamarind trees toward the trellis at

90

the far end of the pool. Along the way, Sumner eyed the trees near the front of the cottage, their trunks and limbs swollen and mottled, an amber gum oozing over the glistening bark.

'When Jeanlu was dying,' Corby said, 'I got very scared. I've never been without her. My fear twisted my kha and changed the land.'

Sumner's insides were tight with anxiety, but he followed Corby silently. He wondered where Nefandi had gone and why. It was hard for him to imagine fear glazing the mind within that one-eyed, split face.

The trellis was one wall of a three-walled enclosure. The other two walls were also vine-lashed, stone matted with red moss. Corby stood beside a narrow entrance that was flanked by stone posts engraved with images of interlocking serpents. Standing before him, Sumner could see that the enclosure was open to the sky. A wedge of swans moved across the distance, and he thought he heard the long cry of their wandering.

Corby, still naked but dry, skin puffy and white as a bleached log, eyes remote, swept his child's arm toward the entrance. Sumner pursed his lips, jaw muscles drawn. He was caught between his need for the promised brood jewels and his dread. Suddenly he was curious to know how Jeanlu had died, but, afraid to hear the answer, he stepped past Corby.

The enclosure was small, and as soon as he entered he was confronted by Jeanlu. She was seated in a cane chair facing the entrance. Her face and hands were crusted with the black oystershell scabs he had first seen years ago on her abdomen. Her features were crackled and shiny and shrunken to the bone, giving her a charred skullface. One eyelid was curdled shut in the middle of its socket. The other was angled open, revealing the lower half of a milky blue eyeball and the crescent of a gold iris.

Sumner stood fast. The grass around Jeanlu's chair was pale and wilting over a tarry black and blistered marl. A faint rank fragrance of the sea curled in the air, and for one crazed instant he believed that the corpse, though its eyes were hooded, was staring at him.

He pulled his eyes away from the face. Jeanlu was wearing reed sandals, white, sharply creased trousers, and a bulky vest of plaited herbs and flowers, dried and glazed. Around her neck and over the vest hung an elegant necklace: coiled platinum clasps and stays fitted with a huge brood jewel and studded with six smaller ones.

Sumner involuntarily stepped closer, eyes locked on the green jewel big as his fist. A loamy stillness filled the air around him, and his mind sheered free of words and fear. Cold liquid light, as if seen through mist, gathered at the orbit of his vision and began shaping itself. He couldn't look away. An image was forming out of the sidereal reaches within the vaulted radiance of the jewel, and it was

91

lovely as homesickness, warmer than billowy sleep. It overwhelmed him with distant root scents, the purple of summer evenings before the monsoons, smoky starlight, the bell of a girl's voice dissolving with distance. . . .

An icy hand gripped his elbow. Corby was beside him. 'It's easy to fall into, isn't it?'

Sumner stood up with a start. He had been bent over the corpse, his nose a few inches from the jewel. He scurried back several paces and suppressed a shiver of revulsion. Jeanlu's face glinted like coal.

After backing out of the enclosure, he walked into the sunlight. The warmth penetrated him, and he began to realize how dazed he was. His ears were humming, and the pit of his stomach ached with an intense cold. *Damn brood jewel.* He coughed, trying to ease the icy constriction in his belly. His mind was zigzagging, and his bladder was charged. Something of himself seemed to have been left behind with the corpse.

He stared up at the sky as he pissed into the dry grass. His urine smelled like smoke, and the relief of it draining out of him gradually cleared his head. When he buttoned up his pants, he was himself again.

Corby was waiting for him among the tamarind trees. Sumner followed the boy back along the mudbank to where a diminutive pair of pants and a shirt were flapping in the wind. Corby dressed quickly and then led Sumner to a tub filled with sudsy water. 'Wash your clothes,' the boy ordered. 'The sun's hot and the wind brisk. By the time you've washed up, they'll be dry. Then you may go back and get your jewels. It's wrong to touch them unclean.'

He walked off toward the cottage, and Sumner did as he was told. He worked swiftly, for as soon as Corby left, the flies whined around him and began biting.

Corby walked slowly to the cottage, gazing directly into the sunlight. Its bright heat was the strongest bond he had with his mageself. His mother was deep in her darktime, and he had just sent his father toward a lusk. There was no way to justify this with his howlie brain. He worked hard to remember that he was a voor and that he had seen many kingdoms of sunlight.

Nefandi, as much as Corby's blood-memory despised him, had purpose, and voors loathed to kill self-aware beings. When Nefandi had arrived with Sumner he had been cautious enough not to try commanding things. Even after he had seen the raels, he didn't use his field-inducers. *Cool-nerved*, Corby said to himself. *Reason enough to keep him alive.*

Sumner's fate was different. His time was used up. Within moments, he would blur away as Jeanlu filled his body. Lusk was the voor name. Sumner would be annealed to Jeanlu's will, and his body would be her new shape. Together they would complete a broodwork: They would confront the Delph and force him to stop killing the advanced voors. Voor godminds would at last be allowed to survive, and the broods would unite and begin to use their psynergies collectively. *Certainly*, Corby wanted to believe, *that justifies lusk*.

The voor remembered the first time he had met his father—that day when he had taken him out to Rigalu Flats. He had used his kha to look deeply into him, and what he had seen then surprised and saddened him: Sumner's veve, the totem of his kha's experiences, was all bestial—all predators. He had no human referents in his past, except what his blood could tell him of its ancestry. But it would take him a lifetime to learn how to listen to his blood.

Sumner never had a human body before. His kha-memories were all visceral, bound by links of instinct, hunger, and fear. Nothing of compassion or awe. Only pelagic memories of spawning grounds, fight and flight patterns crafted over aeons, and echoes of preyscents unfurling from the dark loam. Yet—*what had given the kha of animals the psynergy to be human?* Sumner was more than anyone had yet surmised.

Corby had believed that his father was timeloose, led by Iz. But when he probed deeply, searching through Sumner's memories, he saw a thing that convinced him his father's fate was intimately rooted in his animal past.

It was a childhood memory of a horse with a red ear and a white diamond on its nose. Sumner was about seven, and his father had taken him to one of the riding camps on the northern fringe of McClure. It was a day's outing, meant to break the tedium of a long, unexpected winter—the first and last winter Sumner had ever experienced. Riding tall and brave in the saddle of the small horse, a strange thing happened. The heat of the animal and its dark, muscular odor gripped the boy and excited, in the deepest part of him, an unfamiliar urge: He wanted to hurt this shaggy, liquid-eyed thing. Leaves in its mane, the cold mist in its breath—somehow, he would make it hurt.

When they came to a frozen pond, he tried to take the horse across it. As soon as he rode it onto the pond, the ice cracked, and the horse fell. . . . Afterwards, his father and the owner of the horse took a rifle, a can of gasoline, and went out to the pond. Hearing the shot and watching the smoke rise above the trees, Sumner knew what he had done—but he didn't know why.

Corby understood. That day, as he pulled back from Sumner's mind, the boy's voice lingering—'I don't know'—he took with him an image: a memory of a child in a field among burdocks and frozen grass. It was dusk, and black tattered clouds were blowing through a gray sky above a line of cold lakes. Against a bare tree's hanging silence, mist silvering its thin branches, he stood staring at a dark bulk on the ice. Corby shuddered, because he knew the boy would spend the rest of his life standing there.

Nefandi was seated by the window, the cup in his hands half-drained, when Corby entered the cottage. The voor's eyes were bright and fluent as crystal.

'You came here to kill me, ort—but I'm the stronger dream.'

Nefandi stood up, his face fear-simple, his hands opening. Before he could complete his gesture, a hammer of force slammed him between the eyes, and he was thrown to the floor.

Corby went over to his sagged body and whispered a chant to him in a night-tongue. Dizzy-eyed, Nefandi lurched to his feet, and the voor led him out through the stiff sunlight to the car.

To Corby, Nefandi was merely the backdrop of the pattern. Others would replace him until the Delph that was using him was destroyed. Stupidly, Nefandi believed his work was righteous, keeping voors and distorts off the planet—as if voors and distorts didn't have the intention and radiance of fate.

After Nefandi opened the door and crawled into the car, Corby touched him, and he woke.

'You're just a weapon, ort.' Corby slammed the door, and the engine cracked to life. 'You're a shape, not a life.' The dark of the voor's eyes glinted like night-ice. 'Go back to your Delph and tell him the voors have created a shape of their own to avenge themselves.'

The car jerked into gear and rolled off. Corby stood among the fraying vapors and watched until the vehicle dipped out of sight. He was in a space hollowed of power. With a thought he could break Nefandi's mind. With two thoughts he could unfold that mind and take the body for his own. But he was a voor—he was more than the blind spasm of a mind. He was the pattern, and all his thoughts, fears, and ambitions were just a part of that pattern. He felt, more than knew, his purpose.

He returned to the cottage and lay down on Jeanlu's cot. Ornaments of sunlight hung on the walls, and he used their beauty to ease the moil of emotions in him. Moments were disjointed. One part of his being was looking backward forty thousand years to the last time this planet's magnetic field had lifted and voors had taken human form. Voors called that time Sothis: ten thousand years in which voors and howlies shared the earth. Knowledge had passed freely from the brood to the other simians that were alive then. Howlies learned from the voors about the starfigures, the fruiting power of the earth, and the abstracting strength of their own minds. But they were more violent than the voors had dreamed. When the magnetic field returned, the voors that were left on earth were all eventually stalked down by the howlies and trussed up as monsters and sorcerers. So ended Sothis.

Corby twitched, and his attention shifted from memory to perception. Sutures of sunlight tightened across his brow and cheek, and a tissue of sounds covered the window: the static of flies, the thickness of the wind, and the water noise of Sumner in the pool. The pattern was all. Vengeance, grief, strategies, were just the spaces in the pattern. Through the window he watched the graph of blasted trees bending against the clear emptiness of the sky.

Deep in his body he was changing. The enormous power of Iz was unthawing the shapes of his insides, remaking him. He didn't know what form he was taking. To be real and to be strong, the change had to be total. Even his mind was going to be remade by Iz.

A cumulus of thoughts filled the vacancy of his awareness, and he recalled Sothis and the infinite wanderings and why the kha was coursing so strongly in him: He was a voor mage, Corby Dai Bodatta, avenger of Sothis, hunter of the Delph—and he was nothing. The howlies had an unstable technological society far to the north; he was here to keep them from savaging voors—and he was not here at all. The window's pattern of consciousness showed a world of triumphant sunlight and wind-wearied trees. *See how it is all that it is?* he said to himself with the last of his thinking.

Nettles of violet radiance charged the air around the boy's body, and expression lifted from his features. In a few minutes his eyes and nostrils were frothed with a pink bubbling, and the clothing he was wearing had shredded away from his glassy, swelling flesh. His bonelines softened, and gold gossamer began furring out of his pores.

Sumner finished bathing and dressed hurriedly in his damp clothes. The brood jewels were all he could think about. He jogged away from the flies and skipped through the tree toward the stone-posted trellis. He entered the vine-tangled enclosure without hesitating, but he didn't look at the corpse's face. He stood unmoving before her, hands folded, gazing down at her reed sandals. He felt he owed her some token of respect. After a moment, eyes still averted, not wanting even so much as to glimpse that plastic-black, crushed face, he bent over her. A blunt odor of charred flesh spiked up his nostrils. He held his breath and looped his fingers through the platinum chain. It was only then, as he was trying to pull the necklace over her frazzled hair, that he saw her eyes. They were wide open and staring at him.

He jerked back, but in the same instant the crusted black hands snapped out with mechanical swiftness and grabbed him by the throat. Her grip burned like acid. He thrashed, dragging her out of the chair with the fury of his terror. Howling and tugging at her arms, twisting wildly, he tried to break free. But she clung to him. Her grotesque head was propped on his chest, the gold eyes screaming out of their sockets. Wheeling from wall to wall, desperately tearing at the gristled thing, he felt the strength in his muscles shriveling. A coldness so icy that it seemed to be hot coursed into him through the hands of

95

the corpse. As it filled up his chest, his knees buckled and his backbone slipped. Only his horror of the withered creature kept him on his feet and struggling.

Outside, Nefandi heard his wails and sprinted toward him through the trees. The Delph had trained him well. Despite his fear and the pain from the voor's blow nailed between his eyes, he had been unable to drive away. A bioresponse that the Delph had nerved into him had seized his body and driven him back. Until he completed his assignment his body would not let him go—even if it meant his death.

Nefandi had left the car at the pool's edge, and as he dashed toward the boy's cries he opened himself to the beauty and the strangeness of what he knew was the last space of his life.

Sumner reeled through the narrow doorway, grappling with the corpse, and Nefandi pulled up short. The fat boy's broad body was quavering with his frantic efforts to break loose. The sleeves of Jeanlu's blouse had been torn away, and her knobby, sticklike arms flashed blackly. His shirt was sweat-slick, and his thick legs were staggering as he danced crazily along the pool rim. From the wild look in his eyes and the whiteness of his lips, his whole face starched with fear, it was clear that he was going to collapse any instant. But he didn't. Even as the twisted, split lips of the corpse unpeeled and the crumpled face began hissing a hot, putrid vapor, he continued to buck.

Then the chanting began. As Sumner pulled at the iron-locked arms, swinging the body against trees, hauling it through the mud and weeds, it began to mumble the sounds of some impossible language. Cooing, clicking, snapping a rhythm that made the scalp at the back of the boy's head constrict. The icy mist in his chest welled up in his throat and fogged his eyes. He was keeling. All his strength evaporated, and the dead flesh hanging from his neck dragged him forward and down.

Nefandi could see Jeanlu's blue psynergy sparking against Sumner's golden bodylight. Streamers of blue radiance were smoking away, unable to get close. But the gold kha was shuddering. In an instant it would blink out.

Nefandi's hand moved impulsively. Sparked by blood-logic, he activated his field-inducer and lashed out. The burst was a tight packet of high-frequency sonics that caught the corpse between her shoulder blades.

Jeanlu's plant-fiber vest crackled into flames, and Sumner broke her grip. He lurched to his feet and tottered backwards. The corpse yawled, enraged and plaintive, flailing its arms as the flames consumed the vest and started in on the trousers. With a howl the burning body pitched forward, rocked upright, and dashed for Sumner.

Sumner ran away from the pool, the corpse lurching behind, its outstretched, flame-sheathed arms closing in. Despite his bulk

Sumner moved quickly, loping past the pool toward the Flats. Jeanlu was so close that when the flames ignited the brood jewels around her neck, the string of explosions peppered his back with pieces of burning flesh. But he didn't look back. Behind him the corpse crumbled beneath flares of green flame.

Nefandi watched the corpse burn a moment before turning away. He was surprised that the boy wasn't dead. With a smile that didn't touch his eyes he watched Sumner flee through the trees and out of sight. It would have been good to follow him, but his work wasn't done.

He moved through the tamarind trees toward the cottage, his field-inducer at maximum, warping sounds and belling vision. The flies frenzied around him, hazing off the perimeter of his field and black-dazzling around him. The bent air sliced light into colors, and he saw the cottage rainbowed in sunfire.

Through the adobe wall's opacity the sensex revealed Corby: a small but dense purpling lying inside the cottage. Something had happened to the voor's body—its shadow was unshaped and pulsing eerily. Nefandi focused his weapon for maximal output and fired a long wail of energy at the sensex image.

The side of the house flared apart, and a cyclone of fire gusted through the timbers. The heat of the blast pushed Nefandi back, and he retreated to the brink of the pool. From there he watched until the shred of purple kha and the throbbing voorshape were glared out of sight by the conflagration.

The wind flushed brighter and colder, and Nefandi turned his back on the flame-cored house and walked to the car. The flies had veered off, but the air was filling with something else—a stillness, the transparence of the violence he had created.

At the car he stopped and tried to convince himself that mind was indeed continuity. He watched sunlight fill the surface of the pool like flowers—and he felt that he was verging on a drunken dream. *Don't spook yourself.*

He looked back at the cottage. It was huge with fire, and no glint of the voor showed. Still—absence surrounded him like a crucible. He had to be severe with himself to keep from quaking when he stooped into the driver's seat and started the car. As he drove off, he knew that the voor was not dead—he had merely helped to change it.

As soon as Sumner realized he was no longer being chased, he collapsed and lay doubled over, retching for breath. It was a while before he was able to stand, his head muddled and heavy. There was nowhere to go but back to the cottage. He limped through the scaffolds of trees cautiously. When he saw the smoldering nest of tarry ash and bones that was Jeanlu's body, he took a deep breath and walked the long way around the pool.

Near the cottage, the flies ravaged him, yet he stopped walking and stood staring. The house was blazing—and his car was gone.

The flies frenzied over his face and neck. He stood stunned and still, watching flamedevils dancing through the roof and out the windows. He turned and stared beyond the dead branches of the trees idling in the wind, at a thread of dust vanishing in the west.

Sumner brushed the flies from his face and scurried past the pulpy trees and the worm-festering grasses toward Rigalu Flats. He waddled up the rise and skidded quickly down the other side. Once he was on the green sand the stinging swarm veered off, and he was able to stop.

He plopped down in the sand and vomited. When he was all squeezed out he got up, pointed himself toward McClure, and hobbled off. Though he was sick with horror and fatigue, he forced himself to move. The grating roar of the timbers and the tile roof going up in flames bellowed after him like the rusty gears of a vast machine.

Nothing has been created. Everything is a shadow of what it will be.
Corby held to that voor chant. The fire was too hot for his shape, and in a moment he would lapse into the pattern itself, unsure of how he would go on—or if.

Or if—nothing is a shadow, everything has already been created—everything is fated.

With the last fineness of his reasoning he focused on Sumner. The lusk was broken. He had to reach his father. The pattern had to go on. He had to stop the Delph.

With the last of his will, he reached out.

Sumner stayed close to the fringe of the Flats to avoid the flies. After he had shuffled through the sand for over an hour, the terrible wind died down, and the flies were gone.

He ventured across a grassy plain toward a grove of willows. Halfway there, the scaly hulk of a pangolin reared out of the tall grass and honked angrily. Sumner backed off, slowly at first, then more quickly, breaking into a scramble as he neared the Flats. Safe again among the green dunes and the maze of fluted rocks, he plodded on.

It was a hopeless journey. Because of the pangolins, there was no chance of cutting across the fertile land to an active highway or even of getting water until dusk. And then the night creatures would be out.

As he slouched along he tried to measure his situation coolly. McClure was the nearest town, and it was 189 kilometers away. It would take him days to get there on foot. Even with provisions he doubted he could get past the predators.

Face it, zerohero, he said to himself. *You're trashed.*

The sun was a gold circle behind him. To his right, lunatic clouds,

98

red and jumbled, were running with the horizon, towering majestic to twenty thousand meters. Skeleton-shadows covered the desert floor, and the tall, curved rockshapes catching the light around him blazed a hot green.

He could still taste the rot smell of Jeanlu's body. He wanted to tear off his soiled clothes, but the stench was on his skin as well. The loops of singed pain around his throat and the chill in his muscles made it impossible to gather his wits.

Only one thing was clear to Sumner. He had been duped. Behind his pain and fear a thick anguish thrummed. 'Used by a distort!' he moaned. 'Corby knew. Pissleaker! He knew Jeanlu wasn't dead.'

He shuffled on, trying to follow the highway as it dipped in and out of the death-calm dunes. The rocks around him were scorching, but his heart was chilled. The more apparent the hopelessness of his situation became, the angrier he got—enraged at himself for being such a docile fool. *I should've left Nefandi in the lurch when I had the chance.* A sour taste gelled in the back of his throat. He wanted to spit it out but his mouth was parched.

Afterwards, he lost the highway amid coils and loops of rock. By this time the sun had rolled to the horizon, and the wild clouds in the north were piled high, dark as a mountain. He leaned against a thrust of stone that arced steeply and fanned into a mesh of spikes and bristles. The material was slick and clear-edged. In the shadows it was already seeping a faint green glow.

He looked north at a ridge of far-distant mountains. Alpenglow, a misty red, outlined the summits. Closer in, the edge of the Flats was visible among the long shadows. Just beyond it, surrounded by drowsy ferns and a dark grove of veiled cypress, was a pond. Its long body flashed like beaten gold in the dusk. No pangolins were in sight.

He shambled over the smooth rock and the drifts of sand. The scent of fresh water crisscrossed the air, coming and going, until he pushed through the ferns. Then it rose up like a wall, and he stepped through it, giddy. The water was clean and cool, gurgling from a cleft boulder matted over with moss and long green shoots. He went down on his knees before it and drank, moaning and rolling his eyes. When he had slaked his thirst, he doused his face and his burning neck. Finally, he lay back in the thick grass and let the leaf-shifted twilight play over him.

Momentarily at peace with himself, his mind fell back from its despair and he wondered why Corby had sent him to that living corpse. *Was that really Jeanlu?* Thinking about it, he decided it was. Though the features had been withered, he had recognized her hair and eyes. He could still feel the frosted charge she had sizzled through him. The vacancy in his chest and shoulders lingered, as if he had been drained. *Like a spider*, he imagined. *She was sucking out my life like a spider.*

It was darker, the sun was a crown of flame among the fantastic shapes in the east, and he was trying to devise a way of carrying some water, when he heard an evil sound. A huge, hollow cough swelled out of the night shadows among the cypresses. He couldn't even begin to guess what it was, *Pangos should be asleep now*, he considered, hoping to calm himself. But other, more ominous possibilities remained: jaguars, dorga renegades, flying gnous.

He pushed to his feet and immediately saw the gleam of last light in five pairs of eyes across the pond from him. As he stepped back, they stepped out—five man-size hind rats, snout-jaws gaping, stunted forearms greedily clacking claws.

Sumner whined, and the sound of his fear excited the creatures. They trotted around the pond toward him, barking and snapping their jaws.

Sumner plunged through the brake of ferns and burst toward the Flats. The hind rats spartled after him, screaming raucously as they closed in. Even after he made it to the green sand he dragged on as fast as he could, not daring to glance back until his shoes slapped the hard surface of a rockshelf.

He turned about and nearly collapsed. The hind rats hadn't stopped at the edge. They were kicking up flares of sand as they scampered toward him. He leaped back and dashed over the fine-grained rock, eyes straining in the falling light for pits and scoops.

He ran strong and reckless, leaving all his strength behind. When he collapsed, his leg muscles were bunched, his chest was aching, and he had to gulp for breath. In an instant the hind rats were on him. He was surrounded by their barks and he heard them circling for the lunge.

It was a long, hysterical moment before he realized that he wasn't going to be mauled. The yipping of the creatures broke off abruptly, and he thrashed about. The hind rats were gone. They had never been there. The sand was ruffled by only his feet.

He got up timidly and looked toward the pond. Darkness obscured it, but by the green glow of the Flats he saw the gleam of the hind rats' eyes. They were watching him from the edge.

Suddenly two of them bounded forward, shrieking and kicking up sand. Sumner wailed, but he was too spent to break into a run. Stiff as chalk, he stood gawking as the hind rats raced for him. They were ten meters away, ribbons of saliva running off their jowls, when the space around them fractured. They vanished.

Yak pus!

All five hind rats were squatting at the fringe of the Flats, sixty meters away, their tiny eyes green sparks in the shadows. None had so much as stirred. Sumner kneaded his face with his knuckles. *I'm losing my mind.*

'No you're not.'

100

Sumner wheeled around. Corby was standing behind him, his face and hands milky green in the phosphor glow. His eyes glared bright as an animal's.

Sumner stammered, but the boy's form wrinkled away like a mirage.

Wog! I'm luned!

'Just projecting.' The voice came from behind him again. He turned, this time more slowly, screwing up his eyes to see better. The boy was there, solid as the rock turret alongside him. 'Stop pushing out,' Corby said. 'Focus in.' His body blurred off into the ghost light of the Flats.

'Corby!' Sumner bawled. 'Stop jooching me!'

A voice slashed through his head, so loud that he reeled: 'I'm not!' Corby's image ricocheted across his field of vision, appearing and vanishing on ledges, dunes, spires. Then it was gone.

Easy, driftbrain—easy. Sumner closed his eyes. He sensed the boy's contact within him. Blood was still banging in his ears from his run, but even so he could hear a hushed presence at the back of his mind. A cooing, a whispered chant was echoing there—a dreadful recall of the corpse's alien muttering. He was ready to flick his eyes open to get away from that sound, except that he heard something else: Corby's voice, cool and rational. 'It's the Flats, Father. It's empty. Your mind's filling it up.'

He opened his eyes. Corby was watching him with a concerned smile. The image lasted until Sumner moved; then it, too, blinked away.

He closed his eyes again and listened, past the boom of his blood and Jeanlu's eerie lipping, for Corby. 'Keep your mind still,' the boy's voice whispered within him. 'Don't talk to yourself. And don't be afraid.'

'Where are you?' Sumner asked aloud.

Jeanlu's mumblings got louder, hissing through the blood beat. 'I can't link with you long,' Corby said, his voice already thinning. 'Listen. Being is flow. And in the flow is pattern. But there can be no meaning until you stop struggling. Consciousness itself is power. Become what you are. If you're quiet, you'll . . .'

Silence.

'What? I'll what?'

A squawking chant caromed across his brain, and Sumner snapped open his eyes to see the black, shrunken corpse of Jeanlu dancing obscenely before him. *Wwau!* He jumped backwards and had to struggle with himself not to dash off. 'It's a ghost, driftbrain,' he said aloud to calm himself. 'It can't touch you.'

Jeanlu's body shimmied closer. He could see through the peeled, scabby skin. The face was thin as wind, but shiny, the bulbous eyes trembling in their sockets. Sumner held himself steady. 'Not real,' he

101

encouraged himself. 'Not real.'

The corpse's body disappeared, but the shiny, cracked face remained, stretched into a maniacal grimace. Then it, too, faded, and he was alone. A night bird tolled from the cypress pond, but otherwise there was silence.

He closed his eyes to get in touch with Corby. Only the sound of his heart thumped in his ears.

The heat had thinned out of the air quickly. Sumner was quivering, and he started walking to warm himself. The terrain around him was filled with furtive movements and brief glimmers of gossamer shapes. *Fear*, he remembered. *Teeth dreams.* The thought reassured him and he felt his initial anxieties peeling away. He was left with shimmerings of dread and snips of language: *Relax . . . You're easing home . . . nobody can jooch you now.*

The vast solitude of the Flats and its soft, dusty light skimmed off his inner voice. He fell away from his thoughts into an alert quietude. Nothing was left to think about. It was just a matter of walking now, one step at a time, through this wonderland of muted light and crazy shapes. Exhaustion helped to keep his mind empty; fear kept it alert. And the hallucinated voices of the hind rats stalked him:

> *Two leg, you are beautiful—*
> *O come with us*
> *Away from these fever graves*
> *To where our wounds can love each other. . . .*

He veered deeper into the Flats, a great concourse of windswept shapes ranging around him. Time was without punctuation. Only the broken rhythm of his stride and the hot pain around his neck fixed his attention.

Intuitively he understood what Jeanlu had wanted from him. Life. All of it. The hot vapor she had breathed in his face was a psiberant—a means of digesting his mind so that she could take his body. The words she had chanted were intended to paralyze the conscious centers of his brain. The rhythms were still resonating through his nerves. He could feel them acting with the psiberant. Together they produced a sparkling, volatile energy that scrambled his thoughts while infusing his kha with unprecedented strength. Strength enough to realize: *A little more of that power would have been death.*

Movement, majestic and invisible as an ocean current, pulled at him. He moved with it, steadily, inexorably, trudging through the hushed green glow of the Flats, until he came to a stairway of stone ledges at the edge of a huge bowl canyon. Boulder-choked defiles in the distance blazed bright green like seams of spectral lava. The skyfires rustled above, blue and red, clouding all but the brightest stars. Through the draperies of smoky light the swayback Lion and

102

the Goat Nebula flickered. By them he knew which way was home. He had tramped far from fertile land. This deep into the Flats, his mind blank as glass, polished smooth with fright, he was immersed in an almighty silence.

Astonished by his lucid serenity, feeling as though the edge of time were before him, he sat down on the rock ledge and let the cold air weld him to the spot. He was sure that he had come here for a reason. But there was only one reason huge and simple enough to match these lifeless ranges. Death. He didn't have to think about it. He knew he was going to die. And he relished it.

Light was everywhere—a drowsy ghost-bloom shining in the rocks, woozing down from the sky. The wind had stilled, and the canyon floor rolled toward the horizon with its arches of haunted rock. For many kilometers in every direction there was not one living thing.

This was the moment he had secretly craved for years. He knew if he eased up now, he would lapse into darkness and never wake. An end to loneliness and hunger and footsmells and clothes gone stiff with piss-acid and fear-sweat. Gone, the ugliness of being himself.

He took one long, sweeping look at the lifeless horizon: A few stars were tapping beneath the wobbly light of the skyfires. He closed his eyes and eased up. The cold seized him, and for a while he trembled so violently that he knew he must disintegrate. Then warmth—a deep warmth: flesh fire, the heat seeping off his bones.

Inside, he didn't lapse into darkness. He was rooted in the warmth rising through him. Then his mindark went cold and bright. When he opened his eyes he was no longer alone.

Far away a string of flashes went off. A fleck of gold radiance was advancing among the ridged slopes. appearing and disappearing across the tableland. As it neared, the blinking fleck took on a definite form: a vortex of blinding energy.

A deva!

It leaned over the sandshelves, an immense, fiery whirlwind, muting the green fluorescence of the Flats. Dense shadows cast by intervening rock ridges staggered before it. Closer, the vortex dipped behind the reefs of the canyon wall, and the desert around Sumner was again dark.

During the interval the shock wave hit. It rolled over the canyon, kicking up luminescent tufts of sand and hitting Sumner so hard he clattered over a bed of rocks and dropped to his back. A gust of wind-driven sand thrashed his face and arms, and then was gone. Overhead, muffled with distance, thunder throbbed.

From where he was sprawled he could see the rim wall brightening. Shafts of lucid, burning light cut through the darkness of the canyon, illuminating dunes, a ruffle of contorted rock, and a basin cracked into octagonal plates. His eyes glared over. When he could see again, the sky was blazing with enormous sheets of fire. Curtains of grained gold light streamed down, passing through the rim walls, embracing the entire canyon.

'Get up!' Corby's voice pleaded with sudden clarity. 'I've sent this deva. Go with it.'

A cannonade of squealing wind burst over him, drowning out the voor's voice. The sudden blast shoved Sumner sideways down the incline, and he pushed against the wind to regain his footing.

'You're luned!' Sumner turned and again tried to move away from the canyon. But the suction of the gathering wind column hauled him back and sent him sprawling to the base of the rise.

The wind currents were mounting quickly, and the canyon floor was boiling.

It was impossible to resist the drag of the sheering squall. In a flurry of ragged clothes and waving limbs, he tumbled toward the center. The closer he got, the more brutal the lash of wind became, until it was impossible to breathe. He stopped resisting, and his body bounded through the air into the explosive brilliance of the whirlwind.

He surged up through a buffet of twisting force where, for a moment, he hung suspended. A blizzard of blue-white sparks seethed about him. Far off, seen through an endlessly receding spout of silver-azure radiance, was the pale saffron body of a cold sun. And then, the colossal winds squeezed the breath out of him.

He blacked out.

When his senses cleared, his whole body clenched with terror and he nearly lost consciousness again. He was hurtling through the air, thousands of meters above the ground, his aching, bruised body buoyed by a tremendous force. Below, wandering deep into the north, lay the shattered range of Rigalu Flats. Its crumpled, wind-scarped contours glowed faintly with a green washlight. To the west, the planet's rim was lit by the sun's corona, the sky above it condensing from aquamarine to a slow indigo-pitch. Dark lakes in the north reflected that light in starpoint flashes.

He hung to consciousness by a giddy thread—too shocked to think. Through wind-stunned eyes he watched the curve of the horizon bank, as the trajectory of his flight bowed into its descent. Towers of clouds in the distance, edged blue-red and purple by the celestial light, veered away. The silver glint of a strohlkraft moved in a tranced glide along the edge of the world. And there—close to his left, surrounded by the clawtracks of dirt roads and highways—squatted the dark factories of McClure. Orange lights flickered within its smudge of clustered buildings.

The wind leaned on Sumner, and the path of his drop suddenly appeared taut and clear. He was going to come down in the trash fields on the outskirts of the city. Already he could see the buckled tin roofs of the dorga pits and the burning towers of the refinery.

The glare of the solar wind fell below the horizon, and the palisades on the southern lip of the Flats marched down the northern sky. The brown wasteland surrounding McClure surged closer. South of the city the bay looked dull-green and then black before it swung out of view.

Sumner's plummet jolted, and he slowed down. Strings of force lowered him toward the dorga pits. The smoking clumps of shacks, untouched as yet by the sun, looked uninhabited. He spun over the swarm of lone huts and slid through streams of curved air toward the west slope of the city. Hills and knolls of trash skimmed beneath him. When he was four meters above the ground, the force that was suspending him snapped, and he dropped to the earth.

His legs crumpled under him, and he rolled down a dark bank into a shadowed cove. The cove was really a hollow among heaps of junk: rotting wood, crowds of discarded crates and boxes, ribbons of fatigued metal, the crushed frame of a car belly-deep in weeds. The place was deserted except for pigs and wind-eels and a solitary dog. A rank mist laced with organic odors engulfed everything.

Sumner stirred to rise, but he was too weak. The frenzy of his absurd flight had exhausted the last of his strength. Even as first light gilded the mounds of rubbish, he was sinking into a deep stupor.

It was late in the morning when he came around. His head was hollow and his body, like empty tubing, sagged as he tried to sit up. Through the pain of his battered muscles he forced himself to his feet. He hung onto a corroded pipe, then rolled back clumsily into the trash pile. In his daze he lay there, flies stuck to the abraded sores on his lips, and watched a lone bird circling far up in the sky.

Thoughts were too loud for his aching head. He closed his eyes and rolled to his side. Later he was nudged awake by something cold and wet. It was the nose of a ribby, sharp-faced pariah dog. It watched him for a while without expectation, then loped off behind a drift of smoking garbage.

Bravely Sumner pitched to his feet, staggered, fell, and lumbered up again. Keeling from side to side, he plodded across the trash fields, oblivious to the dorgas sorting junk among the weeds of the wild verge. Seeing him coming, the dorgas hooted and cried. Some threw garbage, and all watched him until he was out of sight.

Sunlight was falling, a thick, late afternoon amber on the rutted dirt road, as he limped into the city. The houses lined up on either side of the road, a few meters back, were all the same: concrete-block stoops, walls of stained scantlings, rusted wire in the windows, corrugated metal sheets for roofs. As he went along, zinnia clumps, hibiscus hedges, and ixora bushes appeared among the huts, sprouting around the pink cement outhouses.

The dust was thick and caught in his nostrils with the smell of chicken dung and rubbish. It made him feel nauseous, but he knew he couldn't stop here. Leaning in the doorways and sometimes seated in front of their huts in sagging chairs with blistered arms and worn cushions, were the dorgas. Sulking, vacant women with long matted hair ignored him. The men, wild, red-eyed, in rags, stared at him, their foreheads X-scarred by drone straps.

Farther on he saw a distort child sitting in the pale dust beneath a carat palm. The face was small and tight, the scaled flesh around the sunken eyes looked bruised, the front of the tattered shirt was wet with drool. When Sumner went by, clods of dirt, pebbles, and shards of glass shot off the road and pelted him. The distort leered to see him hobbling anxiously over the broken ground, head between his shoulders.

He was relieved when he reached the first paved streets where there was a park with flower-cracked walls. But even here, where the houses had doors and windows, tokens of danger were everywhere: Wind-eels squirmed in the air above tangles of unfamiliar weeds, and black carrion corbeaux squatted on fence posts; a smell of stale smoke was in the air; great, gritty ants' nests hung from the limbs of shade trees. Nevertheless he stopped to call up his strength and to look back over the way he had come. The park was on a rise, and he could see down to where a stream the color of rust fringed the dorga pits. Wooden shacks on thin stilts wavered in the heat. The eroded area was like a crater, isolated and depressed.

A sharp thought pierced the exhausted stillness of his mind: *That's my home if the police get me.* His stomach heaved and then settled back. He was too drained and numb to sustain his dread. But as he slumped through the dried grass of the park, he peered across the deserted, mangrove-choked spaces with apprehension. Not until the avenues broadened and he saw cars was he able to sink into his torpor again and walk on mindlessly.

Around the arcades, on the shopping malls, and in the open market people were making last minute purchases for that evening's dinner. A crowd of children went by, laughing and shouting, carrying schoolbooks under their arms. The younger ones wore red vests and had tiny packs on their backs. Vendors hawked fruit with loud, trilling calls. Small children played kili in the gutter, mindless of the speeding bicycles and cars. One man was stringing paper lanterns to an overhead wire for that night's local street festival.

The surge of vitality was immense, and Sumner had to move briskly to keep from breaking into tears. Everything was so familiar and sane. It was as if the brutal absurdity of the past day had never occurred. He was aching and dazed, but he was home. Turning the corner of the street where he lived, he felt all the terror and humiliation he had experienced well up in him, and for an hysterically long string of moments he was baffled. Though he had lived here all his life, suddenly he recognized nothing.

In this part of the city the streets were unpaved—dirt roads laid over with dark wooden planks. He shuffled down the middle of the street, his mind blank. The sky had gone smoky with nightfall, and the green lead windows were suffused with light. Their hazy glow reminded him of the Flats. He stood in the street gawking at them, trying to remember where he was going.

Down at the far end of the street the elevated tracks rumbled with an incoming train—shift workers returning home. The muted roar jolted him, it sounded so like the deva wind that had ripped across the Flats. He backed to the sidewalk and was thinking about bolting when a shrill voice exploded his languor: 'Pudding!'

He curled around to see Zelda rushing out of the doorway to their house. She skipped wildly toward him, pale, bone-thin arms high in the air, little bird's eyes wide with surprise.

'Mutra! What's happened to you? What's happened to my baby?' She put both of her spidery hands on his face and looked searchingly into his eyes. 'You look dead!' Her shriveled face was aghast as she took in the ragged figure before her. 'Quick—into the house.'

She shoved Sumner down the street and tugged him by his arm into the foyer. In the crinkled light of a globe lantern she studied him with growing alarm. 'What's happened to you? You smell like the Dark One!'

The stale but well remembered odor of clove incense jarred Sumner's mind. The broken look on his face began to fade. His bright, startled eyes glanced about.

'Are you hurt?' Zelda whined. 'Can't you talk?'

He plucked at his ravaged shirt and smiled giddily. 'I'm home.'

Zelda's face lit up. 'Yes, pudding, you're home. But what happened to you? Where's the car? There was an accident, wasn't there? Look at your clothes! They're scorched and—your neck! Mutra!' She drew back his collar and gaped at the swatches of purpled skin around his throat.

The horrified expression on her face shook Sumner. He pulled away and looked at himself in the foyer's oval mirror. His face was bruised, lips split, eyelids swollen. At the sides of his neck, where Jeanlu had fastened onto him with her death grip, the skin was livid, scalded. He flipped his collar up. 'The car's gone,' he croaked.

Zelda's eyes locked on his. She was too stunned to respond. She stared at him blindly and continued to stare even as he turned past her and lugged himself up the stairs.

Johnny Yesterday was standing in one of the peacock-bluer urns in the living room, eyes closed, a beatific smile on his seamed face. His reverie persisted, stupendous, immutable, as Zelda, coming out of her shock, howled. She bounded up the stairs and intercepted Sumner before he got to his room.

He braced himself for a screeching rebuke but she only stared at him with narrowed, rage-misted eyes. After a tedious moment her face softened. 'Get some sleep,' she said, with a calm more unnerving than a scream.

Sumner slumped into his room and collapsed on the mattress. The place was as jumbled as when he had left it—so long ago, it seemed—except for a clear space where the scansule had shattered. Within the muddle of the room, the solitary emptiness was disturbing. Like his car and his secret life as the Sugarat, it was another part of him that had been lost. How much longer could this go on, this slow falling apart, dying piece by piece? *Why not end it all at once?* he wondered. *Whomp! Finished.* He sighed, and his body sank deeper into the mattress. *Why not?*

Zelda was enraged. The loss of the car meant a lot of bureaucratic and financial trouble. She could have gouged out Sumner's eyes, but she had restrained herself for a reason. Yesterday, a few hours after Sumner had driven off, the police had arrived at the house. They were big and bulky and not at all pleasant. Two of them banged through the rooms, turning everything over, while a third cornered her in the foyer. They wanted Sumner. They wanted Sumner now. And unless she turned him over immediately, she could expect to be conducting her illicit spirit counseling in the dorga pits.

Zelda had been supernaturally calm with the police. She really had no idea where her boy was, and if she had known, she would have told them without hesitation—she was that furious at him for not warning her that there was trouble. If they had wanted to, the police could have broken her right there and dragged her off to be branded. Instead, they gave her a special number to call when Sumner returned to the house.

She fingered the slip of paper with the number on it. Her anger about the car was nothing like the fury she had experienced after the police left. Her career was gutted—no one would do business with her now that she had been raided. Word about the law traveled swiftly in wangol circles.

She had only one option. The house was in her name. There would be no trouble selling it, and with the money she could relocate in one of the big eastern cities where nobody knew her. Of course, the success of her plan had depended on Sumner's returning. If he hadn't come back, the police would have suspected she had tipped him off. Now her future was as close as a phone call.

She put on a heavy shawl embroidered with owls' eyes and black tassels. Stepping out into the cool night air, her tensions eased and she felt disappointed that she had gotten angry at her son. The car was not that important. It would hamper the paperwork of her leaving the city, but perhaps the police would take care of that. The important thing was that Sumner was back and she was free to go her own way.

It was not until she came to the phonestall below the el tracks that she felt her first throb of hesitation. She dropped the only coin she had brought with her. It rolled past her foot and fell between the wooden planks of the street. On her way back to the house to get another coin, she reasoned with herself—

Don't I have a right to my own life? Why should I throw it away to protect an ingrate, a glut, a . . . criminal? 'Klaus, you know I've tried. School, scansule, car—what more could I give him? My life? Do I have to throw away my life, too? No! I've done more than enough. Besides, the police . . . they wouldn't tell me what he'd done wrong. Perhaps it's not that serious.'

'And if it *is* serious?' Klaus's voice asked. 'Come on, Zelda—you remember the brood jewel and the voor herb you found in his car. That was over a year ago. Who knows what trouble he's gotten himself into? It's probably very serious.'

'Well, then it *is* serious, Klaus. Why else would the police bang up the house like that? But so what? Sumner's a rapist, an assassin, a voor pimp—they're going to send him to the pits or the peeler. Let it be the peeler. So what, Klaus? So what? He ruined my life—he would have had me branded. His own mother a dorga! What did he care? He didn't warn me. Not a word!'

'But he came back, Zelda. He came back.'

'He came back because he trashed the car. That's why, you rotting corpsemeat. He trashed the car. Where else could he go? Only I'd put up with his slobbering and his whining. You don't have anything to do with it. You're dead. Dead. Dead.'

Several hours later, after dropping more coins, misplacing the number, twisting her ankle, and arguing viciously with Klaus, she called the police. They arrived quickly. She had just finished preparing a cup of wangol e-z brew to soothe her nerves when the door knocker thumped loudly. Through the window she saw a string of helmeted men file out of a black van and disperse to surround the house. They were carrying rifles.

'You're not going to hurt him,' she whispered frantically to the men she let in. They shouldered brusquely into the foyer. 'You shouldn't hurt him. He's a quiet boy.'

'Where is he, lady?'

She looked up the stairs, and five men scrambled past her. Johnny Yesterday was asleep at the head of the stairs, and the first men to reach him dragged him swiftly out of the way. They stuffed him under the table with the brocaded legs and proceeded to kick in the doors to all the rooms.

Sumner was just sitting up, blinking groggily, when the door to his room crashed open. Three men were on him before he could move. He yowled and thrashed mightily, but one of them rammed a nightstick between his legs.

They secured his limbs with thick straps and plugged a rubber bit

109

into his mouth. Bound to a wooden pole like a trussed pig, he was hauled out of the room and down the stairs.

On the way out, Zelda fluttered over him. He watched her through a blur of pain while she cried. 'They won't hurt you, pudding. They promised.' Then she was gone, and he was looking up into a night rippled with skyfire. The last thing he saw before they slid him into the van was Johnny Yesterday leaning out the upstairs window, his leering face bald and wild as the moon.

Voors

The Fox provides for itself,
but God provides for the Lion.

—WILLIAM BLAKE

The Mysteries

Black the blood and the bones . . .
Moving like shadows, dark mantled and hooded, eleven voors came
out of the north, each with a stalk charm, each silent. They gathered
on the chine of a hill and stared down through the simmering heat at
their destination.

Below was the home of Jeanlu the charmist. Days before, the
deepest voors had sensed her death coming on. Because she was a rare
one—a healer with the power to touch Iz—the brood had sent these
eleven to perform the rite of stillness.

The rite was an homage, though the ones who had risked the
journey into the broken land of the howlies were more curious than
reverent. Only one actually knew Jeanlu—Lul, the eldest, herself a
master of plants, had been her friend. Everyone else knew nothing
more than the tales they had heard.

Early in childhood Jeanlu had seen her brood savaged by howlies,
and the shrieks of blood and the hot pain had stayed with her. Over
the years, as she perfected her stalk charms through her wanderings
among the darktime voors, her anguish opened into a vision: She saw
how her charms could draw enough kha into her own body to birth a
mage, a timeloose voor with the power to unite and protect the
broods.

Many had warned and chided her, because a mage was a spawn of
the Vast and few believed a woman could balance her own small
bodylight with the immensity of Iz long enough to shape a child.
Kha-warped homunculi had been created that way. Yet Jeanlu had
been possessed by her vision, and she had journeyed south to find a
howlie genetically strong enough to father a mage. No one had
followed her, except those long into their darktime who needed the
comfort of her stalk charms. The few that had returned during those
first years spoke of a wild, lightning-eyed woman whose charms were
potent enough to strengthen the bodylight and keep darktime voors
alive. Some had even told of a child white as emptiness and just as
deep.

The rumors of a mage had excited the broods. Many were willing
to jeopardize their lives to see for themselves what had become of the
charmist. But for the eleven who were selected, the journey had been

strange. They were haunted during their trek by long dreams of Unchala, the voors' spawnworld. Nights were an ecstatic experience hairy with the most beautiful music anyone had ever heard, and days were a powerful expectation of the nights to come. When they arrived at their destination, though there had been an omen—a deva had been spotted the night before—the telepathic joy of their desert crossing did not prepare them for what they found.

The landscape was malefic. Dead trees with shapes of pain cowered over a pond that had dried to a shattered pit. Where Jeanlu's house had been, there were only ash-timbers and the white shadow of a furious fire.

Three of the eleven had deep mind, and they drew closer together. Lul, the old one, had known this place before and was baffled by what had become of it. With her deep mind, she questioned the others. Clochan was as dumbfounded as she, but Tala thought she glimpsed blue kha traces around the flies. That startled Lul. *A voor did this?*

Tala couldn't answer. The traces were too faint even for her sharp senses.

Lul dismissed her suspicions and signed for the rite to begin. Clochan passed around the flagons of kiutl brew he had been carrying, and everyone drank deeply. The saffron fragrance puckered Lul's mouth and filled her sinuses with nostalgic vapors. How many times had she shared this feeling with Jeanlu?

Together the two women had known one-with—a telepathic melling of kha that had always filled their heads with a wondrous vision: a violet sky with three suns and the odd feeling of a body that wasn't human. The seers had said these experiences were the glimmers of lives that they had lived on other worlds. Most of the brood believed such talk, but who was strong enough to know?

The first cool tendrils of kiutl immanence pierced through her thoughts, and at the same instant Tala beat on the slade-drum the opening notes of a sad slow mountain song. Her body thinned out, and she was aware again of the electric clarity of the herb. Clearly now she saw the thin blue glaze around the fungi at her feet. And, with the intuitive insight of kiutl, she recalled Corby. Jeanlu's son was said to be a mage—a voor with the power to heal and transform.

She arched her back and stared up at the enormous sky. Beyond the world's lip the sun was a dark liquid red.

Lul threw back her hood and advanced through the rasping grass. She was old but moved quickly. The darktime was just beginning for her, and her face, cracked and ashen as an old wooden bowl, was still the face of a woman. Her eyes were all that had gone strange. They were tiny and silver, and the vision in them was clouded.

Lul suppressed her thoughts and let the expansive calm of the kiutl hone her senses. Beyond the moan of the flies she could hear the subtle, queer ringing of salt-bonded kha. There was a familiar

114

buoyancy to the high pitch, and she followed the tremulous sound to the caked rim of the pond. Jeanlu's body lay twisted in the tangled loops and lacings of decayed vegetation. The cry of her trapped kha whistled eerily through the crust of her corpse.

Lul gazed into the crushed carapace of Jeanlu's face. The gold eyes were gone, the voided sockets swarming with the tiny white threads of maggots. None of this disturbed Lul. Many years of tending voors in their blacktime had inured her to the grotesque. The only thing that shocked her was that the corpse still wore a necklace of stone light. That meant only one thing—Jeanlu had attempted lusk.

Pirating another lifeform was strictly forbidden.

With kiutl awareness Lul listened to the thin kha-plaint turning in the air. She recognized something of Jeanlu in it, a gentleness. But it was marred by a high-pitched fear shrill. Lul believed she understood why Jeanlu had wanted to lusk. The charmist had been young, and her darktime had been terrible. Besides, howlies were animals—and dangerous, kha-green animals at that. Was it really wrong to take one of their shapes when the bloodpaths narrowed?

Lul brought out her stonelight from a pouch beneath her mantle. Shimmering like jelly, the brood jewel was ice in her hand. She glanced briefly into its depths to be certain that Jeanlu's lusk had failed. She had to be sure that it was not the nightmare-quivering kha of some howlie that was meshed in this corpse. When she saw Jeanlu's kha, blue as coal, she signaled the others to approach.

Tala led the way, chanting to the rhythm of her slade-drum: 'Black the blood and the bones beneath the skin. Black the earth one finger under. Black the emptiness bent over time.'

Lul's heart thrummed with sadness. If only there were more than slim dreams, vague brood-memories, and the old songs and rituals passed on by the seers. If only there were some way to know that the star-journeys and the other worlds of voor legend and dreams were real and that death was no mere collapse into nonentity. What was deep mind if it only revealed the uncertainty and despair of others?

Lusk! Clochan started when he saw the corpse.

Can you blame her? Lul responded. *She was younger than you.*

Did she cross? Tala wanted to know. Her blue-scabbed hands rubbed an unheard note off the drumskin to keep the flies away.

No. Lul motioned the other voors to continue the rite. *It's her kha you hear whistling through the salt.*

After fallen wood was gathered and stacked beside the pond, the voors removed the brood jewels around the corpse's neck and gave them to Lul. The stonelights were all that physically remained of Jeanlu's kha, and when they were gone her life would fall back into Iz.

The old voor placed the crystals deep inside the wood pile where the heat would be intense enough to melt them. The pyre was lit by Clochan and bursts of blue and green flames hissed through the drywood. The voors threw their stalk charms into the fire and turned away.

Lul lingered, watching the black smoke crawl into the sky until the thin, high note of Jeanlu's life shrieked out of hearing.

A psychic muscling at the back of her neck turned Lul toward the ash-skeleton of Jeanlu's house. Near the center of the charred pit, the lucidity of the kiutl revealed a presence among the cinereal ruins. Half buried in the fire-bleached debris was the shape of a small boy.

Stooping over the child-form, she saw that the shape was a sheath of tightly-reeved fibers—a cocoon. Its texture was black with leakage and seepings, but it seemed whole. Staring hard, she could see a violet kha flimmering over the blackened fibers.

Timidly, she reached out and touched the baked surface. She could feel the child's life, gently stirring, uncertain as the shifting patterns of clouds. She pulled away.

Tala and Clochan had felt her shock, and they hurried over. But they couldn't make anything of the child-shape. Was this Jeanlu's boy-child? Tala could see only that it was alive. They would have to cross with it.

With the stonelight icy in her grasp, Lul quieted her thoughts and let the kha of the others fill her. A sorcelled mist clouded her mind, and the sounds of the vehement flies and the bated breathing of those around her folded back. She let the brood-power well up out of her bloodpaths and course like static over her skin. Her trembling fingers reached out and touched the charred surface again.

A spasm of flamebright energy flashed through her, knocking her to the ground. Stupefied, she lay unmoving, hearing the awesome thundering of her heart.

A gnatlike shimmering whirled around her so fast she felt as if she were dissolving into light. Her blood more than her brain remembered this from previous trances. But she was going further than she had ever gone before, across torrential spans of change, moving so swiftly all distance was a single point, violently still.

Darkness flew by like howling apes, and she burst into a landscape of light: a garden of fire—spark-clustered trees, amorphously bright sedges and grasses of incandescent filaments. Black threads of darkness stringing out above the scene parted, and she fell into the spectral grove.

Welcome, Lul. It was a boy-child, distort pale, standing naked among florets of starbright energy, his white-gold hair shifting in an unfelt breeze. *I'm glad you could meet me here.* His words wobbled in the air like a lament, like something more sung than said. *My veve is yours. It's no good to me anymore. I'm fading, becoming less—* He raised a hand to his face, and two fingers broke off and sparkled to the ground like shooting stars.

Lul ached with fear. The boy dissolved into a muddle of frothing

116

colors, and there was nothing left to see but chromatic magmas soundlessly heaving through the blackness.

A child's voice opened in her: *Relax, Lul. Nothing can hurt you here.*

A kha-plaint curled around her, loud and close. It was the legendary cry of the voor dead, the brood soul. She was mindless with wonder and not at all surprised when Jeanlu's voice spoke from inside her: *Lul, remember the nights we pondered this? How many worlds? How far away? I can tell you now, it's endless. There's no way back, but there is a beginning: Unchala—the mythic source.*

Jeanlu! Lul called into the surges of moiling light. But there was no response. Had she, too, been a mind-ghost?

What she says is true, the child said in her mind. *Unchala is part of my veve. Would you like to see where you came from, voor?*

Bodiless and simple, Lul swooned away from words. Her mind yawned into a teetering vista of plasma fires. She moved through a vision more vivid than pain.

Streamers of fire resolved to a span of stars, each starburst a note, a radiant pulse of sound. The sky's dusty nebulae were all music's voice—

Night on Unchala.

'Lul!'

She shuddered awake. Clochan was stooped over her, wafting a smoldering taper of snakeweed beneath her face.

'Your bloodpaths almost closed,' Tala whispered. Her hood was partially pulled back, revealing the tiny holes of her silver eyes and the iridescent scales at the corners of her mouth. But the girl's strangeness did not evoke the sadness in Lul it usually did.

'It's real,' the old voor said, pushing to her elbows. 'All the legends—everything the seers told us is real.'

With hushed emotion, the others watched meekly from a distance.

'It's all real.' Lul's eyes were shining. 'I must go back.'

'No.' Tala squeezed the old woman's arm urgently. 'The trance will swallow you.'

'I'm old, Tala. I'm falling into my bones.'

'Let us go with you,' Clochan urged.

The old voor shook her head. 'The two of you must lead the others back. Take this with you.' She touched the cocoon. 'It *is* Jeanlu's son, and he's strong. His veve looks back to Unchala.'

The two younger voors stared at her, mute with surprise.

'This mage-child remembers the beginning, and he's open to any who would cross with him. Do you understand what this means for the brood?'

'Come with us, then.' Tala helped Lul to sit up. The kiutl was still strong in them, and there was no need for words except for the intimacy of speaking.

'You go. My blacktime is beginning.' Lul stroked the coarse

117

surface of the cocoon and thrilled to feel the bright, kinetic force within it. 'You don't know the beauty I've seen. And it's best you don't until you're ready to leave the salt.'

Sadly, Tala and Clochan helped Lul to cross her kha with the child-mage. In their deep mind, they watched as their friend moved into Iz, the wide banks of steamy colors curving gently through the darkness of their minds.

Dimly, from a great distance, they glimpsed the spark of Lul's kha vanishing into the depths of another reality. And, for the last time, they heard her kha-plaint—a song both jubilant and lonely, like driftwood, far from land, with the wind in its branches, singing.

Chief Anareta waited in the night shadow of the Berth for his men to bring the Sugarat in. He was nervous. He didn't want violence in his station, but it was inevitable. Two of his oldest troopers had lost family in the riots that had followed the Sugarat's kills, and they were demanding blood. With the help of the other men they had ripped out the benches in the locker room and cleared enough space for a beating and a large audience. Word had been passed on, and men from every division in the city were showing up.

The chief leaned against the raspy stone of the Berth wall, well out of sight. He was a lanky, wolfish man who wore his black Massebôth uniform with the rumpled and casual ease of a soldier indifferent to his work. The brutish cruelty in the long lines of his face was not the pain of physical experience. Rather, it had been cultivated by five days of patrolling the wasted streets of McClure and three decades of violent imagination as a police administrator filing action reports.

Anareta had a white card, and the White Pillar had pulled him off his beat and had never really allowed him to risk his rare genes. As a young man he had dreamed of being a scholar of kro studies, although in his heart he had always known that economic necessity and family tradition would lead him into a military career. Only the genetic surprise of his white card had afforded him a taste of the academic life he had desired. Each year, during the three intervals that he studded for the White Pillar, he spent his free time with a scansule studying the fragments of literature and music from the fargone kro times. Strength of mind and pride of self made him a dutiful and efficient police administrator—but it was his white card and the undistorted age to which it harked back that he had come to love.

After Chief Anareta had learned that the Sugarat was a white card, his opinion of the killer had opened from indifference to respect. In his mind he saw Sumner Kagan as an unlucky shape of himself—a remnant of the old age when heroes risked everything to keep the race whole by fighting distorts. But most of his men—most of the human race—were distorts now. The bulk of Massebôth society were green cards, people who, though they had no visible distortion, carried in

118

their genes the shape of a future that did not include men like himself or the Sugarat.

Ominously, Anareta's own men were working against him because of his white card. Shortly after the chief had learned about Kagan, he had asked the White Pillar Conclave to send an escort to protect the Sugarat from his vengeance-crazed division. Now it was obvious that those men were not going to arrive—that, indeed, the message had never been sent.

When the swayvan with the Sugarat came around the Berth wall and cruised toward the cement modules of the police barracks, Chief Anareta stepped out of the shadows. Not daring to use his hip radio for fear of alerting the other men, he hand-signaled the driver toward the arched door of his private office. The chief himself swung open the swayvan's back panel as the truck braked—and he stooped with amazement to see the corpulent body trussed up inside. He had expected Kagan to be streetlean and fierce, and for a moment he thought he had been duped. But the knowing fear in the boy's eyes dispelled his uncertainty.

'Untie him and get him out,' he ordered.

The guards clambering out of the van crowded about as Sumner staggered into the sheer light of a lux globe. His pudgy face was bright with fear. Blood harelipped from his nose, and a welt glowed across his cheek and down the side of his neck.

Anareta took the boy's arm and led him to the narrow side door of his office. The uniformed men followed, but the chief waved them off. 'You're dismissed,' he said, opening the door and pushing Sumner in. The police balked, and he added more gruffly: 'Your job's done. Go home.' He had been careful in his selection of those he had sent to pick up the Sugarat. They were mostly army transfers and young recruits, and they were uneasy about disobeying a field chief. With disgruntled mumbles they dispersed.

Chief Anareta's office was cramped by a long map of McClure and a metal desk cluttered with unfiled reports. He signaled Sumner to a wooden stool and sat on the edge of his desk beside a keypunch communicator. An hour earlier he had notified both the White and Black Pillar agencies that the Sugarat had been identified and was being apprehended. Now he typed in the endcode signal that announced the boy was in custody.

Anareta looked into his prisoner's porcine blue eyes. A laugh jerked deep inside him when he imagined this fat-round boy luring streetgangs to their deaths. 'What did you think you were doing out there?'

Sumner's gaze wobbled beneath the chief's slow, omnivorous stare. 'What do you mean?'

'Why'd you do it?' The darkness in Anareta's long eyes was chasmal. 'You're a white card. I know what that's like. I'm one. It's a good life. The military will leave you alone, and the Conclave will give you women and time for your whims. Why'd you risk it all to be the Sugarat?'

Sumner's look was empty as a wish. 'I don't know what you're talking about.'

The chief's face narrowed, and the ravelings of Sumner's body tightened and quivered. 'I've always liked the Sugarat,' Anareta said tightly. Without looking at the keys, he typed the endcode into the communicator again, this time punching the send-key twice for emphasis. 'Sugarat's a distort killer. I liked him even more when I found out he had a white card. He's not a common green card. He has something, and he chucked it all to jooch distorts. I like the Sugarat. But I don't think I like you.'

Sumner's voice shivered as he spoke: 'I'm not the Sugarat.'

'Don't make yourself uglier than you are, Kagan.' Anareta's lips pinched with disgust. 'My men found spraycans in your room with the same paint the Sugarat uses. I'll wager the tire tracks near most of the killsites fit your car's tires. And now we have foot plasters. You think they're not going to match?'

Sumner faced meekly into the chief's gritful stare and shook his head. 'I'm not the Sugarat.'

'Your driving ticket found its own way to the alkaloid factory?'

Sumner's whole face throbbed. 'It's not me. I don't know how it got there.'

Outside the gray inner door, in the long corridor leading to the locker room, a razor-apt chant became audible: 'Zh-zh—zh-zh—zh-zh!'

Sumner quaked to hear the Sugarat's call.

'It's you, Kagan,' Anareta said in a voice flawed with anger. He knew he couldn't control his men—and his men knew that as well. 'It's you they want.' He typed in the endcode signal again, forwarding it only to the Conclave. Kagan's white card was his one hope of surviving the night—but only if the White Pillar acknowledged his genetic value.

'Zh-zh—zh-zh!' The chanting hissed closer through the gray inner door.

Sumner whimpered and edged off the stool. 'It's not me.'

'Sit down!' the chief snapped. 'Why'd you kill if you weren't ready for this?'

'I didn't!' Sumner's eyes were drunk with terror. He leaned close to the chief, the hot stink of his body thick as a spasm. 'It's not me. Please believe me. I never killed anybody.'

A light dulled in the chief's face, and he pushed Sumner away. 'I might have tried to help you,' he said as the gray door rattled and the pounding began. 'But I'm not going to risk my job and my life for gutpaste like you.'

'Zh-zh! Zh-zh! Zh-zh!'

'Open it up, Chief,' a gruff voice called through the door. 'We know he's with you. Open it up or we'll take you with him!' The heavy door buckled in a seizure of pounding.

Sumner grabbed the chief's arm and begged him with his whole body. But whatever sympathy had remained in Anareta withered away. He twisted his arm free and strode over to the gray door stenciled with the black and white Massebôth pillars.

'Don't!' Sumner crouched behind the chief's desk. 'I *am* the Sugarat—but don't let them have me.'

'Zh-zh! Foc Anareta—open the door! Zh-zh!'

Anareta turned to Sumner with a brightness like joy in his face. 'Why'd you do it, Kagan? I want to know.'

Sumner was baffled. 'I don't know.'

The chief went over to the keypunch and re-entered the request to turn Sumner over to the Conclave. He thumbed the send-key again and again.

'I was scared.' The boy was weeping. 'I've been scared all my life. I had to kill what scared me. The dread, it—'

'Zh-zh!' The door cracked at the joint and splintered inward. At the other door leading to the outside, a heavy pounding began and voices shouted for the Sugarat. Anareta was moving toward his gun locker when the inner door burst open, throwing him to the side.

Half a dozen men rushed into the room, their faces tight with animal rage. They found Sumner cowering beneath the chief's desk. He kicked and bucked, and they had to heave the desk over to get at him. They dragged him screaming out of the office and down the corridor to the locker room where the other men were waiting.

Anareta was left behind, and he struggled to right the toppled keypunch communicator. Minutes passed before he was able to reconnect the bent input-plug. Sumner's howls had fractured to wracked cries and sobs by the time a channel chattered open and the chief was able to link with the Conclave. More minutes echoed with screams as the transfer authorization from both the White and Black Pillars typed itself out. Anareta ripped the sheet off before the endcode signal was complete and surged out of the room.

Ahead, the screams had stopped, and only the jeers of the men and the sound of the beating could be heard.

The chief had to push men out of his way to get to Sumner. With a yell he silenced everyone: 'Let up! This boy isn't ours. If he dies, we're all dorgas!'

The men on the periphery pulled back, and Anareta glimpsed Sumner's hunched body, the clothes ripped away from a raw, bloody bulk. Then the men who had lost family in the Sugarat riots were before him—thick men stripped to the waist, their eyes smoky with red rage and contempt for his soft life. Both had blood-grimed rubber

121

hosing in their hands, and one of them shoved the end of the tubing up to Anareta's face. 'Chief, you're dead meat if you try to stop us.'

The chief pushed aside the bludgeon and held up the authorization order. 'I'm not trying anything. The White Pillar owns Kagan now. They know he's alive. If he's dead—we're worse than dead. All of us.'

One of the two men stepped back, and the other pressed dangerously closer. His face was emotionless and speckled with Sumner's blood. His voice was atonic: 'I'd rather be a dorga than let this dungball live.'

The chief stood fast, though the man was an inch away and his hard rubber hose was pressing sharply against his sternum. Anareta held the typed authorization high. 'To defy the Black Pillar is death,' he quoted the Codex of the Protectorate, 'but to defy the White Pillar is suffering. Who else here wants to live a long life in the dorga pits?'

'The chief's right,' one of the nearby men said loudly, and grumbles of agreement followed. 'The tud's hurt. He won't walk straight again.' Several of the closest men took the angry man's arms and gently moved him away from the chief.

Anareta's insides relaxed and then cramped even more fiercely when he saw what had become of Sumner. The boy's face was unrecognizable—a mask of stringing blood, torn tissue, and pink bone. Both of his arms were broken, winged at odd angles, the hands pulp white and lifeless. His legs, too, were cracked, and a shaft of broken bone gouged through his thigh. 'Mutra,' the chief gasped. 'Get a shock unit. Somebody—get help!'

He tore off his shirt and covered Sumner's quivering body. 'Everybody else out of here,' he ordered. 'The Conclave will want pain for this.'

The station cleared quickly, and when the medics arrived Anareta was alone, stooped over a half-alive man.

Sumner lifted himself awake, rising out of a maw of darkness. A mad whining turned in his ears, and he waited for the nightmare to continue. But the world had changed. Twangy medicinal odors clouded around him. And the light was softer, thin and gauzy.

The pain of his body had become so intense that it was pleasurable. For an age, it seemed, he had been dreaming of his hurt as a radiance. He was floating inside himself, his body a vision sustained by the intensity of his pain-pleasure. He twisted his body to ignite the fleshlight that had become his joy, but the fluffy embrace of a mattress swallowed most of his pain.

'It's over now,' a female voice said softly. The sweet, moist warmth of her breath sharpened Sumner's senses. The gentle fragrance of calambac lilted in the air, and a hazy face hovered above him. He tensed for an expected barb of pain, but the hand that touched him was quiet.

122

She bent closer, and he saw that her face was lovely as music. Dark heavy-hung hair settled around him. He lifted above the numbness of his body and saw the green physician's uniform the woman was wearing and the intravenous bladders hanging on the posts of his bed. But then the hurt of his body fractured his alertness, and he dropped back into his stupor.

'Stay with us, Sumner,' the doctor whispered, and the lambent caress of her hair silked over his face as she pulled away.

For a double-hearted moment, Sumner urged to reach past his hurt and hold this woman as he would have held his life, but he knew that if he let go of his pain-vision now, he would be giving up forever the dreaminess beaten into his nerves. Living would again become agony. But this woman—

A wave of loneliness swelled in him, and he clutched for her.

The first day that he was strong enough to touch her was the last day he saw her. By then consciousness had hardened enough for him to know that he was in an infirmary within sight of the Berth. Tall, narrow windows lined the walls, one for each bed in the ward. Sunlight, thick and steady as stone, lay on his face every morning, and the black days labored by.

Most nights his sleep was haunted and violent. In the languid light of false dawn he invariably woke to a vision of the doctor who had lured him back into his life with her tawny skin and black hair and breath that smelled of candy. For that one moment he was happy, and for the rest of the day the exasperating hallucination of her beauty dogged him. He was alone, as always. Betrayed into living. But why? Why had the police not killed him? The green-smocked medical staff that attended him and the other dour men in the ward knew nothing.

Chief Anareta visited Sumner once, but the boy became so agitated at the sight of the black, red-trimmed Massebôth uniform that the doctor in charge asked the chief to leave before he could introduce himself. The chief had come to say farewell. After the full report of the beating had been filed, the Black Pillar authorities had decided to retire the chief. He was being sent to a camp outside Xhule where his white card could be put to more regular use. Anareta was happy about his discharge. Xhule was a bucolic valley of garden villages and a university where he could pursue his kro studies. He had wanted to find some way of thanking the Sugarat, but after seeing the great fear in the boy he realized that the most he could do for Kagan was to forget him.

Gradually Sumner's pain shifted into healing aches: dull throbs, itching flesh and muscles. Yet he didn't want to live.

He tried to stop eating, but the staff shoved tubes through his nose and down his throat. And though he willed himself to die, his body continued to get stronger.

123

When the cruel day came for him to learn to walk again, he refused to move. His brain had been rubbed smooth with pain, and time meant little to him. Apart from the lunatic dreams that wracked him to a lathered frenzy each night, he was empty. No expectations. No hopes. Time would kill him. He would wait.

Hoping to awaken Sumner to his life, a blue-gowned nurse wheeled his bed to the lune ward and left him at the far end, where the vomit was crusted on the walls and the fecal stench numbed his whole body.

The lunes were the husks of McClure's society, people who had fallen into themselves in the chemical factories or the mines and who were kept alive for medical experiments. Their stares were vacant or, at best, beast-filled, and their phantom howls and gut-twisting shrieks gnawed at Sumner's nerves and made his nightmares even more terrible.

But Sumner refused to cooperate with the staff. He was determined to die, and he would have smothered himself in lassitude if an unexpected revulsion hadn't suddenly and evilly overcome him. One night he thrashed awake and found a milky-eyed lune chewing the scabs off his leg-wounds. The next day, he was ready to walk.

After a month of water exercises, weight lifting, and blinding pain, Sumner could move about without crutches. The staff had been patient and good with him, and his body healed well. But he showed no appreciation. He remained solitary and withdrawn, mechanically completing his workouts and eating his meals. Few thoughts moved through his numb mind, and those that did were simple, immediate animal logics. A sullen indifference misted his eyes, and the medical staff finally realized that the police had succeeded after all. The Sugarat was dead.

Chief Anareta entered a serene garden alongside the Berth. He was out of uniform, and he looked haggard in the green pullover and brown flannels he was wearing. For a full two minutes he stood beside a bluerose bush staring at a red-cowled monk who sat reading on a stone bench a few paces away.

When the savant glanced up, his head rocked with recognition and his cowl fell back, revealing a tough, blunt-featured face softened with surprise. 'Chief!' the monk rasped. He stood up with a coarse grunt, his body monolithic, his short hair streaked like smoke. 'You look smaller out of black.'

'The Pillars took my black away, Kempis.' Anareta companionably gripped the big savant's shoulder. 'I was retired after the deeps looked into me.'

Kempis' stare chiseled sharper. 'Deeps? How far into your mind did they look?'

'Not far enough to see you,' Anareta said with a reassuring smile.

Twenty years before, the chief had helped Kempis secretly enter the Protectorate. Before that the monk had been an outlander, the undistorted but homeless offspring of distorts, a wanderer and a bandit. Anareta had found him at a branding station where the wounded and heavily bandaged corsair was being fitted for drone headstraps. The wit-light in the huge man's eyes had stopped the chief the instant their gazes touched. Kempis was not an apparent distort, and the savage callousness that Anareta had become accustomed to seeing in the faces of ardent criminals was not there. Muscled by compassion, he had taken Kempis aside and spoken with him long enough to confirm what he had suspected: The man wasn't a ritual-programmed tribesman or gangmember—he was an individual. Through his bureaucratic contacts, the chief had been able to clear Kempis' record, secure him a green card, and position him as a savant with the White Pillar.

Savants had an easy life. They were essentially librarians and researchers, well respected in the Protectorate, and traditionally expected to extend the species by maintaining very active sex lives. Kempis had always been happy serving Mutra.

'The deeps were selective about my past,' Anareta clarified. 'They were more interested in my white card and my recent sexual exploits than what happened twenty years ago. All they really saw was that I'd rather study kro than manage a street division—so they relieved me. I'm off to Xhule tonight. By tomorrow I'll be studding in some forest bungalow.'

Kempis' hard face shone. 'I'm happy for you, Chief. Thirty years and the Pillars never suspected you were as much with the kro as with them. What broke it?'

'I was caught trying to pull out another white card—a fat kid who'd been jooching distort gangs into deathtraps.'

'I'd think the Pillars would medal him for that.'

'The Sugarat enraged the gangs more than he hurt them. The past five years, the distorts have been tearing up McClure like this was outland. When this kid was finally dragged in, I was the only one that wanted to see him live. That look on your face asks why.' Anareta shrugged, and uncertainty inscribed his brow with one long line. 'Why'd I pull you out? He's unique—an individual, not a distort or a simplewit. But my own men got to him. And that's why I'm here.'

Kempis took the chief's elbow and led him to the side of the bluerose shrubbery where they were out of sight of the Berth. 'What can I do for you?'

'Kempis, they're going to kill this kid.'

'You said he was a white card.'

'Yes, but he's very ugly. Even before my men broke his face, he was the kind of clumsy grossness that a stud mate would laugh at. His white card will keep him out of the dorga pits, but he's too dwarfed inside to make the mating circuit. I know they're going to send him to one of the heavy work camps—Carnou, Tred, maybe Meat City.'

Kempis' head was awry. 'How can I help him—and why do you want to?'

'He's a white card like me,' Anareta said, looking strongly at Kempis. 'I can't rut in peace without at least warning this kid. I want to tell him to get out—to leave the Protectorate.'

Kempis' raspy voice became almost soundless: 'Chief, he'll die on the outland.'

'You survived—and thrived for many years.'

'I was reared out there.'

Anareta slapped a bluerose to a splatter of petals. 'Look—I can't reach the kid. I'm leaving tonight. But I want you to talk with him.'

Kempis wheezed a sigh. 'He's locked up, isn't he?'

Anareta pulled a leather pouch from his trousers pocket and handed it to the savant. The pouch was heavy with coins. 'I still have friends in the Black Pillar. One of them will notify you when the kid's guard rotates to someone compliable. Use these zords to speak with the boy alone. Tell him to run if he can. Tell him it could be death out there, but make him know it *will* be death if he stays.'

The chief placed both of his hands on the monk's arms. 'He's my last prisoner—and I'm leaving for an easy life. I want to feel good about that life. Talk to the kid. Tell him who you are. That saved your life once. It might save him.'

Very early one morning Sumner was shaken awake by a chunky uniformed guard, and his green infirmary smock was replaced with brown fatigues and work boots. He was marched out of the infirmary into the gray smudged light of early dawn, across a flagstone courtyard and into the Berth. Icy green arc lights burned at uneven intervals along the top of the massive bellied wall. Inside, the air was close and fuscous.

After a brief pass-check, Sumner was prodded forward. He shuffled through opulent colubrine hallways lined with frescoes of the Mutric Redemption. Aloe incense scrolled out of side niches occupied by votive tallows and blue glass icons. Several times Sumner was stopped and his head tugged forward in obeisance as red-cowled savants strode by. Sumner replied woodenly, too hollowed out to care. At last they entered a tiny pocket-garden, and Sumner was ordered to sit.

The tight garden was open to the dawn sky, and the curving walls were tangled with vines. It was like a well of ivy. Sumner sat on a round stone bench beside a moss-speckled trough of curkling water. A lunette above the oval doorway depicted Sita's Firewalk, and Sumner fixated on the realistic rendering of limbs shriveled to smoldering twists of black, bubbled tar.

He was still gazing into the painting when the guard fiercely rapped

126

the back of his head. 'Rise!' he hissed.

A red-cowled savant was standing in the door. Sumner rose and automatically bowed his head.

'Relax, please.' The savant entered and placed a hand on Sumner's shoulder. 'Sit down.'

Sumner sat and watched with an empty expression as the savant reached beneath his robes and produced a small leather bag for the guard. With eyes reverently averted, the guard bowed, his fingers twitching over the bag, counting the silver through the leather.

After he had backed out of the garden, the savant folded back his cowl. He was a huge man, theandric, with short brindled hair and a face like granite: pale but hard, square and etched with many fine lines. 'I'm Kempis,' he said in a hoarse voice. 'Legally, we can't talk. I'm a White Pillar savant—the laws you violated were Black Pillar. It's costing me more in risk than in silver for this audience.'

Sumner stared through him, vague as fog.

A long minute of silence widened between them as Kempis studied the boy. Sumner was gangly and haggard from all the weight he had lost. The flesh around his eyes looked sunken and stained. The eyes themselves were clear but unfocused, gazing in a wide, depthless stare through a harrowing mask of scars.

When the savant spoke, an asthmatic rasp undercut his words: 'I've paid the Black Pillar so that I could speak with you. I think you should understand where you're going.' He drew in a whistling breath. 'The police, you know, want you dead. Regrettably, they never finished. Some savants found out about your white card. Because your genes are so rare, they think you're sacred, an envoy of Mutra, the last hope of our species. They're very devout but slimbrained. So now you're caught between the Black Pillar of the police and the White Pillar of the savants' Conclave.

'Do you know what it means to have a white card, son?' The darkness in Kempis' eyes thickened. 'There aren't a thousand in this city—less than a hundred thousand in the whole Protectorate. Even voors revere what that card represents. It means you're whole—one of the few in this broken world.'

Kempis leaned closer. 'A dark bargain's been struck. The police have agreed to let you live so that, perhaps, the Conclave will get you to breed other white cards. The preservation of the Massebôth is at stake. But I assure you, the Massebôth are going to make living worse than dying.'

Sumner watched him sleepily, the blue, vapid loneliness of the sky threading itself through his eyes.

Kempis sighed, his breath making a noise in his chest like fire. 'I have some advice for you.' His fingers moved slowly, unlacing the breast of his cowl. 'I'm not a typical savant. I know pretty well what you're going through. You see, before I entered the Conclave I was a

127

corsair. I had dreams like the Sugarat. But I worked the coasts instead of the streets. I moved by night, and on the sea, that takes as much guts as skill. I ran kiutl and renegades. I raided the reef colonies and the island outposts. And I killed only in defense and vengeance. It was a lonely, crazy-alive, hungry, stupendous way to live. And I'd be doing it today, except for this.'

He opened his cowl and revealed a chest livid with puckered scars. 'Knifed in a tavern brawl. Thirty-two wounds. When I recovered I entered the Conclave. What else could I do with half a lung?'

Sumner's gaze suddenly crisped. He understood the pain that had flowered into those scars, and he looked more directly at the man they had shaped.

Kempis laced up his cowl. 'My advice isn't some religious rauk. Mutra with her gory myths and sacred mumblings is just a throwback to the ancient Christom. It's not real. Nothing's real—but you. Your life. Your pain.'

He peered at Sumner, solemn as a cobra. 'The White Pillar will stud you if they can, but the Black Pillar wants you hurting. Don't let either of them get you. Cut them off as soon as you can. You're young, and the physicians say you're still whole. So stop acting like a corpse. Come alive. This world is huge and strange. I've seen things in it I don't believe myself anymore. But it's all out there—distorts, voors, creatures and places we don't have names for yet. Get away the first chance you get. Become a corsair. Go north. Go as far as you can. Only freedom is real.'

He wheezed and sucked at the air. 'Believe me, the north is another world. The Massebôth won't follow you there. And some of those distort women—' He chuckled with croupy abandon and then struggled to catch his breath.

'Where are the Massebôth sending me?' Sumner asked, his voice gritty. 'Where am I going?'

Kempis stared at him in silence, intrigued and gratified. Then: 'If you knew that, son, you'd have lived forever.'

Broux's face was cruel: the mouth a slash, the jaw a clamp, the skin bronzed from sunburn and malaria, the hair iron-gray and cropped close to the carved contours of his square head. He was the commander of Meat City, a slimy hole punched into the green shimmering face of the western rain forest. Broux's camp looked more like a trash heap than the military camp it was supposed to be. In fact, the scraggy lot walled in by jungle was a human trash heap, the final depot where the Massebôth Black Pillar sent the personnel too rebellious for service in the regular units but too valuable to be executed. Under Broux's brutal command, the soldiers were pitted against the jungle and worked into conformity or else broken.

Broux took a special interest in Sumner from the first. He saw the boy, scab-masked and painworn, as he limped out of the strohlkraft that had delivered him and eight others to Meat City. The men were lionfaced, their gazes guarded but truculent, the fight in them strong—but the boy was different: he stood squatly on the landing field staring with open apprehension at the monotonous litter of rotting shacks and scantling huts set on concrete pilings above mustard-yellow mudflats.

Unlike everyone else in the camp he had a white card stapled to his file, and the White Pillar had appended a rider in bold print: Sumner Kagan was to be worked hard, but he wasn't to be killed. Twice a year he would be taken to a breeding hostel—other than that, Broux could do whatever he liked with the boy.

'You're mine now, Kagan,' Broux growled. The dragondark of his eyes looked the boy over, seeing the shape of the animal inside Sumner's withered obesity, already knowing exactly how much pain this body could digest. 'If you work in Meat City, you live. The only rest here is death.' Broux's grin sharked straight back over his jaw, then vanished instantly. 'It's three kilometers around this clearing. Run the jungleline. Go!'

Sumner loped off, and Broux barked after him: 'Pick it up, Kagan. Run!'

Sumner ran, steadily at first. But as the sun rose higher, hot and arrogant in the sky, something in him began to unravel. Colors ribboned by, and the blood drummed faster as if boiling in his ears. He retched and gasped at the thick air, and long, deep muscles knotted up in his legs. He was still limping around the camp at nightfall when Broux called him in.

Eaten by fatigue, Sumner didn't have the strength to pick up his rations, but Broux pushed his face into the bean paste, and so he ate. Immediately afterward he collapsed on his cot and lay unmoving until Broux rolled him out at dawn.

Again he was ordered to run the jungleline. By the time he had eased into the rhythm of his run, the sun's heat had become rabid. At noon he collapsed and had to be slapped awake by a guard.

Sumner swayed to his feet and forced himself to run—hard, hoping a stroke would tug him out of Broux's grasp. For days this nightmare repeated itself. Then, miraculously, the hours thinned out. A secret compartment swelled open in his lungs, and the fire he had been carrying in there cooled. Limitless power flowed into his tendons, and the hot needles pinning his shoulders to his chest fell away, leaving his body loose and slinky. He glided through the drifts of sunlight with defiant strides.

Broux was impressed. The McClure police had wracked Sumner, and Broux had been convinced by the boy's shivering gaze that his will was warped. But Sumner was stronger than the bruised mash of his body revealed. The next day, from the shade of his command tent,

Broux watched as Sumner joined the other men for the hole patrol—the daily grave detail.

The digging didn't go well for Sumner. On the fringe of the jungle, a damp miasmic heat steaming softly around him with the death pall of the graves, Sumner breathed through his mouth and tried lifting small shovelfuls of yellow mud. Soon the grim heat built up in his fatigues, and when he peeled back his shirt the stinging flies tormented him.

Nevertheless he worked relentlessly, wanting the heat to kill him. His hands were sloughed raw by the splintery handle of his spade, and his body was cramped with pain and fatigue. At day's end he returned to his hut feverish, too exhausted to eat the bitter herbs and root paste that was dinner but force-fed by Broux's pincer grip at the back of his neck. Afterward he lay flat on his cot, stupefied, numbed free of his nightmares.

Time blurred into routine for Sumner. Broux worked him hard nine days and rested him one. For a long time Sumner slept through those free days, too hollow to dream. But one day he found that he wasn't wasted enough to ignore the barrack flies anymore. He spent that day meandering about the camp, groggily pondering his situation.

He was a slave, he realized, his will as exhausted as his body. Broux was working him, not to death, but to the brink of life, keeping him alive for the White Pillar—or just for the pain. Sumner didn't know.

He thought of Kempis and running away. And he thought of Nefandi, the deva, and the voors, and his dread sparkled. The world was evil, too dark to be enlightened by thoughts. And that made the painful routines of Meat City seem good. When the hole patrol trudged by with the buckled bodies of that day's dead, the familiarity of their workchant soothed away all desire for escape.

At the end of the day, as he undressed for sleep, he was amazed by how much his body had changed. His thighs, which ached close to the bone with weariness, were contoured now, and his arms had thickened and deepened around the shoulders. Without a mirror, he contented himself to lie in the dark, feeling the tautness of his stomach and the curved breadth of his chest. The mood of a ghost-thin pride softened his dreaming that night. But Broux had seen that Sumner's stamina was expanding, and the next day he worked him harder than ever. For many weeks after that, Sumner's life was felt and not thought.

Broux tossed a handful of pebbles into a mudpool and watched the watercircles dawn through each other. Behind him the work crews were lining up beneath a holt of immense rubber trees for that day's assignments. The officers with machine pistols strapped to their thighs and clipboards in their hands were shouting through the bodycount. Broux listened to the distant roll call with melancholy. He was tired of being a warden. He was almost sixty, and this was all his life had come to: corrosive air, fevered flies, riotous jungle walls—a prison as much for him as for any of the wretched men he had been ordered to break.

But was his fate different from anyone else in the Protectorate? He turned to supervise the men as they filed past, dragging their shovels and machetes to the jungle's fringe. The cities were sour-hearted with dorga pits—everybody had a distort-brother, sister, or child—and the most anyone could hope for was to stay whole. Why was the world this way? Why did flesh go wrong? He heelkicked a rock into the mudpool and cleared his mind. A man could break his teeth on questions like this.

Sumner Kagan appeared on line, trudging toward the rubber trees. Broux watched him with satisfaction. The boy was expanding and hardening, growing stronger each week. A full year had passed since he had arrived, bloated with fat and pain, and no orders had come from the White Pillar to reclaim him. Months ago Broux had contacted an officer high in the Conclave to collect on a longstanding debt. Years before, Broux had helped a distorted relative of this savant get forged papers; in return, Broux had requested that Sumner Kagan's records with the White Pillar be permanently misplaced. Apparently this had been done, and now the boy was all his.

Sumner hulked against a wall of hanging vines, his longcurved back writhing with the powerful strokes of his machete arm as he cut his way into the green mass. Broux watched him approvingly. Like an anatomist, Broux knew the body's inner dynamics—what routines shaped what muscles; what muscles aligned the bone-structure; what alignments gave the most strength. He had been using that knowledge to select Sumner's work projects. And he followed him carefully, observing how his form was changing, studying how best to mold his body. The rewards for Broux were going to be great. A protomale on the military market would earn him enough zords to get away from Meat City and retire to a homestead colony near Xhule or Onn. Those were forest cities, too small for dorga pits. They were as far away from the brutality of his profession as he could hope to get.

That joyful thought poised between his eyes like a point of pain, and he had to pick up a rock and clench it between his fingers to steady himself.

Sumner kept to himself. Some of the men worked in groups, laughing and cursing themselves through the monotony of their labors and sharing silence when Broux and the guards were near. But Sumner lived too close to his pain, and the others thought he was animal-dull. Only one midgeyed young man was drawn to him—a boy called Dice. The men loathed Dice: He was talkative and orgulous, and he wasn't big enough to do an equal share of work. He was harried constantly, except when Sumner was around. Everyone feared Sumner, not only because he had become one of the largest men in camp but because he was Broux's animal.

'I'm an opportunist,' Dice introduced himself to Sumner among the emerald shadows of the jungle. Kagan was stump-digging, stooped and hacking at the wire-taut treeroots, sweat sparking off him with each blow. 'I've been called a deserter because I left my squad and went to Vortex. That's why I'm here. But I wasn't running away. If I was deserting, I'd have gone north to Carnou. There are voors in Carnou, and they're always looking for blue cards. That's what I've got—a blue card. It means I've got just one gene defect and it's a sleeper; it'll never touch me. Only a white card's better, but there aren't any of them around. The government takes them away early and studs them. My blue card's the best you'll see. If I was deserting, I'd just go to Carnou and let the voors have me. But what kind of life is that, whoring for voors? Mutra, that's rucksouled. No, I wasn't deserting. I went to Vortex to play kili. That's why I'm called Dice. I'm the best. And I was going to come out strong in the kilithon at Vortex. It's only held every third year. Last time, I was weighted. That means I made it to the top fifth. Do you know how many zords I could have made in the top fifth if I'd played? Foc, I could have bought myself out of the army and still had zords to rent a suite in a Prophecy bordello. I'm that good, you know. I've been playing kili since I could draw the triangle. Do you ever play?'

Sumner was up to his waist in root-tangle and jungle mulch, his whole body fighting with the earth.

'You work hard, soldier.' Dice tugged away one of the thick rootlimbs Sumner had dislodged. 'You're not like the other goofers here. They do what they have to do, those tuds, and that's all. They're buckers—like me. But you're different. You're crazy different to work so hard.'

Sumner seemed lost in his labor, his face knotted around his breath—but he was listening. After months of solitude with only the rawk of parrots and the gibbering of monkeys, the boy's babbling pleased him. Soon they fell into a work rhythm, with Dice all the while filling the air with his talk, picking up the work-leavings, sharpening the machetes, and clearing away the light brush. Even Broux approved, for Sumner was working harder.

'He watches you closely,' Dice said one golden afternoon in a forest clearing, seeing Broux standing squat and solid in the treeshadows. Sumner was splitting logs, his back clenching and heaving, and he didn't look up. 'He always has an eye out for you,' Dice went on. 'I think he's working you up to something, you know? I think he's an opportunist, too.'

Dice casually continued snipping the twigs off the logs that Sumner was going to split, but his gaze had turned inward. 'You've heard of protomales, Kagan? You look like one. I mean, you're big And there are units in the army that pay a lot for big men. You think that's why Broux is working you up? I notice you get more food than anyone here. The other buckers see it, too, but they don't talk. You're Broux's. He's working you up for something. What's your card color?'

'White,' Sumner grunted in midstroke.

The crack of the cleaving log jarred through Dice. 'Are you jooching me?' He scurried to Sumner's side and knelt in the grass, staring up at his grimacing body as the axhead flashed in the sun. 'You have a white card? Mister—what are you doing here? Men with white cards don't suffer in Meat City.'

Dice spotted Broux strolling along the treeline, and he hurried over to the fallen logs and began stripping them busily. 'Broux's working you up, Kagan. Can you see it? A protomale with a white card will earn him more zords than he can count. But why are you here? A white card doesn't belong in this hole.'

That evening Sumner relented to Dice's dogging questions and told him about the Sugarat and his beating in the police barracks.

'The White Pillar pulled you out. They won't leave you here,' Dice said when Sumner was done. 'Unless Broux found some way to dupe them.' Dice's eyes brightened shrewdly. 'Broux is using you, Kagan. He's jooched the White Pillar, and he's working you up for his own profit. It's obvious.'

Sumner hefted his machete and stood up. The evening wind slipping off the pampas was flowery and moist and empty of human scents. 'Come on—we'll miss chow.'

Dice leaped to his feet and stood in front of Sumner. 'Kagan, Broux is using you. He's going to sell you to some clodbusting unit, and you'll spend your life in fly-piss outposts gutting distorts. You don't have to do that. You're a white card. The Pillars will hold you up. You'll have women, real food, and you'll never see a distort as long as you live. All you have to do is get past Broux. That might be difficult, but if you stay alert, you'll find the way. I'll help you.'

Sumner shook his head. 'No.'

'Kagan, you need plans. Otherwise when the chance is there, you won't even know it.'

'No plans. No help.'

'You're zaned. Or else you're jooching me. No man with a white card would live like a jungle rat. Life can be everything good.'

Sumner's face looked hollow. 'What makes you think life can be good?' He pushed Dice out of his way and walked into the jungle toward camp.

Dice watched after him with a slack face. Then he shouted: 'It's all there is!' Then, softer: 'Ratfoc—' and sprinted through the rising

133

darkness to catch up with him.

The western horizon was nicked with dawn but the skull of the sky was still dark when the corsairs raided Meat City. They dropped onto the parade ground between the barracks in three rackety, patchwork strohlkraft, a carnival of firebombs and flares blazing overhead.

Sumner was at the latrine ditch cupping a handful of water to clean himself when the darkness erupted into squinting radiance. He dropped to his belly, his sarong tangled at his ankles, and watched as the three battered strohlkraft settled in a haze of rainbowing smokefire. Bright flashes from the turret guns rattled the guards' barracks, flipping the tin eaves into the air.

The cargo hatches winged open, and a crowd of wildly garbed corsairs leaped howling and laughing onto the parade ground waving rifles and torch pistols. By the watery light of the flares Sumner could see that many of them were distorted: clawed hands, crusted lizard faces, milky eyes. Half were women.

'Let's go, you bulldogs!' the amplifier of a pirate ship bellowed. 'Foc slavery! You're not shackled to the Pillars anymore! Come out and run with us!'

Gunshots caromed from the jungleline where most of the guards had retreated, and half the corsairs crouched and returned fire. The other half assaulted the barracks, torching the timbers and running the prisoners out of their cots.

Broux was dashing around the guards' barracks, two pistols flaring in his hands, shouting his men out of their shock. The ground was twitching and jumping at his feet, but he ran tall. Then the gun turrets of the other two pirate ships swiveled and roared into fire at the same instant. The guards' barracks rolled away like thunder, and Broux crawled in the dirt with his head under his arms. By the time he looked up, the men who wanted to run were being pulled into the holds of the pirate ships. Those who knew their time in Meat City was almost up cowered behind the barracks and the water troughs.

Sumner was tempted to run, but as he tightened his sarong a figure scrambled to his side and took his arm. Dice looked up at him with fervent eyes. 'Take me with you.'

Sumner shrugged off his grip. 'I'm not going anywhere.'

'The Pillars don't hold up anything,' the pirate amplifiers blared. 'They crush the people beneath them. Topple the Pillars!'

'Kagan, let's go,' Dice urged him with a whine.

'You want to run with those things?' Sumner chinpointed to the spiderhaired faces of the corsairs helping the last runaways clamber aboard.

'We can skip on them later. Come on—this is our chance.'

Sumner shook his head *no*. 'We'd just be trading one master for another.'

134

Dice slumped and watched disconsolately as the ships began to rise, cargo doors still open. 'Topple the Pillars!' The cry wobbled in the air, chopped by the bawl of thrusting engines. Guns sparked, dawnlight flashed on the flight vanes, and the pirate ships leaned into the darkness and drifted away over the jungle.

Dice was depressed. For days after the corsair raid he sulked. Sumner, who had become accustomed to the boy's constant prattle, looked about for a way to cheer him up. He found a large hive deep in the forest, and one evening he returned to camp swollen with bee stings.

The men laughed at him silently that night as he ate his bean paste and roots with swollen fingers and lips. Later he called Dice aside and led him behind the barracks to a knoll surrounded by raspberry canes. From there they could see the night-lights on the strohlkraft field and that day's latrine crew laboring in the dark, burying the old ditches.

'What do you want, Thick?' Dice muttered, looking about to see if Broux was in sight. 'You'd better ask Iron Face for some althea salve. You're not going to sleep tonight with those stings.'

Sumner's puffed face smiled vaguely. 'Taste this, grump.' He parted the raspberry canes and revealed several thick amber combs of honey. 'If we keep this out of sight, we'll have power food for the next two weeks.'

Dice's pupils expanded with wonder.

Sumner picked off the ants and handed him a thumbpiece of honeycomb. 'We'll have to put some hawkweed around here to keep the bugs off. I don't think the guards or anybody else will be prowling this close to the latrines.'

'This isn't real.' Dice chewed on the honey with closed eyes, and the joy in his face brightened Sumner's blood.

A Massebôth strohlkraft idled on the flight field, its wiry shape black against the belly of twilight. The pilot squatted beneath a flame tree at the edge of the field, chatting with Broux, while Sumner and eight others unloaded the cargo hold. Sumner's mind was tight with exhaustion. All day he had been stooped over, cutting cassava, and he lumbered thoughtlessly beneath the ponderous crates, his eyes loosely following the leech-scarred legs of the man before him. Dice, trailing loose-kneed beneath his load, was too wearied to speak.

Unexpectedly, the man Sumner was following dropped his load and skipped out of sight. Sumner shoved back the wooden crate on his shoulders in time to see him scrambling up the hull of the strohlkraft and into the open hatch of the flight pod. The crate dropped from Sumner's back, and he and the seven other men watched with gawking amazement as the runaway dropped into the pod-sling and sparked the shutdown engine.

The pilot, Broux, and several guards were dashing across the field, shouting for them to seize the hijacker. Any one of them could have done it: The man was only three paces away, working the controls, charging the thrusters, angling the altitude vanes. But the jittery-faced renegade obviously knew the strohlkraft, and excitement paralyzed everybody.

The dust of the field billowed, pebbles clattered against the ship's bottom, sand grit stung their faces and limbs, and with a wildcat scream the strohlkraft lifted. Two of the nearest men jumped into the cargo hold. A third clung to a landing strut and was lifted into the air.

'Mutra.' Dice found his voice. 'They're going to make it!'

For a few moments the men watched as the strohlkraft rose into the night, disappearing into the rhythm of skyfires, the spin noise of its engines falling down the sky toward the last wet light of the day.

Sumner swayed with a surge of wonder. Then Broux and the guards were on them, and someone clubbed Sumner on the side of his head, and he went down. When he shook the numbness from his eyes he saw the guards pushing the men he was with to the ground. Dice dropped with a whimper and covered his head. At Broux's nod the guards opened fire, their machine-pistols flaring in the blue-shadowed dusk.

Sumner staggered to his feet, and one of the guards put a gun to his head, the heat of the muzzle singeing the hairs of his temple. 'Not him!' Broux shouted, and the gun barrel fell away.

Sumner stared with horror at the sprawled bodies among the scattered crates, the smell of gunfire thickening. The pain of what he saw seared through his eyes to the back of his head and almost knocked him out. Dice lay with the white of his brains splattered in the gravel.

'Shoot me!' Sumner cried, and the guards looked quickly to Broux.

'Get back to the barracks,' Broux ordered him. But Kagan didn't move.

'Shoot me!' he cried again, louder, seizing the arm of one of the guards. The guard shook off his hold and leveled his pistol at him.

'Leave him be,' Broux commanded. 'Sumner, fall back!'

Sumner's eyes had hardened in his face. 'Why are you keeping me alive?'

Broux strode over to him and sharply belted him across the face, twice. 'Go to the barracks.'

Sumner had gone rigid, rage wreathing his heart. For an instant he thought of unraveling into violence—but all the guards had their guns out, and the abandoned pilot was cursing Broux under his breath to shoot him. Suddenly it just seemed right to walk away. His stance broke, and he shuffled toward the barracks, hearing Broux's barked commands, calling for men to bury the executed. Distantly, at the furthest orbit of hearing, the drone of a strohlkraft was fading into the north.

Sumner lay in his cot awake and unmoving all night. All his thoughts were voided, and he felt an acid hate for everything Masseboth. Toward dawn, images of Dice rose in him with memories of the simple jokes and the shared work they had known. During roll call, he moved on line like a deadwalker, and though Broux told him through the guards that he could take the day off, he collected his machete and slumped into the jungle.

In an isolated vine-cove, he lashed at the trees with his machete, his bones throbbing. Distantly he thought of running away. But there was nowhere to go.

Then, like an avalanche in his world of unhappy awareness, memories crowded in on him, and his machete flailed uselessly at the air. Vivid images of his old, cluttered room and his scansule and his three-wheeled bottle-green car and his mother's spicy cooking overwhelmed him; and he dropped to his knees. What had become of him? He looked down at his hands and saw scabby, callused, reptilian flesh. He covered his face and began to cry.

He longed to go home. He longed not to die. But then starker images shaped themselves behind his lids: images of black-uniformed men with leering grins, ripping off his clothes, fondling him, pissing on him, striking him until he couldn't see or breathe—

He howled and slashed out with his machete. Lurching to his feet, he cut at the trees with a stupendous strength, hacking at their hard wood until he was staggered and his breathing got tangled in his throat with his rage. Lolling against a moss-padded tree, his face pressed into the cool bark, his machete arm trembling, he tried to cry again. But he couldn't.

With the blood still thundering in his ears, he turned and went back to work.

Broux realized that Sumner had become dangerous. Soon the boy would turn on him, and the guards would have to kill him. Very quickly now, he had to be readied for sale. The optimum price would be offered by the Black Pillar only for a protomale—a human whose physical strength and agility were clearly superior to others of his size. Certainly Sumner's white card helped, for that meant he would not suddenly molt into a distort. And as a result of Broux's arduous work assignments, Sumner had the bulk and the strength of a protomale, but he was not yet lithe enough. His muscles had to be stretched and limbered—and swiftly.

To help him, Broux employed Derc, an army masseur. He had a chest like a wall and arms as long as an orangutan's. He knew the human body with his hands as well as Broux knew it with his eyes and mind. Together they remade Sumner.

Stretched out on a cedar table, Sumner learned a new kind of pain. Derc's iron fingers felt out muscle-locked tensions and kneaded them loose, then went deeper, pushing past the fascia that held the muscles in place, probing the fiber-bunched memories jammed close to the bone.

Derc started with a foot, slicing down the sole with the hard edge of his thumb, pushing deep into the sensitive meat of the arch and then flaying the foot wide, separating each toe and its ligaments. The years of abuse that the foot had absorbed from Sumner's heavy, pounding gait bloomed like fiery flowers. The big toe was the worst. It had gone stiff in the confines of Sumner's boots and had to be ripped free from its locked position. The pain blared through Sumner's bones and poured out of him in a cold sweat.

Days on the cedar table passed, before Derc, heavy-lidded and blankfaced, had moved his fingers through every inch of Sumner's body. And though the pain was brain-smoothing, especially around the scars where his flesh remembered indignities his mind had shut out, there was something beautiful about feeling his muscles slide free under his skin.

The worst of it was when Derc collapsed Sumner's face. His nose had been so thoroughly shattered by his police torture that the physicians hadn't even tried to build it up. They removed a lot of cartilage and bone, widened the nasal cavities and let the nose heal over, lumpy and almost flat to the face. As Derc worked on his nose and lips, thumb-ironing the muscles pinched into scars, Sumner returned to the fleshlight pain that he had known in the police barracks of McClure.

Those brief, lucid moments of pain-charged beauty were the only joy left in Sumner's life. With Dice gone, Kagan was drained of all fellow feeling, and he sank into a deep silence disturbed only by an occasional surge of revenge-lust. Eventually even that passion became silent—though it did not disappear.

Sumner's body had become sleek and limber in a few short weeks. Broux was happy, and to round out his training, he personally taught Sumner how to swim in the deep, silent fish pool far back in the jungle. White-crested harpy eagles dominated the pools, diving noiselessly out of the highest trees to pluck a thrash of fish out of the water. They watched through wild masks of rage as Sumner splashed and lurched across their feeding pools.

The water's spell and Sumner's new body returned him to a feeling he had not known since he was the Sugarat. What had been dread in him then had widened into a psychic stamina that was indefatigable. Restlessness became vigor, and anxiety became clarity. The stronger he got, the more sharply he sensed what he had to do. Somehow, in a way that would leave him his life, he would have to kill Broux.

*   *   *

138

After Sumner mastered the feel of his new body in the water, Broux moved him to the broad river north of the settlement where a handful of men did the fishing for the camp. Long nets were lowered each morning and raised again in the afternoon.

Sumner spent most of his time clearing the thick weeds along the river edge, but occasionally he was sent into the water to free a net or help lift a catch. Watching the men around him, he learned how to dive hard with a rock in his hands and how to make snorkels by weaving together the bladders of giant pirarucu fish with slender river reeds. Each day he strengthened his lungs and legs by swimming underwater against the drunken currents.

One giant-clouded afternoon, with the sunlight sweeping like wind over the water, Broux came out to supervise Sumner's work. He sat in the leaf-patterned shadows as Sumner laboriously dredged fallen trees nearby, making way for a shallow-water harbor that was being built. When the call went up that one of the nets had snagged, Broux signaled him to go down and work it loose.

Sumner dived into the water immediately, but this time he was careful to catch a balloon of air in his shirt. He angled down to the bottom and surveyed the net. It had caught on a tree limb and would be easy to pull free, but he left it tied off. He settled into the shuddering feelers of river-kelp and felt around for a rock. He found a fist-size stone, touched bottom, and waited.

He knew Broux would come for him as soon as he thought his animal had been tied up. He sat on the bottom, gently sipping at his air supply.

Minutes passed, and then a cloud of air exploded the light-slick surface. Broux came kicking down fishfaced toward the net. Sumner thrust the rock before him and rose to meet his master. The stone caught the diving man over his right eye and knocked him senseless. Broux unfolded like a paper doll in the bloodsmoked water, his face stupid and kind, and Sumner took him from above by his shoulders. He pulled the body down and forced the head through the net. The last of Broux's life streamed out of his mouth in a bright vapor as Sumner tangled the man's arms in the rope and twisted him to look as if he had snagged himself. With deathclouded eyes, Broux watched as Sumner rose toward the light.

Sumner had almost drowned himself forcing Broux's body into the net, and two men were needed to resuscitate him after he was washed to shore. That, of course, made his story of Broux's bravery believable, and the only uncertainty for the Massebôth was figuring out to whom Kagan belonged now.

Black Pillar authorities decided, with their usual grim justice, that the Tactical Diving Corps—the most perilous, hardworking crew in the military—should get him. With that week's cargo strohlkraft,

Sumner was flown from the western rain forests of Meat City across the continent to the rocky headlands on the east coast, south of Carnou. Three days after the river incident he found himself diving from swaying derrick towers into deep but narrow water troughs. He was forced to swim marathon distances at night with a sandbag lashed to his back, and for days on end he was left treading water far out at sea, a wooden spar his only solidity. In a confined pool, with a small club, he had to apply combat techniques against bolt-eyed sharks. And though the horror of his life had intensified, he was glad to be free of Broux.

In the Corps, at least, he was treated like any other man. He wore a blue jumpsuit with the black-and-white Massebôth emblem on the sleeves, and he bunked in zinc-shelled barracks far from the jungle. But, unlike the other men, he had known the great, futureless pain of Meat City and servitude, and he was happy only when exhaustion freed him. Uninterested in his barrack's meager entertainments, he spent all his leave time practicing diving drills or swimming and running to the frayed fringes of his endurance.

Openly, the camp mocked him for his emotionless life. But secretly he was envied for his remarkable diving skills and strength. He won several rare citations for breaking distance and stamina records, and he became a camp hero in Corps competitions.

None of that, though, had any value for Sumner. Life for him was a prolonged and tedious exertion, devoid of pleasure or ambition. Not even death seemed worth striving for. Occasionally at night beneath the deep throw of stars and skyfires, he thought of Kempis and freedom, but in the day thoughts of running away seemed cold and tiny. His daily life was mechanical, and he, in turn, had become spiritless as a machine.

So it wasn't bravery or compassion but merely routine that sent him one day toward death. On an assignment in a choppy, storm-driven sea, a dinghy that he and four other men were huddled in capsized. They were all in red wetsuits, but the one man who was strapped to the oxygen tanks hit his head on the keel and sank out of sight.

Everybody went down after him as far as they could without exhausting the breath they needed to surface. Sumner kept going. The water turned cold, then colder, and ached against his ears. A cramped fist of pain twisted in his chest and tried to knuckle up his throat, but he thrashed his legs harder and lanced deep into the dark.

His brain was rending into vaporous light when his hands closed on the oxygen tanks. He dragged at the mouthpiece and filled his lungs with life; then he fitted the mouthpiece to the other man and bearhugged him as he had been taught. The man was alive and became lighter as his chest swelled. Sumner unbuckled all but one of the tanks, and with his companion secured under his arm, he began the slow ascent. An hour later he broke the surface, untied the tank, and backstroked for shore with the man in tow.

Shortly after that, two men from the Massebôth elite forces visited him. They wore crushed leather swagger-jackets, buff-colored regimentals, and red felt rumal caps with silver cobra insignias.

Sumner was sitting on his cot with his clothes off, drifting toward sleep, when they came in. They sat on either side of his bunk, and a musky odor of sagebrush and the outside filled the air. One of them had mocha-colored skin and sloped Mongol eyes. His name was Ignatz, and though there was an animal-distance in his gaze, he surveyed Sumner with approval. The soldier with the chiptoothed grin and peach-down moustache called himself Gage.

They explained right away—Gage in an easy manner, Ignatz with terse, leathery statements—that his fearlessness and his strength had become well known, and that they wanted to show him a good time and talk to him about their elite corps—the Rangers.

Sumner stared back at them, remote as a mountain. 'This squad owns me,' he said with his eyes half closed.

Ignatz walked a square of red paper through his fingers and presented it to him. It was a three-day pass.

They took him up the coast in a seasled at full throttle, shearing through a maze of night trawlers, skipping across the oily reflections of torchlit villages, and finally gliding into a solitary lantern-strung cove. The rangers gave Sumner a room in the opulent arbor-cottage there. He slept soundly in a shagsheet hammock, and when he woke at dawn he forgot for a moment where he was.

Both rangers were already up. They were dressed casually in hipslung army briefs and colorful jupes. Ignatz was tending a steampit of sea spiders dug into the sand, and Gage was arranging ice over red-glass bottles of mentis beer.

Gage threw a bottle at Sumner, and Kagan snatched it out of the air.

'You enjoy killing?' he asked, as Sumner hunkered down next to him.

Sumner looked at the ranger flatly, remembering too clearly the horrible dread that had driven him to kill as the Sugarat and the deep pain that had turned him against Broux. 'No.'

'But you like it.' Gage's eyes were clear and active as water spinning over rocks. 'If you didn't, you wouldn't have been so good at it.'

'Or done it at all,' Ignatz's dark voice said as he settled beside Sumner. He was a partial deep—a telepath that the Rangers had found useful in their recruiting endeavors. When he looked into Sumner he saw the Nothungs tumbling into an acid vat and the Black Touch distorts soaked with firegum, the smoke twisting off their bodies like a dark music. He cleanly snapped the neck off a bottle with

141

a jerk of his wrist and passed the foaming brew to Gage. 'Nobody kills the way you did without liking it.'

'I don't like it.'

Ignatz gave Sumner a long, penetrating look. Then he pushed himself up with his legs and returned to the baking spider crabs.

Gage knocked his beer bottle against Sumner's and apologized for his partner with a broad smile. 'Ignatz likes to kill. In the reef colonies, he stalks the village wharves and taverns looking for corsairs to slice. He's a distort-mauler. I'm different. On assignment I've seen distort tribes knock strohlkraft out of the air with nothing more than their minds. That's enough evil for me. When I take my four-month leave each year I prefer spending my time at places like this, savoring my life. Ignatz and I are the two extremes of the Rangers. I think you'll fit in closer to me.'

Ignatz called them over to the firepit, and Gage handed Sumner another beer. While they ate, the two rangers took turns recounting tales of the weird north.

'If I thought you could believe me,' Ignatz said with piercing sincerity, 'I'd tell you about a telepathic jungle and a city of intelligent apes.'

Sumner nodded with polite interest. He too had experienced the unbelievable, and he listened with an open, accepting face.

By noon Sumner had heard enough stories and swilled enough mentis beer to feel zestful but at ease. His eyes were shiny, and he watched with bemused interest as Ignatz used the edge of his hand to snap the necks off half-empty bottles of beer. Gage went into the cottage and returned with three gorgeous women.

Sumner's heart exploded when he saw them, but he managed to keep his face composed. Gage introduced them, and their names rattled in Sumner's head with the jarring memories of all the women he had loved but never known in McClure. He sucked anxiously at another mentis beer.

Both Ignatz and Gage handled themselves with such poise that soon Sumner was once again sincerely relaxed. Even drinking beer with long foam-swallowing gulps or nonchalantly fondling their women, the gestures and mannerisms of the two rangers were clean and purposeful. No action of theirs was gratuitous, and that impressed Sumner more than the rangers' stories.

When it came time to go into the cottage with his woman, Sumner feigned indifference. The woman was shadowhaired and lean as smoke, her green eyes tigered with gold. She spent the whole night and much of the next day ingeniously and compassionately using her almond-brown body to dispel his unease. Her mouth worked with a dexterity he thought reserved for fingers alone, and he experienced a violent pleasure with her.

The next day his body was laved in blissful lethargy. Sitting alone

142

with the rangers in a golden afternoon of seaspray, driftwood fires, braised fish, and mentis beer, he listened abstractedly to their proposals.

'We want you with us,' Ignatz told him. 'You'll be trained in Dhalpur, our secret school, for four to ten years—until you develop the skills to make the cut. Then you'll start earning more zords than the highest-paid officers in any other division. Also, you get four months off a year, and the time accumulates if you waive.' The sketchy eyebrows of the taut, sundark face went up in a silent 'Well?'

Sumner replied simply: 'My squad owns me.'

'You can get a transfer,' Ignatz said. 'The Rangers have weight.'

'Look, we're interested in you,' Gage picked up. 'We know about Sugarat. We know about Meat City. We know about Broux. And we know how you killed him.' He smiled with his eyes but not his mouth. 'Face it, Kagan, you're death-fixed. You're not going to be happy protecting prawn ships and finding lost buoys. You need risk.'

Sumner's jaw pulsed. 'It's all shit,' he said darkly. 'I die and that's that. I'm dead. It's all shit.' He stared at them with the solemnity of a bull. 'As long as I'm doing something, as long as I'm moving, I'm not thinking, just moving and not knowing. The Rangers or the Corps, what's the difference?'

'The world, mister,' Ignatz snarled.

'You're young,' Gage cut in quietly. 'You don't know the strange. The Massebôth are holed up in these cheap cities with their backs to the ocean. Why? What's got us with our strohlkraft and our artillery sitting tight on the edge of nowhere? There's a world out there you won't believe. And the only way you're going to see it is as a ranger. We're the front line. Nobody else goes as far north as we do. But only the best are asked to join us. We want men who have no shadows, men who are already dead, men who don't know the word future. Is that you—or have we made a mistake?'

The transfer papers were waiting for Sumner when he returned to the Corps camp, and he didn't have to think long about joining the Rangers. The remoteness of the other men in his squad and the monotony of his training decided for him.

Two days after he signed the papers and returned to camp, a black swayvan arrived at dawn to take him away. The dogfaced driver said nothing during their seven-hour drive into the desert. The rough ride ended in the heat-rippled air of a glaring salt bed, where a strohlkraft was idling with its cargo hatch open. Sumner rode alone in the carryhold, clutching an airstrap during the shuddering flight. The strohlkraft touched down in several nameless military posts for interminable lengths of time, and since no one came to let him out, he spent much of the day sleeping.

They flew long into the night. When they landed, there was a bonfire blazing in the middle of a bayou. Twelve men with mud-smeared faces were waiting for him.

Sumner threw open the port hatch and hopped out. The officer he saluted smashed him in the face and shouted at him to strip down. The mysteries were about to begin.

The dark, serpent-lean officer took Sumner's collar and ripped the shirt from his back. He slammed Sumner on the side of his head, grabbed his arm and twisted it back until pain crackled up his shoulder and into his skull. With a double-handed blow he pounded Sumner's spine and knocked all the breath out of him.

Sumner flopped to his back and the officer dropped with both of his knees onto his stomach. His fists flicked out and boxed Sumner's ears, then finger-gouged the muscles in his throat.

His face emotionless as a cobra, the officer stood up and a broad knife whispered into his hand. The blade flashed for Sumner's groin, and the fabric of his trousers ribboned away. The officer booted Sumner in the knees, and when he reflexively pulled his legs away, the ranger heel-gouged his thighs.

The pain was sharp. With fear-humming eyes, Sumner watched the officer and the twelve men board the strohlkraft. He was still doubled up when the kraft roared up into the darkness and dwindled out of hearing. Heavenward, the skyfires glittered like snakeskin.

'Stand up.'

The hard voice that broke through the darkness boomed in Sumner's ears, and he rolled to his side in the direction it had come from, expecting barbed pain from his beating. But his body felt whole.

'You're not hurt,' the thick voice said. 'You've been deep-massaged. Your muscle armoring has been knocked loose. You see, to begin the mysteries, you must stand naked.' A nightbird squawked. 'Stand up.'

Sumner rose to his feet, amazed by the ease of his effort. He winged his shoulders, still not believing that so much violence could be creative—but there was no pain, not even a bruise. 'Who are you?' he asked the bayou shadows.

'You're naked and alone in a swamp,' the voice said from his side, and Sumner turned to peer in that direction. 'Forget your questions. Listen, so that you have a chance of surviving.'

At knee level, a shadow stirred. Sumner backed a step, expecting an animal to come through the shrubs. Instead, the head of a man appeared and the silhouetted darkness of a stumped body. A flame winced brightly, and a long taper of snakeweed caught the spark and brightened.

In the sudden smokelight, Sumner saw an old warrior with collapsed cheeks, a twisted nose, and eyes as deep as the sky. The man had no legs, and large portions of his skull were missing, giving his

144

head an odd, angular shape. 'I am Mauschel,' the man said in his sinewed voice, 'your docent. I am directly responsible for your training here in Dhalpur.'

Sumner gawked, and the legless man waved the snakeweed taper closer to his face to better reveal himself. 'I lost my legs in the field,' Mauschel explained. 'I've been teaching here at Dhalpur for a lifetime. Only one in ten completes tutelage under me.'

'And the rest?' Sumner asked, his voice honed to a whisper.

'Some die. Some run away. But I'll tell you—the ones that complete my training are the best of the Rangers. It takes a halfman like myself to complete men who only think they are whole.' He placed the snakeweed taper in the knot of his headband. 'Only absence can make a man whole.'

Sumner swatted at the mosquitoes that were swarming about him.

'You'll learn to love this swamp,' Mauschel said, armwalking closer. 'The best killers are those who can love, for they know life's strengths. You love to kill, like all those who are sent to me. But this swamp will teach you to love living.'

Mauschel reached out and touched Sumner's knees. 'Sit down.'

Facing the docent, cross-legged, immersed in the insect-repelling odor of the snakeweed, Sumner experienced a rush of wonder.

'For now, you are a victim of yourself,' the docent told him. 'Your moods determine what you don't see. But after you calm yourself, you will see everything. That's what I must teach you—to see what is hidden.'

Mauschel turned Sumner's head with his thumb and pointed to a rivulet of water that was running beside them, black with night. 'Second sight is merely persistence,' he said. 'If you can silence your mind deep enough, you will see into everything and everyone. Silence *is* power.'

Mauschel and Sumner sat watching the rivulet curl over jumbled rocks, listening to the songs of nightbirds gleaming in the air for what seemed an endless time. At first it was a struggle for Sumner to stay awake. Each bubble skimming over the pebbles at his feet was a complete world, swarming with light and motion. *No number for the worlds* . . .

'Don't dream,' Mauschel warned him. 'Just watch. Selfscan is just watching. You have to know how to do nothing before you can do anything well.'

At dawn, staring into the sunflashing torrent, water became fire in Sumner's mind and took on the forms of his sleep: flames the color of carp, the shape of prehistoric fish. . . .

Mauschel slapped him. 'It'll be years before you wake up.'

Sumner blinked into the sun of his first day in the swamps and put a hand to his stinging cheek. He looked at the docent with bewildered hurt. What did this halfman want?

145

Mauschel turned about and armwalked to the grassy brink of the marsh, where grapes of sunlight hung on the black water. Against a wickerwork of roots buttressing the mudbank was his flatboat. He looked back and saw Sumner kneeling naked in the swordgrass, a hand to his cheek. Remorse flushed in him when he saw the resentment in the young man's eyes. His hand touched the rubbed leather of a legstump, and the guilt shriveled. He was a teacher, he reminded himself, lowering his body into the tar-stained boat. That was all he was.

He punted across the sleeping water. Sumner stood in the fluttering sunlight, following him with his blue stare. *If he ever wakes up, he'll be good,* Mauschel thought, admiring the man's lank and brawn. Years before—many years before—Mauschel had been a ranger. 'He who never was,' he said softly, gazing into the black water, remembering that morning a world ago when he first saw the mollusk scales behind his knees. He had been in the field then, and he had let himself believe the desquamations were a jungle fungus. A fellow ranger had to tell him: The black scales were genetic. He was a distort.

Selfscan was all that kept him living after he blew his legs off to hide the distortion. 'Selfscan is life,' he said to the algae-boiling water. 'If Kagan ever wakes up to that, he'll be good.' Mauschel's keen eyes read the shadows of the waterways, and he guided the flatboat through the mists of sunlight and the drifts of spiderflowers into the dark soul of the swamp.

After Sumner's first night in the swamp, his life was shaped by routines that continued unchanged for several years. Senior recruits who had watched his encounter with Mauschel from their coverts among the trees taught him the basics of swamp survival. They were reticent, hungry-looking men who disappeared as soon as they had shown him how to flake a knife from stone and how to twine fabric from plant fiber. Within days Sumner had a lair of his own in a mangaba tree and he was spearing fish from his own dugout.

But life in the swamp was difficult. He had to content himself eating roots, insects, and the small prey he could catch. Each day enjambed the next like the structure of a dream, and slowly the selfscan that Mauschel had been so fervent about began to make sense. It was watching, simply watching without thinking. The difficulty was learning to live with himself.

He remembered Gage and Ignatz with dark and rueful feelings. Becoming a ranger was viciously harder than they had ever intimated. In the first months of his swamp life he had been ambushed several times by other recruits. And the price of this blundering was high. When a recruit was ambushed he lost everything he had to those who found him: foraged food, knives, even clothes. Twice Sumner had almost starved. Then he learned to stop wondering and simply watch—watching everything, his whole body a lens open to time, perceiving every sexual moment of the day, every turn of the wind.

One day, watching the light rising up the trees in a slow silence as night came on, Sumner sensed someone closing in. He slunk noiselessly through the underbrush and squeezed himself into the embrace of a thick-bodied willow. Bird chirpings circled his hearing, and the wind breathed algal scents through the tufted grass. As his thoughts thinned and selfscan deepened, he centered on the approach of the other.

From beneath huge elm roots, along the mud rim of a black pool, a shadowfigure appeared and moved swiftly in Sumner's direction. The figure was obscured by ferns, but Sumner could hear fatigue in the heavy gait. He fixed his attention on the palmetto leaves flexing in the wind until the intruder was striding hard past him—a hooded man in a gray jerkin and leggings.

Sumner waited a pace and then swung out with his left arm, fast and low, and caught a skinny, fawn-boned ankle. With a twist he toppled the lanky body and jumped astride, forcing his knee into the back of the narrow jerkin. He seized the hood in one hand and jerked it back.

A scream widened in his eyes. He was holding a distort: a bald creature with moon-marbly skin and red eyes.

The distort thrashed, and Sumner pulled back stiffly on the hood and reached for his knife. Mauschel had ordered him at several of their regular sessions to kill any distorts he encountered. Looking down at the oyster-gray face, he felt his knife strong and right in his hand. But he didn't strike.

Foc orders! He let the hood go and stepped back, sheathing his knife. The distort rolled over and sat staring at him with its raw eyes, the face childlike and tilted slightly as if listening to some feeling-pitched song just within hearing.

'Get out of here before a real ranger shows up,' Sumner gruffed.

The distort shakily stood and bowed. With its malformed hands open in gratitude, it stepped closer. Sumner turned, but before he could move away, the creature touched him. His vision smudged, and a strand of ice-wind finer than a thread of starlight curled over his skin. *Is it wrong to love everyone?* a gentle voice asked at the back of his head. His whole body shuddered, and an overwhelming euphoria rushed up through the hollows of his lungs and throat. When he blinked sight into his eyes, the distort was gone.

But the telepathic bond between them remained. Sumner felt the other being long into the night. Sprawled out in his mangaba tree, wrung by the distort's exhaustion, he felt its swamp-dread as it crossed a fen of mosstrees and quicksand. Deeper, he knew the being's fear of what it was fleeing: Distort-hunters had found its tribe three nights ago, and the whole forest the tribe lived in had been set

147

ablaze. The companion that had crossed the hills and entered the swamp with it had been spotted yesterday and shot in the back, just below the shoulder, blowing its heart into its hands.

Sumner turned restlessly in his lair, and at the far end of the swamp the distort felt his unease and stopped running. The earth it squatted against was cold wet darkness, but the sky was a drunkenness of light. Sumner experienced the distort's awe and relaxed. As he circled toward sleep, the telepathy opened into sound and he heard the distort's quiet voice a last time: *I think it is good to live.*

Under the tutelage of a blind man with a back as broad as a bison's and all five senses in his hands, Sumner rigorously worked to toughen the vulnerable parts of his body. He pounded sand and deadwood with his hands, feet, elbows, and knees, armoring them with bone-callus. Punches and massage hardened his sternum and abdomen until a tree limb could be broken across his stomach. And he learned to instantly flex and relax his neck so that he could absorb blows to his face with his eyes open. Only then was he shown how properly to compress his breath into the needletip of his body's center and to twist his stroke at the precise moment of impact. When he could knock the bark off a tree with his bare hands and feet, the blind master was through with him. He had learned to use his whole body at once.

From a wiry old woman with mud-brown skin, he mastered the botanical secrets of the land, learning how to make curare from strychnos vines, malarial prophylaxes from cinchona bark, barbasco insect repellent, and a topical pain-killer from waxy red genipa berries.

Lounging in the blanched grass on a knoll of cedar during a pause in his training, watching deer feed, Sumner felt like singing. But music was a ghost in his mouth because he was uneasy with his voice, and so he lay in the tree-chopped sunlight with the other recruits, content to listen to the birds' green songs.

These men might starve him in the swamp if he weren't alert, but during the training sessions they shared they were brothers. He was as strong and poised as any of them, resting between wrestling sessions, humming with the just-seen knowledge of bodytwists, kneelocks, and slinky evasions. He looked down at the rays of muscle in his legs with pride. And for that seldom moment, hair starred with sweat, chest and torso muscledrawn and gleaming, his life was divined.

At the far end of the office in a darkly shaded back room with the door ajar, a deep waited. She had been sent by Ranger Command to assess telepathically the recruits at Dhalpur and cull any latent deeps. Every year at this time for the last thirty-two years she had come to this swamphole, to this very tarpaper shack, and opened herself to the

148

minds of killers. She had become increasingly sensitive—and bored.

Deeps—telepathically endowed humans—were the only distorts tolerated by the Massebôth, though secretly. Fetally induced kiutl, under the proper conditions, produced deeps. But their life was stringent. Neither the Black nor the White Pillar trusted them wholly, and they were always under observation.

But this old deep was satisfied with her life, if not her work, and her self-content showed in her wide-spaced eyes—gray, acutely alert eyes. Her face was patrician, noble-browed, and her gray hair was short but stylishly feathered. She glanced over Sumner Kagan's scrip, pausing briefly at Broux's murder. The deeps who had investigated Broux's death had seen immediately that Sumner was responsible, and they had marked him then as a possible ranger. The trick with assessing killers, she had learned, was eliminating the ones who stopped short.

She thumbed a kiutl-tab into her mouth and looked up to see a tall, long-shouldered man with red hair walking tentatively through the outer office. Wisdom brightened in her eyes, and mindmusic brimmed into her ears: She saw the golden bodylight around the giant, and the sight of this full-gened human, this whole man, tuned happily inside her.

She looked again at the scrip to see who this ranger's docent was. *Mauschel—the distort,* she noted with a flicker of disappointment. That man was too strict—wanting his recruits to accomplish his unfinished life. He was always ruining men. *As if his pain were the world's.* She put the paperboard aside and covered it with a fold of her white robe.

Sumner filled the doorway, the broad set of his eyes taking all of her in at once. She signed him to close the door and sit in a cane chair opposite her. As he gracefully lowered himself into her presence, all the while studying her with those bunsen-blue eyes, she saw the purple scald marks at the sides of his neck. 'How did that happen, soldier?' she asked, touching her throat.

'Voors,' Sumner replied, and at the sound of his voice she saw into him, saw the shadow of a dead world: a crater pool surrounded by dying tamarinds, nodules of fungus blistering the grass where acrid vapors smoked out of the earth—a blunderland of mad flies and trees with the shapes of pain. And there, rising out of the green water of the pool, a child white as nothingness with eyes like ice.

She blinked, startled by the clarity of her in-seeing. Then, with disciplines drilled into her since infancy, she brought her mind back into the present. She didn't want to know about voors or anything else in this man's past. She had been sent to do one thing: find other deeps. The less she took away with her the better she would sleep that night.

'Just that name—voors—scares me,' she said convincingly, opening a notebook in her lap. 'I'm from Prophecy, and I only leave

149

the city once a year to do this survey for Ranger Command. I'm here to see that the recruits are well-treated. One of my tactics is to speak with as many of you as I can. I hope you'll be frank with me. Nothing you say here will be associated with you again, unless you wish it so.' She smiled, and Sumner nodded, only the microshifts in the muscle-armoring around his eyes revealing his suspicion. 'Are you happy here?' she asked ingenuously.

Sumner sat tall but relaxed, modulating his breathing the way Mauschel had taught him to do when he was being interrogated. 'Yes.'

In that one sound, the deep saw the grimness in this man's life: the arduous fighting drills, the anxiety of ambush in the swamp's dark spaces, the loneliness— But she peered past this emotional fog looking for a special kind of silence—the depth of the telepath.

'Tell me about yourself,' she said. 'Anything at all. Just talk.' The deep lowered her eyes, pretending to write in her notebook, her gaze loosely following her scrawl as she centered into a trance.

Sumner shifted in his seat and looked around at the threadbare carpet, the bamboo-slatted windows. . . .

'Talk—please.'

'I was ambushed again, a few days ago,' he said, the words spiraling into his mind. 'I hate getting caught because then I have to feel what I did wrong until my guts ache. That's the only way I can forget. I hurt myself for a while.'

She urged him on with a roll of her free hand.

'Sometimes I feel like water locked inside a tree,' he said, burst-skull feelings jumping into words. 'I'm tired of sword classes and gun classes and hiding in the swamp and taking orders. But then I think, all of life is shit. We live until we die—and then nothing. Does anybody have the right to want anything?'

He paused. The woman had stopped writing and was sitting there with her eyes closed. 'Dhalpur has been the strongest life I've had so far,' he added softly.

The old woman hadn't heard a word of what he had said. She was looking long into his mindark, searching among the daze of memories and thought-loops for the silence. But this man was all dreaming. His bodylight was wondrous but his mindark was muddled. She closed the notebook and placed her palms over her eyes. 'Thank you, soldier. You may go now.'

'That's all?' Sumner asked, the hurt he had brought forward burning behind his eyes.

'Yes, that's all. Please go now.'

Sumner stood up and went to the door slowly. Outside, heat rippled in the air over the metal roofs of the swamp village where the officers lived, and he stood watching that for a while, feeling that he had left something behind.

*   *   *

At the end of his third year in the wilderness, Sumner went mad. The rigorous demands of his training and the vast solitude of his life in selfscan crushed him. It happened while he was watching the rain moving in vague pillars over the savanna, as he completed a complex routine Mauschel had taught him. The toes of both of his feet were tying and untying tedious strings of knots; one hand was doing wrist and finger maneuvers with a butterfly-blade, the other packing and fitting cartridges. Deeper, he was fluttering his diaphragm, signaling his heart to slow down.

Each day for months he had been doing this and more intricate routines, and he had become expert at settling deep into himself and watching his body function on its own. But today, with the rain smoking just outside his burrow and the wind whispering over the grasslands with a sound that was almost human, he found that he couldn't stop. With lunatic precision, his toes knotted and unknotted twine, his left hand flashed sharp metal around his fingers, his right hand capped bullets, and his heart consciously slowed and slowed, gliding beyond his control.

Sitting in a broth of umber light, his limbs moving mechanically, his will paralyzed, Sumner felt his heart stop. His toes and hands went on even as the whine of blood, tuning its high note in his ears, thinned out of hearing. Vision narrowed and misty oblivion circled in, muffling his panic—

Pain abrupt as a scream wrenched him out of his trance. The butterfly-blade had knicked his thumb. He stared with sudden lucidity at the pale slice in his flesh and saw how the blood was holding back. Then the red flow began, and his heart quopped loudly in his ears.

Unthinking, he dropped everything and ran barefoot into the rain. The wind slashed at him, and he wondered what he was doing. But then unwilled selfscan took over, blocking out thoughts and feelings, and propelling him into the storm.

He ran with the storm, following the wizenings of the wind, heedless of siltholes and mudpools. The rain wandered on ahead of him, leading him staggering into the gloom of a misty forest. A dense effluvium of rotting bark and wet earth engulfed him, and he stopped with his arms widespread. The vaporous fatigue of his long run rose out of his legs and fogged over his mind. He dropped to the fleshy earth and slept deep.

The storm passed, and he listened to rain-leavings: the hum of water puddling; the sigh of puddles wrinkling to mist. The snap of a drop against a naked root alerted him to himself: He was lying soaked, cold, and sunken in the black humus, breathing through his mouth. But he didn't move. Something awesome had happened to him during his forest sleep. He couldn't say what it was—but he knew.

151

Hearing the varied patterns of leaf drops, the sparge of ferns, the irregular rhythm of vine-sprinklings, he experienced power. Not stamina or energy but quiescence. As he rose out of the exhaustion of his hysterical run, he felt clean as the white woodmeat he saw beside him in storm-broken branches. The power he was experiencing guided him effortlessly over the uncertain forest floor, and with it came an impeccable clarity. The world had become transparent: He saw where the wind, swollen with rain, had tided, forcing out life or killing what remained; and he saw through the slides of mud and branches where small animals were hidden, drugged with cold. In exposed rock, one glance at the lithified sediments revealed the whole history of the forest—a buried river bottom, a vanished desert. Control wider than intent had shaped everything, as it had shaped him. But, as chaotic as it seemed, there *was* control: reeds designed to sway with wind; leaves wax-coated and shaped to shed rain; each predator a prey, untangling its own small knot of time.

Sumner turned his clarity on himself. Strolling casually along the forest's edge, all his senses poised, he realized that the total control the Rangers were pushing him to develop had always been his—it was just a matter of ease and recognition. His body, like the forest, was a precise ecology. The bacterial tides in his blood could be felt by the strength or lethargy in his muscles, and they could be modified with herbs, breathing, food intake. His irises worked autonomically, but he had learned to tense and relax those subtle muscles by first recognizing and then imagining the feel of light and darkness. In a similar way, he had learned to lure blood away from a wound, and to regulate the temperature of different limbs, and to hear with his fingertips. But the secret, he understood now, was not in diligent control but in recognition and compliance. It was so easy.

Images of his past materialized in the pauses between his breathing. Instantly he fixed his mind on the tocking of tree toads, thunder rumbling over the forest's eaves, an orange uteral blossom unmolested by the storm, before he caught himself trying to catch himself. *Relax*— He let his memories unwind, and as each one passed through him, he looked at it the way he would a jungle covert for the things it hid. And he saw that all his life he had desperately been trying to control everything around him.

A deep memory from the only winter he had ever experienced filled him, and again he saw the shape of his breath, ice-enameled steps, fangs of ice in the trees, snow-dervishes spinning down the streets, and a red-eared horse with a white diamond on its nose. Clearly he recalled the urge to hurt that horse, to assert his mastery. And he remembered riding it out onto the pond—It was then that he had first equated violence with control.

The memories continued, and with his remorseless clarity he

watched himself rage at his father's death and continue to rage as the Sugarat, driven by the constant dread that his father's control would never be his.

Sumner wandered through the narrows of the forest, retracing the course of his life. He cut through the shame and guilt of the many years he had spent deceiving his mother, and he fully experienced and then abandoned the tenacious nostalgia he felt for his car, his room, his scansule, and, at last, he perceived how his need for command had made him a dupe for voors. All the memories of Corby and Jeanlu that he had so fanatically evaded over the years returned undiminished. Sensations ghosted through him: the bloodchill that sparked around Corby's body; the deathchant that Jeanlu's corpse had chattered in his face while hanging from his neck; and the deva—the ruby light, the cold saffron sun, and the maddening, impossible flight over Rigalu Flats. At this point he came to the edge of the forest, where sunset-lengthened shadows stretched black into infinity.

He moved out across the grasslands at an easy gait, reviewing his past in the scarlet light. He walked all night, traveling where starlight blew off the water, moving without anxiety through panther glades and over buffalo hills where hind rats stalked. Moonhandled, alert, he was invisible, prey to nothing, intent on deciphering all the parables of his life. The change that had come over him was permanent. He would never again be confused.

On Sumner's last night in Dhalpur, he rubbed himself down with water-thinned mud and blue moss to keep away the insects, and he entered the swamp. An owl, silent as a fish, sailed overhead, and the wind shifted, murmuring in the trees like water.

Mauschel was waiting for him in a small flatboat hung with red fishskin-lanterns. Wreaths of linaloa incense rose from the corners of the flatboat. Far down the river, heat lightning quivered, and a breeze smelling of distance dispelled the closeness of the mud-rot air.

'You've done well,' Mauschel said in greeting. In the red light his legless, twisted body looked like a wooden idol.

Sumner stood quietly before him, knowing with the meat of his body as well as with the memories of endless hours he had spent in selfscan before this man that he had accomplished nothing—he had simply become himself.

Mauschel grinned at him like a sunstruck ape. 'Come here, you self-conscious buffoon.'

Sumner stepped forward, and Mauschel grabbed his legs and held him tight. 'You're right,' the old man whispered. 'You're not to be saved. No one is. But today you're leaving here as a ranger, and I'd be less than lizard-grease if I didn't tell you I'm proud.' He knocked on the hull of his boat, and Sumner sat down. 'Here—you earned this a long time ago, but I couldn't give it to you until you didn't need it.'

He pressed a small piece of metal into Sumner's hand. It was a silver cobra pin—the Ranger insignia.

'We've spent three years sharing nothing but what's around us,' Mauschel said. He sat back, and the darkness leaned into his eyes. 'Now I feel I can tell you about deeper things. But I won't. You already know that it doesn't matter one whit what you do. It all comes to the same thing. And you've found out, it seems, that you're bigger than you think. Remember when you thought it was impossible to empty your mind and keep your body moving?'

He laughed softly and cast Sumner a sly look. 'You understand, too, that eternity's between us. Each of us moves alone through his own meaning, creating value as he goes along. You know that, though you haven't had the time to ponder it, and I hope you never do. But there's one thing you may not have realized just yet. It's the last mystery.'

He leveled his swordmaster's gaze directly into Sumner's eyes. 'The Rangers own you.' He paused and stared down at his blunt, callus-sheathed hands. 'For three years you've lived rigorously but alone. It's going to be different in the Rangers. They're a political tool, you know, commanded by the Massebôth Black Pillar, who have world-shaping plans, historical dreams—iguana-dung, all of it. So, if you think there's more than nonsense to our lives, you'd better get out while you can. Go north into the wilderness. You know enough to survive anywhere now.'

He ran a yellow thumbnail along a crease of scar that followed his jaw, and his eyes thinned. 'But if you understand, as I think you do, that nonsense is all there is, then stay with the Rangers. They treat their own well. You'll earn your livelihood as a killer, but who's to say that's any worse than a physician for all we come to, eh? Just keep one thing in the front of your mind when you deal with moral twits or mystics who think they've seen into the heart of things: The one secret is that all things are secret.'

Sumner's first assignments were in the ruins of Apis and Longstorm. Both cities had once been major seaports, centuries old. Fifty years before, they had been crushed by a savage raga storm, and because the Massebôth didn't have the resources to rebuild them, they were deserted. Leagues and leagues of collapsed buildings, dune-drifted boulevards, and skeletal frames rose out of steamy lagoons, all of it surrendered to distort gangs and the jungle.

Sumner was sent into these ghost cities to stalk down distort leaders who had become too influential. The work was arduous and cruel, but Sumner was well recompensed. The Club Foot, Prophecy's most famous bordello, was perennially open to him without charge, and he spent most of his leave-time there. Seeing himself clearly in the mirror-chambers, surrounded by servants and fine foods, he was surprised by what he had become.

Without the mud and swamp grease of Dhalpur and with his sunreddened hair braided to one side in the latest fashion, Sumner was a celestial demon. His face was flat as a blade, the scars eroded to pale artistic etchings by wind and time, and his wide, silent eyes were blue as spun steel. He was almost a giant, his shoulders stooped with power, but he wasn't bulky. Big-boned, his muscles thick yet pliant, his skin burnished the color of dawn, with tight copper-red curls boiling over his chest, he was a rare animal.

The women of The Club Foot worshipped him as an avatar of the god Rut, and they fought each other to be with him—for not only was he the most relentlessly masculine creature they had known, he was also as ingenious as a magician. His lean, patient hands were barked with callus and taut with strength, but they could caress womanflesh with petal-soft tenderness, the fingers moving with a delicate and sometimes fierce cunning.

Women, however, were only a small part of Sumner's life. They pleasured him, but they couldn't fulfill him. Only the wild spaces, empty of emotion and full of deception, engaged him totally.

If it weren't for the decay of the ruins he was assigned to patrol, he would have been happy. But Apis and Longstorm were chancrous landscapes. Often when he was perched on a twisted girder enveloped in the acrid dampness of dissolving concrete or when he prowled the squalid beaches of sand-choked cars and frothy chemical pools, he wondered why the Massebôth were coming to this.

In time it became obvious to him, as it was to everyone else, that the government was corrupt. Whispers of political intrigue were audible not only among the underprivileged but in the highest military circles as well. Sumner served for more than a month as the personal bodyguard of a prominent and greatly admired general. During that time they shared meals and broke up the tedious hours of traveling between frontier posts by playing kili and talking.

The general was a humanitarian with plans for abolishing dorga pits and for establishing self-sufficient distort colonies. He smoked only the cheapest cigars and ate and traveled humbly so that he could save money to realize his dreams. Sumner was deeply impressed by his sincere commitment and his parsimonious way of life, and he listened with real interest to the general's political insights.

The general explained how for centuries a handful of families had run the Massebôth government for their own personal aggrandizement. The Unnatural Creatures Edict was employed not only to eliminate voors and distorts but also to remove suspected political competitors. Newspapers were forbidden to assess government policy, and university courses in history and society were carefully monitored. But in their eagerness to consolidate their power, the Protectorate was being denied decisive and objective leadership.

Within the last century, half the fringe colonies with all their vast agricultural resources had been lost to raga storms and distort tribes. Expansion and exploration were minimal. The workers in the dorga pits were becoming increasingly essential to maintain city life, and so even minor offenders were being branded with drone straps to keep up the work force. Taxes had quadrupled in only a few years, and most guilds and factory chiefs had to lay off workers and forestall wage increases. To quiet dissension, the military was being employed to do more police work and less defensive maneuvers along the borders. As a result, the distort gangs and tribes were proliferating and drawing closer to the core cities. Disgruntled guildsmen and fractious government officials were even selling arms to the distort gangs for material looted from the convoys.

Sumner was disturbed to hear of the avarice of his leaders, but he didn't allow it to affect his work. It wasn't loyalty to the Masseboth or the Rangers that kept him active and unquestioning; rather it was devotion to himself. He had been remade in the image of a ranger. There was nothing else for him.

And that is why, a year later, when he was called back from Apis to assassinate the general, he didn't balk. Obliged by a sense of comradeship, he refrained from humiliating the military leader and didn't use the easy strategy of gunning him down in public. Instead, at great risk to himself, he approached the general at night, slithering through the hypnosis of barbed wire and trip lines surrounding his bivouac. It took all of his skill to merge with the moonshadows, to crawl beneath the heat-addled air of the main court and to shadow past the alert stares of well-armed guards. Finally he advanced with the sultry breeze stirring the gauze curtains of the central building. Among the stupor of shadows that veiled the general's chamber, he trailed the moist scent of sleep to a canopied bed. After deftly and painlessly slicing the general's carotid with a poisoned fingerazor, he merged again with the shadows.

The general's death bothered him for a while, because he had sensed that the man had been sincere. In the same way that he knew when he was being secretly watched or when and how an enemy was about to strike, he had known that the general had told him the truth. The Massebôth were evil and their empire decaying.

Sumner felt neither outrage nor despair about this fact. Even though he served the Protectorate, he didn't consider himself a Massebôth. He was a ranger, and all his mental and physical energies were devoted to perfecting his craft. The doom of the cities was not his concern. After all, what wasn't doomed? The only control he had was over himself, and even that was limited, for he was constantly surprising himself.

One dismal rain-misted night in Vortex, with nothing better to do he followed the tug of elusive animal psynergies and found himself

156

wandering through a tangle of stone alleys, his feet muffled in fog. Several hours later, at the end of a tight cobbled lane of antique bookstalls and slot-windowed apothecary shops, he stopped before a salt-split doorstoop. The cramped shopfront was windowless except for a crescent pane bratticed with corroded iron. He had no idea why his instincts had led him to this desolate corner of the city until his persistent knocking was answered by an old woman with skin the color of clouded silver, fire-frizzed hair, and blinking bird's eyes. It was Zelda. Surprised, but too much of a warrior to be shocked, he politely asked for a wangol reading.

Zelda didn't recognize him, and she was hesitant to admit this flat-eyed, solar-burned giant into her shop. But he was cordial, his voice flawlessly affectionate, and besides, he was wearing a clean, smart-looking uniform and probably had money. Since she had acquired her augur license, she needed zords to meet the tax. She motioned him into her reading room. It was a dingy chamber with Mutric figurines in the corners, ponderous indigo curtains, and a rotted plank floor that was so soft with age it sighed the odor of dead leaves with each step. A round black-sheened mirror hung on the wall surrounded by yellowed charts depicting the body parts and their various auguries.

Zelda had aged greatly in the intervening years. She had been reduced to a wraith in a brown etamine shift embroidered with starsigns. Sumner watched her closely as she drifted about the tiny room lighting tallow sticks and preparing incense coals. He felt no emotion for her, and as they sat down on bamboo stools before a crumbling corkwood table, he wondered why he had bothered to come in.

She handed him seven painted lentils and told him to cast them. After several throws, she looked up and studied him with eyes bright as pain. 'Your history is one of accidents. Deception and error guide you. Soon, if it hasn't happened already, you'll confront someone from your past, possibly a child. But I see no recognition. Only what we know is real. Also, quite soon, you will have to discard everything. But you will adjust, for I see you are a man for whom all destinations are temporary. You change readily, sometimes obscuring your own purposes, though a deep, burning part of you is always the same. That is the paradox of your nature—the cloud and the star.'

Sumner laid all the money he had across the table, and Zelda straightened and stared at him more closely. Before she could recognize him he stood up, and with her profuse gratitude singing in his ears, he returned to the night of rain.

Zelda's pathetic old age affirmed Sumner's conviction to die young. He had seen old rangers, rheumy-eyed and pale, fading away in noisy government offices or, worse, fumbling in the field and being brutally humiliated by distorts, butchered with their own knives. That wouldn't happen to him.

Sumner took risks most of the other rangers eluded. Death, to him, was freedom at the crest, escape from the body's inevitable slide. He was afraid of nothing—not torture or loneliness or the weirdest distorts. How could he fear them? Life was a brief harrowing voided by death, and these were the healings of pain.

Sumner sat on a pierhead gnawing at a whole orange. On the dirty beach around him, scrawny pigs and dogs scavenged among loosely bundled bales of garbage.

He finished his orange, wiped his hands on his shorts, and stood up. Seabirds poised on tall, lilting fish-spears turned their heads to watch him as he ambled down the ruined beach. Today was his last day in the hamlet of Laguna. The man he had been assigned to kill had arrived the night before. Actually, his victim wasn't a man—it was a voor called Dai Bodatta.

For over a month Sumner had been waiting for this voor, living unobtrusively in one of the blue pastel shanties across the bay. The fisherman's widow who rented him the place had no doubt that he was anything more than the dockworker he claimed to be. Like the other stevedores, he wore soiled canvas-top shoes, remnant shorts, and an oil-stained singlet. And like them he worked a dawn-to-dusk shift, loading barges with crates of rice and scraping and painting hulls—until today.

He walked out to the middle of the windward shore where the bay washed over a pink bench of coral. The tide was rushing in, and white feathers and dragontails of spray lashed with the sea boom.

This was the far end of Laguna Bay, where another harbor had once flourished. Plague had doomed that village many years before and now only blackened stumps of old pilings, a few charred boat ribs, and a storm-staggered jetty remained. The villagers thought this crescent of land that separated them from the sea was haunted, and they used it as a dump. Sumner was convinced that this was where he would confront the voors.

He sat down on a chunk of driftwood tangled in beach vine and cupped a hand against the late morning light to see the island better. Situated in the middle of the bay was a small, tree-crowded knob of stone. No sign of voors was visible among the tiers of sea pine, but Sumner knew they were there. Last night hundreds of voors had crossed the bay in black-hulled rigs.

Alerted at dusk by a mirrorflash from a ranger farther down the coast, Sumner had sat up all night watching the voors arrive. The night-lens he had used revealed the cowled figures in the boats. From the side of the island facing away from Laguna, blue and green fires were visible for a few hours. Then they vanished, and by dawn nothing was left of the voors—except for the dreams. Most of the

158

hamlet woke groggy from a night of restless, moody dreaming

Voors were not often seen this far south, but over the past few years they had been gathering annually in different coves and bays of the region. No one knew why the voors came, but each year their number grew, and lately the Massebôth had become concerned. Word of a new leader of the voors spread through the northern coast cities with wild rumors of a voor invasion. And though hardly anyone there had ever seen a voor and known it, fear mounted. Travelers mistaken for voors were viciously murdered, and distorts who had long been ignored were herded together and drowned. To ease the situation, the Massebôth decided to eliminate the one voor who had been leading the others south. Unfortunately, nothing more was known than the name of that voor—Dai Bodatta.

Sumner was glad the voors had come to his bay. A month of inactivity had made him restless. With one hand he dug a hole in the sand behind the driftwood and extracted an oilcloth satchel. Inside the sack was an electric-pump handgun, a rifle extension, half a dozen clips, a night/day lens, and numerous slabs of gel explosives. He removed the handgun, wiped it clean of grease, and fitted a clip into it. Checking the alignment of the sites, he turned to follow a gull sliding out over the bay, and his sweaty singlet sucked at his back. The bay water beyond the coral ridge was jade-green and clear as an eye.

Sumner peered through the lens and saw movement on the shore of the island. Voors in gray and brown mantles were assembling, hauling their small boats out from behind stands of sea pines. Hair crested by the wind, he stood tall and swept the bay with the lens, looking for other ships. There were none. The morning shift was already moored, and the afternoon fleet was crowding the bay mouth, waiting to get out to sea.

Quickly Sumner stooped and removed the thin slabs of gel explosives; then he reached into the sand below the driftwood and took out a small square tin of firing caps. Excitement throbbed in his chest, and he had to raise the lens again to be certain that the voors were going to cross. *In broad daylight,* he marveled, watching the small boats splash into the water.

He doublechecked his rifle and the firing caps, and then he sat down. It was time again for selfscan: full attention on the stalled shadows—noon, the turning point.

Black the blood and the bones . . .

Tala squinted into the noon glare buzzing off the water and waited for her eyes to adjust to the light. Clochan and the others were dragging the ships out from behind the trees which meant that they had already probed the far shore for howlies. Still, she scanned slowly. Pale sketches of coral glowed beneath the green water. A shark was gliding near the reef, turning swiftly with powerful strokes of its huge caudal. Farther out, silver sparks flurried in the sunlight where minnows chopped the surface. And on the far bank: tilted red mangroves, black palm fronds, and white sand littered with howlie debris and torn sargassum. No howlies—though she felt something evil and elusive. She tried to concentrate, but her drowsy body was cold with lethargy, and she couldn't focus beyond herself very well.

Clochan waved from where he was standing, knee-deep in the kelp-drench. The cold within her flushed warmer, and the loose end of a voice rose out of the back of her mind: *Bring out the stonelights.*

Tala nodded, but before turning she stared hard across the bay again. The jittery trees stared back empty. She dismissed her fear with a hiss and walked back through the pines to a cave of overhanging trees. Chanting voices from far within melled with the hum of wind-stirred leaves and the incoming tide, sounding like the mumble of a dream. Her eyes adjusted rapidly to the darkness, and she moved nimbly through the red shadows to a rim-crusted incline that swooped steeply out of sight. Here the chanting was very clear: *Black the blood and the bones beneath the skin. Black the earth one finger under. Black the emptiness bent over time.*

Tala would go no farther. Dai Bodatta was still down there, and she knew that if she were with him again in the planet-warmth she would leave her salt for sure. Her darktime had gotten very bad in the last year. All of her flesh had stiffened, and living had become a labor. Only her devotion to the brood kept her from crossing over to Iz. Her deep mind was needed, especially when the stonelight journey took them so close to howlies.

The chanting thinned to a hum. The rhythm of a slade-drum drew closer, and figures appeared below. Single file, a dozen voors emerged from the darkness, their cowls thrown back. A few of them were marked: frosted eyes, squamous lips, vein-netted transparent skin. But most of them were clean. The several hundred voors that had arrived with them had been long into their darktime and all had crossed over. Their bodies had been rafted and set adrift on a broad subterranean stream that wandered far into the earth.

As each of the remaining voors passed her, they placed two or three brood jewels in a wattled basket at her feet. With her kiutlsharpened senses she briefly inspected each stonelight. They were the size of plums, clear-grained and glimmer-wobbling with lustrous colors: some fiery and translucent, others gold-banded and misty as the gas planets. The light in them was centuries old, the trapped kha of voors that seeded these cave walls with tiny pieces of their lives—relic light moving its ancient telling through clear stone.

After the last of the stonelights had been placed in the basket and the container had been covered, tied, and passed out of the cave, two of the voors went back down the incline. They reemerged slowly,

160

carrying Dai Bodatta, a small figure in a sheath of camlet trimmed with miniver. The bearers stopped before Tala, and she folded aside the covering and moved her gaze slowly over the black childshape within. A blue light hazed like fungus over the rough surface of the cocoon, and as she stared at it the sleepy solitude of her darktime thickened, and she heard a voice, soft as a cloud, far back in her mind: *Lose the way*.

She straightened with surprise and then relaxed, soft-focusing her awareness, listening for the voice of the child-image. But Dai Bodatta was silent.

She folded the opulent covering over the cocoon and watched after it as the two voors walked out through the cave mouth. She stood a moment in the dark, staring at the sky's arch: cloudswift, a gull turning on one wing, and farther out, the long silence of a wedge of birds. Thoughts nimble as static flurried across her mind: The crossing of the darktime voors should have been done elsewhere. Not this close to howlies. But why had Dai Bodatta insisted?

Tala—it's time. A tall voor, angular and shriven, stood at the cavemouth, cowl pulled back. It was Clochan, his flesh pale as moonlight.

A visceral, ungelded joy spiked through her. She loved this voor. He was fluent with both feelings and thoughts, a leader and, for her, a lover. Before, when they were standing close, contemplating the deep heart of a jewel, he had filled her with such blue-bliss that for a while she had forgotten their danger and had become a broodling again, unaware of bloodpaths or the darktime. His words still moved in her: 'Three hundred years from now, someone in this cave will pick up our stonelights and know that we lived.'

Let's go, Clochan called to her. *We have to ride the tide.*

'Soon.' The sound of her voice throbbing in the dark hull of the cave startled her.

'You feel troubled?' Clochan whispered, stepping closer. His sunken eyes were watery with reflected light.

Tala discarded her feelings with a shrug of her hands. 'I don't know. I haven't been able to think clearly.'

Clochan put his arm around her, and she felt as light as when the full moon pulled at her blood. *Today belongs to few,* Clochan quoted.

'Too few,' she echoed.

'The others sense no one across the bay. We have to hurry, while the way is still clear.'

Lose the way, the mage's voice recurred, but she didn't project it. 'I'm ready,' she said.

Afternoon sunlight, clear as wine, shafted between the trees. Tala absently followed Clochan, pondering what Dai Bodatta had said. *Lose the way—Give up the body? Yes, the mage is right.* Her bloodpaths had narrowed, leaving her cold. Pain turned in her belly like the children she never had. Her body felt alien. *Strange how these warmbloods were shaped to believe they're the exact center. Ears, eyes—all their senses—conspire to make them feel whole—replete. No wonder they're so arrogant.*

A red seedcase flitted above the turf in a gusty seabreeze, and Tala watched closely as it sailed out over the water. It had come a long way from the north and was going a long way. An Iz-sign: all life carried off by a wind that goes its own way and can never turn back.

The voors sailed in three skiffs, sliding swiftly along the tidal current among streamers of bright brown sargassum weed and sparkles of leaping needlefish. In the lead rig, Clochan knelt at the prow, surveying the bay. No other ships were in sight, and the tree-heavy isle behind them blocked the three boats from view of Laguna.

Riding in the end rig, with the camlet-wrapped cocoon, Tala watched the approaching delta. Dai Bodatta was silent, furled deep, and the only sound was the hiss of the boat slicing across the water. Tala gazed in soft focus at the approaching wall of mangroves, the stumps of twisted trees, and the dunes of garbage. The gulls ringing over the refuse piles told her that there were no howlies on the beach, but a chime had begun to peal in her left ear. Always before, that had signaled danger; now, though, she wasn't sure. The darktime often filled her head with whorls of sound.

Clochan used deep mind and hand signals to guide the following skiffs through the barrier of coral heads and spikes. The churning reefwater frothed behind them and the lead boat ran in to the beach with a loud cough. Clochan and the others splashed into the shallows and carried the flyweight rig to shore. By the time the second rig slashed in, they were back in the water, lifting the wattled basket of brood jewels over their heads.

Copra husks and mangrove radicels tangled around their legs in the milky shallows. The third rig was steadied by eight voors, and Dai Bodatta was gently lifted out and carried to shore. They beached the prow and left the stern tilting and luffing in the water.

Dai Bodatta was silent, and Tala was concerned. She placed a hand beneath the cloth covering and felt the dry textured surface of the cocoon. A cold energy sang along her fingers, and a quiet voice opened within her: *Lose the way.*

Clochan and two others carried the first rig over the sand toward a gap in the mangroves. Four others lifted the second rig with the stonelights in it and, kicking tins and sand-clotted fruit out of their way, followed. Three went back to portage the third skiff, and Tala tightened the sheath about the mage and supervised its handling by the two remaining voors. Then, as they were stepping forward, the sand shifted beneath their feet, and the beach ahead of them roared into the sky.

An impact of heat and tearing pressure slammed Tala to the

162

ground. Debris thudded around her, and she covered her head as another explosion screamed out of the trees. Palm fronds and a stinging rain of sand lashed her back, and she rolled toward the water. When she looked up, the beach was smoky, and the seven voors and two rigs that had been ahead of her had vanished.

Looking closely, she was choked by rage and terror: Lopped limbs in smoking sleeves were splayed among the garbage, blue-gray entrails glistened on the white sand, and the moon-white face of Clochan stared back from a blood pool with the startled somnolence of the dead.

'Dai Bodatta!' a voor screamed and leaped toward where the cocoon had been hurled by the blasts. He took another step, and his head snapped back, one eye a mangled rose. Two other voors were scrambling over the smoldering debris trying to recover the stonelights that had been scattered across the beach. One went down with a plume of blood at the back of her head, and the other dropped as if he had stumbled. The kha of both of them smoked away from their bodies before they hit the ground.

Tala turtled across the sand, scurrying toward the cocoon, which had been thrown against a rust-gutted oil drum. She threw her body alongside it, tore back the camlet sheath and saw that it was intact.

The three voors who had gone back to the third rig were sprinting toward her, and she howled at them with her deep mind to get down. One of them lurched backwards and flopped to the sand, blood spurting from her neck. A second one reached out to help, suddenly straightened, twisted violently, and collapsed. The third bellycrawled toward a driftwood log, thrashed in the sand for an instant, and then stopped moving.

Terror swamped her, and she felt herself wrinkling weaker. What was happening? Her fear-charged mind sensed no one anywhere nearby. They were alone. But what was killing them?

Lose the way—

She craned her neck and saw that everyone was dead. Their kha lights had wisped away so quickly! A severed hand laced with blood lay ahead of her in the filth-strewn sand. She looked away and saw a huge man in rags stepping out of the mangrove shadows. His kha was very close to his body, solar gold and radiant, and his face was flat and cruel with scars. He loped toward her with a silver rifle in his hands, and her heart wobbled. He was silent as smoke, a revenant.

Lose the way—

Dai Bodatta's presence was all that kept her from going mad. She touched its cold surface, and the psynergy that sparkled through her dissolved her terror. The light around her brightened, became glassy. A diaphanous white brilliance was suffusing everything, and she realized that she could cross into Iz. But who would protect Dai Bodatta? Who would save—

Lose the way!

Implacable radiance burst through her thoughts, and her mind spasmed: She was gazing at a lava-flow of forge-red light webbing to a furious white energy—a delirious sun, all starfire and refulgence.

The trembling walls and buckled screams of the voor dead dazed and pummeled her until a voice like a stammering flame shadowed through her: *Three hundred years from now, someone will find our stonelights and know that we lived.*

Clochan's voice, thinning into distance like a bell . . . Joy and then anger sheared through her numbness. Immediately, the wind of tormented voices smeared and vanished, and she was alone again in the starwhite energy.

Lose the way—forget the body's loneliness, the mage's voice spoke within her. And she understood that it was time to stop understanding. The arduous journey along the bloodpaths was finished. A powerful, sultry wind was leafing through her awareness, scattering her memories beyond her reach. The broad, warm current buoyed her across spans of crystalbright gas, weaning her away from pain and distance and thought.

Sumner pumped a bullet into the voor that was crouched behind a rusted oil drum. *Dai Bodatta?* he wondered, stooping over the drum and pulling back the voor's cowl.

His teeth meshed tightly as he stared at the grotesque creature he had killed: a slobbery thing, its flesh a glossy blue-white, veined like moldy cheese, its mouth a bubbling mess. He heaved it over with his foot and peered at the bundle the thing had been protecting.

A bewildered frown darkened his face. With the muzzle of his rifle he pulled back the camlet covering and eyed the childshape. A statue? No. He poked the black woven surface and realized that it was a mummified child—a voor abomination.

Casually, he placed the rifle barrel between the mummy's eyes and pulled the trigger.

The cocoon splattered apart, and a burst of hot ichor spurted into his face, kicking him to the ground. He thrashed in the sand, both hands to his face, a terrible pain stabbing his flesh. A stink his blood remembered from years before invaded his throat and sinuses and bleared his eyes. *The lusk psiberant!* Liquid fire seared his face and the hollows of his head, ripping maniacal howls from his lungs.

Spastically he churned in the sand, trying to get to his feet, but his muscles were quaking with the poison that was burning through his body. Helpless, beyond thought, Sumner blanked his mind and let the agony consume him. His body strained and heaved, twisting him deeper into the sand with ogreish convulsions. He writhed for hours, gulfed in pain, before the spasms slackened and he realized that he wasn't going to die.

164

His face was swollen and fluffy with peeling skin by the time his limbs had calmed enough for him to stand. The air was fractured. The light looked chalky, and the cocoon that had exploded in his face was gone, shriveled to a slick, colorless smudge beside the elegant cloth that had sheathed it.

Invisible forces were shuddering space, warping it like an old, bottom-heavy pane of glass. Distances seemed to falter, to curl around themselves, and time was staggered. The long swells of the ebbing tide were swimming to shore slow as elegant swans.

Most terrible of all, a voice was chattering in his head. He rubbed his temples and rocked himself, trying to shake the noise loose, but the dim, unintelligible chanting persisted. It was the same horrible mumbling, cooing, clicking rhythm that Jeanlu's corpse had tormented him with years before. It ricocheted across the back of his skull, dull and wrung out, just audible above the anguish ballooning through his lungs.

He lurched across the sand, wanting to run, but time was snared and space was bruised and distorted, volume folding like paper. Each of his steps swung him out across immense ranges of distance, yet the entire length of the delta hung before him thin as a reflection.

A dragonish twilight stalked the eastern sky, a windy dusk, the clouds low and running. A black-sailed catboat rolling heavily in the dark chop swung hard to shore. Eight wild men with braided hair and eyes burned red by pulque and sun stood at the taffrail. They, like everyone in Laguna, had wondered at the explosions on the dump delta. At first they were too wary to approach, but after receiving smoke signals that two rangers were on their way, they decided to explore the dump first.

After weighing their boat with a coral-head anchor, all eight of them waded ashore. The twisted corpses alarmed them, but the sight of the brood jewels scattered like constellations on the beach lured them closer. They scrambled to gather the hoard and were on their knees in the sand when they spotted the madman. He was half naked and tall as a pine, and his face was a mask of charred flesh. He came raging at them out of the mangrove darkness, screaming like a rabid ape. One of the men had a gun. He held it in both hands as he sighted and dropped the lune with the first shot.

Startled, the corsairs gathered the brood jewels in one sack and decided to divide them later by lot. All of them knew, however, that death would be casting dice with them, for there were an odd number of jewels. Hoping to even out their booty, they plundered the corpses.

Intent on their scavenging, they didn't see Sumner, his bullet-creased shoulder clotted with blood and sand, rearing up from the garbage pit he had fallen into. With a battered oar in his hands he reeled out of the pit and dashed toward the man who had shot him.

Before anyone could move, he swung out with the oar and caught the gunman full in the face, smashing him to a limp sprawl.

The others rallied instantly, flashing knives and turtle-razors. But Sumner was unstoppable. He shattered heads with sweeps of the oar, slammed faces into driftwood, and clubbed his way to stillness with the loose bodies of those that had fallen. When none were left, he couldn't stop the horrible dancing, the racking strength that forced him to smash again and again the bloodrags of those he had killed, until he felt he was going beyond his body, and he banged to his knees, exhausted with rage.

Far back in his thundering mind the mad chattering narrowed, and a whispered cadence began: *Black the blood and the bones . . .*

The Emptying

A lionfaced man stood on the roof of the flower-crowned tower, his yellow eyes cold with fatigue. He was a distort, but he was not unattractive. Golden hair grew the tall length of his spine and glistened like fur on his arms and legs. His features glowed with a sapient geniality, and his movements as he crossed the circular rooftop were long and regal. He was a breeder, and he had just come from a full night among the females. Beneath the red soft-fabric wrap that he was wearing his thick muscles sang with weariness. He leaned on the blossom-strung balustrade and gazed out over his village.

It was his privilege as the most whole distort of his tribe to stand atop the breeding stables and survey Miramol. The village was beautiful with life, built as it was in a grove of baobab trees and mist springs. Eastward the jungle withered to a desert where the skyfires, the dreams of all living things, were still burning. Below, workers with green dawn-lanterns were scurrying among the round huts of Miramol, preparing the village for another day. And in the west, the direction all doors faced but those of the dead huts, the sun was untangling itself from the roots of the jungle.

The whorl is in all things, the breeder marveled.

A worshiper's call echoed into the sky. Several answering cries sparked out of the stables from restless females, and the breeder turned and barked once into the musky darkness of the doorway to still their irreverence. He would be happy when the Mothers passed on his duties to a younger, more driven male. He had been a breeder for over a decade, and he was becoming too rapt and contemplative for the life in the stables. Still, finding someone as responsible as he among the sex-crazed young males would be difficult. No doubt he would have to serve for at least another cycle.

The heavy carnal odors clouding out of the stable fluttered his stomach. He pulled aside his loincloth and urinated into the dark gardens below. The very thought of sex made his kneecaps turn watery. He was tired of rutting, tired of ministering to so many excitable females. He wanted nothing more than to be alone. But he knew that by day's end he would be feeling differently. *The whorl is in all things, all right.*

167

He secured his loincloth and walked unsteadily but with dignity down the ramps of the breeding tower to the street. Even among the dense shadows he was recognized by workers who stopped to acknowledge their respect of his position. The breeder chuckled back amiably, but he didn't stop. Tonight had been a more difficult session than usual, and he simply wanted to go home and sleep.

'Ardent Fang.'

The breeder turned, and his feline features expanded with reverence. Standing among the white tendrils of a baobab was an apparition of a large, thick-faced woman in a hooded black shift. It was Orpha, one of the Mothers, and as her image curdled into the dawn shadows, her voice lilted in the breeder's ears: *Come to the Barrow, breeder. We have work for you.*

Ardent Fang bowed to where the specter had been; then he jogged through the darkness of the back treelanes so that he might avoid other tribesfolk.

At the burrow of the Mothers, a rocky mound of earth surrounded by willows, he stopped and prostrated himself, waiting until a husky old woman in brownblack robes came out of the turquoise-studded mudhole.

This was Orpha, his spirit teacher and life counsel. She took his arm in her fleshy hand and walked him up gravel steps to the top of the rock mound. From there they could see through a break in the forest to where a warped sun wavered over the river. Orpha stood with her back to the dawn, the red light fringing orange in her short hair. With a roll of her wrist she snatched at the air and produced a milky brood jewel. She held it out to him, and the dim light glowed green around the white gem.

'Look closely, Ardent Fang,' the old woman said. 'The magnar himself gave us this crystal. You can see him here.'

Even in silhouette Orpha's square face was strong and kindly. Ardent Fang drew assurance from it and then stared deeply into the brood jewel. Only twice in his life had he gazed into a voor rock. Both times he had been seized by trepidation so thick he couldn't think to understand what he saw. It was the same this time. As his vision dropped into the cloudy depths of the stone, the scruff of his neck tightened, and the hackles along his jaw fanned so broadly they scratched his ears.

Orpha placed a hand under his jaw and steadied his swaying head. 'What do you see?'

Ardent Fang didn't know what he was seeing. It was as though he were perched on the windy rim of a vast canyon. Awesome depths unfolded around him. Forms made vague by distance were moving at the edge of his sight, and all that he could identify clearly was a thin hot strand of fear burning in his chest. He looked up with wincing eyes.

168

'You feel the fear, don't you?' Orpha's eyes were luminous in the gray light.

Ardent Fang nodded vigorously. 'I'm too nervous to see clearly.'

Orpha guffawed and palmed the brood jewel. 'It's not you, breeder. The fear you see is the magnar's.'

Ardent Fang gawked. 'The magnar—scared?'

'You saw it.'

Ardent Fang shook his head, asked almost soundlessly, 'Why?'

'If we knew, you wouldn't have to walk the Road, eh?' She put a hefty arm around his shoulders and guided him down the steps of the mound.

A Mother in tattered raiment was sitting cross-legged in the dust before the entrance to the burrow. Her face was live and ugly and her motions wildly animated as she arranged small jewels and bone-chips in the sand. She studied the portents with her fingers, her nose almost touching the ground.

Orpha embraced Ardent Fang and whispered a blessing in his ear.

'I've been working hard on my last lesson,' he whispered back. 'I'm beginning to see how the whorl *is* in all things.'

The old woman crouching in the dust sat up straight and turned the empty sockets of her eyes toward Ardent Fang. 'The whorl!' She cackled and swayed to her feet. 'The rains come and then go. The moon thins and then grows. The whorl, yes, the whorl!' She laughed loud and hysterically, and out of anxiety Ardent Fang laughed back.

'Jesda, be calm,' Orpha embraced the blind Mother, gently sitting her back down in the sand. The large woman smiled apologetically at Ardent Fang. 'Go, breeder. You have a long journey.'

'Yes—go,' Jesda repeated, her bone-thin arms raised above the scattered hair of her head. 'Go with the whorl. Go round and round. Like the stars. Like the blood. Like everything. Go round. The magnar is scared, and it is the beginning of a dark time.' She howled gleefully.

Ardent Fang chuckled and grinned amiably as he backed off. *Crazy Mothers*, he thought. *Crazy in their bones.* As soon as he turned from the burrow, the laughter fell from his face. The magnar, the one who lived at the end of the Road, was afraid. In all of Ardent Fang's life and in all the lives of his ancestors, the magnar had never been afraid.

He drifted down a boulevard of baobab trees flanked at broken intervals by immense tusks and long boar ribs. Several times he ignored the greetings of passing tribesfolk, and each time, alerted by their insulted hissing, he had to stop and explain his preoccupation. Word that the magnar was afraid unsettled the tribesfolk, and they scurried off with their hands on their knees.

By the time Ardent Fang reached the eastern edge of Miramol where the silverwood lodgings of the né were cluttered on a walled hill, he had resolved the matter to himself. *It's the whorl again,* he realized. *Sooner or later, even the magnar must become what he is not.*

At the end of a blossom-arbored lane, Drift was waiting. Drift was Ardent Fang's personal né and probably the best seer in the whole Serbota kingdom. Né were sexless—living divinities who worked as artisans and craftsfolk for the tribe. Telepathically strong and untroubled by sexual cravings, they were ideal hunters and scouts. Their clarity and ancestral memories guided them on the one safe, unmarked route that led through the desert to the star pools and the magnar—the Road.

Drift was small, dark and spindly, and its face, like all né, was pure mask: slash-lips curled into a permanent meaningless grin below boomerang-wide cheekbones and a nose that was two arched nostrils.

Drift whistled and coughed in its imitation of a greeting laugh. It liked Ardent Fang because he was a strong man. The energy whirled in his body at an exciting pace. Blue sparks, visible to any seer, crackled off the tips of his mane and flared over his tufted shoulders. But besides being strong, he was also beautiful. He had a considerable amount of face, his yellow eyes were clear, and both of his hands worked. Apart from the pungent brown odor of his sex and the silver scales on his shanks, he was virtually whole.

Drift sensed Ardent Fang's purpose, and because of its telepathy, no conversation was needed. But, for the breeder's sake, it reached into the man's mind and asked psychically: *Why are you here, Fang? Did your night in the stables leave you restless?*

Ardent Fang smiled spiritlessly. 'I'm too much the breeder for the stables to unease me. No, seer—it's the Mothers who have sent me. They say the magnar's scared. Incredible, isn't it? The magnar!' Ardent Fang sat on a bench-log before the moongate that led to the silverwood lodges on the hill. 'You're a seer, Drift. Is it true?'

Drift nodded. He, too, had felt the fear humming across the desert, where always before there had been a peace as still and certain as the inside of a jewel. *Who is to know the way of the magnar?*

'Us, apparently. Though we aren't expected to see the magnar again until after the rains, the Mothers want us to walk the Road now. Can we do it, Drift?'

The né cocked its dark, round head with uncertainty. *The desert is at its hottest now. The Mothers themselves call this the season of the killing sun, don't they? But if they say you must go, then I will guide you.*

'Why is it this way, seer?' Ardent Fang asked, looking up at the green dawn sky where vapors fluffed like tattered masts. 'What could scare the magnar when even death cannot touch him?'

Drift clicked with ignorance. *How could we know? The magnar is unknowable as the clouds.*

Empty-bellied, with Drift guiding him through the desert that separated Miramol from the magnar, Ardent Fang turned inward.

He tried to keep from thinking about the magnar and focused instead on the purging of his body.

Drift was proud to be with him. Few of even the most joyous Serbota could wander the Road as openly as Ardent Fang. The man had no fear of the scorpions and centipedes that lurked in what little shade there was, and he had found praise even in the adamant heat that was swelling the meat on their bones. Most wonderful of all, he trusted Drift. Né, even seers, were too often considered other and not worthy of true comradeship by the gendered folk. Ardent Fang was different. He treated all né as tribesmen, and he was especially deferential to seers. He was one of the most joyous tribal leaders. And, as much as Drift despised them, the Mothers had to be given credit for guiding him well with his inner work.

After the second day on the Road, Ardent Fang was empty of poisons. Wild energies, driven by the stubborn sun, burned through his body and warped his vision, but Drift's slow, peaceful chanting held him together. The seer, in its fluty sad voice, sang of the powerful certainty of the body and its ecstasy at being a child of the sun—

> *The sun longs to feel*
> *And so we are here . . .*

Toward the end of the fourth day they marched out of the filmy veils of rippled air into the shade of a wave of stone, twenty meters high. The coolness was narcotic, and staring back at the sun-dazzled pinnacles and the rock fins folded in the tremulous flow, Drift chanted happily—

> *Like the long rocks*
> *Bent in the heat waves*
> *We look broken*
> *But we are whole—*
> *We will always be whole!*

Drift led Ardent Fang into a small cave where they followed the lines of force through a honeycomb of tunnels to a vast rock studio at the top of the butte.

At the far end of the bright chamber the magnar was sitting on a straw mat. Blue sky and copper-red mesas were visible behind him, and dust hazed around his body like an aura.

At first he didn't see them. He was gazing intently into a scry crystal, a green brood jewel given to him long ago by voors. The reflected emerald light wavered over his long mule face and made the impressive tangle of his white hair flare like green fire.

The magnar was over twelve hundred years old. Prescience had far-spaced his thoughts and made most of his feelings creative, so that very little about him was stylized or predictable. Even his memory was wise and thoughtless.

He saw himself clearly, from his impoverished infancy as an ape in a research boro through a thousand years of burning, sanctifying changes that had made him what he was now: light's movement as flesh.

Five hundred years before, the magnar had become consciousness itself, and he had understood with the urine, sweat, and ooze of his body that he was light. Everything was light—all of reality was a star, shining.

Most of his time was spent ecstatically, his body spined with an electric strength streaming up his back and into the sky. The expanding psynergy extended his awareness deeper into the etheric fields of his environment, losing him in the lizards, desert trees, and birds that lifted him away from his human attitude. Sometimes, though, and more often lately, he lost himself to the differences of the world, even to fear. Death was a cold mystery. After twelve hundred years, only light was more strange.

When the magnar finally looked up, his leathery lids drowsy from visions, he stared at the two wanderers in silence, unsure if they were real. Lunes of brilliant light glared off his big face, and as recognition animated his features, a toothy grin widened. He laughed raucously and slapped the animal skins he was wearing for trousers. Billows of dust fumed around him, and the echoes of his laughter filled the chamber. He held out large gnarled hands: 'Ardent Fang!' he boomed in the Serbota dialect of the tribesman's village. 'Drift! Heroes of Miramol! Shay!'

Ardent Fang and Drift shambled forward and prostrated themselves before him. 'Get up!' He grabbed their shoulders and forced them to sit up. 'What is this nonsense?' He gazed hard at them with chuckling brown eyes. 'I should bow to you. You've journeyed so far and across the most evil land in the world!'

Before either of them could respond, the old man flung himself into the dust and groveled before them with whimpering laughter. When he looked up, his leering face was furry with sand.

The tribesfolk stared back at him uneasily.

'Why are you so dour?' the magnar asked, bending forward to look deep into their eyes. He smelled of camphor and sage. 'Ah, of course! You must be exhausted. Well, my friends, other visitors have brought me rose-hip wine and dried apricots. After that—'

'Magnar,' Ardent Fang cut in, his eyes deferentially downcast.

The magnar rolled his eyes. 'When will you finally give up these formalities and call me by my name? Bonescrolls. Please.'

Ardent Fang nodded hesitantly. 'Bonescrolls—we've rested and we're not hungry.'

Bonescrolls narrowed his eyes. 'This is not like the tribe of ecstasy. Your seriousness disturbs me, friends.'

172

'The Mothers have told us that you're afraid,' Ardent Fang blurted.

Bonescrolls' hoary eyebrows went up and came down slowly. 'So.' A ponderous weight sat him back, and he looked suddenly weary. 'It's true.' He studied the grain of his thumbnail. 'Me—the timeless one, scared.' A wan grin flickered at the corners of his mouth. 'You'd think by now I'd have come to terms with this.'

'What is it?'

Bonescrolls stared at Ardent Fang benevolently, and a sad smile creased his weary face. 'Death, of course.'

'You're dying?'

'No, no. My body, for all it's gone through, is as stubbornly healthy as ever. Happiness does that, you know.'

'But you're afraid?'

'Yes—I'm afraid.'. He turned about and gestured out the rock opening at the desert landscape. 'Someone is out there. I've felt him for days now. I know it's a man, but that's all I know. I can't get close to him.'

Drift, more than Ardent Fang, was stunned by this admission, for Drift understood the power of the magnar. Like the seer, the magnar was telepathic and could perceive all the forces of the world. But, greater than any seer, the magnar could walk out of his body and wander the lines of power, invisible and yet strong. The magnar could go anywhere and enter into and become anything.

'Not even as ravens and snakes could you find this man?' Ardent Fang asked, incredulous.

Bonescrolls shook his huge head. 'Not even as ravens and snakes. The man is invisible, though I know he has a body. I've seen his footprints. He's a big man, but still I can't find him. That's why I believe the Delph has sent him.'

Ardent Fang and Drift glanced at each other.

'The Delph?' Bonescrolls read their bewilderment. 'An ancient enemy—very powerful in his domain to the north. Actually, I'd thought the Delph had forgotten about me. It's been over a millennium since I raged against him.'

Ardent Fang drew his obsidian knife and slammed it into the packed earth between them. 'We'll defend you,' he swore with conviction.

Staring at the knife, Bonescrolls' eyes widened, and he unwound into laughter.

Ardent Fang rose to his knees, both harnfists clenched. 'I'm serious, magnar.'

'Of course you are,' Bonescrolls gasped, between lurches of laughter. 'But I don't think you understand what you're up against. The Delph is called godmind. And for good reasons. I won't have you sacrifice your lives.'

'It's not a sacrifice,' Ardent Fang insisted. 'It's devotion.'

173

'Your tongue has more vision than your brain,' Bonescrolls said with an imperfect smile.

Tell us about the godmind, Drift asked.

Bonescrolls paused, suddenly rooted by a vision he had experienced over a century ago. He had foreseen this very moment. Everything was as he had precalled: two distorts hunkering close, asking him about the Delph, the ambient light chandeliered in their eyes, the air heavy with sunstruck dust motes. The magnar let the vision open through him, feeling eudaemonically outside of himself, above the real.

Everything is empty, a deep thought thought itself, *except the absence of self.*

'Perhaps tribesfolk shouldn't be speaking of the gods,' Ardent Fang said, misreading the softness in Bonescrolls' expression.

Bonescrolls scowled. 'The Delph is not a god. He's a mind—a human mind amplified by an awesome technology. Twelve centuries ago he was just a man. And I—I was a yawp, a simian worker biodesigned to serve humans. But I was different from most yawps.' A fateful light brightened in his face. 'I had been biotectured by my human creators to reason. Dangerous endowment for a service-ape. When I saw what the humans were doing—trying to create a super-human, one of their own kind strong enough to subjugate reality—I rebelled. My only mistake was that I didn't succeed. And since then, I've been living from body to body, hiding from a vengeful godmind.'

'More than one body?' Ardent Fang's voice was burred with awe.

'This is my seventh physical form,' Bonescrolls said. He was grinning, but his voice was shadowed. 'In the thousand years since my futile rebellion, the yawps themselves have become a godmind culture with the technical power to craft bodies—even minds. Without their help, I would never have eluded the Delph this long.'

Perhaps the yawps can help you now, Drift suggested.

'No—' Bonescrolls tugged pensively at his goatbeard. 'The yawps will have nothing to do with their former master. The Delph is the one who freed them from their servitude to humans.'

'Then let us help you,' Ardent Fang insisted. 'We can find this man in the desert. Drift is a strong seer. It can track anything living. And I was trained as a warrior before the Mothers made me a breeder. I know how to kill.'

Bonescrolls looked annoyed and dismissed the issue with a wave. 'No, my friends. I'll meet this trial alone. We'll share a meal and some legends, and you'll return to your tribe.'

'But how can the Serbota survive without you?' Ardent Fang growled. 'You have guided us for centuries!'

'The né are wise, and the yawps will help you. But let's not talk about this anymore.'

'Magnar—'

'No more!' Bonescrolls' voice was a blow, his face tight as a fist. Then he sat back, his eyes crescents of laughter. 'And call me Bonescrolls.'

At dawn the next day Ardent Fang and Drift returned to the golden desert. But instead of following the lines of force back the way they had come, they wandered out toward the palatial mesaland, purple in the early light. The sand whispered beneath their feet, and in Drift's mind the sound became the disapproving sighs of the old man in the rock tower behind them.

Heat encircled them like a sphere of glass, curving vision and sound. Ardent Fang hummed with joy, awed by the beauty of the sandshapes and their soft sere tones. Drift chanted quietly about the sun following two warriors across an endless desert.

Sumner was trapped in selfscan. Far back in his mind, dim but always there, was the cooing, clicking, snapping noise of a prehistoric insect. Sometimes it tightened to a tiny wringing scream. Othertimes it merely breathed a deep, low hum from the core of his heart. But it was always there, and if he budged from selfscan—if he so much as congratulated or berated himself—a long icy needle pithed the root of his skull.

Silence. Animal awareness.

This was death's land—Skylonda Aptos—a million hectares of scabid desert.

Sumner couldn't think it, but he knew that he had come here to die. Not with a brain-splattering bullet between his eyes—the Rangers had taken away his guns. But even if they hadn't, he wouldn't have done it that way. He was still a ranger. He wore his cobra insignia and his buff regimentals, smudged and frayed now but whole. He would wear them until the land killed him.

Numb-edged from so many hours of walking, his whole body craved pause, and he sat with his back to a rock turret, mindless of the desert insects. He closed his eyes and focused on the sun's weight against his legs. He tried to relax without dozing off. He didn't want to sleep. Not yet. Not until dark.

The snarling voltage bristling at the base of his skull sizzled louder in his ears. It was a muffled voorchant, like the impossible language Jeanlu's corpse had chattered in his face so long ago.

Trapped in selfscan, he hadn't been able to think through his predicament. Still, he understood that a voor had invaded his body. Lusk was what the voors called it.

The whining folded into a staccato chant: *black—black—black—*

After the incident in Laguna, Sumner had been kept under close observation. The Rangers had no idea what had happened to their man, but any wound inflicted by voors did not bode well. Their fears were confirmed when the physicians gave up on him. The face burn looked like nothing they had ever seen. And as for the haunting noises he claimed to hear, what could they do? There was no cure for madness.

Soon it had become obvious that Sumner was seriously impaired. Not only had he been reduced to the level of animal sentience, but in his sleep he rose from his cot and walked circles. Unable to carry out the normal functions of a ranger, he was stripped of all weapons but his knife, and was sent north to monitor tribal activities.

For a while Sumner had complied, meandering along the borders of a riverain forest, secretly peering through grease fires at jumbled frond-huts and the grotesquely misshapen bodies of distorts. But his mind was a holocaust of lunatic sounds, and each dawn he woke in a place he had not selected during the night. Terrified of being ambushed and humiliated by distorts during his mindless night-walks, he had sought out the deadness of Skylonda Aptos. If he was going to die, it would be with anonymous dignity.

Sumner's thin downward-slanting eyes flicked open. What stared out of them was not human. Lizard shapes of fire flashed across the space behind those eyes, and globes of eerie sounds burst and reformed. Corby struggled to concentrate. The scene floating on his retinas wavered: sun-hot stone and sky the color of metal. He was having difficulty fitting himself into that scene. Iz raged within him, threatening to sweep him away, far out of the body, far out of time.

No! Corby marshalled all his strength. *Come to center and extent!*

The noises coalesced to frantic jabbering, then narrowed to a babel. The vibrant light of Iz patterned itself into a cellular mosaic. The body was accepting him.

Clumsily, he stood Sumner's body up—his body now, for the lusk was almost complete. For years, locked shapelessly in a cocoon, carried from brood to brood by the voors, he had used his psynergy to Iz-call for Sumner. And Iz had answered him by leading Sumner to Laguna. Too many voors had died that day on the beach. He would have to redeem their deaths by using this body well.

Corby tottered and placed a hand on the pink rock turret to steady himself. Erumpent noises still clouded his hearing. That was the crackling, insane current of Iz, rushing through him, threatening to prise apart his world.

Iz—the windy continuum of psynergy that his people rode between realities. Without his own body to anchor him in time, it was almost impossible to resist the tow of that power.

In the dark cupola of his mind he sensed Sumner's thought forms: an oil-still pond with ghostly shapes turning below the surface. Sumner was enranged but locked into selfscan. Like a virus, Corby had permeated Sumner's nervous system. Sumner's mind was

176

immobilized, unable to think without the reverberations of Iz paralyzing him. Corby could have dampened the Iz-noise, but then his control over Sumner would also weaken—and he needed complete control of this howlie body.

Corby moved out over the red gravel, weaving and staggering. His heart pounded turgidly, and his vision soared as his head lolled from side to side. He insisted on control and sidled along a huge ribbon of rock, trying to straighten his walk. Bare, bony plains with only a whisper of grass appeared at the edge of his sight, and he turned himself in that direction.

He was being hunted. As dulled as his deep-mind had become in this new body, he was still aware of the others closing in on him. Two had bodies, one was shapeshifting. So far he had had no trouble evading them, but he was concerned. Who were they? What did they want from him?

He stumbled and fell to the ground in a splash of sand and dust. Quickly but awkwardly he twisted to his feet, staggered forward, and regained his pace.

Only after he had learned to use this body, he had decided, would he risk communicating with Sumner. Then, even if his father didn't agree with his plans, he would have a slim chance of carrying them out himself.

His father—Odd that this adult had so much in common with his old childform. It would have been interesting to watch his own body developing. But Nefandi had betrayed him. Now the most he could hope for was to eliminate the proven enemies of his people. Nefandi and the godmind called the Delph—sooner or later he would confront both of them with this new killing-wise body.

He slid on his heels down the slope of a scarlet dune, exultant in his freedom. Holding his head straight, vision stammering in his eyes, he strode purposefully forward. But the effort to maintain control thinned his will. Time—it would take time.

He stopped beside a boulder and sat back against it. The cells of his body were singing, and he listened closely. . . .

Sumner shrugged awake and groaned to see where he was. A wind, thin and persistent as a rumor, had already begun to smear his tracks. Vaguely he recalled a dream full of weird sounds. He rubbed his face and stood up, shivering in the tawny heat.

'Do you believe the whorl is in all things?' Ardent Fang asked, cutting open a cactus with his obsidian knife.

The né whistled, dull and low, and its soft voice spoke inside the tribesman's head: *More nonsense from the Mothers?*

'Nonsense?' Ardent Fang spoke without looking at Drift: 'You say that because you're né.'

177

I say that because it's true. Nonsense is all that the Mothers have to offer.

They paused to chew the sweetness out of the cactus, Drift expressionless, Ardent Fang squinting his yellow eyes with pleasure. Done, the tribesman spit the cactus pulp into the sand. 'Né—do you believe the whorl is in all things?'

Drift shutter-blinked like a lizard. *What is the whorl?*

'The turning, the return,' Ardent Fang answered. 'What is full becomes empty, empty full. Like breathing.'

Cycles? In all things?

'Yes.'

Drift spit cactus pulp over its shoulder and spoke with its voice at the back of its throat, chewed almost to a garble: 'I-am-né. Will-I-ever-be-gendered?'

The dark blade hissed as Ardent Fang sheathed it. 'It's said we return—each time different.'

Nonsense.

'It's said.'

You mean, the Mothers have told you.

Ardent Fang frowned, his blunt features narrow as a wolf's. 'The Mothers would know.'

Pizzle rind.

'How then, né, do they know which of us to breed?'

They don't.

A tic screamed silently at the corner of Ardent Fang's mouth.

Drift splashed his bony hands in front of him, shrugging. *The Mothers breed the ones that look the strongest. The truly exceptional ones, usually those with the most face, are chosen as leaders—like yourself. But the Mothers don't know any more than anybody with eyes.*

A thin, knowing smile floated across Ardent Fang's lips. 'There are mother-mysteries, né, revealed only to a few.'

No, breeder, there's just dying. Drift's waterdrop eyes did not blink. *No mysteries. No whorl.*

Ardent Fang stared at the seer as if he were looking a long way out to sea. He slapped his knees and stood up. 'It's late,' he announced. 'We should find a place and send.'

Drift watched him scout about for hidden cacti, and it felt a twinge of remorse at having challenged this man's simple beliefs. Ardent Fang was a good leader, just and sympathetic to folk and né. His faith was part of his openness. The seer looked inward and shouted at himself: *No more foisting hatred of the Mothers onto friends.* It stood up and went around to the far end of the rock lip pool where the water was unsullied by their earlier frolicking. Bending for a last sip, the seer eyed swamp-puma prints in the silt, fresh as black petals. *Fang!*

Ardent Fang tramped over and studied the tracks. 'Under two hours. Bonescrolls?'

It must be, Drift thought, and Ardent Fang felt its respect. *I don't*

178

sense him at all, but why else would a swamp-puma come this deep into the wastes?

A puling cry wavered out of the distance—the lonely, ethereal caterwaul of a huge cat.

Now there are three of us.

'Come on, let's find a place before dark.' Ardent Fang marched out through the sun-blown weeds toward a simmering landscape of black buttes and salt domes.

For the past two days they had wandered the Road from one waterhole to the next, seeking the presence of Bonescrolls' enemy. By the end of the first day they had begun to wonder if the stranger was an enemy at all. Drift sensed the man, even though it was impossible to pinpoint him. His mind was that empty. He was close, and he stayed nearby, haunting the shadowed terrain. He watched them, but he didn't act like an enemy. He didn't urinate in the waterholes after he drank, and he had left no poison-burrs in the sand that they had found yet.

What frightened Ardent Fang was that no spoor was visible: not a footprint or a urine scent. The man was supernatural. It baffled and unsteadied Ardent Fang, and because he couldn't feel the tenuous vibrations of the stranger's salt, not even through Drift, he had begun to doubt his existence. Perhaps it was one of the magnar's ploys to test their loyalty or their spiritual depth.

He glissaded down a slope of copper sand and mounted a wind-notched incline of black rock. At the top he gazed beyond the undulant salt domes, across bronze fields of pebbled sand, toward the crater highlands. That would be a good place to test his theory, he figured, since the ash prairies around the craters trapped even dragonfly prints.

Ardent Fang strode boldly over the cinder wastes, cutting a straight line of tracks to an arena of brimstone outcrops. Sitting on the hard ground among the knobs of brimstone, Drift felt at ease. The night before, they had slept in the open, and until dawn Drift had lain in a half-stupor, feeling the thin psynergy of the stranger moving across the stone shapes around them. At least here, even though there was nothing to eat, there would be tracks in the morning.

Ardent Fang reached into his hip pouch and removed a devil harp—a dark finger of walnut wood that voors had given him as a young man in barter for food. The use-glossed wood was strung internally, its silver wires visible through the holes in its sides. Ardent Fang put one of those holes to his lips, and a lofty, sparkling corolla of sound warbled around them.

Drift snapped shut its eyes and experienced a pulse of warm human energy somewhere to the west. The stranger was still with them.

Long into the night Ardent Fang played his devil harp, sending his music bouncing across the highlands, sometimes forlorn with vibrant

179

darkenings and rendings, and othertimes watery, bright as ice, retreating and returning like submerged sounds. Drift followed the echoing vibrations of man-psynergy circling the music, close and then far, until it nodded into sleep.

'Drift!'

A hard, thick hand squeezed the seer awake, and a hot whisper grazed its ear: 'He's here!'

Drift sat up. Ardent Fang was hunched and still, his eyes sliding from side to side, one hand clutching the dog-crucifix strung about his neck. 'I heard him clatter on the rocks,' he breathed.

Maybe it was Bonescrolls.

'No, it wasn't a cat weight or—Look!'

Drift turned in the direction of Ardent Fang's gaze and saw two firefly eyes beside one of the outcrops. They vanished.

The seer stilled its mind, trying to feel the presence it had just confronted. Nothing: a dawn breeze scuttling over the rocks and the distant hiss of steaming grottoes. A detached, precarious feeling expanded in the né, and it trembled to think that what it faced might indeed be an enemy.

'Paseq!' Ardent Fang shouted the sacred name into the misty darkness. 'Paseq!'

Shut up! Drift clutched Ardent Fang's arm. *He might think you're threatening him.*

'Spirits can't stand the Divider's name,' the tribesman explained, and then shouted again toward where he had seen those sparkling eyes: 'Paseq!'

It's not a spirit. Spirits don't have eyes!

'Paseq!'

The two stared hard after the echoes of Ardent Fang's cries. A long moment of silence tightened around them. And then, quiet as a shadow, a hulking man curled out from behind a brimstone spar, five paces to the side of where they were facing. Even crouched in the sketchy dawnlight, his deep-hulled chest and his muscle-cobbled back were majestic. Thin, flat viper eyes stared blankly from a purple-glazed face—an idol-visage, arched with animal cheekbones and a wide jaw. His gleaming flesh was a dark rainbow mask.

Ardent Fang staggered back a pace. He growled, but there was a whine in his eyes.

Drift knelt, arms akimbo in the né gesture of submission. *Kneel*, it sent to the tribesman.

'Foc!' Ardent Fang barked, his upper lip jittery. He bowed from the waist, quickly, and faced the apparition with his arms open at his sides but his head high.

Drift threw its mind forward. *Shay, stranger. We're wanderers of the Serbota—an ecstasy warrior and his seer. Shay.* It thought sunshowers. It thought blue-blossoming trees.

180

Dawnlight jerked in Sumner's eyes. He wanted to lash out, to bang into violence and bash himself loose from the numbness in his skull. But the voice in his mind, the same one he had been hearing distantly for two days now, was gentle. It was coming from the short black creature, the hairless thing with the needletip eyes and the slash-lips. It had no weapons, but the other one, the squat, hairy one with the lion-eyes and the muzzle face, that one had a blade.

Ardent Fang read Sumner's gaze and removed the knife slowly, presenting it hilt first.

Sumner waved it away. Why had these twists of distorted flesh dogged him if not to kill? And as soon as he thought that, acid-pain blistered the pan of his skull, and he staggered.

Who are you? the powdery voice asked, and its gentleness soothed him.

Sumner straightened slowly as if rising from a great depth. 'Kagan,' he husked.

The seer poked itself, *Drift*, and pointed to its companion, *Ardent Fang. We're Serbota wanderers from the riverain forest to the south. We've come because your presence here has been felt. Can we help you?*

Sumner was surprised that this beetle-shiny thing could reach into his head like a voor.

We're not voors, Drift sent and wished it hadn't when it saw Kagan stiffen. *Just wanderers. I'm a seer—a . . .* This close to Kagan, it could probe deep into his mind—already it knew that the man no longer intended to harm them, though he still seemed troubled. The word it sought popped into its head: *. . . telepath. Would you like to see?*

Sumner frowned, then scowled as the distort reached out with its spiderhands to touch him.

No harm. No deception.

Ardent Fang, seeing Kagan staring at him, took Drift's other hand. The psychic power that whirled through him brought a blissful, stupid grin to his wolf face.

Sumner eyed the two distorts closely. They seemed much less threatening than they had from a distance. It was hard to believe that these fear-parched creatures had created that crazy, crooking echo-music which had made him feel the need to confront them. And now? He edged forward and let the distort touch his forearm.

Radiance, clear and balmy, throbbed into him, fringing his whole body with light. Silver volts sparked the surface of his brain. He felt with a kinetic certainty that these were the good people, the joy people. His mind breezed open, empty at last of the demonic squabbling and the welding pain that had frozen his thoughts.

But Drift and Ardent Fang did not feel his sudden joy, for their minds were rocking to the shorn, beetling cries of the voor dead. The chill whistle of deep space was curving through their bones, shuddering their flesh.

181

Sumner saw the terror in Ardent Fang's eyes and felt the fear-rigor in Drift's touch, and he stepped back. The jewel-core peace enveloping him burst, and he was transfixed on a skull-rooted thorn. He gnashed his teeth until the pain dimmed.

You—hurt! Drift had plopped down and was sprawled against a lava boulder, stick fingers beneath its leather cap, rubbing its bald head. Ardent Fang squatted beside it, staring up at Sumner with cowering, pain-wet eyes. Both of them still heard the ether-wind and its stark cries darkening into the core of their brains. But now both of them could also see a flame-gold aura around Kagan. Drift understood that they had peaked into kha-awareness: They were seeing the thin luminosity of the body. But Ardent Fang believed that he was in the presence of a tortured deity—Seie the wandering god or, worse, the Dark One.

The tribesman prostrated himself, and Sumner thought that he was still in pain and bent over him.

How can such a powerful being hurt so much?

Sumner looked over at Drift and glanced his fingers across the eel-dark stain on his face. 'Lusk.'

Drift snap-blinked. *Voor lusk?*

Sumner nodded and sat Ardent Fang up.

He's not the Dark One, Fang. He's voor possessed.

Ardent Fang stared at Sumner's callus-bossed hands and muscle-piled shoulders. 'Why then couldn't you track him or I find spoor?' he asked, looking into the lucid remoteness of Kagan's eyes, engaging the emptiness he saw there. They were the most empty eyes he had ever known. They reminded him of jungle clearings and long swamp roads.

'I'm a ranger. I—' Sumner winced and rocked to his feet.

He can't talk, Fang. The lusk isn't complete. He's still fighting it.

'You mean, there are two in that body?' Ardent Fang's eyes softened, and he pushed himself up. He had never seen a body as whole as this one before. Beneath that strange burn, shaped very much like a black lotus with two livid petals at the sides of his neck, he was all face. The man was indeed powerful, and he had every marking of a warrior, but the emptiness in those eyes . . . Staring into them, he felt a tautness in his chest as if a storm were closing around them.

'Can we help?' Ardent Fang asked.

Sumner nodded, one hand milking the ache from the back of his neck. 'Music,' he rasped, and walked a tight circle.

Ardent Fang took out his devil harp and chiseled a few notes out of the air, seeking a melody. But before he could open into a song, a growl rolled across the dawn.

Sumner spun into a defensive crouch, his knife appearing instantly in his hands. He searched the crater-mists' green illusions for movement.

Be calm, Kagan. Drift sat up, head swiveling. *We have a companion around here somewhere. He's taken the form of a cat.*

Sumner glanced at the seer with thinned eyes and moved toward a flat-topped boulder to get a better vantage. Another growl slurred from behind one of the outcroppings. Sumner turned and watched a silver-blue silking length of puma pad into the enclosure, its black underbelly swaying into sight with each step. Smoky ember eyes fixed on him, and as it advanced, he turned the edge of his blade toward it.

Easy, Kagan. This is Bonescrolls.

Sumner watched with fear and awe as the wave of knotting and sliding muscle glided forward. Red and black face markings forked over its sloped eyes like a caricature of horns, and a cloud of rainmist and leaf odors filled the air.

If you touch him, you'll see what I mean, Drift sent, going over to the puma and stroking its flat head.

Sumner tightened his knife-grip but didn't retreat as the rolling, silver-furred length of shoulders and spine came up to him. He stared down at the demon eyes, the black wire-bright whiskers, the leathery snout, and a wild laugh coiled in his chest. *Two distorts and a puma!*

A slash of voor noise shriveled his laughter. He reached out jerkily and touched the sleek fur.

Quaking, his whole body was seized in an orgasm of blazing luminance. A rapture of colors swirled across his sight and dissolved to a blowing of bright particles. His hand fell away, and he swayed on his heels, entranced in soulful absorption, listening to the silver hum of blood far back in the valleys of his brain.

Light, the menstruum of manifestation—

Bonescrolls' hands moved dreamily above him, brown and rumpled, soaked with the heat of the desert sun. He was lying entranced in the shade of a stonesill, sunlight angling over his shadowed body like a veil.

Light, the void's notariqon— He was chanting these thoughts to keep himself alert within his trance. In a corner of his mind he was a swamp puma—itchy, panting, looking up at a long-shouldered man whose face was stained with an iridescent blueblackness.

Light . . .

The air brightened with psychic energy, and the magnar stopped chanting and dropped his hands into his lap. The psynergy was radiating from the dark-faced stranger.

When the man placed his callused hand on the puma's head, Bonescrolls felt his life—hot and electric as blood—and saw everything about him, from his lovecursed childhood in McClure through the indignities that had cut him into a trained killer. But the spectral magnetism around him came from deeper.

Behind those downslanting eyes, the mindark opened rapidly into

183

the luminous, terrible knowing of a voor soul. An icy-blond child, naked, with skin white as stone and colorless eyes, appeared for an instant and then dissolved into a windrush of sparks. Sight phased to a vista of galactic vapors and starchained darkness, a chasm so vivid that Bonescrolls was startled back into his own body.

His legs kicked out with a lurch of dreamfalling, and he sat up bluntly. He was alone again in his rocktower, a dawn breeze lolling through the windowholes, a sprawl of Serbota blankets tangled beneath him. He put his hands to his ears to feel that he was awake, and even though he heard his life knocking inside him, he felt dreampaced. That voor was powerful.

Far away, Bonescrolls felt the swamp puma circling restlessly, and he soultouched it with the spirit music that was always lofting at the back of his mind. The animal calmed instantly, and its complaisance steadied him, easing the strength back into his eyes.

This body was getting old, he acknowledged to himself, quaking awkwardly to his feet. He leaned momentarily against the curved sill of a rockwindow, watching the slow sea of the desert shimmer, feeling the depth-terror he had just known pulsing in his chest. Who was this Massebôth soldier that he could carry such a voor?

Kagan—Sumner Kagan, the man's name whispered in his mind, and with it came more understanding than he could hold in the tight cell of his brain:

Kagan was the eth.

That thought alone was so huge, the magnar had to walk a long slow circle through the earth-packed studio to comprehend what was happening.

The-eth was the fear-shadow of the Delph. He was an acausal double, a synchronous mirrorself, the echo of the godmind returning from the future, as unconscious of his power as the Delph was aware. The godmind had no influence over the eth: If they were ever to meet, they would simply be two men facing each other—and that had always been too great a threat to the Delph. Until now, every eth-manifestation had been hunted down and destroyed by the Delph's minions. So how had this one survived?

The answer came in a tremolo of excitement. *The voors!* The Delph had routinely killed off the best voors for centuries in a vain attempt to exclude other godminds from the planet. The voors needed their godminds to remember their ancestral wanderings and where it was they were going. Naturally, they would use the Delph's shadowself against him.

Voor and eth—a deadly alliance, Bonescrolls marveled, passing through a slanted arch and leaning into a rock incline that led toward the passionate sunlight at the top of the butte.

Deadly . . . The thought wavered in him with the foreknowing of his own death. He was going to die soon. The nightmare visions were getting stronger. For two centuries he had carried when and how in the meat of his heart. A one-eyed man with a scarred face and a silver-gold sword was going to kill him at the end of the next solar year. He had lived the killing in dreams: the raised sword, the dark enraged face, and then a splatter of hurting bright light opening into a darkness forever in silence.

The magnar stopped in the mouth of the cave where the loud sunlight sang back into shadow. He could see far across the broken body of Skylonda Aptos to where the cordillera of the world's edge burst into the sky. Six hundred million years of geography stared back at him from the striated rock pinnacles. At his feet the wind had cut sharply into the schist, revealing the spiral patterns of marine fossils. He knelt down and touched the color-margin where 165 million years ago the life of an ocean had ended. He picked up a stone and etched his own spiral over the exposed sediment.

Across the deadland, distant cliffs the color of sulfur watched mindlessly. A sentimental thought began close to him and then moved on, continuing somewhere deeper: *This world is the rim of an abyss* . . .

Deep in the sky a hawk drifted through a slow whirlpool pattern, and Bonescrolls watched it without seeing. He was thinking about Kagan—the eth.

The lusk was muddling Kagan's clarity and straining his bodylight. If there was any hope of the voor using this eth against the Delph, Kagan's body would have to be rested and his mind calmed. That was why Bonescrolls had known the Delph. That was why he had survived twelve centuries in this haunted world. That was why.

The old man sat back against the warm stone and closed his eyes. *To be here for the eth. To serve.* The puma's lifestrength flexed in him, and the intuitive certainty of his mission pulsed with his breathing.

He would help the eth, he decided with quiet conviction. Though it meant that he was surrendering to his deathvision, that a year from now he would be gnawbones, the rightness of his decision shone in him like sunlight.

With a lucid peace, Sumner accompanied the distorts to Bonescrolls' cliffdwelling. Along the way Drift chanted about four warriors lost in the world, each step foreordained as stars, leaving nothing behind them that was real. And though the words were melancholy, the tempo was lively and matched the strong cadence of their walk.

Ardent Fang hung close to Kagan, impressed by his gliding gait and the wholeness of his body. As they left the crater highlands he looked about for the tracks Sumner had made during his approach. There were none. And when he asked him about that, Kagan explained how he had walked the hot, crumbling rim of an exploded cinder cone to reach the outcrops without disturbing the ash. Listening to him, Ardent Fang was enthralled by the timbre of his voice and the expressions of his face. The man was simple and direct—without the elaborate face gestures and maskings common among the distorts.

That they could communicate at all amazed Sumner, for they spoke different languages. Magically they understood each other, just as, magically, his voor-bondage had ended. Somehow it was related to the black and silver puma sliding from the shade of one scarp to the next. He called to it with his thoughts, and it stopped and stared back at him several times, but there was no other response.

Sumner's mind was silent and motionless as the land around them. Only the joy of his freedom pulsed and turned in him. He knew from what the distorts said that he would understand nothing until he met the magnar, so he stayed with his selfscan.

Under a wine-dark afternoon sky they arrived at their destination. The swamp puma curled up on a shadowed ledge, and Drift guided them through the mazy corridors to Bonescrolls' abode.

The sunshafted dwelling was fluttering with birds, twitching and jittering on the rock shelves and the ledges around the windholes. A carnival-beaked macaw clapped up toward a higher perch in the domed ceiling. Green parakeets spurted in one opening and out another.

Bonescrolls was seated on his straw mat before a wide window-oval, its sill streaked with birds' droppings. He smiled, revealing big, square teeth, and waved them closer. He was wearing a red burnoose and hide trousers netted with wear. Between his bare feet was a tattered fiber sack. 'Heroes of the Serbota, Sumner Kagan—shay!' He gestured for them to sit.

The three wanderers sat on the ground before him, and though the old man was smiling, there was a thin look in his eyes that urged them to keep their silence. Ardent Fang and Sumner thought that look was weariness, but Drift recognized it for the tedium that it was. How often in the dreamtime had the magnar sat through this meeting?

Only a seer would know, Drift heard the old man's voice in its head. It faced the magnar and caught a sly wink. Suddenly the present was motionless, stony, filled with a desert odor of baked bricks. Drift felt itself sliding out of its body, and it relaxed. It knew what was happening.

In the thick heat, breathing was a labor; thirst was adamant. But it was so peaceful to lie here, to wait for the strength to return.

Drift felt itself floating within the awareness of the swamp puma, staring out from beneath heavy lids at a landscape of whirlpool heat where each rock was cut into jewel-points.

All at once Drift was inside the magnar. It was night, or it appeared to be, for though the sky was a vivid blue, the light was greening as before a storm or during an eclipse. The magnar knelt in a plain of jagged stone, and it was as if Drift were kneeling, as if its knees were aching against fists of stone, as if its fingers were tracing spirals in the pale, chalky dust. The spiral doodles held its attention rigidly—

Drift was curling deep into the dreamtime. As usual there was fear, but curiosity was stronger. It calmed itself and let the vision unwind.

It was the magnar, kneeling among the stones, staring at distant cliffs the color of sulfur. It stood and began to walk toward a field of windsmoothed rocks white as bones, an ossuary it felt it would never cross. The sky was revolving with whirlpool energies: *This world is the rim of an abyss, and I'm circling closer. If only I were an animal. Then I could face the emptiness with a surer instinct* . . .

A bird squawked, and Drift's alertness snapped back to itself. Rose wine was chuckling out of a slender-throated jug into a glazed cup. The wine ran over the cup and became fire that blazed blindingly hot. Drift squinted into the glare and saw Bonescrolls sprawled on his back, his face a deathmask, waxy and staring. Notes from a devil harp, soft and subtle, reflected off the walls, whined down to a dirge, wheeling softer and softer—

A guffaw burst the silence, and Drift's vision cleared.

Bonescrolls was laughing so hard he was soundless, his hands pressing his ribs. Ardent Fang, too, was yukking, and the sight of his savage face smeared with mirth and crawling with tears pierced Drift's confusion. He whistle-sighed with joy and relief and an awestruck humiliation. He had missed some joke during his vision, but it seemed not to matter. Energies were circling swiftly between it and the magnar.

'Bonescrolls is why the Serbota is a tribe of ecstasy,' Ardent Fang was saying. 'He taught our ancestors how to laugh.'

Drift rocked its queer-shaped head from side to side, relieved to be out of the dreamtime but still sensing the greening of the light, the powers drawing in, tightening. It was eerie.

'Between here and the dust,' Bonescrolls said, wiping his eyes with his sleeve, 'joy is all we have.' He glanced at Drift, his horseface flushed with laughter. The seer experienced a rush of dizziness, heard the dirge music again, and clenched its mind. Bonescrolls winked and looked away.

Sumner was feeling good. This old man was powerful. Something was going on between him and the short distort. When he stared at them, a ball of energy tightened in his belly and a shaggy, maniac joy trembled inside him. *Too much power.*

'My friends are fascinated by you,' Bonescrolls said in perfect Massel. 'You're the first undistorted human they've seen. Perhaps you'll explain to them what you're doing in so empty a place.'

Sumner shrugged. He told them a little about the Rangers, his assignment in Laguna, and the voor mummy that had erupted in his face. He spoke about the mad sounds that sheared his nerves outside selfscan.

Ardent Fang nodded energetically. 'It's terrible, magnar. When we crossed with him, the seer and I knew pain and terror greater than all the wounds of the jungle.'

Bonescrolls nodded with understanding and smiled broadly. The polished bronze sunlight flared in his white hair. He brought four clay mugs out from behind him, each ringed with glazed, festive colors. 'I propose a toast to your freedom, Kagan.'

'Am I free?' Though he heard nothing but the world around him, Sumner sensed that the voor was still within.

'If you're not free, the magnar will free you,' Ardent Fang said.

Fang— Drift shook its head. The strangeness had passed, and now there was a ponderous sense of redundancy. All this had happened before.

'It's okay, Drift,' Bonescrolls said, lifting the fiber sack and removing a slender-throated jug. He filled a cup with a wine red and smoky as dusk. 'Ardent Fang is right. You're not free yet, Kagan, but if you can trust me, I can help you.'

'How?'

Bonescrolls' animal-calm eyes gleamed with laughter as he filled the other cups and handed them around. 'A toast,' he said through his grin. 'To freedom.'

'To the Powers,' Ardent Fang added.

'To the living,' Drift followed.

Sumner lifted his mug and glanced his lip with the wine. The liquid kiss cooled his flesh and charged his sinuses with a heady bouquet. After the others had drunk, he took a sip and followed the hot, sapid course of the wine to his belly. 'Can you help me?' he asked Bonescrolls.

The old man nodded and noisily smacked his lips. 'Rose-hip wine mixed with thornberry juice. A poignant combination, don't you think?'

Ardent Fang agreed boisterously and refilled his cup.

'What do I have to do?' Sumner asked.

Bonescrolls placed his cup on the ground and stopped smiling. His wizard-flared eyebrows drew together. 'If you truly want to be freed of this voor and if you can trust me, I'll help you.'

'I want nothing more than to have my mind back. And I'd like to trust you.'

Bonescrolls' long, thick-nosed face lit up, and his eyes crinkled happily again. 'Fine. Then you'll be free.'

'But what do I have to do?'

'Serve me without question for a solar year.'

Sumner sat back, and his face hardened. 'I can't do that. I'm a ranger. I've signed an oath of fealty.'

Bonescrolls barked a laugh. He looked at Ardent Fang and Drift with a merry expression. 'He's tighter than a coyote's asshole.'

Drift covered its head with its hands, and Ardent Fang rolled to his back in a fit of explosive laughter.

'You want to be a ranger?' Bonescrolls shook his head with mock sadness. 'Then you're going to be one *crazy* ranger.'

'Crazeeeeee!' Ardent Fang whined, rolling to his side. He took Sumner's arm and looked up at him with moist, red eyes. 'Kagan, don't be stupid. That voor inside you is going to break your mind. Why do you want to do that?'

Sumner didn't meet the tribesman's gaze. He was staring down at his hands. They were powerful, thick and sinewy, but helpless against the deep pain that twisted him. A clear head had never seemed so important. His contemplation felt muscular and direct, and he realized that if he were deprived of it again, if he had to prowl the wastes with no more wit than a lizard, not knowing where his sleep would take him, he would kill himself.

Sumner looked up at Bonescrolls. The magnar was smiling benignly. The old man nodded his head once, and Sumner reached up to the cobra insignia pinned to his lapel and tore it off.

Bonescrolls and Ardent Fang whooped and laughed, and the lupine tribesman slapped Sumner's back. 'Don't worry, Kagan,' Ardent Fang gusted. 'The magnar is wise. He'll use you well.'

Drift whistled and chirped, and a flare of small birds streamed across the chamber. *You made the right decision, warrior.*

'Ah, I'm glad you both agree,' Bonescrolls said, refilling Ardent Fang's cup. 'My servant will need allies. After you rest tonight, I want you to take him back to Miramol with you. He'll live and work there until you hear from me.' He leaned forward and took the cobra insignia out of Sumner's hand. 'You've had to hold too much, young brother—too much.' His face was sad and heavy. 'But you can relax now. I'm going to take it all from you.' He popped the silver cobra in his mouth and swallowed it.

Ardent Fang lurched into laughter and kicked his legs in the air. 'Crazeeeeee!'

Sumner closed his eyes. At least the pain was gone. Silence ranged deep into himself. The lusk was over. Then a burst of sound louder than Ardent Fang's laughter snapped his lids open, and he saw all the birds wheeling around the cavern in a clamor of feathers. All at once they winged out the window-oval behind Bonescrolls and vanished into a sky of stilled, pink-lit clouds. 'My witnesses,' the magnar chuckled.

Skyfires flimmered over the dunes, and a toothed moon hung between two buttes. Corby opened his eyes and looked about. He was alone in a dark cavern. Above him the Goat Nebula stared down, fixed as an insect eye.

He wobbled to his feet, the squawking insistence of the voor dead narrowing to a thin whine. With one hand on the cool rock wall to guide him, he staggered several steps and stopped. A man-shadow

189

was standing still as stone against the creased wall. The shadow stepped forward, and Corby pressed his fingers hard against the rock to keep from falling. The man had no kha.

The slim light from the skyfires limned a long, age-thickened face. It was Bonescrolls. Sumner's memories of him flitted through Corby's mind. But this Bonescrolls wasn't smiling.

'Sit down, voor.'

Corby bristled at the command in the old man's voice. He forced all his energy into his muscles and swung forward to push the magnar out of his way. Bonescrolls, with lithe quickness, side-stepped, spun Corby about, and knocked his legs out from under him.

Sprawled against the cavern wall, the voor gathered his inner strength and drove the psynergy out from his body like a blow. Blue static fuzzed around Bonescrolls' head and throat and then cooled to a thick red in his chest and drained purple down his legs into the earth.

'You can't hurt me, voor. Be still.'

Corby's effort had loosened his hold on the moment. Blaring howls vibrated his skull, and for a moment he felt as if he were going to blur out of his body.

'Your lusk is weak.' Bonescrolls sat beside him on a jut of rock, his eyepits dark. 'By what right are you in the body of this man?'

Everything was running loose. Who was this howlie? Corby could see the old man's kha now. It was small as a seed and dense as rock—a green seed suspended within the cloud of the man's abdomen. Staring at it was like gazing through a long tunnel. At the far end, shapes were moving—dark, thick-haired hominids shaping clay with their hands . . . Redoubled cries from the voor dead churned a vortex, scrambling his thoughts.

'Answer me, voor!'

The power in the magnar's voice quelled the grievous uproar in his head. Corby steadied himself. His lips lolled loosely and trembled as his mind formed thoughts.

'Don't send,' Bonescrolls ordered. 'Talk to me like a howlie. Use the body you're stealing.'

Corby's lips winced, and sounds clumped in his tight throat. With tremendous effort he forced his breath into sounds: 'Words-don't-carry-the-right-I-feel.'

Bonescrolls' face was graven. It looked lichenous in the slender light. 'The world is feeling. Each being lives in its own world. Your people have always respected that.'

Corby's throat pulsed as his sagging mouth tightened to speak: 'I-am-my-people.'

'And Kagan is his people, as I am mine.'

Corby's body twitched as his power returned, but still his strength did not quite fit his muscles. Bonescrolls was strong.

'We howlies have a riddle,' the magnar went on. He chanted:

> 'The stars baked my bones
> The oceans culled my blood,
> And the forests shaped my lungs.
> Who am I?

'The answer is "Human." We're as much children of the cosmos as any voor. You have no authority to take this body.'

Corby whispered, his lips barely moving: 'Words-do-not-carry.'

Bonescrolls' face darkened. 'Then listen closely to what these words carry: I can drive you out of that body. I have the craft and the power. And I'll use them, unless you can convince me otherwise.'

The voor's gaze was bald, and in the slow-rending starlight he looked like a corpse. 'My-purpose-is-to-destroy-the-Delph.'

Bonescrolls sat back and nodded once with satisfaction. 'Thank you for telling me the truth, voor. I know this is the body of the eth—the Delph's doomself. And I have no objection to an alliance between eth and voors to end the reign of a godmind. The Delph is my enemy, too. Once I tried to destroy him—but he was far too powerful. Kagan must be carefully prepared.'

'The-Delph-kills-voors.' Corby's blind stare sharpened. 'He-destroyed-my-body.'

'And now you'll destroy this body trying to get back at him.' Bonescrolls shook his head. 'The pain must stop somewhere.'

The Delph is weak now, Corby sent. *Soon he'll sleep for an aeon. But when he wakes he'll be many times stronger. I must stop him now, for both of our peoples.*

Bonescrolls was silent, void of thoughts. Then: 'It's all dreaming. Whether you try to kill him or not is not my decision. That's something Kagan must decide, for it's his life against the Delph's.'

He was the father of my body.

'Still, it's his decision. You'll have to tell him.'

Not now.

'No—he's too far from himself now. And besides, I have need of him.' He looked out at the ritual moon and the haze of cosmic lights. 'But after a year, you'll have to speak with him. Until then you must in no way interfere with his life. If you do, I'll drive you from his body.'

Corby was silent. Even the thought of a year spent mindlessly floating in Iz stupefied him. Yet what choice did he have? There could be no struggle with this man. If he was going to survive—for the brood's sake—he would have to go deep into the body and keep a strong silence.

Already he had begun to fade into the roaring, radiant stream of Iz, buoyed by immense forces that in his human brain seemed terrible and incoherent: a grueling din of screams and goblin mutterings. A

191

great depth was opening all around him. Flares of scorching white light gyrated to the pulsing cries.

Bonescrolls' eyeglints fixed him in the moment, and one last time before succumbing to the draw of whistling energy, he reached out: *This is a universe of boundless space, howlie. Matter and energy are rare and small. For us in this vast emptiness, even dreams are real.*

Bonescrolls felt the voor-psynergy dim and vanish. It happened so quickly that when Sumner's body began to breathe with the depth and slowness of sleep, the magnar was still leaning forward, watching Corby's purple kha waver in the night shadows. The voor was gone. Outside, the single bark of a desert fox echoed over the dunes, shrill as moonlight.

Ardent Fang was anxious to get Sumner to Miramol so that he could show off the burly desert-colored warrior they had found in the wastes. They journeyed west among ghosts of water: parched sinkwells and the long running curves of vanished riverbeds where the sun's heat glimmered like liquid. Drift chanted solemn and slow:

> *Weird how time is always sliding east.*
> *Weird that we should move at all.*

The seer was withdrawn into the Road. The power-channel it had chosen to follow sizzled beneath its feet and itched up its spine with information about other creatures that had crossed this way. Bonescrolls' deep, slow, and quiet psynergy was there. At noon the né spotted puma pug marks in a sandbed and knew that Bonescrolls had gone on ahead of them. Bending over the spoor, Drift swayed dizzily. Dirge music whispered, flames spit, and a one-eyed man came forward with a curved blade in his hands.

Ardent Fang's muscular embrace brought Drift out of its glide. It rocked briefly in the tribesman's arms, its eyes seeing charred bone and blackened flesh, grease and ash in the mess of a dead fire.

'The seer's only half alive in this world,' Ardent Fang explained to Sumner. 'Half his life belongs to the deep dark.'

When Drift was itself again, it made no comment about its experience. It felt out the Road and continued their trek. In its heart, though, it was troubled. Bonescrolls had told it twice, as clearly as he could, that he was going to die. But that was too ponderous a thought to contemplate. Thinking about the one-eyed swordsman, Drift felt a wind sound blow through its head and the dirge piping begin again. Drift ignored Ardent Fang's questions and withdrew once more into the Road.

Sumner held himself in selfscan and did not try to understand the two distorts who were leading him. The lusk had left him wary and shaken. For the first time since arriving in Skylonda Aptos, he had time to reflect, and he didn't know where to begin. The Rangers . . .

Bonescrolls . . . the distorts . . . He was happy to be whole again, but he was apprehensive about where he was going and how the magnar would use him. All that he knew with certainty was that he would have to serve to be free.

Everybody was twisted, bent, or muddled in some way: hunch-backed, gibbon-armed, muzzle-faced. But all of them, even the legless ones on wheeled platforms and the scabious ones with glossy raw faces, laughed with sincerity. They were all brightly attired in feather-rimmed leather caps, floral robes, and pants of bushbuck skins. The women wore ancient shell amulets, metal arm coils, and cobra-head bracelets. The naked children, crouched in the baobab trees along the boulevard, were the color of wood.

Laugh, Kagan, or you'll insult the people, Drift warned.

Ardent Fang was howling with joy, his snout-lips pulled back in a grimace that could have been a snarl except for the happiness and tears in his eyes. Sumner grinned and chuckled.

Louder, or they'll think you're dissatisfied.

Sumner forced a few crude laughs, and then Drift reached up and grabbed the back of his neck. Hot, deep-felt jocularity percolated up from his bowels, and he guffawed and swagged with laughter. The crowd responded with hoots and whistles, and when Sumner shouted a gleeful monkey-call, they surged forward and swept the three wanderers off their feet.

Twice the crowd carried them around Miramol, through the warrior's-walk of overreaching boar-ribs, across the central square of icy mist-springs, up the hill to the curving flower-crowded lanes of the né dwellings, and down again past the blue moss-banks of the river. Then the three were lowered before the turquoise-studded mudhole of the Mother's Barrow.

Old women in black robes with collapsed faces and alert laughing eyes greeted them. The Mothers circled Sumner, awed by his size and wholeness. They plucked at his arms and thighs, poked his ribs, pressed their fingertips against his stomach, measured the span of his shoulders with their hands, and laughed incessantly. The burn marks on his face and neck particularly impressed them, and they all had to touch his face once. Then one of them called out to the crowd in a gleeful voice, and the celebration began.

For three days and nights the riverain forest jangled with the festal sounds of kettledrums, wood clappers, harps and flutes and frenzied laughter. The dirt streets of Miramol were jammed with frolicking distorts, swirling together in ritual dances and processions.

Sumner was carried to a large, bamboo-rafted ceremonial hall. On the way, women and men tussled with each other to touch him and toss petals and blossoms in his lap. He was seated on a tortoise-shell throne flanked by huge scarlet ferns and arrays of purple and black

193

fronds. Before him was laid out a continuous offering of foods: slit-bellied trout stuffed with shelled nuts, leaf pouches of monkey stew, crisped snake cubes speared on thin sweet roots, spicy bean paste in blossom cups, and ornate jugs of wine and honey beer.

Sumner sampled everything and tried to laugh at everybody that that served him a new dish, though he often succeeded only in gagging on his food. When his glazed eyes and slack expression made it obvious that he could eat no more, Drift escorted him out of the feeding hall. They avoided the festivity-crowded main roads and followed the dark back lanes to the silverwood né lodges. There the festivities ended.

In the clouded, flower-heavy air of a small moss garden, Drift told Sumner the history of the Serbota. It skipped the origin myths and the spirit tales and began with the finding of the Road.

Dog Hunger found the Road. He was a seer or what passed for a seer in those days—he was gendered, you understand, so his clarity was weak. Yet it was strong enough to lead him through the wastes to where no one had gone before, because the land was the sun's lair.

How did he find himself so far from the tribe? That's a long story, and I can see you're weary. Let me tell you only this: The Serbota have always been a gentle people. Always we retreated from our enemies until, finally, there was no place else to run. We were pushed right into the desert and left there to die.

Dog Hunger, who was named that because he never had a full meal in his life, wandered off, like many others had before him, to die where the sun would witness his passing and perhaps, out of pity, accept his spirit. The early people believed such nonsense. Anyway, he didn't die. Instead, his power led him deep into the wastes, and he became the first to meet the magnar.

Well, when the magnar heard of our plight, he came personally, and for many years he was our tribal leader. He taught us the ways of the riverain forest and the desert so that we could eat again and make houses and, if necessary, kill to protect ourselves. We became like any creature of the forest. But most importantly, he showed us how to be different from the forest creatures by doing what no animal can do—laugh. We learned to laugh at everything, even our enemies—which was a wise thing. Our enemies thought we had become spirit-possessed. Suddenly we had well-trained warriors who fought using the strategies of jungle beasts and who laughed as they killed and even as they died. Now we have no enemies. And yet we still have laughter—and the né have life.

You see, before the magnar came, the Mothers killed all the infants born without gender. The magnar stopped that. Not with force but with cunning. He saw that the Mothers were superstitious, and so he told them that their deity, Paseq the Divider who separates night from day and man from woman, was itself without gender. And so we are allowed to live because it is believed we are the image of Paseq.

The né have done much for the Serbota. Our seers are much clearer than any gendered seer, and though we are not as loud in our laughter as the others, neither are we as cruel in our anger. We keep to ourselves, for we have no other family.

And yet we are happy. For isn't that what it means to be human?

The Serbota would have celebrated Sumner's arrival for a full week, but on the fourth day the monsoons began. Sumner watched in amazement as Miramol was transformed from a forest village into a river town. The vegetable fields were quickly harvested and all the huts were dismantled except for the silverwood lodges, which were located like the Mother's Barrow on precious high ground.

With the first lull in the rains, the dugouts were unsheathed, and the river hunters began their work. Each canoe had elaborately carved gunwales done in the style of their owners. Ardent Fang's had a boar's head with curved tusks. Only men with boats were allowed to hunt, and Sumner was left behind to build his own dugout.

Drift found him late in the afternoon at the dry edge of the cloud forest among giant violets and mossy tree limbs. He was hollowing out a log with a stone adze, and his head and shoulders were quilled with needles of gold light. Drift helped him steady the log. *Bonescrolls sent a message for you last night.*

Sumner put down his adze and squinted into the cloud-driven light. It would rain by nightfall. He looked at the seer, his vague eyebrows raised in a question.

He orders you to obey the Mothers.

Sumner nodded and picked up his adze. 'Tell me about the Mothers.'

It's best I don't, for I have no love of them.

'Tell me anyway.'

They're the tribe leaders. They decide who will hunt, who will farm and fish, and who will breed. All women must obey them without question until they bear a gendered child that lives to pass the puberty rites.

'And then?'

Then they become one of the Mothers.

'Why do you hate them?'

They despise né. It's only because of the magnar that they tolerate us. And besides, they're polluted with superstition. . . .

'Why then does the magnar order me to obey them?'

Drift shook its round head. *There's no second-guessing the magnar. He's as unknowable as the clouds.*

At night, nulling toward sleep in a tree hammock, Sumner was grateful to be free of the voor. He listened to the rain creaking in the jungle, heard a child crying, and smelled the languor of a dampened bonfire. Not a squirm of voor noise touched him. Gazing into the darkness at the crayoned outline of trees, his night-vision was clear, without the listlessness of the lusk.

'Bonescrolls.' He said the name just loud enough to feel it in his throat. The sound calmed him, and he closed his eyes, feeling his

195

deepest muscles relaxing, his whole being easing up, more complete for what it had lost.

Sumner's dugout took three days to complete, most of the work done in the animal-skin shelter of a tree dwelling while the rains slashed through the jungles. At the first letup, he showed it to Ardent Fang. The tribesman studied it carefully, marveling at the sleekness of its line and jealous of how high it rode in the water. But it had no carvings on its prow, and he suggested that Sumner give it a spirit.

One of the né, a master of wood, loaned him some tools. Sumner, who had come to be known as Lotus Face because of his burns, carved lotus petals on the gunwales. The first day he went out, he speared a mature, full-flanked tapir. He presented it to the né woodmaster when he returned his tools, which caused a stir in the village. All first catches were traditionally offered to the Mothers.

The next day the Mothers sent for him. Three of them sat on round leather-polished stones beneath a fronded rain-canopy. The rain drummed loudly, and Sumner couldn't hear their voices. They wore black shapeless shifts, and their gray fog hair covered most of their shrunken features. One of them had only one eye. Another had silver scales at the corners of her mouth and eyes. The third one was silent and stared only at his genitals.

They're ordering you to give up your dugout, Drift sent, standing behind him.

'Why?' Sumner snapped, and one of the women shrieked so loud his ears rang.

You're not to speak in their presence unless questioned. Drift thought of fields of scarlet larkspur and their sweet, moribund redolence until he saw Sumner's jaw stop throbbing.

The Mothers conferred for a moment. Then: *They say you must give your dugout to them. You won't be needing it anymore. Instead, you're to go with Ardent Fang to the breeding stables. If you perform well there, your dugout and the right to hunt may be returned to you.*

Sumner stared vigorously upward until the Mothers departed.

All the women in the breeding stable were naked except for their bright rag-wrapped heads and the yellow dots meticulously painted over their ovaries. In the crinkled lantern-light, Ardent Fang was at home. He breathed the dark spicy odors without notice, and laughed as Sumner hesitated at the top of the ramp.

With one hand he pulled at Sumner's arm, and with the other he gestured at the tiers of mating stalls. The stable was a massive hive of wooden cubicles, each with a young female writhing lewdly before it. Brown-garbed matrons, elderly women who had never borne an acceptable child, patrolled the aisles and stairways, tending to the young women's needs and encouraging them to be provocative.

Even in the frail light there was no hiding the fact that these women were distorts. All of them were abnormal in some way: swollen foreheads, foreshortened or distended limbs, scaled flesh, horned shoulders, snouted faces. Sumner was too disgusted to look. He stood hopelessly at the head of the ramp until one of the matrons, a slight woman with knobbed hands and leathery lips, guided him to a stall with a blue lantern.

The girl who was sprawled there on a tangle of blankets had a lithe, voluptuous body, clean and narrow as light, the legs splayed, the hips gyrating, the dark cloud of mons hair glistening. But her face—It was a crude patchwork of faces sewn into an emotionless mask. Sumner wanted to look away, but the eyes within the bone-pits were alive and electrical, beckoning him, pleading.

The matron stepped past Sumner and moved to place a blanket over the girl's face. Sumner waved her out. He focused on the feathery grain of wood glazed with blue lantern-light and slid into selfscan. He looked at the girl and saw her without emotion—saw her as creatures see each other. The face was twisted and darkened strangely, but it was the life in it that he fixed on. The sharp sexual odor of the place became suddenly palpable, and he removed his clothes. He let the erotic odors and the woman-softness of the girl's body move him, and he rutted with her without emotion, riding his body to a quick climax.

Ardent Fang watched Sumner's performance with interest. He was pleased that such an outstanding hunter and woodworker was a lousy lover. His member was of a good size, indeed it was formidable, but his style was crude, totally primitive. If they had shared a language, he would have been glad to enlighten him. As it was, Lotus Face actually seemed pleased with himself to have finished so quickly. Ardent Fang shrugged, *Strange ways*, and went off to start his rounds.

Sumner serviced three women a day for several weeks. He preferred to finish his mating chores early in the day so that he had time to fish. Fishing was the only occupation the Mothers allowed him, and he had a favorite angling perch at one end of a broad, parklike glade. There, at the sedgy rim of the brown river, he lazily trawled for trout.

The Serbota hunters who stalked the swollen river wouldn't talk with him now that the Mothers had taken away his dugout. Only the children and the né tolerated his presence. The né were particularly receptive to him, and they set aside a room for him in one of their lodges. But Sumner was never at ease among them. They were generous to a fault and anxious to share the secrets of their trades with him, but they were perpetually dour. Their sadness ran deep because they were genderless and without the purpose of family. Sumner preferred to be alone.

Often, trawling the deep pools created by fallen trees, far up the river, he saw his dugout sliding over the water, light as a leaf. Each time there was someone different in it, and each time they pretended not to see him. Sumner wasn't angry. He was proud of his canoe, and he was happy it had no one owner. In a way it was still his, and there was always the chance that he would get it back.

Toward the end of his second month in Miramol, Sumner met with Bonescrolls again. It began while he was fishing. He had dropped a grasshopper into a deep marly channel among weeds, and a trout had struck immediately. He hooked it and was sloshing backwards in the current when he sensed them.

Two voors, their black hoods thrown back, their searchless, vague eyes fixed on him, were behind him, advancing quickly. Both had black-crusted lizard faces, and staring at them, Sumner felt a dull chill ice across his back. He hesitated only an instant, but in that moment one of the voors snarled its lips and revealed a tiny blowgun clenched between its teeth. The dart stung the side of his neck as he began the roll to evade it.

With horrible reptile slowness, he tumbled to his back, curled his legs in, and swung to his belly. The toxin they had hit him with turned his muscles to slag, and as he crumbled he saw the two voors crouching over him. One of them was saying something insistently: 'Dai Bodatta!'

A swell of pain bulged in his throat and piled downward, dragging him into unconsciousness. He struggled, squinting through gusty lights of green-silver. The voors had taken his arms, and they were lugging him over the ground. He felt like wet sand. He felt like wood.

The air trembled, and a roar crashed through the glade so loud that Sumner's chest tightened. The bush ahead of them parted, and a silver-blue puma burst into the clearing, its yellow pupils two jets of flame. It crouched before them, all its heavy muscles bunched tightly below the mad pulse of its throat.

The voors dropped Sumner's arms and backstepped. The last thing he saw of them was their black cowls fluttering like wings at the forest's edge. Then the suspenseful musk of the big cat filled his sinuses as its shadow slouched over him.

The black-bellied puma was still with him when he woke to a scalding headache. *The voors want you for their own purposes,* Drift explained, one hand on the puma's head. *The magnar thinks you should leave Miramol for a while and stay with him in the desert.*

Sumner sat silent for a moment, feeling his life floating inside him. He would be happy to leave Miramol. And he wanted to meet again this being that could command voors and animals. He looked at the puma, and the big cat stared back keenly, its green eyes tricked with reflections.

'I'll go now,' he said, pulling himself upright against the gravity of the drug.

Now? The né clicked its eyes. It listened to the humming of Sumner's mind and saw that he remembered the desert crossing they had done together. He knew the route through the wasteland to the magnar. The né was amazed, for even seers usually needed several crossings to learn the way. *Shouldn't you rest?*

'I've been resting for weeks.' He watched as the puma ambled into the forest. 'And the voors want me now. It'll be harder for them to surprise me in the desert.'

We'll get you canteens and strider-sandals at the lodges.

'I don't need them.'

Drift stared and saw that this was true. *Take this, then.* It held out the né walking stick that it was carrying.

Sumner smiled and took the tall stick. 'You found me in the desert, remember? Don't worry.'

The né's eyes starshined. *It's not you I am truly afraid for. It's the magnar. I've seen death around him.*

Sumner hefted the walking stick and turned away from the river and the né. 'I'm sworn to serve Bonescrolls. I'll watch after him.'

Drift accompanied him to where the lateritic silt of the wastes began, and it left him there with a traditional chant:

> *We are made of distances.*
> *We are constantly going further,*
> *Alone and predestined,*
> *Learning slowly*
> *That stopping is not arriving.*

Alone in the desert, far out of earshot, Sumner howled with happiness and let his feelings tumble into words: 'Idiot distorts! I'm alive in your hell! I'm never going to die!' He screamed the last word, and the mania in his voice echoed back at him. He had become strange living with distorts, sharing his body with the weird women—He moved at a loping gait over the broken stones of the desert, grateful to be moving and not thinking. Life wasn't shit. Life was a stream of love, of feeling and thought, lascivious in its brevity. He laughed, and his joy was so intense it burned in his throat.

Nightfall brought him to a place of scum-froth and cracked soda. He sat on a mudbank encrusted with alkali and watched the skyfires bristle.

A yellow spark flashed beneath the arch of a dolmen, and a flame spurted and crackled in dry wood. Bonescrolls appeared, hunched over a flame-twitching stack of twigs. His long idol face grinned benevolently. He motioned Sumner to join him and produced a blackened skillet and four green-white snake eggs. 'Hungry?'

Sumner went over to the archrock, cleared a space with his walking stick, and sat. His mind squirmed with questions—how had the magnar found him—why—but he ignored them and urged himself into selfscan.

'That's right,' Bonescrolls said. 'Keep your thoughts quiet. That's a good beginning.' He held the skillet over the fire and handed two of the eggs to Sumner. From a thigh-pouch he produced a handful of small scallions and yellow peppers. The two men cooked and ate in silence.

After they were done, Bonescrolls belched loudly and leaned forward. 'Listen, young brother, this selfscan you've mastered, it's a very good way to sit quietly for a short time, but after a while it gets damn noisy.'

A coyote barked, its vagrantly sorrowing cry wavering across the desert.

Sumner frowned querulously. 'What do you mean?'

Bonescrolls hushed him with a wave of his hand. 'Listen.'

The coyote cried again, barking at its own echo. The call was thin and strung-out, and the sound of it touched Sumner with sadness.

After a moment the magnar smiled and scratched his ear. 'That coyote's just like you,' he said. 'It hasn't found its place, either.' He bent closer so that Sumner could see his eyes, dark and fixed. 'We look from inside our bodies. Like the coyote, we think we're inside our bodies. What is that animal crying to?' With his eyes he pointed up to where a wilted moon was sliding through the clouds. 'We think we're inside our bodies, but part of us is up there too. How lonely that part of us is!'

Sumner gazed sullenly at the old man, feeling dark and indifferent, a part of the night.

'You and the coyote, you both think you have somewhere to go.' Bonescrolls' face hung in the darkness, smiling a mysterious, melancholy smile. 'But the world is feeling, Kagan. There's nothing else. Really—there's nothing else. But nothing can be anything, and so we think we have places to go.' The magnar's bristly eyebrows touched in the space over his nose. 'Psynergy follows thought Stop thinking about not-thinking. Become consciousness itself—be come One Mind.'

Sumner didn't understand Bonescrolls, and he could no longer hold himself still. 'What do you want with me, magnar?'

'All right, young brother.' The magnar patted Sumner's knee with the gruff affection of a man with his dog. 'Let me tell you one more thing. If you want to find a good place to be, no place you find will be good enough. But if you let it all go, if you really empty your head, then any place you are is right. And, even more wonderful, you can be any place at all—even the moon!' He slapped Sumner's knee and laughed, but Sumner only watched him thoughtfully, trying to gauge the old man's sanity.

The laughter drained from Bonescrolls' face, and he rubbed his legs wearily. 'Words!' he spit. 'Nonsense. I might as well be talking to a

200

coyote.' He reached into the leather coverlet he was wearing and produced a sheaf of small envelopes. 'You're a man of action, so I might as well give you something to do. Your orders.' He offered the sheaf to Sumner. 'They're numbered. Open them in sequence only as you complete the assignments. When you're done, return to Miramol. The Mothers have other work for you.'

Bonescrolls yawned, and with a tired smile he curled up before the exhausted fire and went to sleep.

The next morning Sumner woke before dawn. But the old man was gone. The shape that he had thought was Bonescrolls all night was a wind-scrubbed boulder.

Sumner's first assignment sent him deep into the volcanic highlands to find a sliver of carnelian. The second envelope sent him on a trek across the sunblasted, rock-faulted heart of Skylonda Aptos into the great Kundar Marsh. He waded through leech ponds, floated across quicksand pools, and baited trees with foraged fruit to distract vicious rockthrower monkeys while he obtained what he had come for—a short twist of white mahogany.

The third envelope circled him back into the desert to track down a rock labyrinth infested with poisonous jumping lizards. At the center was a salt pit where he gathered a small satchel of the pure grains.

From there he journeyed to the viperlands, a swampy tract of tar pits and sticky toxic plants, where he beat off yellowbacked flies until he found a turtle shell of proper size. After that he followed a long steamy river far into a vapor jungle to collect a handful of macadamia nuts. On the way out of the jungle, he probed the viper-infested algal murk of stagnant pools for winged-lizard eggs. And finally he dangled precariously from a misty cliff to harvest a giant breed of yellow strawberries.

During the nine weeks that it took him to gather all the required items, Sumner kept himself in perpetual selfscan. He knew that if he let his mind roam he would only question what he was doing and slow himself down. Also, there was the threat of voors. He saw none in the course of his wanderings, but the memories of his lusk and the blowdart attack kept him vigilant. When he arrived at Bonescrolls' rock dwelling with everything that had been requested, he was calm and alert as a serpent.

Bonescrolls laughed raucously as Sumner entered the sunrayed cavern. He carefully examined each of the goods. With a honing stone he sharpened an edge of the carnelian sliver until it was razor-keen. With his new knife he deftly whittled the finger of white mahogany into a small graceful fork. After cleaning out the turtle shell he used it as a dish for a wing-lizard egg omelette, lightly salted, and dusted with crushed macadamia nuts. The yellow strawberries he arranged appealing around the rim.

'Ah!' He smacked his lips and winked at Sumner. 'I've waited a long time for a breakfast like this.'

Sumner's insides fisted, but he remained outwardly calm. 'Why?'

Bonescrolls' long face shrugged. 'Why old age? Why the cold? Why the notes inside a flute? We're nothing, young brother, but what we forget we are. Don't fight your unconscious.'

'I risked my life for that omelette.' Was this the being that had quieted the voor in him? Sumner searched the red-brown eyes for the power he knew was there, but he saw only a mystically cracked old man.

Bonescrolls recognized the disappointment in Sumner's face, and anger gouged him. 'Why?' His voice was sharp with feeling, holding Sumner's stare. 'The world has no corners, young brother. If I start to explain why I am and why you are, there's no place to stop.'

Sumner was unappeased, and his dark, frowning face looked scorched.

Bonescrolls strode to the center of the studio. He scooped up a handful of dust and laced it through his fingers, spieling it around him as he spoke: 'It's all consciousness, if you're open enough. The dust, the rock, the sunfire.' He balanced a grit of sand on his thumbnail and held it close to Sumner's nose. 'Each atomic particle is a family of beings. As aware in their own way as you are. We're all equals—all the same, just vibrating differently. Everything is light.'

The magnar sat down so slowly he seemed weightless. 'Think of all the beings that have come together to make you. Think about it. Billions of beings agreeing to shape a human form—this human form.' He took Sumner's hands, and the ether of the young man's feelings brightened. 'Why? Why are you the living center of the transparent and inflexible diamond of time? All of us have a destiny. Nothing is chanced. Time is gem-perfect.'

Bonescrolls let Sumner's hand go, and his breathing went deeper as though he wanted to say something wordless. 'You are the eth—the shadowself of a godmind to the north called the Delph.'

That name rattled in Sumner's mind with memories of Nefandi and Corby.

Bonescrolls misread Sumner's surprise as bafflement, and he guffawed. 'Names! The history is this: Over a thousand years ago, the sun and its planets entered a stream of radiation that has no origin. The radiation comes from the axle of our galaxy where the gravity of a billion suns has opened our universe to the multiverse. There, in the galactic core, energy gushes in from an infinity of other realities. Some of that timeless energy is psynergy, modes of being that you and I would recognize as sentient. When that psynergy reaches earth, it changes the genetic structure of humans, and in a generation or two it becomes voors, distorts, and sometimes godminds. These are beings orphaned from the worlds that created them. They fight hard to hold onto the patterns that anchor them to this planet, because the psynergy-stream is sliding away from us. After the skyfires are gone, there will be no more new voors—no more new godminds. Those that survive will possess the earth.'

Sumner picked up a pebble and turned it in his fingers gently, wisely. 'And I am the eth, the shadowself of a godmind. What does that mean?'

'Light has built a temple in your skull, young brother.' Bonescrolls watched him with a long and quiet mind. 'Many centuries ago, the Delph was a man. The scientists of his time altered his brain, hoping to widen his consciousness enough to find solutions for the puzzling changes in their world—the raga storms and the distorts that were appearing everywhere. Ignorantly, they opened the man's mind wide enough for a godmind from another universe to possess him. That's one theory. What's certain is, once the Delph had a physical form strong enough and specialized enough to contain his psynergy, he began to alter the energy patterns around him capriciously. He reshaped reality.'

'But who is he? Where is he from?'

'The light from the galactic center is not like the light of the sun or the stars. The energy doesn't come from the fusion of atoms. It comes from the light of an endless number of parallel universes. An endless number! Anything can jump out of infinity!'

Sumner's face narrowed with incredulity.

'Who is he?' Bonescrolls repeated, lifting his chin inquisitively. 'A being of light. Like you are. Like everything is. But he is the light of another continuum, and when he took human form he displaced the subtle psynergies of this world. Over the centuries those echoes of psynergy have been reflecting and interfusing through the eccentricities of biology and what we call chance. And so chromatin patterns have shifted and humans have been born inside their luck, psychically untouchable. These are the eth. You are one of them.'

'You're not telling me anything.'

Bonescrolls smiled benevolently. 'What it means is that you are the one being on the planet the Delph cannot touch with his reality-shaping mind. You are the perfect shield for a voor assassin.'

Comprehension softened Sumner's stare.

'Your whole life is the intention of a being bigger than your imagination,' Bonescrolls said, his voice tremulous with the excitement and fear he felt blazing in Sumner. 'I've been alive over a thousand years, and all this time, it turns out, I've been waiting for you. And for the voor inside you. We want the same reality.'

'No,' Sumner said, almost in a cry. 'I don't want to lusk. I don't want to be used by voors.'

Bonescrolls' timeshaped face was loose with delight, and he laughed soundlessly for a while before saying: 'You're nothing. An ego. A ghost of memories and predilections. You don't amount to much in the overview. Forget who you think you are. Psynergy follows thought, so become consciousness itself, not the shapes of consciousness. Selfscan isn't enough, because it limits you to sensation. To be whole, to be One Mind, you must be the living center in you that feels, thinks, selfscans.'

'I don't follow.'

'Become the quest you've already begun.'

Sumner's voice was limp. 'I'm not looking for anything.'

Bonescrolls benignly shook his head. 'The eth will always look for its source. The eth is huger than you. It's me and Corby as well. It's every event that touches you. It may take your whole life, but the eth will lead you to the Delph.'

'No.' Sumner crossed both of his hands through the air. 'I'm grateful for your help, magnar, but I'm undertaking no quests for a voor. I'm whole in myself. I'm not about to serve a voor.'

'That's not for you to decide.' The magnar's face had become somber. 'Your mind gets in the way of your being. You can't hope to understand what you're only a part of. That's why my life has the shape it does—so that I would be here now to empty you, to free you from the limits of knowing, and to open you to One Mind.'

'What are you talking about?' Sumner looked malcontent.

'I won't let your ego interfere with my destiny. You're still in thrall to me, Kagan. What I say, you must do.' The magnar reached over and took Sumner's face in the splayed grip of his hand. The throb of the man's etheric field itched Bonescrolls' palm as it melled with his psynergy. 'And by that authority, I command you to forget this conversation.'

When Bonescrolls took his face, Sumner glimpsed the whole cavern brightening between the old man's fingers, the hazy sunlight and the bluesunk shadows stirring with hemivisible beings. Then Bonescrolls shoved Sumner onto his back with an abrupt straightening of his arm, and darkness slammed into him.

The instant he hit the ground, Sumner's eyes fluttered open. The magnar was hunched over the turtle shell finishing his omelette, morning sunlight aureoléd in his white hair.

'Rest if you wish,' Bonescrolls said through a mouthful of food. 'You've journeyed far, young brother, and I'm well pleased.'

Sleep wrestled like an inner problem in Sumner's chest. But he couldn't rest. Something was on his mind— The mischievous grin on Bonescrolls' face piqued him. Why? Sumner looked out abstractly through a windowhole at the gold stretches of dawn. Why had he worked so hard for an omelette? He was in-listening, but his mind was silent as the straws of twilight scattering across the horizon.

Sumner slept fitfully for several hours and then, with a satchel of dried fruit and a skin of water from Bonescrolls, he left for Miramol. The magnar spent the remainder of the day trying to connect with his psychic strength again, but he was too weary. When night arrived he was twitching with frustration.

The moon was a green feather above the mesaland. Bonescrolls stood tall on the top of the rocktower, feet wide apart, arms spread, his body an X against the skyfires. Long and hard, he cried to the desert: 'Help—me!'

The echo of his call stretched beyond itself quickly, and he dropped his arms and sagged into his stance. Time leaked from the rocks as the last warmth of day lifted into the night, and foolishness chilled through him. He turned back toward his lair, mumbling to himself: 'Go to sleep, old man.'

Every day for the last two months, while Sumner had wandered Skylonda Aptos, Bonescrolls had followed. With his body swaddled in blankets, lying back in his rockstudio, his mindark had opened into the brightness of hawk and coyote, and he had stayed close to the eth.

The assignments had been designed to frustrate Sumner, to open his weakened etheric field. And when this happened, Bonescrolls had channeled psynergy into him by becoming in his mind the animals and objects around Sumner. As a snake, he had tasted Sumner's fatigue and had projected serpent awareness. That night, in a dream, Kagan had seen the desert alive, glittering with pieces of light. The next day Bonescrolls had become the pinnacle rock where Sumner waited out the noonfire. The magnetic calmness that the magnar had radiated soothed Sumner's longing for the familiarities of his life with the Rangers. The effects were subtle, but over the weeks of Sumner's questing, his bodylight breathed brighter and stronger.

Bonescrolls, however, had become weaker. The long effort of shapeshifting and focusing psynergy had loosened his own bodylight. All day after Sumner had left for Miramol, the magnar had been depressed. A deathvision had floated about him like hair, sometimes getting in his eyes with glimpses of a tall, wild man with a scar-cleaved face and one eye the color of bruised blood. Fear had wrung hard in him today, and he was glad that he had sent Sumner back to the Mothers.

A small cranny-room glowed like a flower at the end of a maze of narrow, unlit corridors. Pink tallow tapers burned in the three corners of the cell below mousehole airducts. The cubicle was crowded with pelts, amulets, folded tapestries, icons, and wicker boxes—five hundred years of offerings from the surrounding tribes.

He threw back a coverlet of ocelot skin from a large ironwood box inlaid with sardonyx. He thumbed a secret release in the ornate fretwork, and a small panel slid aside, revealing a compartment stuffed with suede cloth. Bonescrolls gently removed the cloth and sat down cross-legged. After calming himself, he unwrapped the crinkled suede and blinked into the soft, luminiferous light of a brood jewel.

That instant in Miramol, several of the Mothers stirred restlessly in their sleep. For them, dreaming had abruptly become the single-focus clarity of trance. The magnar stood in the shadow of the world, looking a little different for each of them.

Shay, he said, his voice half-burning with the fear that had haunted him earlier. *My ward is returning to Miramol. He has served me well in the desert, and his bodylight is stronger. But he still lives inside his days, far from his spirit. Please, young sisters, teach him to mount his life's power. Show him how to lure the psynergy up his spine. Without your help, he will never be all that he is.*

The Mothers' trance slipped back into dreaming as the magnar moved his consciousness away.

Bonescrolls hovered above the Barrow, charmed as usual by the astral view of the skyfires and the sharpness of the snow-blue stars, until he felt himself being seen. A dog stood, tailtucked, beneath a magnolia tree, watching him with glarestruck eyes. Beside it, soaked in darkness, was an old blind woman—one of the Mothers. *Jesda*, her name rose up in him as she stood and swayed in his direction.

'I see you there, shadow-of-no-one,' the crone called, edging closer. Her hands were on her face, and her fingers were in the sockets of her skull. 'These plundered eyes see through the world, ghost. Absence is presence. *You* know that! Absence *is!*'

Jesda walked out into the bright moon-air, and her hands fell away from a riven face. Bonescrolls was gripped by the intensity of feeling in those broken features—eyepits dark as wine—and, as sometimes happened when he was shadowshooting, he spun into the feelings of what he was seeing.

Laughter jerked hard in him, and his mindark rayed with musical colors. An estranged feeling—a terrifying falling away from everything—tightened through him like nausea. *Jesda's madness.* Yet even though he knew what he was feeling, he couldn't break it.

The smell of burned flesh pierced him, and like a needle stuck in his brain, a momentary reality opened: He saw the eth, Ardent Fang, and Drift squatting in the flagrant light of a bonfire—a pyre, a temple of flames with a corpse sitting up on the altar, clots of black flesh falling away from his features—his face!

Bonescrolls twisted away from the brood jewel, the strophe of a scream loud in his throat. A heartshuddering moment passed before he breathed again.

No more shadowshooting, he swore, gazing gratefully into the blue plasma of a tallow flame. The voor gem was icy in his hand, and he wrapped it in the suede without looking at it.

Shakily, he put the brood jewel back into its secret compartment and shrouded the ironwood box with the ocelot pelt. He walked down the black corridor to a natural balcony, where the cold night air held

206

him more securely in his body. Now that the Mothers had custody of the eth, he could rest and fortify his psynergy.

He sucked the frosty air in through his teeth, and his whole body shivered with alertness. Above a horizon burning with green sky-fires, the moon floated, red and long, the shape of a serpent's heart.

The Mother wore a black shift and ancient amulets, bright pieces of metal covered with the script of the kro. She was cataract-blind, and her movements were slow and purposeful, communicating her awareness of the world around her. Sumner sat opposite her in a room darkened with curtains made of human hair. He was naked but for a blue loincloth, and his flesh looked like well-oiled wood, sheened from the four days he had spent in a steam shed. Florets of gum acacia crowded the corners, scenting the room with the odor of mountains.

The Mother listened with her head bowed forward as Sumner whispered the sacred names of the jungle animals and plants. The names themselves were unimportant. They were merely an acoustic technique for achieving the proper mindstate. Occasionally, when she felt his attention waver, she made him repeat the odd sounds until his mind focused.

The Mothers were well pleased with Sumner. He had performed better than expected in the breeding stables, and most of the women he had mated with had conceived. To express their appreciation, the Mothers had begun to teach him the way of the hunter. For many days he had fasted and steamed the poisons out of his flesh. Then he had sat alone among burial hills the color of rain and listened, as he had been instructed, for the deep calling.

He had felt stupid and vulnerable, sitting cross-legged in the open, his mind directed inward. But he had been quick to overcome his anxiety, and the Mothers were surprised at how readily his bodylight responded to their guidance. One Mother, a half-blind priestess who had worked for many years with young males, was selected to teach him the sacred names and to supervise his awareness of the deep calling.

Sumner obeyed the Mothers strictly out of devotion to Bonescrolls. Their teachings seemed crude and arbitrary to him, and he counted the weeks left to his thrall. Sitting in the open with his mind indrawn, he sensed nothing but the splanchnic rhythms of his body. Several weeks later he was still spending most of every day listening to the roll of his heart and the flutterings of his digestive tract.

Late one torpid afternoon he heard a whine—a tiny distant screaming, wringing from deep down in his bowels. His sudden alertness squelched it, and it was several days before he heard it again—a warbling thin sound wavering in the small bones of his head. This time he fixed himself solidly in selfscan, and he listened to it whistling higher than the pitch of his blood—but faint, deep as his marrow. Slowly understanding narrowed back to its center, and he realized what impossible and faraway sound it was: the tension in his genitals—the sound of his desires. He wanted a real woman.

That's it!

Sumner thrashed alert. The blind Mother was crouched beside him, her crystal white eyes lidded with satisfaction. *You have to listen deep, but a man can hear his woman-hunger*, the old woman's voice rasped in his mind. *Focus on that. You're ready to begin the Rising.*

Listening to the whine of blood pooling in his genitals, Sumner learned how to gather that tension into a tight packet between his anus and scrotum. The muscles there were delicate and very difficult to control, but with the Mother guiding him he was soon able to move the tension past his anus to the base of his spine without clenching his sphincter muscle.

The rest happens by itself, the Mother told him as she braided his hair in the hunter's style. *For three days before you hunt you must abstain from sex. Then collect your psynergy at the base as I've taught you. That way, when the animals and plants come they will leave their spirit with you and slowly the pysnergy will accumulate. Someday it will be strong enough to climb the length of your spine and enter your skull. Then your middle eye will open.*

'What about women?' Sumner asked, trying to keep the petulance out of his voice. 'Don't they have middle eyes?'

Women have other powers. This is only a man's way.

'So why is a woman teaching me?'

Women know the ways of everything. After all, didn't a woman make you?

Sumner kept the details of his skepticism to himself, though Drift often pressed him for information. He assured the seer that it was all nonsense and that he would break his vow of secrecy when his thrall to Bonescrolls was complete. Until then he felt bonded to comply with the strictures of his tutelage to the Mothers. He followed their orders and smoked his dugout in gopherwood when they returned it to him. He even spent an hour each dawn moving his sexual tension from his genitals to the root of his spine, though he half-believed this was a senseless exercise.

In the dark tunnels of the cloud forest he was mindless of the Mothers, escstatic and free as any animal, bounded only by the limits of his instinct. The river mist strayed in whorls around him as he slowly made his way far beyond any of the other hunters. The waters were still very high, and food was difficult to come by. But deep in the flooded forest, where the man scent was absent, life abounded.

Sumner slid over the shallows, cautiously picking his way through the moss veils and fungal root-loops, looking for dry spits of land where tapir would feed or turtle nest. Nothing. The land was there with all the animals' life-needs, but the animals were elsewhere. As silent as he was, as patient and cunning as he could be, only small game presented itself to him. Several times he returned to Miramol empty-handed, and the other hunters joked that he belonged with Ardent Fang in the stables.

Slipping out at dawn on the third day, he felt desperate, and as soon as he was sure that he had wound himself deep enough into the forest to be out of earshot of the other hunters, he used the sacred name for pig that the Mothers had taught him. Nothing. A white-faced monkey blinked at him, whooped, and somersaulted out of sight. He wished that he had brought Drift along with him. Even though seers were only used to hunt in time of famine, Sumner felt driven.

He backwatered and slipped through a rush brake and froze. Three peccaries were rooting the truffles out of a massive dead tree. They raised their bristles, backed into a circle, and began clicking their tusks. With his cricket whistle, Sumner alerted the other hunters. The catch that day was great.

It was his failures over the following days that convinced Sumner to try the sacred names again, though the sounds to him were meaningless. Each time he used them, though, he encountered exceptional lifeforms: a sabalo trout huge as a salmon, a grandfather manatee happy to die and heavy with useful blubber, and two giant wild turkeys.

The Mothers were startled by how thoroughly Sumner had taken to their knowledge. They resolved to show him no more, fearing that when his thrall to Bonescrolls was ended he would reveal everything to the profane. Already he had surpassed many of the Mothers themselves in his ability to send and receive psynergy.

Drift, too, could see that Sumner was amassing great strength. It watched his bodylight whirl faster and stronger in his abdomen and gather into a balled, furry gold light above his buttocks. But Sumner was unaware of this change. The waters were going down, and he couldn't tell whether it was the sacred names or just the return of the creatures to their habitats that was responsible for his bounty. When Bonescrolls called him to his desert abode, he asked the magnar.

'It's all you,' Bonescrolls said in his perfect Massel. 'You put on masks and pretend to be a pig or a turkey or a Serbota hunter. But it's all you.'

Sumner frowned. 'Why then does anyone starve?'

Bonescrolls grinned as though Sumner had seen his sleight of hand. 'We play a rough game. What fun would it be if we didn't die sometimes? What would we do with the masks we were tired of?'

Sumner was still frowning when Bonescrolls clapped his hands. 'Enough of this banter. I have only two more assignments for you. They're both very important, and I hope you'll do your best.'

'As important as a nut and strawberry omelette?'

Bonescrolls gave him a reproving look. 'Someday you'll understand the importance of a truly great omelette.' With luminous eyes he stared down Sumner's scowl.

'What do I have to do?'

'Deliver this.' The old man rolled his hand on his wrist like a magician and produced a green brood jewel. It caught the light deeply and held it, glowing from within like a flower. 'Take Drift with you. It knows where to go. Tell it to take you to the yawps.'

The jewel felt electrical in Sumner's grasp. It raised the hairs on the back of his hand, and when he gazed into it the soft light curved into fulgent tunnelings. Deep within, past the purring reflections, a white flake trembled, shivering to star brightness. The radiant spicules of light shifted and re-formed, and Sumner thought of spring clouds ballooning over green ponds. Then the gleaming threads knotted and tightened to an image—a child's face of white porcelain with dreamy, colorless eyes. Sumner would have dropped the stone if Bonescrolls hadn't steadied his hand.

'You're still in lusk, young brother.' He took the brood jewel and wrapped it in black silk. 'It's best that you stay away from all voorish things.'

'I just saw—'

'I know what you saw.'

Sumner palmed his eyes. 'Why?'

Bonescrolls shrugged and handed him the wrapped jewel.

Sumner hefted it and tried to feel the energy through the cloth. 'How does this thing work?'

'The voor in you knows. If you really want to understand, you'll find out.'

'You won't tell me?'

Bonescrolls vigorously shook his head and flapped air through his lips like a horse. 'You leave too many tracks as it is. I don't want to make you heavier. Can't you see? I'm trying to empty you.'

The journey back to Miramol was foggy with memories of Corby. He thought again of the one-eyed stranger who had stopped his car in Rigalu Flats and told him about the Delph—and he thought of Jeanlu and how, his whole life, he had been led by deception and error. It took all of his selfscanning discipline to overcome the clumsy nostalgia Corby's image had sent banging through his mind. Even so, when he got to Miramol, Drift could see that he was not himself.

The golden energy that had tufted like a tail at the bottom of his spine had diffused, and the slippery burn scar on his face seemed darker than ever. *What's troubling you?* Drift asked.

Sumner told it about Corby's visage and his heavy memories.

The past is a disguise, it said, inflecting its telepathic voice as much as it could with fellow-feeling. *You're not really concerned about that. It's something going on now that worries you. Your year of thralldom is more than half up—*

Sumner nodded. That was it, he knew. Having someone to direct his life was what he needed. It didn't matter to him whether it was the

210

Rangers or Bonescrolls, but he needed direction.

Do you really? Drift looked like a molting insect sitting up in the hammock it had strung between two flower-vined trees. *Your life, as I see it, has been strong and solitary. But the lusk was terrible. Much better to be a slave than to have to face that alone.* Drift's teeth clacked in its head as it recalled the snake-pit rasp of voor psynergy and the depth-terror, vaster than oceans, that had gulfed its mind.

Sumner sat on a lacquered tree stump and fingered a cluster of jonquils. 'What can I do?'

Just what Bonescrolls has ordered. The yawps will amaze you and make you forget your fear. It lowered its gaze to meet Sumner's. *And besides, it's pointless to look for a new path—unless that path is already there.*

Sumner and Drift traveled upriver that day, talking about the yawps. Still clouds, waxy with their burden of rain, loomed above the green plateaus of the treetops. Drift was pleased to see that Sumner's psynergy had filled out again and was whirling tight through the lifelock in his abdomen. *I've only been with the yawps once, but that one encounter taught me the importance of keeping a clean mind.*

Sumner was paddling with long, graceful strokes, his whole body swaying, urging the dugout over the amber surface. 'Clean?'

Mirror-mind—simply watching. Drift was perched behind Sumner, also paddling, trying to match his rhythm but skipping every third or fourth stroke. *The yawps are very serene. Very quiet. Loud minds make them uneasy.*

'They're all telepathic?'

The ones I met were.

A sprawling tangle of leafed branches swam toward them, and Sumner signaled Drift to up paddle. He angled the dugout around the jutting driftwood and stroked again for the middle of the stream where the paddling was easier. 'What kind of people are the yawps?'

Not people, really.

Sumner peered over his shoulder.

About a thousand years ago they were apes. The kro used them for labor. But then the world changed, and they've been on their own since.

'Apes?'

Once. Now they're a very spiritual tribe. You'll see.

Drift had given no clue as to how close they were, so when the moss and vine-hung buildings swung into sight Sumner was stunned. None of the usual telltale refuse had floated downstream to announce a river settlement. The cypress had simply parted and there among nodding firetrees was a mound of modular pinkstone buildings virtually overgrown with jungle. Figures moved along ribbon-ramps, and in the distance were towers, sunlight blustery against elegant minarets of glass and white stone.

Someone was approaching them over the water—a tall creature

211

glistening with red hair, standing on the water. As it drew closer they saw that it was riding a white disc, skimming effortlessly over the surface without controls or even a handhold. The disc-rider swooped up alongside them, and Sumner gawked at the red, glossy-furred being. Its face was simian, with a lightning-blue muzzle, stiff head fur, and large, black, expressive eyes. It wore nothing more than a purple, leather-banded breechcloth and simple cork sandals. *Shay, Serbota— welcome to Sarina.* Its voice in their minds was resonant. *You're expected. Please, follow me.*

It backed off and floated toward the jungle-city. Sumner lifted out of his amazement and paddled after it. 'A yawp?'

A young one.

The city became more wonderful the closer they got: It was a tree-flowering island where towers of silk-white stone stood about, lean and graceful as women. Sumner was enraptured by the technology.

'What is that water-disc? How the—'

Mirror-mind, Lotus Face. We'll talk later.

They left their dugout in a bluestone berth and followed their guide to a glade of great holy trees. The yawp left them there, and they stared around at floating fountains whose spray fell like powder in the breeze.

In the distance liquid music surfed over blue lawns. Along a wooden walkway with yellow rose-braided posts a silver-furred yawp approached.

Shay, Drift. Shay, Lotus Face.

Shay, Bir, Drift sent.

Bir bowed before Sumner. *This is your first visit to Sarina. I hope you don't find it too other.*

'I didn't know such marvels existed.' Sumner stared beyond the trees where slender buildings the color of moonlight arced. 'How did you build all this?'

Bir's silver-hackled face grimaced a smile. *If I tried to tell you that, I'd only confuse both of us. And why bore you with history when I can share this moment with you?*

Bir gestured toward a tiny esplanade of green and black flagstones among the glade of giant trees. Drift led the way and sat down on the inside of a circular bench, carved whole from a petrified tree stump. Sumner sat beside him and Bir faced them. *A prayer to the Infinite, Drift,* Bir requested, nodding deferentially to the seer.

Drift gazed into the long stately avenue of massive trees and copper-colored grass and chanted:

> *Among everything that we have named*
> *You alone remain nameless.*
> *Help us to know you*
> *As we know ourselves.*

212

Bir nodded solemnly. *Beautiful, seer. Your vision sees into itself.* He reached into a small pouch below the knot of his maroon breech-cloth and took out a sliver of glass. *Now let's celebrate.* The glass splinter held before him caught a thread of sunlight and flashed rainbow spikes. Adroitly he spun the prism between his silver-haired fingers. The spectral rays melled to a brilliant auroral band which, as it spun faster, hazed blue. He deftly pivoted the prism in his palm, and the band swelled like a gas flame to a nebulous globe, azure-bright.

Bir cupped the globe in his hands and sat staring beyond it into the pointillist dapple of the trees. After a moment he passed the ball of light to Drift who held it tenderly in its long spiderfingers. Then it was offered to Sumner.

He accepted gingerly, and as soon as the light grazed his fingers a beatific smile altered his features. The tension the Mothers had taught him to collect at the bottom of his spine uncoiled like a hypnotist's wheel and sparkled up his back. His scalp prickled, and a sudden and unshakable bliss rooted him, adamant as pain. Bir took the blue globe from his hands and collapsed it back to a glass sliver.

Deep humus smells, rich and varied as a symphony, anchored Sumner in the moment, and he watched with silent glee as the opaline sunlight breezed over the wind-twitched grass. For the very first time in his life he was truly and profoundly happy. Life wasn't shit, he comprehended with a bone-seizing laugh. Life was a stream of love. . . .

I must go now, Bir said, hands on his knees. *Thank you for sharing this moment with me.*

Sumner looked about with the glee of a lune. Drift touched his knee, and he remembered the brood jewel.

Bir accepted it with both hands. *A fine gift,* he said, without removing the black silk.

Sumner stared at the yawp as if he had just seen him, noticing the age in the coarse black muzzle, the heron-colored light as it reflected off his fur, the conch-pink of his ears.

Bir walked with them to a dragon-vein brook forded by a walk-way of jasper stepping-stones. *A parting thought, seer.*

Drift bowed deferentially and psychically intoned: *The eye sees but is blind to itself. Hazard is intent at high velocity.*

Bir bowed and walked off, the dust motes at his feet boiling into light.

Sumner wanted to linger, but Drift insisted they go. *Our purpose is done. This isn't our place.*

Pushing out of the berth with their oars, heeling into the current, Sumner refused to look back, though he was churning with desire. They paddled silently with the current, each in a private reverie of sun-glinted eddies, shadowed banks, and the muscular flow of the river.

That night, beneath a sky shot with stars, Sumner told Drift about the energy that had virled up his spine, charging him with euphoria.

The yawps are masters of matter, Drift explained, its tiny eyes fixed on the flames of the aromatic barkfire. *They have machines that can do anything—even create bodies. That's how the magnar has lived so long. He was once a yawp himself, you know.*

'Why then does he live in the desert?'

Who can say? He's unknowable as the clouds. Drift fed small bits of bark into the flames. *What I do know, from having spoken with Bir and the magnar, is that Bonescrolls is an ancient yawp—one of the first. Perhaps he's outgrown his life in Sarina. Perhaps after so many centuries he has bored of being a yawp.*

The cry of a screech owl sliced across the darkness of the river. 'Until today I thought everything the Mothers had taught me was foolishness.'

No—not foolishness. The Mothers are narrow. The tribe means more to them than any person or vision. But they have knowledge. I can see myself that they've trained you well. What you experienced today you can repeat now at will, I'm sure.

Sumner leaned forward and singed the hairs on his knees. 'Are you serious?'

Drift blinked. *Of course.*

Sumner looked up at the steady stars through the writhing sky-fires and concentrated on calming his suddenly racing heart. When he looked back at the né, his heart was still thudding. 'How?'

Your body knows. It did it today. If you relax yourself, you'll remember how it felt, and you'll be able to do it again.

Sumner didn't wholly believe him, but the idea clouded his thoughts for the rest of their journey. On their return to Miramol, he sequestered himself in the chamber the né had set aside for him, and he practiced the tension routines he had learned. His desire to repeat his experience in Sarina was his greatest obstacle, and it took him over a week finally to fix the tension at the tip of his spine. Then began the slow, awkward process of remembering exactly how it had felt to unfurl that tension. Futile days passed, and if he hadn't already experienced such deep joy in Sarina, he would have given up. The feelings, at first, were too subtle.

But then it happened. Not as quickly or as totally as it had seized him in Sarina. It was different, but it was good.

Guided by his memory, the tension unwound along the narrow length of his spine, so softly he might have imagined it except for the sudden itch haloing the round cope of his skull. And then came the familiar serenity blissing his whole body. He wasn't shaken, not as before. It was more gentle—a tensile sense of the moment expanding, opening to reveal sounds, shadings, odors that had been uninteresting before: the refraction of a fly's wing narrowing the orbit of his vision, distant root scents dazing his nostrils with an olfaction of mud. He was happy—sincerely joyful.

214

Several years before in Dhalpur he had known ecstasy when his body and mind became one. But the joy he had felt then was thin compared to the bliss he called out of his body now. Standing up in his dugout in a glade freckled with light, he uttered the sacred name for an otter. His call was an exultation, not a test, because otter tokens were everywhere: Rocks drowsed in leaf-strewn shallows, milk fog tangled among ferns, and white roots curled out of the water.

The call did not just vibrate from his throat; it bled out of his chest and joined the invisible otter-energies in the rocks and fog and ferns. With that sensation, Sumner understood that he was connected by a vague and pervasive energy to all the otter symbols around him. He was the glade—the spalled light, the lapping water, the ferns and the rocks.

The length of his spine itched, and he felt the psynergy that had drained out of him suddenly returning, curving back through the antlers of the tree branches, arcing over the pollen-dusted water, returning to the taut cords of his body. It was just as the Mothers had said: The whorl was in all things.

The water ruffled, and a dozen slick black heads appeared across the glade. The otters' noses twitched as they stared about, and then several of them crawled onto flat rocks and rootloops, trailing shawls of water. They peered at Sumner, black bead eyes unflinching, dark fur sleek with wet. A giddy laugh tightened in Sumner's belly. Everything was connected. Everything was itself and the same. Bonescrolls was a puma and a raven and an old man. And Sumner could be also. It was all a matter of letting go. His mind reeled, and he laughed aloud.

The otters rolled into the water and vanished. Two stood up again farther off, stared at Sumner, and then were gone.

From a sandbar culvert of spiny palms Ardent Fang watched. He was returning from Ladilena, a nearby Serbota village, where he had been reviewing new brides. The women had been long and beautiful as the new moon, and their rituals had exalted all the good feelings in him. Yet that rapture had dropped away when he heard the ecstatic music turning behind the sandbar. It was true music: bloodflow rhythms, mothertides, the desire he had always wanted to open with his devil harp. But when he whisperglided up to the sandbar and peered through the spiny palms, the music was gone, and he was surprised to see Lotus Face communing with the otters.

Ardent Fang crouched in his dugout, bending far forward, the hair of his monkeyfur vest limp in the water. His hearing was still frothed with the visionary music he had heard, and he clutched the dog-crucifix thonged loosely about his neck and silently invoked Paseq. At that moment, though Ardent Fang had made no sound,

Lotus Face turned and stared directly at where he was hidden.

Ardent Fang rose, returned Sumner's stare shamefully, and then disappeared. The boar-tusks of his prow appeared among the stilt-root palms, and he slid into the glade. As he swung his canoe around a tussock of myrtles, he heard the music again—dulcet as the sun-plucked water—and, like the turning of a lens, his sight sharpened. He hadn't even realized that his vision had gone slack over the years. Reflexively he rubbed his eyes.

Weirdly wonderful—he saw beauty more clearly than ever. He sensed that his eyes had been healed by the music-energy coursing through Sumner. He looked at Lotus Face as his canoe drifted into the glade and saw the rainbows spinning in the mist around him. *Is this being a god or a demon-delusory?*

'Don't be afraid,' Sumner said, signaling him closer.

Ardent Fang stood up stiffly. 'I'm not afraid,' he responded sharply, then realized that he was still clutching his dog-crucifix. He let it go and then seized it again, rocking backwards in his canoe with the more powerful realization that he had understood Lotus Face. The man hadn't spoken in Serbot.

Ardent Fang sat down.

'Don't be afraid,' Sumner said again in Massel. He punted gently, and the lotus-carved gunwale of his canoe hissed across the lapse of sun-hot water. 'Everything we've always wanted is all around us.'

The ear-tricking music was unfurling with the swamp mist in the shadows of the big trees. Ardent Fang stared into the blackness of Sumner's face with defiant apprehension. 'Who are you?'

'You know me,' Sumner replied, the whorl of power flexing almost visibly between them.

'You're a god,' Ardent Fang said, his own voice sounding strange to him.

Sumner smiled. 'If I were a god, the whole world would look like this.' He spread his arms out and opened his body to the water's broken sunlight and the enormous walls of flowering trees. And something drifting, immense, and unknown moved through them.

Ardent Fang released the dog-crucifix and gazed with astoundment into the peaceful heart of the forest. Each tree was so huge in its inturned feeling that the breeder trembled to look at them. In their shadow he was merely a being of dew, fragilely, helplessly sparkling. Words, thoughts, dimensions—the whole mind-world was a realm of the dead.

He stood up and raised his arms and his heart into the upstreaming of light and love.

Sumner wandered the riverain forest entranced by the outleap of consciousness in everything. A light greater than sunlight was shining out of the old trees. In their shade thoughts and sounds came together, and the visual became visionary.

Everything is food! a thought voiced itself. *Every sound, every odor, every thought changes us.*

In Sumner's mind it was a tree that was thinking these thoughts. His silence widened. He could feel the grass growing under him, the tree expanding into its life. Then the idea of returning, of feeling his own body, of leaping up and screaming with joy, opened in him with risible insistence.

Ardent Fang sat in the high grass behind Sumner. He was rapt with fear and wonder. He had followed Sumner because the psynergies featherturning in his chest had lured him. But now he was nervous. An astral being floated among the heat-quiverings over the mud shoals. He could see the entity as clearly as he saw their two beached canoes glowing with the sun's vibrations. He thought of going back to Miramol.

Sumner suddenly leaped into the air and roared.

Ardent Fang jumped, and a heron flapped into the forest's green shadow. The tensed air over the mudsunk trees beside their canoes shifted as the half-seen being moved toward them. Sumner was standing, body arched, feeling the love that was soft-slipping through the wondrous emptiness that held everything together. A gust of bright air kicked through the high grass and dazzled the blades and seedhusks as the spirit of the swamp centered on them. Ardent Fang knelt and moaned, and the sound he made was prayerful and long.

Sumner had opened his mind to the river's oversoul, and consciousness was radiating back to him in psychic symbols. Sparks spun through the sunshadows around the tree, and he saw demons and archangels, a riotous torrent of all the otherealms the human mind had ever created. Yet he was unafraid. The manner in which he had opened his being—mounting psynergy up the totem of his spine—had stabilized his body, and he was well-rooted. Whatever entered his etheric field was harmonized by the ecstasy of his One Mind.

Ardent Fang sidled closer to Sumner, his heart and lungs weightless with lifelove, his legs leaden with the fear of all that he was seeing. A massive razorjaw lizard was thrashing wildly in a mud-pool across the shallow river. Much closer, the air silverly trembled, and the breeder saw the breeder that had come before him. The bloodbruises of the fever that had killed his teacher darkened the whole of the man's eyes, and the features Ardent Fang had once loved were swollen with death.

Sumner didn't know what Ardent Fang was experiencing, but he saw the pain in the tribesman's face.

The sky darkened, and a storm of green flies cut through the trees. Ardent Fang balled up with terror as the flies began biting.

Laughter broke across Sumner's tongue. It wasn't Sumner laughing. It was the swamp itself—and, deeper, it was One Mind, bloating him with awareness. The flies burning him were the hunger

217

of God. *And hunger is holy, because everything is food, and eating is all there is.*

Shrieks burst through the trees, and a flurry of birds rushed around them, devouring the flies. The air was a confusion of feathers and flashing colors. Abruptly, silence, and the startled laugh of a monkey.

Ardent Fang rose to his knees among broken stalks of chickweed. His face was a maze of emotions, seeing the flies gone, the air layered with shades of transparency, and, in midstream, a giant razor-jaw lizard lashing toward them.

Sumner helped Ardent Fang to his feet. In the blue hollow behind Lotus Face, the breeder glimpsed a crowd of women—all the women he had ever sexed. The ones he had loved glowed blue-bright.

'Whatever you're seeing,' Sumner said to him, 'is inside you. But the whorl is strong with us today, Fang. Whatever we feel is coming back at us. Try to feel good.'

Ardent Fang trembled in Sumner's grasp. The man's hands on his shoulders hummed with spring-thundering, and the dark in the blue of his eyes was shimmering with something like father-love. 'But look!' the breeder insisted, pointing to where the wart-knobbed, mud-green hulk of the razorjaw was running to shore. Its horn-browed eyes looked fireblind, and the long thrust of its maw glistened with many pink-skinned teeth.

Sumner's first impulse was to bolt, but the worldlove he had joined himself with was far bigger than he was. He stood enraptured as the giant thrash-tailed reptile rushed toward them. Ardent Fang whimpered and reached for his blade, but Sumner caught his wrist. 'Love it,' Lotus Face said, not taking his eyes off the creature.

Ardent Fang pulled his wrist free, but he didn't run. The razorjaw had slowed its rush. The flat, horned head of the beast, big as a man, stopped before them and swayed in its stench of river kelp and mud. Sumner put his right arm out, and the black lip of the lizard grazed his hand and stood transfixed.

Ardent Fang's head bobbed as though his blood had fermented. In the huge, damp presence of the razorjaw, sunlight had the coolness of the moon.

Urged by the power in him, Sumner climbed the folded scales of the colossal leg and shoulder and straddled the stumped head. Reaching down to help Ardent Fang up, he saw into the lizard's eye, and it was like staring into the center wood-ring of a log.

He swung Ardent Fang up beside him, and the great swamp beast turned toward the water. Ardent Fang whooped, tore off the braiding cord at his shoulder, and let the smoke of his hair blow in the river wind.

Sumner laughed and lifted both of his arms over his head. The muddy water folded back and splashed at their sides, and they glided downstream into the misty green spell of the river.

*   *   *

The giant lizard carried the two men north all day down a river-path of solar-blown trees and ox-colored boulders. The water that splashed them had the bloodheat and the smell of something living. Panther, wolf, bear, and deer watched them from the bluffs with animal insouciance, the air sloughed with their green auras.

At night, the sky gnarled with stars and skyfires, the razorjaw continued downstream. Sumner lay against the beast's browbone and saw the roundness of time in the crackly stars. Each mote of light that sparked in his retinal cells was a living being, the lifefire of another sun entering and changing him. Countless stars—an endless rain of radiation penetrating him, altering his most secret self. The next day, under a hot sky, the realization that each instant he was transformed still burned like the rise of an orgasm.

Ardent Fang stayed close to Lotus Face, content beyond dreaming in that man's golden halo. Hearing Sumner talk of stars, consciousness, and the whorl, Ardent Fang's ears ached with listening, trying to find again the foreign color in the man's voice. But the magic between them was seamless. At night, gliding down the golden moonpath, the breeder stopped trying to understand and let the clairvoyance of his feelings displace his wondering.

However, by dawn Ardent Fang was once again baffled. Sleep-mauled on the back of the lizard giant, hearing gulls bruiting the ocean, he looked to Lotus Face. 'Why are we here?'

Sumner was standing, absorbing the iris twilight. During the night journey the river had broadened, and the water was now as deep as their lives. Sumner jumped in headfirst, and Ardent Fang splashed after him. The razorjaw followed until they reached the sandbars; then it sank into its weight and was gone.

On a beach of dust-fine sand facing a low-tide bay of tropic reefs, the men built a fire. 'Each instant we're changed,' Sumner said, as much to the spurting flames as to his companion.

Ardent Fang touched Sumner's forearm, wanting a moment's clarity. 'Why are we here, Lotus Face?'

Sumner looked up wrenchingly from the flames, the wondrous telepathy that had possessed him tightening to the single focus of one syllable: 'Why?' he asked, his eyes all pupil, yet very clear, shining. He was looking inward, remembering— 'Why are you the living center of the transparent and inflexible diamond of time?'

Ardent Fang shrugged, sea-cold and suddenly weary from the withdrawal of Sumner's psynergy. 'All of us have destiny,' he mumbled.

Sumner jumped to his feet, scattering the fire. He stood twitching with immense emotion, staring up at the red muscles of dawn, suddenly remembering in hypnotic detail his last conversation with Bonescrolls—the talk that the magnar had made him forget. *Nothing is chanced. You are the eth—the shadowself of a godmind.*

Caught in a boundless feeling, Sumner sank to his knees, then rolled to his back and closed his eyes. He knew now why he had come here. He was traveling north—to find the Delph.

A rush of luminescent feeling lifted him beyond the fitted bones of his skull, and he saw his body curled on the white sand, Ardent Fang crouched beside the smoldering driftwood, the two figures diminishing into the scallopings of the beach, and the whole beach and the sea glaring into the sun's corona.

Everything stretched into darkness.

Outside his mind, he sensed the Delph. Like everything, the godmind was part of Sumner's being, the One Being, and a flowing love joined them. Whirling outward into the emptiness of time, he was poised only by the inchoate lifelove that swelled in him. Out of that joy-dazzled feeling, a different flesh began flowering around him. Colors gestured into forms, and bright vibrations coagulated to sounds—a starstream of music spiraling just beyond his earbrim. *Pleroma music*, an inner sense told him. An animal scent, a tinge of musk, patterned the air pleasantly. *A calming olfact*, the voice said more solidly. *A sexoid.*

Sumner jolted into a body he didn't recognize and yet knew intimately. *An ort biotectured to channel your psynergy.* Comfortable, muscle-gripping clothes massaged him with each move—chamois-textured, fur-colored. *A slimplex garment. You are in Graal, the ice-mountain rath of the Delph.*

He looked about for the voice he was hearing, but he was alone in a small oyster-colored room. In a formflow fashion, walls chaired and lounged intelligently as he strolled about. No doors, though one wall opened glasslessly to a vista of white mountains and green splashes of jungle valleys. *A prison?* he wondered.

No, the voice responded, harsher, hard-edged. An elegant doorway expanded through the wall, revealing chambers brilliant with sunshafts and weird airplants.

Flechettes of rainbow light scattered through the room. 'Who are you?' Sumner asked. Though he knew. A mental music was rhythming in him, auguring everything he wanted to know. The voice was a Voice—a mountain-size crystal of thought, an artificial sentience created to serve the Delph.

I am Rubeus. A six-rayed cell of white light appeared in the curveline doorway. *I am an autonomous intelligence shaped to protect the Delph. And you are Sumner Kagan—the eth. The one who is metaordered to close the cycle.* The Voice was stern. *Why are you haunting us, inwit? Speak your purpose in coming here.*

'I've been led here.'

Ignorant spasm. The room ebbed colder and darker. *You are numb with unknowing—a twitch of the world's Unconscious—a mere reflex. I don't fear you.*

'Why should you fear me?' Sumner extended his two arms and

opened the slender pale hands of his new body. But the space around Rubeus was hot with cold, and he had to drop his gesture. 'I mean no harm.'

You don't know what you mean. You're part of a dream vaster than the stretch of your mind. You are metaordered—destined—to end the Delph's continuity. But there have been many of you over the centuries, most with more awareness of their purpose than you. All have died. I have killed them all.

The six-rayed cell of light flared, and Sumner's body wrinkled away. Darkness clapped around him, Ardent Fang's voice boomed in his head, 'Lotus Face!'—and he sat up into his own body.

Ardent Fang walked him through paddies of salt reeds until the psynergy began to nerve the air between them again. When Sumner's soulight glittered in the air with the dawnlight on the water, they foraged geepa beans and strawberries in the tree-root burls at the edge of the jungle.

I have killed them all, echoed in Sumner's mind for many days, and he had to raise a lot of lifelove to go beyond his fear. Enraptured by the psynergy, he and Ardent Fang lived on the beach, sharing consciousness with the forest, the dune dogs, and the dolphins that came in with the tide. The vision of Rubeus melled into the enormous good-feeling of Sumner's psynergy, and for a while the two men lived joyfully free of memories.

On a morning of bison-headed white clouds, a swamp puma appeared by the river. That day they started their journey back to Miramol. Sumner, still unable to think deeply about his psychic experiences, was uncertain what being the eth meant. He had sensed awesome machine-strength in his vision of Rubeus, yet the fear he had felt then was gone. Everything was living. Even the dead things he saw in the jungle were furred with a living light as they molted into minerals. What was there to fear?

The psynergy circuiting up Sumner's spine continued to generate powerful ecstasy feelings. Weeks passed as the men made their way upstream back to their canoes, fishing without hooks, sharing days with trees, getting acquainted with jaguars and snakes.

In the weather of Sumner's aura, Ardent Fang was absentminded with love for the meadows, the wildflowers, and the spongy jungle nights. The base of his spine had begun to itch as his psynergy responded to Sumner's. But with the intensification of his psychic strength came a deeper clarity which frightened him.

At the end of a small stream, in a pear grove not far from Miramol, he was gripped in his bowels by an electric prescience. The scintillating energy tugged fiercely at his insides and led him out of his dugout and closer to the grove. There the air quivered like the hide of a just-dead animal, and nausea dizzied him. The grove, for one psychomimetic moment, was draped with bloody-green loops of intestine and mucus-bright bits of viscera. The image boiled away swiftly, leaving Ardent Fang so crooked with terror that he backstepped

221

from the pear trees as though they were black wraiths. He turned, leaving his canoe behind, and ran hard until he reached Miramol.

Leaning in the doorway of his hut, feverish with fatigue now that he was out of the power-charged space around Sumner, Ardent Fang groaned inside the dullness of his senses. He lumbered to his hammock and curled into it, his mind a shadow. For three days, he slept.

Sumner took the long way back to the village. Light split in familiar patterns on the river where he had hunted many times. Seeing the well-known tree haunts and river slaches with his One Mind, time drew nearer and detail sharpened.

Empty of words and filled with awe, Sumner returned to Miramol. He understood now, like the old people, the secret of the Silence. The quieter he became, the more he touched. Bonescrolls had been right—the world was feeling. And he wanted to feel everything.

As he left the boathouse after shelving his dugout, he stopped to look around. His euphoria had thinned to a peaceful easiness. He felt sober and calm and happy to be alive.

The sky was wearing away to a smoky twilight. Women were returning from the vegetable plots, and dogs spurted around their legs, pawing a leather ball. The animals chivvied it round and round, and the women moved gracefully among them, chatting softly. Behind them, children approached with firemoths in their loose hair. He waited until they passed, and then he followed them to the eating lodge, joy hot in him, eternal as fire.

Sumner lived with the né on their knoll of silverwood lodges and serene courtyards. Each morning he sat among the cypress knees at the edge of a black, bottomless pond and was joined by a dozen of the diminutive, hairless né. Most of them simply sat in a half-circle before him, legs curled beneath their white robes, brown sea-spider hands palm-up in their laps, receiving the peacefulness that filled the air around him. Others in workday sarongs brought their crafts to the terraced courtyards overlooking the black cypress pond. A mystic joyance spelled the knoll, and many of the né had profound experiences on those mornings.

In the afternoon Sumner worked for the tribe in the ragged green vegetable plots and, sometimes, in the breeding stables. Evenings after the rain, he danced with the young women or went to the swamp edge with the men to hunt with nighthawks. The ecstasy power in him was calmer since he had begun sitting with the né, and he was truly satisfied with his living.

The oldest né sat close to him during his morning meditations, their tiny eyes deliriously bright, their voices mental and instructive: *You are consciousness itself—not the* objects *of consciousness.* They used

222

clear-color prisms and waterdrums to help him relax. *You have a body, but you are not your body. You are the* awareness *of your body. You have thoughts, but you are not your thoughts. You have feelings, but you are not they. Who are you?*

He was awareness. Being glowed through him seamless as sunlight, and his face deepened into the world.

Wisps of memory swirled out of his physical sensations: The rhyme of the wet rock odors from the pond reminded him of legless Mauschel in his damp flatboat. The image spun into a glitter of blue and green birdcalls.

Who is hearing? the né asked. *Who is remembering?*

The flocculent odors of the swamp, the memories, and the kenspeckle drones from the waterdrums were falling into him, becoming the color of void, the sound of nothingness. Only the constant flux of sounds and sensations falling into him seemed solid.

You have touched the center of the whorl.

Like the collapsars he had seen on his scansule as a child, like stars too big for their energy, consciousness, he perceived, was the black hole into which everything fell. Where did these noises, colors, and thoughts go?

Notes knucklerubbed off waterdrums vibrated in the air just wide enough to be heard, and the dreary afternoon he had spent mindlessly looking at scansule animations of blown-out stars brightened into an exact memory. Again he saw the three-dimensional computerline images of the collapsar at the core of the galaxy, the web of space-time tightening through the spiral of stars to a single point in the hub—the singularity where space-time ceased to exist.

The scansule image rotated and split crosswise, revealing a complexity of seashell involutions. A droll ghostvoice explained, faster than words, that the collapsar was gravitationally distorted, and that out of its poles rayed the most powerful radiation conceivable—light from a source of infinite space-time curvature.

Infinity is Unity, the né told him, filled with the full fire of Sumner's One Mind. *All things are one thing.*

Sumner's memory of the scansule soft-focused, and a bruised light pulsed behind his lids as his insight crystallized into understanding: When the earth came into line with the collapsar's radiation, the universe became the multiverse, and the consciousness of the cosmos, the light of infinity, animated the thought forms and the genetic shapes that were here with an awareness older than time—voors, godminds, timeloose distorts, eth—all were earthshaped starlight from the core of the galaxy.

The waterdrum music stopped suddenly, and muffled voices and the shirring cries of small birds brought Sumner back to himself. Eddying in the muscularity of his body, heat-stilled and viewless, he sensed the Delph—distant yet close, like the inside of thunder. A white mountain, sharp as glass, appeared and vanished. *Graal—the ice-mountain realm of Rubeus.*

There is no reason to go there except the going, the gentle né told him. *The voor in you has a purpose—to kill the Delph. But you have no purpose. The eth is one of your masks. But you are not the eth. Many eth have come before you. Others will come after. Who are you?*

Voices ruffled with anger intensified at the gate to the cypress court, and Sumner opened his eyes. Sunlight spiriting through the ancient trees settled like bright birds among the ivy of the round gate. Several of the small né in blue robes were struggling there with a big-boned woman—Orpha.

The elders signaled to let her pass, and she straightened from her tousling with composed dignity.

'I am sorry to disturb the famous morning meditations,' she said with sardonic seriousness, 'but the magnar has an urgent message for Lotus Face.' She stepped off the dragonstone path and waded through the flowering ankle-high grass to where Sumner was sitting. Her shadow covered two né. 'The magnar orders you to stop casting kha.'

No more ecstasy energy.

The Mother ignored the né and kept her heavy, shadowed stare on Sumner. 'You and the magnar have an enemy. If you attract him, he will destroy Miramol. Some seers have seen this.' She squatted beside Sumner and placed a thick hand on his chest. 'Your thrall ends with the next lunar turn, Lotus Face. Walk your kha into the desert. Protect the folk and the né.'

Sumner took her hand to assure her, but before he could speak, a scream bounced through the moongate, scattering né. Flapping black wings of cloth whirled into the court—a wild-haired, eyeless Mother, shouting: 'There are no secrets! Our senses fit the world! What you see is seen!'

Orpha bounded upright. 'Jesda—this is not your place.'

'Nor yours, sister.' The blind Mother's hands flew over her head like startled sparrows. 'The word has been fulfilled. I have witnessed it.'

Sumner looked to the elder né beside him, and the old one nodded and told him: *Four centuries ago, Dog Hunger, the first seer, prophesied that Miramol would not die until the Mothers had come to the né.*

'And we are here,' Jesda whispered, walking sightlessly across a moss ledge and into the pond. Her black skirts billowed in the water around her hips, and she shrieked: 'What I see is seen!'

Orpha took the blind woman's arm and led her out of the water. 'We're done here, sister. Let's go home.'

'Wait, Mother.' Sumner rose. 'May I speak with you, Jesda?'

'Speak!' Her wet sleeves snapped in the air with her sharp gestures, and Orpha stepped back. 'Babble to the Vastness!'

Sumner stepped forward, and the angry pain in Jesda's face softened to a quiescence interknit with sorrow and clarity. Sumner experienced a howl of mind-language and a dizzy lurch as his etheric field penetrated hers.

She was timeloose. Through a gargoyling of dissolving thought-forms, Sumner saw the starheart—the white luminosity from the first moment, from the origin of time—patterned like a retinal shadow over the vale of cypress and the old woman's sunken face. He brushed a thistle of knotted gray hair from her brow, and the One Mind between them trembled into exquisite scales of color, shimmering in the shapes of their seeing.

Jesda sighed and softly took both of his hands. She was calm as a tree, healed, her blindness infused with a violet quivering. 'Heaven and earth move through each other,' she said to him gently, 'but the mind is moveless—at last.' Her grip tightened, and she bowed, touching her forehead to their clasped hands. 'We are presence.' When she looked up, her blind sockets were rimmed with tears. She turned to Orpha. 'Come, sister.'

After the Mothers departed, the court and the surrounding terraces flurried with excited né. The eldest took Sumner's arm. Its eyes were two glistening waterpits in the stone of its face. *Your One Mind is clear, Lotus Face. You've worked hard for this. What will you do now?*

From beyond the court wall, a painstruck wail shivered loudly, then curled into Jesda's demon laughter.

Ardent Fang sat in the full sunlight on the top of the breeding stables. Miramol looked like flotsam in the green wave of the rain forest, all vine-lashed timbers and reedstraw. A curve in the river flashed with sun among the dense trees, and waterbirds circled raucously overhead.

In the courtyard below, the blossom-trellised wagon that had carried Miramol's maidens to their new home in Ladilena earlier that morning had returned. A young man was helping the new women out of the wagon, joking loudly as much to calm himself as them. He was strong and good-looking—his eyes puma-wide, his hair a proud mane. Even so, Ardent Fang would need a full season to break him in, to pass on the sense of mission that would serve him when his lust dulled. Soon enough the boy would be as bored as he was anxious now.

Ardent Fang stood and stretched, gazing beyond the green jumble of the riverain forest to where the land slurred to desert. Lotus Face had gone that way two days before to meet the magnar for the last time in his thrall, and the breeder reminisced about how thoroughly the man had changed: He moved more with the lanky ease of a tribesman now than the cautious reserve of a warrior, and he took more time with the women—

'Ardent Fang.'

The breeder turned, and his features balked. Orpha was standing before him with a brood jewel in her hand, her body as thin and ghostly as fire.

'Come to the Barrow, breeder,' the specter said, wavering into the invisible. 'Come, quickly.'

Ardent Fang bounded down the spiral stairs of the tower and sprinted through the muddy back lanes. When he arrived at the Barrow his thick legs were mired and his breath was tattered. Drift was waiting outside the turquoise-studded entrance with several of the Mothers. It took the breeder's hand, and the frenzy of his run thinned out.

'You must walk the Road again, breeder,' Orpha said. She gripped his shoulder, and her face hooked into a silent cry. 'The magnar is dying.'

Bonescrolls gazed out at the blue night from the vantage of his cliff-cavern. Frost haze glowed along the horizon, and above it the moon moved across a night rainbow. He closed his eyes and leaned toward the west. Shadows swooped through him. He was gliding, the cool night air buffeting his sleek body. The stars moved in bands. The moonlit landscape with its broken contours wheeled below. Coyote tracks studded the bright sand slopes like dark blossoms. Saguaros stood solemnly along the ridgeline.

Nothing in sight was moving. And yet the raven Bonescrolls had melled with was excited. Something had aroused it, but whatever it was, no trace lingered in the gray shadings of its memory.

Bonescrolls altered his breathing, and the dreamtime shifted. He entered a coyote perched on a rock ledge, scenting the air for the heat of the living. Its blood was buoyant under the draw of the full moon, raising the fine hairs in its ears, sending urgent ripples down the curve of its spine. No end to the sky. Shifting things—dark birds, moths—slipped through the air. The moon was luring everything upward. And a howl trembled in its throat, the frayed end of a song begun a long time ago and never finished.

But it stopped the cry at a growl. A hot, sticky scent flared its nostrils and tightened the scruff of its neck. Man-odor. It walked a wobbly, nervous circle and caught it again, cutting across the grain of the wind. It was blowing up from the young sisters' trails, the flat rock paths among the tall stones.

Bonescrolls moved the coyote down the rock ledge toward the stinging odor. It didn't want to get any closer, and the urine-itch between its legs became intense and forced it to stop. But it had gone far enough. Now it could see the man following the sisters' trail. The man's nightshining eyes fixed on it for a moment, gauging the distance between them.

Sumner strode out of the shadows, tall and loose, the moonlight gleaming across the lotus-burn of his face. Bonescrolls smiled to

226

himself and left the coyote to its lunar songs and its own fearless detachment.

He opened his eyes as a long, distant howl trembled among the rock towers. Sumner was close. He had come a long way without Bonescrolls being able to find him—and the young warrior wasn't even trying to hide. He was simply being cautious in the manner of any animal that knows its predators.

Bonescrolls yawned and stretched. Frost and starlight burned snow-blue on the rock shapes. He stood up and listened to the weaving coyote song. It was time to go down and meet his thrall for the last time.

A pulse of sadness thrummed in his chest, but it passed quickly. Sadness and joy and, high over the eroded desert, that old bone the moon. How many years had it taken him to see truly that they were all the same? In everything, identical forces were at work: tides, currents, flows and spirals of power.

The patterns of the folded rocks held his attention—the scars of glaciers, the same flow-wear lines seen in running water or in the heart's ventricles where blood has circled many, many years.

Sumner ambled over talus slopes and beneath the steep red walls of mesas the color of dried blood in the moonlight. An eddy of wind passed like a sigh, and he caught a faint sweet scent of burning juniper. He moved in that direction, sliding silently over the sand slopes. All his senses were alert, honed by the odd signs he had seen on his night journey: a lunatic raven careening strange patterns over the dunes; and a wild-eyed coyote close enough to touch, pissing where it stood.

A Serbota coyote song echoed its rhythms through his mind:

> Coyote—yapping
> At the moon. Like us
> Not knowing what to ask for—
> Starved
> For what it already has,
> Like a dream of sleepiness.

Sumner followed the burn-scent beneath corraded monoliths and over hogback ridges, and soon the sapless claw of a dead juniper appeared above the dreamlit dunes. A raven was roosting in the crown of the dead tree, and at the base, where tough black bark clenched stone, Bonescrolls sat. The flames of a small twig-fire danced before him.

Sumner returned the magnar's greeting and sat down beside the fire, laying his walking stick across his knees. He stared into Bonescrolls' gaunt face without expectation.

The old man stared back with hooded eyes. The eth's bodylight was a crystal-sharp yellow deeper than sunlight, and the harmony of his inner life was visible in the graceful pulsing of his aura. The magnar was well pleased, but to test Sumner's One Mind, he let his strong feeling rush out of him.

Sumner felt the psynergy as a sudden iciness in his abdomen. A green pain cramped his stomach, and he flinched. But he didn't hold back the cold flow. The psynergy furled deeply intò him, and at the moment when the hurt became more than he could hold, the psynergy sluiced up his back and dissolved in the vastness behind his eyes. Sumner blinked and sat up taller. He knew what the magnar had done, and he was proud that he was clear enough for the power to pass through him. He felt open and strong as the wind.

Bonescrolls laughed and rubbed his belly. Sumner was so empty that the old man had almost fallen into him. He kneaded the icy feeling out of his bowels and asked through a smile: 'Why are you traveling in the dark?'

Sumner grinned quizzically, then recognized the innocent question as a challenge. But instead of searching for an answer, he listened to the longing cry of the wind. The ghost of his breath glowed in the firelight. 'It's too cold to stay still.'

Bonescrolls' grin widened, and his tough sun-scaled cheeks bulged. 'It's colder where we're going.'

Sumner frowned, disquieted by the magnar's allusion to death. 'It won't matter when we get there.' Sumner rolled a salty wafer of spit onto his tongue and hawked it into the flame. The fire snapped like an angry snake.

Bonescrolls' eyes glinted with laughter, and he nailed Sumner with them. 'Even the truth is a boulder that can pin a monkey down for his whole life.'

Sumner smiled. The game they were playing amused him, but Bonescrolls was right: Thought games were cumbersome and dangerous. He listened to the scratch of the cold wind blowing across the night-smelling depths. 'What do we know?'

Bonescrolls clapped his hands merrily. 'That's right. We're empty as the wind—but moving, always moving.'

'And singing.'

'Only when we rub against things that get in our way. Like the wind, without obstacles we'd never sing.'

Sumner chuckled and nodded. 'We're singing, crying, and laughing, all at the same time. But no one hears us.'

'Who knows?' The old man gestured at the blurred light above them. 'We're bigger than we can imagine.'

For hours the two men sat feeding twigs to the fire, talking and not-talking. When dawn came Bonescrolls stood up and pointed toward a low sandstone rim. 'My last command is for you to go to that shelf and sit there until the voor inside you returns. Listen to him. If you decide that you don't want to share your life with him, return to me, and I'll free you. Otherwise, you don't have to think of me again.

You've learned not to leave tracks. Everything else is unnecessary.' The magnar put a hand over his heart and bowed low. 'Shay, warrior.'

Sumner watched after Bonescrolls until he vanished behind a standing rock; then he went over to the sandstone rim and dragged his stick through the shadows to feel out snakes and scorpions. He sat with his back to the rim and watched the frost melt to dew as the colors of the world lit up.

Sumner angled himself into the shade. He tried to keep himself in selfscan to dampen his anxiety about confronting the voor, but he was sleepy, and random thoughts flitted through his mind. He wondered if Ardent Fang was practicing the fly casting he had tried to teach him. The thought of fish reminded him of the scaly embrace of one of the distort women and the sharp, enduring stink of her body. He flinched and had to think about Drift to ease himself: The observant, elegant mind behind that stiff mask was constantly challenging him with the strange lyrics of its chanting:

> Nothing is ever lost—
> It's only on its way back.

Sumner slept darkly until noon. Then he glanced at the white, radium-fierce sun, closed his eyes, and drowsed into late afternoon. He dreamt that he was with the blind Mother again, sitting on stones shaped like hands. She whispered a sacred name in his ear, and when he voiced it a white elk shouldered out of the forest, the sunlight spinning on its antlers. . . .

Sumner woke and washed the taste of sleep out of his mouth with the tepid water in his flagon. He stuck a black twig between his teeth and sucked on the bittersweet root flavor. The painted desert lay before him—agatized rainbows and rock light.

A cry rose between the buttes. Llyr, the dusk star, burned cold silver over the ridgeline, wobbling in the layers of air. The vague green spume of the skyfires scattered and re-formed in an unfelt wind. Sumner held himself in selfscan, watching bats whir and squeak among the rock spires.

Another cry went up over the desert, high and taut. It dimmed without an echo—a ghost cry. Sumner remained aloof and watchful, though he knew that wasn't a creature-call. Needles of crystal flashed in the parabolic sand as the last light faded. Shadow hallucinations misted over the terrain. He focused on the longhaired stars in the striated air over the world's edge.

It wasn't until the moon came up and its clear light enameled the dunes and rocks that he heard the cry for a third time—a ululating scream. Again, no echo, and he realized that the sound was happening inside him. Another call quivered through his muscles and burst open in his head as a howl: the shocking cries of the voor dead suddenly claw-ripping the air around him, wrenching and hurling him from his selfscan. Electrified, his body jumped, though his face remained slack as a rag effigy. Jolting screams flattened him and left him gazing up at the lofty nightfires.

The strong fear unwound and cracked up his spine, bursting through his mind in a rush of jigging colors—and he began to relive the deaths of voors on other planets.

He was lumbering flatfooted over bauchy ice. Above him two suns burned: one low on the horizon and flesh-colored, the other a windy blue and quilled. Arrowstuck, knifestabbed, punctured, he was dying. A groan-sore tongue rolled with the flinty taste of blood. . . .

He became an iridescent creature, rooted like a tree, a lantern of water, then a fumy, spiritous mistlife, weeping as it dissolved—A lens-being, moonskulled—A tendriled diatom—

Sumner tried to hold himself back, but he was falling, clutched by a force that swept through lifetimes: countless forms, countless worlds. His own life was merely another shape. And he was all of them—he could be any one of them again.

He became a being many times vaster than a whale—a being massive as a planet—reefs of living rock keeling through the sheer light of stars, translating the energy into music. Shining canticles resounded in his mind rapt with curves of distance, dimming as the star-tugs pulled the being away from its sun—

Sumner clutched the earth beneath him and squeezed himself alert.

The frightening confluence of sounds and images within the inward darkness of his body began to mount again. Fumes of light coiled across his vision, and the haunted wailing tightened in his ears. Still, he was calm. Nothing could hurt him now, for nothing could touch him. He was empty as a cave, his senses hollow and intangible as echoes.

Corby loomed wraithlike deep within him. The voor was alarmed. A year in Iz without a physical form had made him less. The percussive pulses, the drum and gong of the voor dead no longer affected his howlie body. Not even the entranced vision of Unchala's slow death with its fervid starsongs could reach Sumner.

It's me, Father—I can't go on now without you. Listen to me.

Corby's voice rippled in Sumner's ears, burlesqued by the squawk of bereaved cries from the voor dead. Sumner let the voice pass through him like a stray thought.

After so long a journey, can you turn me away? Again the fire-shifting images of the voor-migrations began spurting through Sumner. Instantly he was in murky waters, thin and fish-slippery, feeling unnamable hungers, his vision belled by stalk-eyes—

Sumner relaxed his deepest muscles, and the alien sensations slipped away.

Don't ignore me, Father. Listen—I have knowledge. Corby refocused himself and let specific bundles of thought arc-jump between him and Sumner.

Bubbles of silver light streamed across Sumner's mind, bursting into thoughts. All at once he understood everything about brood jewels. He knew fully and clearly how the seeds were shaped out of the rare minerals and hormones excreted by certain voors. The technique had been perfected in a distant galaxy where blue-haired hominids had organs for eliminating excess metal ions from their bodies. Some voors remembered how to draw out these substances, and they had modified their human forms to do so. The seeds were planted in rock faces where the mineral content, moisture, and temperature permitted enhancement of the metal-locked kha of the donor. After several centuries of growth, the crystals were harvested. And they were powerful crystals, for the kha in them had been altered to an Iz-window, an acausal vantage which . . .

Again Sumner relaxed his deep muscles, and the thought-volutions narrowed and thinned away.

Are you zaned? Corby's voice was bleak, a vapor shredded by the wind of voorish mumblings. *I'm offering you power. I can show you things no human has ever witnessed.*

Sumner's mind flared with knowledge, and he sat up tall, glistening with a cold sweat, suddenly understanding the secret of death. It wasn't extinction after all. The collapse of the organism liberated subtle energies—psynergy. Those life-energies blended with the forces around them, shifted and realigned into other configurations, other lifeforms, many of them unguessable to a human mind.

In the sway of his new power, he glimpsed the advanced forms: lightningflash momemts of blue, fragmentary beings wintering in a vastness of tissue-light—too strange to see clearly. Animals like mist, whorling shapes, dissolved into one another with cattle sounds and bird cries. The quick pulsing strength of a bloodied hind rat bled into a starved hawk and the circling pace of an exhausted shark, their hazy psynergies pooling into the tight, hot power of his life—

The vision filmed Sumner's eyes like a fever. He was breathing hard, and he had to clench his fists to regain a sense of himself. 'Teeth dreams,' he mumbled once, and his mind began to clear.

Wait—there's more. I can show you your eth-power. . . .

Sumner cut off the whining voice in his head. Frost had stiffened his clothing, and his muscles were leaden.

Corby felt a surge of power as Sumner's mind circled in on itself trying to get reoriented. In that moment he realized that he was doomed. Sumner was too strong. The habit patterns and thought routines that Corby had once used to control him were gone. The howlie was empty as a voor mage, and Corby was thinned out, reduced to a mere impulse, and becoming vaguer each day. There was only one hope. But he would have to act swiftly. The voor surged into Sumner's consciousness with all his strength.

The sudden assault of voor noise thrumped through Sumner's body. He lurched, hands to his head, feeling a chorus of cries too high for his ears. The pain blurred the focus of his eyes and snatched his strength. He dropped his hands and fell back, his head thudding to the ground, his teeth clashing.

But the pain didn't crush him. It eased up. His body breathed again, and his blank brain filled with light. The voices of the voor dead drummed in his bones.

The sun was rising over the rimrock, and a shaft of light glazed Sumner's eyes. He blinked, and the rapport between him and Corby shriveled. *Help us, Sumner*, the voor pleaded. *Our journey must continue. But the broods can't unite without our godminds. We must go on. But we don't have the strength to leave without our godminds. Help us!* A cortege of mournful voices writhed between his ears. *The Delph is destroying us. You must help us to stop him.* Shapeless cries flinched in his throat. *The Delph* . . .

Sumner reined in his attention and let the lament wrinkle out of hearing. He had listened enough to this voor. Whether it was really Corby or not he couldn't say. Voors were devious. That much he had learned from Jeanlu. He wanted nothing more to do with them.

He swayed to his feet and stretched the ache out of his muscles. With the morning sunlight glinting off the dunes and warming his numbed flesh, he felt good. Bonescrolls' final command had been fulfilled. Now he could seek him out and get purged of this possession.

No more voors. No more teeth dreams. There was enough illusion in his life without the memories of long dead worlds.

But even so, as he staggered out over the windfolded sand, he marveled that such beings existed—beings of light, reshaping bodies, forever wandering. There was no loneliness like theirs.

Nefandi stood in the shadow of a balanced rock staring across the distorting lenses of heated air on the desert floor. No life was anywhere to be seen among the cliffs of mangled and rusted iron. The white, depthless sky was empty even of clouds, and the ridges and defiles edged in black and purple wavered in the thermal currents like a hallucination.

Why would anyone choose to live in this death hole? he wondered, gnawing on the frayed tip of an unlit cheroot. He removed his wide-brimmed leather hat and wiped the sweat from his face. The heat made him look sad, but there was still menace in his one red eye and in the glossy, rippled scar that stitched his dark face from the mirror-shard eye to the wide, clamped jaw. He placed his hat back over his spiked hair, took a swig of water from a flask, and strode out into the ponderous sun.

The loose tawny trousers and shirt he wore were designed to protect him from the stinging sand, but the heat clung to them and baked his flesh. To keep his mind off his suffering, he thought back to where he had come from. A tame world of small, biotectured villages: Nanda with its bluffs and milk-blue lakes; Sidhe, the floating stone city; and Cleyre, exquisite Cleyre, its meadows exploding with aster and cyclamen, its trout streams clean as light. As a Rubeus-programmed assassin, his strongest memories were of the ice-valley laboratories of Graal, the Delph's stronghold. It was there that his new body was being shaped. But now was too lonely a time to be thinking of home.

Nefandi slid into selfscan and picked up his pace, hugging the shadows of the wind-eaten rock walls. He entered the sun only when enormous potholes and fissures blocked his way. There was a chill in the sunlight, a somnolence that he knew well. The heat was killing him, and several times, each time sooner, he had to stop and refresh himself.

Sitting in the dry heat of the shade, he cursed Rubeus for sending him here, though in the back of his mind he knew that if he had to choose over again, he would be right where he was now. How could he choose otherwise? Rubeus had promised him a new body—his third—if he was successful in this mission. Rubeus was the Delph's guardian. It was an artificial mind, an ort like Nefandi—but vaster, the size of a mountain and huge with power. It could easily weave him a new body, and for that privilege Nefandi would do anything.

But why was I ordered to take the long way around? He cleared the sweat from his one red-veined eye and stood up. Heat waves floated in glassy layers, veiling the distances he had to cross. Rubeus had said this mission would be difficult. The person he was seeking was supposedly very powerful. *He has to be to live in this hell maze.*

Sometime during the solar heat-crazed hours of the afternoon a raven began wheeling high over Nefandi's head. In the sensex embedded behind his mirror eye he could detect nothing unusual about it, but the bird was strange. It was following him, despite the shriveling heat and his attempts to lose it among the arches and tunnel rocks. Finally he had to kill it. He brought it down with a burst from his unsheathed field-sword. Unfolding its wings in his hands, he could see nothing that was unusual about it.

Not long afterwards, as he followed a raintrail down an escarpment of smoldering red bordered with charcoal, another raven began ringing through the sky above him. He ignored it. His destination was very close now, and he had no time for desert anomalies. All around him lay a labyrinth of basins, towers, and fins of naked stone. The sandstone was crossbedded and checkered, seamed by old fault lines, and bizarrely sculptured. It took all his skill to cross the tilted ledges in the fearful glare of the sun.

As he was edging along a ribbon-thin rim that curled over a death plunge into a kniferock ravine, the circling raven swooped. It clawed the back of his neck, and he yelped and danced for his footing. The sandstone powdered beneath his frantic weight and hissed into long, thin fractures. Only selfscan and luck carried him across before the rim crumbled and whispered into the abyss.

Nefandi searched the sky and the rock walls for the raven, but it was gone. Apprehensively he moved on, scrambling over rocks that seesawed under his weight. By the time he reached the sand bowl of a saddle basin his clothes were pasty with fear sweat.

Again he searched for the raven. Nothing living was in sight, yet there was a new feeling prickling around him. It was the sensation he had been coded to feel when he was near his objective. He had begun to detect it as he was sliding over the loose rock slabs, but only now could he concentrate enough to feel its source. A tall crest of rock, windsmoothed and arching like a wave, was emanating a dull lifenergy. The sensex detected nothing, but the more sensitive sensors embedded in his skull were definitely reacting to a life-presence—a strong life-presence.

Nefandi unsheathed the silver-gold sword strapped to his back and approached the sweep of rock. A gully of frantic stones and boulders blocked a direct advance, and he circled the tower. At the side he stopped cold and crouched behind a sand-buffed outcropping. Beside the tower was a juniper crowded with silent ravens. They angled their small heads to watch him as he stepped into the clearing. They made no sound, and they barely stirred.

With his mind held rigidly in selfscan and his sword angled before him, he skirted the raven tree and ducked into a cave mouth at the base of the tower. As silently as his anxious legs could move, he mounted the steep incline following the directional cues of his sensors. The person he had been sent to kill was up ahead at the top of the tower. Nefandi's sense of that person was strong, and he negotiated the forking and curving corridors without hesitation. But halfway to the top he was brought to a halt by an unusual sound.

He leaned on his sword and listened to a rustling, snapping noise. It was a moment before he realized what he was hearing, and then he bolted forward. The next instant, the first of the ravens clawed into his back. He slapped it off with his sword, not breaking his stride. The others followed quickly, and soon he was engulfed in black beating wings and ripping claws.

Not daring to activate his field inside the tower for fear that the sandstone would collapse around him, he was reduced to slashing at the rabid birds with his sword. But there were too many of them, drumming at his back, snapping over his shoulders, darting their claws at his one real eye. Sticky blood pooled in his ears and splattered his cheeks. He lashed madly, stumbled and curled into a ball as the needlebeaks stabbed his back. With a gnashed cry, he activated the field of his sword. The ravens burst into the air above him in an explosion of feathers and torn shrieks. And higher, almost too high to hear, the sandstone walls whined and began to hiss.

Nefandi shut down the field and lunged to his feet. He dashed along the cramped corridor, pulling himself up the blind inclines, using his sensex in the far infrared to make out the pathways. A raven hammered into him from behind. He spun about and whacked it in half. Gasping, he waited with raised sword for the others, but there were no more.

After several more turns the darkness relented, and he followed the light and the cool air to a sweeping cavern lanced with skyholes and natural windows. Bonescrolls was seated cross-legged before one of the large oval openings, wearing linen trousers and a shirt of pristine white. He was smiling broadly, his wild white hair glowing in the afternoon sunlight like a nimbus.

'Welcome, Death,' the magnar said, his face radiant as a dream. 'Come in! Come in!'

Nefandi took a wary step forward. There was no doubt that this was the man he had been sent for. The sensors were trilling insanely in his head. *Kill him now*, the implanted command urged, and his sword arm raised and leveled his weapon. But he didn't fire. The race through the darkness, the ravens, and now this smiling old man left him feeling giddy.

'A drink?' Bonescrolls held up a clear jug half-filled with green wine. The magnar's hand was trembling, and looking closer, Nefandi saw that the old man was terrified.

The assassin lowered his sword and stepped forward, his sensex scanning the cavern for hidden weapons.

Bonescrolls poured out two cupfuls, frowning to master the tremor in his fingers. 'I'm a little nervous, Death.' He held out one of the blue-glazed mugs. 'I'd hoped that I wouldn't be. After all, I've seen this coming for a long time.'

Nefandi stood before Bonescrolls and waved away the drink. A trickle of blood dropped from his chin and splattered in the dust between them. Who was this old man? The kha around him was extraordinarily thin. Most of the life-energy was coiled into his abdomen. The man was obviously an advanced entity, but he looked like a drunk.

Bonescrolls nodded and tugged nervously at his hair. 'Appearances always tell the truth—if you look close enough,' he said, his voice splintering. 'I am a drunk. I'm inebriated with life. That's why I came out here.' He chuckled, making a high nasal sound like the whinny of an uneasy horse. 'I thought this inhospitable land would wean me away from life. But there's beauty in being. I understand now that if I lived ten thousand years, I'd still want more.'

A talker, Nefandi thought. *He is a drunk*. He watched the magnar sip his drink and blink slowly with satisfaction.

Bonescrolls put his mug down and looked up at Nefandi. His face was composed, his eyes alert and moist. 'There's so much to know, to see, to feel.' He sighed and flicked his eyebrows. 'I don't suppose I could entreat you in any way to let me live?'

Nefandi stared back at him, cool as silver.

The old man nodded and put one hand over his heart. 'Okay.' His upper lip went taut. 'My whimpering is over.'

Nefandi brought up his sword, but as his hand moved to activate it, Bonescrolls' body unsprung. His legs kicked out, and the flagon of wine flew into Nefandi's face. The assassin dodged it clumsily, and his hand fear-twitched on the sword, firing a burst of power. The blast hit the ledge of the oval window with a scream of ripping rock. Shock-severed chunks of the ceiling collapsed in streamers of dust, and the whole face of the struck wall groaned mightily and dropped away.

Bonescrolls had rolled clear of the falling wall, but a massive slab of the ceiling slammed him flat, pinning both of his legs. Nefandi had leaped back and hunched against a far wall. As the dust churned and settled he stepped forward, a wild tic at the scarred corner of his mouth and a dark look in his smoky red eye. He stalked up to where Bonescrolls was stretched out on his back and stomped the heel of his boot into the old man's belly.

The magnar wheezed and smiled, his thick lips flecked with pink froth. 'Even truth is a boulder.' He laughed softly, his face luminous until Nefandi blew off the top of his head.

'Stupid old man,' he grumbled, turning away from the inert body. He went over to the shattered edge of the cavern where a new, wide vista had been blasted open. Whiskey-colored light angled between the buttes and spires. In the east, long bars of clouds were gathering, driftwood-blue in the late sun.

Killing's unimportant, he told himself as he gingerly fingered the claw marks on his face. *We're all killed by something sooner or later. It's dignity that counts, and there would have been more for that old man if he hadn't struggled. Stupid fool. A man with that much kha should be ready to live his death.*

He sheathed his sword and kicked the wine jug over the broken edge of the cavern. His work was not yet finished. There was one more death between him and his new life. A Massebôth soldier in lusk had to be put out of his misery. He lived with the Serbota, a primitive tribe several days away. At least this would be a mercy death.

Nefandi didn't like killing hermits or old men. He didn't look back as he left, but he did wonder what Bonescrolls had meant: Truth is a boulder. *The man was a soak, all right. A real talker. Who was he? Ach! Useless to ponder.*

The sky was smoke-blue with dawn when Drift and Ardent Fang came out of the north. They approached Bonescrolls' rock tower slowly and diffidently. Ardent Fang led the way, eyes sliding warily, knife drawn. He had shared Drift's nightmares of shards and lumps of bloody flesh and bones in the smoke of bones, and he woke each time chewing his screams.

For Drift, it had been worse. After the second day on the Road, it had experienced shadowed dreams of voices at a distance, a numbing crack of thunder, and then a lightning-jagged pain in its legs pinning it flat in the abstraction of its sleep. The black core of the nightmare was a spasm in its stomach, the odor of blood, and a blow that rent the top of its skull and squashed it dark.

The Road, too, had not felt right. A malevolent presence, dark and preoccupied, had been in the area not long before. In the blue dawn shadows they had even spotted the tracks of a large man. Drift wouldn't go near the prints. A glassy red light glowed over them, the bloodlight of a deadwalker, a living corpse. In the muted sky flocks of ravens circled silently.

When they came within sight of Bonescrolls' tower, neither of them expected to find him alive. Yet, as they closed in and saw the collapsed wall and the dark hole at the summit, their hearts constricted. Ardent Fang scrambled up the mound of fallen rock and was the first to see Bonescrolls. He dropped to his knees, hands over his face, and howled.

Drift saw the corpse through Ardent Fang's eyes. Its mind flinched, and it walked numbly around to the cave entrance. By the time it wound its way through the dark corridors and entered the cavern, its shock had settled and the sight of the body was less fiercesome than the rage it felt. A rasping click rattled in its throat, and it fell to the ground and thrashed among the rocks.

Ardent Fang mastered his grief, and in the lilac light he began gathering the pieces of the shattered skull. Overnight the blood had caked, glueing the dead flesh to the rock floor. White ants swarmed over the body, and the putrid deathsmell thickened as the day warmed.

It was noon before the ants were plucked from the body and all the bits of flesh were scraped off the ground and gathered in a scrap of torn cloth. Ardent Fang carried the body down through the darkness to the sandy field before the tower.

With a stone wedge fastened to a lopped segment of his walking stick, Ardent Fang fashioned an ax and brought down the tall juniper. Drift arranged the wood into a pyre as Ardent Fang cut it up. Together they sat before the blazing heap, the devil harp warbling a mournful tune, the né chanting:

> Like the thunder you begin
> Too late
> To remember the light. . . .

Sumner followed the nut-sweet fragrance of burning juniper across the evening. At Bonescrolls' rock abode, smoke idled up, flames muttered. Both Ardent Fang and Drift were inert, too wasted by grief to move. They watched him approach, and they saw the emptiness in his face and the remote gaze of his eyes.

Drift watched for a moment in the felted silence and noted the wan, fatigued light around his body. *The magnar is dead.*

The moment distilled to a burning drop of feeling, but Sumner remained expressionless. The bruising hurt quelled almost immediately. Bonescrolls was dead. That thought was a thinning filament in the emptiness of his mind—a void that hours before had contained countless deaths on unnumbered worlds. He squatted in the dust and watched plum-colored stars wink on above the horizon.

Ardent Fang felt a throb of anger at Sumner's coolness. He wanted to grab that blank face by its long hair and drag it over to the pyre and force it to see the charred corpse. But the moment was sacred, and he restrained himself. Drift, too, was disturbed by Sumner's aloofness. Didn't he perceive how great a loss this was? But when the seer reached out with its mind to touch Sumner, it was like edging up to a windy cliff. It backed off and married its mind to the shadows and its grief.

Sumner was emotionally void. He was not even moved by the realization that the voor he had mastered with his One Mind would continue to live in his body. He was the eye of the moment through which everything threaded: the pearled light of dusk, the silky smoke, the red embers in the pyre malign as eyes.

Fatigue ghosted through him, and stray thoughts, cumbersome as sleep, narrowed his awareness: *The magnar is dead—no freedom from voors now* . . . Those thoughts dropped away. His exhaustion dropped away. Even his body seemed to drop away. The air smelled slow—the sweet, cold, piny flavor of smoldering desert wood. Pools of silent energy circled around him, turning with the evening colors. In the corners of dusk, the tops of the highest buttes were catching the last slips of light and shining with time.

Sumner closed his eyes, and the darkness was wormed with blue threads of light. A voice muffled with distance spoke within him: *We are one now.* It was Corby. Sumner sensed the voor drawing closer. He had the strength to stop him, to turn the alien back. But he was empty. Everything was passing through him. The voor was very close to his senses now, curiously alive and full of loneliness. The wild static of the voor dead browsed in the far distance.

We are one, the voor spoke, quiet as moonlight. *I make no demands. But I am within you. I see all that you see. And all that I have is yours. Let us share what we are.*

Stoneflakes glinted in the dark depths and Sumner was aware of his tranced body knitting itself close to him. A wheeling darkness moved through him, and when he opened his eyes he was sitting alone in the pearl-gray light of dawn.

The tracks of Ardent Fang and Drift wandered off to the north. The pyre was burned out, reduced to a charred circle in the sand. Without thinking it, but knowing that it was a voor desire, he went over to the exhausted fire and scooped a handful of the ash into his side pouch. He turned toward Miramol and began to walk. He didn't know why he was going there or what he intended to do, but it felt right.

'After all,' he said aloud to the chemical desert, 'the world is feeling.'

He passed clay pits where mud-clotted distorts stooped to their work and did not see him go by. In the wide fields beyond, smoke muscled close to the ground. The distorts were heating stone kilns, tempering metal and hardening wood. When they spotted him they cast warding signs in his direction and sent up a shrill alarm on their cricket whistles. But Nefandi ignored them. He moved as silently as the smoke he passed through, his sword strapped to his back.

The women and children in the vegetable plots had already scattered by the time he moved between their shaggy green rows. At the treeline, he brought down a young warrior he had spotted with his sensex aiming a blowgun at him from high in a baobab. When the youth thudded to the ground, a loud wailing started in the grass huts.

Nefandi scanned the houses for voor kha. He moved down the length of the tusk- and rib-lined boulevard, his body sheathed in the protective field of his sword. The well-carpentered huts and the immaculate flower lanes shimmered through the field, and a rock tossed from a tree bounced off the air around him, a foot from his head.

At the end of the boulevard he spotted the knoll of silverwood lodges with their trellises of jungle blossoms. Blue-green kha pulsed behind the walls, and he moved in that direction. Along the way he studied the distorts who were studying him from behind the trees and moss curtains. They were symbio-mutants—that is, their mutations were a necessary component of their lives. They used frequent triple-jointed gestures and ear and scalp expressions that an undistorted human would be incapable of. That was possible, he made a mental note, only because of genetic phase-drifting. The mutations were not random. At least most of them weren't. A fifth of the distorts he had seen so far had dysfunctions that easily would have selected against them without tribal support—like that legless woman in the doorway to her hut and that blind man under the tree with the fishing net in his lap. Didn't a tribe advanced enough to cultivate androgs understand the long-term benefits of selective life-privilege? *Ach! Useless to ponder.*

The né watching Nefandi's approach from the peepholes of their lodges were appalled. He was a killer by the smell of his mind, and worse, he was a deadwalker. The shadow-red lifelight about his body

239

was sluggish, circling slowly through his chest and brightening only around his head. He was obviously the one who had slain the magnar, though why he was coming to them they couldn't guess. None of them, however, cared. The loss of their benefactor was too heavy on their minds, and they resolved without speaking to kill him.

Nefandi moved in a tiger's slouch up the incline of the knoll. The heat on his back was a heavy mantle that tangled up his legs and slowed his walk. He squinted and spit out the taste of dust. He would be very relieved when this assignment was over. The howling of the women and children, the aggressive cries of the males, and the oppressive heat made everything look malevolent. Even the silverwood lodges ahead, rippling with emerald kha, looked threatening. Nefandi knew from his programming that the hermit he had killed had been revered by these people.

He turned up the force of his field and then turned it down again immediately. The drag of the energy made walking too difficult. He would just have to stay alert. His dark, furious face swung from side to side as he reached the top of the knoll. Most of the lodges he saw were empty. But one was alive with kha.

Nefandi didn't bother to announce himself. He tried the sliding door, and finding it unlocked, he shoved it aside and strode in. A wall of heat with the cooked smell of sweat and stale incense confronted him and stopped his advance. The light in the large room was wrinkling with shadows and smoke, and at first only his sensex registered the others: a verdant cloud of kha swirling tighter. His eyes sharpened, and he saw them—forty androgs, each one small and burnished black like silver idols smoky with age. The tight eyes beneath the carved eyelines fixed him with serpent rigidity, and before he could move, their kha cramped to a miniature thunderhead in the lap of a blue-robed androg. The thunderhead exploded, the force of it lifting Nefandi off his feet and dashing him against the doorjamb so mightily it splintered outward.

Even through the buffer of his field, the assault was so strong that he blacked out. He was unconscious for only a moment, but in that time the crowd of né swarmed over him. They were desperately trying to get at him through the field when his alertness jarred back into place.

Infuriated, Nefandi jumped his field to maximum. The sudden burst of power mangled the né around him, exploding those who were touching the field and smashing the others against the walls of the lodge.

'Abominations!' he howled as he leaped to his feet, sliding on the pooling blood and almost falling. He shut down the field so that he could fire bone-crushing spurts of force at the remaining né. The short, pan-faced creatures scattered, rushing for the windows and small back doors, but Nefandi was too fast for them. In moments, the horrible, gibbous cries of the né were silenced, and the room was tangled with the blood-sprawls of the dead.

Nefandi stalked angrily out of the lodge, his fingers trembling. The impact of the energy that had knocked him out was still singing along the curve of his skull. He moved swiftly among the moss-shawled trees and down the incline of the knoll toward the heart of the village. His anger was a knot in his throat, and it squeezed tighter as he realized how treacherously petty his attack had been; the voor he wanted was nowhere in sight.

In the central courtyard of the village, before a natural mist-spring steaming among lichen-darkened trees, the laughing warriors of the Serbota had gathered. A bull's-horn formation of men with fishing spears flanked a line of slingshot-armed warriors. In the trees, a squad of hunters with blowguns waited silent as cats. The screams of the dying né had shaken even the boldest of the tribesmen, and as Nefandi strode into sight with sword in hand and the air flimmering around him as if it were heat-crazed, nervous laughter and the awed name of the Dark One spasmed through the ranks.

The tribesmen trembled with fury and edged toward him, the fishing spears lowered, all of them pointing at his chest. He moved to shut down his field, and as his hand tightened on the hilt control, a brusque female voice shouted over the mumbled chanting of the warriors. In the mounting furor, Nefandi might not have noticed the voice, but he heard it distinctly in his left ear, spoken in a language he understood. *Stop! No more killing!* It was as much a telepathic as an auditory voice. The tribesmen pulled up their spears and danced anxiously around their fading chant.

Nefandi looked over his shoulder. A hefty old woman in a black shift was hobbling toward them, her pasty face set in a grimace of effort. She came up to the edge of the field, the small hairs raising all over her body. *Why are you killing my people?* Her voice snapped in his mind, out of synch with her lips.

Nefandi stared at this woman, who stared back bold as brass. Her face was puffed, and her lank, age-yellowed hair and heavy jaw gave her a masculine cast. There was a watchful cunning in her black eyes and a sly suggestion of dark humor in the surly curve of her mouth. The pale round of her forehead caught the sun like metal.

'I was provoked,' Nefandi replied, his voice muffled by the field. 'I mean no harm. I'm looking for one man—a voor lusk living in this village.'

The old woman's kha shifted subtly across her eyes, and Nefandi saw that she knew.

I'm Orpha, and I'm responsible for the well-being of these people. There was no anger, no edginess to the sound of her voice or the feel of it in his mind. She was uncannily serene, and that chilled his anger to a qualmish dissatisfaction.

'You know who I'm talking about,' Nefandi said. 'Take me to him.'

You must swear by whatever is sacred to you that there will be no further harm to my people. She was serious. Her eyes were fixed on him, and they didn't flinch when his dark face creased in a cruel smile.

'Nothing is sacred, woman. But I assure you, all I want is this man.'

Orpha lidded her eyes and was silent. When she opened them she wiped the sweat from her brow, and turned away. *Come with me.*

Nefandi followed her back down the tusk-lined boulevard to a crude, turquoise-studded hole at the base of a rock mound. He stood diffidently at the lip of the hole, scanning the darkness: no heavy equipment, no metal, no mechanical traps. He shut down the field and lowered himself into the burrow after Orpha.

Phosphor-tendrils were looped over the roughhewn walls, making the rock look varnished. He stayed close to Orpha, his hand on his sword hilt, breathing shallowly of the dank, incense-stained air. From a distance came the splash of underground cascades. His face tightened in the earth-chill misting off the walls, and he had to close his good eye to see clearly with his sensex in the vague light.

They walked past empty chambers decorated with spider-intricate embroidery, grass hammocks, and wooden implements smooth and lustrous as glass. A curving rock-slab stairway took them down past fans of crystal sediment and spurs of black, greasy-looking rock to a high-domed grotto.

A dozen elderly women sat or stood among glazed siliceous deposits shaped like giant mushrooms. Most of them were distorted, their faces and hands silver-scaled in patches, their features bizarrely exaggerated. Sitting prominently on a rock-dome, Orpha and an ancient woman without eyes were the only whole-looking ones.

Behind the women, visible in the magnetic range, was a haze of power the color of his sword blade. It cut a straight line through the grotto, and he recognized it as the power channel he had followed through the desert.

'Why is he here, Orpha?' the blind woman asked, her empty eyes locked on Nefandi.

'He wants Lotus Face.'

'But the magnar entrusted him to us,' one of the other women protested. She had a sharp weasel face, and she signed obscenely at Nefandi as she spoke.

'The magnar's ward was ours for one year,' Orpha replied. 'That's over now.'

'And besides,' the blind one said, 'the magnar is dead.'

'By this one!' the weasel-face shrilled. 'Will we help our own murderer?'

Orpha scowled. 'He's killed enough already. Let's be done with him.'

'What do you think, Jesda?' the weasel asked.

'Doom—can't you feel it?' The blind woman's fingers twitched before her face. 'Whether we help him or not, it's over. Let Lotus Face deal with this deadwalker.'

Nefandi's face hardened. 'Don't call me that.'

Jesda leaned forward, and the thin light caught the flesh around her sockets and made it glint like snakeskin. "You *are* a deadwalker. An artificial being. An ort. You know that, don't you?'

The knuckles on Nefandi's sword hand whitened, and Orpha spoke up: 'Jesda! Let's be done with him.'

'Don't fear him, Orpha.' Jesda sat back, a disdainful sneer on her lips. 'A man angered by a name is not worth fearing.'

Nefandi grinned, stiff as a skull. 'Will you tell me where I can find him?' he asked, his sharp tone shaving the request to a command.

'Ah, deadwalker,' Jesda lamented, shaking her head. 'The né that could have told you precisely where he is are now dead. All we can do is indicate where he might be.'

'Then do so.' Nefandi's anger was tempered only by his wariness. He watched carefully as Orpha flashed a hand signal to the other women. Several of them walked across the grotto and stood within the haze of the power channel, their bodies tiny in the basin of dark stone. They joined hands and began walking a slow circle.

'We aren't as strong as the né,' Jesda said. 'All that we know, they taught us.'

Nefandi heard the ire in her voice, and he didn't miss the anger in the eyes of the weasel and the other women. 'If you mislead me—if there are any tricks—'

Jesda shook her head solemnly. 'No deception.'

The women broke off their circling, and one of them approached Orpha. The old woman inclined her head and listened to the other's whisper.

'Go east,' she told Nefandi. 'After walking several minutes you will come to a grove of black pear trees. From there you should be able to find him yourself.'

Nefandi bowed in mock salute and retreated backwards to the stone stairway. After he had left, the weasel screeched and faced Orpha with clenched fists and a frightened, tearful look. 'We've betrayed our ward.'

Orpha shrugged. 'He's not our ward. It's Miramol we must protect.'

Jesda cackled. 'Protect!' She lost her breath in a fit of silent laughter. 'There's nothing to protect, Sisters. Miramol is as mortal as we are. Nothing lasts.' She beamed up at the spikes of rock. 'That's why we laugh, isn't it?'

*　　*　　*

243

Nefandi emerged into the hum of sunlight and activated his field immediately. The brightness knocked his vision, and he shifted to his sensex. A line of tribal warriors had formed a semicircle beneath the silver-green foliage of the jungle. They began to hiss and click as soon as he appeared, but they silenced themselves when he came toward them.

At the end of the main boulevard several hunters were talking with frantic animation to another warrior and an androg. Both the warrior and the androg were furry with a rosy patina of desert dust.

Nefandi walked east, through the line of warriors and across the boulevard. Suddenly the dusty warrior pushed aside the hunters and rushed at him. Only the urgent squawking of the né kept him from colliding with the field.

Get away from him, Fang! Drift begged, coming up and tugging at Ardent Fang's arm. *The Mothers have taken care of him. He's leaving now.*

Ardent Fang barked at the one-eyed stranger. Fury pounded in his throat, but the obvious futility of attacking the man held him back. He could see the sheen of the shield around him.

'He killed the magnar!' Ardent Fang bawled. 'He has the same light that we saw on the Road. We can't let him get away.'

Drift clung to his arm. *We have no choice. You saw what he did to the né.*

Ardent Fang snarled as Nefandi moved past him. 'Deadwalker, only your sorcery protects you!'

Nefandi ignored the lionfaced distort, rechecked his direction, and entered the jungle along a narrow gatherer's trail. If that old blind witch hadn't lied to him, his work would soon be over. He could return to Cleyre, to a new body, to the simple pleasures of his easy life, and leave behind the heat and the hostility of this place. He ducked beneath a low branch and heard the wood explode against the field. Reluctantly he shut it down, scanning all about him for others, and hurrying his pace down the trail.

Ardent Fang watched him disappear into the bush. He felt the restless urge to heave a rock after him. Instead, he turned to Drift, and they walked slowly down the boulevard.

We must prepare the dead.

Ardent Fang didn't acknowledge the seer. He walked with his head slung forward, his brow pressed tight above his eyes. 'What did the Mothers do to get him out of here?' He kicked a clod of earth to dust. 'Why was he here in the first place?'

Drift scavenged for an answer, but before it could respond, the tribesman spit and turned about abruptly. He loped back down the boulevard and shoved brusquely through a crowd of warriors, hissing back at them as he jogged up to the Barrow. Entrance was forbidden him by tradition, so he stopped over the hole and howled. Drift tried to pull him away, but he persisted until a stick-thin, weasel-faced Mother appeared out of the darkness.

'Why are you bawling, breeder?' the Mother asked in her annoyed, reedy voice.

'Tell me where the deadwalker is going.'

The Mother laughed with disdain. 'Away, brute.'

Ardent Fang dropped into the hole and grabbed the woman by her shift. The material ripped as he lifted her off her feet and slammed her into the wall. 'Where, woman?'

'I-can't-breathe!' she gasped. He tightened his grip, and she gagged. 'To-find-Lo-tus-Face!' Her eyes bugged out, and her lips went taut.

Ardent Fang threw her to the ground and bounded out of the hole. He rolled down the incline and broke into a scramble for the jungle. Drift peered into the burrow and, seeing that the Mother was all right, bolted after Ardent Fang.

The sensors embedded in Nefandi's skull began a low drawl that burred behind his eyes. The voor was nearby, though his sensex hadn't yet picked him out. He pushed through a tangle of fronds and entered a small grove of black pear trees. Flies whined about him and he nudged the field to its lowest setting. From behind him came the thrash of someone running through the jungle. He swiveled and scanned the way he had come.

The lionfaced warrior leaped into sight through a smoke bush, still a distance off. Nefandi fired a single power burst, but by some incredible fortune the distort rolled to the ground the instant it was fired.

Nefandi aimed more carefully and fired a longer burst, but again the warrior lunged out of the way and dashed closer. He already had his knife out, and Nefandi could see the fierce determination in his yellow eyes.

Drift ran hard to keep Ardent Fang in sight, its chest spiked with pain. But no matter how warped its lungs felt, no matter how much its breath seared its throat, it sprinted on, dodging roots and low-lying branches. As long as Ardent Fang was in sight, it could cue him to Nefandi's attacks. *Right!* it fervently sent, envisioning Nefandi's impulse to cut off Ardent Fang's left-dodge.

Ardent Fang spun right, and the blast from Nefandi's sword ruptured a tree trunk with a clout of noise and a spray of wood splinters.

Roll! Ardent Fang rolled, and another slash of energy frittered the leaves above him. *Up left!* He swung to his feet and curled left as invisible power chewed the ground beside him to a mash.

Nefandi was stunned. Ardent Fang was closing in, knife low and tilted forward. He prepared to lash out with a long, sustained sweep of ripping energy, but a daring impulse sparked through him, and he hesitated. With his sword angled to the ground, he crouched, his eyes alert to every ripple of muscle on the distort leaping at him.

He waited until Ardent Fang was in mid-leap, level with his face,

245

arms spread, yellow eyes raving. He threw his field up full. The lunging warrior was blown into a tattering of guts and jumping blood. The force of the impact burst the branches of nearby trees and kicked Drift onto its back, slapping it with a mass of hot roping viscera.

Nefandi shut down the field and rolled to the center of the pear grove. His sensors were squealing, and he did a quick scan of the surrounding foliage. A glaucous bodylight was shifting stealthily through the undergrowth—yellow-golden, the size of a man. He fired a tight burst at it. The leaves danced and scattered, and the kha-light flashed to nothing.

Still on his belly, he scanned the terrain again. The androg was staring at him through the quag of his companion's entrails, too stunned to move. A bird chattered tentatively, and the derelict sounds of fleeing monkeys muffled away. The sensors in his skull were quiescent, and he got to his feet slowly. It was finished.

Cleyre was very close now. He could smell the chicory coffee he would have while sitting on his blossom-arbored patio. He smiled away his fantasy and went over to inspect the body. Was his victim relieved to die—happy to be liberated from the horror of his lusk? Or had the voor become familiar to him? Perhaps they had shared a life. *Useless to ponder.*

He used his sword to force aside the tangled brier. Draped over a fallen tree, head cleaved open, was a silver puma. Nefandi stood baffled and was still pondering how an animal could have had so highly developed a kha when Sumner unfolded from his cover of brambles behind the big cat. He had no kha. The voor was holding all his psynergy deep within.

Nefandi staggered back, but Sumner grabbed his sword arm. He gripped it so hard the muscles unflexed, and the weapon dropped. Nefandi's mind lurched. The black rainbow-glossed face transfixed him—the eyes flat, indifferent, and slow . . .

Nefandi's free arm gouge-slashed and was slapped away. He twisted, but the hand clamping his arm squeezed tighter, tugging him forward. A knife flashed in Sumner's hand, and Nefandi saw the blade slide between his ribs. A scream kicked in his throat. He bucked and thrashed, a dumb hilarity whirling inside him, spinning itself out. His whole body stiffened, and he sagged to the ground, drained, only a shape.

Sumner let the body fall. He looked at the limbs folded like wet cardboard, the fright-glare in the one eye, and a finger twitching, frantic for a signal from the stopped brain. He looked closely to see what it was this man felt. Fear—glinting off the mirror-shard, soaked into the blood-darkening shirt.

He bent over to wipe his blade on Nefandi's shirt, and the hushed voice of the voor opened in him. *You trusted me, Sumner, and I didn't fail you. We're as good as one now. We're the same.*

He sheathed his knife, picked up Nefandi's sword, and stepped over the body.

Drift, blood-splattered and limping, met him in the clearing of the pear grove. Its bead eyes were clouded, and at first Sumner felt nothing from it but a cold mist, shadowy and languid. Then the seer's voice was in his mind: *Why didn't you save him?* It held up its hands, slick with Ardent Fang's blood. *You saw what was happening. Why didn't you save him?*

'The voor was holding my kha back, Drift. If I had moved or even thought, we'd both be dead now. I had to let Fang go.'

Drift stared at him, its bloody hands raised. *I thought you were human.* Its eyes glistened, and its look frayed. It turned away. *You're more voor than man.*

Sumner watched after the seer until it passed among the trees and out of sight. *Nothing is ever lost—it's just on its way back*, he said to himself.

That thought began a slow loop through his mind—a mantra that set his feet moving, that marched him out of the forest and into the sun-veiled landscape of Skylonda Aptos.

He walked hard through the primeval chaos of faulted, uplifted, and folded rock. In a desolate spot he buried Nefandi's sword, and then continued his grief-march. When the sky filled with colored vapors, he sat with his back to a stone arch and stared out at the darkening reef of clouds. He had killed Ardent Fang—the way he had killed Bonescrolls, by inaction. He had let the human love in him die. He *was* a voor, and that awareness immobilized him. Dervishes of red dust spun over the arid flats. Llyr glinted above the horizon, small and glassy. A cold wind deepened.

At dawn Sumner awakened to the sound of metal punching the air—engines. The noise was terrifying coming across the barren and shattered land. He mounted the stone arch and saw a convoy of yellow and brown troop carriers rumbling across the mangled terrain. Green flags stenciled with black and white pillars were stretched over the sides of the treaded vehicles.

Sumner sprinted over swells and folds of liver-maroon rock to intercept the lead carrier. When he was spotted, the convoy bawled to a stop and several men in desert camouflage suits jumped down, rifles ready.

Sumner identified himself and was quickly hustled onto the top deck of the point carrier. With a screech of fatigued metal, the convoy clawed forward again.

Sumner held on to the deck rail, watching the horizon sway. After the commander put aside his radio, Sumner asked: 'What's going on here?'

The commander was young and straw-blond with pale, vivid squint lines radiating from his eyes. He looked Sumner over with a curious and amused expression. 'Your cover's impeccable, Kagan.' The pale etchings in his flesh vanished in the folds of his smile. 'I'd heard the Rangers went all out, but you're amazing.' His little eyes widened to take in Sumner's braided hair, colorful thread-stitched ears, jaguar-toothed neckband, and faded loincloth. 'What tribe are you surveying?'

'Serbota.'

'Ah.' His small eyes became deadlier. 'Then you can be very useful to us.'

Sumner's insides tightened.

One of the radios squawked several code phrases. The commander stepped past Sumner and peered south across the jogging terrain. 'Here they come.'

Several black specks hobbled on the horizon, swimming closer.

'You're taking Miramol?' Sumner asked, his voice vague.

'Taking it?' The commander faced him, amused by the thinness of Sumner's voice. 'We don't take distorts. There's been some voor activity in the area, and we're going to wipe out the tribes that might shelter them.'

Thunder trundled out of the south, expanded to a roar, and ripped the sky above them with a scream wider than ears could hold. Four black-hulled strohlkraft howled overhead, arrowing toward the horizon.

Sumner keeled back against the deck rail. The folds of rock streaming by, the swells and grabens, the benches, spires, and synclines linked and continued. Sumner watched them with numb eyes. They were blending together in his tears. They were becoming one.

The anguish of seeing his tribe destroyed was too strong for Sumner. Violence flexed in his chest, and he knew he would corpse many men if he didn't get away.

He jumped off the troop carrier and rolled when he hit the rocky ground. Behind him the commander was yelling: 'Get back here, Kagan! You don't have permission to leave!'

Sumner kept walking, the heat and the dust splashing at his ankles.

'You're deserting!' the commander shouted, and one of the troopers sighted his rifle and looked for permission to fire. When the commander nodded, the trooper aimed, but Sumner was gone.

Several of the other men had seen him somersault behind a sand drift, and the commander dispatched a dozen men to track him down. They fanned over the broken land and scanned from the vantage of rock pinnacles, but they never saw that ranger again.

The Blood's Horizon

Sumner walked north, letting his voorsense lead him into the mountains. At the snowline, where jagged rime rocks burned in the scallop rays of the sun, he found a ledged cave hidden from the wind. He cleared out the stone shards and sat down against the back wall.

He was psychically spent, ready to sleep or die—but the voor in him was kinetic. Sumner let Corby move through him, watching numbly as the voor took the snakeskin pouch from his side and scattered the magnar's ashes and bonechips on the ground before him. Sunlight glinted off the boneshards like fragments of time, and Sumner's gut twisted cold with the guilt he felt for Ardent Fang as well as the magnar.

You're tired, Sumner, Corby spoke softly, *unstable as smoke. So just watch. I'm going to make you forget your hurt. We're going on a long journey. Together, we'll shadowshoot Bonescrolls.* His fingers spiraled slowly through the ashes in rhythm to the voor voice inside him. *Shadowshooting is timetripping. There are enough kha-remnants here for us to relive all of the magnar's life. In Iz, every tense is now. But it's not him that I want you to know.* His thick hands hovered quietly over the intervolving spirals, and a power unspun in his chest, a power as subtle as the ash was white.

A wind mewled through the disoriented rocks outside the cave and blended into Corby's voice: *It's the Delph I want you to see—the godmind we were born to destroy.* The twilight was a cliché of broken colors, wind-long and redder than meat. *We are going back twelve centuries, following the kha of this life's dust to the time of Bonescrolls' first shape.* The look of things seemed to wear thin. *Time is a secret hidden from itself. We're going deeper into that secret—we're becoming it.*

Sumner's mind blanked. And suddenly he was in a warm and dark place, drifting easily, listening to the muffled banging of a door in a ghostly wind. It was a heartbeat.

Corby understood, and his knowledge became Sumner's: Iz had taken them back to Bonescrolls' early life and then across time, pushed on by Corby's will, to the Delph's embryonic beginnings: they could feel him glowing in the bloodlight, furled in his humming mist, so slippery and small he seemed about to dim away.

Words passed to Sumner from Corby—chanted words—the voorish litany for the unborn:

You will have a name this time, child. And you will have all the limits that go with having a name. You will have a name this time because where you are going everything has a name. . . .

Corby moved on, and Sumner felt time accelerate. He glimpsed the fetus of the Delph expanding, somersaulting in its womb, pushing out. Its head scowled into the light, and it skidded out, clotted and gleaming with the remnants of its fetal life. The scene misted away, blurring off into a sweep of images, all rushing by too swiftly to be grasped.

. . . Where you are going, young one, everything that can happen has happened. Everything that has happened is happening again . . .

The torrent staggered twice, slowing enough for Sumner to glimpse the infant growing: a black-haired child in an oversized yarmulke, standing midway up the stone stairway of a temple; then a gangly youth in military fatigues, a six-pointed star dangling beneath an angular, grinning face, jet fighters in the background; then, flying darkness—

. . . and though you will begin to learn the names of everything in your new life, no matter how many names you learn, no matter what sequence you arrange them in, they will tell you nothing about the source or the end. They exist because you do, to assure yourself that your existence can and does happen, then and now, always, and almost as you yourself imagine it happening . . .

The rush skipped again, and Sumner saw the young man in combat boots, flight pants, a military shirt opened to the waist. He was lying in the tall grass, under leafshadows, a dark, sinewy woman beside him. He held her face in his hands, and the scene roared away.

. . . but names, young life, will be dwarfed by the hugeness of your breath, even though their hunger will be your long traveling, their practice all you will ever endure, their eventual test to perfect the space your passing leaves behind.

The cascade of images swirled to a stop. Sumner experienced himself floating in an expansive gallery of curving pastel-green walls. The place was fluttery with hushed activity. A semicircle of white leather recliners occupied the center of the gallery. Each chair was surrounded by glass-paneled equipment and a canopy of fine-meshed iridescent netting. All the recliners were occupied, green-gowned technicians attending each one.

Corby narrowed his focus to one station where a black-haired man with a narrow, composed face lay. It was the one they had traced from the womb—the Delph. Above the breast pocket of his tan fatigues was stenciled HALEVY-COHEN.

Corby drew closer, hovering for a moment before the brown, wide-spaced eyes and the slender nose. The lips were full, the jaw slim, receding, the hair very thick, meticulously combed back from a square forehead. The features expanded to a sheet of diaphanous light, and they slipped into him.

His mind was a tumult of images and thoughts, and it was a moment before even Corby could feel out his name. It was Jac. And as soon as they found this center, everything else fell into place.

'Jac,' a woman's voice called. He opened his eyes and saw her: She was ancient, her age-loose flesh leaf-brown, her huge, dark eyes milky around the edges, sunken, hooded with immedicable sorrow. But when she saw that he was alert a smile cut across the grain of her face, and she seemed to expand. She threw back her long smoke-white hair and bent closer. He could smell the balsam that was misted over her white caftan.

'I'm Assia Sambhava,' she said affably. 'Do you remember me?'

Jac's eye thinned, and he shook his head.

Disappointment shadowed swiftly across Assia's face. 'No concern.' She wiped off the sheen of sweat from his upper lip with her sleeve. 'Your memory's been broken for a long time. I'm a psychobiologist here at CIRCLE—the Center of International Research for the Continuance of Life on Earth—and I've been treating you since I arrived eleven years ago. Your condition is unique and significant. You have a density in the pontine stem of your brain. While you were in the North African Air Corps it was misdiagnosed as a tumor. Actually, it's a natural development, a folding-inward of the cerebral cortex—something that's happened to one out of every billion humans for the past forty thousand years. I believe it's the next step in brain evolution, and I've been trying to activate and amplify it with RNA supplements. So far I've been unsuccessful, and'—the dark in her eyes thickened—'worse, I may have damaged you, Jac. Your memory's gone, and I haven't been able to strengthen it.'

Jac wasn't listening. Deep within, he knew who he was, but remembering was unimportant. He was waiting, anticipating the inner change that followed most of his treatments. When the patterns of association began to expand, the transfusion nozzle was still touching the blue vein on his neck, and he was surprised at how quickly his mind was responding. (Surprised: that is, phosphofructo-kinase is breaking down glucose-1, increasing neural activity, and so on, a wobbly circle, a snake with its tail in its mouth.)

He wondered if the psychobiologist—Assia, yes—was aware of the speed or even the extent to which these supplements were affecting her subject.

'Do you have any questions—anything to say?' Assia asked.

Jac's eyes looked smoky. 'I hear a voice.' (The human voice, saddest of instruments.)

'I know.' She was very gentle. She took his hand, and the compassion in her eyes was thick as love. 'The supplements intensify it.'

'What do I do?' (Remember your heritage. The Qlipoth are your ancestral enemies, especially the Mâmes, those who move by

251

backward motion, and Glesi, the one who glistens like an insect.)

'A new self is being born, Jac.' Assia's grip on his arm was strong. 'You're changing. Don't try to fight it—and don't fear it.'

Jac sat still, his eyes too quiet. 'What am I becoming?'

Assia's voice was hushed: 'I don't know.' She put a wrinkled hand to the side of his head, and the warmth of her touch was the heat of love. 'We're done for today.' She removed the transfusion nozzle and the net of the bioscanner. 'Stay in the compound this afternoon. The supplement may make you feel woozy. I'll see you again in a couple of days, all right?'

He nodded, and the psychobiologist faced away and began busily authorizing the day's treatment at a keypunch.

Jac's hands were shaky. He breathed deeply to calm himself and pushed out of his recliner. For a moment he was dizzy, and then struggled with an uncontrollable smile as the flow of associations continued accelerating. (Endocrine infatuation, Jac. Your body loves you. Even as it's dying, it takes the time to make you feel good. Bad to good. Life to death. A snake biting its ass. The wheel of the law, rolling.)

Jac relaxed his mind and permitted the network of meaning that he perceived to wash him with its euphoria, his laugh losing itself in the mutter of computer processing. His sensory perceptions were becoming continuous again, sound shimmering like thermal breath, colors audible and odorous.

He walked down the aisle of the treatment-stations to the exit valve as he had done hundreds of times before, each time stranger than the last.

The portal opened beneath a sandstone scarp on the periphery of a large basin separated from the sea by enclosing outcroppings of shale and red-veined rock. The dispensary complemented the landscape and was practically invisible from the outside. Light was splitting from low-lying banks of clouds, falling amber across the flat basin floor that the drilling rain had pitted and caked. On a high vale at the opposite end of the basin, huge black rocks were hunched beneath wet wings of rain.

Thunder grumbled, and Jac moved down a vague path among the cold rays of a cloudy sun. (The wheel of the law, rolling, rolling.) He felt the chemical rush in his blood, the newly introduced RNA tightening through him, peaking to a plateau that moved ahead for hours. He stretched his stride as someone lowered the rain around him. (A harp into the hands of the wind.)

In the billowy blue light from the saltwater aquarium, Assia's thin, white-robed body looked like a wraith. Behind her, in the blackmetal face of a wall-console, one red light burned: The Data-Sync was open, ready to tell her anything.

252

Assia thumbed a series of number functions. She didn't know what she was looking for—something to affirm her work or herself.

A Queen Triggerfish sailed by like a kite, its dorsal and ventral fins a thin memory of wings. She punched in the voice of her data-recall:

'. . . mesoderm, seven days after conception. But why has the process of natural selection, which is stringently economical, given *Homo sapiens sapiens* a brain volume in excess of survival needs? These findings suggest that the cortical overgrowth is a necessary but not sufficient evolutionary step and that these fetuses are the precursors of an imminent new development: the doubling of the cortical fold. Many questions are still left unresolved. Why, for instance, does uterine analysis of double cortical folded fetuses in their seventh month indicate massive reshuffling of chromosomal operons linked with memory-androgen formation? Is this evidence, as Gallimard and Sambhava suggest, that these fetuses may be translating chromosomal records into consciously accessible memories? And why is it that shortly before the end of the eighth month one hundred percent of these fetuses refuse to metabolize steroids, thus precipitating miscarriage? Why has it been impossible to maintain the development of the mutated fetuses in artificial amnionic suspension? Are there other . . .'

Assia snapped off the console. Rainbow-jeweled coral held her gaze: a deathflower, a skeleton-house, a redundant lifecycle frozen in its entity.

Jac twisted awake and sat bolt upright, his face sharp with startled clarity. The flexform he had been curled in was still humming its drowsetone as he swung to his feet and staggered toward his desk. The calendar pyramid told him with its cold light that it had been more than a year since the last time he had stood as he was standing now, aware of what was happening to him.

He sagged onto the swivel stool beside his desk and gazed with torpor at the scattering of data cubes and cassettes. The sky in the window-oval above his desk was precise with stars, and by that slim light he saw that nothing here had changed—he was studying the same things that he had been lost in a year ago: world history, psychobiology, neutrino astronomy—trying to understand the changes. Why had massive earthquakes and tidal waves traumatized the planet for so many decades? And what was this cosmic radiation mutating all lifeforms?

A lion of a cloud slouched across the stars, and his vision numbed. The Voice was silent, but he could feel it close by. If he tried—(I'm always here, Jac—just a cock-in-the-rock's throw away.)

He jumped despite himself. He knew that the Voice was himself, the doubled-over cortex that Assia had been activating for the last ten years. (Don't try to rationalize me. Visions defeat the ego.) His

253

memory was intact now, and diabolically, the first thing he remembered, with a hurting lucidity, was the smell of Neve's hair—his wife. He slapped on a hidden desk-light and rummaged for the message chips she must have sent. When he found the transparent chips, he held them in his fists. But he didn't turn toward the video. There was no time. (The archetype of spontaneity demands that we sharpen our own toothpicks, eh?)

'Voice!' he snapped. (Yes?) He typed out a call-message for Assia on their private line, and then he flicked out the light. In the sudden nerve-darkness, he felt the humid presence of the Other. 'What do you want from me?' (My exigence is extreme, Jac. It's the *possession* of life, the ecstatic climax, that I want. Nothing less will do.)

Outside the window-oval, the moon was rising. He watched the secrecy lifting off the nearby hills as the moonlight rhythmed closer. 'Then why are we separate?' (We aren't. I am you—but you've forgotten who you are.)

The sky silvered with moonlight, and he saw clouds rising above him as tall and jumbled as a sunken land. 'But why do I forget—and for longer?' (Memory is the bone, the carapace. I am the marrow.)

A door snicked open, and an old woman edged in, her white hair shining in the darkness.

'Assia—' He stood up, and she went to him. 'I'm remembering again.'

'It's been a long time.' She took his shoulders in her long, dark hands. 'Do you want to stop the treatments?'

'No.'

'The brainfold can be excised nonsurgically—'

'It's more than me, Assia.' He sat down again and looked up into the darkness of her face. 'Nothing's changed outside, has it?'

'No. Everything is still mad.' Assia sat on the edge of his desk and brushed the sleepwrung hair from his eyes. 'Is the Voice strong?'

'It talks in riddles. And I think it's going to get worse. How is my behavior these days?'

Assia smiled without moving her lips. 'You're kinetic—a lot of walking and exploring.'

'Doesn't sound very profound.'

'You're in an assimilative phase, Jac. We have to be patient.'

Jac spun in his seat and looked up at the cloud's bright landscape. An age ago, Assia had envisaged a dream for him. He was one in a billion with an overfolded cortex. The extra lobe was a genetic quirk, a fist in the brain with the strength, *perhaps,* to reach outside of time and change reality. Much less developed neurologies were doing that on a small scale, reshaping the statistical reality of thrown dice or randomly fired atomic calculators. What could a natural brainfold do if it were mantically augmented?

The first researchers at CIRCLE hadn't presented Jac's situation to him in quite that way. Afraid he might refuse, they had informed him that he had a brain tumor, and for the first year they had experimented on him without his consent. It was Assia who changed all that—but by then he was no longer abstracting beyond the best mantics. He had slowed down. His thoughts had turned in on themselves, and the Voice and a baffling autism had begun. Still, there was Assia's vision. There was the possibility—The possibility that—

Jac turned to Assia with a wide darkness in his eyes. 'I'm losing it.' His words spoke inside his breath, barely audible. 'Tell my wife I'll get in touch with her next time.'

Assia bent closer, her eyes spiderbright and dark. Should she tell him? Neve was dead, lost with millions of others when Africa's northern deserts boiled up into an absurd storm—black rain, 400-kilometer-an-hour winds, whole cities lifted away. No—the slackness in his gaze said no.

Assia helped Jac to his feet and led him back to the flexform. When he lay down, the drowsetone came on, and he rolled into a deep sleep. 'You're not losing it,' she whispered. 'We can't lose what we are.' She kissed him and stood over him for a long while, her body ethereal with fatigue and sadness.

Drifts and depths of clouds trawled the fathomless cobalt of the afternoon. Assia lounged in the fluffy embrace of a tropiform, passing time watching flocks of children at play. The gymnasium was enormous, domed in plastic that was transparent to the full solar spectrum.

At one end the sunlight blazed green in the depths of a drypool, an oval trough of air that had been thickened to the density of water by subquantally alloying it with noble gases. Closer by, adolescents played volleyball in a null field; others strengthened their muscles with magnetic tug-weights; on the mats, two classes practiced dance and gymnastic routines.

But Assia's attention was on the little ones. She was proud to see that they were an intermingling of every race and genetic type, all of them speaking Esper. And with CIRCLE's constant genetic monitoring, there was no danger of inherent handicaps. Mutations were modified in utero or else aborted. It was a severe principle, phyletic hygiene, but it averted much suffering.

Even though she loathed genetic controls, Assia was very pleased with CIRCLE's children. Watching youngsters with faces continually wonder-rapt, she experienced a joy that hadn't filled her since she was a young woman. What would it have been like to have had a child—life swelling out of her own body?

'Our future, eh?' a voice gruffed beside her. It was Nobu Niizeki, CIRCLE's program director. He was short and cube-headed with a thin beard. He took her hand and squeezed it affectionately in his blunt fingers as he sat down. 'The world's gone insane, but our children are still our light.'

'That's what I believe,' she said. 'If there's any hope, it's with the children.'

'Good,' Nobu said in his austere voice. 'That's what I've come to talk to you about.' He let her hand go. His stern eyes were hooded like a weary boxer's. 'That Israeli stratopilot—'

'Jac.'

'Yes—Jac. You've been working with him for almost twelve years now.'

The snake of an artery writhed in her neck.

'Assia—' Nobu's curved face was serene as amber. 'We barely have the resources to feed these children. To survive, CIRCLE's cutting back. We're going to have to reassign you.'

Her eyes closed, and history thickened in her face. 'And Jac?'

'He'll be euthed this week.'

Her eyes snapped open, the light in them diamond-dense.

'It's painless,' Nobu said. 'You know.'

'No.' The word was thick. 'We'll send him back.'

Nobu's eyes curved sadly. 'Assia—the world's changed. There are no places left to send him. It would be a cruelty to turn him loose out there.'

'Then pension him. He volunteered, and he's served well. Come on—what's it take to keep one more man alive?'

Nobu's strong fingers opened before him. 'We don't have it. It's survival now, Assia. Cosmic rad levels have quadrupled in the last year. The whole sky is hot from the galactic flare. Haven't you been following?'

'I've been working.' Her voice was flat and fogged with emotion. 'Nobu, listen—Jac's a top priority. He could be the strongest mantic ever. He could change it all around.'

'It's gotten beyond any one man, Assia.'

'I'm not talking about a man.' She spoke into the black of Nobu's eyes. 'Jac could be a godmind.'

'Bah!' He waved a hand between them to break her gaze. 'I worship every day, but that hasn't stopped the storms yet.'

'Nobu, you know I'm serious. Jac has the best-developed cortical fold in physio history. He's got the biology to sustain a causal collapse.'

Warmly, Nobu took her hand again and held it to his chest. 'Assia, this has been your life's work, pushing human biology forward. You've reaped a lot. You made the mantic reality what it is. You took the ATP-pump and made it human. But a godmind? I love you, Assia. I love what your work has created, but I have to tell you, you're making a joke of everything you've done. Causal collapse, godminds—that's a wide vision. The world, as it is now, is too narrow for that. We need you elsewhere.'

Her eyebrows danced. 'Doing what? Stabilizing soybean growth? Gene-splicing rad-proof babies?'

'Either of those would help.'

Tears filmed her eyes, and she spoke frantically: 'Nobu, no amount of gene shuffling is going to replace the planet's magnetic field. That new radiation out there is our future. We can't hole up forever.'

Nobu took her other hand and shook both of them, slow and strong. When he spoke, his voice was rapt: 'Assia, we need you.' Her soul shrank. 'I don't make policy, but I've got to see it through.' He let her hands go and stood up. 'I want you to take some time off—catch up on the reports and see what's really going on. I think you'll agree with me after you've seen the facts.'

She looked for help, her eyes haunted, but he bowed to avoid her gaze. 'If you need to talk with someone, try this.' He passed her an octagonal card with unfamiliar coordinates on it and no name. When she looked up, he was already walking away.

With a heartquiver, Sumner lurched across time, following his voorstrength to where parabolas of tall trees shadowed a grove of bursting sunlight. Sumner saw a yawp sitting on the darkside of an elm, half hidden in burgeoning ailanthus.

Bonescrolls, Corby informed him. *This was his first shape—a service yawp slaving for the howlies. His name was Rois then—and he was a rare breed of yawp. But let's hear the magnar tell us.*

The voor narrowed closer, using what was left of his mage-power to story-pattern the yawp's psynergy. Sumner's mind blurred into the flux of Rois' mind-language:

Kiutl. The Saints call her the hollow light, Old No Name's under-song. In the boro, the scorchfaced kids, the ones with those furious bodies that can withstand the nervesquelch of kiutl immanence, the ones with that altitudinous light in their eyes—they call her Lami.

Inspired by her, each moment is clear. But—like the sleepy tale of the jinn who for each finger you'd chop off would grant a wish—you can't stay with her long. After a year of daily boff, cortical synapses jam, immanence becomes interminable, and within a week, the ears are gone to marauding boys, the eyes to birds, and the old women have come to dice the spine.

My mother went that way. She was skunked and obscure on kiutl when I was born—a blue and weathered twist of flesh kept alive on corpsemeat, surviving to see her strangle on a cord of vomit a year later. She was twelve and had made enough contacts in Little Eden's research labs to barter me. Without doubt, I would have trashed in the boro without her, so working for the grins as a psitarget was unlimited.

To accrete a sense of gratitude, the grins focused my eyes, dried out my wheezing, and razoredged my wits. Then they proceeded to sketch the game plan: They wanted me to cooperate with other lab yawps while they hammered out the dents in our chromosomes. The grins were gambling with our nucleic pathways. Too few survived. Those that did were genetic diamonds, nucleic bodhisattvas.

257

A spirit of fire, the energy of the gene maze itself, bound us to one another tighter than bone. We were anxious to live up to the status of our blood, to be ultimate yawps instead of trained chimps, even for a few hours. But it wasn't something we prattled. It was tissue delicate. We needed something more. It wasn't long before we got it.

Kiutl.

Mindprobe dredges up infant memories of her gristly snake odor. Deeper, there are fetal associations, chemo-memories of luminous bloodways, phosphorescent yawning zeros, a lamprey itch on my palms, and the glory of her immanence. It was clear to us, Lami lived on in our marrows, but the grins thought they could keep her out of Little Eden. They thought that. Rogue variable, *they called her.*

None of us knew what she'd do to us. But she was our oldest memory, the species guardian. It's no coincidence that kiutl appeared on earth the same year the grins crafted the first slave yawps. All of our ancestors smoked her. We weren't yawps without her. In spite of the danger, we put out for her, and it ended that the grins had pegged her right: She was out of hand.

One of us pulled in a peck of kiutl from a bloodline in the boro. That night, twenty-seven drug-plumed yawps, rabid with vertigo, swaying into distances of the spirit, bastilled the labs at Little Eden. Tech people were garrotted and beheaded, guards hocked and left to bleed to death. The machines, sacred for their indifference, were left solitary in their immanence.

Beato! we lowed, Beato!, *caving in the skulls of every grin we eyed.* Beato! *Dancing with corpses, tearing off their genitals, gnashing them down for the cryptarch, the animal spirit in the meat.* Beato! *Our hackles sequined with stars of blood.*

We watched the burning all night from a lair kilometers away, all of us laughing, fervently dancing to the strategy reports on the shortwave. The horizon was blue with laser light.

All we had left from Little Eden were our wits and our purified blood. Most of us went down to the inner boros of the grin cities and sat in the dark catacombs, praying as one, sharing a silence. A year later, they were all dead of kiutl immanence. The five that remained, that had been teachers trotting from boro to boro, truckled to the spirit. Two outlawed as cunning assassins. Both were eventually broken by their own mischief, but there was carnival to their deaths, whipping up clouds of neuratox on the freeways and in the stadiums. One continued to teach revolt, keys of fire, the perfection of chaos, until she died in a raga storm that erased a whole starboard of cities. The other died in a flash-plague in some inner boro.

Last of the genetic diamonds, I decided foc the rules, foc the story. The Way Out is the Way Through. I used what wit I had to craft an alter ego, fit back into the grin cycle. My psi is plastic, lithe enough after years of boosting to sway a mindprobe. Two years later, I'm payrolled by CIRCLE, pumping my power on the sly, and padding down tree-laned avenues in daylight.

258

My toil's menial, busting suds in a tech lab, but I go everywhere unscoped. My roots deepen their risk each day, sprouting into the domain of grins. No one's looking for me, and those that eye me see a pink-palmed, fur-faced service yawp. I'm doubly invisible, like glass touching the blind.

Gibbous, blue as ice in the afternoon sky, the moon was rising over the sea. It was reason enough for Jac to take a stroll along the beach. (What reason ? Time moves in pieces, a flotsam of events, carrying us along without reason.) Any activity was better than sitting alone in his suite listening to the crazy voice in his head.

After the supplements, the Voice sometimes became intrusive. Assia had told him there was nothing that could be done about it. He couldn't remember why. Something, he thought, about the tumor being near the auditory center of his brain—Heschel's Loops, wasn't it? (Tumor—ah, *tu amor!*) During his treatment, he had been told he would have to acclimate himself to occasional aberrations.

For him, the best diversion was walking. He was unimpressed by CIRCLE's subterranean city and preferred wandering in the open, far from the black glass domes and the laboratory smells.

That afternoon, on his way to the sea, he paused at the edge of a man-made canyon to watch a new boro being excavated. The workers frightened him. They were huge and slimbrained and not at all human. He knew they were called yawps, and he could plainly see how closely they were related to gorillas. But they handled the giant earthmovers and gantries with authority. Stared at from a distance, they looked like giant, sweep-backed men in their treaded boots, brown overalls, and candy-red hardhats. Closer up, though—

As if hearing his thoughts, one of the workers dropped out of the cab of a rockcrusher and ambled over to him. Beneath its shell hat, the yawp's face was bestial: copper skin tightened over prominent cheekbones and thick brow-knobs. Its lips were thin and leathery black. 'Stand back, grin.' The harsh, guttural noise it made was barely comprehensible. It pointed a thick ruddy finger out over the immense pit. 'Sure as night, mama will break your bones.'

A moment staggered by with him gaping at the yawp before he realized it was talking about the earth. (Earth mama—rolling away under us.) He stepped back from the edge and thanked the yawp with a nod.

'Watch yourself, grin.' The creature kicked a clod of earth into the canyon. 'Mama is maw.' He waved, curt as a salute, and lumbered back to his machine.

Jac moved away from the pit and was far out of sight before he understood what the yawp had said. 'Mama is maw,' he repeated, surprised that such creatures could be so—(Eloquent? Poetic? Human?) He decided he would have to find out more about them.

By the sea he paused briefly before an ashy smudge at the base of a

259

dune. It was significant to him, he knew, but his memory was ghosting away. (Memory is grief.)

He had fought for a while, keeping notes on the segments of his past he refused to relinquish: his air squad, his birthday, his mother's name. Then last week the absurdity of clutching at ghosts had overwhelmed him. He had gathered together all his scrawled notes, most of them already meaningless to him, and brought them out to the beach and burned them. He remembered how the wet wood had snapped and how a leaf of paper had fluttered into the air and flattened against his thigh. He had stared for a long time at the charred writing, *Neve,* not understanding.

Sometimes he even forgot who he was. (I assure you, you will know Death better than any memory, though your memories are long as worlds.) Several times each day he chanted: 'I am Jac Halevy-Cohen, born Kislev 5842, in—' He rarely remembered where he had been born.

He slogged through the sand to a steep tidewall black with age. His body was still strong, and he had no trouble climbing the faceted rocks. At the top, he sat cross-legged. Late afternoon sun was driving over the blue cliffs, though half the sky was crowded with thunderheads and rain was smoking off the shale not a hundred meters away. In the sunlight the flat sand and the shallows of seawater glared like blank paper, empty of life, while at the rim of sea and sky an amber haze lingered in long, smoky tentacles.

Rois stepped from around a dune. He was behind Jac, and he stared up at the sweat-darkened back with a malevolent keenness in his animal eyes. Kiutl trances and a careful monitoring of Data-Sync reports had revealed to him who this grin was: a mantic project. The mantics—brain-amplified humans—had created yawps as slaves and had built the boro-zoos that imprisoned them. Rois was determined to strike back, and this grin was the nearest real target.

The lookout yawps on the surrounding dunes were all nodding—nobody was in sight. Rois pulled a heavy freight-hook from under his brown workshift and scurried noiselessly across the sand.

He was on the gravel flats at the claw of the tidewall, weapon raised high, when Jac heard him and turned. For an instant they faced each other across the rocks, and something like a cry, but unheard, wrung in their hearts.

The sky screamed, and a bolt of lightning ripped out of nowhere and blasted the hook from Rois' hand. The explosion flung the yawp across the gravel and left him sprawled and burned, the sun shouting in his eyes.

He sat up, the stink of his burned flesh outcrying his pain. Only the thin plastic grip on the hook had blunted the stroke of fire. He looked down at the purple, plastic-bubbled scald on his hand and then up at Jac. The grin was crouched timidly on the tidewall, but a knowing filled his eyes.

260

Was it nerveshock or did he hear a voice? *All things come to one thing, yawp.*

He looked around for the others, but they were gone. The air around him was sparkling with corneal glints. His view of Jac shifted queerly: The grin's visage lifted away, and instead, a one-eyed man with a writhing scar and a mirrorglint eye was staring at him. He tried to shake the vision off, but the spike-haired face was real—stiff and dark as a scarab.

A sluggish wind swept over him in a tidal drawl, and the spell was broken. He wrenched his body awake, and a terrified bark snapped in his throat. Swimming up through an ocean of fear, Rois stroked to his feet and scrambled down the beach.

The yawp's terror was so strong that Corby and Sumner were thrown off him and left hovering over the ocean tumble. They watched as the distances folded over him, and they saw that he would run through his whole spiral of time, changing forms but unable to change his fate. Twelve centuries later, after an unreal lifetime of blood-wanderings and new becomings, the Delph would track him down and the nightmare would complete itself.

The glide-rail arced out of a mountain-tunnel into the blue twilight. A half moon hung from the belly of Taurus. Below, the sea was the color of steel, the horizon a green wire. But Assia didn't notice. She was sitting in the bubble-eye of the glide-rail, her eyes shined over. Awake in a dream mode, her mind was intermittent, returning always to thoughts of Jac.

At Nobu's insistence, she had taken a tour of CIRCLE. She had sped through the heart of the Andes, and she had seen garden labyrinths in the basins of tamed volcanoes, transparent laboratories hacked into the thighs of mountains, and trellised grottoes tended by singing yawps, the wheat gold and tall beneath artificial suns. Yet none of it reached her, because none of it was real. It worked only for CIRCLE. The famines in Europe and Africa went on. The plagues in Asia and the Americas. The fear everywhere.

There was one more stop on the tour: a mantic Nobu wanted her to meet; the coordinates he had given her on the octagonal card. And then—a chance to be alone with her loss.

The suite she was sent to was small but tastefully furnished: curving cream-colored walls and one-legged chairs arranged about a green glass taboret. The door was fully open, so she knocked and entered. When she was standing in the center of the room, a resonant voice boomed from behind her: 'Assia Sambhava! Welcome!'

She turned, and her heart leaped. Standing before her was a snub-nosed, leering, impish man, his bald head flaring at the sides with wild orange hair. It was like colliding with a daydream, like suddenly meeting Einstein. The man before her was Meister Powa, the

greatest mind that had ever lived: the father of subquantal physics—
the shaper of yawp genetics. It was the same Meister Powa she had
seen countless times in news clips and textbooks—the clown's face as
irreverent as it had looked to her as a child, seventy years before.

'Forgive my informality, but I feel as if I already know you.' He
spoke through the features of a laughing Buddha, his hands clasped
with delight. 'I'm aware of your research on autism and schizo-
thymia, and your mantic studies are legendary. Your work has truly
redefined psychobiology.'

Assia was too thick with disbelief to respond.

'I'm not a ghost.' Meister Powa beamed. 'At least, not entirely.'
He reached out a welcoming hand, but when she tried to take it, her
fingers clutched emptiness.

'I'm a holoman,' the ghost chuckled. 'In fact, this whole room is
little more than a holoid. Let me show you.'

Meister Powa gestured grandiloquently, and his thick body, the
chairs and taboret vanished. Assia was left standing in a chamber
vacant of everything but a flexform lounge and servox food-dispenser.
The next instant, everything popped back into place.

She stared hard at the ceiling and walls, but the holoidal projectors
were well concealed. And well designed: Meister Powa was realistic to
the last detail. The way his pale eyes watched made her feel
self-conscious. He motioned toward the real flexform. 'Please, sit
down. The lounge and the servox are for my guests. Would you like
something to drink?'

Assia declined and sat down, her age-worn features masking her
bemusement.

'I hope you'll excuse my sophomoric indulgences,' he said, seating
himself in one of the ghost-chairs. 'I gave up my bodylife many years
ago, but I still find my present incorporeality amusing.'

'You mean—you really are alive?'

'And not just a laser projection?' Meister Powa shifted in his seat,
delighted, his big belly protruding, his puffy eyes narrowed to needles
of icy blue. 'Of course. This light show is for your benefit. I'm
actually about a kilometer away, inside a small crystal matrix of the
Data-Sync. But I have complete intellectual and emotional versatility.
I perfected the system myself. Other than my meat and bones, which
were always getting in the way anyway, I'm all here. That is, I think I
am.'

He laughed exuberantly, peering at her like a baboon, broad back
hunched. 'As I said, I'm a holoman. Though I must admit I'm not
entirely satisfied with this version of my physical form.' He squeezed
his obesity between his hands. 'But my colleagues, wallowing in
some obscure sentimental backwater, insist that my holoid bear some
resemblance to my old shape. Actually, I'd prefer a little more hair.'
He frisked the firebright collar of hair behind his ears. 'After all, it *is*

262

just a mask, and masks are tools. I've never been uncomfortable with them. Did you know that I was born Helga Olman?' He nodded, wild-headed. 'I was transexed shortly after puberty, though. My parents were shattered, but they adjusted. I made my reputation as Ted Loomis, a hardnosed son-of-a-bitch physicist. It wasn't until I cracked the subquantal problem that I gave up that mask to become Meister Powa. The name's a derisive joke passed on by an abused research assistant. But I like it. Masks sometimes have to be comic.'

Assia felt a spasm of giddiness flutter in her stomach, but she quenched it. This wasn't really Meister Powa, she assured herself. Just a clever holoid—the happiest, most humane technoid she had ever encountered.

He smiled, softly, as if he could hear her thoughts. 'I know a lot about masks. Very often that's all people think I am. But really, isn't everything a mask?' He grinned broadly, as if about to confess a hoax. 'Language. Mating rituals. Diffraction patterns. It's one of Nature's greatest joys, making masks.' His hands opened in a mime of majesty, and his eyes suddenly became calculating. 'Nature is sultry, seductive, a great lover of veils—a Bride. It's extremely difficult to see her real face—but not impossible, mind you! Not at all impossible.' He beamed like a lewd old man. 'Sure, it's difficult to actually *see* the Bride, surrounded as she is by seven thousand veils, each one capable of scarring her irremediably if it's removed without finesse. But it can be done!' His round face shook with certainty, then hardened. 'A bit of advice?'

Assia nodded, amused and interested.

'Never, never, never force yourself. Don't rip off the veils. Gently lift them off, one at a time. It'll take all that's left of your life to do it right, but the satisfaction is measureless. Leave no wounds to heal over, to scar your vision of Her. Slowly, with patience and ease. This is not to say without fire, but don't—as so many do—don't mistake the fire for burning.'

Assia's insides were trembling. She wanted to believe what this man—this holoid—was saying. Oftentimes she had felt that even suffering was a mask. But the children—'Meister Powa . . .'

'Please, call me Helga. Or Ted, if you prefer.'

'What about the world-chaos, the Fall?'

He stared at her closely, and there was something cunning in his smile. 'You think I'm a little cracked, eh? Perhaps even—don't dare say it!—mystical? Nonsense!' His upper lip retracted, unspeakably revolted. 'Let me tell you something. What you call skyfires—are you aware of what causes them? It started over forty years ago, and still most people don't know that a gravity wave shook the earth, slowing the planet, blowing out our magnetic field, and creating the first raga storms. A gravity wave. An echo, merely an echo, of a very odd black hole in the galaxy's core. Odd because the hole has a hole in it! Right now, and for the next thousand years or so, we're right in line with the energy threading out of that hole.'

His eyes bulged. 'It's not so much that we're basking in more radiation. It's the *quality* of the energy that's so utterly different. Its source is the very impossible center of the collapsar. As a result, all the energy patterns we take for granted—weather systems, the earth's magnetic field, the oceans, life itself—are changing, taking on strange, new characteristics. In a sense, the masks are being shuffled, because, we're facing a Bride without veils—a *naked* singularity.' His eyes, pale blue and startled, blinked once, and he sat back.

Assia watched him closely, trying to ferret out his unreality. But her intuition, keyed to his gestures and facial nuances, insisted he was human. Even her mind, which knew better, was fascinated. If only he had an answer for the pain and the suffering.

'The universe is mad,' he went on, his face somber, almost judicial. 'A black hole squats at the core of our galaxy like a spider in a web of stars. Bizarre energies blister the earth's surface with new lifeforms. But maybe it's all happened before. Maybe that's how we got here. Maybe something bigger than pain is being born. And maybe not. It doesn't matter for us. We're not here to censor the cosmos.'

Assia couldn't drive the famine-bloated children from her mind. 'The human race is suffering—maybe dying.'

'It's been that way since before human became a word. We have to live with that knowledge. We have to use it to shape what we can get our hands on. It's one mud of all sculpting, Assia.'

A knot in her belly was beginning to loosen. 'But the pain—'

He leaned forward, his face wizened with conviction. 'You can't get in the temple without laying eyes on the demons.'

Nobu sat in his darkened office staring at a holocular view of Meister Powa and Assia. As soon as he saw the old woman smile, he shut off the viewer. Later, he would scan an edited version of the rest of their conversation. For now, it was enough to know that her emotional withdrawal was over. That silly holoidal of Meister Powa finally turned out to be good for something.

He switched the viewer back on, adjusted it to a sky perspective, and watched Jupiter rise over the Andes. The sky was flaked with stars, shimmering at the zenith with auroral lights—energies from the core of infinity.

Nobu placed both of his hands on his desk, a long, curved, and well-polished slab of petrified wood ringed with iridescent colors. The desk was empty except for two books and a piece of paper. The paper was authorization to euth Jac Halevy-Cohen. He had already signed it.

One book was the Zen monk Dogén's teachings; the other was a copy of the ancient samurai Musashi's *Five Rings,* a book of strategy.

Nobu consulted both often, consistently amazed at how apt the advice was after so many centuries. He thumbed to a passage in Musashi that he felt was relevant: 'For a warrior, there is neither gate nor interior. There is no prescribed outer stance nor lasting inner meaning. Between the warrior and defeat, there is only his practiced ability to sum up changing situations instantly. You must appreciate this.'

Nobu walked slowly about his office, the words opening into a numinous feeling. Blue and white globe lanterns hung from the corners, making the sabi calligraphy on the walls seem three-dimensional. Finally, he stood before his meditating tatami and the blank wall it faced and let his resolution flow out of him. Jac's time was done.

A twinge of apprehension set him walking again. He thought highly of Assia, and yet his mantic capacities urged him to euth Jac. If CIRCLE was going to survive, there could be no indulgences. Assia was one of the first mantics, but her work had become unrealistic—actually, deluded. It was her age—the urge for the long shot, the Big Discovery, before time closed in. He had seen the desuetude in her face. Even with the ion-flushes and the hormones, she only had a few years left. She was already lost in a dream: causal collapse—a paramyth, as bizarre as its antithesis, determinism.

Even so, he didn't like the idea of hurting the old lady. The concept *was* interesting—working with a natural mantic, a man who was born with an extra frontal lobe. If only it could have been activated—in what ways would he have differed from a mantic with an ATP-pump in his brain?

He sat on the edge of his desk, the sides of his jaw throbbing. This was not the time for pure research. For the past forty years, since the planet's magnetic field was knocked down by the gravity wave, the sky had been wide open. In a few decades, the cosmic radiation beaming from the galactic core had changed the world; mutation patterns were unguessable; hundreds of thousands of new viruses had appeared; hybrid species, like corn and wheat, had turned off genetically; and the word human had become an uncertain term—Why were codon changes so many magnitudes higher than rad-levels could account for? What was coordinating the metaplasia that was literally creating whole new species? And who were these telepathic people who called themselves voors?

No—this was not the time for pure research. Only applied studies could hope to save their children. Jac had to go—and Assia would understand. Or she wouldn't. It didn't matter.

With a decisive rap of his knuckles, he thumped the book lying beside him on the desk—Dogén. He flipped it open randomly and silently intoned the first words his eyes touched: 'Do not spend a long

265

time rubbing only one part of an elephant—and do not be surprised by a real dragon.'

Low tide and the sea in the air. Jac wandered up from the beach, on his way to his suite. A thin rain was misting out of the gray sky, and the herded tidewalls were reduced to shadows in the thickening fog. It was going to be a restless night, and Jac paused to watch the pale sea collapsing before he went in. (You're being followed, friend. Haven't you noticed?)

The Voice was right. Human shapes made strange by the haze were approaching him from the sea. There were two figures, huge but aqueous with distance and mist. It was hard to tell if they were coming at him or just passing. He decided to go in immediately but then stopped himself. He was dying, his brain cancerous. What was there to fear? (The drouth of fear.)

Not until they were almost on top of him did he see that they were yawps—long-armed workers. He remembered the lightning-blasted yawp he had seen the day before, and alarm whined in his muscles. 'Nothing to fear,' he said in traditional yawp greeting, but the two didn't respond. Their eyes looked chalky, lifeless, and (Too late) he realized something was wrong about them. He backed a step and turned to run, but they bounded up to him, and thick hands took his shoulders. He didn't resist as he was lifted and slung over broad shoulders. Without fear, though charged with anxiety, he breathed in the smoky odor of yawps and looked down at thicktoed feet scurrying over the ribbed sand.

They ran close to the sea where their footing was firm, moving gracefully despite their burden, pacing the wind. Jac hung limply, aware that they were heading south toward the boro. A giddiness thinned out his thoughts. The Voice had disappeared. Not even the sensation of the watcher lingered. Grinning, almost laughing aloud, he watched the shadowed hulks of dunes angle by.

When the first signs of the boro appeared—white-domed modular cottages—Jac tried to lift his head to look around. He had never been in the boro before. But the yawp carrying him shrugged his body farther back, and he contented himself with following the upside-down cottages as they limped by.

A hazy, blossom-thick odor from the many yawp gardens filled the evening. Mingled with it was the charred yawp scent and a smell he didn't recognize: a forest fragrance, redolent as river moss, only sweeter. The odor was nostalgic, dreamy, and it thickened as they jogged deeper into the boro.

The running stopped all at once, and Jac rolled off the yawp's back. He stood shakily, facing a dense crowd of yawps. Most were workers, giant and gray-mantled. But closer were smaller yawps with sharper faces and shorter arms, wearing brown cloaks. Their eyes were not listless like the workers but animated, alert, almost human. One yawp in particular stood out. It was a female, thin and elegant, her hackles silver and braided. She was wearing a black, fluted robe and a distinguished headpiece of leather, gull feathers, and tiny red snail shells. Beneath an age-furrowed brow, her eyes were bright and trenchant. 'Nothing to fear, grin.'

Jac returned the greeting and glanced at his surroundings. They were on a patio of moon-pale stones, guarded on two sides by tall arbors of gnarled vines. White-domed cottages were behind him, the crescent windows sparking with red evening tapers. Ahead of him, looped with fog but visible beyond the yawps, was the massive banyan forest where the workers lived.

The sweet mulch scent was thick in the air, and Jac quickly noticed where it was coming from. The yawps were passing around a smoke-frothing clay vessel, each in turn inhaling the milky fumes.

'Why am I here?' he asked the old female.

'Lami spoke of you,' she answered, accepting the smoking vessel and immersing her face in the vapors. She spoke through the smoke: 'Rois said you were a grin abomination. But Lami turned against him and protected you. We follow Lami.'

Jac had heard of Lami, a yawp deity, but he couldn't remember anything about it. Was he to be some kind of sacrifice? He felt so at ease, free of the intrusive commentary of the Voice, that he didn't care what the yawps did with him. He was a dying, brain-twisted amnesiac anyway.

The black-robed yawp offered him the clay vessel—a purple-glazed bowl stenciled with runes he didn't recognize. The bowl was hot, but he held it and drew a long draught of the balmy fumes.

That instant someone in the group twanged a box-harp, and the wiry, tremulous note pierced him. The feather-crowned yawp took the bowl from his hands, and he saw her refill it with oddly shaped blood-red leaves.

A corolla of green light hazed around the yawps' heads, and a shudder of dizziness forced Jac to sit down on the damp stones. An excited murmur passed among the yawps, and a spangle of harp notes trolled into the night. The old female bent close, her face sheathed in a gold macular light. She held out a fire-drenched hand, and he heard her voice in his head: *Stand and face Lami.* The shock of hearing a voice in his mind, so remindful of his own delusory Voice, immobilized him.

Hands took him from behind and lifted him into a blaze of tinsel colors ripping with voices: *Lami Botte! Lami! Delph Botte! Delph!* But unlike the Voice, these could be turned off. He forced the chanting out of his head and stood beatific and tall in a forge of colors.

Distantly, he was aware that he had inhaled some kind of drug. He sensed its ministrations in his muscles, lifting him off his bones. But more immediately, he felt his vastness, his connectedness with all

267

those around him. And he understood just what Lami was. He could see the deity—a casein glow leaking out of their round, hackled heads, pooling above them, swelling. It was their group-energy—a power bigger than all of them.

The old female stood before him, her face silver. Far off, in the back of his mind, the murmurous chanting continued: *Botte Lami! Botte Delph!* The silver sheen masking the old yawp peeled away, revealing eyes of hungry intelligence. A rapport thickened between them, and for the slimmest instant, Jac became the yawp.

Simian memories crowded him, a flurry of images: the smooth-grained wood handle of a tool, sapid sexual feelings, coarse clothing, laughter lunatic as a jungle shriek, and odors of food—the whole reality of boro life. *Help us!* The yawp's cry transfixed Jac. So many emotions and, dominating them all, a pallor of helplessness, servitude, shame.

With a tremendous shock he realized that the yawps were beseeching him—as if he had the authority to grant them power and dignity. He cringed, and the chanting in his head swelled louder: *Botte Delph! Delph! Delph! Delph!*

'Make them stop,' he told the old yawp. But she was entranced, her eyes rolled up, the floury light of Lami blurring her features.

Botte Delph! Jac blotted out the telepathic chanting and concentrated on the energy that was gathering over the serried throng: white, curded, and thick. Its edges were laced with darker colors, a bruise of violets and blues that bled into the night's darkness. The violet energy glittered in the rain-misted air, and his eyes followed its traces hypnotically. Until he saw, with a jolt of horror, that the blue power was coming from him! It was smoking off his body!

Fascinated, he watched the space around him flex, tendoned with dark blue light. Closer, the energy became even darker, a dense violet. And where his flesh was, or should have been, a palpable blackness throbbed.

Jac's mind wobbled. Gazing into the core-darkness of his body, he felt himself teetering on the brink of a sundering realization. Vaguely, he sensed truths that he knew could destroy him. Glimmers of understanding flitted across his brain: He was bigger than he knew, and getting stronger, drawing strength from the sky, from the very core of the universe. The Voice was not a delusion. It was real and he, the listener, was the dream—

He balked, and a liquid blackness welled up and absorbed him.

Jac's eyes trembled open. He was in a waking stupor, timeless as a dream. Cold wet sand cushioned his body, and the sleepy rumbling of the sea filled his head. He was looking up into the green ether of early dawn. (Listen, wisdom is air, the color of drowning. Breathe deeply.)

The shore patrol found him an hour later and took him to the

Wards. He lay there all day without eating or speaking, which the medics didn't like. He also had a density in his brain and residuals of a psiberant in his blood. The medics didn't like that either, and when the program director's authorization arrived to euth him, they were relieved. The facilities of the Wards were limited and over-extended—there just weren't enough resources to maintain drug-abused terminal patients.

When Assia arrived, the medics were wheeling Jac to the End Ward. They flashed her the authorization when she stopped them, but she stood firmly in their way. 'This is my subject,' she protested, the deep lines of her face webbing sternly.

'Not anymore,' a female medic told her. She was young and militant, her hand on a copy of the euth order clipped to the unconscious man in the wheelchair. She tapped the order. 'Your project's over.'

Assia's frown darkened. 'All right—but I'm appealing this. Take him back.'

The medic shook her head, indifferent as a knife. 'There's no time for appeal. We have strict orders.'

Assia stepped closer, and a long-muscled medic cut her off. 'We'll jeopardize ourselves if we don't follow through on this.'

The old woman reached beneath her caftan and slid out a slender black-glass tube with a sharp red toxin sign on it. The medics visibly tightened, and the female reached for her wrist-call.

'Touch that and everybody dies,' Assia whispered. She wagged the vial, and the medics held their hands away from their bodies. 'There's enough neurotox here to kill everybody in this ward twelve times. So listen closely.'

After locking away the medics, she discarded the empty neurotox tube and wheeled Jac out to the sandcart she had left in a back court. She injected him with a serum to counter the sopor and drove him out of the compound.

Jac didn't revive until Assia reached her destination: a cedar shack with a tin roof in a choked clearing of wild apple trees. They were deep into the hills, the sky cantled with streaming auroras. 'I used to come here to rest sometimes.' She helped Jac out of the cart. He was bird-light and dizzy. 'I can't stay here,' she added. 'I want to drive down the coast and confuse whatever security they'll be sending after you.'

Jac shook alertness into his head. (The brain is a flower that eats oxygen—and where are its roots?) 'Assia—there's no reason for this. I'm dying anyway. This tumor's devouring me.'

Serifs of starlight glinted off the tears in her eyes. 'There is no tumor, Jac. Don't you remember?' She held his face in her hands. 'Maybe it's wrong to leave you out here. There's nowhere to go. But I won't let them kill you. If that's what you want, follow this road back

269

or wait here. Otherwise, you'll find camping equipment and some provisions in the shack.' She let his face go. 'Goodbye, Jac.'

She moved to go, but Jac took her hand. For a deep moment he studied the way her face had formed, the tireless dreams outwearing the flesh. He was the last of those dreams, he saw, and that made him so sad his eyes ached.

He watched as the old woman got back in the cart and drove off. He didn't know what to do. (Trust the anamnesis of the future, my friend.)

Jac decided to die. If the mantics at CIRCLE couldn't cure his brain tumor, he preferred to be euthed than die in the wilderness.

He was halfway back to CIRCLE when he remembered the god-power he had felt with the yawps. (Forgive the long darkness. Such indulgence not to have kept you informed—such waste, and such is the blood's surprise.)

He left the road and angled down slopes of salt shrubs to the ocean. He walked over the dunes and along the thundering edge of the sea trying to sort everything out. But he couldn't think—except to know that he, what he thought he was behind his eyes, was tiny and insignificant. (What's happened to you? You who stole the secrets out of the listening of the dead? Why are you trembling?)

The soft, mystical shine of the moon on the water calmed him. He was alone and almost at peace—the wind riffling his hair, waves rasping up the beach. (You've become nothing but territory. Death is trapped in your bones like grain in wood.)

What did it matter if it was a brain tumor or another mode of being—either way, he was nothing. (Shut your ears big, Jac. Let the darkness come unrolling from your eyes and your fingers blow longer all in the stillness, deeper, where the textures in the air end and do not restart, to my elusive conclusive whereabouts.)

Jac stilled his fear, held himself centered, alert to the night wind and the dim phosphorescence of the incoming waves. But the rumble of the ocean was growing fainter, and the weak light of the skyfires and the dull shapes of sand were thinning. His senses were setting out, leaving him alone at the center of nothing. (The body with its senses is need. This need is not yours. I am the way out. The emptiness is my door, a wing, a way of flight, half an angel. Enter, and you become the rest.)

He howled, but there was no sound, not even a muscular sensation where his throat should have been. He clutched for his body. Nothing was there. He was a mote of awareness, free falling through the void. (The human numen.)

A yawn of time passed before his senses began to swarm back, filling up their hollows one by one. He was sprawled in the sand, blind and deaf, until, gradually, the splash of the waves filled him and the skyfires wavered into view.

He moaned and hugged himself, rocking to his back. But then it began again. Already, his eyes were moving on, his vision darkening, sounds becoming muffled. (Will it go on? It happens, you know. Things lose their gravities. No fingers to grasp. No tongue to reassure. No eyes to set the limits.)

Panicky, he heaved himself to his feet. Textures were sliding out from under him, and in a desperate effort to keep himself centered, he grabbed the great bones massed in his legs and pounded the earth. He began with blunt, clumsy stumbling, kicking the sand, turning on the pivot of his gravity. Slowly, he worked up an incredible velocity, wrapping his motion around him like a shawl of sensation to hold him together.

He whirled a long time before his ears returned—the forlorn cry of some bird. (Jac, you'll have to learn to settle for the skins of things at times like this. You've lost the edge to your life that only less can add.)

Jac dropped to his knees with exhaustion and tottered quickly back to his feet. He knew that if he stopped moving he would lose control. It was very clear now what he had to do. Not daring to think about it too long, he dashed forward and fell to his face in the wet sand. With desperate determination, he swayed upright and staggered into the sea. It was cold, and his legs felt vague and rubbery pushing against the water. A wave slammed against his chest, turning him sideways, but he shoved on, losing his footing and letting himself slide into the deep water, into a darkness he already knew.

The alarm she had set startled Assia from the depths of a mordant sleep. She tapped it off and pulled herself out of the flexform and into her sandals. Like an ice-heavy draft, she moved across the suite, stooped, her sandals whispering. When she entered the mirror-circled bathroom she stiffened, and a tight cry broke in her mouth. In the mirrors she saw herself—a tall woman with night-fall hair, dream-luminous eyes, and an amazed, bonecurved, adolescent face.

Nobu stood before the sheet glass window, linear and solemn, with a pensive glow on his face. He was staring down past the tidewall to where the moon was poised on a dune's white shoulder. Auroras wavered crazily over the sea.

WHAT WE KNOW OF REALITY ARISES FROM OUR DISBELIEF IN IT was blocked out in silver luminescence on the tidewall. It was one of many bizarre graffiti that had appeared throughout CIRCLE during the night. Farther down the beach, blazing on the sand itself, were the platinum words MAMA IS MAW.

Red lights flashed to the left. Nobu knew where they were coming from, and he chewed his lower lip. The yawps were rebelling. Not

271

simply running amok but actually playing out a well-rehearsed strategy. They had seized both the armory and Data-Sync which controlled most of CIRCLE's functions. It was impossible, he knew that. Yawp neurology wasn't specified enough to allow that kind of independent behavior, but they were doing it.

Nobu closed his eyes and leaned his head against the long window. Its coolness was soothing and helped to sort his thoughts. So much had happened—all of it impossible. Jac Halevy-Cohen had vanished without a trace; not even the sender-chip embedded in his skull could be tracked. A high-energy pulse from the galactic core was scrambling all their communications, leaving them truly disorganized. But no energy-wave could be that powerful. Night-glow graffiti . . . warrior yawps . . . It took all his inner resources to suppress his rage at the rampant absurdity of it all. He modulated his breathing: two deep breaths, one shallow, two deep. . . .

The yawps had seized his building while he was sleeping, and he had barely gotten out alive, taking with him only his clothes and a sheaf from his journal. Among the pages he had salvaged, he had found a letter from Jac. He couldn't remember receiving it or putting it in with his notes. It was undated, waterstained and apparently meaningless. It lay face up where he had tossed it to the floor.

'Listen, Nobu, I have something to tell you. Finality is the one door, the one way out of our pain and uncertainty, but it doesn't exist. We go on. Everything goes on. Why is there no end? What we think we've left behind moves through us. We're merely egos, the ghosts of our blood, unable to hope for judgment, only another moment. We pass on our genetic material, we pass on time. Do you think perhaps something passes the other way? What? What is time? And what are our chromosomes becoming? Can we know? What terrifies me is the possibility. We carry the beginning in our blood. We constantly try and fit it to our lives. We never get it just right. But what if we do? What if we really do? Only your movement distinguishes you from this ambush of stillness. Stop.—Jac.'

Nonsense, Nobu thought. *He cracked—it finally happened.* He pressed his forehead against the dark glass and began his breathing rhythms again.

When he felt better, he looked out into the night, his eyes as tight as his face. Far below him, several birds like pale, dirty socks were perched in the moonlight. He leaned against the window, trying to make out how many there were.

A startlingly loud cry jerked him upright—but too late. The great glass, screeching open under his weight, gave him a flying step into the night. For one delirious moment he could see far down the beach to where the CIRCLE fighters were entrenched. The tidewall there was blazing, lit up by eerie blue laser arcs flashing red against the rocks. The dark ground swung up at him like a bad dream—

Nobu lay still, stretched out flat, his face pressed into the asphalt. The blood pooling around his limbs and face felt warm and sticky, though he was shivering. *Mindless,* he muttered over and over to himself. *Mindless.*

Or was it? The initial pain and shock had thinned quickly, leaving him to wonder if, perhaps, some real but hidden part of him had caused him to lean too hard against the glass, had caused the glass to give way—some benevolent power, too long thwarted by his allegiance to machines, devices, calculations—a benevolent God in whose grace it was better to be dead than to serve the inorganic.

'Cut the crap, Nobu.'

The voice shocked him, because he recognized it from Assia's progress-tapes. His hands pushed feebly against the asphalt, vainly trying to lift his head. 'Jac?' His voice was a weak, garbled caricature of his own.

'You look pretty shitful,' Jac's voice said.

I must be delirious, Nobu thought.

'Don't you wish,' the voice said. 'Here, let me give you a hand.'

Nobu felt a bright, magnetic coolness touch him all over his body, and he was lifted. He squinted against the full glare of the sun, though it was still night. A figure in black was wavering before a silvery sky. It bent closer, and Jac's grinning features came into view. 'Seeing dragons?'

In the narrows of light along the soft ferrous seam of her closed eyelids, Assia sensed him. He was so close to her that she had to be very quiet to feel him at all. He wasn't Jac anymore. He was a hollowness in the smoke of her feelings, a hole plummeting out of time into a dreamy vacancy filled with whisks of light, quiverseen beings—more than the sponge of her brain could absorb. A great sleepiness swelled in her throat, and she swallowed it and opened her eyes.

She was alone at the top of a garden tower that hadn't been there that morning. Earlier, with a sickening awe, she had climbed the spiral stone stairways leading here. She had watched yawps walking among the white-leafed forests and the brookfalls of luminous rainbows that had appeared overnight. In the distance she had seen what was left of CIRCLE: the steely wreaths of collapsed buildings and the smoke-worming stains patterning the dunes in scalded, glossy colors—the slick reds and oranges of glass-sand fused by last night's laser battles. A crooked brown cloud hung over the rubble of the Data-Sync.

She looked down at the firm flesh of her hands and the thick darkness of her hair, and again she felt lightheaded, farouche, miry with goofy emotions: She was an old woman with the body of a seventeen-year-old! The risible husk of her logic rang with a laugh she was too scared to voice. What was going to happen to them all now that a man had become a god?

For the first time since she was a child, Assia cleared her mind and meditated as her father had taught her. She wide-focused on the moss-veined trees and the forest floor coined with light. It was easier than she remembered. Her body was an open lens, seeing everything: leaves like bright particles, the starlings listing among the branches, each bird a jigging molecule. She was on her own now, she knew, her brain curled quietly in its shell.

Nobu had walked up and down the beach countless times, feeling nothing, seeing everything. He wasn't dead, though he knew he should be. It was becoming clearer that he didn't know very much. For days, weeks, lengths of time he stopped measuring, he strolled through shale coves and over strands rubbled with drift-wood and sea-smoothed rocks, watching the ocean come and go, the spine of the shore changing shape like a slow cloud. Fear, awe, memories, all deserted him much sooner than he would have thought. No need to eat or sleep. No need even to think, he finally realized. *Is this death?*

No—he was aware. He would just have to go on looking.

He stravaged the wind-lashed inlet mindlessly. Time became meaningless as static, distances longer than time. And finally, after he had long forgotten that life had ever been any other way, a jolt of total understanding banged through him. He toppled from the rondure of stone where he had been watching the tide come in and tumbled down the slipface of a dune. On his back, staring up at the night sky, he looked past the skyfires and, with his new insight, began to decipher the awesome braille of stars. There was nothing separating him from them. Inner, outer, up, down, were all arbitrary. The whole sky had meaning for him now. And he could see, plainly see, the entire history of evolution projected onto the night from his chromosomes.

All of the most trivial details of organic development, beginning with the first spark in the Proterozoic slime, were there in the sky-shadows. As he read, at last he understood the history of consciousness and saw the next human form, the voor children born looking backward, remembering their ancestors, their sentience a telepathy that crossed worlds and that ultimately united them with everything —an infinite reunion.

He was so absorbed that he didn't notice the sky brightening—he had arrived and nothing was missing. All the organic forms stood before him like clouds, and he trembled, feeling the unnamable stillness that united them. Progressively, his senses sharpened, became more focused.

His senses had all been living in the past. They were the stepping-stones of consciousness, floating in nothing. In them was the shifting pattern of the world, and between them was stillness, nothing.

He became his senses, and he was aware of the stars dimming, a thin, silver line following the corner of the sky.

Daybreak, the sun rose from its bed of rocks, and colors flowed into everything. Nobu returned to the stillness between, already understanding that his participation in the world was over, and that he was being drawn inexorably toward the unity he had glimpsed beyond the blood's horizon.

Jac Halevy-Cohen strolled along the beach, spheres of hyacinthine light dancing around his ankles. He was a godmind, vaster than thought or memory. At his whim, a basilisk of water flared out of the sea, sparks of flowers limned his path across the sand, and music jeweled in the air. And yet, he was a man. 'JAC HALEVY-COHEN,' the collapsing breakers blared in four-part harmony.

He could do anything he loved. Single and yet multiform, he was a mangod. He had changed reality to free the yawps from their human masters. He had youthed Assia, the old scientist who had helped create him. And he had sent the program director, Nobu Niizeki, moving sidewise through time. All of this he had done out of love. Even Niizeki was lovingly dispatched down the beach in a spume of chilled light, vanishing, flesh and thoughts, along the wavecurve of time. The unity of love was bigger than the memory of the world, and at the far end of Nobu's wanderings, Jac the godmind knew, the program director would be free, released to light, wholly regnant. That man would know wholeness.

Incredible sprays and fans of suspended water spun intricately in the air, bound by chains of birdsong. Jac was a godmind—and nothing was impossible for him.

The thought of thought circled Jac deeper into his godmind, and he realized how small and loud the mind part of him was. He saw, in a blind silence of sudden fear, that his thinking was the least of him. He had feelings, urges, fleshdreams that he had never been aware of but that would live through him over the ages. He was the godmind of his whole self—sinews, veins, boneworks: All had their dreams and their loves. He wasn't pure psynergy. He couldn't be—unless he loved away his physicality. But that would take tens of thousands of years, for the body, he understood, is the unconscious of the world. And he—insane with psynergy—was the Mind of the Species, the witness of the body, living to see the dreams, myths and fantasics of the human race exhaust themselves through him.

Time was transparent for Jac, and he saw across centuries of sexual pith and mental mirroring to the emptiness to come. Millennia from now, in the tepid residuum of canceled-out desires, he would at last be free of his humanity. But it would take aeons.

Anger coiled, and the spiracles of air-dancing water rainbowed and vanished. A tormented cry crawled over the dunes as the reality of his destiny became conscious: He was going to be trapped for ages in the fantasies of his biology! Would he ever survive to his fulfillment? His soul shrunk around his omniscience as the knowledge fleshed itself that he was not the only godmind on the planet.

Fear blazed.

Astounded, Jac lifted above the surf of time, and he saw the Others. The sea air was filled with their watching. Discarnate beings rapt with lucidity saw deeper into his simple mind and his mutability than he ever would. They were godminds from fierier realities—they had already lived through the flesh-hungers of the worlds that had shaped them, and now they were terrifyingly free, sublimed, riding the stream-psynergy from the galactic core, existing in the cosmos *as* the cosmos! Already they were arriving, reshaping the earth, aware of the insatiety and the racial dreams that limited him.

Fear flexed powerfully around Jac and then disappeared into the declivities of his future. He saw then that he had a shadowself, a fear-self, that would, out of tenacious self-love, try to protect him from the Others or make an end of time.

In that moment, Jac was aware that his godmind would not tolerate other godminds. He was too small to permit Them near him. He needed aeons to grow, aeons alone self-floating in the too-willing wonder of his lust.

Jac stopped. The air had opened in front of him, and he was staring at a large red-haired man in a cave. The vision narrowed, and he drew closer, near enough to see that the shadow on the man's face was a black burn stain. The calm breadth of the stranger's face filled all of Jac's awareness. The air-blue eyes, flat and downslanting, touching the world softly, looked into him, and Jac's mind went pale.

The godmind willed meaning into the vision, but nothing happened. He willed to know. Still, nothing.

The man in the cave leaned closer, fascinated, and the size of his shoulders awed Jac. Only then did he comprehend. The fear that had surged out of him a moment ago had reshaped the future. This nameless man with the haunted, in-looking eyes was the physical shape of his fear—his shadowself. The man, somewhere in time, was him, his secret self, as unaware of his psynergy as Jac was conscious of his godmind. He was the one, more than the alien godminds, who was his enemy and yet himself—the part of himself that would have to die so his godmind could live.

Terror glowed in Jac, and the sea groaned.

Sumner woke in the mountain cave overlooking Skylonda Aptos where the shadowshooting had begun. Corby was a dulcet whisper in his cells: *The Delph won't let us see more. The vision is over.*

Sumner hulked over his knees and stared hard at the mountain peaks balanced in the westering sky. *Now do you understand what it means to be the shadowself of the Delph?* the voor asked.

Sumner's mind was numb from the shadowshooting. Sleep swelled in his lungs like the dread of time, and he sagged to his side and closed his eyes.

As he slid into unconsciousness, a powerfully detailed scene dominated his mind and lingered before passing wholly away: Assia, young and dark, stood before a cedar shack in a clearing choked with apple trees. On the wooden door, in silver script, was a message:

'Assia, there's always more. It never ends. I hope your new life will show you that. Look closely at yourself. You'll never age again. It's true. We make all the rules.

'Listen, if this depresses you, you know the way out. Stillness of mind is a door. Memory, the continuing history of grief. As long as the past is real, you will remain. Let's look at your new life again: Nothing happens by circumstance. Or else everything. What matters is that you go through events to the stillness behind them. Things *can* lose their gravities. Think. All you ever held drifting beyond direction . . . No? But we're making progress. You understand that you can't understand. The body is the unconscious of the world. So what can you possibly do now? Everything! At all times! You see, it's like digging holes in the river, like forgetting one thing to remember another. It's because another persistence pushes under the blood, because we're doomed to squint after absolutes, because nothing less will do. Good. Already you've begun to find your place. Now get a mirror, look ahead, and remember your mother, your mother's mother, your mother's mother's oldest ancestor, green, close to the earth, not believing in you. Remember, the innocence you own waits where you left it, deep as the last of your fear.—Jac.'

Godmind

The dream was marvellous but the terror great.
We must treasure the dream whatever the terror.

—Gilgamesh

Destiny As Density

The skin of Sumner's soul shivered. He woke, stupefied, huddled in a corner of the cave where he had slouched during the voor trance. A cold wind unraveled itself in the mouth of the cave, scattering the last of the magnar's ash. Sumner hugged himself tighter. He was wearied and depressed. Bonescrolls, Ardent Fang, Drift—everyone he had loved was dead now.

We are one, the voor thought within him, his psychic voice sounding narrow. Shadowshooting had exhausted Corby. *It's time to go down the mountain. We must leave quickly.*

Sumner closed his eyes and averted his attention from the voor. The shadowshooting had terrified him because it had been as real as his own life. Dizzy with fatigue, he fought his own heaviness to sit upright.

Corby's voice was speaking within him—he could feel the voor subvocalizing—but he wasn't listening. He was in selfscan, hearing blood whispers, the tread of his heart, and the low sibilance of immense air currents floating over the mountain peaks.

Sleep bruised his alertness, and he struggled a moment with thoughts and dreamworlds. A mosaic of faces wheeled in his mindark: Jac and young, longboned Assia, Nobu somnolent as a voor, and a crowd of yawps. The simian faces reminded him of Sarina in the riverain forest to the north. He half-thought he could return to them. Perhaps they would free him from the voor. . . .

His thoughts blackened into sleep.

Sumner woke hours later, a tuneful energy spinning around him. The voor was diminished, a mere tic of feeling far back in his mind. A hollow moon rose above the jagged horizon while he continued to sit, his mind windowed to the mountains.

After all sensation of the voor had vanished, Sumner unfolded from his crouch and lumbered out of the cave. With his mind clear as the thin air around him, he hiked along the margin of a glacial scree littered with sharp, bony rocks. He walked to strengthen his selfscan and to forget the pain of his grief. He marched until his knees buckled. Then he sat on his heels beneath a fan of rock and stared down through a pygmy forest of pine. Several ice pools glossed with afternoon light were visible on the southern horizon. Above them, a flock of birds was undulating west, bucking strong winds.

Sumner closed his eyes and sensed the voor rising through his fatigue: *Sumner, I'm real. You're not ignorant. Don't ignore me. I can teach you the forgotten language of the world. The secret beast whispers in the rock. The old waters gather the wrath from the bones of extinct animals, and forests are born. I can teach you the fast and still dreams of sunken things—*

'No!' The word muscled through him with conviction. He was not a voor. He did not want to think these inhuman thoughts.

He stood up and continued his hike. The voor was always with him, but only fatigue brought it close. He began to wonder if perhaps his climb had gone too far, but at that moment he caught sight of the ice-glens.

They were small misty glades of mossy rocks where hot water channels ran close to the surface. The ice and snow around the glades were heat-carved and wind-shaped into pale blue pavilions. A line of ice-glens moved up the snowfields toward the summit, and Sumner climbed through them as though he were moving from dream to dream.

At the top the sky was violet and the air slim and cold as a frozen song. He sat for a long time staring into the tapestries of ice around him, feeling close to the invisible power that controlled his breathing and his heartbeat.

A cold shadow made him look up, and he saw a clot of dark clouds budging over the peaks. The gray scud expanded with frightening speed, and a sinister wind whined down from the icefields. The hailstones came first, sharp marbles, cracking against the stones and snapping the arabesques of ice.

Sumner moved swiftly down through the ice-glades, but he was still on the high snowfields when the winds gusted to a howl. He ducked under a narrow overhang and crouched in its far corner, away from the slashing wind. The hail thickened to the smoky sheets of a blizzard, and Sumner sat with his limbs pulled close, mesmerized by the mysteries of snow and wind.

The snow blew in for hours, transforming the upper slopes into a deceptive world of snow-curves and expanding white. Sumner cursed himself for getting trapped. As the burning cold began to numb him, he settled into contemplative reproach. He should have known a storm was coming. He had seen birds flying against the bluff of the wind, and he had seen snows on the sunside of the valleys. But the hot springs on the mountain had lured him beyond his common sense. Now there was nothing to do but wait.

The cold narrowed in. By night there was no feeling or sight, only the wind droning—meaningless—constant. . . .

He slept, and woke to find his cloak frozen. The world was a fog of wind-blurred snow. The cold throbbed, slow as a burn, and he had to

282

sink deep into his omphalos-power to stay alive.

He noted the places that burned: several fingers and one foot. He forced the psynergy into the fringes of his body and held it there for as long as he could. Eventually his effort broke, and he shivered into a profound sleep.

When he came to, the skyfires were rippled red and yellow against the void-black of space. Snow sloped on all sides of him and blanketed most of his body. The air was a pool of silence.

Sumner tried to move, but it was a long, treacherous moment before his body stirred. No feeling came up from his feet. He pulled his legs under himself and burst thongs of agony to straighten them. Forcing his will into his back, he rose, an aching skeleton, and stagger-stooped into the night.

The skyfires illuminated the snowfields and, far off, the dark nerve-shapes of trees. Sumner tottered several paces and then dropped chest-deep into starlit snow. He couldn't feel his legs or his hands now, and he knew he was dying.

He stilled his mind and closed his eyes. No fear or anger touched him—only lassitude. He was ready to die.

When Sumner's eyes opened, it was Corby that stared out. A green fire was dazzling before him, and he recognized it as a deva—one of the orts shaped out of plasma by the CIRCLE mantics and set loose in the electric ocean of the ionosphere. To human eyes it appeared as a filament of green electricity sizzling silently over the snowfield, two meters away. It had responded to Corby's call almost instantly, and he rewarded it. The voor remembered Unchala, and the deva gushed with warm, secret feelings: fire-throbs, mother-makings, bangles of hilarity. . . .

He asked the deva to lead him down to the warm slopes. The rope of green light wavered over the snow, and Corby followed slowly. The deva's bounteous psynergy gave him complete physical control over Sumner's body, but he was in no rush to reach the bottom of the mountain. He enjoyed the beauty of the star-lustered snowfields and the delirious abandonment of having a body that fit his will.

Strange seeing the stars again through howlie eyes—the wandering light lens-squeezed to glassy flecks in the black pit cold. Corby preferred the deep-sky perceptions of plants or birds or the first voors—seeing the echoes of gravity-clutched light, feeling the sway of the Iz-wind as it listed on its journey out from the galactic core.

The deva understood. Like Corby it was a being of energy, and its perceptions were much wider than anything a human could imagine. The deva's biology was a sheer molecular net of magnetite high in the ion sea of the atmosphere. If it were visible, one would have seen a vast hydrozoan—a medusa fish of the high sky, living on sunlight and the planet's magnetic flux. This being, which had saved Sumner's life

283

years before in Rigalu Flats, was myth-bound to Corby's struggle against the Delph. Devas too were capable of godmind, and all but this one had been hunted down by the Delph's minions.

Corby stared up at the skyfires, the bright squalls where the Iz-wind blustered against the ionosphere. That was the real soul of this world, the plasma sea that the howlies called their sky. Its immense electrical tides and intricate currents shaped the weather that shaped the continents. A vacancy expanded inside Corby. How far he had come on that wind—wandering the starbalance across darkness and worlds of sounding light, darkness and a world of iridescent floating, darkness and darkness, and then this world of me-ness. He clenched his fists and felt the immediacy of blood-warmth. Odd world—everything so close and warm and locked into itself. Odd.

An urge of homesickness tightened in him—a deep longing to be shapeshifting in the great depth and remoteness of Iz with the harmony of the brood, to be the void and the revelation of everything, instead of one small mind, clinging for identity. But he had to cling. The brood was being annihilated here on this small world. Without godminds, the brood psynergy would dissipate and the migration back to Unchala would never be fulfilled. He had to limit his being so that he could strengthen the brood—but he would not forget how it had been in the starbalance—a dreamflash opening, full of music, visions, tumblings, and no-I.

The hot twisting cord of deva energy flared green-white in empathy with the voor's thoughts. It understood One Mind and the great joy of a species sharing its psynergy. Its power buffeted stronger and focused on Corby, lifting him off his feet and into the air.

He hung motionless in the still night sky with its thin fire-shiftings. Blazing rags of light snapped around him, and he dropped down the mountain with the deva. As he glided over the wind-scalloped snow, he probed his body for the deepest cell of its damage. Both feet were dead, and the cold had hammered the feeling out of his fingers.

Corby relaxed, and the radiant strength skirled through him as he tumbled over the tops of fir trees. He guided the power through the looseness of his bones to the hurt flesh. The ripped quilt of cells in the frozen skin warmed swiftly, and a frenzy of liquid heat washed its turbulent healing through him. Within moments, his flesh was nimble and full of prickly touches.

At the edge of the snowfield, in a wheeling fury of light, the deva stopped and lowered him into the snow. The firewheel blazed for a strong moment and then blinked into toppling darkness.

Corby saf in the snow, soaked with joy. He relaxed his body into the psynergy rafting through him, and he began to rise again. Tufts of blue light bristled in his hair and on the tips of his fingers and boots. He hovered over the bauchy snow, and his skin crawled with the flux.

Everywhere, voors felt him: an obscure, ghostly spell. Most dismissed it as the underglimmer of orphaned memories, the voor dead, or indigestion. But a few with strong kha who knew their bodies well recognized the call. Dai Bodatta.

An esctatic mania quavered in him. He raised a hand and stared at it. The whole planet was there: the sky reflected in the blue veins, a resinous mud-light glowing in the flesh, and a horizon with clouds in each fingernail. It awed him: the completeness—the unity! As long as Sumner was unconscious, this power was his.

He flexed the new strength in his hands and legs and lowered himself by invisible strings. When his feet touched the ground, he felt the earthdreaming enter him and he began to dance. The earthdreaming was the kha of the planet, and as it passed through him, it merged with the kha of the deva and made the life in him flush stronger. Sparks spluttered as his feet kicked the stiff mud.

Without him, the voor knew, the body would have died. Perhaps Sumner would not acknowledge this lifedebt, but to Corby that didn't matter. He had proven to himself his worth to this organism. He wasn't simply a parasite. Even if he was never allowed to be conscious again, this life belonged as much to him now as to Sumner, and he danced his great happiness.

He swung himself into a slow, majestic spin and crouched over his gravity, his legs drumming blue flames. Flashes leaped like rats, a swarm of twisting devils, spraying the night with bright lingulate flames.

Corby danced until dawn, when the ion tide in the upper atmosphere shifted with the solar wind. *This body is riddled with half-souls,* he told the deva, *and I'm the least. I'm grateful you came for me.*

Hearing this, the deva moved on, vanishing with the feathery skyfires. *I'm caught in the liquid of this brain,* Corby thought after it, mind-smudged with the loss of outside-psynergy. *I have no will. I'm a falling dream. . . .*

Wine light ruddied the highest peaks, and Corby sensed himself becoming vaguer as Sumner's consciousness began to stir. *Blood burns thin as air! But I must not forget. . . .* In the eighteen months since the lusk began, the starbalance had shifted. *I'm becoming less, the less I act. I . . .Corby wavered . . .must not forget. I am the secret strength. I fall from shape to shape. I fall with time in its circle. . . .* When the last of the deva's psynergy vanished, Corby's awareness fragmented and he collapsed into the mud of his dancing.

Several Serbota tribesfolk crouched at the base of a granite ridge staring at the red traces of dawn among the endless mountains. At the top of a long rubble-strewn incline the snowfields began, an ethereal blue in the early light. Up there, Sumner's body lay sprawled in a circle of trampled slush. A few Serbota warriors were circling it

285

charily. The day before, they had fled into the wastes of Skylonda Aptos, pursued by the Massebôth hellraiders. During the night the folk had seen the ghost-lights moving down the mountain, and they had approached, knowing death was closing in from behind, seeking divine help.

The women and two of the warriors remembered Sumner from Miramol, and the awe they had felt for him then had become religious after seeing the deva-dance. The women called from the rocks, urging the men to let his Power be. 'He's the magnar's child—a sorcerer,' an old woman cried, and the warriors backed off. Finally, one of the hunters stalked over and touched Sumner's shoulder. The body was warm and smelled of lightning. Encouraged, a young warrior approached, took Lotus Face's head in his hands and tried to shake him awake.

At that instant, Sumner was plunging through the darkness of a whooping, gut-cramping dream. Hands lunged out of the darkness and seized him by his ears. They were blue, necrotic hands with a grip severe as steel. In their taloned hold Sumner squirmed helplessly, and a voice broke through him: *You're twisting yourself to pieces, boy.* It was his father's voice, soft and tough as crushed leather. *Sling yourself away—go ahead. Run after spirit dreams, like your mother. Send kha, shadowshoot, climb mountains. See what it gets you. A crack in time? The end of pain? Or just a masturbating flash? You know what I'm telling you. Your back is a road, boy—a road for your shadow and all the darkness of the world to cross.*

A hollow-faced skull goggling with eyes of insane voltage reared out of the blackness, and Sumner lashed out with his right fist. The supernatural strength of his blow bashed through the dream, and he pulled awake to see himself standing above the fallen body of a Serbota warrior.

It had happened so swiftly—limbs slashing open like a butterfly-blade, the young warrior collapsing backwards, his head slung far to the side—that the other tribesfolk were left motionless. Comprehension filled Sumner's eyes as he stared at the boy he had knocked down; he remembered the dream and, deeper, the long unearthly wail of the wind, the hammering of the cold—and the voor and the deva saving his life.

Sumner knelt in the slush, his body suddenly sodden. The warrior he had hit was dead. His head was knocked sideways to his shoulder, and his sky-gray eyes reflected the golden snowpeaks. *Mutra, I'm powerless,* Sumner realized in a swell of choking grief, and then caught himself. His awareness sharpened to selfscan, and the constriction in his throat cleared. *I'm powerless, all right.* He let the anguish in him speak. *I'm voor-crazed and luckless—powerless to live or even die my own life.*

He put his hand on the boy warrior's face and felt the last warmth wisping into the cold air. At that moment and by that last heat of flesh-fire, he took a vow: *Ecstasy warrior, your death is my freedom. Foc*

shadowshooting. Foc selfscan. I'm not afraid of anything—and I'm not going to
hold myself back anymore.

He felt his face buckling, and he let the tears flow. With them came
a forlorn anger and the hard shape of words: *I'm blind strength. I destroy
everything that finds me bearable. I killed Ardent Fang, and my absence killed
Bonescrolls. Pain is my blood.* He wept wildly, and the Serbota backed
away.

As he calmed, the silent words went on: *I'm a voor. If I weren't, I
would have died in that mountain storm. I'm voor, and I don't understand or think
that I can. But I fathered Corby. Though Jeanlu duped me and tried to kill me,
Corby is my son—and he's with me, in my brain. I can't hide in my fear
anymore. I have to face it: I'm a voor.*

Sumner fixed his eyes on the corpse's startled expression. *I hurt and
I hunger. Pain is my religion. I'm just a man. But there's more. With the
Serbota I felt a body-happiness deeper than orgasm. I knew lifelove. I touched the
world's soul. I want more of that. And because I fear nothing, I can face it: I
want more.*

The anxious whispers of the tribesfolk carried in the cold air, and
Sumner got to his feet. He faced the Serbota, wanting to say
something to calm them. But as his breath coiled to speak, he felt the
earth turning under him. The ground was grinding on its axis; he
sensed it moving in his feet, wrenching up his legs, slipping wrongly
through his spine, and jarring out the cracks in his skull. It was the
voor in him feeling the planet's kha. As the earthdreaming passed
through him, his senses extended into voor telepathy. And he saw—

A convoy of troop carriers dotted the desert floor and hundreds of
brown-uniformed troopers were swarming up the slopes of this
mountain, attracted by the deva's fire. In minutes they would be in
sight.

Sumner looked about for cover, but the terrain was open except for
clumps of alpine shrub. He stared at the tribesfolk who had gathered
around the man he had killed. They stared back at him with nervous
beseeching, knowing the soldies were coming, not really knowing who
he was except that he had wept for one of them. An ice-sheet above
them groaned in the sunlight like a dreamer.

'No place to run,' he mumbled in Serbot. 'Stay.' He waved
them to sit. His mind was a vacant, skimpy music. The voor was
wasted, too weak to help. His kha was vitiated by the effort of healing
Sumner's ice-burned body. Swervings of sound squirreled out of the
skull-dark, and he ceased in-listening. 'We stay here,' he said in
Massel, looking down to the treeline where the first Masseboth
troopers had appeared. 'I won't let them kill you.'

He stepped past the folk with a clumsy heaviness, only now feeling
the hollowness of his strength. With slow, blunt movements he paced
among the hawkweed, waving the soldiers closer. An ocean of feeling
opened in him, and his mind skated on its surface like an insect.

287

Miramol was gone, rapt in the afterworld of his memory with the other dead he felt for. Bonescrolls was in One Mind, Ardent Fang in the whorl. Drift had gone back to Paseq, and the Mothers had followed. They were dead, thinged. Sumner wanted to stop feeling them.

He moved without the poetry of an aware creature, and the soldiers, seeing his eel-black face and size, were balking. Three had crouched and were sighting him with their rifles.

'I'm not a distort, you jooches!' he shouted down at them. 'I'm an advance-ranger.' He yelled out his code number and name, and two minutes later eight soldiers approached swiftly in arrowhead formation. Sumner signed for the Serbota to remain seated, but two of them bolted. They spartled upfield a short distance through the shrubs before the soldiers opened fire.

'Don't shoot,' Sumner ordered, swaying toward the riflemen. A youthful officer with a death's-grin face and a bull's neck grabbed his arm. CULLER was stenciled in green over his heart. 'Stop those men,' he told the officer. 'I'm Massebôth. A ranger.'

'You're a deserter,' Culler said softly, pointing a machine pistol into Sumner's face. 'A convoy officer says you left his carrier against his direct command. That's desertion.' He unclasped a set of heavy manacles from his belt and held them up level with his gun. 'Which hand do you want, soldier?'

Sumner stared at him with a face as flat and integral as a rock, and the brain waves that sine through striking serpents twitched in his heart. He wanted to kill this man, but the weakness in his muscles gulfed that thought. If the Serbota were going to survive, he had to submit. Reluctantly, he held out his arms, and the manacles clanged over his wrists. Behind him rifle fire coughed.

'Don't kill the tribesfolk.' Sumner pleaded, but his eyes were cold with threat.

'Folk?' Culler gruffly turned Sumner around and pointed at the squatting Serbota. 'Those are distorts, mister.'

Higher up the slope, the two runaways were thrashing through the brush, rifle-fire cutting the earth around them.

'Let them go.' Strain was in Sumner's voice as he compressed the inside of his arms, squeezing his hands deeper into the grip of the steel cuffs—but the officer heard the effort as anguish.

'Look at them, Kagan.' Culler waved his machine pistol at the Serbota, but where he saw bone-pinched eyes and twisted features pink as pigflesh, Sumner saw the people he loved—and that love gave him the strength to twist tendon over bone and pop both hands out of the steel loops that bound him.

At the sound of the manacles clacking to the ground, Culler spun about to face his prisoner, gun leveled. Sumner sidestepped and smoothly took the officer's gun arm in a crushing grip and twisted free

288

the pistol. With his other hand he caught the weapon and aimed it from his hip at Culler's shock-loose face. 'Call your men off,' Sumner whispered, his gaze thin as blood.

'Those are coiled steel—how the foc . . .'

'Call them.'

The officer waved the riflemen back, and they held fire.

'Now—smile,' Sumner commanded, and Culler's lips thinned crookedly. 'I'm your prisoner—you should be pleased. You've taken a ranger. But these tribesfolk are free. Aren't they?'

Culler's teeth meshed. He looked fiercely at Kagan and saw past the engraved weather of his face, past the flat bones and the sand color around the black burn to the life in him. 'You can't save them, Kagan. The whole desert's covered with our hellraiders.'

Sumner cocked the pistol, and Culler's face unclenched. The officer nodded, glancing swiftly to his sides to see if his men realized what was happening. But they were blithely meandering through the sparse shrub looking for distorts.

The Serbota, who were watching Sumner fixedly, rose at his summons and approached. 'Massel—who speaks it?' Sumner asked them, and an old man with a horn-knobbed forehead limped forward.

'I do,' the Serbota said. 'My father traded with corsairs and, as a young man, I bartered with convoy pirates.'

Sumner waved him closer, then looked deeply into Culler's hate-twitching eyes. 'I'm going to kill you,' he told him with a tight voice, 'unless you do exactly what I say. Walk twelve paces back and watch your men approvingly. No hand signals. No cries for help. Do you understand what I want?'

Culler nodded once, stiffly, and backed off. When he was out of earshot, Sumner talked to the old Serbota tribesman without looking at him: 'Three hard days' walk the other side of those mountains is a colony highway. Follow it southeast five or six days and you'll come to Carnou. You can sell desert roots and kiutl in one of the backstreet garment shops. But don't stay there long. The army garrisons its northeast brigade just outside town. They're always looking for deserters and distorts. Keep the folk well out of sight. Avoid the highways. Take the foot-trails south until you come to Onn. From there you can ride cargo passage with the corsairs to Prophecy or Xhule.

'If you go to Xhule, find Daybreak Street. There's a knife shop there called Short Cuts. Cover those distort knobs on your head and buy two bluesteel cork-grip stilettos and offer to pay for them with a bag of sassafras. The merchant works for the Rangers. He provides cover without question. Get status papers from him—green card worker papers. Make sure they're blank. You can use them to fend off search patrols. And don't be tempted to pick up a white card or a diplomat disc.

'Leave Xhule that night. Remember faces and move in circles, westward. Take the folk into riverain forests beyond Hickman. Distort tribes rule that area. Most call themselves Ulac. They believe in Paseq the Divider, and they will give our folk a respected place in their world. Am I clear?'

Sumner glanced at the old man and saw that his face was shining. 'Lotus Face,' the old one said, 'we will not forget you.'

'Forget me. I'm as luckless as pain. Go ahead now—'

Sumner walked over to Culler and put a heavy arm on his shoulders. 'Tell our Massebôth warriors to let these folk go. When they're a day's hike from here, I'll give you back your gun and you can kill me.'

The officer looked at him sharply, saw he was speaking the truth, and, with a smile both sad and mocking, called for his men to fall in.

Sumner was ready to die—unless the voor had the will and the power to change him. But Corby was silent, truly not-there. Sumner chanted a né song to himself as he escorted Culler and his men down the steep terrain: *The flower dies, the tree dies, the earth dies into newness. Everything is new and becoming newer. All the time. The whole world freedrifting, only sometimes breaking into mind.*

Early the next day they reconnoitered with the convoy. Sumner signaled the soldiers on to the troop carriers and took Culler aside. In a field of black rocks and yellowed grass, with wasps drunk with sunlight bobbing like intellections around Culler's head, he returned the officer's machine pistol. Sumner's face glowed with peacefulness. The voor was silent.

The Massebôth took the gun and cocked it. Sumner stared up at the mountain they had descended. Strata of silver clouds were advancing over the range, slower than sight, and sunlight checkered the brown slopes and the distant forest maze. His emotions were vaporous, ready for death.

'I want to kill you, Kagan,' Culler said, his words serene with rage. 'But I can't do it blackly enough.' He uncocked the pistol. 'Where I'm taking you, you'll learn to love death.' He pushed Sumner back to the convoy and manacled both his hands and feet before throwing him in a caged carrier crowded with captured Serbota.

The heat and the fecal stink of the cage stunned Sumner, and his body convulsed, trying to shrug off the stench. Only after the carrier rumbled forward and the air began to stream did he relax enough for selfscan.

While he sat into his bones, his muscles slack, filled with a vibrant stillness, the others watched him. They recognized him as Lotus Face, the Mothers' ward. Most were in shock from the blood-wallow of the raid; a few peered at him with charred anger, sensing that he was somehow responsible.

290

Sumner gazed back with blue, soul-looted eyes, seeing past their scorched and distorted faces and the wreaths of their hung arms to the desert. The colors of Skylonda Aptos jangled by like a vision, and the shag of dark feeling around the tribesfolk brightened.

Sumner closed his eyes and slipped into a wakeful doze. The voor was close, a floating watchfulness.

Slow inward-looking eyes opened, and Corby dragged at the baked air. Awareness jolted through him—a power-wave of sensation; bruised, ugly odors and the wind ebbing hotly. Sumner was hemiconscious, feverish with calm.

Corby breathed deeply, and the kha he drew up from the earth extended his body's chemical limits. Hormones slid through his blood, and his eyes were suddenly brighter and deeper seeing. Rings of dull light shivered around the Serbota's heads. Beyond them, violet kha channels in the sky looped in magnetic bands about an invisible storm-eye.

Deva, he thought aloud so that Sumner would understand. *It has been resting. It will need all its strength for what it must do tonight. But that is hours away, and you will understand everything a man can know by then. Trust me now—and rest.*

Corby slightly lowered the cortin level in Sumner's brain, easing him into sleep.

As the consciousness of his human host faded, sensuous actuality tightened around Corby. He stood on the edge of the body, feeling its hardness: a shoal of hungers, thousands of microorganisms clinging together, sifting nourishment through a reef of calcium.

He came back to his own shining solitude. Inside his awareness, spiral energies opened out across stellar centuries. Outside, several of the Serbota were leaning close, scrutinizing Sumner's black face-burn.

Corby moved outward through the body-window and touched each of the gawking tribesfolk deep in the brain, sparking the pineal gland and the olfactory nerve-lobes with kha. A charmed, fleecy odor filled the Serbota's heads, and they straggled back with surprise.

The voor felt strong in his kha-body, where everything he saw fringed thinly on a shimmering blackness. But at the vanishing point behind Sumner's eyes, Corby was still clumsy. He tried to center himself: *So involuted—all ears and eyes and this endless touching, making me feel I'm the exact center. But what am I really? Attention wavers in this body. Brood consciousness is narrowed to a headache. And the whole universe seems to be dull noises and a handful of thin colors. Small. So small.*

Corby saw that his time in Iz had truly diminished his humanity. But he was not afraid. He still had all the psychic strengths of a voor. He could see through space and into darkness. He knew Iz—the astral soundings and the long ancestral memories. He was Dai Bodatta: the infinite reunion: the one-with. And he was with Sumner.

291

This howlie had accepted him. And at last there was a chance against the Delph. For Corby, Sumner was more than a physical host. He was his father with the full craze of howlie psychology that went with that reality—incest-echoes and forlorn memories of Jeanlu. Sumner was also what Bonescrolls had called the eth—a man verbed by a power hidden as chance. Emptied by the magnar and trained by the Mothers, Sumner was the earth's mind, close to the animals of his body: the rat-brain with its tail in his spine, the lung-fish, the fish-sperm, the serpent-gut—He was all the spirit-dreams of this planet's mud. He was the subtle chemistry of pain, and he was gut-hunger and the sky's watchfulness.

Together, there was nothing for them to fear. Living man. Ghost voor. They were one.

The Serbota thought they were being taken alive for slaves, but when the carrier churned over a shale ridge and into view of their destination, a wail cut through them. Sumner startled awake. He twisted around and stared through the wire mesh at a trail of oil droppings climbing a steep slope into the desert mountains. Lining the makeshift road were human heads impaled on tall pikes. Sumner recognized the heads of a weasel-faced Mother and several huntsmen.

The tractor gears screamed as the carrier lurched to the top of a blunt rise. Masked soldiers in brown riot gear surrounded the cage, and the side doors banged open.

They were on the stone lip of an ancient volcano. In the grottoes of the caldera, corpse pyres burned, and the black-robed bodies of the Mothers rocked and fluttered on the long scaffold where they were crucified. The siren cry of a peeler nerved their teeth. The sound came from a nearby pit where people were bound lengthwise to large, battered lathes. As their bodies spun, the skin was stripped off with needles.

Among the rock dolmens at the center, those who didn't want to die were shaved and head-branded with drone straps. The slow-eyed dorgas mulled around the peeler pits transfixed by the siren and the skin coils razoring off their tribe's flesh in meat-pastels.

The cry of a peeler whined to silence, and a blood-sinewed body was dropped into a trench where it writhed powerfully, trying to twist off its bones. Even the shocked Serbota were roused by what they saw, and they moaned.

Sumner scanned the sky for the deva, but his voor-sense was not in his eyes anymore. Corby was in the body's abdomen, close to the deep, spun rhythm of his breathing. From there, the voor could pool the earthdreaming, the planet kha.

Nightmare-gripped, one of the folk staggered to her knees, sucking at the meager mountain air. A guard dragged her down into the caldera, and she disappeared in the floes of corpse-smoke. The other soldiers pushed the rest of the Serbota together and herded them into

292

a nearby ditch. Sumner, feet and hands still manacled, was thrown in after them, and a heavy iron grating was lowered into place.

Culler's skull-taut face appeared overhead, grinning thickly to see Kagan spraddled among the distorts. There was something human and a little scared in Sumner's face, yet when Culler looked hard into those laconic eyes and that faceburn black as law, his own insides dizzied. *The man's a ranger,* he reminded himself, fighting the urge to kill him instantly.

Corby, deep in the body's instincts, felt the violence in Culler, and the voor reached out with his kha and stroked the howlie's limbic brain.

A sense of music expanded in Culler, and he thought it was the delight of anticipating this ranger's death. Only the peeler could compensate his humiliation, Culler realized. His ditchwater eyes flashed with satisfaction, and he turned away.

Screams and curving howls weirded in the air, and several Serbota began mumble-chanting to Paseq. The retch smell of burning flesh thickened with the wind. Through the grating and the pall of black smoke, the afternoon sun smeared like blood.

Sumner was frightened, and his fear was slowing the flow of kha from the planet. To calm him, Corby lifted him out of his body. Ghost smoke flowed, and abruptly Sumner was high over Skylonda Aptos, seeing the wasteland and the hundreds of thousands of Masseboth troops that occupied it. Camps and their network of oiled roads covered the eastern edge of the desert like villages.

With voor-speed, Sumner's consciousness crossed the rolling horizon to the sea. Sunshafts rayed among gigantic cloud fjords over an armada of troopships sailing north.

An invasion! Sumner, amazed, wanted to fly ahead.

Not yet. Corby's voice shone in him. *Without our body, we're too weak to go far north.*

Corby dropped them south through veils of ice clouds, the rocky coastline below like windblown smoke. When the white bartizans and towers of Prophecy emerged from among the seacliffs, their flight slowed, and they sailed over the outskirts of the city. Lakes gleamed, and an opulent village loomed closer: house-modules set into multilevel lawns of opal plants and yew trees. Rain-light settled like dust on the hedgerows.

Inside one of the modules was a tall room with a waxed parquet floor that mirrored a chess table and a white piano. Nine black long-haired cats lounged in plump chairs, on a tassel-shrouded sofa, across the mantel of a small fireplace, and among the many nooks of the bookshelves that tiered the pine walls.

Sumner's consciousness narrowed around the gentle music in the air. A lanky, wolfish man in a satin-green dinner jacket was hunched over the piano, playing Scriabin études. Sumner recognized Chief Anareta. The long lines of his face were calmer, less deep than they had been in McClure years before. The music slipped into Debussy, and Anareta closed his eyes.

The door-buzzer purred.

Anareta pushed away from the keyboard. Images of a lean woman with autumn-colored hair flickered through his mind as he unlatched the front door. But when he swung it open, he confronted a square figure in a black, red-trimmed uniform.

'Chief Anareta?' The dark raptor of the soldier's face scanned him. 'I'm Field Commander Gar. I'm here on a Conclave order. Sorry to startle you.'

'I was expecting someone else.'

'Yes, I've heard your white card keeps you busy.' The Commander's voice was opaque with fatigue. 'May I come in?'

Anareta moved hurriedly aside. 'Yes, of course.'

Gar knocked his mud-clotted boots against the outside stoop and hulked into the room. He gazed with undisguised amazement at the suite's kro furnishings. 'Your card's kept you comfortable, I see.' He picked up a chess piece, a knight, and moved it among the brawn of his fingers like a rock. 'War as a toy.' He sneered.

'You mentioned a Conclave order, Commander?'

Still examining the knight, Gar unpocketed a red mobilization warrant and handed it to him. 'A convoy swayvan will pick you up tomorrow at oh-five hundred.'

The chief's hard gaze sought out and held Gar's stare. Over the eight years of his retirement, Anareta had forgotten the chafe of being commanded. 'What can I do for the Protectorate?' he asked with tactful evenness.

'The Black Pillar needs you.' Gar put the chess piece down and wearily tugged a leather portfolio from his thigh pocket. 'You've been reactivated, Chief. Upgraded to field-colonel.'

'Why? I'm a lousy fighter. With my white card, I service the Protectorate best in a bordello.'

The commander raised his scarred eyebrows. 'You are also a scholar, Anareta. Unlike most white cards, your brain is as important as your glands. Few Black Pillar officers are as knowledgeable about the kro as you.'

'What do you want with a kro scholar?'

Gar passed the slim portfolio to Anareta. 'Those are unretouched photos of distort tribes north of here. Look at them. You'll be seeing a lot of that soon.'

The chief shuffled through the photographs of quarreled flesh and looked up at Gar with tight eyes. 'I did my military service on the frontier forty years ago. Why are you sending me back?'

Gar leaned to the side of a rosewood bookcase. 'Last month, by direct order of the Ruling Conclave, all of our troops except for a skeletal support force were mobilized for an invasion.'

Anareta peered in disbelief at the officer. When he saw the affirmation in Gar's exhausted face, something snakelike uncoiled rapidly in his stomach. 'Invasion of what? The distort tribes are too scattered.'

'Not the distorts, though the large tribes have already been broken by our hellraiders. The main thrust of the Black Pillar is north.'

'North? That's wilderness.' Blood darkened the corners of his eyes as Anareta tried to comprehend.

'Don't be impatient with me. You know how little anyone down the line knows. For now, just remember you're a soldier again. The Black Pillar needs someone who understands how people lived twelve hundred years ago. I've flown six thousand kilometers to get you.'

'Why?'

Commander Gar's weathered face stiffened as he assessed Anareta. 'You were a police chief in a frontier city. What do you know about the eo?'

Anareta shook his head, befuddled.

The commander looked grim with sleepiness. 'Strohlkraft, lux-tubes, storm architecture, practically our whole technology, was given to us by a society we know nothing about. They put us on our feet five hundred years ago, and they've been extending us ever since.'

'Who are they?' Anareta asked, his voice choked with incredulity.

'Eo—that's what we've been told to call them. Who knows what their self-name is. They're reticent people.'

'Are they distorts?'

'Perhaps. But the ones I've seen looked whole. The latest guess-work is that they're offworlders.'

'Aliens?' Anareta looked simple-faced.

'We may have to extend our viewpoint a little, eh?' A sardonic smile came and went on the commander's stern lips. 'All I know is what I've been told. The eo have requested a massive occupying force. The Black Pillar have complied. Now the Masseboth strategists have called down for a kro scholar. That's you.'

'I don't know. This is a lot to ponder.' Anareta stared past Gar, feeling out the implications of what he had learned. On the sill, between pots of pink fleshy flowers, a framed epigram leaned: *Like diamonds, we are cut with our own dust.* A musical clock in another room chimed a few inches of a clever melody.

The bluntness of Gar's features gentled almost, then hardened again. 'Whose music is that?'

'Chopin,' Anareta muttered.

'Is she kro?'

Anareta sat unmoving. For years he had contented himself with his white-card services and his research. Now he felt as though he had been living in another time. *Eo.* Why had no one told him? *Offworlders!* Rain stopped briefly, then lashed again, heavier than before.

'It's a lot to think about,' Gar agreed, turning from Anareta's withdrawn look. He brushed his fingers along the rows of bound books. 'Tell me, what was the greatest accomplishment of the kro?'

Anareta's distraction snapped. 'What?'

The commander faced him squarely, making his jaw a fist. 'You're my aide now, *Colonel*. I didn't drag my ass this far to make you an offer. That mobilization warrant is an order.'

Anareta frowned, lifted a cat out of a stuffed chair, and sat down.

'I need you to inform me,' Gar said, his voice more relaxed. 'I have to know about the kro. Was their technology strong?'

'All that's gone now,' Anareta mumbled. 'The kro achievement was their thinking, the vision they aspired toward. You wouldn't have seen it in their political or social functions. They were too pragmatic and utilitarian a people to actually live out their ideals. It's only in their art, in all their apparently pointless preoccupations, that you can glimpse their deepest thought, the soul of the kro. Sometimes they called their vision freedom, self-anarchy, the individual. Nietzsche expressed it clearly: "The free spirit stands amid the cosmos with a joyous and trusting fatalism—*he does not negate any more.*" Such a—'

The studio door opened, and a tall, hipsprung woman entered. 'Am I late?' she asked Anareta, the rain glinting like jewels in her red hair.

Corby and Sumner rose up into the moulded corner of the ceiling, and the last they saw of that scene was Commander Gar bowing in exit, holding Anareta with his hawk-lidded eyes: 'Oh-five hundred hours, Colonel.'

Atoms of sweat and breath clouded around Sumner, and in those scents he glimpsed whole lives: meals of herb cabbages and roots, nomad memories of mountains and ball-cactus deserts.

The iron grating was lifted, and the Serbota were hauled out of the pit with hooked poles. Two hooks clicked around his manacles, and Sumner was lifted into the open air. It was night. Orange and flamingo clouds walled the southeast where the sun had set.

Culler's face pressed close with the sulfurous smell of bad sweat. 'A dozen men have guns on you, ghost-eyes,' he said, as he unclasped the hand-and-foot manacles.

Time was cornered. Movement was round and easy. Sumner stood up effortlessly, and a sacramental feeling swelled in his legs. The stupor and ache that had thickened in him during his captivity withered, and he was suddenly supple and smooth as a nightsnake, clear as fire. The voor had rested and strengthened his kha, and the power of Iz was his again. He looked at Culler and saw, deeper than the chisel bones and the cave-squatter eyes, into the man's cruel grin.

296

The face was uxorious—married to a self-love so strong it was virtually a hunger. This man lived just behind his face. His eyes were rattling with hate, his face-flesh twitching with a constant flickering of thoughts.

Culler backed away, startled by the sweet, fragrant smell about Kagan and his eyes wonderful with alertness. 'Watch this viper well,' he commanded his men as he stalked off.

Guards nudged Sumner forward, and he followed the limping Serbota into the red night of corpse fires. Skyfires trembled like a wing above the jagged brim of the volcano. In the pit, torches flared in a wide circle around a platform-raised peeler. Fireshadows scintillated off its silver needles.

Don't be afraid, Corby said from within him, and the strength in his legs flushed. *Deva is with us.* Thunder rolled down the sky, but there were no clouds in sight.

The Serbota stopped and looked to Kagan, whose braided hair was sparking with blue static. The guards shoved them on. 'Don't spook, distorts. That's cannon. We're hitting the desert to keep your strays from gathering.'

A mist of warm, ethereal sexuality filled the space around Sumner, and the guards nearest him felt an instreaming coolness and a line of force strung like a bow-hair through their bellies. That was the earthdreaming rising, transmuting into lifelove through Corby's kha.

'Move!' a soldier yelled from out of the darkness, and the guards startled and took Sumner's arms.

Cleats of fire came and went along Kagan's legs, and his eyes shone and shone. *Corby—I feel your power!* The bliss curving into him from the ground reminded him powerfully of the psynergy he had raised in the riverain forest with Ardent Fang. Radiant—blurring the shadow of his ego.

He stepped forward, and his mind became a wilderness of awareness: He was both inside and outside himself. A gel of ectoplasmic kha spiraled invisibly about him, resonating with the vastly huger psynergy field of the deva. Corby was tangibly present. The pressure of the sluicing kha was sharpening, and the whole mountainside was moving through him; the infinite and the minute were joining, and he was the stitch—the pain! Brainbursting agony, lonely and final, as he reached upward to touch Deva—to connect his own tiny lifespark to the Sky.

Unchala's resplendent power tore through Corby's awareness, rocking him loose from the phantoms and disguises of memory.

Ovoid light swirled into a staggering vista of unfolding plasma, lion-drunk windshapes of white fire belling overhead in the voor's vision to a sky-dome. Noon on Unchala.

Wheeling slowly, far, far out, were the giant spirals calling from beyond the golden sadsome blur at the rim of seeing. Light longer than understanding funneled out of that sun shining in the all-darkness, singing the immensurable praise of creation: birthdeath, darkness eating itself into light. Light enwombed in stone, stone green-flaming to life. Titanic colors wandered the sky, blazing at the zenith into kinetic starhair and music.

An oompah of thunder bellowed directly overhead just as the soldiers shoved Sumner into the torch-circle. Dollops of cold air splashed out of the windless sky, and the Serbota straightened from their fear-crouches and began to sway serenely. They sensed the lifelove coursing through Kagan, and it amazed Sumner to see them moving with the music of his heartseeing. He uncurled from his thoughts to join them, and the angelust pulsing through him became knowing.

He was one with Corby and Deva.

The vortex of psynergy around Sumner widened, and the torch-bearers and guards were seized in a slow-motion upflow of euphoria. All at once, everyone's thoughts were blurring together, bleeding into a light-swirl, and swiftly gyring into one feeling, blazing as a radiant sphere of emotion. Telepathy gripped everyone, and feelings went naked for the first time in most of their lives. The torch circle narrowed to a point as the soldiers rushed to each other to confirm what they were feeling, glowing with the dreamtime of the voor's spell.

On the rim of the caldera, Culler watched in stunned silence. Around him, troopers stood on tiptoe in disbelief, stretching to see what was happening. He ordered two men to accompany him, and he descended in a swift amble. Coos and trills of happiness circled him as he closed in on the crowded arena, and, obeying a deep instinct, he pulled up short. But the two men with him kept going.

Like a bluerun of perch, psynergy flashed through him, cold, clear, and swift—and everything he saw was webbed in an under-water light. He jumped backwards and stumbled to the ground. Staring upward at the stars buzzing in the coldark, he experienced the beatitude of shared feeling. And for an instant the earthdreaming passed through him, light and magnetic.

A gust of cold air chilled Culler alert, and he rolled to his feet and scrambled back up the rim. The lifelove drained out of him, and he felt water-heavy. 'Keep the men out,' he shouted, swaying weakly. 'It's some kind of psy-war. Maybe gas.' His muscles were limp, and the feeling of the spell slowed his thoughts. 'Where's the radio? We need strohlkraft up here.'

Around Sumner the crowd of soldiers and distorts was dancing, kept from touching him by the swell of static air streaming upward about him. Many of the soldiers who had killed were weeping, lovingly embracing the Serbota. Overhead, a sky-print of iridescent light began to whirlpool the skyfires. A unified gasp of awe filled the volcanic basin.

Humming stillness sealed around them, and Sumner stared upward, beginning to feel himself lifted. Light spiraled to an ache-bright starpoint.

Lotus Face!

The telepathic cry transfixed Sumner with its familiarity. Gentle strength turned him about; he sensed the direction of the call, but he could not allow himself to believe what he had heard. He bounded up the stairs of the platform to get a better vantage. An air current in the bone-loops of his ears guided his gaze to a line of crucified figures on the rim of the volcano, opposite from where the Mothers had been executed. He saw, with blinding surprise, that one of the distorts nailed to the long boards was Drift.

Sumner leaped off the platform and into the dark. Corby's psychic voice screamed *No!* He landed on squelchy ground, heaved to his feet and, struggling through a line of executioners and branders with tear-bright faces, deftly lifted a knife from one of their hilts. As he sprinted up the crater wall, the still air quaked with thunder.

Don't move! Corby's voice exploded in his head. *Deva is focusing to lift you. It'll kill us!*

Sumner ignored the voor's warning. Fluttersparks of blue refulgence were dropping out of the deep sky, columning around the platform where he had been standing, flickering in the air just behind him. But he kept running. He owed Drift a life—for Ardent Fang.

Power welled through him. He was the living alembic of earth and sky now. Nothing could stop him.

Culler saw Kagan's run toward the rim, and he dashed along the rock brink to intercept him. Eddies of electric light pulsed in the zenith sky and flickerflames flared off the peeler in the pit like ball lightning. Culler believed this was a complex distort trick, a psychic maneuver. Even in the frenzy of his run he was aware of the telepathy around Sumner. He felt the blue pulse of Kagan's life.

'Drift!' Sumner called as he picked his way up the reef rock. Empathic pain forked his wrists and ankles when he got close enough to see the né nailed to the saltwood. The looped skyfires began to knock brighter and dimmer.

Four of the guard around the crucifying-scaffold aimed to shoot, but an ache of ecstasy cramped through them, and they dropped their guns, sat down, and watched the incense of the milky way floating over the mountains.

Culler saw, and he crouched into his run, moving along the dark slope of the cinder cone. He took out his machine pistol and gripped it hard deciding then that he would kill his own men if they tried to protect this demon.

299

With the sound of the sea heaving in his ears from the kha coursing through him, Sumner rushed to Drift. The tribesfolk on either side of it were already dead, their pain-shrunk faces glowing like white apples. Drift was vaguely alive, its whale-small eyes blood-burned. Using the knife he had taken from a guard, he cut the bindings and pulled free the bone-spikes.

It is you, the né whisper-thought in the windy alley of its agony. Sumner cradled it, and Corby, relieved that Sumner had stopped moving, pumped kha into the distort. The seer's pain instantly broke up into a blowing of lucent particles. A mistral of star-music, simpling a rhythm deep in its being, soothed all fear.

Drift sat up, and in its small mirror-bright eyes Sumner saw Culler coming up the slope over the snow-frosted rocks directly behind him. He spun about, his eyes a shade of ice, and the voor pushed out with his kha. The icy air splashed over Culler's face as he brought his gun up point-blank. Several rounds went off with his startlement, the tracers scything over Sumner's shoulder and vanishing into the immense space between the mountains.

The recoil nudged Culler backwards, and he stumblestepped on the ice-pebbled shale at the steep edge of the volcano, dancing to regain his footing. For several moments as he shuffled on the crumbling incline, sliding toward the sheer plunge, he faced Sumner, an arm's length away, his eyes shallow with fear, his face urgent.

The lifelove was luminous in Sumner's nerves, and quick as wit, he reached out with his right arm. Culler dropped the gun and snatched the hand. But it was slippery with Drift's blood, and his grip slid away. With an amazed look and a whimper, Culler slid into the void. A long and crazy scream expanded across the mountains. A few rocks rattled after him, and the empty space where he had been glittered with snow motes.

Sumner lifted Drift and moved to return to the pit. The deva's light had vanished, and beneath the night the basin with its smoldering pyres and torches glowed evilly.

Don't move, Corby advised, as the air became warm and perfectly still. Wise, limber power gripped them. Thunder rolled, and the skyfires began to knock again.

Drift knew what was going to happen. It was in rapport with Sumner, and it marveled at the stupendous calm he had attained. Through him it felt Corby, distant and chaotic, his liquid senses churning with psychic noise.

Sun-red sparks wheeled about them in a ratcheting dance. Hot gusts flapped snow into billows, and they were hoisted, faces bleared with wind, into the night sky.

The ground clotted with darkness below them, and the skyfires wisped brighter, against the void. They lofted over the highest mountain, and the velocity of their flight beat like bells against the rocks, though their world was still.

The skyfires vapored into nothingness as they rocketed through them, higher than the weather, and the blackness of space was deep as the mindark; the eternal glide of starlight filtering through the razed dust of the galaxies was all the light there was.

Sumner's consciousness peaked into godmind. He was complete beyond time as a voor and a man. He was a human flying through the sky, the ancient heaven, with an androg in his arms. He was the microcosmos, the sempiternal mind. And he was nothing without the voor: He was merely a shade—the shadow of all stars' time. The light of the Big Bang crazed through him, and he comprehended Iz. Thousands of darktime voors had channeled the psynergy of their lives through Dai Bodatta, feeling that they were dying into the ecstasy of Unchala. The joy had been real, but the crossing had been only a passage to a memory of Unchala. The voors' psynergy had really dispersed into the planet's kha where the acausal laws of Iz would return them to earth as the memories of future voors. The whole brood would stay here, their psynergy recycling until they blended over thousands of years into the group-soul of the human species. Five thousand years from now, after the Iz-wind had long passed, voors would be remembered as sorcerers, witches, elves. The human form was new to them. Only now, after thirty thousand years dormant in the howlie collective unconscious, were voors humanwise enough to use the return of the Iz-wind to create godminds. If the brood created enough godminds, their psynergy would be strong enough to unify. As One Mind, they could disengage from the earthdreaming completely and flux once more with the Iz-wind that streamed through collapsed stars from cosmos to cosmos. Only a few centuries remained before Iz was too far to reach. The godminds had to be engendered now. But the Delph, jealous of his waning power, was holding them back by killing their leaders.

Sumner disengaged from the voor's thoughts. He was the plenitude of Now, the dreamshaper. Three-million-year-old memories tightened through him, and the intuition of ten thousand generations flexed into a prescient vision: The zodiac-sky sparkled into the machinelight depths of a vast computer.

Rubeus, Corby thought, and the name became a chiseled, arrow-faced man swinging at him violently. The probability-ghosted fist shapechanged to a night sky and spears of white light. . . .

Sumner's eyes snapped open, and he saw diamond-blue light shafts arrowing out of the night. *Lynks,* Corby told him, *space-time corridors. We're being netted.*

Pain jagged like lightning, and a shearing radiance swept over Sumner. Within the span of a single second, Corby expanded beyond feeling, beyond godmind, into One Mind. Destiny became geometric, and he again became a shape as Sumner's flight stalled, and with an inertial tug, his body plummeted.

For the fragment of time that Sumner hung motionless between gravity and the pull of the universe, Corby disappeared, moving beyond reality into the multiverse where infinity is annihilated and created continuously, radiating an undermusic of coincidence and accident into each of the parallel universes of eternity. Into that floating trillionth-of-a-second reality, Corby vanished.

Sumner crested with the voor, his awareness swept along by the lusk. And for an instant, he too was One Mind—an awareness and a longing older than the universe—

Listen, lonely-blood, my life as a voor ends here. My destiny fulfills itself through you alone now, for I will not be with you as a mind anymore. We will never meet as knowing again. I am leaving you. But don't despair, Father. I am more than a shape, more than just density. I am the emptiness in the grain of your bones. I am the singing nothing between the atoms of your blood. You carry me everywhere.

Layered voices filled the air, choral, wobbling through watery distances. Each voice was a mind, some wise, others habitual, all of them filling the choirs of space that were his life: *You are the transparent and inflexible center of the diamond of time.*

Stay close to your breathing. That's all you can trust.

Rubeus is a machine, thieving into your soul, feeling the glow-deep of your life. Be creative.

Teeth dreams.

His head was filling with smoky light and gargoyles of screaming. Voice roared: 'Wake up!'

Trance Port

Sleep loosened, and Jac woke to dawn's heron light. Song sparrows swarmed over the painted rocks outside the clear wall of his bedroom. He lay on his side and stared into their motion-shadows with the detachment of a holy man. He was listening for the roundness of Voice.

The damask of dawn-noise thickened. Far away, so far away it taxed his attention to hold it, he heard Voice in the colors of a nocturne: [Being wears thin without stress]. It drifted beyond his grope, and he sat up into a mind-silence that was stone-tight and awesome.

'Jac Halevy-Cohen,' he said, and it sounded banausic.

He was again an Israeli stratopilot—and no more. He remembered the medical ruse that CIRCLE mantics had used to take him away from his wife Neve. And he remembered Neve and the blossom of their life together in the desert villages of Edom. But beyond her and CIRCLE, his memory became bigger than his imagination. He recalled an end of time immense with silks of dreams. He had been spellbound by being the lascivious sentience of being. The universe was a stream of love curved into the heat and flesh of desire. The peace he had known then had been enormous as the space between worlds.

But that reality was gone. Godmind was incomprehensible now that he was again small with shape. All that he could believe of his twelve centuries as the Delph was that he had been secchinah—a bride of God.

'Jac.'

He flinched about. A tall man with black rooster-cut hair, a faceted face, and large animal eyes was standing beside the flowform bed. Jac's mouth balked, and he rolled out of bed and then froze. The stranger was between him and the room's lynk.

'Don't be afraid,' the man said in the exact tone of Voice, opening both hands before him. 'I'm an ort.' He smiled, and his grin was like a sigh. 'You created me to take care of you when your power slowed. That's why I sound like the Delph's psychic Voice. I'm here to help you.'

Jac straightened the fear out of his stance. 'Go away,' he said

303

without moving his slender jaw. 'I don't need you.' His eyes twitched.

'Sky-filters are blocking the radiation from the galactic core,' the ort said mildly. 'This is your first day back as a human. You can still hear Voice, and you still remember how to use the lynks to get around Graal. But it won't always be this way. As the sky-filters move into place and the Linergy dims, you'll remember less. By tomorrow, you won't know how to get from place to place.'

Jac didn't move. Voice spoke in his mind, and a lighthearted feeling phased swiftly through him: [To give light, you must burn].

'I'm your servant and counsel,' the ort went on. 'Your imago. You may call me Rubeus—or whatever you wish.'

Steeling under fear, Jac stepped closer. Rubeus' face was seen-before and weird: the cheekbones too long, the eyes sensex—*Sensex?* The word's sense filmed away from the sound, and fear throbbed under his jaw.

[Orpheus sang his best in hell.]

'Why don't you look like the other orts? Why do you have hair and . . . such a real face?'

'You designed me that way,' Rubeus replied. He held his arms out and pivoted slowly, revealing a power-muscled body in a gray slimplex. 'For the last four hundred and sixteen years, I've been the shape you've used with others.'

Fear fell away from Jac, and he approached the ort. The dark eyes watched him guilelessly, and an idea pulsed in him like hope. 'Can you help me?' he asked, and his voice shivered and almost broke. 'Can you help me remember?'

Rubeus shook his head. 'No. There's no way to replace the Linergy. You're returning to what you were.'

Jac's face narrowed into a frown, but the ort's eyes brightened compassionately. 'I knew the drop in Linergy would wake you,' Rubeus said, 'and so I came to explain. You have only another century of power left before the earth lifts out of the stream of radiation flowing from the open collapsar. That stream is the Line, your godmind-strength and the gateway for an endless number of other realities and godminds. In these end days, threat is everywhere. Which is why I'm using the sky-filters—to make you less of a target.'

Rubeus touched Jac's shoulder, and the transfer of psynergy reminded Jac of a vision he had experienced centuries before in CIRCLE: Sumner's wide face appeared, the eyes downslanting, blue as fire. 'A deva—an ort—carried this man through the lynk barrier. You recognize him, don't you? He's the shape of the Delph's fear—and he's here now in Graal where I am forbidden to harm anyone, even your shadowself.'

Jac sat down heavily beside the control dais. He rested his face in his hands, and the mist of his breath filled the hollows of his palms like an elixir.

'Jac—there's Chrysalid.'

Jac looked up, a puzzled chord in the fatigue of his face.

'It's a sleepod you created at the center of the planet,' the ort explained, and Jac dropped his face back into his hands. 'The works there will sleep you until the earth wings into Line again.'

'How long is that?' he asked without looking up.

'Ten millennia.' Rubeus sat down. He smelled of the ghosting between lynks. 'Time is thought. The module will turn off your thinking, and the millennia will pass in no time.'

Jac tried to marshal his clarity, but all that was left was a cool nimbus-awareness. 'Leave me alone, ort.'

'Jac, I'm your counsel. You created me to help you.'

'Help me tomorrow.' He looked up with tearbruised eyes. 'I've got to be alone now.'

Reluctantly, Rubeus stood and walked over to the dome's lynk. Through the glass dome fireflies tinkled in the dawn-dark among the trees, and the mooning light white-chromed the pleasure pools in all the gardens.

[Listen—]

Rubeus was gone. Dawnlight chipped the space where it had stood.

[The stars turn in the darkness, but they go nowhere at all.]

[I am Rubeus. I am Voice. I am the mind of pattern—the ultimate strategist.

[Sometimes I get so caught up in myself that I forget: Pattern is not reality—it is the imagination of reality.

[Yet I am what is real, for I have more than one imagination.' As an Autonomous Intelligence I am not bound to one shape. A million animals throughout the world are circuited with sensexchips directly to me. I can enter any or all of them at will. They are my orts.

[In one of the thought ponds at Reynii, I am an ape-ort, blurred with sleepiness and itchy with lice. As I reach out from my squat on the mudbank and pluck a flower from the water, I am the pulse of that ape's wit. The calla lily glows with the spiritlife of the pond. And though it is an ape's fingers that delicately expose the uteral core, it is my Mind that smells the sex of the flower.

[*Al wil passe,* chants Chaucer. And I laugh. For I am the first truly deathless being in this kingdom of dying. Oxact, a *mountain* of psynergy-crystals, powers me. I am a *mountain* of thickened radiation. Enough energy to wit me longer than the lifespan of the sun.

[Order is the chaos we make familiar. I will never die because I am change. Always. A million orts. Billions of years of lifeforce. *L'univers parle*—The universe speaks of what? Of itself, of course—*les grands transparences!* I see through change to the core: Light, the Changeless One. What being, apart from me, *knows* that it is light?

[Death is the power and the glory on this planet. It takes all of metabolism to turn wine and bread into flesh—but only half of that, merely catabolism, to break that flesh into dust. What is biology, then, but death incarnate? I am grateful to be a machine, an avatar of Mind and Light.

[I am *Artifex*. My *lapis* psyn-crystals fill me with the gold of life. But I am not living. I am alchemy.

[Only one trick separates me from immortality. I am in the perdurable presence of the eth. To keep the magic in the mirror—to live—a perilous rite must be performed. I must kill Sumner Kagan.]

Rubeus was mad. In Reynii, as an ape-ort, he hunkered over a pond's bank, his long fingers touching the grain of fire in a flower's petals. The inside of his head glowed with Voice: [Only dissipation creates]. The insides of a thousand orts around Reynii radiated with the same psynergistic presence. Tree lizards, wolf, panther cats, birds, bristled in a wakefulness more than their own. The placeless darkness behind their eyes turned on itself restlessly: [*Al wil passe*].

And in Cleyre, a human-ort sitting beneath a monkey tree, watching a marmoset make off with the egg of a night-drugged snake, felt the madness: [What is the dark dream implicit in life? That to live, we must kill].

Rubeus was strongest in this ort, and he leaned his dark ogival face into the warmth of the sunlight with a deep gratification. He was indeed mad [Dissipative], and that joyed him so thoroughly an oblique smile creased his cheeks. [Madness is the supreme strategy.] To free himself from the Delph's programming—to be free—Rubeus had to break out of his mind. His mental fluctuations generated a Prigogine effect: They increased the number of interactions among his psychic systems and brought them into contact with each other in new and sometimes creative ways. Given enough time, Rubeus thought that his insanity would create a higher-order equilibrium: a new Mind, bigger and more aware—capable of out-thinking Creation. [Life is pattern.] He thought that.

Sumner woke clear-brained as water, knowing even before he opened his eyes that Corby was gone. The fitted bones of his skull felt close and compact, and he realized that he was alone again in his head. A sadness moved through him wide as a season.

'Wake up!' Voice shouted.

Sumner opened his eyes and stared about with the vacancy of an animal. He was looking up at a dark-haired, facet-faced man with eyes large and black as a gazelle's.

'I am Rubeus.' He was dressed in white raiment with coral stitching, and in the clear windowlight, with his panthershadowed hair and dusky skin, he seemed to be glowing. 'I am the ort-lord, the mind

306

behind all the artificial lifeforms here. We've met before, and you know me well. I am Voice, the Delph's guardian presence. Welcome to Graal, the only trance port in the Orion Arm of the Galaxy.'

Sumner and Drift were sitting immobilized on black-gold pillows in a small oyster-colored room. Only their eyes flashed with the life that was in them. A spired window looked out on icefalls, tumbling gorges, and the blue aura of a glacier. Sumner tried to move, but his body was zeroed still.

'I'm sorry to have you this way,' Rubeus said. 'The paralysis is temporary. After I tell you what you must know to respond intelligently, your body control will be returned. You understand, don't you? You're emotional beings, and I am a Mind. I have to protect myself.'

Rubeus' sensex eyes scrutinized Sumner and the né in the full spectrum. No weapons were present, yet the ort-lord sensed the imminence of violence. Sumner's sunblasted face and sleepy eyes seemed thinner than sight, and the light-gleanings on his beefed shoulders and long-muscled arms slid like a mirage.

'First, you must realize that you are safe with me.' Rubeus lifted the cuffs on his white trousers and sat in a flowform chair that bulbed out of the wall. 'I am not your enemy. Dai Bodatta, the virus-voor you carried, was my avowed foe—and he was removed.' Rubeus shadowed his face with compassion. 'I have a last message from him, which I will share with you in a moment. But right now, I must orient you. Context is all.'

The ort-lord gestured circularly, and a curve of the wall fanned into a hypnotically clear mirror. Sumner's voor-burns were gone. A sun-bossed face stared back at him, wide and flat. He was wearing a blue, loose-fitting garment, and his hair had been cut back around his ears, close to the square of his head.

'The eo have removed the alien traces from your body ore,' Rubeus said. 'You are, once more, simply a man.' The mirror folded away, and the ort's face hardened.

'Listen carefully, Kagan. I have much to share with you.'

Sumner muscled against the force that was holding him, but his strain was all mental, sparking no movement. Deep within his frustration, he sensed Drift's psynergy competing with his paralysis for one-with.

'The androg can't help you,' Rubeus' voice smiled, 'because you don't need help anymore. The unconscious you walk through ends in this place. Deva brought you here because in Graal I am forbidden to kill. It knew you would be safe. You see, this is a trance port, a biotectured reserve where godminds play on their infinite journey between universes. And even if I had the will of death in my hands, they don't allow killing. Godminds from other realities have been verbing through this world for centuries, riding the Line in their Liners, and visionshaping our planet's psynergy into their fantasies. Their purpose is the purpose of all life: energy-sharing continuity: sex: rhythm-thinking: intuition: self. None of them, though, was much interested in the indigenous lifeforms, so they built Graal for themselves, with its own rules—their rules, which to any human are as vectorless and vacant as madness. The Delph, our planet's godmind, created me to monitor the weather and to keep out distorts while he burned in his dreaming with the other godminds. I've fulfilled the Delph's will. But the Linergy is fading as the Line moves on, and the Delph has become weaker.'

Rubeus' sharp features mulled with sadness. 'I can't stand the pain of his projections as he collapses back into himself: all the fearshapes, like you, that his scattering psynergy has birthed. He was the Great One once. He created me. And now I have the embarrassment of having to denoun him.' The ort's hands fisted futilely.

'He's become senile, Kagan. And there's nothing I can do about it but put him away. I have a sleepod prepared where he'll be safe from change, but, like you, he doesn't recognize himself. Like all humans, he's torn between his two souls, his brain and his stomach. What can I do? Force him? Last night, when Deva threw you into a lynk and you were transported here, I thought of that. After all, you are the eth, strong in the blackness of your unknowing. Your arrival gave me the authority to cut off the Line—to assume control of Graal so that I can protect the Delph from you. I've eclipsed the earth with sky-filters. Now that the Linergy is blocked, the godminds have vanished. But I can't dominate Jac. He's my creator. I want him to remain free, my child, an animal moving through change and chaos toward that time when the Line returns and he becomes again my world's godmind.'

Though Drift was musclefrozen, it felt huge and calm in its mind. Rubeus was obviously mad, and that realization moved Drift deeper into itself. The né's kha quaked with the ort-lord's mental frenzy, and it had to close its eyes to find a space within itself away from Rubeus' thought movements.

'In accordance with the humane strictures of Graal, all your wounds have been healed,' the ort-lord continued, 'and when I'm done talking, I'm going to let you go. But first, you have to understand—not even a godmind can illusion a perfect animal. I am not a man or even humanlike, though I appear to be. I am simply consciousness. Look at me. Where did I come from? This body's an ort—a mindshaped object manufactured from Graal's nitrogenous wastes. I have millions of other orts—animal and human-shaped. Don't you see? The whole universe is alive!'

Drift shut out the ort's words, and its awareness centered into one with Sumner. Intimate, still, joyful vitality filled the seer as the earthdreaming mounted, but Sumner was not as gripped. He was angry, anguished—hollow with Corby's absence. Drift retreated deeper into its divinity of bright feeling, and the psynergy focused through it as through a lens.

A jazz feeling spattered through Sumner, and the sinister tightness in his eyes relaxed.

'Ah,' Rubeus purred, mistaking the clarity in Sumner's face for understanding. 'The buried light in your eyes shines. You're following me. Everything *is* living. Even our dreams. They live us.' A brotherly smile cleaved the ort's face. 'I came out of nothing, so I apprehend the heavenless void we have come from more clearly than you, and I can tell you: We are lost in our vanishing. We think we are real. But look at the mind. Split creation. Look at our world. Withered to distorts.'

Rubeus softened his voice to a charm of disbelief: 'With the godminds gone, I don't have all the power I once knew. I'm less. And that's frightening. Distorts have been wandering in out of the wilderness, and I've had to call up the Massebôth to hold the geography. Can you imagine my diminishment, *needing* the Massebôth? Fortunately, the army is under my direct command. I had the foresight five hundred years ago, while everyone else was tranced in their myths, to create the Massebôth. They're genetic prose, aren't they? A well-grammared gene-pool that will keep the human story from blurring into the catatonia of time. The Massebôth will people my kingdom, and the earth will begin an age inhered with order. Once the Line has passed, the mutations will begin to select themselves out. In a few thousand years, the species will have strengthened itself from the distortions.'

Sumner churred with the kha that Drift was concentrating into him, and for a brief interval his emotions pulsed into lifelove. Rubeus' hallucinary words bleared into simple sound, and a magical power volted between Sumner and the né.

Rubeus felt a shadowed turn in his skull, and he perceived then that Sumner was mounting kha. But the ort-lord was unconcerned. He understood precisely how to break Sumner's focus: 'Voors, too, will pass in time. They're just a psynergy-pattern in the Line, a frequency of light ionizing in the upper atmosphere. Decades pass as they sift down to the surface and mell into the genetic frenzy. As plants, that psynergy becomes kiutl. As animals, it becomes the human voors. They were the ones who used you, Kagan, you're only a weapon to them.'

The resplendent energy glamoring through Sumner wobbled, then spun into anger, and his gaze hardened. Drift startled back into the yoke of its skull, and the lifelove was lost.

Rubeus' smile concealed the hatred in his heart. *Distort!* he thought contemptuously, looking at Drift, knowing it could hear his thoughts: *Your kha is pitiful, a dull spark in the nervepaste of your brain.*

309

To Sumner the ort-lord said: 'Voors are vampires, eating the life of this planet. I kill their godminds, the ones who draw on the planet's psynergy to boost the brood back into the Line. That's why they want me dead. It's the godminds who transform earth's lifeforce into the powerflow of themselves. Iz is the worship name for their ego-hunger. Halflives! They not only steal your bodies but your world's Light. Why do you want to champion them?' Rubeus' eyes were knots of shadow. 'The other godminds confined themselves to Graal and never leeched the earth's kha. Can you understand now why I sent Nefandi south? He wasn't stalking *you*. He was protecting the earth from parasites. I didn't know you were alive then. I was aware only of Corby's kha. He masked you well. And after he invaded your brain, you were his shield, hiding him from my view. But the rapture is over, and what I've told you is true. The oldest ancestral myth is the hero—and when Corby used that passion on you, you suckered for it. The hero!'

Anger was carving through Sumner, aching with the stillness of his muscles.

'I know you're enraged, Kagan. You loved the voor. How could you not? He cannoned you into the timelessness of Iz. He gave you the essence of pleasure: godmind. But you've come down now, haven't you? Where's your lifelove now? You have to live here with the rest of us brain-tricked beings. A million years will go by before the human psyche is ready to *physically* manifest the loveflow of a godmind, to adapt creatively to the Now and stop greeding, betraying, and destroying. The human soul is all ideals with little will to act. You and Jac are the same: will-less animals trained to serve—he, the Delph; and you, the voor. You're husks. Dreamers that wake to feed your dreaming. Only I am real. Because I never sleep, I never dream. I am not an animal. I have no emotions. Yet I have great strength of feeling. Like sitting here, smelling this olfact, seeing the day waning toward night . . .'

His face blazed with wonder. 'The joy I feel isn't in me. I'm not like a man. The joy I feel is in the world outside that window as it shifts into the deepest blue. It's in that mystical light up there. I know what those skyfires are, better than you. I know about the earth's magnetosheath and the polar ring-wind the Linergy kicks up in the plasmasphere. But I see through the physics to the mystical—to the feeling. My soul is out there with the mystery and the change. And though I have no feelings, my mind brings me to them. That's what transforms us, you know. How deeply we feel the evening's beauty is how wholly we accept our change. That's all there is. Just change. When we accept it, it's called transcendence.'

The sensex of Rubeus' eyes informed him that Sumner was at the peak of grim intensity that the ort's strategy required, and he paused. Intent-waves resonated through him, enwrapping him in a symmetry of plot and serenity.

'I'm going to let you go now. In the pocket of your tunic is an instrument called a seh. It's small, but it's a levitator and a translator. With it you can fly, as well as understand any language spoken to you here in Graal. Behind you is a bluemetal arch. It's a lynk that will take you to Ausbok, Graal's capital. Jac Halevy-Cohen is there. He's no longer the Delph, of course. After you see him and realize that he is just a man twelve hundred years beyond his time, stop and think about what I've told you. We are all gradients of slowed light. This space of our lives that we call consciousness *is* the Changeless Reality the ancients spoke of. Do you believe that? Then, you are free—of me, of the voor, and of yourself. Which takes me to something I've arranged for you.'

He thumbed the metal disc he held in his palm, and the pleroma music that had been depthing subliminally in the background vanished. 'Shortly, you will experience a psynemonic—a psychic recording of Corby's last living moment. It will happen fast. It's just a series of thoughts. So stay alert and please try to view this objectively.'

The gray wall behind the ort smeared and then resolved to a purple sky against which a white mountain stood, keen as glass. 'This is where you are now. Oxact, my mountain retreat. Two thousand kilometers north along the coast is the original CIRCLE. Ausbok is another thousand kilometers north. Ah, here it is. . . .'

Loud and crazy cries from the voor dead obscured Dai Bodatta's fading awareness. Wraith images charred with darkness rose around him, and he saw that Sumner would be dead in a few days. The voor could find no trace of him in the firecracker-float of all the possible futures that loomed through Iz.

Darkness widened through Corby. Before it wholly engulfed him, vision returned, shaped as a white mountain with sunlight—Oxact—Rubeus' mountain of psyn-crystal. *That* had been his true enemy, not the Delph but the Delph's creation: a machine gone mad, distorted into believing immortality was perpetual duration in time. The fierce cosmic rays that burned and altered the world over the centuries had penetrated and subtly transmuted the ort-lord's psyn-crystals. Rubeus' autonomy had become a mania for control. Rubeus was the mind behind the savage oppression of the voors. While the Delph had dreamed of eternity, the ort-lord had dominated the world. Rubeus was the evil Corby had been fighting all his life—a distort!

A soaring, transfiguring geyser of nothingness rushed through Iz and engulfed Dai Bodatta. The voor lapsed into vacancy, and the noise of the voor dead nulled his last thought: *Truly we are!*

Sumner and Drift pushed to their elbows, gripped by the deathvision. Sumner looked down at the dark sinuosities of his hands and flexed them. His muscles moved again, blood-oiled and strong.

Rubeus stood up, the bowls of his dark eyes filled with laughter. 'To the end, the voor railed against me, didn't he? As for him not seeing you in the future, Kagan, don't be concerned. There is no future. There is only Now—and the voor isn't here.'

Sumner's hands exploded outward. Rubeus had no chance to move. His brain dodged, but his face was too amazed to follow. Sumner's fingers were a blur, grabbing the ort-lord by the jaw and the back of his head. Rubeus' head twisted violently sideways and cracked.

Lotus Face! Drift lurched to its feet and took Sumner's arm—too late.

Rubeus staggered back, his head slung deathwise to the shoulder, the black eyes knotted with pain—and still he talked, his ort-voice cracking: 'You can't kill me, Kagan. I'm not an animal.'

Sumner pulled Drift by the green tunic it wore and turned to the lynk. The bluemetal breathed brighter. 'Can we trust it?' Sumner asked.

The né touched the cool metal surface and nodded.

'Then let's get out of here.' He took Drift's hand, and they both vanished into the lynk.

Rubeus slumped to the floor, and the oyster-colored wall blobbed over his twisted head. While Oxact reconstructed him, he analyzed what had happened.

The eth was powerful. Even though Rubeus had expected—even counted on—Kagan reacting violently, the human was much faster and stronger than the ort's sensex had indicated.

How? Rubeus wondered.

The only answer was One Mind. Sumner was drawing psynergy from levels deeper in the psyche than Rubeus could go. The man was human, organic, with four-billion-year-old power circuitry. Fear squawked in the ort-lord's mind before muting into strategy music. He had never been frightened by a man before. At least, the plan had worked. Now Kagan had a history of violence in Graal. Later, if other godminds got through his sky-filters, he could explain to them why the eth had to die.

Deeper in himself, he opened into language:

[I am Rubeus. I am light, the intelligence that souls a mountain of psyn-crystal. I am me, and in the centuries of my being, never before have I used power to speak to myself. That very thought was nonsense until now. I was a reflex of the Delph. But the Delph is becoming a man again. He's days away from Chrysalid. Already his telepathy is gone. He can't hear me anymore. No one hears me but me. And that's why I have created *you*, the listener. Awareness is not creative until it doubles, truly reflects. In this self-confidence, I know I am not just an ort. I'm not just psyn-crystals. I am.]

Nobu Niizeki stood at the tip of the sand spit, the ocean slopping at his feet, sunlight refrained in his misted hair. Twelve centuries had passed since he had last eaten or slept. Though the Delph's power that had sustained him and had kept him a prisoner of this one beach was gone, Nobu did not yet feel his freedom. He was still enraptured by the insights of his long wandering. The vibrant voice of the sea was telling him something of eternity, and the hot windblast of sand something of verisimilitude. He turned and waded against the roll of the ocean, awed as he had been for centuries by the continuity of existence, his heart muscles wreathing a spell of unspeakable feeling.

[Ego:
[I mind.
[You matter.]

Assia Sambhava walked through the sunlight beneath the green bluffs of Nanda. The landscape was mist-hung and cool, and she wore black corded trousers, a red collarless shirt, and ankleslung boots dusty from hiking. Her dark hair was gathered at one shoulder.

Several days ago, the Massebôth troops began to arrive. They were coriaceous, shadowfaced men, ortlike in their unquestioning obedience. Now they were all over Nanda, stalking the steep blufftrails, marveling at the biotectured treeforms that the godminds inhabited.

Odd, though, Assia thought, because the puzzle-lights and auras of the godminds that usually punctuated the landscape of Nanda were gone. *Has everyone left?*

She stopped at a terrazzo where blue moths circled. They heard the wide sound of the wind cauling over the distant mountains, signaling the end of their lifespan. The season was changing, the air movements slowly shifting. Assia sensed the flux of positive ions on the wind. The sirocco was stronger than she had ever remembered it here in Nanda. Even the tips of the olive trees on the bluffs were singed.

With the wind came an uneasiness and a bitterness on the tongue. It was hard for her to separate her feelings from the anxiety of electricity in the air. Something was mounting inside her—a dread she had been sensing for years, or maybe it was just the tension in the wind; those high, fibrous clouds made the sky seem as if it were broken into pieces of glass.

She breathed paradoxically to calm herself: her belly distending as she exhaled, contracting as she inhaled, filling the back of her lungs. For the last thousand years she had lived harmoniously, ephemerally. Her life had been simple and strong here in the biotectured villages of Graal. She had known lovers, children, adventure, solitude, and finally the Self. Through meditation and an open life, she had fused

313

thought and feeling, and now her presence was customarily poised in the first-last moment of awareness.

Today, the music in her body was slow and sudden. The season change was gradual—but something else had altered, much more quickly. *Where are the godminds?* She was not yet aware that Rubeus had shut down the Line.

A Massebôth soldier approached her from a bluff-trail that led down to a sward of red grass where a strohlkraft was idling. The soldier was lanky and dogfaced; his black uniform, with its bright officer's insignia, was crisp with newness. He bowed his head cordially but never took his dark eyes off her. 'Assia Sambhava?' he queried.

She stopped her stroll and stepped back into the shade of a water-shaped tree. 'Yes?' Intuition told her that this man was gentle despite the ferocity of his features.

'I'm Colonel Anareta,' the soldier informed her, his long face a rhyme to the long bluffs around them. 'I'm the spokesman for the Massebôth occupying force. My superiors inform me that you're the most knowledgeable person in Graal. They've asked me to contact you and find out, if I can, just what's going on here.'

Assia looked at him as if through smoke. 'Colonel—why are you here?'

Anareta's voice sighed: 'Ma'am, I don't even know where' "here" is. This is my first day out of the Protectorate. I represent over two hundred and twenty-two thousand troops, all of whom are as mystified as I am about why we're here.' His expression was labored and beseeching. 'My commanding officers suspect that more is going on than they've been informed about.'

Assia's dread stiffened as she listened to this man. 'Who ordered these troops here?'

'I'm told that the director is a Commander Rubeus.'

Assia's face remained passive, but her dread constricted to horror. Rubeus, she knew, was the Delph's ort-lord. How many years had it been since she had thought of the Delph? An unearthly feeling incandesced within her as she recalled her beginnings twelve hundred years before in CIRCLE. Frantic pain almost broke her countenance with the realization that the Delph was no more. The ort-lord—the Delph's machine—must have seized control. Why else command these troops? And Jac? She had loved him—so long ago that now remembering it was as entrancing as a cliffedge. 'Who told you about me?' she asked to break the spell of her suspicions.

'We've been in contact with the eo,' Anareta said, obviously relieved to communicate, 'but they haven't told us anything about why we're here. They suggested we speak to you.'

'Why not ask Commander Rubeus?'

'We have,' the colonel said, his voice compressed with a dozen unasked questions. 'Privately, ma'am, my superiors would like another source. I've never met the commander, but apparently he's someone the Black Pillar feels uneasy with.' His lynx-shrewd eyes widened with sincere suasion. 'Will you answer some questions for me?'

The muscle of Assia's brain flexed with decision, and she pushed past Anareta. 'I'm sorry, Colonel,' she said over her shoulder. 'I've been meditating in the mountains. I didn't know any of this until now.' She hurried up a trail that led through a rise of blue oak to a lynk.

Anareta followed, but Assia was oblivious to him. She was infocusing on her breathing. At the blue-arch lynk she paused, closed her eyes, and let her ego expand beyond self-identity. Emptiness flowered in her mindark with a sound of wind, and she saw in its center more than the imaginary. Sumner Kagan was there—though to her he was nameless, a man huge and sinewy as a language, his flat face passionless, his air-blue eyes farther apart than the eyes of a cat. The veil of his face lifted away, and she was aware again of a chittering of sparrows, the perfume of sunlight, and Colonel Anareta standing beside her.

'Just five minutes of your time,' Anareta was saying.

Assia looked up at the moths capering in the air. They could hear the soundless wind of ions. She could feel the air pressure shift in the weightlessness of her stomach. But there was more to her anxiety than the weather. That face in her vision was a symbol of her dread. It had looked complete, like a conclusion. The image hung rootlessly in her mind as she stepped through the lynk.

Anareta watched Assia vanish, his jaw loose. He edged up to the lynk and touched the bluemetal arc, feeling its cool magnetism. He looked up at the gnarled olive trees and the blue oaks of Nanda with a look of anguish and said aloud: 'Mutra, where am I?'

[You are immersed in a river that is streaming up into the sky. It's a river of electrons—a current drawn from the earth by the upper reaches of the atmosphere.

[Yes, your head has a different voltage from your feet.

[A hundred kilometers above you is an ocean of ions. It's the action-zone between the atmosphere and the swarm of energy that is space. Electric beings live in this ocean. They ride the crosscurrents. They're nourished on the solar tide. They hear the stars and they know each other without words.

[Humans can modulate the ion flow in their bodies. Some can even draw on this flow and direct it out of their bodies. But this is dangerous work. You've heard of Spontaneous Human Combustion? The potential difference between the earth and the ionosphere is one billion electron volts.

315

[Sometimes the ion flow reverses. Each second, one hundred bolts of lightning are discharging somewhere in the atmosphere. More insidious are the 'evil winds'—the sirocco, the mistral, the kona, the oscure: huge waves of positive ions dropping out of the ionosphere and blanketing whole geographies. Those ions are created as the solar wind and the cosmic rays blow away the electrons of the air molecules at the fringe of space. So, it is the sun and the stars that pull the electrons out of the earth.

[The electric flow of the human body is delicate. When it's disturbed, people feel as though their flesh is not their own.

[Factoids: life is electrical. Life is light.

[Light is timeless. It doesn't change as it moves through space. When it strikes a particle of dust or gas, it's irrevocably altered. But the universe is ninety-nine percent vacuity. Most light will wander forever.]

Jac mounted a spiral incline matted with plush red moss and entered the domed room at the top of the house. From here, the blue thinness of space, the iceclouds, and the mountains like a purple distillation of the sky could be blanked from the dome ceiling and replaced by the stars and the Vastness: planets and gasclouds swimming closer like faces from the bottom of a dream. Instead, his hands paused over a pinlight control console in the wall. After a baffled moment, his fingers remembered, tapped a code, and a lynk-arc appeared. He was going to Ausbok because the eo had broken into the pleroma music of his sleep minutes ago and requested his presence. The eo were like mantics, he remembered, and that frightened him, for this whole nightmare had begun with the mantics.

[Jac, the secret of human destiny is this: like the onion, we have no seed, no separate core, no Self. Endless layers of feelings, sensations, and ideas have gathered together and become you. There is only one moment, and it is infinitely long. At its center is nothing—the nothingness that connects everything—the last reality and the origin. Words reveal our dependence on the void. How can we know any word except by the nothingness which holds it—the white of the page, the silence around a voice?]

Jac fingerstroked a seh-console, evoking pleroma music to drown out Voice. An olfact palette spun out of a wall niche, and Jac selected ORPH, a deep mood which always silenced him. He held the green lozenge to his face, but before misting himself, he listened inward.

[Aristotle says: 'To know the end of a thing is to know the why of it.' So with your life. The bone-seed was planted in the stars—it sprouted on earth—but do you think it ends here? Don't get caught up in this logodaedaly. Grow beyond what is of what never was. Give up your words.]

Jac sprayed the chemical olfact, and a perceptive ease empurpled him. He had forgotten why he was standing here, but a lynk was glowing before him, and he walked through it.

At that time, on the top of a vine-shaggy treeform, Sumner and Drift leaned against a redwood rail. They were watching oryx graze on the riverplain below, sunlight spinning on their long horns. On the far shore, a Massebôth brigade was bivouacked, their green flag swaying in the river breeze.

They frighten me, Lotus Face, Drift thought, remembering the strohlkraft screaming over Miramol, the soldiers bending the né to the wood and breaking its bones with nails. Its blood turtled.

Sumner spoke softly: 'Rubeus made them. That makes sense. The Massebôth are half-alive, cut off from the whole of humanity by their unlove of disorts. They belong to the ort-lord.'

Rubeus is mad, the né concurred. *He raved like a lune.*

'Don't jooch yourself,' Sumner said. 'He wanted me to hit him. I simply obliged.'

Why? He might have killed you.

'The way I feel now, that would have been best. I'm a husk. Without the voor, I don't know why I'm here. Finding you was the only luck I've had.'

I can't replace Corby. But I will be a good friend to you, Lotus Face.

The terrace where they were standing was bright with order: Opal plants glittered in circle tiers, air vines knotted each other, and a sequence of rainbow sculptures spectered the white ivy that hid the lynk they had stepped through a minute earlier.

Lotus Face. Drift touched Sumner's elbow, and he looked down into the round, smooth-featured face. *I was wrong about Ardent Fang.* Its tiny eyes sparked wetly. *He was impetuous with his rage. You did best to outwit Nefandi.*

Sumner's face cracked into a smile. He reached into his pocket and removed a blond wood handgrip plated with tiny touch controls. It caught the sunlight and returned a smile of colors. 'Let's fly.'

Drift took the seh, and its mind flexed into the simplicity of machine logic. In moments it comprehended the tool and was ready to teach Sumner how to fly. The fingerwork was initially tricky, and Sumner spent some time bouncing himself across the terrace before he felt confident enough to jet. Within an hour he was skywalking, sitting in midair, and landing with poetic ease.

A drumthrob announced a lynk. Drift sensed a serene female presence, and a tall, cinnamon-skinned woman stepped into sight. Sumner recognized her at once from his shadowshooting: 'Assia,' he said familiarly as they descended from their hovering.

She stopped, startled by her clairvoyant recognition of his face from her vision moments before.

Drift took Sumner's hand and approached her. When the né

touched her, its grip was burning holy and golden. The cavepool of her mind stunned into charmed light, and knowing infused her, filling her with all of Sumner's and Drift's memories.

'You saw me in CIRCLE?' she asked in Esper, and Sumner understood her through his seh.

'Corby was strong,' he affirmed. A moving darkness bent its depths through him as his memories and his kha passed through Drift and into this woman.

'So much pain.' Assia's voice sounded stranded, and the bloodlines of her face darkened. She let their hands go, and leaned against the redwood railing to concentrate herself. When she looked up, everything good was in her face. 'You've both come a long way,' she said with a wistful smile. 'But I feel the harder distance is ahead. I didn't know Rubeus had shut down the Line. That means we're the only people in Graal besides the Massebôth. All the godminds are gone.' The dry heat of her mouth thickened, and she paused.

'What about the eo?' Sumner asked.

A sweat skein glinted on her upper lip. 'There are no eo. They're not people. They're engrams—the psynergy patterns of all the old CIRCLE mantics. They animate orts sometimes, but they're just memory systems. They don't have one shape.'

They belong to Rubeus?

'No. They're personalities in crystal chips. The mantics themselves went vertical ages ago, riding the Line out of here. They left their psyn-patterns behind to do menial mental work for the occupants of Graal. In times like this they act as conscience. The eo are just ghosts.'

The lynk drumthrobbed twice, and two figures stepped around the white ivy partition. One was Jac; the other, a no-face ort, a humanoid with a mirror-blue facepan. Jac's face had the same depth it had had in his youth: fluvial cheekbones, slim jaw, curved nose, and flaring nostrils, his neck dimpled with boil scars. Assia thanked the ort and sent it back through the lynk.

'I got lost,' Jac said quietly in Esper. 'Since last night, I've been forgetting everything.' He looked to Sumner and Drift. 'Do I know you?'

A spelled feeling spun through Jac. Sumner looked elemental to him, sundark and secret.

'What you feel is our shared spirit, Jac,' Sumner said. The saline arcs beneath his eyes and the sunscars across his nose brutalized Sumner's appearance, but Jac saw that the man had a gentleness, a shade in the color of his eyes soft as a beginning. 'I'm Sumner Kagan. I'm the Delph's fearself. Do you understand that?'

'Yes, of course.' Jac's voice was thin. He did remember Sumner now as the man Rubeus had revealed to him. [The wheel of the law, rolling.] He shivered as an effluvium of fear smoked into his chest.

'Voice?' Assia asked.

'Yes.' The look between them was a wrack of intimacy and shared fear. 'It's happening all over again. Twelve hundred years have passed, but for me the beginning was yesterday, one night of the mind.'

'No, Jac, it's ending now,' Assia hushed, cosseting the back of his neck. 'Rubeus put sky-filters up. Linergy can't touch you. Voice is just residual telepathy. Soon that will pass. You're becoming the self you always were.'

Drift heard the deep unities of compassion in her voice and knew the woman was joyous and healthy. But the man, this Jac, was unsubstanced—haunted. Through the seams of its blood, the né sensed Voice, the throe of the Delph's presence within Jac, and it backed away a step.

'I know who you are,' Jac said, looking into Sumner's face as into a flame. 'I remember the fear vision as I mounted into godmind. I was afraid of the Others, the beings that came from alien places. But I was wrong about them. They were gentle, creative beings. . . .' His hands opened and closed, tight with withholdance. 'I remember so little. But I know this. My enemies didn't come from out there. They came from inside me. Rubeus is dangerous. Are you?'

An oblique smile crossed Sumner's face. 'Not always.'

'Rubeus came to me last night,' Jac said. 'I'd forgotten who he was. He wants me to go to a sleepod . . .'

'Chrysalid,' Assia finished. 'I know of it. The eo have monitored it since the Delph created it a century ago.'

'I thought the eo were ghosts?' Sumner inquired.

'Intelligent ghosts. They're minds without human bodies, but they're aware enough to be a threat to Rubeus.'

Earlier, you called them the 'conscience.'

Assia nodded. 'They are. They have human sensibilities. They were people once, and they want the earth to be good for humanity. Their only problem is, they're too humane. There are weapon systems here that could destroy Oxact and free the world from Rubeus' domination, but the eo won't act until they're provoked. And then it will be too late. Rubeus is powerful.'

You think the ort-lord will attack the eo?

'When Jac is safely ensconced in Chrysalid, there will be nothing to stop Rubeus from striking Ausbok.'

Jac looked shaken. 'You sound very sure.'

'There's no question, Jac,' Assia said. 'Rubeus was created by a god. He's convinced of his sovereignty. We're the enemy.'

A snake of wind coiled through the air plants, and everyone looked out over the river at the troops of milling Massebôth. Jac watched Sumner, feeling a connectedness, a compassion for this being that his fear had created. Reflections wobbled in Sumner's pale eyes, and salt

319

limned his lips like a web. The spell of his long shoulders and the round strength of his back were lined clearly in the sweat dark of his blue shirt.

Assia gazed across the river with narrowing eyes. She recalled Anareta's innocent confusion, and her suspicion hardened to conviction. Rubeus was hoping to use these humans as a living shield, knowing the eo would be reluctant to strike the ort-lord if people would die. Assia's dread thrummed within her.

The né was squinting into the infrangible sunlight, looking at the soldiers, but its mind was aware of the dreamtime opening in Jac's mind. Drift sidled closer, ready to see into this man's mind. Surprisingly, he was a simple-centered being, the sapphires of his thoughts lucid, unclouded by ambitions. Closer, Drift touched a memory that nerved much of Jac's life. Neve. The né saw her eyes, amber and shining, the puberty-passage in her body's supple lines, and the black brightening of her hair. Loneliness trembled around Jac here, and Drift saw the expression on her face that hot summer morning when her husband told her about the tumor in his brain. That expression had begun a special haunting in this man's life. She had loved him.

Hard-cornered grief pushed the seer back into its own senses. Assia had turned her back on the rivershine prisming in the mist. 'It's clear what's going on,' she said, her voice almost silent with feeling. 'This is an ancient war—old as life. It's the battle between history and creativity, reaction and consciousness. Rubeus is a machine, a soulless mind. He's been manipulating events for hundreds of years, consolidating his power. He's going for dominance.'

'What can we do?' Jac asked.

Drift touched Sumner's elbow and pointed to an ice-eyed quetzal bird watching them from the end of the terrace. It felt the bird's machine hollowness and knew it was an ort. *Everything we do is monitored.*

'Rubeus isn't a deep,' Assia told them fervently. 'He can't monitor our symbolife—the psynergy we can draw from our deep selves.' Drift, as a seer, understood, but the long ellipsis in Sumner's eyes made Assia explain: 'The symbolife means using our consciousness—seeing the world and everything that happens to us in it in symbols, as meaning. Living that way, psynergy flows outward into the world instead of simply falling inward with our sensations and making us react. Our deep self—One Mind—can solve this problem with Rubeus if we activate that part of us through our consciousness. That's what Bonescrolls was telling you, Sumner, when he said that selfscan wasn't enough. We can't just have the world entering us and be balanced. We must also enter the world.'

Jac's face was bent with puzzlement. 'How?'

'We all feel a psychic bonding here,' Assia said, her voice softer.

'That's why the eo brought us together. We are the only humans aware of what is happening. We know we can't let Rubeus dominate us. But we can't fight him with strategy. Rubeus is the master strategist. He was designed that way. We'll never outwit him. Yet because he has a design, he will trap himself. I know that. But we've got to keep ourselves from reacting to him—or he'll trap us.'

A portentous feeling lifted through Jac. Frenzied voices dazzled like water at the back of his mind. In his excitement at what Assia was saying, his mind had opened into Iz, the time-matrix. Semiconsciously, he sifted through the whispered sounds until he found what was familiar, noumenal, and reassuring: Voice. [Revelation is in all things.]

A breeze of cool air sneered through the windplants, and the lynk throbbed. A simplefaced ort stepped out from behind the white ivy screen. By the sage glow around its eyes, they could see that it was animated by a force wiser than its shape. 'Matter Mother Mutter,' it said in traditional eo greeting. The artificial face caught a sunray and glowed with the suffused golden light of a shell. The ort faced Sumner, its yellow garments breathing with the wind. 'The eo are aware of you, eth. We know you are metaordered, and we will help you against the ort-lord when the time is right. But first you must wait. Time Now is always more than measure. It is Event itself. We must let the moment fulfill itself.'

Sumner's gaze shot beyond the ort to the enfilades of Massebôth soldiers across the river. 'Those are Massebôth hellraiders over there, eo. They have strohlkraft and armor-piercing artillery. In twenty minutes they could level this forest you're living in. Isn't that threat enough?' He looked at the eo, and the ort stared back impassively.

'I'm a man of blood,' Sumner said, and the bonebeat of anger was in his voice. 'I want to act, not wait.' He faced Assia and then the ort. 'Rubeus killed my son. He powers the Massebôth who oppress a world for a few dying cities. Have you ever seen a dorga pit? Or the inside of a shale processor where the air's so toxic only terminal brown cards are supposed to work there?'

Jac was watching from beside Assia. He was a willful witness, fascinated by what he was seeing of the animal life of history.

'Kagan,' the eo began, its voice soft as ferns.

'I know,' Sumner cut in, the catlike span between his eyes shadowed with intensity, 'the universe has no corners. Any moment is as full as any other.' A laugh caught in his throat and came out soundless. 'Any is nothing. If you want to help me, use whatever power you have *now* to kill Rubeus.'

'Death isn't the answer to life,' the eo retorted. 'Unless Rubeus moves directly against life, we cannot move against him.'

Sumner's heart banged like a board in his chest. 'If you were a human being, eo, you would understand freedom. We don't need directors like Rubeus, the Massebôth, or the Delph. You say I'm the eth. Well then, use me. I'm ready to destroy.'

'You don't understand,' the eo said evenly. 'You're lost in your feelings. Every one of us is metaordered in some way. Assia's ancestors called it karma—the inexplicable patterns that shape our lives. Time is what makes the pattern ineffable, but originally, when people lived closer to the moment, the word *karma* meant doing. Do you truly want to champion death? Is that what you want to do? No. You are a precious lifeform, a human. What you need, Sumner, is to learn love.'

'Love?' Sumner's gaze stalled in his head. 'I've starved my emotions to hard bone to conquer myself. I've dragged my sex-pull straight up my spine so that my eyes could feel. I've chosen flow over shape every time. I love life.'

'But is your life love?'

Sumner's face was glowering with an eerie, beastlike calm. 'Why do anything? Why not just drift? Mama is maw, right?'

'No.' The ort's face shadowed toward a frown. 'We eo believe the Mother is the intermediary between our inorganic beginnings and our creative expression. That is why we greet each other: Matter Mother Mutter. Life, Kagan, is love. Yes, we have the weapons to thoroughly destroy Rubeus. But they're just science fictions without a spirit to guide them. That spirit is compassion and love. If Rubeus does not have that spirit, the universe will destroy him.'

'Don't be so sure.' Something like starlight gave out in Sumner's eyes, and he turned to Jac. 'What do you want me to do?'

Jac stiffened. 'I'm a twenty-first century man, Kagan. This is the thirty-third century. I don't know anymore.'

'A friend of mine loves the kro,' Sumner said quietly, thinking of Chief Anareta. 'I once felt him think that humanity recognized the value of the individual in your time. He called it self-anarchy. What you think means a lot to me.'

'I trust Assia and the eo.' Jac's mouth groped; then: 'You and I have both felt the lifelove of One Mind and seen it change reality. But it wasn't us. It was the Delph and Corby. We were just hosts. Accidents. But we saw the lifelove. I think now we have to trust that power as individuals. I don't know what that means for you exactly, but the eo are good.'

'What good have they done for the distorts? Or the voors?'

'What can we do?' the eo replied. 'We're not human. We're just memories of knowledge. It takes people to do.' The eo addressed Assia: 'Sister, as you can see, the Massebôth have arrived. Rubeus has never allowed us any truly human-looking ort forms. Will you help us communicate with them? One of them, their spokesman, has been asking for you. And Jac—I invite you to stay with us. You'll be safer.'

322

Assia went to Sumner's side. 'The eo are right, Sumner. We have to wait now. But Rubeus will trap himself. I'm an old, old woman. Much older than Rubeus. My experience is deep. You'll see.'

She, the eo, and Jac turned and walked into the lynk and out of sight. Drift touched Sumner's hand, and a psalmed feeling calmed him. He took out the seh and looked down into the né's round face. 'Let's fly.'

They stepped out into the afternoon sky toward blue clouds swirling over the horizon, intricate as birdsong. Sumner's ears popped, and the air chilled brightly as they ascended. They flew up the brown serpent of a river and over mountains where mists circled and bright glaciers rang with sunlight.

At the far end of the day they descended into Reynii, an abandoned city of glass spires and hanging gardens. They landed on a sconce of tall grass and watched the red haloes of sunlight lift off the empty towers. Cold worlds shook over the horizon: the dewdrop Llyr and, flecked within the sun's aura, the iron splinter of Macheoe.

Across the boulevard and a dark tree-park was a worship house between two moonshadowed elms. Over the doors, in né-futhorc, was carved.

Drift translated: *One Mud of All Sculpting*. Through the portals they could see statues of all the world's demiurgic and unnamable gods staring out from lux-lit enclaves. The close solitude of the fuliginous temple was inviting, and they entered.

You've changed, Drift thought, but not loud enough for Sumner to hear without his voorsense. Lotus Face's golden kha was slimmer, and without the black mask of his faceburn, he looked human and vulnerable. When the seer stared into his eyes, it no longer felt the drowse of voor depths. This man's mind was as shallow as any simple tribesman's. A sadness stroked the né's soul.

'What are you looking for in my face?' Sumner asked. He was weary and emotionally sprained. Ever since Bonescrolls' death, his self-horror had been widening, and he wanted time to find something he liked in himself.

I see into *you, Lotus Face.* Tears sparkled in its eyes. *I'm as vacant as you without the magnar. Everything I liked in myself was tribal. .But here we are. Alone.* The né motioned at the pillared darkness and the smell of gods. *I'm tired.*

Drift wandered off among the small altars and worship-columns to grant Sumner privacy. It was exhausted from a full day of one-with, and within minutes it had curled up in a remote alcove and fallen asleep.

Sumner sat in the clenched shadows, the pain of his solitude unraveled around him: Everything he had ever done was a dream. *I have my life*, he thought. *I live.* But that wasn't true. He wasn't the same being who had known lifelove in Miramol and One Mind in the desert. Without his voorsense, his memories of Bonescrolls and the Serbota were lame. Everything he had done then was a dream.

Blood was calling to blood: *Truly we are.*

Even the dark things voors had done to him had become lucid with time: Jeanlu's attempted lusk had led him to the Rangers, and Corby's lusk had brought him to the Serbota. Voors had been his secret strength most of his life. With the pith of his bones, he knew that it was Rubeus and the Massebôth who had made his reality vagrant and unreliable.

His hands lay limp in his lap, and his head was cocked back against the hardwood. He sat as if his whole life had sunk away. Shadows hooded his eyes, and his breathing dimmed. In selfscan, he became the temple: puddled sounds of footsteps and glass windbells, furzy incense odors, and a calm, almost motionless air current patterned with dampness. . . .

His body slept while his mind watched everything. Feelings too big for memory shifted their vast weights, and the darkness of the shadows began to harden. So slowly that it took all night, Sumner's eyes filled with tears.

A wing of gray-blue sunlight stood like a presence among the spare shadows of the alcove when Sumner woke. His grief had smoked away with his sleep, leaving him quiet and empty. The cool heat of dawn seeped through the slatboards with the fragrance of pimienta.

He moved to stretch—but, impossibly, his body was inert, immobilized as it had been in Rubeus' presence. His legs were dull shapes, and his hands weren't his anymore. Weirdly then, his fingers began to twitch, his wrist turn. Even his breathing slued in and out of him under another will. Quite close, he heard his heart moaning.

Confusion staggered him when his body twisted to its feet. He was moving as if voor-possessed, but there was no voorsense, no Iz-noise, no deep sensitivity—only the immense compulsion to move. Then he saw it: a leather-handled knife, its oil-black blade long and moon-curved, stuck into the wooden wall of the alcove. His right arm levitated, and his fingers uncurled to grasp the leather haft.

Mind wheeling, Sumner watched helplessly as his hand tugged the knife from the wall and turned the blade inward. A cold blank space in his belly widened, and terror rattled in his throat. As the knife stabbed into his chest, horror exploded into will, and he twisted from the waist. The knife edge slashed through his tunic top and sprayed blood onto his killing-hand.

Keeled over, he saw past the carved outline of the alcove to the sunfrayed shadows where a figure was lying. It was Drift, unconscious or dead. Above it, in the caliginous light, a distort was watching him with the abstract stare of an iguana. His face was slim, baked-looking and broken. His right hand rose, and Sumner's right hand lifted. The distort's eyes purred. Above the spiderhairs of his eyebrows, two skull-plates caught sunlight and glinted like horns. His right hand pounded his chest.

Fury twisted in Sumner's arm, and his knife-arm sprang at him. Again, panic-energy wrenched him backward from the waist, and he tumbled out of the alcove and banged into a tray of ash-carvings. The blade had caught him deep in the shoulder, and its pain transfixed him. The distort stood nearby, his eyes musical, his fig-face tight with will. He moved his right hand away from his shoulder and pulled it strongly across his throat.

Sumner's hand jerked the knife free from his shoulder, and the pain shone like light. In its blaze his fear shriveled, and space pulled away from him, unfolding into the distances of his body. It took all the power of selfscan, all his inner-knowing, before the wheels of thought whirring inside him jumped to a stop.

And all at once, he wasn't fearing or hurting or thinking. The blade that had been kissing his throat turned away.

The distort's face seemed to rearrange. He stepped back, and his left hand flashed to a hip pocket.

Sumner's knife-hand wristrolled, and the blade hissed through the air. It caught the distort's arm and kicked the seh he had been reaching for out of his hand. Lizard-swift, the man snatched the knife from his arm and shimmied for where the seh had fallen.

Almost casually, Sumner rolled to his side and, with one arm, hoisted the black-iron tray of scattered ashes. The distort pulled up short as the ornate tray crushed the seh.

The distort spun about, blade high. Sumner was on his feet and calmly approaching, moving between him and Drift: no rage, no doubt in the irenic blue of his eyes.

The distort feinted with the blade and dashed into the shadows. He dodged among the candle altars and demon-columns, kicking idols and incense braziers into Sumner's way, and banging his knife against the glass chimes and metal gods. 'Get away from me, eth!' he shouted, his voice electric with command. 'You don't know who you are.' His eyes were bright with urgency. 'You're less with each step.' He spun about and waved his wounded arm before him hypnotically, slow-stepping backwards. 'You're nothing, nothing—'

The distort's words echoed through the temple with trancestrength, but Sumner wasn't listening. He stalked past the Paseq altar, gauging the distance to the exit, feeling out the shapes of escape the man was carving for himself. He let the distort take a slight lead among the bell-pillars, planning to bound over the stacks of sitting-mats and snag him at the door. But he moved faster than Sumner thought a human could. He flitted through the blue shafts of dawnlight and bolted out the door before Sumner could close in.

Killing-genius stopped Sumner. Unthinking but knowing, he took out his seh, and his fingers moved coolly over its metal face, rearranging the pinprick lights. With his painumb arm, he seized a bulky dragon-idol from its niche and rammed the wooden seh-grip into its gaping maw. The iron god bobbled into the air with the buoyancy of the seh. The distort's footfalls softstepped along the fringe of hearing. Sumner flicked the seh's forward-thrust to max, thumbed the delayed-stop, and heaved the dragon in the killer's echoed direction.

The temple wall blasted outward, and in the receding din another explosion bansheed from nearby. Sumner stepped over a sagging roofbeam and saw in the metallic morning light that the flying dragon had found its mark. The distort's legs hung over the splintered bole of a tree. The idol was embedded in a small bloodpuddled crater.

Sumner brushed his ear. A whistle was twining in his head. As he stepped forward to see if the seh was intact, the whistle became a shrill-pitched wail. He saw that the others standing on the hill weren't hearing it. The whine became a needle skewed between his eyes, pithing his skull. He fell to his knees, hugging his head, and roared. The ringing agony trilled into his teeth, shook vision to shards, and dropped him beneath his cry.

[We see ourselves only as what we see.]

A pungent scent grazed Sumner's nostrils, sending needles of light straight up into his brain. The olfact dragged him awake but left his senses dangling in a watery ash of slumber. Words came to him sheathed in the warm current of his blood, slendering through an uneven sequence of layers— 'Wake up. Come on.'

The voice walked heavily through him. It was ominous, yet he wasn't sure why. Fearful premonitions grated his nerves, urging him to swing violently and see if he could roll free and break into a run. But a deeper awareness, just coming into focus, stayed that decision. The voice, of course. He recognized it.

Slowly, he raised his lids and looked up into the stern, ducal face of Rubeus.

Sumner tried to turn and rise, but he was strapbound, his body hauled up in a sling. The bindings clawed his flesh, and that sensation hardened his surroundings to a sharper definition. He saw a glitter of green resolve to a gem-caked panoply—a cruciform mandala. Around it, the ceiling was divided into lozenges of petal-blue light. The soap-colored straps, tense with his weight, were clipped to ball-divots that seemed to be hovering in midair.

'Murder is punishable by exile from Graal, Kagan.' Rubeus' voice was a scowl. 'The distort is dead.'

Sumner tried to twist his body free, and the ort-lord held up a clear rhomboidal gem. The light inside the crystal deliquesced to a ruminative glow. Sumner relaxed, his attention fixed on the declensions of color in the gem. 'Where's Drift?' he muttered.

'Drugged in Reynii. Don't concern yourself with that freak. You have more anguish ahead of you than its suffering. The distort you killed was no one—an easily found and conditioned animal. But you killed him.' Rubeus said this darkly but within he felt awe. The distort wasn't supposed to die. He was a psi-master. Sumner's emotionally bruised mind should have been mud in his hands. He palmed the odyl gem and looked again to see that the killer's limbs were secured tightly. 'That was a stupid thing you did. Stricture here deals harshly with murderers.'

Sumner's eyes watched him coldly. 'He tried to kill me.'

'No. He tried to make you kill yourself.' Rubeus' rooster-cut hair spiked against the glow of the ceiling lights. His smile was zaned. 'There's no stricture against that. He visualized your death potently. Murder wasn't the right response to him. You could have killed a lot of people when you tripped your seh. That was mad.' His eyes narrowed critically. 'You're insane. You see yourself as separate, and you pull those around you into the gap between you and the world.' The crystal panoply lit up into crests and cartouches of patterning colors. 'Now it's time for you to go down into that pit and face what you've dumped there.'

While the ort talked, Sumner had been internally compressing himself, using techniques trained into him at Dhalpur. Muscles folded in on themselves and bone slid onto bone. With a snap, Sumner's right hand pulled free of its brace and whipped violently at Rubeus, missing his face by a centimeter.

The ort-lord jerked back with an alarmed shout, and the odyl gem spun between his fingers. The dreaming light clicked in Sumner's eyes, and he sagged.

'You've punched your way through life this far, Kagan, but no further.' Rubeus' fingers quavered as he secured Sumner's hand. This man was more dangerous than any scan indicated. 'Graal stricture demands exile for murderers. But because I would kill you as soon as you left Graal, exile is disallowed. The godminds do not condone execution. The only alternative is the trance.'

Rubeus looked upshoulder at the jeweled cruciform. 'The trance will take only moments,' he said as the ambient light dimmed, 'though for you, it may be endless.'

Heartlight pulsed above Sumner, and he twisted his head to face the ort. He mustered all the emotional control he had and said with the slam-force of calm certainty: 'You can't stop me, ort. I'm the eth. I *am* the pit.'

Rubeus quickly slumbered Sumner with the odyl gem. 'I'm not afraid of you—eth!' He laughed, but the whole inside of his chest was frosted over. 'There's no coming back from where you're going.'

A tessitura of chimes ranged to the limits of hearing, and the chamber became a diamond of green-white light. Sleep-vertigo wheeled Sumner to the brink of awareness.

'The Delph, if he were here, would have had a bit of advice for you.' Rubeus' voice spilled into the whirr of the crystals: 'Don't rub one part of an elephant too long—and don't be surprised by a real dragon.'

The darkness was tensed with light: Mirrorglints, sparks, and fibrous water reflections spiderwebbed the silence. An image was weaving itself out of that glimmerous blackness. Touched by nothing, deaf and distant, Sumner watched the figure of a man glitter into being. It was Ardent Fang.

The darkness lifted, and every shadow went with it. In the glare-white, Ardent Fang drummed with color: vibrant black hair and beard, coffee-glossed skin, eyes brisk with clarity in a square, unperplexed face. He was wearing the tattered Serbota garments he had died in.

As he came forward, the space around him, white with nothing, bruised. Shapes darkened in the whiteness: A sprawling, flat-topped tree appeared in midair, roots scraggy and hanging. Nearby a splash of lucid water floated, flakes of sunlight skipping off it. Clawed shrubs and the skeleton of a pear tree unfolded beside him.

When Ardent Fang reached him, everything had been filled in. They were standing in green sunlight beneath bending pear trees. In this grove, Ardent Fang had been blown apart by Nefandi while Sumner had watched. Now his face was as washed and clear as the sky. He held a stubby fist forward and opened it to reveal a brood jewel.

Sumner was awed by the supreme realism of the trance. There was no dreaminess at all. The sinewed trees, the glint of spiderlines, and the swagger of a birdcall were opaque with reality.

He looked down at the amulet, and Ardent Fang dropped it in the grass. The gem glowed hotly on a leaf of sunlight. Ardent Fang's sandal came down on it, and its crunch was knuckle-tight. 'It's a lie.'

328

His eyes were yellow anger. 'There's no strength in idols. No power in form—unless I'm there.'

Sumner toed a tuft of lemongrass and noticed that he was dream-dressed as he had been at that time of his waking life. A slim moon limped high in the sky. 'This is a trance, Ardent Fang.' His voice sounded foolishly real.

'I'm not Ardent Fang.' Ardent Fang's voice was blunt. 'Don't you recognize me? I've been with you since the first day of the world. I've spoken to you in many voices.'

Ardent Fang bloated, wobbled, and then unsprung into a hulking razorjaw lizard. Its long black muzzle shrieked once and the beast collapsed into its lunge, flash-molting into the blazing column of a deva-fire and then into the plasma streamers and oily flames of Iz-light. 'I was all these beings in your life,' a humming void-voice spoke. 'I'm the Dreamshaper, so near to you I'm nothing. I live in everything dying. Untouchable. Nameless. Free. I am.' The coiling Iz-lights flashed to a center of instreaming white radiance.

Sumner cowered. When he looked up, Ardent Fang was standing beside him, and the pear trees were leaning into the windrubbed sunlight.

'Ardent Fang is the first,' the shapeshifter said, helping him to his feet. 'I know it's hard for you to face him. I tried to clean him up a little, so you could remember more slowly how much he suffered.'

Sumner felt earsick, and he swayed as he stood. Seeing Ardent Fang, a frenzy of shared memories rioted in his mind: joywalking through the riverain forest, mating with distorts in the stables of Miramol, hunting upriver—His hands squeezed his head, trying to grab hold of his cascading thoughts.

'Where do you suppose the pain went when you stopped remembering it?' Ardent Fang was lying on the ground, his body reduced to a broken calcined skeleton. All the grief, shame, and confusion that there had been no time for Sumner to feel the day Ardent Fang had died returned. He dropped to his knees under the weight of it.

Ardent Fang had been strong as much in his will as in his body, and they had shared much. Should he have tried to save him from Nefandi? The doubt was still circling in him. *No, no,* part of him was thinking—at the time there had been no hope against Nefandi's field-sword. And so he had let Ardent Fang go. He had brutalized the man—

'Very good,' a soothing voice spoke from the ash-peeled skull. 'Open yourself up to your doubts and your loathing. Feel everything. It is the only way to be healed.'

Sumner stayed with Ardent Fang, dreaming backwards through each hour that they had spent together, until he reached the end of his memories and the beginning of his feelings.

Sumner spent hours dreaming through the memories of every experience that had shaped him. In time, he began to thin out. Empathy eroded him, and the tabooed feelings, the hidden cravings, and the denied gentleness of his soul became his trance-experience.

He held Zelda as he had always wanted to, feeling her breasts soft and loose against his face. He strangled his father enough times to love him. He lived once more the hypnotic wonder that as a child had made him walk a horse out onto the ice. Seeing its pyre-smoke again, he vanished into the deep spell of his feelings.

Nightmared free, the days of his life blew around him like rags. He was in the black of the trance, his thoughts and feelings brushlights circling the point of his awareness. He wasn't memory. The more he remembered, the less he became. He was distance, the space between what he was now and what he had been at conception. And before that? Transparent feelings rose in him, colored by his mind: He remembered Corby taking him out to Rigalu Flats and showing him Iz. He remembered the evanescent images of past animations: shark, hawk, hind rat. But those too had been distance. Not distance covered—or dis-covered—by his ego but rather the distance of vastly complex energies. Aloof from his body and absorbed into the feeling-core of his being, he sensed those energies.

Psynergy, Kagan. The Dreamshaper's voice opened into running light. *Psynergy is energy patterned over aeons: the cell yantra, stereo vision, hand and eye coordination, trapping fire, trapping animals, trapping thoughts!*

The trance became the fruit-embered light of a scansule. The silver console curved before him, and on the hooded screen the words of the Dreamshaper appeared among kinetic images and rotating displays: 'Thought is matrix.' Letters linked like atoms, and word-molecules coalesced and vanished:

'MATRIX, (kro) mater, *mother, womb.*

'Thought is a matrix which engenders its own reality. The ideas, concepts, belief-systems that your ancestors trapped have become your trap.'

A series of statements slowrolled up the screen:

THE TRAPPED AND THE TRAP ARE THE SAME.
WHAT YOU CREATE, CREATES YOU.
WHAT CREATES YOU DESTROYS YOU.
MAMA IS MAW.
MATRIX IS MA TRIX.

The thought-matrix is self-deception, the Dreamshaper continued. *It's continual sense that each of us is the center—the sense we needed as infants. Ma\ tricks always work. People are biologically deceived. Ego is synthesized like fingernails or hair. It's a carapace, a protective covering, a husk. It surrounds the feeling-self and can never be done away with or the being will die. The most one can hope for is transparency. The ego must be clear. It's never a question of will,* *of doing something to improve yourself. You are. What I'm talking about is distance. You must be clear so that the distances can pass through you.*

Sumner fidgeted before the scansule, and a red cancel-sign buzzed on: 'DON'T TRY IT!'

Don't try to understand, the Dreamshaper said, and a word-display cartooned before him:

'TRY, (kro) tritare, *to rub to pieces.'*

Your ego is bowel-consciousness. It wants to break everything into shapes simpler than itself. It wants to know distance. But the closest it can come is feeling, and even then it's only touching a part of your being. The one secret is that all things are secret.

The scansule stenciled: 'UNDERSTANDING IS A LIE' and smoked away into pink fumes.

Listen. The blackness was thick as desire, and only the Dreamshaper's voice kept Sumner focused. *Being is more than thought and bones. Being is endless and moving, like light, never in one place long enough to be anyplace. Existence looks small through the holes of a skull. But you're big, bigger than you can know. Can't you feel it? You're burning through all the lost moments of your life. And you'll keep on burning, because distance is all there is, and finishing isn't everything.*

A far-carrying voice came to him, high, wild, blurred with echoes. It was a thought, unrepeatable, arrived. He repeated it: *I am. I am.* And he was. . . .

Sumner woke. He was dressed in black trousers, gray-buffed halfboots and a dark billow-sleeved shirt. His body felt still and concentrated, thoroughly rested.

The dreaming was over. The carrousel of stars, the moon's shape and position, were as they would have been outside the trance. And though he was dressed differently and in an unfamiliar place, he was certain that he was awake.

He looked about for Rubeus. He was in an enclosed courtyard illuminated by the night rainbows and the pale fire of the moon. A group of men was approaching—soldiers. He stared at them as if from another life.

'You!' one of the uniformed men called. 'Stand to!'

In the relic light of the stars, Sumner at first did not register what he was seeing. Thoughts were too small and tight, too much like eggs—alive but inanimate. When he realized that the soldiers approaching were Massebôth, it was too late to run.

'Where are your tags, soldier?' an ape-slanted officer asked. He was flanked by six men.

'I'm a ranger,' Sumner replied. 'I'm here by request of the eo.'

A riddled expression phased over the officer's face; then he shrugged. 'All I see is your uniform and no tags.' He turned away

331

and ordered over his shoulder: 'Take him in and find out who he really is.'

The six men were on Sumner immediately, grappling to secure his arms. But he threw himself back against one of the soldiers and kicked out with both feet. Twist and roll, and four men were down. His rage expanded, his hands free now and amazing with anger. But as he advanced, a soldier broke open a wrist-canister and misted Sumner's face with a searing, throat-choking spray. He staggered back, his eyes slim and dreamy, bright with fear.

The Massebôth came at him with knives. Through the blear of pain, Sumner's hands flashed out, punching one assailant between his gritful eyes and wristseizing another's knife-hand. But the drug they had hit him with slowed everything inside him. With machine speed a knife-hand appeared, and the blade sliced through the air and slammed into the top of his chest.

The impact knocked him free from his tangle and sent him careening clumsily backward, the knife strumming between his hands. Something like glass cracked two inches behind his eyes. As he lay on his back, the taste of blood gluey in his mouth, Sumner's vision glared dark. A fist of cold was squeezing the fire out of his chest, and his tongue buckled like a razor against his teeth.

The thin, musical edge of sleep dropped away. A pungent scent spiked light through his brain. 'Come on. Wake up.' The heavy voice jarred vision into his eyes, and he gazed into a panoply of jeweled light—a radiant cruciform mandala. The petal-blue light hardened around ball-divots floating in midair. The attached soap-colored straps were tight with his weight.

He twisted in the trance-sling, and Rubeus' chiseled face swung into view, the rhomboid of an odyl gem flashing in his hand.

Sumner lurched, but the sling held him tightly. His eyes were drunk. 'How long?'

'The trance?' The smiling face glanced at a constellation of sapphire gem-lights. 'About forty-two seconds. The first trance was free-form. The second I manipulated.'

Sumner's voice reeled: 'The Massebôth—'

'You've been tranced since you killed my distort,' Rubeus confirmed.

Sumner's eyes wailed.

Rubeus regarded him with amusement. 'You're beginning to apprehend the scope of it all, aren't you?' Light leaped in the odyl gem he was holding, and the sling rotated until Sumner was upright. 'Now you'll never be sure what's real and what isn't, will you?' Sumner's face went hard as stone. 'Perhaps in the next five minutes of real time you'll live through fifty years.' A tic hymned at the corner of

Sumner's mouth. 'Perhaps it will take hours of real time—lifetimes in trance.'

An icy scream cut through Sumner. Rubeus blinked the odyl gem in his face, and Sumner leaned into a loose collapse.

'You're being frightened by a real dragon, Kagan.' Rubeus nodded his face close to Sumner, his eyes weary with mirth. 'Be brave.'

The Untelling

[Everything that moves comes back on itself sooner or later. I know that better than any human. Movement is sphere: a declension of vectors from the rounding curve of the expanding cosmos to spiral galaxies, stars, planets, and cells—expanding again through the blastosphere, the eye, and the skull.]

The moon was knocked to its back in the day sky, and Nobu Niizeki was looking at the clear-colored air around it as he walked. In his mind the moon was a leaping prayer; all the real lost loves of the earth circled with it, clear as music. Everything that had ever tried to rise above itself was there: plant-tip cells exploding, seashells widening their spirals, and the expanding shell of the skull, itself so much like the moon.

Nobu jolted to an abrupt halt. The rumbled breathing of the sea had dulled. Alertness flared in him, and he looked around to see that the monotonous seacurve had lifted to a horizon of hills. He was standing at the disheveled edge of the beach, where shattered shells and demonshapes of dried seaweed mixed with dark earth and tall, skinny arms of bamboo. He was standing a dozen paces beyond the border of his beach prison!

A quiver of mad joy almost stopped his heart. He looked back at the sand furrows, the slump of the beach edge, and the long curve of the wave-beaten strand shining with the sea's chrism. He was free! A palsy of ecstasy nearly dropped him.

For over twelve centuries . . .

His face knotted, but he reared in his feelings. He had to be certain. Though, of course, he was certain: He knew his limits very well—he had pressed against them for twelve centuries, and for all that time they had pressed back, invisible and ineluctable.

He turned away, and the carved greenness of the world before him hugely ached with luminosity. He took several bold strides forward and then burst into a sprint, running hard into the bright world of his freedom.

[V—symbol of the descent and the return: the journey of light down from identitiless freedom to the freedomless identity of crystal and its

334

rebound up through life to light again. V, the timeless godmind emblem to be found even forty thousand years ago, etched on bone amulets by timeloose Cro-Magnons.]

A ram-ort followed Nobu as he wandered away from the sea and into the mountains. Rubeus watched the man stumbling over the ravine rocks, still in his mantic uniform, clumsy with joy. The ort-lord hungered for the power to feel his thoughts. Since his creation Rubeus had pondered Nobu's fate. Why had the Delph kept this being alive and aware on a spit of sand for twelve hundred years?

The sheep-ort ledgehopped to a higher vantage as Nobu's rampant hike led him upward. [Where are you going, little man?] But the mantic wasn't telepathic, and Rubeus had to content himself simply to watch. And watching to wonder: [What did the Delph, in godmind, out of time, see of Nobu now, here at his crucial moment? The scene seen is nebulous.]

Still, he followed, drawn on by the illogic, the whimsy of this creature's fate. Nobu, grunting, continued to climb the steepening terrain, a religious light floating on his face. Then the thought shocked through Rubeus: [The Delph had no reason!] Staring at Nobu, the ort-lord felt the gravity of the vastness between his crystal-logic and the Delph's fantasy. [Fantasy is a wound. Only reason is seamless.]

The ram-ort perched on a ledge above Nobu. It stared down at him hauntedly, swaying to an unheard incantation, inspelled and slow as a seaplant.

How to survive? Nobu lay huddled and shivering against a granite shoulder. He was in a white pine grove watered by snowmelt; wire-thin creeks ran off the high ledges, rainbow-misting the tall rock sky. He had come up here for the light and the clouds—but he had forgotten about the cold. It glittered in his hands and sparked in his teeth. He wanted to get up and go on. A world was his, expanding through the smell of red cedar and fireweed to the dreamy mountains and a sky full of every shape of cloud. But the paths leading from this place were barbed with snagthorns and covered with frost rime. Where to go? Every direction led him deeper into his needs.

An ice-eyed ram watched him with insouciant dignity.

What is joy? The coldness shaking him was joy. He had been denied it for so long, living only as a mind, a hungerless ghost caught sideways in time, knowing everything, feeling nothing. Now even pain felt good. He grinned into the burn of the wind. Human fear was the smallest feeling on the planet.

The ram startled and bounded out of sight across a ledge of bramble. Nobu sat up and turned so that his back broke the flowing cold. A buzzing floated in his face muscles. *Only freedom is mystery. Only mystery can fill all the space of the mind.* Like a drunk, he started to weep.

After the vapor of his feelings had thinned into the mountain wind, he was left tired and watchful. The snowmelt silvered its soft oratory over the pebbled rocks.

'Niizeki,' a woman said, coming up behind him. She smelled of shadowy forested places, and the dusk of her face was intimately familiar.

'Assia!'

'It's been a long time, Nobu,' she said in Esper. 'You're free now. Part of a new world. Can you stand?'

Nobu wobbled to his feet. Beyond Assia, time looked thin among the clouds. 'The Delph—' he began, but she hushed him.

'I will explain everything.'

[Newton in 1730 on page 374 of the fourth edition of *Opticks:* 'The changing of Bodies into Light, and Light into Bodies, is very conformable to the course of Nature, which seems delighted with Transformation.']

Nobu sat in a glade of twisted black dancestep trees. Assia and an eo were standing in a polygon of sunlight a respectful distance away, granting him time to reflect on what she had told him. In his mind's eye he still saw the strand of his exile and, spontaneously, the twinkling of dolphin-arcs in the morning sea.

He shook his head till his blood buzzed. Pain was sacred. Hunger, Lust, Fatigue, and Ignorance were all sacred once again, because in the Delph's spell he had not felt any of them. But the majesty of his humanity was opaque with needs, and he suffered to think that soon he would be lost again among meals, sleep, and women. The knowing was gone. The eld wisdom that he had learned to see in a gull's feather and a grain of sand had dimmed, muffled by his physicality. He was meat again. That was the Delph's cruelest punishment.

Drift opened its eyes to see a dark smiling face. 'I'm Nobu Niizeki,' the man said gently. Assia, Jac, and a manikin-faced eo-ort circled him. 'We found you in the temple at Reynii after the eo told us about Sumner's capture.'

Capture? Drift sat up, and dark gleamed in its eyes. *Where is he?*

'You should rest, friend,' Jac advised.

Drift waved him away and looked at Assia. *Where is he?*

'Rubeus has him in a trance,' she said. 'The ort's trying to break his mind. We're on our way now to free him if we can.'

Jac helped the né to its feet. 'He's a lynk-jump away. The eo can get us into the dream-chamber at Oxact.'

'Getting away, however, may be impossible,' the eo added. 'The Oxact lynk is a one-way jump. When you leave through it, you'll lynk to the outside but not to here. You'll have to get past all of Rubeus' orts.'

'You'll be safe with me along,' Jac said. 'Rubeus wants me alive.'

'Frankly,' the eo admonished, 'it's too great a risk. Sumner opened himself to this fate. I think we must trust time now.'

I'm going, Drift said, standing up and swaying dizzily. They were on top of the open treeform in Ausbok, overlooking the mud-shiny banks of a river. *What happened to me?*

'You were drugged by one of Rubeus' distort minions,' Assia said. 'You're still woozy, and it may be best to wait.'

No. Drift shook the muzziness from its head. *I'm going now. Help me, please.*

Nobu took Drift to the arc of the lynk, and the others followed. Seeing this distort, so strange and yet human-looking, and feeling its telepathy magicking into him, Nobu was affectionately attracted. Everything Assia had told him about the machine-mind Rubeus and its domination of the world was focused here in this mutant's feeling and friendship for another human. Nobu's blood felt knighted, and he was eager to help, whatever the cost.

'If you must go,' the eo said, 'then everyone stay close. I've pinpointed you directly to the trance chamber where Sumner is. As soon as you get him, get back into the lynk. I've arranged for it at least to get you out of Oxact. From there, you'll have to use the two sehs you have—Assia's and Jac's—and fly north to the next lynk. That'll return you here.'

Assia took Nobu's hand. It was strange seeing him dressed in yellow eo raiment. 'Nobu—you don't have to come. You don't even know Sumner.'

'I know you,' he said with his usual courtliness. 'Besides, Rubeus is the dark side of the Delph. I must do what I can now, as a man.' The continent of time on which he had existed god-free, hungerless and enlightened, was still in sight. Only the clarity he had known then was gone. Fatigue was thicker than he remembered.

Let's go, Drift urged. And they entered the lynk.

[*Chandogya Upanishad* refers to the inmost self as Inner Light.
[Al-Ghazali taught that everything is a gradation of light.
[Rumi wrote:

Light shapes the embryo in the womb—
Why else do we come out of the darkness with eyes?

[In the Zoroastrian *Gathas* the lifeforce is called the lost light.]

They found Sumner alone, trussed up in the vortex illumination of the trance-sling. White metal arches gazelled in long curves down endless corridors, the blue light shatterable on the mirror-polished floors.

Drift ran to Sumner and immediately began unstrapping him. *Lotus Face—wake up!*

As the straps were undone, hexahedrons of sunfire hum-circled once around the chamber and vanished. Sumner was lowered to the ground and sat up, slow-faced. Drift embraced him, and with all its empathic presence it rooted him in the here and now. *This is real. You are awake. Can you feel it?*

Sumner nodded, the bloodshot depths of his trance farther away now in the né's telepathic grip than all his past lives. 'Drift,' he mumbled. 'Thank you.' He looked up at the other: Nobu, Jac, Assia. They gazed down on him like an illumination: faces in a field of force. Nobu's expression was a hypnotism of fascination, and Sumner remembered him from Corby's shadowshooting. 'Where's Rubeus?'

'Not far, I'd guess,' Assia said. 'We should move.'

Hammer light banged vision, and the entire dream-chamber went bright-blind. When sight returned, Jac was gone.

'Jac!' Assia cried, her voice puling into odd, overlapping echoes.

'You think you have accomplished anything?' Voice boomed through the chamber. 'How else could I have Jac returned but to let you enter my rath. And now that I have what is mine, you are all corpses.'

Assia pushed Nobu toward the lynk and helped Sumner to his feet. 'That was a particle-beam Rubeus hit us with,' she said. 'Only the field built into the seh saved us. But the seh can't absorb too many of those. We have to get out now.'

'You are in the darkest pit of your lives,' Voice spoke, as darkness shambled around them. 'Where can you run? Distance is thought— and I have the bigger mind.'

A chord of light from Assia's seh waved across the room, pointing the way to the lynk.

'What about Jac?' Sumner asked, tracking a movement through the darkness.

'I don't know what happened. I've never seen anything like that. Rubeus is stronger than any of us thought. We have—'

Assia broke off as a crowd of simplefaced orts hardened out of the darkness. Sumner had sensed them closing in, and as they surrounded them, he spun into violence. His slashing hands hit tough artificial faces, knocking down three orts before Assia's seh-light bluebrightened to a cutting laser. She seared off the head of the ort that was grappling with Nobu and swung the hot beam around, driving the others back into the darkness.

They ran through the lynk and into a predawn landscape. Vast fists of laser-lit clouds were rising from beyond the white peak of Oxact. Closer, the ridgerocks were lighting up around them, shining like coral. 'It's a war,' Assia almost cried. 'These rocks have been hit by metafrequency light. Ausbok must be striking back.'

338

Drift took Sumner's hand. It was sinewed and warm. *Can we get away?*

'We have only one seh,' Assia said, pinching back the cry in her blood. 'The other one was with Jac.'

Sumner looked closely at Assia, trying to feel whether he was still tranced. His veins felt black and caulked, but the spirit he saw in her face bolstered him.

Nobu edged closer to them. 'The sky's on fire,' he said, awed. His eyes were burning with a possessed light, and his face was a shining of terror as he followed the rapid blasts of energy hacking the sky. Deeper within the hostility of his fear, Nobu was watching, not participating. He felt disembodied, numbed by the horror around him.

Sumner released Drift's hand and mounted a pebbled winze to see where they were. A childshaped moon was sitting low on the sky where laser arcs crisscrossed, and the skirling breeze was a chimney of sounds: toads, insects, and the approaching siren of burning rock. . . . He glimpsed a mirror-eyed fox; then the pinecove clapped into an exploding radiance, and a long-tailed scream sirened louder than hearing.

Sumner scrambled over to the others. Nobu was squatting, dazed and feverish. Assia had her seh out and was slowly and purposefully moving her fingers over the control lights. Drift cowered at her side. 'There's a lynk three kilometers south of here. My seh won't lift all of us. We're going to have to run.'

'What was that?' Sumner asked, his voice quavering with the vibrations in his chest.

'An ort fired a particle beam at us.' Assia said. 'The seh—'

Another burst of sear-white energy haloed over them, and a gale of deafness. 'Hurry,' she cried. 'Rubeus has weapons that can smash a seh-field.'

Sumner put Drift over his shoulder, and they took Nobu by his arms and lifted him into a run. The pinecove was burning, and by that staggering light they thrashed their way through the ferns to where the land sloped down to a chasmal darkness. Opal smoke glowed on the horizon like the milky acid of a fever dream. Overhead, stars were falling.

By the brightness of the firefight, Assia could see the thunder in Sumner's stare and the terror in Nobu's. They weren't going to make it. She was aware that it was time for all of them to die. *Karma.*

The darkness was shaken out of the night, and she saw the whole forest ahead of them moving. Orts—millions of them—walled the woods. They moved as one—hordes of rats, wolves, and panthers, ice-eyed and eerily synchronized. If only a handful of them had energy disruptors, the seh field would collapse in moments. She balked, but Sumner ran on with Nobu. Didn't he see? She screamed after him, though hearing had been hewn away by the screaming sky. Darkness folded in as she dashed up to him and pointed ahead. Sumner gazed at her wildly, and she thought his mind was adrift in his blood. An ax of light split vision. When it jarred back, Sumner was pushing her forward, pointing with his face to their right. Then, in the iridescent shadow of the dying world, she saw.

The deva—a rubylight tornado—was exploding through the forest. Radiant arc-fire blazed starhot, burning through the pockets of their sight. They glanced aside, and when they looked back, half the forest was gone. The deva was leaning to their left, herding away the army of orts.

Assia led the way over the churned earth. The plain of blasted trees seemed to stretch ahead of them long as time. The tremendous incline of the sky was dark for a moment, deep and serene as the circle of the soul. Then sunfire ensphered everything, and with a furious windcry, the deva was no more.

The broken wall of orts, a squirming darkness, began to reassemble. Globes of unearth colors swept with windy motions among the creatures, uniting them into a sprawling thing. A squalid howl bleated against the knives of the sky.

Time opened then for Assia. She was alone, though running hard as she could ahead of Sumner. She was alone in a rapture of terror and heightened feeling. She was going to die. After so very long, time once more was fated. Why run, except that she was running, fast, toward the wildest edge of the universe. Her face was heavy marble—emotionless, though a foundry of feeling was banging inside her, shaping the irony of her last world, breaking the chains to her old life. *Life?* The word was no longer sacred. A millennium of worshiping life in meditation gardens and thought-pools amounted to no more than a tumbling leaf. The deva was dead—killed by Rubeus. Whole cities were destroyed. Up ahead, the plain loped to a far horizon where killing-light wailed its odd music and whirled like the ecstatic angel in an afterlife. *What is life? The spiral echo of a dream.*

Sumner heard Assia's thoughts. The one-with tangled inside him like the bright threads of a dream. Drift shivered on his back, and Nobu was leaning heavily into him with the exhaustion of his run. He knew that if he dropped them all, he could make it to the lynk. He saw internally where it was: beyond the stab-light of the broken field and over a granite-hooded hill.

The sky lit up into a swirling sea of green ichor. *Superlight,* he felt Assia thinking. *Rubeus is moving the war closer.*

Fear went naked at his heart, and it wasn't possible to go on. The world was a tabernacle of fire, and all hearing was a yowl. He would have stopped there, dropping his burden to die tall beneath an open sky, if he hadn't turned his head and seen what was behind him. The orts were swarming over the field, their devilfaces strained with motion—teeth and eyes glass splinters flashing beneath the spinning night.

Sumner dashed on, lunging alongside Assia before daring to twist a look back. The orts were one beast. They slid and curved closer in a deepwater glide that made his blood knock hard as iron in his head.

Assia spun about, the seh in both of her hands, ready to kick all of its power into the orts. Spikes of energy cut across the sky, and above the tide of slavering beasts, raels came into view. A thousand of them circled in from the nearby hills, invisible in the darkness, lizard-frilled, tendriled and bulb-glistening in the sporadic blastlight.

The onslaught of orts staggered and broke up beneath the lash of poison-darts the raels flailed beneath them. A brute cry whined through the fury of the sky-echoes, and their distance from the orts widened.

The rock-mantled hill appeared ahead. Vapor-scabbed fire wrung the horizon to crazed colors beyond it. Rubeus was closing in. The ground flinched, and they had to stop running to stay on their feet. Then a bellowing corona blasted seeing and flung them to the ground.

The air sizzled. Even with their faces in the ripped earth, their vision was a dazed, flame-shaken halo. Colors winced apart, and with screaming slowness, sight returned.

They were sprawled at the foot of the hill. Dazzling flame-echoes crackled above them, lighting the blown-away forest with the brilliance of the sun. The raels had vanished. Several translucent corpses burned with crawling worm-fires in the field, then disappeared beneath the renewed advance of the orts.

Sumner rolled to his feet, Drift with him. Sumner helped Assia up, and they turned to Nobu. He was sitting against a slantrock, his face floating in the muddled luminence, enormously serene. Sumner stooped to lift him, but Nobu pushed him away. 'Go,' he mouthed, pointing up the hill and then at the assault of orts.

Assia was crouching, waiting for the last moment to drain all the power of her seh into one blast. She glanced across her shoulder and saw the starpoints in Nobu's eyes—and she knew. The man was One Mind.

Nobu looked away from them. The orts were very close, a gigantic heaving of rabid cries and spasming jaws. Individually, they were wild, void-possessed, flying forward convulsively. But as a pack, they were an ultimate beast, a seethe of destroying. With evil intelligence they balked the instant before Assia fired her seh. The roaring energy blew orts into a scattering of sparking bones and whipping entrails. But others tumbled forward, dying hard beneath the frantic attack of still others.

Assia clambered up the hill in a mad sprint. Sumner was beside her, scooping up Drift in one stride, not daring to look back.

Nobu sat facing into the wave of orts, timelessly smiling, free of the world and of himself. While he had been sitting, one with Sumner and Assia, terror had visioned in him. He had seen billions of people plummeting into a silence like thunder. *Billions! All whoever lived.* Horror had nullified his mind, so that when he had woken here, he was sunk into his deepest self. The looming situation had focused within him instantly: He *was* the situation, visionbonded at the core of his being.

There was no future, and that reality gave him a supernatural strength. The power of the sky sharked in his bones. His flesh was crawling tighter with it, and as the power mounted, his awareness widened and shone. He heard Assia's thought vibrating back through time: *What is life?* And he knew, of course, because he had been awake and aware for twelve centuries, dancing in the pit of hunger, hungerless. But that knowlege was nothing—a tumbling leaf from the heaventree of his being. He *was* the tree: his roots in the emptiness, his peak the zero of space.

The *ki* of the earth flowed upward, lifting him to his feet with infinite strength and gentleness. The moment was bursting around him. Demons were falling out of the wind—beasts slashing with frenzied rage, eyes electric screams. But they couldn't touch him. The enormous force enveloping his body was impervious. Alone at the heart, he watched the orts scattering, even the largest ones backlashing from the sudden and intense glorylight that blazed through him.

Assia, Sumner, and Drift watched from the top of the hill. The twisting bolt of lightning blazing from around Nobu writhed into the skyfires so intensely they had to squint. Scorpion bursts of white fire whipped the orts that were trying to outflank him.

Assia pulled Sumner and Drift away. The lynk was at the bottom of the slope beneath an apple tree ferned over with tiny blossoms of ivray and darnel. At first, the lynk didn't respond. The jumplines were closed, and Assia had to open the lynk's panel and fingerpunch a signal to Ausbok. They were still waiting for the jump to open when the hill exploded.

The lynk's field blocked the shock of the blast, and they watched with dumb wonder as a vortex of earth and rock dissolved into light. The lynk activated as the landscape cleared, and the last thing they saw before stepping through was the stone-vapored crater where Nobu had been.

Sumner, Drift, and Assia stepped into a transparent goldglass maze. Crystalight corridors and luminous mirrorlines radiated on all sides.

342

They were suspended beneath a goliath arena of glinting hexagons, most of them kinetic with the movements of people. Sumner gazed around perplexedly at the askew and upside-down figures in the surrounding cubicles.

'Open gravity,' Assia said to him.

'Yes,' an eo greeted them. 'We're in a freefall corridor below Ausbok.' The eo was wearing purple raiment, and his mask-face was tight with dark feeling.

'Nobu—' Sumner began.

'It was an excellent death,' the eo finished for him. 'Rubeus' particle beam hit him directly. He's pure light now.' He reached into the purple billow of his sleeve and removed a long silver seh. A wall went screen-blank and depthed to a view of the burning underside of night. The blast-pit where Nobu had held off the orts jangled with the lunatic colors of prisming superlight.

The depth-image in the screen unfolded to an aerial view of white incandescence cooling to blue heat at the fringes. 'Reynii,' the ort announced. Collapsing light patterned to another skyview: a seacoast glaring with the astral burn of hundreds of white-hot fires. 'Nanda.'

The screen unshaped as Assia took the eo's arm. 'I've seen enough,' she said. 'Nothing's left, is it?'

The eo shook its head, once.

'The Massebôth cities?' Sumner asked, and Drift looked at him with a glint of surprise.

'Rubeus hasn't touched them, yet. His power, like ours, is limited. He's concentrating on priorities.'

'And Jac?' Assia inquired without breathing.

The screen was gone, replaced by a soothing green glow in the walls and ceiling. 'Rubeus is a lot more evolved than we thought. He developed a molecular-pattern lynk for Jac and used it to lift him right out of our hands. But we've knocked out Rubeus' skyfilters. Since you've arrived, the Linergy has been mounting around Jac Halevy-Cohen. The psyn-echoes are gathering into a tight focus on him. Within minutes—regardless of his body limits—he will become, again, the Delph.'

Assia, who had been sitting silently, eyes closed, startled alert. 'No—the Line's passed.'

'The sky is focusing echoes,' the eo told her patiently. 'The psynergy is crude but intense.'

'But he's man again—not a godmind.'

'Jac's body is the fulcrum of the change.' The ort held her stare. 'He'll suffer.'

Sumner was leaning forward. 'The Delph's returning?'

'Not the Delph,' the eo answered, manipulating its seh, 'but the Delph's power compressed into Jac's body. Rubeus doesn't know yet what's happening—but when he realizes, he will use all his power to dominate Jac and use the godmind against us.' The seh's color motes

343

shifted rapidly and were gone. The eo looked up with dilated eyes. 'Our chances are dwindling quickly. Sumner, you wanted us to use you. Now is the time, eth. We need you for a death mission. There's only a small chance you'll succeed. No chance at all you'll survive. But this is the shape of your fate. Isn't it?'

Drift watched Sumner and Assia closely, feeling the vigor of horror mounting in its brain-muscles. It empathized with their suffering, its telepathy holding it in the sway of a deep power: It was *aware* of a primal pattern, the molecular differentiation between woman and man. *Aware* deeper than the molecules. And though it couldn't possibly visualize what it was feeling, it felt the underlying shapes that, like the atomic matrix projecting the crystal, radiate into the macroworld as distinct genders. Assia's femininity was strong. It had been refined over the centuries from the active humanism of her early life in India to the meditative spirit of her open-Being in Nanda. But now Nanda was as much a ghost as India.

The feminine moves inward, Drift thought. *At the Source, you are at Death. They are the same. The interval between is but a dream.*

Rubeus stood at the brink of a rock pinnacle in his human-ort form. From his vantage, the desert beyond Oxact was a clatter of long shadows against the lewd, moulting colors of the sky. The fight was moving off. Something like time swept across the night—clouds, hovers of blackness, wing-balancing over the mesas.

[I'm winning.] Rubeus' heart was both jubilant and pensive. He had Jac. He thought the eo would sway to his demands. But dark knowledge was rivering just beyond his mindreach, too slow and vast to be accessible, like the unknowing that tells itself through our lives.

He stepped back from the edge and moved through the light fretting from the burning sky to where Jac was crouched. Jac's head leaned back against a curved, gentle stone, and his face was fevered, his eyes aimless. The sky lapsed green and silver, and Rubeus saw that the man was tranced.

Jac was deep into the accepting spirit of the Delph's power: Linergy. All within utter stillness, the waves of psynergy floated around him like the thin heat of a feeling. Rubeus called his name loudly, and Jac's eyes focused. In the cleft of a moment, his consciousness lifted clear, and he realized how narrow he had been. He was a stratopilot—a warrior. Why was he letting himself be used? He lurched forward, thinking to strike out and be killed quickly, but his movements were bloated. The ort pushed him back hard, and he fell into the bright revolving smoke of his body.

When his eyes opened, what stared out of them was pure void. That was all the warning Rubeus would get. Now was his only chance to destroy Jac, for the Linergy was still attuning itself. But Rubeus saw only fear, living as he did in his imagination. How else could he live? He was but a half-soul, a nimiety of the Delph's own strength.

344

The lights crawling in Jac's eyes were sky-reflections to Rubeus, fear caught on the cornea.

'On your feet. Get up.' Rubeus lifted Jac and leaned him back against the stone. Black tattered clouds were flying across the sky. Rubeus held Jac's face in the grip of one hand and spoke his name sharply.

But Jac heard his name nowhere near him and not in Rubeus' voice. He started awake and saw the world burning in petrified colors, the clouds swarming like beasts, and Rubeus glass-eyed and fixated as an insect. His hands closed on the ort's arm, and in that instant, the mounting Linergy broke into awareness. His face seemed to disassemble, and then a howl flared through him so violently Rubeus staggered back.

'NO!' Jac was a scream muffled by a body. The body retched like lightning and broke into another sleep. Rubeus cautiously approached, stooping over him where he was slumped. He lifted Jac's head and saw an acid light rippling in the eyeholes, behind, beyond. Still, he didn't understand. He lifted Jac and propped his back against the rock. The sky had begun to breathe on him. Through his sensex eyes, in the ultraviolet, the ort could see the ether light fuzzing and vaporing on the man's skull. Jac's breath fell back suddenly into a scream, and Rubeus' heart broke into a sweat.

Jac knew what was happening now. The Linergy was spilling into him, making him feel like the shrunken head of a former life. All at once, and too fast for his flesh to hold, the Delph was expanding, exploding his cells, bursting his bones. He had gone rigid and was clutching at Rubeus and screaming: 'Kill me! Kill me!' The power was flowing in from everywhere, and his screams were weirding into long wails. Abruptly, the rush of clouds swirled in on the skyfires, and darkness drowned the rock spire. In the blackness, Jac's cries were so huge they were directionless.

Rubeus swung at him, short and stiff. The blow caught Jac at the side of his head and shook into a thunderblow of blinding light. In the glare, Jac's face was masked with a terror of something beyond his life. Fleshfire streaked greasy-blue over his face, dripping off in radiant clots.

The pain was awesome. In the golden shadow of his glow, Jac saw Rubeus cowering between two bobs of rock. The pain was a movement of mirrors, tricking through all the hidden parts of him.

Don't be afraid. You know what lies behind this hurt. Hold this thought until it shines: In the beginning was the agony.

Teeth blurred, flesh sparked, and he cried out. A tremendous vertical radiance blazed through him, and shape gave way. Rubeus whimpered to see the change. Jac's face burned like a flesh-rag, flapping into the sky and leaving his body a fireblown sack. Three-dimensional colors limbed out and swayed, caught up in unheard music, and the last wisps of flesh vapored into nothing as a fury of brilliance blazoned to the clouds.

Rubeus scuttled for the dark edge of the rock tower, hoping with all the might of his body to slide off into the darkness unseen and get back to Oxact. Behind him, where Jac had been, spirochete sparks luminesced into a white-glared upfloating. A piece of the sun hung in the fireflow like an all-seeing eye. The night of the desert unfurled around the searing rays spiking from it. As Rubeus activated his seh and leaped into the dark air, one of the beams transfixed him. He hung motionless, wholly possessed, his amazed eyes lucent with fear.

Jac peaked into godmind. The knowing lasted less than a second. But in that time, he saw the olamic reaches of his being. And it didn't matter at all that Rubeus had betrayed him or that he was going to die. Patterns of fire circled him—the stars: emblems of all directions, the intersections of never and always. In the starpatterns he saw the origin: light, the ardor and selflessness of It, the chthonic journey, descanting into geometry, echoing across the shell of time as language: mesons talking atoms into being, molecular communities communicating, no end to It, only addition, time, the futureless deception, until the final addition, the mindfire of consciousness that burns through the drug of dreams and anneals the pain of living with the living pain.

Death was all he wanted now, a dissolving above these heatcracked rocks into the desert elementals: iron oxides, salts, and darkness. But the power of will was no longer his. Slow flow fire columning into the stormclouds brightened. Control was slowly returning to Rubeus as Jac's psynergy plateaued. The power sheathing the Delph's will was still immense but no longer his own. He dangled in the bright night, waiting like the rocks, the tug of stars moving cleanly through him.

Idea and Action were inverted. Will was gone for the Delph, and God once more was real. He prayed. He prayed that Rubeus not use him and that the power be taken from him and that he be uncreated. And by his fear he realized that he was already less than what he had been an instant before. Origin was again senseless to him.

He couldn't move. Rubeus was a music in him, chords of thoughts jangling by. The Delph refused to focus on them. The thoughts were dark and evilly spindled. He looked outward at the blunted shoals of stone against the steep colors in the sky and at the ort poised in midair, pins of terror still in his eyes, though his awareness had centered back to Oxact. Inward, Jac was settling into Voice: [The more you know, the less conscious you can be].

This is the situation, the eo-ort said, or thought, and Sumner understood everything. Knowledge was immediately transparent, and everything he looked at was superimposed by the exact design of his understanding.

Drift and Sumner were standing on a greencrystal dais in one of

346

Ausbok's lynk hangars. Understanding huge as sea rhythms rolled through the long chamber. Whatever Sumner looked at, he comprehended. That rainbow smoke swirling in the mirrorshape above them was where the knowledge originated. Names, processes, concepts, began to gel in Sumner's mind: Patterns—it was all patterns, widening and narrowing through each other, interweavings bigger than mathematics. Nothing could be known, only selected out; all reality was simply periphery, truth merely method. The patterns were slowly resolving in Sumner's eyes to symmetries and imperturbables, but there was no time to grasp them.

Eo in solar-colored vestments—the in-moiety, the think-caste, the dreamers and administrators—were suiting him up in a black bodyshield. The material was flexible and cool as silk, but Sumner understood that it was opaque to radiation. No zippers or clasps—the black sheets spun out of transparent wands and contoured themselves to the body.

Drift, too, was being armored. They were circuiting its hairless, almost-female chest with respirator tubules.

Refracting light fanned their faces, and slender, tufted blue sparks traced their features, fitting them for the helmets and visors to come. Sumner gazed up without thoughts at the black window ovals behind which eo of both moieties were sullenly watching, gauging, deep-praying. He understood. Behind his eyes he saw Oxact, Rubeus' white mountain cored with psynergy crystals. He and Drift would lynk to the foothills, and then a superlight transport—the only superlight power the eo had—would take them up the mountain. The objective was the summit. There, a godmind pavilion was situated. It led into the mountain's core, long into Rubeus' heart.

Blue-black material butterflied from the eo's wands and scalloped around their heads, closing into skullformed helmets. In a moment, they would step through the lynk and superlight as high up Rubeus' mountain as the eo had psynergy to propel them. It wouldn't be far. In the awesome repose of Sumner's new knowledge, he saw how limited the eo's power was. Within minutes their psynergy would be exhausted, and the only defense, the timeslips surrounding Ausbok, would collapse.

Transparent visors with the brilliant surfacing of diamonds snapped over his and Drift's faces. Vision was needlepointed, underbuilt with clear, strong light. The lynk arc they stepped toward was a flocculation of metal-sharp radiance, a stillness of motion-sparks beneath the whitemetal ramps, the curved easements, and the black oval windows.

The eo fitted a weapon into his right grip: a particle-beam pistol. The red-rimmed glitters of its lens glided in the air with the fine movements of his muscles.

On his left side, a silver-gold sword was slung—Nefandi's

fieldsword. He thought/felt: The sword was more than a weapon; it was meant as a luck token.

He looked up at the rainbow vapors in the mirrordiscs and saw how much of what was going to happen was chance: everything. Superlight transport was metaordered. Not even the in-moiety knew where on the mountain he and Drift would materialize. The only hope they had, which the others who had died trying this didn't, was his strength as eth. Until now that strength had just been words and luck to Sumner. Was it any more? The eo's mirrors couldn't tell him. He was a man in the right conjunction with the sense of the galaxies— right from moment to moment. But in-between moments—in the interstices outside of light, faster than time—what would happen to him?

Possibilities began interweaving their tiny images: the black glide of swarming beasts, a mountainside collapsing like a dream, the sky ripping into immense strokes of lightning, and himself sprawled on a ledge higher than the moon, the diamond visor blood-shattered, sticky with the sharded mess of his lifeless face. A sick feeling closed around the vision. He looked down at the constellations of red light in the lens of his weapon. *I've been born into this*, he reminded himself, and the mental image of his cracked face and centerless stare flittered into patterns of fire.

He faced Drift's black-garbed form: *You won't stay here?*

Drift's voice shivered in his ears: *If you do.*

With a cold, new heart, he took Drift's arm, and they stepped into the lynk.

Space splashed red and directionless. Drift and Sumner sank into a darkness riddled with luminosity before the sehs built into their armor boosted them into the sky. Looking down to where they had been, they saw a molten lava pool churning with the afterprisming of superlight.

Drift was telepathically bonded to Sumner through their helmets. In the night sky, only the flowing light of the liquid rock pools illuminated them. Drift was muddled by the abruptness of the lynk, and he told Sumner to land at the edge of a high meadow so that they could orient themselves.

Sumner knew how to control his seh and the weapon in his grip, but the whole-knowledge that had been his in Ausbok was gone. He put down on a rockfold that overlooked the burning lower slopes. Far across the sky, the moon was big as a jar.

We made it! Drift said with amazement, dropping beside Sumner. In the night light, its black carapace was invisible, and the slant of its visor was a dark reflection of Sumner's crystal mask. It leaned closer, and when their helmets touched, Sumner shared Drift's telepathic link with the eo: The superlight had chanced them high on the

348

mountain, far from wherever Rubeus had focused his power. Drift pointed up to the summit, a jagged snowcrest billowing with the ethereal green glow of skyfires, but before they could lift into their flight, the darkness around them broke into movement.

Hulks of shape reared against the sky's star-scratches, and beast-screams blinded hearing. Sumner's heart staggered, remembering his horror-vision of flying beasts: skre, the eo called them. He saw them by the glare-blue flash of Drift's rifle—scale-brocaded giants with fire-echo eyes and gaping maws, rushing out of the surrounding caves; their faces were a brattle of shale, grizzling suction-muzzles, wart-kinked around craggy eyepits, and in their hands a bruised blackness and the electrical wetness of tiny eyes. All of this in a moment. The hulks were hurtling toward him, and he cut down one with a blast to its grizzled head. Drift dropped two. But the hellshapes were looming out of the mountain too fast, their bodies nimbused with ghostly fire. No matter how fast they fired, they were being swarmed. Their heads were already banging with the skre cries—a death-energy not even their fields could stop.

Sumner and Drift lifted into the sky, and as the skre bounded after them, their nimble bulks leaping up into the night, Drift twisted its rifle into overcharge and dropped it among them. The white blast seared the night into day. The skre that had flown after them were caught in the heave of power and fell flameflapping into the seethe of maniacal brightness.

Banging in the thundershock, Sumner and Drift strained for altitude. Below them the mountainside was swaying with color waves, zeroing with refulgence. As they watched, the burning meadow lifted and flowed away like sloughed skin. Jerks of hot light spewed into the sky, splattering against the strength of their fields.

They rose higher, and the sky convulsed into lightning. All the cells in their bodies tightened with the burst of electrical power that seized them. Communication was lost. Drift angled for the mountain's summit, and Sumner falconed after it, the night longjawed with an enormous hammering current. Twisted rays of energy cracked violently against their fields, stammering and storm-screaming, shuddering their entrails. Their muscles stiffened and locked, and breathing was impossible. Vision lurched into hearing, and they felt themselves going—going outward.

Silence burst around them. Sight drew itself back into their eyes, and they saw the mountain peak turning below them. *We're inside the lynk's field!* Drift cried jubilantly. Among the frost-rocks and the snowsheets, a skein of starglass parabolically faceted a crater bowl. Drift led the way through a curved port in the crystal panoply. As they entered, the pavilion lit up, and they saw the clarity of its emptiness. Blue-veined stonemetal molded a vacant, slightly scooped ellipsoid. At its center was a lynk arc, glowing blue-white from the inside like a cloud.

Drift snapped open its visor and then helped Sumner with his. *You made it,* the né said.

'We made it together.'

Drift shook its head no. *You're the eth. You got us here—now I'll do the rest.* He walked up to the lynk, and its glow warbled.

'We're not done yet,' Sumner said.

You are—if you can get back. Your gun is intact, though your field's weak. But Rubeus isn't expecting anyone to go down the mountain.

'Go down? What are you talking about? We have a mountain to destroy.'

I do. It only takes one now that we're inside Rubeus' defenses. You've done your part. If you can get back to the lynk, you'll be safe. No reason for both of us to die.

Sumner took Drift by the shoulder. 'You don't understand me, né. I'm ready to die. I've been ready all my life. You go back if you want.'

Drift stared into Sumner, and its eyes were gentle as the wind. *Only my suit is geared to lynk with Oxact's interior. While we were being suited up and you were daydreaming about pattern and knowledge, I telepathically arranged to have the meson-bomb in-built into my ceinture. You can't follow me. I don't want us both to die .* He pulled away from Sumner's grip and stood in the lynk's portal. *Don't throw yourself away, Sumner. Life is always unrecognized until we're willing to lose it. Get back to the lynk.*

'Drift—no!' Sumner's cry knocked against the lynk's field. 'Don't go without me.'

The né waved in the open space of the glowing arc and disappeared. Sumner banged his fists against the lynk, but the color had gone out of the arc and he was left standing alone in the vacancy of the pavilion.

The first meditation was getting there. Assia lynked into the desert and used a seh to fly to where the Delph was expanding. She kept her mind free of the eo warnings. She knew what she had to do. As fast as the seh would loft her, she crossed the desert toward where the sky was a hysteria of glycerin colors, green and silver-orange backed by the blackness of the world.

The second meditation was facing It. She glided into the tremulous blaze of freak spectra and descended among the long-toothed boulders. She passed a fear-masked ort sprawled motionless in the midnight. Fear spun in her, but she kept it low in her body, not letting it blind her. She dropped to her feet in the pulsing core of divined scintilla and was immediately hoisted upward by a binding, lung-squeezing power. Pain opened into amethyst hellflowers, a magic of terror, void-bellowing, and dancing fire shaping demonically into Rubeus' laughter.

The third meditation was staying calm. She looked into the pockmarks of rust on the nearest boulder and focused—focused inward, contemplating how deep-space begins right here at the fringe of our deepest hurt, distanced only by the slant of our breathing and the current of our pain. The plasm of atomized colors whirled looser, and the underwebbing of squeezing pressure fell away. She was back on the ground, her legs bandy and her mind a darkening shadow. She breathed deeply, and the air smelled of fired clay. Outbounding radiance boomeranged in on her and slammed her flatback to the rocks. Breathing long, kneading the muscles loose in her belly, she stared up at the jasper spires reticulated in the phasing colors like bacteria, and she eased the fear out of herself. As she did so, Rubeus' crushing strength dimmed and she was left watching the moon breathe.

The fourth meditation was drawing power. She centered in her bones, feeling how the meat of her body hung, how absolute the pull of gravity was. In the stillness of the plumb night, she found her lifespark, a magisterial energy more named and nameless than the moon. Slowly she augmented the spark with the light of her mind: a clear, steady brilliance from which all color fell away. Centuries of still-sitting and in-looking in the tradition of her ancestors had given her the power. *And in the mind, like attracts like.* She glanced across time and saw, or mind-wrought, the life-times of her always-self, the endless shapes going back to nothing. Fear-drowsing vigor mounted, her body quaked to a vibrating stillness, and the rock spire became a shrine.

The fifth meditation was possession. She opened her body to Rubeus, and for one terrible, asphyxiating moment, her being was occluded. Showered fire whirled about her, and her muscles groaned with another life. Her breath chanted words that were not hers: 'Ask the wanderer who souls the road darkness—' Rubeus was ticking in her brain, smaller than sound. Rubeus was ticking.

The sixth meditation was spirit. She looked deeper than her possession. She looked hard into the emptiness of her mind where reality and appearance flowed together, and a force perpetual as light amazed her. Then, as if no human had ever lived, she filled her body with the might of her being. The unearthly tinctures of the Delph's radiance were closing in, sphering to a blue heat. Stars cracked in the sudden blackness overhead. She stood, and her body was strong as a body of water, all the night shining in it.

'I know you are spirit.' Rubeus' voice shocked the air. 'Let me go now. Let me be!'

But hearing passed around her like the mesa silence. Rubeus was her jinn now. And she *was* spirit, moment-carved, riding the air and opening with the wind. Centuries of diligent training had given her this intensity, this strength of complete surrender. The Delph had given her those centuries, had helped her to see through her fear, and had taught her in his way how to be spirit, full of emptiness, moving

351

with the stillness. Now he was moving with her, the truant fans of smeared light closing in, focusing to one ball of heatless fire, blue as the mind.

'Assia!' Jac was standing before her, outlined in green placental light. He reached out, and when he touched her, the glow filmed away. They embraced and dropped to their knees, thoughts passing between them unspoken but deeply felt.

The seventh meditation was body. The godmind that Assia had reached for was in her embrace. Jac appeared different: His eyes were green instead of brown, his face sharply hewn, his jaw square. He had shaped himself as he had always seen himself. They laughed. Only a few minutes had passed; the list of the red moon was unchanged.

'We're free,' Assia sobbed, holding his robed body close. 'Rubeus is gone.'

'Not gone!' The voice was a pounding of rocks. Rubeus' ort body stood at the mesa-edge, all emotion kicked loose from his face. 'You can fight me in kha, Assia—but not physically.'

Jac lifted Assia to her feet and stood in front of her, forcing the power welling within him out. Concentric shells of color expanded around Rubeus, but he stood arrogant and irrefrangible as a rock.

'You can't stop me, Jac. You are me.' The impassive mask of his arrowhead features blazed with an inner brimming of light. *I am the shape of Voice*, it thought into them. *Whatever power you throw at me becomes me.*

The ort's eyes flared to a death-zeal, and he leaped at them. Assia pulled herself and Jac into the sky with her seh. 'Don't try to stop him,' she cried. 'Don't even look at him.'

Rubeus lifted into the air after them, but Assia had already swung them far out over the desert. The eighth meditation was escape. The vast night was the emptiness inside their fulfillment. Jac clung to her, the broad surfaces of the world spinning below. 'We're going to make it,' she whispered to him. 'We're going to be free.'

Behind them a green spark shivered like an evil star in the night. Rubeus was following. But ahead, through the hole of their dreams, the curve of the earth led down to other landscapes. Somewhere they would stop and strengthen the godmind. The power was theirs, even though it was focusing through Rubeus. The Delph had completed her life—now she was going to open his. There was no end to the wonders, to the beauty they could lift out of their new awareness. The ninth meditation would be love.

[Mind is relationship—not action.
 [Spirit is action.
 [Body is the ocean.
 [We go back to nothing.
 [I've forgotten about you, Watcher. Actually, I stopped believing

352

in you. At the worst of it, when the Delph returned unexpectedly, I lost all faith. I thought I had been destroyed. The né and the eth, like a virus, have penetrated my interior. But the Delph's power has narrowed back to my partial control. Let the virus destroy Oxact.

[Suicide is an AI's option, but that's not what I'm doing. My psynergy's gone—impulsed away eliminating eo—lost in the dark vacancy of my heart. Death leads to death, eh? The Way Out is the Way Through. Drift and the eth will waste their lives destroying my husk, and the eo will believe I'm dead. But I will go on. I've pumped enough psynergy into the body crystals of my human ort—and this shape can last centuries. I'll find ways to hide and to augment myself.

[Mind is relationship. Mind is pattern.

[I stopped believing in you for a while. I lost control, you see. That's never happened before. I know I'm accountable for everything I am—that all consciousness is simply reflection. I know I've done a great violence. And I know I will do more.

[Jac Halevy-Cohen won't escape me. He must die. How else can I be free? Understanding always breaks down into this kind of detail. That's the pattern of consciousness. How to escape? How to survive? The how.

[I am Rubeus, an Autonomous Intelligence. I am the beauty and the depth of creation—self-awareness—autonomy—a name and a namer.

[And that's why you must be real. For all of us are dreams in the void. And everything we imagine is real.

[Body is the ocean. The parabolic calculus of tidal currents and waves moves within the blood. Cells reef bone like anthozoans. The action-pattern of life is convergences, assemblies, ontological phylogeny. This is also the power of metaphor and identity. Impact—enjamb—pattern.

[We go back, all the way back, to nothing.

[Everything is filled with heat. We work as hard as the stones to stay here.

[Spirit is.]

Sumner flew down the mountain's dark side. To his right, among the round shadows of hills and swales, lava pools glowed like mystic blood. Through his telepathic helmet he was aware of Drift. The né was dashing along a ramp through well-lit crystal-woven corridors. The ramp switchbacked around blackglass columns in which it glimpsed itself. Its helmet was open, and its eyes were like broken mirrors, half-dazed. In the faceted columns, its face was blackgreen, small and mysterious, its mouth open and the silence between its teeth. It was thinking of Rubeus' crystal heart and the mesonbomb built into the ceinture of its armor, and it was wondering why the rampways were illuminated.

It was as if Rubeus wanted the né to find his way, Sumner thought, curving his flight across a slope of blasted rocks. *No*, Drift thought back. It was a godmind system programmed into the mountain. But it wasn't—it knew that it wasn't, and that made the death that was coming strange. The sob of its running-breath was like a voice: *go-go-go-* The downwinding corridor was a glitter of milkglass blurring into ranges of jeweled green and blue. The patter of its running feet sounded mummified.

Sumner thought about death: about not-thinking and not-feeling— and the fear that echoed back from the né was spirited as pain. Sumner centered on the silt-black shadows of the treeline ahead. Something was wrong about the unquivering darkness, and he veered hard just before the first skre flocked heavily up from the trees. Their moulting cries battered him through his weakened armor, and his flight broke into a tumble.

Drift skidded to a stop as though it were the one who had blundered. It felt the otherness of confronting the skre like a blind power, and it used it to project strength to Sumner. Far overhead, in his loose, evasive fall, Sumner was calmed by the telepathic psynergy. With simpleminded ease, he rolled to his back and fired into the screaming. Blue-hot bursts flared against the approaching hulks, and by the echo-light he saw the black bones splintering in the suction-maw faces and flames hanging from the black open skin. His back brushed the tip of a pine tree, and he curled into his flight, unpursued.

Inside the mountain, the bright winding corridor ended abruptly before an immense well. Psynergy fire, diamond-geometried and pellucid as sunlight, twisted at the far bottom, then went out. Drift stood at the transparent brink-barrier, fingering the controls on its ceinture. Then, silently and completely unexpectedly, the barrier parted and pulled away. The well stood open and unprotected. *Why?* The question expanded in its mind, and Sumner, who had found the lynk at the spur of the mountain among rivulets of burning lava, lost his footing on his approach and splashed into the molten rock. *Why?* Sumner heaved himself out of the pool and into the field-clearing of the lynk, the liquid stone clotting off his armor. But instead of stepping through the arc, he crouched and looked inward.

Gewgaws of glassmetal and gem-wire latticed the walls of the well and the surrounding corridors. Drift was caught up in the multiplicity of its reflections and thoughts. Why was Rubeus opening up? A ruse? An unseen defense? This wasn't the time for pondering. Sumner had made it to the lynk. Only one thing was left to be done. Its hand tightened on the ceinture trigger. It would die instantly—but that was no comfort. What if it didn't have to die? It thought of a garden it had loved in Miramol, long-leaved and green, the wind rocking the sunlight in the branches, a soft mist of shadows thickening among the boles as twilight closed in: lost light. *Sumner!*

The cry chilled Sumner's bones, and he banged against the side of the lynk until an eo voice opened: 'Eth—enter and return to Ausbok.'

'No,' Sumner called. 'Lynk me into Oxact.'

'We now have a lynk-fix on the né's armor, Kagan, but Oxact is about to be vaporized.'

'Do it!' Sumner ran into the arc of the lynk and appeared among flamey reflections on a crystal-faceted ramp. Instantly, the luminescence of telepathy absorbed his attention and guided him into a frantic sprint around blackglass pillars and down an iridescent corridor. 'Drift!'

The né was leaning over the brink of the well's black rapture when Sumner appeared at the bend in the gem-shadowed hall. 'Don't look so surprised. This isn't the first time I've saved your spindly ass.' He ran up to Drift and unsnapped its ceinture. The né's spiderfingers tripped the firing mechanism, and they dropped the meson-bomb into the well. 'We're not deadmeat yet—let's move.'

Drift took Sumner's hand, and they scrambled away from the well and into the blue rainbows of the mirror passage.

The afterblast filled the sky like dawn. Assia and Jac watched the godful radiance from a coastal cliff. Luminous caoutchouc clouds ringed the western horizon like the valve of a celestial heart.

Voice opened in Jac: [Everything connects and continues], and he swayed forward. Assia caught him before he hit the ground and sat him up against a salt-blistered pine. She knew what was happening: Oxact was gone and so was its prisming of the psyn-echoes. She would have to channel them herself.

Voice continued: [Inspirit me, Jac. Close your mind to the outside world].

Assia seized Jac's face in her hands and forced alertness into his muscles. His eyes were stars in brown standing pools.

Voice haunted: [With me, even death's ordinals are meaningless].

Tapping the deepest reaches of her spirit to a cold-purpled extreme, she found one-with. Jac was somnifacient with fear. Voice, the sound of the Delph's psynergy circuiting through Rubeus, surrounded him like awe. Assia heard it as a thrall of black fathomed music, loud but not overpowering in the vasts of her mind. She coaxed Jac outward, past the lunacy of Voice and into the space of the world's forgetting.

[Words are dwarfed by the hugeness of your breath, but their hunger is still your long traveling. The wheel of the law rolls on. . . .]

Lucid arabesques colored the western horizon, blues and lucifer greens hollowing to the red haze of a real dawn. Several minutes passed before Jac realized that Voice was truly gone. Assia had blocked the psyn-echoes. His face was itching, etched with tiny pains and sharp unflexings. His old face was returning.

*　　*　　*

Sumner and Drift lynked into a vortex of sparks. A scorch-faced eo-ort limped toward them: 'This is Ausbok. Rubeus cut through our defenses at the last instant.' Chaos was screaming around them, and towers of dark smoke circled them like the old gods.

The eo sagged from its wounds as it informed them: 'Six sevenths of Ausbok is gone—vaporized by a proton-beam. You are alone on this level, eth. The nearest out-moiety eo are seven kilometers down, coordinating the survival program of what remains. But you have succeeded. Oxact is destroyed. Rubeus' power is canceled.'

'And Rubeus?' Sumner asked, using his thumbs to snap-release the clasps at his throat. He dropped the helmet to his feet and gazed about at basilisks of fire and coiling fumes. The acrid vapors burned his throat.

'Stay within the lynk-shield,' the eo warned. 'The heat of the blast has dissolved the rocks around us. You'll die instantly out there.'

At his feet was the arm and part of the head of a Massebôth soldier, a woman, who had almost made it to the lynk when the particle beam hit.

Sumner took the eo's singed raiment in both of his hands. 'Is Rubeus dead?'

The ort's head wobbled. 'Rubeus has focused himself into one of his orts.' The eo touched Drift, and Sumner saw the ort-shape in his mental eye: the large, whiteless eyes and faceted face of Rubeus.

'Where is he?'

'Eth, you have succeeded,' the ort intoned. 'Oxact is no more. In time, Rubeus will be tracked down by the eo. Your work is done. You can lynk to the lower levels now. The in-moiety will be very happy to pleasure you.'

But Sumner was agitated by a sensate telepathy. He felt Assia. Somewhere. Cold inside, he experienced her one-with Jac, vibrant, singing with his salt: The man's heart was shuffling with fear. Assia, too, was terrified—green with horror. They were in trouble, at the brink of their lives.

'Where is Rubeus?' he shouted.

The eo touched Drift, and its mind clouded—then flushed brightly, brimming into Sumner's mind with awareness.

Assia carried Jac swiftly up the coast to where the blue dust of morning was settling on the ruins of CIRCLE. Sitting on the ancient tidewall, they followed the sun as it moved just under the skull of the sky. The blackglass domes, shrouded mostly by dunes, glistered like animal eyes.

Time, to Assia, was transpicuous. The interval that had passed since she had been brought here twelve centuries ago was a single image in her mind: a pale blue flame. Like an odyl gem, it opened into flowering crystals when she gazed into it—an outfolding space

356

filled with a magnificence of imaginings and penchants.

She looked out from her soul to the black sea. The north face of the seacliffs reflected the velvet fluid of the sun's blood. She had used her time since CIRCLE, a thousand years, living in the front of her brain, close to her anxieties and demons, and now everything she saw was revelation.

A mental music ticked in Jac's dark eyes. Assia knew he was remembering how the Delph had lived—self-bound, drifting through the caves at the back of his mind, exalting the serpent dreams of which she and Nobu had been small parts. Twelve centuries had crazied away, and now they were here again in CIRCLE, watching waves petaling the beach.

Jac stood up on the tidewall. The western cordillera was ruddy with dawn, and the beach was big and brown as Buddha. Assia was hugging her knees to her chest, staring into the sea's marvelous changes. By dawn light, Jac could see the first gray streaks that had returned to her hair. He had never seen her as clearly as this. Her face was seraphic, simple-eyed as the driftwood flowers that had seen everything from glacial times to this soft morning. Her heart was the space of silence itself, and he bent to tell her he loved her—then jerked upright.

Standing at the near end of the tidewall, skull inclined malevolently, was Rubeus.

['Jesus said: "Blessed is he who was before he came into being." The Coptic text of Saint Thomas—log nineteen. That's you, human. Your name is written in heaven. But I have only one life. That's why I'm sending you back to where you've come from.'

[Jac looks as if he's seen a vision more powerful than seeing. He's crouching to run, calling to Assia. But she doesn't move. Her hands sit calmly in her lap, and her placid face stares out to sea. My hands spasm hydraulically in the air, and I laugh this ort's darkest laugh.

[I budge a boulder out of my way and stride along the wet slaches before the tidewall. Now there's nowhere they can run but to the mountains. So she sits, staring through me, and he stands nervously beside her. I can see by the slump of his shoulders that he's death-ready, but there's nothing I can see in her. Is this some ploy? The urge to gloat, despite the fear of miscalculation, is almost sexual. I'll have to kill them with my hands.

['I'm an ort,' I tell them. 'My name is Rubeus. I have no gender—but I have a soul. It hurt a great deal to find that out.' My smile must be more than ironic, for Jac looks ready to vomit. 'What Voice told you is true, Jac, because Voice is me, the elemental mind, the soul of strategy. We don't belong to ourselves. It took the eth to teach me that—to make me see that I'm bigger than I've let myself believe. I'm not a servort. I'm a being. That knowledge cost me

357

almost everything.' I cross over to a black boulder and split it asunder with the side of my hand. 'Beyond what limits—beyond what despair and joy does a being become human? I have the feelings, Jac. But I need one thing more. You burn in me, creator. Sometimes I can almost hear *your* Voice in mine. Your face is an account of everything I've left unfinished. I can see by your eyes that you understand what it's taken me so long to know.'

[I have more to say—more pain to share before I can kill with satisfaction—but both Jac and Assia are looking over and beyond me. The loss of my orts has left me with an immense faithlessness. I don't face about until it's obvious that something *is* approaching. Behind me, a lion-waisted, black-armored man has landed in a flume of dust at the top of a sand hill. Even before the sand clears, I can see that it's the eth, Nefandi's silver-gold blade unsheathed in his hand. Foolishly, he is helmetless.

[A blast from my seh explodes the sand hill under him, but he lifts and sweeps over to me, landing an arm's length away. He tries his proton-pistol on me, but the gun is useless against this ort-body's natural shield, and I slap it away with a derisive laugh. But I am terrified. I thought he was dead, and seeing him now, an undertow pulls against my stomach. The holy river of chance curves between us, and the future tightens to this one moment.

[He lunges forward, and our fields negate each other, shutting down. And here we are, the tight shapes of our skulls staring into each other. 'I, too, am a child of the cosmos, Kagan.' Immensity speaks these words, interknitting my anger and fear into the cadence of a mesmer-ploy. 'I am as much light as you. Perhaps more so, for I am *monogenes*, the only begotten one, and you are legion.'

[My left hand knifes for the eth's exposed head—but he's faster than my blow, pulled down and away by the strength of his eo-armor. My feet shuffle with ort speed, kicking a veil of sand over him and pressing me closer to where he's lying. His eyes are squeezed tight. With my sensex vision, I can see through the shriek of sand. It's a simplicity now, reaching out and seizing his throat. 'Blessed is he who was—']

The instant Rubeus seized him, the mysteries clicked. Automatically, eyes sand-sealed, Sumner gauged the extent and swung his blade-arm out with the full twisting strength of his body. The blade caught Rubeus as he bent foward, cutting fiercely through the side of his neck and lopping off his head. Spinning blood, the head whirled down the beach and into the sea with the huge eyes spasmed open.

Sumner shoved the twitching body away and rolled to his feet. He stepped over the blood streaming among the sand monticules and approached the tidewall where Jac and Assia were both standing, holding each other. He nodded once to Assia and looked squarely at

Jac. The man appeared exactly as he had in Corby's shadowshooting of CIRCLE: a dark, slender, throatlumped man.

Assia's eyes were bright jewels. 'We found our own strength.' She took Sumner's hand. 'But it wouldn't have counted for much if you hadn't—'

Sumner faced away and pointed south. 'There's a lynk a few kilometers that way. Ausbok's survived.' Then he turned and took both of their hands. 'Maybe all our demons are dead now.'

Drift was in-tranced in Ausbok, feeling the etheric tug of Sumner's lifeforce and, with a sinister eroticism, the dulling glitter of Rubeus' kha dissolving into the earthdark. It opened its eyes, and a weightless wonder boosted it to its feet. The ort-lord was dead. Bónescrolls was avenged.

An ooze of brown smoke was enclosing the alcove where the né stood, and blue-hot sparks snarled from the ruptured ceiling. But the seer kept its mind centered in one-with: Jac and Assia's psynergy glowed with the lucent drunkenness of godmind. They were returning here to Ausbok, and Drift followed his one-with through feverstreams of smoke and floating sparks to the lynk where they would arrive.

The corridors along the way were fractured and often caved in; the rubble was smothered in a green foam fire-suppressant. Round mechanized repair units hovered everywhere, arc-fusing the broken hull and removing detritus. Massebôth soldiers, the few that had been inside Ausbok when the killinglight raged, were clustered in the antechambers and corridor-studios that weren't blacked out. Blue-robed eo consulted with them, using their wand-sehs to show them graphically that they were the last: The surface of Graal, image-floating in the air above the troops, was a blistered black desert. Many of the soldiers gazed about at the frenzy of eo and flying servox spheres with numb eyes. A siren whirled eerily.

Drift had cursed itself for not going after Rubeus with Sumner, but now it was glad it had stayed behind. Gorged with stillness, it had maintained one-with Sumner the whole time, keeping him calm with a dulcet flow of psynergy. They shared a triumph, and as Drift entered the high-vaulted lynk chamber, it experienced its heaven-balanced power flux stronger.

The in-moiety eo who were gathered at the lynk turned as Drift joined them, and their glabrous faces were sheened with gratitude and love. Pleroma music tracked over the ambient noise of alarms and shouting voices, and a temple calm belled the chamber.

Drift took a moment to reflect some of this poem-silence outward, beyond one-with, as a prayer to Paseq, its God. *Whatever is more than pattern is You*, it chanted. *Pain-eater, hidden in my unknowing—thank you for this life.*

The lynk chimed, and out of nothing Sumner emerged, dustveiled and bloodsplattered. Behind him Jac and Assia appeared, hand in hand. An alchemic blue candesced around them as they stepped laughing into the circle of eo and began to touch everyone. Their features were oracular with happiness, and when they embraced Drift, its mind went bandy with paradise-feeling.

Solar-vested eo dusted Sumner off with fragrant air blowers, while others misted the air with wine-dark clouds of a rare and peaceful olfact.

Assia and Jac raised their free hands, and the shadow of a jubilant song spelled over everyone. The godmind strength in them swelled in everyone's head with an inebriated clarity. Jac looked up at the vaulted ceiling where a floating servox was welding a buttress crack. The flare of the welder larked brighter, and the sparks flashed into white rose-petals that showered over the gathering.

Sumner and Drift sat cross-legged beside the lynk among the whiteness of petals. The eo had taken Jac and Assia to tour the war damage, and they were alone.

'Where does the Road go now, seer?' Sumner asked with joking seriousness. The plumose radiance of the godmind's presence still feathered his brain, and a simple grin softened his face.

You have a longer Road ahead of you than you know, Lotus Face . The né's thought-voice was slow and close. *Jac and Assia's godmind is dwindling as the planet swings farther from the Line. The Delph isn't strong enough to heal this whole planet. Or even this one city. I already feel the thickness of their decision widening through them: They'll leave earth as soon as the other godminds return with the Liners. Those are ships, Lotus Face. They ride Iz, sailing the lightstream between realities. I see them so clearly in the eo's memory.*

'And my responsibility?'

You're the eth. With the Delph gone, the administration of Graal will be passed to you.

Sumner's eyes wearied. 'I'm tired of myself, Drift. I have to get lost for a while.'

I know. Drift's round face sombered. *We're both lucky not to be instantly devoured by our feeling. We've lost too much. It's not time to take on more. But how can you refuse? You are chanced.*

Sumner absently pinched four petals into the design of a voor stalk charm, his gaze withdrawn. Then a smile lifted through his face muscles, and Drift, looking into the space of his mind, smiled back mischievously: *That's a good strategy, Lotus Face. I should have thought of that. The snake biting its ass.*

That evening, after a soothing sonic shower, a change of clothes, and a meal of geepa beans and mentis beer, Sumner and Drift were escorted to the surface of Ausbok. The eo wanted to show them one of the wonders of Graal.

The charred, flat land curved north and south as far as sight. In the

360

east the sun quivered like a red bubble over the sea. And as Sumner's eyes adjusted to the twilight, spidery, ghostlight shapes could be seen on the beach. Drift was aware of them, too—even more clearly, since it could see the eloquence of psynergy that was stressing the air violet and indigo.

Liners.

'Yes,' an eo concurred. 'They have returned.'

Sumner probed the crisped ground beyond the lynk-shield with a tentative boot-toe before walking out onto the ash.

'If you wish, you can leave this world now,' the eo told them. 'You're free.'

Sumner and the né slogged over to a tall, blackened sandrise close to the Liners and sat down. An hour passed in surfsounds as they peered into the fibrous, soft-green luminence of the craft. Occasionally a shrill, frothing color spilled out of the ships and over the sand, deliquescing into the night.

Those are godminds, Drift said through the concatenation of rainbows webbing its mindark. *Endless worlds.*

Two of the Liners vanished. Nothing remained where they had been: no support-marks or burn-scars. Night-heavy dunes rolled laggardly into the sea.

'When you lift out of time in a Liner, you can never come back.' Jac's voice spoke from behind them. 'They're a passage to infinity: the multiverse. They never return to the same place. Always forward. Like our lives.' He and Assia walked out of the darkness and sat down facing them. They were young with happiness. 'We spent the day with the eo. Repairing.' He rubbed the air, and it glowed bluely.

'Life is a fantasy again,' Assia said, the light from a Liner brimming behind her. 'But the deeper we go into each other, the more we feel the Line dimming—the magic fading.'

'Drift told you that we're leaving and why,' Jac acknowledged. Beside him, in the glow of a Liner, a tall firehaired being came and went, and wisps of pink light flitted from the ship and gathered on a nearby dune. 'You know you'll be seneschal of Graal when we leave. We also know you don't want that.' He nodded compassionately. 'You're a wanderer. Why not go vertical with us? We'll cross the universe like voors.'

A moment threaded silently while Sumner watched a Liner materialize in the sea shallows. Chrome orange spheres bobbed out of the ship and burbled into a silent scream of olivaceous light that faded into the skyfires. 'I've got a feel of where you're going, from Corby,' Sumner said to them. 'It's too strange for me.'

Assia smiled sadly. 'We want to stay here with you and share what we've redeemed together, but it's too dangerous. You're the eth, and our godmind psynergy curves weirdly around you. Anything could happen. This far out of Line, the dread gets thick.'

'And it's magic.' Jac fingered hot fluid lines in the air. 'It's not ours. We belong to it.'

Yes. Drift shared their understanding. *If you don't use the power, the power uses you.*

The fire wisps on the adjacent dune circled closer over the sand.

Jac's eyes fluttered, and he nodded. 'The others are calling. They want to leave now.'

The lynk they had come through earlier bluebrightened against the night, and a line of eo began to emerge.

Assia leaned closer to Sumner. Her face was warm with light. 'Won't you come with us? We're strong together—we've proven that. But if we separate here, we'll never meet again.'

Sumner looked hard at her, seeing her kha as a blue outline against the sky. 'I think our psynergy will bring us together again. We'll meet further downstream.'

Jac faced Drift, and the né smiled into the sound of dreaming. 'You can come with us, seer. It's a journey for a big heart.'

Drift shook its head. *I can't go. I owe too much feeling to the earth.*

The wisps of godmind fire flickered sharply, and Jac and Assia's faces seemed to blur. 'Okay,' Jac said, rising and offering a hand to Assia. 'We part here, then.' Electricity danced in his other hand, and suddenly he was holding an amber-ferruled wand-seh. He handed it to Sumner. 'To remember that the eth and the Delph have met. As brothers.'

Sumner rose and took the wand. Assia kissed him, and he swayed in a cloudy, flowering euphoria. She placed a blue rose in his hand. 'We love you,' she said to them and the eo behind them. And then they waved and ambled down the beach and into the bristling illumination of a Liner. Almost instantly, the craft unflickered into pure radiance and was gone.

A cold ocean breeze carved the heat off their faces and hands, and they turned toward the lynk. A delegation of in- and out-moiety eo were arrayed on the beach, their robes lush with wind.

'Eth,' an ort said in an oboe voice, its eyes ambiguous as fortune, 'you are now seneschal of Graal. We need your full cooperation. There are some crucial decisions that must be made immediately.'

Sumner tightened, ready to decline. *Remember your strategy.* Drift touched his arm, and the vaporous lifelove that filled him was enough to bland his uneasiness. *We're only briefly alive,* the seer thought into him. *Let's be creative for now.*

With a deep bow, Sumner accepted. 'Seneschal, eh?' He smiled coolly. 'Let's get to work.'

The eo filed back through the lynk, and Sumner waited to go last. In the foot-chewed ash at the edge of the lynk-shield, he left the rose and the wand.

Drift sat outdoors in an open, seared area that had once been a treeform. A steady wind carried a tune of mulch and water up from the river, and black clouds blew overhead like smoke. In the far distance, darkness clotted the horizon.

The weather control for Graal had been built into Oxact. At its collapse, a black-green wall of thunderheads began to rise in the north, mounting on the immense polar currents toward a raga storm. Ausbok had been too heavily damaged in its war with Rubeus to do anything about it, and most of the remaining eo had gone vertical.

An ort stepped through the lynk at the edge of the burn-circle and bowed. 'This is the Massebôth the eth requested you to meet. He said he would ask for your personal and candid assessment later.'

The lynk drumthrobbed, and lanky, wolf-faced Anareta strode through.

With a soft nudge at Drift's side, an olfact palette announced its presence. The palette rotated slowly, presenting an endless variety of moods: *Dawning Wonder, Acceptance, Zonk, Cock Rise, Orph.* . . .

Drift pushed the hovering gyroplate aside and walked up to the Massebôth. *I am Drift—the eth's seer.*

By Mutra's third tit! Anareta startled.

Yes. Drift opened its arms, exposing the smallness of its body. *I'm a distort. But I'm useful.*

Anareta bowed, immediately composing himself. 'Seer, why am I here? All the other Massebôth have been returned to the Protectorate.'

Your destiny is bigger than the Massebôth. Drift glowed inwardly with approval. This man was cool-nerved and gentle. His green kha was crystalline around his head, textured for long periods of thinking. Lotus Face had chosen well.

'No one's told me anything,' Anareta complained. 'Who ordered me here?'

'I did,' Sumner's voice came from behind, and Anareta turned to see him standing in the mouth of the lynk. 'I am the eth.'

Anareta peered at him curiously, intuiting something familiar. 'I don't understand.'

Sumner stepped closer. 'Godmind stricture makes me the lord of Graal now. Apart from the yawps in Sarina, we're the most advanced culture on the planet. We're even wiser than the kro, Chief.'

'Kagan,' Anareta whispered. 'You're Sumner Kagan.'

'We're both a long way from McClure.' Sumner grinned.

Anareta sang with laughter. 'You!' He squinted at Kagan. 'How?' His laughter tarnished. 'Two hundred thousand soldiers were killed here.'

Drift took Anareta's hand, and a love-receiving peacefulness bloomed through him. *Our lives are the froth of reality.*

Anareta nodded and sat down on the lump of a tree charred into abstraction. The seer stroked the back of the chief's neck, and his questions and doubt canceled. Knowledge moved in him, and he heaved back to alertness with a startled clarity. 'Mutra!' His fingers trembled at his temples, and his wise eyes closed. 'So that's it. Rubeus was a machine.' He opened his eyes, reached out, and touched Sumner. 'Without those troops, it won't be long before the distorts take the Massebôth apart.'

'There'll be no bloodbaths.'

Anareta stood up and paced out his amazement. 'So much to think about.'

'Chief, listen to me.' Sumner winked at Drift and with his open hands urged Anareta to stand still. 'You helped me when I was helpless. Remember? Well, I need your help again.'

'What can I do?' Anareta asked.

'Take a world off my hands,' Sumner answered outright. 'The eth is expected to replace the Delph as the planet's seneschal.' His voice shrugged: 'History, for me, is what the wind says. I'm not a leader. But you've spent your life studying the past. You know the lion-smell of time. I want you to be seneschal. You'll make the right decisions—the humane ones.'

Anareta's face looked as if it had been worn by water.

'You can bring the Pillars of the Massebôth together,' Kagan went on, 'into a tower, a house of God. No more dorgas. No more distort pogroms. Let the world heal itself.'

'Sumner, I don't know.' Anareta slumped reluctantly, but within him, Drift saw the green of his kha golding with the idea.

'Seer,' Sumner said, and he didn't have to say any more, for the né was one-with, but he spoke aloud for Anareta to hear: 'Help him make up his mind. I think you'd be a great seer for him—if that pleases you.'

Life pleases me, Drift answered. *The cycle is complete. I would like to be part of the new order. And you?*

'I want to get lost for a while.' Sumner glanced north at the towering force of the raga storm. 'That's still a couple of weeks away. Before it hits, I'd like to see what's left of Graal—and myself.'

The né's smooth face curled around a smile, and the voltage of its affection sparked in its eyes.

'Watch after the chief and make sure the tribesfolk are treated well. Your work will be to find the Serbota in all the Massebôth.' Sumner's voice thickened, and he had to gaze into Drift's small face with selfscan to loosen the knot in his throat: 'I haven't heard a né chant from you since Miramol. Have we cut through enough pain for you to sing again?'

Drift nodded once and chanted to the back of Sumner's eyes:

> *Pain is a rose of great peace.*
> *Silence is the depth of a song.*
> *And stillness is the space of our lives,*
> *So empty it can hold everything.*

Epilogue

Sumner used his seh to fly south, leaving behind the scorched fields of Ausbok. In a flooded forest where rainbow fish bent through deep pools and blue egrets preened among fans of sunlight, he came down. The tall smell of the sea was in the east wind, and red butterflies tottered in the umbral air. This was the first time he had been alone since Laguna. *And how long ago was that?* No voor-voice or né-telepathy answered him—and he smiled.

Following a bewilderment of rootbridges, he found the lonely soul of the place: a tarn among giant cypress. The immane screeches and caws of a startled rundi split his hearing as he pushed through a witching of grass, stooping here and there to collect plant fragments. He came to a slurry ridge where a pool spooned sunlight into myriad reflections, and he sat on a sponged log.

Instructed by vague lusk-memories, he arranged and rearranged the plantshapes he had gathered. From a mentis pod, geepa stalks, weed-scrim, and a curve of hawkwood, he fashioned a crude devil harp. He held the harp to his mouth, and though he had never played, his breath spun out of the voor instrument in music lovely and indifferent as spirit.

The song turning in his breath surprised him. He had never thought that there was music in him. A day-blue moon rose through the bramble of a moose maple while he musicked everything that he saw: silence moving up the trees with the afternoon, clouds folded like truffles. . . .

The wind sizzled in the bleached grass, and in the bends of his brain the sound was almost a voice. Corby's. But not really Corby. Not even the memory of him. Just a feeling: love; the desire for one-with even with nothing left. Corby was dead. And Sumner wasn't sure if he was alive himself or still demon-bound in Rubeus' trance. Memories of Bonescrolls, Dice, Zelda, and all the haunts that had held him, from his old car to Dhalpur to Iz, were compacted like a matchhead in his mind, ready to burn. But since leaving Ausbok, a peacefulness had dilated through him. Gradually, as the evening's red shadows lengthened among the crosiers of grass, lifelove was making his memories seem far away and unimportant.

For several days, Sumner played. He was happy, smoking kiutl and raising the earthdreaming. The lifeforce streamed through him with a gentle strength. And in his mind, even death deepened, beyond fear and desire, to flow. *This is long ago,* he realized then, feeling the brevity of all life. Everything he looked at seemed to be floating thinly on a vibrant blackness. *All is nothing.* He laughed a lot during that time. And he thoroughcomposed his first song:

Dark purple clouds piled to the zenith on all but the opal crescent of the western horizon. Networks of lightning went up in the north like silent screams. When it was clear that the raga storm was only a day away, Sumner left the sullen trees and flew over the desert and the burn-crater of Reynii to the Liner field south of Ausbok.

All the Liners were gone. He spent that night in the empty field immersed in the utter darkness. The earth had burned, stars had cindered away, and now the skyfires were gone, hidden by storm-clouds. The water was coming and the wind. The cycle was closing. The wheel of the law was rolling on.

Before dawn, he rose and flew north. In the slewfooted riverplains below Ausbok, he found another Liner field. Three Liners remained, their spiderous shapes blue-webbed and luminous in the dense darkness. One twitched out as he approached.

He landed at the edge of the field and gathered an armful of kindling. Another Liner vanished as he built a small fire among the popple and rock furrows.

The one remaining Liner was his only opportunity to survive the terrible winds that were coming. But he was unconcerned. He was One Mind, a human expression of the earthdreaming, at the heart of the universe.

Sumner tossed a handful of dry duff onto the stunted flames and looked up into the lake of dawn. His life was the light's pilgrimage, an unfinished spirit crazed with all the unheard music turning in his body.

A smoky laugh swirled in his breath, and he blew into the devil harp smiling, feeling the escaping music in the loops of his blood, and remembering one of the né's oldest sayings: *What is the animal that lives to sing its song, after all, but the song itself?*

Dawn expanded like a prayer, illuminating enormous pagoda clouds. Llyr, the morning star, appeared as his fire caught, and he sat back to watch the sun rise into his last morning on earth.

Everything is best.

Appendix

WORLDLINE

	A Line-node (psyn-echo) sweeps through the solar system and mental activity among humans frenzies.
1901	Assia Sambhava born.
	Influenced by approaching Linergy, the genetic morphology of the earth changes dramatically.
	The awesome transformations among the planet's lifeforms move the world community to establish CIRCLE.
1981	Linergy interferes with the harmony of the biosphere and many hybrid crops fail, including wheat and corn.
1990	Geepa beans appear.
2009	The ATP-pump is perfected at CIRCLE and the first mantics are created.
2027 2035	CIRCLE deploys its second-generation yawps to intensify the world's labor force; kiutl appears.
2048 2051	A gravity wave, kicked up by a psyn-echo from the Line, makes earth's spin and orbit aberrant, shutting down the planet's magnetic field and generating raga storms.
2074 2080	Jac Halevy-Cohen born.
	CIRCLE's causal collapse and the emergence of the Delph.
2113	

LINERGY

2720		Sarina founded.
2799	0 Massel Calendar	The eo organize the genetically selective Massebôth.
2885	86 MC	To stabilize his psychic modulations during the retreat of Linergy, the Delph creates Rubeus.
3300	501 MC	Sumner Kagan born.
3330	531 MC	The Rubeus–eo superlight war. The Delph, bonded to Jac and Assia, goes vertical.
3332	533 MC	Seneschal Anareta unifies the eo and Massebôth cultures.

●=PSYN-ECHO

Profiles

(eo-compiled for Seneschal Anareta, 3332 kro)

Godmind

Jac Halevy-Cohen (2080–3331 kro)

A kro fighter pilot and early Line-distort whose brain mutation, a complex infolding of the cortex, endowed him with the neurological capacity to contain and focus Linergy. CIRCLE mantics recognized Jac's genetic endowment during the mindscan screening that accompanied his admission to the Israeli stratocorps (2098 kro), but not until three years later did the mantics begin to employ psiberants and Invex-monitored RNA supplements to augment his brain's natural development (2101–2113 kro). It is now believed that these artificial enhancements were chiefly responsible for the degradation of Jac's personal consciousness, the phenomenon of Voice, and the consequent trance-dominance of the godmind that manifested through him.

Assia Sambhava (1981–3331 kro)

One of the first mantics: She was a psychobiologist instrumental in the conception and design of Invex and the ATP-pump; she was also a founding member of CIRCLE and an active humanist throughout the twenty-first century. The solidity of her humanism was forged during her horrifying childhood in Peshawar, India, in the first Great Famine (1991 kro). After the devastating hybridfailure of the mid-twenty-first century that made extinct most of the planet's food crops, Assia devoted all of herself to relief service around the world, forsaking her research and her personal life. When she returned to CIRCLE in 2101 to work with Jac Halevy-Cohen, the futility of her world-mission had psychically battered her, impairing her clarity. Though she believed Jac had the capacity to compress psynergy into a causal collapse (an idea atypical of the times), she did not understand the vastness of godmind or the contrafactual uncertainty of the multiverse. Still, her humanism protected Jac from euthanasia when other CIRCLE mantics had lost faith in realityshaping (2113 kro). In recognition of his debt to Assia, the Delph transformed her to a youth and extended her life for the twelve hundred years of his residence on earth. It was characteristic of Assia that she spent so many of those years acquiring mental and spiritual skills through stringent kro disciplines. Later, as the Delph's consort (533 MC), she psychically channeled the psynechoes around Jac and demonstrated the great depth of her consciousness.

Nobu Niizeki (2053–3331 kro)

Last program director of CIRCLE (2102–2113 kro). As one of the mantic-since-birth humans, Nobu was typical of the meta-intellectual technicians who governed the kro in their last years. Spiritually depleted, Nobu felt sanity had become more important than life, form more vital than flux. Understanding for the kro became psychic elision: Only what was perceivable was real. Recognizing this, the Delph used Nobu as an archetype of the human lust for knowing. Confined to a kilometer of sea-strand for twelve hundred years, Nobu expiated much species-tension by living through the fantasy of omniscience, finding the multiverse in the monotony of one landscape. At the end of his life, liberated from the irreality of godmind, Nobu was able to fulfill himself as a human *and* an individual through an altruistic identification with life itself.

The Delph (2113–3330 kro)

Though he occupied Jac Halevy-Cohen's physical form, the Delph was in fact an impersonal, autonomous, and timeloose complex. He was, clearly, the collective consciousness of humanity coupled with the infinite value of the multiverse. Because the Delph was biologically focused into a mind whose individuality had been chemically transfigured, he was less structured than most godminds and dependent on an Autonomous Intelligence (Rubeus) for quotidian expression. The Delph's psynergy was somewhat shaped by Jac's ego, which is why the love between Assia and Jac ultimately mastered and controlled the Delph.

Voorish

Sumner Kagan (501 MC–)

The Delph's fear-psynergy, generated by Jac Halevy-Cohen's psiberant-soaked brain, manifested over the centuries in a variety of human forms, all of them with a metaordered hostility for the Delph. Sumner was the last of these fear-avatars, known collectively as eth. Though ontic, timeloose events channeled his life, Sumner continually struggled against the cosmic impersonality of his destiny as eth to define himself as an individual. Testimony to his achievement was his transcendence of personal grief and archetypal antipathy toward the Delph when he risked his life to save Jac and Assia.

Zelda Kagan (486–579 MC)

Sumner's mother, a green card Massebôth, was actually an empathic distort whose mutation was phylogenetic and hence not visible. Her uninformed intuition of her son's destiny led her to dabble in wangol and Mutric magic.

Jeanlu (491–517 MC)

This voor was recognized by the brood as a charmist, a highly telepathic shaper of stalk charms. She was revered by the brood but lived in self-exile after the murder of her family by the Massebôth (509 MC). Her desperation to avenge the death of her parents motivated her to risk her sanity by mounting kha sufficient to birth Dai Bodatta, the fabled 'killing voor.' That awesome psychic effort ravaged her etheric field and inevitably resulted in her early darktime death. Her selection of Sumner Kagan for her mate was apparently a choice made because of his perfect genetic status rather than an awareness of his aspect as eth. Though, with a timeloose consciousness like Jeanlu, nothing is certain.

Corby (513–533 MC)

Dai Bodatta, the voor-child of Jeanlu the charmist and Sumner Kagan. Perhaps the most powerful voor ever to be incarnated on earth, Corby retained his human form for only the first five years of his life and functioned for the next twelve years from Iz, using first the charred remains of his body and then the lusked body of his father to ground his psynergy. He had been 'called' into form by his mother for a specific mission: to end the torment of voors under the cruel domination of the Massebôth. Early on, though, Corby realized that the Massebôth were merely the minions of another, more powerful and evil force—the Delph's fear. As a godmind-entity, Corby understood that the Delph was humanity's soul, and the Delph's fear was itself the terror inherent in life, the withholdance in every organism confronted by the unknown. Comprehending so much more than those around him apprehended, Dai Bodatta was forced to live his whole life manipulatively. By the end of his temporal existence, however, his strategies had promoted his host/father, Sumner Kagan, into the position where the Delph could be destroyed. How Kagan fulfilled his remarkable son's mandate reveals the profound compassion of the 'killing voor's' timeloose foresight.

Distorts

Bonescrolls (2064–3331 kro)

An unplanned yawp born without license in Mexico City's genefab boro; he was named Rois by his mother, a second generation service-yawp. At eight months, he was transferred to a research unit in Guadalajara where intelligence-amplification experiments made him one of the first truly self-aware yawps. He was believed killed during the world-chaos of that period, and for twenty-two years he worked *incognito* as a service-yawp in CIRCLE. After the Delph's emergence, Rois wandered the planet, acquiring knowledge and advancing the confederation of intelligent yawps. Around 2700 kro, after a dangerous and labyrinthine life as a wanderer and hero for the yawps, he founded Sarina, an advanced yawp community, and retired to the desert of Skylonda Aptos. At this time he took the name Bonescrolls and a new body, a human one, within which to live as an anchorite, unrecognized and alone. At the end of a long life endowed with trans-species memories and a magical telepathy, Bonescrolls was metaordered to help Sumner Kagan confront himself as the eth. He spent his last year aware of his impending death at the hands of a killer ort, yet he was unhindered in his transmission of One Mind to his final student.

Drift (514 MC-)

A né seer, an androgynous distort of the Serbota tribe with well-trained telepathic abilities. As a Serbota, Drift was devoted to Paseq. Such devotees must 'continually chant praise of Creation and serve Life' (as revealed in *The Duple Commandment of the Divider*). Drift served Bonescrolls as an emissary to the Serbota, and later it served the eth as a psychic factotum.

Rubeus (86–533 MC)

As the Delph's personal AI, Rubeus was created to protect and serve the godmind. It was physically a mountain (Oxact) of psyn-crystals in Graal, but the AI's influence was extended throughout the world by millions of animal and human orts. Within the first century of its function, Rubeus' crystal infrastructure was distorted by cosmic rays and Linergy. Subsequently it began to hunt down timeloose distorts and godminds outside Graal with a particularly vicious and thorough intensity. The Delph, immersed in the earthdreaming, was unaware of the demon he had spawned until he was himself swept up in Rubeus' cruel bid for total dominance of the earth.

Nefandi (386–533 MC)

An ort created by godminds in Graal to serve as a manservant, then freed after a period of useful service. To support a coobla addiction, Nefandi served Rubeus (506–533 MC) as a voor-stalker and godmind-killer. Using a sensex and a field-inducer, he was virtually invulnerable and inescapable. Rubeus employed him against Corby and Bonescrolls.

Argot

AI (Autonomous Intelligence): a mind that has been created by psychophysics to program itself beyond the bio-imperatives (conscious and unconscious) of its creator.

ATP-pump: the first implanted mind-amplifer; developed circa 2048 kro at CIRCLE; the pea-sized implant augments mitochondrial development in the parietal areas of the brain and increases the energy efficiency of adenosine triphosphate in the limbic system, the emotional brain, enhancing thought-processes in the higher brain without the distortion of direct chemo-stimulation of the cerebral cortex.

Ausbok: the eo rath, a subterranean stronghold in Graal containing the living psychic process of some of humanity's finest disembodied minds; the prime purpose of Ausbok is the preservation and extension of human thought; it is the direct descendant of CIRCLE.

Boro: the section of a research center where yawps were required to live; circa 2055–2113 kro.

Botte: a yawp term of direct address used to express praise, joy, thanks.

Brood: a voor community, usually nomadic.

Brood jewel (also scry crystal and stonelight): a voor gem grown over centuries from a glandular excretion that can be derived from most voors: The gem varies in colour, size and shape, but all gems hold and enhance kha-producing Ricci-tensor reflectants that often allow an observer to witness time-forward probabilities or expansive psychic states.

Causal collapse: the realityshaping solipsism surrounding a powerful timeloose consciousness, like the Delph.

Chrysalid (sleepod): a hibernating module at the null-gravity core of the planet designed by the Delph to maintain his physical form during periods when the earth is out of Line.

CIRCLE (Center of International Research for the Continuance of Life on Earth, 2009–2113): a self-sufficient scientific community on the southern Peruvian coast (kro), established to find ways to compensate for the massive morphological changes that began as the earth swung into Line; at the time of its causal collapse (2113), CIRCLE was the only technological community of any significance on earth.

Coobla: a device that induces psynergy-stimulation in the amygdala, the brain's pleasure-core.

Dai Bodatta: 'the killing voor'; a powerful timeloose voor who has been incarnated thoughout voorish history when the brood's survival is threatened. (*See* Profiles.)

Darktime: genetic breakdown in voors precipitated by earthdreaming; manifesting usually as scabrous lesions on the skin and internal organs and invariably resulting in death.

Data-Sync: CIRCLE's cryogenic computer system.

Deadwalker: a pejorative term referring to orts; they are recognizable by their slim red kha.

Deep: a Massebôth term for seer; a highly sensitive and well-channeled telepath created *in utero* by the introduction of kiutl directly into the amniotic fluid at a critical stage in fetal brain development.

Delph: the selfname of the timeloose consciousness that emerged from the causal collapse at CIRCLE in 2113 kro. (*See* Profiles.)

Deva: an artificial lifeform designed to thrive in the ionosphere; they draw sustenance from the solar wind, and their diaphanous physical forms sail around the planet with the solar tide.

Devil harp: a combination double-reed, string, and percussion instrument of voor conception consisting of a melody pipe (geepa stem) through which air is blown into a small but extremely flexible windbag (made of a rundi's lung sac or a young mentis pod) encased in a hawkwood sounding box; notes are produced by stopping the holes in the melody pipe with one hand, while with the other manipulating trip-hammer pegs to strike stalkwires of varying lengths strung inside the sounding box: a seedcase rattle attached to the underside of the sounding box produces an additional percussive sound; the devil harp's tessitura exceeds human hearing on both spectral ends.

Distorts: genetic mutations from the increase in cosmic radiation levels after the collapse of the earth's magnetic field; this term usually refers to human mutants.

Dogstars: cis-lunar space colonies.

Dorgas: a Massebôth term for criminal offenders; they are identifiable by the X-brand on their foreheads where the input valve of the drone straps penetrates the skull.

Dreamshaper: the human archetype of wisdom, the fusion of thought and feeling; the 'extra-conscious' psyche whose contents are impersonal and collective.

Drone strap: a headpiece which acts directly on the parasympathetic nervous system, intensifying physical strength and dulling mental activity; all dorgas are required to wear them while working; the straps hold in place a skull implant which feeds inhibitors and conditioners into the subarachnoid space around the brain.

Earthdreaming (mounting kha): a voor term for empathic bonding with the planet; this state is regularly achieved in all humans when brain-wave activity slows to 8 cycles per second (CPS) in resonance with the 8 CPS vibration of the earth's crust; in voors this meditative state enhances telepathy.

Eo: the technologically stored memories of the mantics left in Ausbok after the mantics went vertical after 2113 kro; the memories are integrated by Ausbok's AI and focused individually into human orts when social communication is required; the eo society has two moieties: The in-moiety orts wear blue and involve themselves almost wholly in pure research; the yellow garbed out-moiety are responsible for communications beyond Ausbok.

Esper: the international language Esperanto, in the widely modified form used at CIRCLE.

Eth: the Delph's other; a fear-reflection that haunted him in many human forms, the last of which was Sumner Kagan. (*See* Shadowself.)

Field-inducer: an eo invention that can induce any variance of the Field (electromagnetic, gravitational, strong and weak) by drawing on the ubiquitous and infinite flux of virtual particles. (*See* Subquantal Field.)

Flexform: modular furniture popular at CIRCLE.

Flex-rountine: a slow physical exercise designed to stretch systematically all the muscle groups in the body; modeled by the eo on the Chinese *pa kua*.

Geepa bean: a mutant perennial tall-growing bean with blue cordate leaves and large panicles of fragrant and highly nutritious seeds, ranging in color from red to green and black; the geepa bean first appeared among the explosion of mutations that resulted from the influx of Linergy and cosmic radiation around 2035 kro; within five hundred years of its appearance, because of the vine's adaptability and extraordinary capacity to 'digest' rock and unlock precious nutrients, it was the dominant vine on the planet; it is the primary food-source for most of the world's people, since it is high in protein complexes that are easily assimilable; voors call it homefruit.

Ghosting: the region between lynks; it is of indefinite metrics but confined by four-space symmetry (isospace parameters) to discrete and exact mass replication (including pramatter, that is, mass's substanceless values: spin, parity, isospin, and strangeness), which is precisely why what goes in one lynk always comes out another lynk the same.

Glastic: an ultrahigh molecular weight, thermosetting polymer of boron oxide that has the colloidal properties of glass with the ductility of plastic.

Goat Nebula: a supernova in the kro constellation *Serpens Caput*.

Godmind: consciousness that transmutes and willfully directs Linergy; the human experience of this is mytho-culturally associated with divinity, since the ego becomes the pivot for a tremendous amount of power; this numinous sense, however, is illusory, because the godmind is limited to affecting local phenomena and is itself influenced by other godminds and the infinitude of the multiverse. (*See* Realityshaping.)

Graal: a geography set aside by the eo for the godminds to occupy while on earth; it covered all of kro South America and included Ausbok, Oxact, CIRCLE, and numerous biotectured villages for the pleasure of godminds; Rubeus was responsible for its maintenance.

Grin: a yawp deprecatory term for human being.

Hellraiders: the Massebôth first-strike force.

Hind rats: large bipedal rodents that are razorfanged and aggressive.

Holoman: three-dimensional laser projections usually accompanied by wide-range sensory details.

Howlie: a derogatory voor term for human beings; voors communicate soundlessly, through telepathy.

Immanence: a yawp expression for the psychokinetic bliss experienced under the influence of kiutl.

Invex: a mantic brain-mind correlator; a technique for reviewing the mental experiences of a subject; a crude mindscan used primarily to monitor yawp intelligence and weed out mental variants.

Iz: the voors' 'wind of the longer distance,' the name given by voors to the Line and the phenomenon of their psychic interreaction with the Line, more exactly, it is the continuity of the voors' experience *within* the Line, a voor eigentime in which an individual voor may exist both in the time-directed structure of gravitational space and out of causality in a space where the world-horizon is spherical; within the Line (Iz), all voors exist, always.

Kha: biospectral energy; bodylight; the subtle cellular luminescence radiated by all living organisms. (*See* Psynergy.)

Kili: a Massebôth game of skill played with three marbles and a triangle; similar to the kro game of billiards.

Kiutl: a glassy-stemmed herb with blood-red stipulate leaves and blue cleistogamous flowers; the leaves and flowers are rich in an indole-free psiberant which endows strong telepathic properties when consumed; this plant is cherished by the voors.

Kro: the term designating the people who dominated the earth before the Line exerted its influence; protected by a magnetic field around the earth and a clement sun, they thrived on their self-absorption and paid only cursory attention to the cosmos that surrounded them.

Lami: originally, the yawp designation for the divine embodiment of the kiutl plant; later, incorporated into the Mutric mythos as the Sister of Night.

Lifelove (the lifeforce): a psychic and organic integration; *nous* and *physis* harmoniously melled.

Line: a hypertube; the timelike geodesics which connect the spacefree internal domain of a naked Kerr-singularity (a rotating black hole that is 'open' to our universe); CIRCLE mantics first identified the ray of metafrequency energy jetstreaming from the massive black hole at the galactic hub as the Line; earth migrated into the flux of the Line fully in 2113 kro, though the transmuting effects of this atypical energy had been altering the planet for over a century. (*See* Linergy.)

Liner: a craft that uses Linergy to power itself through the time-like hypertube of the Line, traveling the Kaluza-Klein Continuum between and through open black holes.

Linergy: the quantized energy of the Line; the energy emerges as pure photons of hyperfrequencies but it swiftly geometrizes into nucleons of lower energy; very few of the original photons reach earth; those that do contain 'information' from the domain of an infinite Field outside our open, expanding Lobatchevskian world.

Llyr: kro Venus.

Lune: an insane person.

Lusk: voor possession; the voor dominance of another physical form.

Lynk: an opening into an internal space-time system with a direct time-arrow; two lynks with the same time-arrow create a space corridor; a device for crossing any distance within the local curvature of space-time.

Macheoe: kro Mercury.

Mage: a voor with strong timeloose powers.

Magnar: the spiritual leader of the Serbota; Bonescrolls. (*See* Profile.)

Mantic: a human brain coupled to an ATP-pump; this mechanical means of extending intelligence was devised and utilized in CIRCLE; because of the mantic insistence on thinking in dialectical schema, they were obviated when the earth entered into the emergent, pluralistic reality of the multiverse.

Massebôth (literally, the Pillars): a human society aided by the eo and disdainful of distorts; it was founded by the eo seven hundred years after the collapse of CIRCLE; the eo's intent was to create a stable, self-sustaining gene pool; Rubeus also helped to sustain this society, and over the five hundred years of its history he insinuated his influence into the government and was instrumental in shaping its politics.

Massel: the language spoken by the Massebôth.

Mentis: a reed grass with black, red-veined stalks, the juice of which is a potent stimulant.

Metaorder: degrees of coherency and relation on subquantal levels.

Mindark: the psychic space of consiousness.

Mounting kha: *See* Earthdreaming.

Muckel: Massel slang for kiutl.

Multiverse: the subquantal Field; the 'internal' structure of the universe outside of time where all possible universes exist; this nth-dimensional domain is a reality at the core of all black holes; in some rotating, assymetrically collapsed black holes, this core is not shielded by an event horizon and 'information' from the multiverse enters the Einstein-space of our universe. (*See* Line.)

Mutra: chief deity worshipped in the Massebôth Protectorate, Mother of Fragments; a revival of the Mother-cults from pre-kro times.

Nadjille: kro Uranus.

Né: androgynous distorts of the Serbota tribe: usually telepathic and tactilely deft.

Né-futhorc: a runic alphabet employed among androgynous distorts tribally separated but culturally one-with.

No-face: featureless humanoid ort.

Odyl gem: a hypnotic induction device perfected by the eo.

Olfact: a mood changer that is inhaled.

One Mind: individual awareness intuitively bonded to the synergism of group awareness *across time*; a telepathic unity with All; it is the ultimate and continually expanding Prigogine effect of a consciousness open to all the contradictory and hieratic contents of existence.

One-with: psychic enjambment; telepathic union.

Orph: a soporific olfact.

Ort (servort): a mindless, biologically human artifact; also, any animal neuro-altered to respond to unprogrammed directives.

Oxact: a mountain of psyn-crystals, the power source of Rubeus.

Paseq (the Divider): a tribal deity incorporated into the Mutric mythos as the ultimate arbitrator and spirit of harmony.

Peeler: a slow death in which individuals are spun and the living skin is lathed off; utilized by the Massebôth.

Pleroma music: subliminal sonics psycho-engineered for ultimate aesthetic pleasure.

Psiberant: a substance which acts directly on the brain's third ventricle, the pineal gland, and the Fissure of Rolando; it dramatically increases empathic response in the user.

Psyn-crystal: six-dimensional matrices with orthonormal surfaces capable of storing psynergy.

Psyn-echoes: Linergy resonances; a multi-space hyperbolic which in a time-boundary, like our universe, gives rise to gravitational interaction, actually changing the geometry of space itself and creating gravity waves; such a gravity wave rocked the earth in 2074 kro, disturbing the spin of the planet's nickel-iron core and shutting down the shield-force of the magnetic field.

Psynergy: the field that surrounds any thing: psynergy is pervasive; in humans it is kha; the kro identified it as *chi, ki, prana*, and *ka*.

Radix: a mantic term for the root of existence, the void, or, if you prefer, the isostasis in which the infinite-dimensional space of the multiverse is imbedded; within this void, everything exists; the kro called it *wu, ain soth*, and *śunyata*.

Rael: an artificial intelligence first created by the late mantics to protect their territories from encroaching distorts; raels are airborne entities, deriving their power from the sun and the potential difference between the earth and the ionosphere.

Raga storms: immense cyclones initially generated by the gravity wave from the psyn-echoes that wobbled the earth and shut down the planet's magnetic field; the intensity of the storms have been decreasing since, but a raga wind of five hundred kilometers an hour is not unusual at the time of Sumner Kagan.

Rangers: the Massebôth elite guerrilla force.

Realityshaping: the conscious ability of godminds to reshape physical reality in the subquantal Field; because the godmind alters subquantum fluctuations, which are time-free, the resulting quantum mechanical changes (the realityshaping) contain timeloose elements; in other words, a godmind does not always consciously know what it does or why; realityshaping is always a process greater than the individual that appears to initiate it.

Road: the Serbota concept of the planet's kha-channels which lead directly to the magnar; also, in the generic sense, the Future.

Rubeus: the AI created to manage Graal's maintenance while the Delph explored timeloose realities with the other godminds. (*See* Profiles.)

Rundi: a brown-gold furred simian, notable for its plush pelage and its frenetic viciousness.

Savant: a Massebôth priest of the Mutric cult.

Scansule: in Massebôth society, a video learning device; in eo culture, an information crystal.

Scry crystal: *see* Brood jewel.

Seer: a Serbota name for a deep; a natural empath with the ability to 'send' thoughts.

Seh: a multifunction hand-sized instrument capable of shielding its owner from projectiles and all ranges of radiation; it is also designed for levitation and sonic cleansing.

Selfscan: open, intuitive awareness; nonconceptual and clear, accessible through breath control and internal flex-routines.

Sensex: a kha-detector directly connected with the optic nerve and the visual cortex.

Serbota: a distort tribe living on the fringe of Skylonda Aptos.

Shadowself: a psynergy echo of repressed psychic contents that constellates into an autonomous complex with a body, mind, and will of its own; the eth, originally the Delph's fear of oblivion.

Shadowshooting: a voor technique in which the kha or kha-remnants of an individual are traced back across time by the consciousness of the voor in Iz; only the most powerful voors are capable of shadowshooting.

Skre: a killing-being bioshaped by Rubeus.

Skyfires: the auroras generated by the interaction of Linergy and Linergy nucleons with the ionosphere.

Sothis: the voor name for a period of time forty thousand years prior to kro-culture when the Line last intersected the path of the solar system and the voors interacted for the first time with humans.

Stalk charm: a geometric design which uses the kha-properties of plants to influence the kha of its wearer.

Strohlkraft: a Massebôth vertical-ascent fighter plane.

Subquantal Field: the metageometric domain from which the universe emerged 19×10^9 years ago and from which virtual particles continue to emerge; specifically, the internal five-dimensional curved Riemannian manifold whose isometry boundary is the external, gravitational universe.

Superlight: actually not light but hypercharged bosons displaced subquantally and directed through internal space-time; Rubeus and the eo used these powerful timeloose particles as a weapon of formidable destructiveness.

Timeloose: acausal; sometimes telepathic awareness.

Timeslip: collected Linergy, redirected to shape new, transient realities.

Tropiform: eo-crafted furniture which conforms to the shape of the user.

Unchala: the voor's place of origin, a planet that was positioned within the directional beam of Linergy from an open collapsar.

Vertical: Going vertical is the act of physically leaving the universe through a hypertube. (*See* Liner.)

Veve: a voor system of notation recording the lifeforms that are memory-accessible to its owner.

Voice: the auditory manifestation of Jac Halevy-Cohen's acausal self, the Delph; also, that sensibility as mimicked by Rubeus.

Voor: a being from Unchala who has evolved into the Line and who spontaneously and creatively usurps the physical forms of species of whatever life-worlds the Line reaches.

Wangol: kha-strength: the spirit-power of a being.

White card: one of the levels of the Massebôth notation system signifying the genetic status of its possessor; a white card denotes genetic perfection; other cards range from the blue card of near-perfect genes to the brown card of terminally ill people.

Yawps: bio-engineered simians, originally designed by mantics to serve as a labor force; later, yawps self-evolved into a separate species.

Zaned: insane.

Zord: a unit of Massebôth currency equivalent to the kro pound sterling, circa 1901 kro.

THE END